# The World's Finest Mystery and Crime Stories

*Second Annual Collection*

## Forge Books by Ed Gorman

*Moonchasers and Other Stories*
*Blood Games*
*What the Dead Men Say*


(as editor)
*The World's Finest Mystery and Crime Stories*
*First Annual Collection*

*The World's Finest Mystery and Crime Stories*
*Second Annual Collection*


(as E. J. Gorman)
*The First Lady*
*The Marilyn Tapes*
*Senatorial Privilege*

SECOND ANNUAL COLLECTION

# The World's Finest Mystery and Crime Stories

*Edited by Ed Gorman*

FORGE®

A TOM DOHERTY ASSOCIATES BOOK

NEW YORK

THE WORLD'S FINEST MYSTERY AND CRIME STORIES:
SECOND ANNUAL COLLECTION

A Forge Book
Published by Tom Doherty Associates, LLC
175 Fifth Avenue
New York, NY 10010

www.tor.com

Forge® is a registered trademark of Tom Doherty Associates, LLC.

ISBN 0-765-30029-X (hardcover)
ISBN 0-765-30101-6 (trade paperback)

First Edition: October 2001

Printed in the United States of America

0   9   8   7   6   5   4   3   2   1

*Dedicated*
*to*
*Janet Hutchings*
*and*
*Cathleen Jordan*

# Acknowledgments

Thanks to Jon L. Breen, Edward D. Hoch, Maxim Jakubowski, Thomas Woertche, Lucy Sussex and David Honeybone, and Edo van Belkom, for their informative summaries of the mystery field, and of course, to my editor at Forge Books, Jim Frenkel, and his able staff.

# Contents

# The Year in Mystery and Crime Fiction: 2000

*Jon L. Breen*

Call 2000 "The Year of the Puzzle." Even what century we were in was a puzzle: Was this the first year of the twenty-first, as millions of January 1 revelers including me chose to believe, or the last of the twentieth? (The answer has something to do with a binary system versus a decimal system, but I'm no mathematician.) Then there was the more significant math puzzle, with elements of the jigsaw: Who exactly was elected president of the United States? It took an extended squabble over dimpled chads, flexible deadlines, doctored absentee voter applications, and dueling supreme courts to decide.

But what, aside from providing promising plot material, did these real-life puzzles have to do with those created by writers of crime and mystery fiction, where the deductive puzzle beloved of traditionalists has been declining for decades? Though the formal detection of Ellery Queen and John Dickson Carr didn't make an unexpected comeback, that most maligned, patronized, and (with book buyers) popular of Golden Age icons, Agatha Christie, had a big year. She was voted the best crime writer of the century by the membership of the Anthony Boucher Memorial Mystery Convention (Bouchercon), held in Denver, and her Hercule Poirot novels were voted the best series. One of the year's secondary sources was an encyclopedic guide to her works, while another was a deconstructionist reconsideration of the plot of her most famous book. Christie even had a new novel this year—sort of. *Spider's Web* (St. Martin's Minotaur) was the third in a series of novelizations of her plays by Charles Osborne.

Meanwhile, at the same mile-high convention, the Private Eye Writers of America gave their lifetime achievement award to master puzzlemaker Edward D. Hoch, a writer more associated with impossible crimes and fair-play clues than blows to the head and rye bottles in the desk drawer.

Giving hope to the more literal-minded traditionalists, no less than two authors, Nero Blanc and Parnell Hall, were practicing the crossword-puzzle mystery, invented by Dorothy L. Sayers in the 1920s but produced since by the late Herbert Resnicow and few others.

With the growing blockbuster obsession of the major corporate book publishers, many readers and writers of bread-and-butter mystery fiction confronted another kind of puzzle: the maze they had to master to find each other.

Finally, one of the longstanding puzzles of crime and mystery fiction, but I don't know if it's a math puzzle, a word puzzle, a political puzzle, or (for those involved) another maze: Why have American and British markets shown such resistance to crime fiction from other languages and cultures? And why does the whole world seem to view the crime novel as an Anglo-American art form?

Early in 2000, during a visit to a national park in Chile, my wife and I learned that our tour guide was a mystery enthusiast who enjoyed a number of

English-language writers in the original or in Spanish translation. After recommending some other writers she might enjoy, I asked her what contemporary Latin American crime writers she could recommend. She was unable to name a single one, indeed seemed to doubt there were any. The only one I could think of was Mexico's Paco Ignacio Taibo II, several of whose brilliant and offbeat novels have been published in the U.S.A., but surely there must be others.

It's true that the French, with Emile Gaboriau, Maurice Leblanc, and Gaston Leroux, have been accorded some historical importance, and at least some foreign-language writers have enjoyed a brief or extended vogue in Britain and America: Maigret's Belgian creator Georges Simenon, of course; the German author of *Night of the Generals* and other World War II fiction, Hans Hellmut Kirst; the Italian author of the bestseller *The Name of the Rose*, Umberto Eco; the Swedish police proceduralist team of Maj Sjöwall and Per Wahloo; and a pair of Dutch authors, Robert van Gulik and Janwillem van der Wetering, both of whom wrote in English. Numerous others have at least occasionally cracked the English language market in translation: the Italian team of Carlo Fruttero and Franco Lucentini; several Japanese writers (Seicho Matsumoto, Masako Togawa, Edogawa Rampo); the French Frederic Dard (Sanantonio) and Hubert Monteilhet; the Russian Yulian Semyonov; the Spanish Manuel Vázquez Montalban; and the Scandinavians Poul Orum, Jan Ekstrom, and K. Arne Blom. Among the prominent foreign-language writers currently being published in English are Holland's Baantjer, many of whose DeKok novels have appeared in trade paperback translations from Intercontinental, and Sweden's Henning Mankell, whose novels about Kurt Wallander are published by The New Press. But the fact remains that the balance of trade in crime fiction has always favored English-language works.

In December 2000, Club Med sponsored a mystery-novel conference in the Bahamas that drew such distinguished American writers as Ed McBain, Donald E. Westlake, James Crumley, and Nevada Barr. Several foreign-language writers were also invited: Taibo of Mexico, Leonardo Padura of Cuba, Santiago Gamboas of Colombia, Laura Grimaldi of Italy; Thierry Jonquet, Chantal Pelletier, and Dominique Manotti of France; and José Angel Manas of Spain. A check of Amazon.com shows that of this group, only Taibo has any books available in English translation. The formation of the International Crime Writers Association a few years ago, and its English-language anthologies, have helped to bring some international writers to the attention of English-language readers, but English-speaking countries continue to have a resistance to foreign writers that does not exist in other countries where English-language books in translation are popular. While you could say the same about English-language motion pictures, at least the best of foreign film can be expected to turn up with subtitles at the big-city art houses. No such equivalent exists for foreign crime fiction.

## THE WEB

The discussion of internationalism leads conveniently to the increasing importance of the Internet as a source of up-to-date information. Quite often I get news of the mystery field in the U.S. and Great Britain first from a Web site that is maintained in Japan: Jiro Kimura's The Gumshoe Site (www.nsknet.or.jp%jkimura). Another useful site, The Mysterious Homepage: A Guide to Mysteries and Crime Fiction on the Internet (www.webfic.com/mysthome/mysthome. htm) is maintained in Denmark by Jan B. Steffensen.

Some other sites I've found particularly valuable are Tangled Web U.K. (www.twbooks.co.uk), a great source of British reviews by H. R. F. Keating, Martin Edwards, Val McDermid, and other well-known author-critics; and the Thrilling Detective Web Site (www.thrillingdetective.com), a good stop for lovers of the hardboiled. My most exciting recent find, though, is Michael E. Grost's A Guide to Classic Mystery and Detection (members.aol.com/mg4273/classics. htm), which includes some contemporary subjects but is most valuable for its historical coverage. You'd be hard-pressed to find a print source that covers in such detail writers of the past like Lee Thayer, Octavus Roy Cohen, Burton E. Stevenson, Helen McCloy, and Lawrence G. Blochman.

## BEST NOVELS OF THE YEAR 2000

The superlative "best" refers to those novels I have read and reviewed, which do not necessarily include all the worthy crime fiction of the year. However, I can recommend the fifteen books below without reservation, and I doubt anyone could find fifteen better. There's no common theme this time apart from the literary: The novels of Collins, Doughty, Engel, Stansberry, Taibo, and Westlake deal in a major or minor way with the doings of novelists, not such a surprising topic for novelists to be writing about.

Sarah Caudwell, *The Sibyl in her Grave* (Delacorte). The late author's final novel about Professor Hilary Tamar, whose gender must remain a mystery, is a literate, seriocomic puzzle for fans of Michael Innes and Edmund Crispin. Has any writer gained as formidable a reputation as Caudwell on the basis of four widely spaced novels?

Max Allan Collins's *The Hindenburg Murders* (Berkley). The creator of the Saint, Leslie Charteris, is the sleuth in this recreation of a 1937 disaster from our best fictionalizer of twentieth-century mysteries.

K. C. Constantine, *Grievance* (Mysterious). With Rugs Carlucci succeeding Mario Balzic as central character, the series about the Rocksburg, Pennsylvania, police continues to feature complex relationships, extraordinary dialogue, and unconventional mystery plotting.

Thomas H. Cook, *Places in the Dark* (Bantam). To say this cleverly crafted, lyrically written, time-shifting saga of two brothers from small-town coastal Maine bears comparison with the author's earlier *Breakheart Hill* and *The Chatham School Affair* should be recommendation enough.

Val Davis, *Wake of the Hornet* (Bantam). Archaeologist Nicolette (Nick) Scott, a specialist in the examination of historic aircraft, investigates a Pacific island mystery involving the Cargo Cults. This series started strong and has gotten better with each book.

Louise Doughty, *An English Murder* (Carroll & Graf). As the publisher's enthusiastic press releases emphasize, this is not your parents' English-village mystery. Subversive or not, it is a sensitive, complex, and remarkable novel.

Howard Engel, *Murder in Montparnasse* (Overlook). The sights, sounds, smells, and tastes of 1920s Paris come to life in this tale of the literary expatriate colony, first published in Canada in 1992.

Nicolas Freeling, *Some Day Tomorrow* (St. Martin's/Minotaur). An amazing novel from the viewpoint of a troubled, quirky, and brilliant retired Dutch botanist suspected of killing a teenage girl. Freeling always has been a specialized taste, but I'd recommend this one even to readers who could never warm up to series cops van der Valk and Castang.

Stuart M. Kaminsky, *The Big Silence* (Forge). Chicago policeman Abe Lieberman, one of the great characters of contemporary crime fiction, confronts a variety of personal and professional problems.

H. R. F. Keating, *The Hard Detective* (St. Martin's Minotaur). Tough woman detective Harriet Martens seeks a Biblically obsessed serial killer in a splendid police procedural from an unusual series—previous titles include *The Rich Detective, The Good Detective, The Bad Detective*, and *The Soft Detective*—joined by theme rather than a continuing character.

Elmore Leonard, *Pagan Babies* (Delacorte). Locales from Africa to Detroit and a pair of likably bent central characters combine for a model comic caper with a serious undertone.

Domenic Stansberry, *Manifesto for the Dead* (Permanent Press). A remarkable pastiche set in early-seventies Hollywood approximates Jim Thompson's style, while featuring the troubled novelist as the main character. (Another publication of interest to Thompson fans from the same small press is Mitch Cullin's chilling book-length poem, *Branches*.)

Paco Ignacio Taibo II, *Just Passing Through*, translated from the Spanish by Martin Michael Roberts (Cinco Puntos Press). A playful, unconventional, and astonishing documentary novel details the author's search for the truth about a Mexican anarchist and labor leader of the 1920s.

Donald E. Westlake, *The Hook* (Mysterious). In the grim vein of the author's great 1997 novel, *The Ax*, this tale of ghostwriting and murder brings the cutthroat publishing scene to life—and death.

Laura Wilson, *A Little Death* (Bantam). Three cases of mysterious death spanning half a century in the life of a British family form the puzzle in one of the most original whodunits of recent years. Presented in the U.S. as a paperback original after a 1999 publication in Britain, this first novel is my choice for book of the year.

## SUBGENRES

Private-eye buffs had plenty to enjoy in 2000, including Amos Walker in Loren D. Estleman's *A Smile on the Face of the Tiger* (Mysterious), as distinguished as ever in style; newcomer Joe Barley, the academic gumshoe of Eric Wright's *The Kidnapping of Rosie Dawn* (Perseverance); Sharon McCone in Marcia Muller's *Listen to the Silence* (Mysterious); Ivan Monk in Gary Phillips's *Only the Wicked* (Write Way); Spenser in Robert B. Parker's tongue-in-cheek racing mystery *Hugger Mugger* (Putnam); the Nameless Detective in Bill Pronzini's *Crazybone* (Carroll & Graf); and Sam McCain in Ed Gorman's *Wake Up, Little Susie* (Carroll & Graf).

Fans of the amateur detective should seek out Simon Brett's *The Body on the Beach* (Berkley), first in a new series about the English village of Fethering; Joan Hess's satirical *A Conventional Corpse* (St. Martin's Minotaur), in which bookseller

Claire Malloy ventures among the crime writers; Val McDermid's *Booked for Murder* (Spinsters Ink), a case for journalist Lindsay Gordon first published in Britain in 1996; Lee Harris's latest holiday mystery, *The Mother's Day Murder* (Fawcett); and Nora DeLoach's *Mama Pursues Murderous Shadows* (Bantam), about small-town South Carolina social worker Grace (Candi) Covington. Though Dorothy Gilman's *Mrs. Pollifax Unveiled* (Ballantine) concerns a spy rather than a sleuth, it fits well in this cozy company.

Those in search of the classical puzzle-spinning of the "Golden Age" can look to Parnell Hall's Cora Felton in her second crossword case, *Last Clue & Puzzlement* (Bantam); and Francis M. Nevins's Loren Mensing in the Queenian *Beneficiaries' Requiem* (Five Star), plus a bunch of British cops: Paul Charles's Christy Kennedy in the locked-room problem, *The Ballad of Sean and Wilko* (Do-Not/Dufour); Peter Lovesey's Peter Diamond in *The Vault* (Soho); Graham Thomas's Erskine Powell in *Malice in London* (Fawcett); and of course Colin Dexter's Chief Inspector Morse in his final case, *The Remorseful Day* (Crown), though it's more notable as a character study than a puzzle.

Police detectives from outside the classical tradition who were in strong form include James Lee Burke's Dave Robicheaux in *Purple Cane Road* (Doubleday), and Ken Bruen's Brant and Roberts in the satirical *Taming the Alien* (Do-Not/Dufour).

Historicals continue to have a growing mystery-market share. Anne Perry's two Victorian series, though not at their peak, were well enough represented by *Slaves of Obsession* (Ballantine), about William Monk, Hester Latterly, and Sir Oliver Rathbone; and *Half Moon Street* (Ballantine), about Thomas Pitt with wife Charlotte mostly offstage. A good addition to the continuing Watsonian pastiche industry was Val Andrews's *Sherlock Holmes at the Varieties* (Breese), one of several from this prolific author and publisher. Conrad Allen's Cunard Line detectives put to sea again in *Murder on the Mauretania* (St. Martin's Minotaur), about a 1907 maiden voyage. Steven Saylor's *Last Seen in Massilia* (St. Martin's Minotaur) is an exception to the general rule that Roman detectives like Gordianus the Finder shouldn't venture out of town. In an example of the past/present hybrid, William J. Mann's *The Biograph Girl* (Kensington) speculates that pioneering movie star Florence Lawrence didn't really die by suicide in 1938.

Considering that the second edition of my *Novel Verdicts: A Guide to Courtroom Fiction* (Scarecrow) was published early in the year (officially 1999 per the title page), I spent surprisingly little time in the company of the lawyer detectives, but I can recommend Andrew Pyper's first novel, *Lost Girls* (Delacorte); and Gini Hartzmark's noncourtroom *Dead Certain* (Fawcett) to my fellow legal buffs.

## SHORT STORIES

The best book in an extraordinary year for single-author collections was Carolyn Wheat's *Tales out of School* (Crippen & Landru), which displays the lawyer-author's astonishing craftsmanship and versatility to maximum advantage. Close runners-up were the first two collections by Clark Howard, published within months of each other: *Crowded Lives and Other Stories of Desperation and Danger* (Five Star) and *Challenge the Widow-Maker and Other Stories of People in Peril* (Crippen & Landru).

Others of special merit from Crippen & Landru included Michael Collins's second volume of Dan Fortune private-eye stories, *Fortune's World*; Edward D. Hoch's *The Velvet Touch* (Crippen & Landru), about thief-of-the-valueless Nick Velvet; Marcia Muller's *McCone and Friends*, in which members of the San Francisco private eyes' extended family of co-workers take center stage; and Hugh B. Cave's *Long Live the Dead*, gathering the venerable writer's *Black Mask* stories. Among Five Star's notable offerings were Barbara D'Amato's *Of Course You Know that Chocolate Is a Vegetable and Other Stories*; Lia Matera's *Counsel for the Defense and Other Stories*; Dick Lochte's *Lucky Dog and Other Tales of Murder*; and two collections by Evan Hunter/Ed McBain: *Barking at Butterflies and Other Stories* and *Running from Legs and Other Stories*. Other publishers got into the act with Lawrence Block's 754-page *The Collected Mystery Stories* (Orion/Trafalger); and Peter Sellers's *Whistle Past the Graveyard* (Mosaic).

It was also a strong year for multiauthor collections. As you might expect at the close of a century, chubby historical reprint anthologies were numerous. Tony Hillerman and Otto Penzler edited *The Best American Mystery Stories of the Century* (Houghton Mifflin). Anne Perry edited a British equivalent, *A Century of British Mystery and Suspense* (Mystery Guild), to which I was honored to provide an introduction. Ed Gorman and I edited *Sleuths of the Century* (Carroll & Graf), which included authors of both nationalities plus Georges Simenon.

Star-studded original anthologies of note included the Adams Round Table's *Murder Among Friends* (Berkley); the Private Eye Writers of America's *The Shamus Game* (Signet), edited by that organization's indefatigable founder, Robert J. Randisi; the Mystery Writers of America's *The Night Awakens* (Pocket), edited by Mary Higgins Clark; and *Crime Through Time III* (Berkley), edited by Sharan Newman. More concentrated on newer names was the Brit noir volume *Fresh Blood 3* (Do-Not/Dufour), edited by Mike Ripley and Maxim Jakubowski.

The Tennessee publisher Cumberland House became a key player in the anthology game with theme volumes both original (*Murder Most Confederate*, edited by Martin H. Greenberg; and *Murder Most Medieval*, edited by Greenberg and John Helfers) and reprint (*Opening Shots: Great Mystery and Crime Writers Share Their First Published Stories*, edited by Lawrence Block; and *Murder Most Delectable*, edited by Greenberg).

My favorite anthology of the year, combining old stories and originals with an editorial apparatus of genuine reference value was Mike Ashley's *The Mammoth Book of Locked-Room Mysteries and Impossible Crimes* (Carroll & Graf). As with other volumes in the publisher's Mammoth series, though, I wish it were in more permanent form, i.e., hardcovers and better paper.

See Edward D. Hoch's bibliography for the year's full story on both anthologies and single-author collections.

## REFERENCE BOOKS AND SECONDARY SOURCES

Book of the year in this category was surely Marvin Lachman's *The American Regional Mystery* (Crossover Press), a criminous cross-country tour by one of the most knowledgeable, readable, and reliable commentators on crime fiction.

Also of note are the collection of Charles Willeford's essays, *Writing & Other Blood Sports* (Dennis McMillan); Hugh Merrill's *The Red Hot Typewriter: The Life and Times of John D. MacDonald* (St. Martin's Minotaur), which has undeniable value despite indifferent writing and a lousy title; Martha Hailey DuBose's *Women of Mystery: The Lives and Works of Notable Women Crime Novelists* (St. Martin's Minotaur); Otto Penzler's *101 Greatest Films of Mystery and Suspense* (Simon & Schuster); and Matthew Bunson's *The Complete Christie: An Agatha Christie Encyclopedia* (Pocket), doing a job you may think is redundant, but doing it well. A more original Christie volume, though one less likely to appeal to a wide readership, was Pierre Bayard's *Who Killed Roger Ackroyd?* (New Press), translated from the French by Carol Cosman—if you can wade through the academic jargon, Bayard has an interesting theory to promote.

*They Wrote the Book: Thirteen Women Mystery Writers Tell All* (Spinsters Ink), edited by Helen Windrath, is both a valuable technical manual for writers and entertaining reading for fans; while the Independent Mystery Booksellers Association's *100 Favorite Mysteries of the Century* (Crum Creek), edited by Jim Huang, provides a good reading list, heavy on authors of the '80s and '90s, with commentary.

Again, Ed Hoch's bibliography will provide the full story.

## A SENSE OF HISTORY

Rue Morgue Press publishers Tom and Enid Schantz continued to reprint worthy writers of the past, including the first American edition of Joanna Cannan's 1939 novel *They Rang Up the Police*, an outstanding piece of classical detective fiction that can stand comparison with Allingham, Marsh, Sayers, and other Golden Age icons; and Juanita Sheridan's *The Chinese Chop*, the 1949 novel that introduced Chinese American sleuth Lily Wu, whose other three cases are on Rue Morgue's future schedule.

Five Star brought us new editions, with an introduction by the author, of Donald E. Westlake's first two Mitchell Tobin novels, *Kinds of Love, Kinds of Death* (1966) and *Murder Among Children* (1967), originally published as by Tucker Coe; while Vera Caspary's 1943 classic *Laura* became the first in a series, edited by Otto Penzler for ibooks, of mysteries that became Hollywood films. The e-books/books-on-demand phenomenon allowed contemporary writers like Stuart M. Kaminsky, Dick Lochte, Annette Meyers, and Loren D. Estleman to make their backlists available to readers, a trend that can be expected to grow.

## AT THE MOVIES

The quality of 2000's crime and mystery movies was far below that of 1999's bumper crop, but there were some good ones, mostly playing the art houses rather than the multiplexes. Best crime film released in the U.S.A. during the year was probably the 1998 British film noir *Croupier*, directed by Mike Hodges from Paul Mayersberg's script and boasting a great performance by Clive Owen as the title character, a bored writer who takes a casino job that leads him into a web of crime. *The Virgin Suicides*, directed by Sofia Coppola, who also wrote the screenplay from Jeffrey Eugenides's 1993 novel, is a dark coming-of-age story about the hidden horrors of suburbia and a rare example of the pure whydunit. Writer-director Rod Lurie's *The Contender*, like his 1999 film *Deterrence*, shows him as a nimble plotter in the political thriller vein. *Under Suspicion*, directed by Stephen Hopkins and scripted by Tom Provost and W. Peter Iliff from (via an earlier French version) John Wainwright's 1979 novel *Brainwash*, may be somewhat stagy in feel, but it's cunningly constructed and makes a great vehicle for the talents of Gene Hackman and Morgan Freeman. Gregory Hoblit's *Frequency*, written by Toby Emmerich, is a suspenseful mystery/science-fiction hybrid: time travel meets get-the-serial-killer.

Some of the crime films I admired during the year were less well-received by critics, so take these recommendations with a grain of salt. The Harrison Ford/Michelle Pfeiffer vehicle *What Lies Beneath*, directed by Robert Zemeckis from Clark Gregg's screenplay, struck me as an admirably tricky variation of the *Before the Fact* am-I-married-to-a-murderer plot. Director Nick Gomez's *Drowning Mona*, written by Peter Steinfeld, is a tongue-in-cheek small-town black comedy asking which of several reasonable suspects murdered the poisonous title character played by Bette Midler. *The Yards*, James Gray's downbeat film of civic corruption (scripted with Matt Reeves), had a terrific cast and should have done better at the box office than it did. *Where the Money Is*, the enjoyable caper movie in which ex-con Paul Newman impersonates a stroke victim, had three screenplay writers (E. Max Frye, Topper Lilien, and Carroll Cartwright, from Frye's story) and was directed by Marek Kanievska. (Is Newman embarked on a series of senior-citizen variations on crime-fiction conventions? This one follows his 1998 "geezer noir" private-eye vehicle, *Twilight*. I liked that one, too, though not everybody did.) *Up at the Villa*, directed by Philip Haas and scripted by Belinda Haas from a Somerset Maugham novella, qualifies as a crime story and a highly entertaining one for those who value the sedate and understated approach to high emotion.

# A 2000 Yearbook of Crime and Mystery

## compiled by Edward D. Hoch

### Collections and Single Stories

(Anonymous). *Herlock Shomes At It Again*. New York: The Mysterious Bookshop. A single twenty-page parody first published in 1918. One of the Mysterious Sherlock Holmes series.

BISHOP, PAUL. *Pattern of Behavior*. Unity, Maine: Five Star. Fourteen stories, including one new novelette, from various sources, 1982–2000.

BRACKEN, MICHAEL. *Bad Girls: One Dozen Dangerous Dames Who Lie, Cheat, Steal, and Kill*. Berkeley Heights, NJ: Wildside Press. Twelve stories, two new, from *Mike Shayne Mystery Magazine* and other sources.

————. *Tequila Sunrise: Hardboiled P. I. Nathaniel Rose: Bullets, Booze, and Broads*. Berkeley Heights, NJ: Wildside Press. Seven stories, two new, from various sources.

BREEN, JON L. *The Drowning Icecube and Other Stories*. Unity, Maine: Five Star. Seventeen stories, 1977–99, mainly detection, including three parodies and one mystery-fantasy.

BRETT, SIMON. *A Crime in Rhyme and Other Mysterious Fragments*. Burpham, West Sussex, U.K.: Frith House. A rhyming playlet and seven brief pieces supposedly written by well-known authors.

BRIETMAN, GREGORY. *The Marriage of Sherlock Holmes*. New York: The Mysterious Bookshop. A 1926 parody of twenty-eight pages, translated from the Russian. One of the Mysterious Sherlock Holmes series.

CASSIDAY, BRUCE. *None but the Vengeful: Classic Pulp Crime and Suspense*. Brooklyn: Gryphon Books. Eight stories and novelettes from the pulps, 1948–52. Introduction by Gary Lovisi.

CAVE, HUGH B. *Bottled in Blonde: The Peter Kane Detective Stories*. Minneapolis: Fedogan & Bremer. Nine tales from *Dime Detective*. Introduction by Don Hutchinson.

————. *Danse Macabre*. Norfolk, VA: Crippen & Landru. A single short story from *Clues Detective Stories*, 4/37, in a pamphlet accompanying the limited edition of *Long Live the Dead*.

————. *The Lady Wore Black and Other Weird Cat Tails*. Ashcroft, BC, Canada: Ash-Tree Press. Nineteen fantasy tales, some from *Alfred Hitchcock's Mystery Magazine*. Introduction by Mike Ashley.

————. *Long Live the Dead*. Norfolk, VA: Crippen & Landru. All ten of Cave's stories from *Black Mask*, 1934–41, with an introduction and interview with the author by Keith Alan Deutsch.

————. *Officer Coffey Stories*. Burton, MI: Subterranean Press. Two stories from *Dime Detective*, 1940.

COEL, MARGARET. *Stolen Smoke*. Mission Viejo, CA: A.S.A.P. Publishing. A single limited-edition short story, fourth in a series, about an Arapaho Native American sleuth. Introduction by Marcia Muller.

COLLINS, BARBARA. *Too Many Tomcats and Other Feline Tales of Suspense.* Unity, Maine: Five Star. Eleven cat stories, two new and one in collaboration with husband, Max Allan Collins, who contributes the introduction.

COLLINS, MICHAEL. *Fortune's World.* Norfolk, VA: Crippen & Landru. Fourteen stories, one new, one first American publication, 1965–2000, about private eye Dan Fortune. Introduction by Richard Carpenter.

———. *The Dreamer.* Norfolk, VA: Crippen & Landru. A single Slot-Machine Kelly story from *Mike Shayne Mystery Magazine,* 9/62, in a pamphlet accompanying the limited edition of *Fortune's World.*

D'AMATO, BARBARA. *Of Course You Know Chocolate Is a Vegetable and Other Stories.* Unity, Maine: Five Star. Twelve stories, 1991–99, from various sources.

DE NOUX, O'NEIL. *Hollow Point / The Mystery of Rochelle Marais.* Brooklyn: Gryphon Books. Two new police stories and a historical mystery from *EQMM,* all set in New Orleans.

DOYLE, ARTHUR CONAN. *The Surgeon of Gaster Fell.* Norfolk, VA: Crippen & Landru. A pamphlet containing the original magazine text of a Doyle novelette, later revised for book publication. Afterword by Daniel Stashower. A limited edition published for Malice Domestic XII.

DUNDEE, WAYNE D. & DEREK MUK. *Tuck Tip & Three Parts.* Brooklyn: Gryphon Books. Two private-eye novelettes by Dundee, one new, teamed with three stories by Muk about San Francisco cops.

ESTLEMAN, LOREN D. *The Midnight Man.* New York: ibooks. Reprint of a 1982 novel with an Amos Walker short story, "Redneck," appended.

FASSBENDER, TOM & JIM PASCOE. *Five Shots and a Funeral: The Short Fiction of Dashiell Loveless.* Los Angeles: Uglytown. Five connected stories by fictional author Dashiell Loveless.

FORTUNE, DION. *The Secrets of Dr. Taverner.* Ashcroft, BC, Canada: Ash-Tree Press. Complete collection of all twelve stories about an occult detective, six published in *Royal Magazine* (London) during 1922. The third of a continuing series, Ash-Tree Press Occult Detectives Library, edited and introduced by Jack Adrian.

GILBERT, MICHAEL. *The Mathematics of Murder: A Fearne & Bracknell Collection.* London: Robert Hale. Fourteen stories about law partners and their firm, some new, 1995–2000.

GORES, JOE. *File #9: Double-Header.* Norfolk, VA: Crippen & Landru. A single unpublished DKA story, later rewritten as two separate stories, in a pamphlet accompanying the limited edition of *Stakeout on Page Street.*

———. *Stakeout on Page Street and Other DKA Files.* Norfolk, VA: Crippen & Landru. All twelve stories about the skip-tracers of Daniel Kearney Associates, mainly from *EQMM,* 1967–89.

HOCH, EDWARD D. *The Gold Buddha Caper.* Norfolk, VA: Crippen & Landru. A single Ulysses S. Bird story from *EQMM,* 12/73, in a pamphlet accompanying the limited edition of *The Velvet Touch.*

———. *The Velvet Touch.* Norfolk, VA: Crippen & Landru. Fourteen stories from *EQMM* about thief-detective Nick Velvet, 1975–99, including eight about Velvet's admiring adversary Sandra Paris.

HOWARD, CLARK. *Challenge the Widow-Maker and Other Stories of People in Peril.* Norfolk, VA: Crippen & Landru. Twelve stories, 1980–94, mainly from *EQMM.*

———. *Crowded Lives and Other Stories of Desperation and Danger.* Unity, Maine: Five Star. Nine stories. 1967–89.

———. *The Killing Floor.* Norfolk, VA: Crippen & Landru. A single new short story in a pamphlet accompanying the limited edition of *Challenge the Widow-Maker.*

HUFFMAN, BOB. *Legal Fictions.* Berkeley, CA: Creative Arts. Fourteen very short stories about the American legal system.

HUNTER, EVAN. *Barking at Butterflies and Other Stories.* Unity, Maine: Five Star. Eleven stories, 1953–99, three published for the first time in America.

ILES, ROBERT L. *The Burning Woman and Other Cases from the Files of Peter B. Bruck, Private Investigator.* Brighton, MI: Avid Press. Thirteen connected stories and a novella.

JAMES, DAVID. *Sherlock Holmes and the Midnight Bell.* Romford, Essex, U.K.: Ian Henry Publications. Five stories.

LANSDALE, JOE R. *High Cotton: Selected Stories of Joe R. Lansdale.* Urbana, IL: Golden Gryphon. Twenty-one stories of crime and suspense.

LEINSTER, MURRAY. *Malay Collins, Master Thief of the East.* Bloomington, IL: Black Dog Press. Three stories from *Short Stories Magazine*, 1930.

LOCHTE, DICK. *Lucky Dog and Other Tales of Murder.* Unity, Maine: Five Star. Nine stories from various sources, 1988–99.

LOVESEY, PETER. *The Kiss of Death.* Norfolk, VA: Crippen & Landru. A single new Peter Diamond short story in a Christmas pamphlet from the publisher.

MARIAS, JAVIER. *When I Was Mortal.* New York: New Directions. Twelve stories by a Spanish author, mainly criminous, including two fantasies and a whodunit.

MATERA, LIA. *Counsel for the Defense and Other Stories.* Unity, Maine: Five Star. Nine stories from various sources.

MCBAIN, ED. *Running from Legs and Other Stories.* Unity, Maine: Five Star. Eleven stories, 1956–2000, three previously unpublished.

MCCABE, PATRICK. *Mondo Desperado.* New York: HarperCollins. Ten short stories, some criminous, published as a "serial novel."

MORRELL, DAVID. *Black Evening.* New York: Warner Books. Fifteen crime and horror stories from various sources, several fantasy.

MULLER, MARCIA. *McCone and Friends.* Norfolk, VA: Crippen & Landru. A novella and seven stories about Sharon McCone and her various colleagues at the detective agency, 1993–99.

———. *The Time of the Wolves.* Norfolk, VA: Crippen & Landru. A single short story from a 1988 anthology, in a pamphlet to accompany the limited edition of *McCone and Friends.*

NOLAN, WILLIAM F. *Down the Long Night.* Unity, Maine: Five Star. Twelve stories, 1957–2000, one new. Introduction by Ed Gorman.

NYE, E. R. (TED). *The Adventure of the Teddy Bear's Ribbon and Other Tales.* Dunedin, New Zealand: Halvon Press. Eleven Sherlockian pastiches.

PARKER, T. JEFFERSON. *Easy Street.* Mission Viejo, CA: A.S.A.P. Publishing. A single short story in a limited edition, with an introduction by Elizabeth George and an afterword by Robert Crais.

PAXTON, WILLIAM C. *The Hidden Adventures of Sherlock Holmes.* Chillicoth, MO: Community Press. Two novellas and two short stories.

PRONZINI, BILL. *Night Freight.* New York: Leisure Books. Twenty-six stories, 1971–2000, one new. Some fantasy and horror, nonseries except for a single Nameless tale.

————. *Oddments: A Short Story Collection*. Unity, Maine: Five Star. Fourteen stories from various sources, 1971–2000, including one each from his Nameless and Quincannon series and one science-fiction tale.

RENDELL, RUTH. *Piranha to Scurfy*. London. Hutchinson. Nine stories and two previously unpublished novellas. (U.S. edition: Crown, 2001).

RHEA, NICHOLAS. *Constable Around the House*. London: Robert Hale. Nine untitled stories.

ROZAN, S. J. "The Grift of the Magi." New York: Mysterious Bookshop. A single new story in an annual Christmas pamphlet from a New York bookstore.

SHAW, MURRAY. *Anatomy of Two Murders*. New York: The Mysterious Bookshop. A new Holmes pastiche in the Mysterious Sherlock Holmes series.

SMITH, JULIE. *Mean Rooms*. Unity, Maine: Five Star. Thirteen stories, 1978–99, from various sources.

STRAUB, PETER. *Magic Terror*. New York: Random House. Seven stories and novelettes of mystery and horror.

SYMONS, JULIAN. *A Julian Symons Sherlockian Duet*. Ashcroft, BC, Canada: Calabash Press. Two Sherlockian tales, edited by Jack Adrian, as a Christmas gift.

TREMAYNE, PETER. *Hemlock at Vespers*. New York: St. Martin's. Fifteen stories and novelettes about seventh-century Irish sleuth Sister Fidelma, some published for the first time in America.

WEIGHELL, RON. *The Irregular Casebook of Sherlock Holmes*. Ashcroft, BC, Canada: Calabash Press. Five stories of Holmes's encounters with the supernatural, three new, one revised from a shorter version.

WELLMAN, MANLY WADE. *The Third Cry to Legba and Other Invocations: The John Thunstone & Lee Cobbett Stories*. San Francisco: Night Shade Books. All the John Thunstone occult detective stories, volume one of the *Selected Stories of Manly Wade Wellman*, edited by John Pelan.

WHEAT, CAROLYN. "Life, for Short." Norfolk, VA: Crippen & Landru. A single short story from *Sisters in Crime IV*, in a pamphlet to accompany the limited edition of *Tales out of School*.

————. *Tales out of School* Norfolk, VA: Crippen & Landru. Nineteen stories, one new, 1989–2000.

## Anthologies

Adams Round Table. *Murder Among Friends*. New York: Berkley. Eleven new stories, one also published in *EQMM* and another in Block's *Opening Shots* (below), in a biannual anthology series.

ASHLEY, MIKE, ed. *The Mammoth Book of Locked-Room Mysteries and Impossible Crimes*. New York: Carroll & Graf. Twenty-seven stories, fifteen new. Foreword by David Renwick.

BLOCK, LAWRENCE, ed. *Master's Choice, Volume II*. New York: Berkley. Thirteen mystery writers choose a story of their own, paired with a story by a writer who inspired them.

————, ed. *Opening Shots*. Nashville: Cumberland House. First published short stories by nineteen mystery writers, 1952–2000.

BREEN, JON L. & ED GORMAN, eds. *Sleuths of the Century*. New York: Carroll & Graf. Twenty-five stories and novelettes, one fantasy, 1905–95.

CASMIER, SUSAN B., ALJEAN HARMETZ & CYNTHIA LAWRENCE, eds. *A Deadly Dozen*. Los Angeles: UglyTown. A second anthology of stories by members of the Los Angeles Chapter of Sisters in Crime.

CHIZMAR, RICHARD & ROBERT MORRISH, eds. *October Dreams: A Celebration of Halloween*. Abingdon, MD: Cemetery Dance. Ten new stories and ten reprints, mainly fantasy and horror, with essays and artwork.

CLARK, MARY HIGGINS, ed. *The Night Awakens*. New York: Pocket Books. Ten new stories in an anthology from Mystery Writers of America.

CRAIG, PATRICIA, ed. *The Oxford Book of Detective Stories*. Oxford: Oxford University Press. An international selection of thirty-seven stories, two new.

DZIEMIANOWICZ, STEFAN, ROBERT WEINBERG & MARTIN H. GREENBERG, eds. *Crafty Cat Crimes: 100 Tiny Cat Tale Mysteries*. New York: Barnes & Noble. One hundred brief tales, eighty-three new.

EDWARDS, MARTIN, ed. *Scenes of the Crime*. London: Constable. Fourteen new stories and one reprint in the annual anthology from Britain's Crime Writers' Association. Foreword by Natasha Cooper.

ELLIS, ALICE THOMAS, ed. *Valentine's Day: Women Against Men*. London: Duckworth. Stories of revenge.

FOXWELL, ELIZABETH & MARTIN H. GREENBERG, eds. *More Murder, They Wrote*. New York: Berkley. Fourteen new stories in the third volume of an anthology series.

GORMAN, CAROL & ED, eds. *Felonious Felines*. Unity, Maine: Five Star. Nine new stories and three reprints in an anthology of cat mysteries.

GORMAN, ED, ed. *The World's Finest Mystery and Crime Stories, First Annual Collection*. New York: Forge. Thirty-eight stories published during 1999, with a review of the year by Jon L. Breen and a bibliography and necrology by Edward D. Hoch.

GREENBERG, MARTIN H., ed. *Murder Most Confederate: Tales of Crimes Quite Uncivil*. Nashville: Cumberland House. Thirteen new stories and three reprints set in the Confederacy during the Civil War.

————, ed. *Murder Most Delectable*. Nashville: Cumberland House. Eighteen tales of culinary crimes, with pertinent recipes.

GREENBERG, MARTIN H. & RUSSELL DAVIS, eds. *Mardi Gras Madness*. Nashville: Cumberland House. Eleven new mystery and horror stories.

GREENBERG, MARTIN H. & JOHN HELFERS, eds. *Murder Most Medieval*. Nashville: Cumberland House. Twelve new stories of murder in medieval times, with one reprint by Ellis Peters.

GREENE, DOUGLAS G., ed. *Classic Mystery Stories*. New York: Dover. Thirteen stories, 1841–1920.

HAINING, PETER, ed. *Great Irish Stories of Murder and Mystery*. New York: Barnes & Noble. Twenty stories from various sources, some fantasy.

HESS, JOAN, presented by. *Malice Domestic 9*. New York: Avon. Thirteen new stories and an Agatha Christie reprint in an annual anthology series.

HILLERMAN, TONY & OTTO PENZLER, eds. *Best American Mystery Stories of the Century*. Boston: Houghton Mifflin. Forty-six stories from various sources.

HUTCHINGS, JANET, ed. *Crème de la Crime*. New York: Carroll & Graf. Twenty-seven stories from *Ellery Queen's Mystery Magazine* by award-winning authors.

JAKUBOWSKI, MAXIM, ed. *Murder Through the Ages: A Bumper Anthology of Historical Mysteries*. London: Headline. Twenty-five stories, all but one new, ranging in time from the tenth century B.C. to 1941.

JONES, STEPHEN, ed. *Dark Detectives: Adventures of the Supernatural Sleuths*. Minneapolis: Fedogan & Bremer. Ten stories, three new, plus a new story cycle in seven episodes by Kim Newman.

LAYMON, RICHARD, ed. *Bad News*. Abingdon, MD: Cemetery Dance. Eighteen new stories and a new one-hundred-page novella by the editor, mainly fantasy and horror.

MCINERNY, RALPH & MARTIN H. GREENBERG, eds. *Murder Most Divine: Ecclesiastical Tales of Unholy Crimes*. Nashville: Cumberland House. Eighteen stories, 1911–1998, from various sources.

NEWMAN, SHARAN, ed. *Crime Through Time III*. New York: Berkley. Eighteen new historical mysteries. Introduction by Anne Perry.

O'SULLIVAN, MAURICE J. & STEVE GLASSMAN, eds. *Orange Pulp: Stories of Mayhem, Murder, and Mystery*. Gainesville, FL: University of Florida Press. Eight stories and novel excerpts, one previously unpublished, plus a 1963 novel by Don Tracy, *The Hated One*, all set in the state of Florida.

PENZLER, OTTO, ed. *Criminal Records*. London: Orion. Fifteen original novellas, three separately published in individual editions.

PERRY, ANNE, ed. *A Century of British Mystery and Suspense*. Garden City, NY: Mystery Guild. Thirty-eight stories from various sources. Foreword by Jon L. Breen.

RANDISI, ROBERT J., ed. *The Shamus Game*. New York: Signet. Fourteen new stories by members of the Private Eye Writers of America, one previously published in England.

———, ed. *Tin Star*. New York: Berkley. New stories of crime-solving in the Old West.

SELLERS, PETER & ROBERT J. SAWYER, eds. *Over the Edge: The Crime Writers of Canada Anthology*. Lawrencetown Beach, Nova Scotia, Canada: Pottersfield Press. Fourteen stories, three new, by Canadian and American members of CWC.

STEVENS, SERITA, ed. *Unholy Orders: Mystery Stories with a Religious Twist*. Philadelphia: Intrigue Press. Eighteen new stories by various mystery writers, some fantasy.

## Nonfiction

AUERBACH, NINA. *Daphne du Maurier, Haunted Heiress*. Philadelphia: University of Pennsylvania Press. A biography of the author of *Rebecca* and other romantic suspense novels.

BAYARD, PIERRE. *Who Killed Roger Ackroyd?* New York: The New Press. The conventions of detective fiction as shown in Agatha Christie's novel *The Murder of Roger Ackroyd*, with a new "solution" to the mystery.

BLEILER, RICHARD F. *Reference Guide to Mystery and Detective Fiction*. Englewood, CO: Libraries Unlimited 1999. An annotated listing of reference books in the mystery field.

BOOTH, MARTIN. *The Doctor and the Detective: A Biography of Sir Arthur Conan Doyle*. New York: St. Martin's. A new biography of Sherlock Holmes's creator.

BREEN, JON L. *Novel Verdicts: A Guide to Courtroom Fiction, Second Edition*. Lanham, MD: Scarecrow Press. An annotated bibliography, greatly expanded from its first edition.

BUNSON, MATTHEW. *The Complete Christie: An Agatha Christie Encyclopedia*. New York: Pocket Books. Biography, novel and short-story plot synopses, character listings, film and TV listings, etc.

CASH, WILLIAM. *The Third Woman: The Secret Passion that Inspired 'The End of the Affair.'* London: Little, Brown. An account of Graham Greene's adulterous affair with an American woman, which figured in several of his novels.

CHANDLER, RAYMOND. *The Raymond Chandler Papers: Selected Letters and Non-Fiction, 1909–1959.* London: Hamish Hamilton. A new selection of letters and papers, edited by Chandler biographer Tom Hiney and the late Frank MacShane.

CHAPMAN, DAVID IAN. *R. Austin Freeman, A Bibliography.* Shelbourne, Ontario, Canada: Battered Silicon Dispatch Box. An eighty-four-page listing of Freeman's books, magazine appearances, etc.

COLLINS, WILKIE. *The Letters of Wilkie Collins, Volume 1: 1838–1865, Volume 2: 1866–1889.* New York: St. Martin's. A two-volume collection of letters by the author of *The Moonstone* and other early mysteries.

DOYLE, ARTHUR CONAN. *The Quotable Sherlock Holmes.* New York: Mysterious Press. Hundreds of memorable quotes from all the Holmes novels and short stories, assembled by Gerard Van Der Leun.

DuBOSE, MARTHA HAILEY. *Women of Mystery: The Lives and Crimes of Notable Women Authors of Mystery Fiction.* New York: St. Martin's. Biographies and minibiographies of eighteen leading mystery writers, with others mentioned briefly.

DUNCAN, PAUL. *The Pocket Essential Film Noir.* Harpenden, England: Pocket Essentials. A ninety-six-page paperback examining seven films in depth and listing hundreds more.

———. *The Pocket Essential Noir Fiction.* Harpenden, England: Pocket Essentials. A ninety-six-page paperback examining nineteen writers in depth and mentioning several others.

GOTTLIEB, SIDNEY, ed. *Hitchcock Annual, 2000–2001.* New London, NH: Hitchcock Annual Corporation. Eight new essays, an interview and reviews concerning Alfred Hitchcock's films, television series, and books pertaining to them.

HAUSLADEN, GARY. *Places for Dead Bodies.* Austin: University of Texas Press. Locales used by more than thirty leading mystery writers.

HAZZARD, SHIRLEY. *Greene on Capri.* New York: Farrar, Straus & Giroux. A memoir of Graham Greene's frequent visits to Capri and the people he knew there.

KING, STEPHEN. *On Writing: A Memoir of a Craft.* New York: Scribner. An account of King's early life, the writing of his books, his views of other writers, and his near-fatal accident.

———. *Secret Windows: Essays and Fiction on the Craft of Writing.* New York: Book of the Month Club. Twenty essays, book introductions, interviews, and short stories on writing, including a long excerpt on horror fiction from *Danse Macabre*. Introduction by Peter Straub.

KRAMER, JOHN E. *Academe in Mystery and Detective Fiction.* Blue Ridge Summit, PA: Scarecrow Press. A bibliography of 483 mystery novels, 1910–1998, with college or university settings.

LACHMAN, MARVIN. *The American Regional Mystery.* Minneapolis & San Francisco: Crossover Press. A detailed survey of regional mysteries, with chapters covering each state as well as major cities and vacation areas.

LANDRUM, LARRY. *American Mystery and Detective Novels: A Reference Guide.* Westport, CT: Greenwood Press, 1999. A history of the genre and its various subgenres, with sections on major authors and reference works.

MERRILL, HUGH. *The Red Hot Typewriter: The Life and Times of John D. MacDonald.* New York: St. Martin's. A biography of the mystery writer, creator of Travis McGee.

NICHOLS, VICTORIA & SUSAN THOMPSON. *Silk Stalkings: More Women Write of Murder.* Blue Ridge Summit, PA: Scarecrow Press. An expanded survey of series characters created by women mystery authors, 1867–1997.

NICKERSON, CATHERINE ROSS. *The Web of Inequity: Early Detective Fiction by American Women.* Durham: Duke University Press, 1999. A study of early women mystery writers in this country.

PASCAL, JANET. *Arthur Conan Doyle.* New York: Oxford University Press. A new biography of Sherlock Holmes's creator.

PENZLER, OTTO. *Cornell Woolrich, Part II (William Irish & George Hopley).* New York: The Mysterious Bookshop. A descriptive bibliography and price guide to first editions. One of a series of booklets for collectors.

———. *John P. Marquand's Mr. Moto.* New York: The Mysterious Bookshop. A descriptive bibliography and price guide to first editions.

———. *101 Greatest Movies of Mystery & Suspense.* Garden City, NY: Doubleday Direct. A listing, with credits and extensive commentary on each film.

PHILLIPS, GENE D. *Creatures of Darkness: Raymond Chandler, Detective Fiction, and Film Noir.* Lexington: University Press of Kentucky. An analysis of Chandler's work in fiction, screenwriting, and on film. Preface by Billy Wilder.

SALLIS, JAMES. *Chester Himes: A Biography.* New York: Walker. A biography of the creator of Harlem detectives Coffin Ed Johnson and Grave Digger Jones.

———. *Difficult Lives.* Brooklyn: Gryphon Books. Revised edition of a 1993 study on the life and work of noir authors Jim Thompson, David Goodis, and Chester Himes.

SARJEANT, WILLIAM A. S. *A Policeman In Post-War Paris: The Saturnin Dax Novels of Marten Cumberland.* South Benfleet, Essex, England: Geoff Bradley. A forty-four-page booklet about the series.

THOMAS, RONALD R. *Detective Fiction and the Rise of Forensic Science.* Cambridge, England: Cambridge University Press. How the development of forensic science was intertwined with the evolution of the detective story.

VANDERBURGH, GEORGE A. *R. Austin Freeman: The Anthropologist at Large, Thorndyke Scholarship and Pastiches.* Shelburne, Ontario, Canada: Battered Silicon Dispatch Box. Volume 11 of The R. Austin Freeman Omnibus Edition, containing a 1980 biography by Oliver Mayo together with nearly one hundred articles by various authors, reprinted mainly from *The Thorndyke File,* and four pastiches.

WILLEFORD, CHARLES. *Writing and Other Blood Sports.* Tucson, AZ: Dennis McMillan, Essays, interviews, and reviews, eleven previously unpublished, by the late crime writer.

WINDRATH, HELEN, ed. *They Wrote the Book: 13 Women Mystery Writers Tell All.* Duluth, MN: Spinsters Ink. Essays on how they write.

## Obituaries

STEVE ALLEN (1921–2000). Comedian and talk-show host who published ten show-business mysteries (at least some ghost-written), as well as three collections of short stories, some criminous.

EDWARD ANHALT (1914–2000). Oscar-winning screenwriter for *Becket,* who also published some twenty-five crime stories in the pulps, most under the name of "Andrew Holt."

THOMAS BABE (1941–2000). Mainstream playwright who published two suspense plays in the 1970s, *Billy Irish* and *A Prayer for My Daughter.*

CONRAD VOSS BARK (1913–2000). British journalist who published seven novels about sleuth William Holmes, 1962–68.

DAVID BEATY (1919–1999). British author of eight thrillers, notably *Cone of Silence* (1959), plus three others as by "Paul Stanton."

KENNETH BENTON (1909–1999). British author of eight intrigue novels, notably *Spy in Chancery* (1972), plus two others as by "James Kirton."

H. S. BHABRA (1955–2000). Indian/British banker residing in Canada, author of two suspense novels under his own name and two others under the pseudonym of "A. M. Kabal."

LEONARD BODIN (1911–1999). British author of a single crime novel, *. . . And the Body Came Too* (1946).

ARTYOM BOROVIK (1960–2000). Russian journalist and mystery writer, head of the Russian branch of the International Association of Crime Writers.

ROBERT (WRIGHT) CAMPBELL (1927–2000). Novelist and screenwriter who published some thirty mystery novels, including five as R. Wright Campbell and one as "F. G. Clinton," notably the Edgar-winning *The Junkyard Dog* (1986) and *In La-La Land We Trust* (1986).

MORRIS CARGILL (1914–2000). Jamaican journalist and radio commentator who coauthored three mysteries with John Hearne, under the pseudonym of "John Morris."

SARAH CAUDWELL (1939–2000). Well-known British lawyer and author who produced four well-received novels beginning with *Thus Was Adonis Murdered* (1981). The final novel, *The Sybil in Her Grave,* was published posthumously.

MARIAN COCKRELL (1909–1999). Coauthor, with her late husband, Frank, of a 1944 suspense novel *Dark Waters,* based on her film script. She also published a solo suspense novel, *Something Between* (1946), and later was a scriptwriter for the Alfred Hitchcock television series.

ROBERT CORMIER (1925–2000). Acclaimed author of novels for young adults including the suspense novel *I Am the Cheese* (1977), as well as the adult suspense novel *After the First Death* (1979).

SIR JULIAN CRITCHLEY (1930–2000). Member of the British Parliament and author of two suspense novels in the early 1990s, unpublished in America.

ALICE CROMIE (1914–2000). Travel writer and widow of bookman Robert Cromie, she wrote a single mystery novel, *Lucky to Be Alive* (1979).

GUY CULLINGFORD (1907–2000). Pseudonym of British author Constance Lindsay Taylor, who published nine mystery and detective novels, notably *Post Mortem* (1953).

FREDERIC DARD (1921–2000). Journalist who wrote more than 150 novels in French about Paris police superintendent "San Antonio," using his character's name as his pseudonym. About a dozen have been translated into English.

L. SPRAGUE DE CAMP (1907–2000). Famed science fiction author who published a collection of short stories, some criminous, *The Purple Pterodactyls* (1979).

NORMAN DONALDSON (1922–2000). British/American author of *In Search of Dr. Thorndyke* (1971, revised 1998), a biography of R. Austin Freeman, and a 1972 Thorndyke pastiche.

DAVID DUNCAN (1913–1999). Science-fiction writer who published five mysteries, some with fantasy overtones, notably *The Madrone Tree* (1949).

PETER EVERETT (1931–1999). British author of six suspense novels, notably *Negatives* (1964).

WILLIAM FAIRCHILD (1918–2000) British screenwriter, author of a mystery play and a single suspense novel, *The Swiss Arrangement* (1973).

STEWART FARRAR (1916–2000). British author of five mysteries, 1958–77.

TERENCE FEELY (1928–2000). British author of two mystery plays and a single suspense novel, *Limelight* (1984).

PENELOPE FITZGERALD (1916–2000). Mainstream British author whose first novel was a crime tale, *The Golden Child* (1977).

LUCILLE FLETCHER (1912–2000). Author of six suspense novels and numerous plays who achieved her greatest fame with the *Suspense* radio thriller "Sorry, Wrong Number," filmed in 1948.

FRANK V. FOWLKES (1941–2000). Banker and government advisor who wrote two suspense novels, 1976–86.

MARY FRANCIS (1924–2000). Wife of best-selling mystery writer Dick Francis, recently revealed to have been a collaborator on his novels.

THOMAS GIFFORD (1937–2000). Author of a half-dozen suspense novels under his own name, starting with *The Wind Chill Factor* (1975). He also published seven novels under the pen names "Dana Clarins" and "Thomas Maxwell," and collaborated with Edward D. Hoch on a contest novel, *The Medical Center Murders* (1984).

EDWARD GOREY (1925–2000). Artist famed for his criminous illustrations and books in a humorous vein.

WILLIAM HARRINGTON (1931–2000). Author of more than two dozen mystery and suspense novels including some historical mysteries and a half dozen novels about TV sleuth Columbo. He is also credited with twenty-one novels ghost-written under the name of Elliot Roosevelt, and acted as a "research collaborator" on some novels by Harold Robbins and Margaret Truman.

ANNE HEBERT (1916–2000). French-Canadian author whose work included at least two crime and murder novels, *Kamouraska* (1970) and *In the Shadow of the Wind* (1983).

SHEILA HOLLAND (1937–2000). Author of a single suspense novel, *The Masque* (1979).

LAURENCE JAMES (1943–2000). British author of seven suspense and intrigue novels as "Klaus Netzen," bylined in the U.S. as by "Klaus Nettson." He also collaborated with John Harvey on a suspense novel *Endgame* (1981) as by "James Mann." He is said to have published 160 novels under twenty-one different pseudonyms, including crime, historical, romance, western, horror, and science fiction.

ADRIENNE JONES (1915–2000). Coauthor with Doris Meek of two mysteries, 1953–56, one each as by "Mason Gregory" and "Gregory Mason."

TERENCE JOURNET (19??–2000). New Zealand author of four suspense novels, 1967–74, unpublished in America.

NORMAN KARK (1898–2000). Editor and publisher of The London Mystery Magazine (later London Mystery Selection) from 1951 to 1982.

JOHN KOBLER (1910–2000). Journalist and true crime writer, best known for *Capone: The Life and World of Al Capone* (1971).

DUNCAN KYLE (1930–2000). Best-known pseudonym of John Franklin Broxholme, British author of thirteen thrillers beginning with *A Cage of Ice* (1970), one of them under a second pseudonym of "James Meldrum."

ELIZABETH LEMARCHAND (1906–2000). British author of seventeen detective novels about Detective Superintendent Tom Pollard, notably *Death of an Old Girl* (1967), *The Affacombe Affair* (1968) and *Cyanide with Compliments* (1972).

Peter Levi (1931–2000). British author of three mystery novels beginning with *The Head in the Soup* (1979).

John V. Lindsay (1921–2000). Former mayor of New York City who published a novel of intrigue, *The Edge* (1976).

Edward (Ed) Linn (1922–2000). Baseball writer who collaborated with bank robber Willie Sutton on *Where the Money Was* (1976) and also wrote a single suspense novel, *The Adversaries* (1973).

Roger Longrigg (1929–2000). British author who published one crime novel under his own name but was better known in the field for his nine thrillers as "Ivor Drummond" and others under the pseudonyms of "Laura Black," "Frank Parrish," and "Domini Taylor." Perhaps his best-known novel was the noncriminous schoolgirl farce *The Passion Flower Hotel* (1962), written as "Rosalind Erskine."

J. J. Maloney (1940–1999). Author of two suspense novels starting with *I Speak for the Dead* (1982).

Atanas Petrov Mandadjiev (19??–2000). Mainstream Bulgarian author, at least ten of whose novels and stories are in the mystery genre. Cofounder of the International Association of Crime Writers and head of its Bulgarian branch.

William Maxwell (1908–2000). Longtime *New Yorker* writer and editor, whose books include a single murder novel, *So Long, See You Tomorrow* (1980).

William McCleery (1911–2000). Author of a single play about Perry Mason, *A Case for Mason* (1967).

Vincent McConnor (1907–1999). Author of eight novels, 1965–89, and numerous short stories in *EQMM, AHMM* and elsewhere.

Michael McDowell (1950–1999). Author of eight mysteries under his own name, but better known for a series of four gay mysteries under the pseudonym "Nathan Aldyne," cowritten with the late Dennis Schuetz, notably *Vermilion* (1980). The team also published two mysteries as by "Axel Young."

Neil McGaughey (1951–1999). Author of at least two detective novels beginning with *Otherwise Known as Murder* (1994).

Eloise Jarvis McGraw (1915–2000). Author of mystery, fantasy, and historical fiction for children, winner of the Edgar Award for best juvenile mystery, *A Really Weird Summer* (1978).

Fred McMorrow (1925–2000). Author and editor who published at least one story in the British edition of *Suspense* (6/59).

Charles Meyer (1947–2000). Author of the Reverend Lucas Holt mysteries, beginning with *The Saints of God Murders* (1995).

Patricia Moyes (1923–2000). Well-known British author of nineteen novels about sleuths Henry and Emmy Tibbett, notably *Dead Men Don't Ski* (1959), *Down Among the Dead Men* (1961), *Johnny Under Ground* (1965), *Murder Fantastical* (1967), and *Many Deadly Returns* (1970). A novella and twenty short stories were collected in *Who Killed Father Christmas* (1996).

N. Richard Nash (1913–2000). Playwright best known for his mainstream drama *The Rainmaker*, who also published three suspense plays, one as "N. Richard Nusbaum," a crime novel, and the espionage novel *East Wind, Rain* (1977).

Earl Norman (1915–2000). Pseudonym of Norman Thomson, author of nine paperback mysteries with Japanese and Hong Kong settings, 1958–76.

Emil Petaja (1915–2000). Science fiction and mystery author who published thirteen novels and more than one hundred short stories, including some two dozen mysteries in pulp magazines of the late 1930s and 1940s. One of his last crime stories appeared in *The Saint Magazine*, 4/67.

TALMAGE POWELL (1920–2000). Pulp writer and author of some 500 short stories and sixteen crime and western novels, one each as by "Jack McCready" and "Anne Talmage." He also ghosted four Ellery Queen paperbacks and was a frequent contributor to *Alfred Hitchcock's Mystery Magazine*. Twenty-five of his *AHMM* stories were collected as *Written for Hitchcock* (1989).

KEITH ROBERTS (1935–2000). British science fiction author and illustrator who published a single mystery, *The Road to Paradise* (1988).

ROSS RUSSELL (1909–2000). Author of at least thirteen pulp crime stories, in *Double-Action Gang Magazine* and elsewhere.

HOWARD R. SIMPSON (1925–1999). Author of seven mystery-intrigue novels, 1965–88.

CURT SIODMAK (1902–2000). Fantasy author and writer of more than seventy screenplays including *The Wolf Man*. He published four suspense novels, notably *Donovan's Brain* (1943) which has been filmed three times.

JOHN SLADEK (1937–2000). Science fiction writer who also wrote a prize-winning short story and two novels about locked-room sleuth Thackeray Phin, *Black Aura* (1974) and *Invisible Green* (1977). With Thomas M. Disch he collaborated on a suspense novel, *Black Alice* (1968), under the pseudonym of "Thom Demijohn." They also published three Gothics as "Cassandra Knye."

ANDREW L. STONE (1902–1999). Director and screenwriter who published novelizations of three of his films, 1956–58.

NIGEL TRANTER (1909–2000). Pseudonym of British author Nye Tredgold, author of thirty-seven adventure and crime novels. All but *The Stone* (1948) are unpublished in America.

MILES TRIPP (1923–2000). British author of more than thirty suspense novels beginning with *The Image of Man* (1955), plus three under the pseudonym of Michael Brett.

A. E. VAN VOGT (1912–2000). Famed science fiction author who wrote two suspense novels, *The House that Stood Still* (1950) and *The Violent Man* (1962).

PHYLLIS WHITE (1915–2000). Widow of well-known mystery writer and critic Anthony Boucher and guiding spirit of the annual Bouchercon conventions, who contributed ten poems to *EQMM*.

PETER WILDEBLOOD (1923–1999). British author of a single crime novel, *West End People* (1958), unpublished in America.

NORMAN ZOLLINGER (1921–2000). Award-winning Western writer who wrote a single mystery, *Lautrec* (1990).

# World Mystery Report: Great Britain

### Maxim Jakubowski

Any literary year necessarily has its up and downs, and the first year of the millennium adopted a familiar pattern in Britain, with a surprising number of impressive new authors emerging, older names confirming the breadth of their talent, and the best-seller breakthrough of a handful of writers, some straight from the starting gate and others an ironic overnight success, when the overnight actually took a dozen years or more.

On the other hand, menacing clouds hover over the publishing horizon, with many of the innovative smaller, independent publishers of the last decade under serious threat from radical new purchasing policies at the Waterstone's chain, which could have a sorry impact on smaller houses with fragile margins. This is a definite worry as these publishers (the Do-Not Press, Allison & Busby, Harvill Press, No Exit Press, Serpent's Tail, and others) have proven a fertile breeding ground for newer talent of an often unconventional nature (despite adverse financial returns Serpent's Tail and Harvill persist in translating overlooked foreign-language mystery authors), and have repeatedly taken risks that larger publishers, many of whom are part of multinational conglomerates, can't afford to. At year's end, Bertram's, one of the U.K.'s largest wholesalers, also warned of major cuts in their stock base, which can only work to the detriment of smaller imprints. Already author John Harvey's courageous Slow Dancer Press has called it a day, faced with the poor sales and difficult distribution.

As a former publisher myself, I realize similar gray clouds have been dominating the British book scene in one form or another for ages now, but with the changing pattern of the retail landscape (and the coming of age of e-retail), I am distinctively worried about the future and the growing obstacles for newer talents to make a mark on the scene, whether inside or outside of the crime and mystery genre. On the other hand, maybe any change in existing patterns should also be viewed with guarded optimism, as none of us can accurately read the crystal ball of the future. After all, the collapse of the British public library system a decade or so ago did result in many established crime writers who catered cozily to that market finding themselves both out of print and without publishers, and this was no bad thing, leaving openings for new voices and the flowering of a harder-edged school of British crime writing and a distinct elevation of literary standards. So only time will tell who is right. Just like a whodunit, in fact!

On the awards front, the year began in a jolly mood with Colin Dexter and Lindsey Davis winning the annual Sherlock Awards for best detectives, followed by Peter Lovesey being awarded the Diamond Dagger by the Crime Writers' Association. The CWA's end-of-year awards as usual evinced some degree of controversy because of the number of American writers on the short lists (Jonathan Lethem, Donna Leon, and Boston Teran won, although Scottish author Denise

Mina took the Short Story Dagger), but the big commercial news of the year was Ian Rankin's swift ascent of the best-seller lists, the debut of his character Inspector John Rebus on television (portrayed by John Hannah), and his ensuing crowning as a television pundit. Couldn't have happened to a nicer person or more worthy author!

Still on the small screen, Inspector Morse followed his literary demise in the adaptation of Colin Dexter's final novel *A Remorseful Death*, and Julia Wallis Martin and Gillian White also saw novels adapted for television alongside perennials like Reginald Hill, P. D. James, R. D. Wingfield, and Ruth Rendell.

On cinema screens, British gangster and crime films were sadly both unpopular and most unwelcome during the first half of the year due to a glut of bad, independent productions (many made possible by Lottery money) cobbled together with all the worst mercenary intentions in the world in imitation of the success of *Lock, Stock and Two Smoking Barrels*, mistaking blood, guts, foul language and violence for plot. Many a critic and spectator sighed at least once a month at how low some filmmakers went in the process. Unwilling to give these terrible films further publicity by even mentioning them, all I can advise you is to ignore any British crime films dated 2000 with the exception of the pithy *Ordinary Decent Criminal* (with Kevin Spacey), which took a curious lens to a tale already tackled in a more political perspective of a gang leader in Ireland. Our patience was saved by the bell, though, when Guy Ritchie's follow-up to *Lock, Stock,* emerged in the autumn and confirmed that he is a real talent (and also now Madonna's husband, of course) with a unique approach in which material (violence, obscenity, and video-style jump cuts) can mesh into an outrageously appealing whole: *Snatch* is a hoot and an able demonstration that East End gangsters don't have to be boorish and leaden. To confirm this view, Jonathan Glazer, a new director, also from the world of advertising and pop videos, had a great end-of-year debut with *Sexy Beast*, which gave British bad-boy perennial Ray Winstone a worthy role as a Brit gangster retired to the Spanish coast whose tranquility is shattered by the arrival of a past nemesis, hilariously if worryingly played by a less-than-saintly Ben Kingsley, far from his Gandhi image. So all is not lost on the cinematic front, with some further nuggets already in the can and awaiting release, which I've had the opportunity to view at festivals or private screenings.

Film and TV also played a major part in one of the year's major events, the Crime Scene Festival held at London's National Film Theatre on the South Bank in July, and now scheduled to be an annual event. Run by Adrian Wootton and Maxim Jakubowski, who used to organize Nottingham's Shots on the Page and the Nottingham Bouchercon, the event combines both literary events and screenings. This year's events attracted thousands of delegates, to meet American authors like Dennis Lehane, Elizabeth George, Robert Crais, Jeffery Deaver, and George Pelecanos and the crème de la crème of British crime writing, alongside many major film previews and retrospectives (and a Margery Allingham radio play performed on stage by Simon Brett and other thespians). The July 2001 Crime Scene will feature a major Agatha Christie section. Nottingham's natural successor, Manchester's Dead on Deansgate, was also a success and took place in October with a familiar blend of panels and events, making British crime fans spoiled for choice in the availability of events featuring their favorite authors.

Likewise, the British crime-magazine scene still thrives with all publications still going: *CADS, Crime Scene, Shots*, and *Crime Wave*, with varying degrees of regularity. Slipstream magazine *The Third Alternative* also published some crime stories. Similarly, London's two mystery bookshops still cater for all the crime in print, with Murder One now reaching the venerable age of twelve years on the fabled Charing Cross Road, and still the largest specialty bookshop in the world. Covent Garden's smaller Crime in Store, however, only survived through charitable donations openly sought from CWA members, which kept them afloat when closure loomed in the spring.

A perennial bee in bonnet of the crime community is the lack of serious review consideration afforded by major newspapers and publications. This is now very much on the mend, with prestigious critics from the field holding secure positions at leading and influential titles: Donna Leon at the Sunday *Times*, Marcel Berlins at *The Times*, Mark Timlin at *The Independent* on Sunday, Peter Guttridge at *The Observer*, Frances Fyfield and Tim Binyon at the *Evening Standard*, Val McDermid at *The Manchester Evening News* and Maxim Jakubowski at *The Guardian*. Mike Ripley lost his Sunday *Telegraph* platform but moved to the regional *Birmingham Post* following the death of Bill Pardoe.

Like any year, this was also one of regret, with the passing of authors and close friends Patricia Moyes and Sarah Caudwell just months apart. Other casualties of the year include Miles Tripp, Laurence James, Duncan Kyle, Elizabeth Lemarchand, and Roger Longrigg (Domini Taylor, Frank Parrish).

And so to a year in books: 2000 began with a bang with a controversial debut that went straight onto the best-seller lists, Mo Hayder's *Birdman*, a serial-killer novel that was disliked by many but whose dark power reached out far beyond the specialized crime readership (as had John Connolly's *Every Dead Thing* the year before). Mo Hayder was a godsend to publicists with her blond film-star looks, murky past, and shy demeanor, but I reckon she is a major talent and here to stay. Another left-of-field blockbuster appeared in the Spring as a paperback original: Jake Arnott's *The Long Firm*, a sardonic and powerful tale inspired by the notorious Kray brothers East End empire of thuggery, with a strong gay, ironic voice that made it very much a word-of-mouth success. This was soon to be followed by J. J. Connolly's *Layer Cake*, another first-person tale of a career criminal whose world is collapsing around him, another literary debut sparkling with zest and originality. All three books, although undoubtedly belonging to the crime and mystery genre, were not marketed as such, which allows a pause for thought, but then neither of the authors originated within the crime community. This is a trend that is accelerating in Britain, with so many new, younger authors adopting the genre as matter of course, regardless of clichés and traditions. A healthy trend, if you ask me.

The year also began with Ian Rankin's *Set in Darkness*, the twelfth Inspector Rebus, and the novel that established his unchallenged domination of the best-selling lists, where most of his backlist camped throughout the year. (At one stage his novels occupied eight of the top fifteen positions on the Scottish best-seller lists!) Many other well-established writers came out with new books: Michael Gilbert, still active in his eighties, with *The Mathematics of Murder*, a short-story collection; Catherine Aird (*Little Knell*); Simon Brett (*The Body on the Beach*); Natasha Cooper (*Prey to All*); Ruth Dudley-Edwards (the comedic *Anglo-Irish*

*Murders*); Jonathan Gash (*Die Dancing*, featuring his new heroine Dr. Clare Burtonall); Paula Gosling (*Underneath Every Stone*); Reginald Hill (*Arms and the Woman*); Sarah Caudwell (the posthumous *The Sirens Sang of Murder*, which sadly only appeared in the U.S.A.); Bill James (*Kill Me*); Margaret Yorke (*A Case to Answer*); June Thomson (*The Unquiet Grave*); Quintin Jardine (with two books: *Screen Savers*, featuring Oz Blackstone, and *Thursday's Legends*, featuring Skinner); Val McDermid (*Killing in the Shadows*); H. R. F. Keating (another recidivist, with *The Last Detective*, and his final Inspector Ghote mystery, *Breaking and Entering*); Nicolas Freeling (*Some Day Tomorrow*); Martina Cole (*Broken*, another of her wildly successful East End gangster moll sagas, which outsell most other better-known British authors by a mile and more); Michael Dibdin (*Thanksgiving*, a haunting, elegiac noir excursion that disappointed many reviewers used to his pithy Inspector Zen chronicles, but which I adored); Roy Lewis (*Forms of Death*); Jo Bannister (*Changelings*); Robert Barnard (*Unholy Dying*); W. J. Burley (*Wycliffe and the Sign of Nine*); Gwendoline Butler (*A Coffin for Christmas*); Ann Granger (*Shades of Murder*); Agatha Christie . . . well, a novelized play by the great Christie expanded by Charles Osborne, *The Spiders Web*; Janet Laurence (*The Mermaid's Feast*); Frances Fyfield (*Undercurrents*); Peter Lovesey (*The Reaper*); Minette Walters (*The Shape of Snakes*); Dick Francis (*Shattered*, which might turn out to be his final book, following the death of his wife, Mary, with whom he collaborated); and Ruth Rendell twice, with a story collection, *Piranha to Scurfy*, as herself, and *Grasshopper* as "Barbara Vine."

The above list would make for an incomparable feast of mystery writing by any standards, but was restricted to well-established writers. To confirm the incomparable choice afforded to British readers, here is another necessarily abbreviated rundown of books published in 2000 by authors who have already made a distinct mark on the crime and mystery scene over the past decade; many of these will be the stars of tomorrow: John Baker (*The Chinese Girl*); Hilary Bonner (*Deep Deceit*); Russell James (*Painting in the Dark*); Carol Anne Davis (*Noise Abatement*); Janet Neel (*O Gentle Death*); Ken Bruen (*The McDead*, the final volume in his White underworld trilogy); Paul Charles (*The Ballad of Sean and Wilko*); Lee Child (*The Visitor*); Judith Cutler (*Dying by Degrees, Power Games*); Leslie Forbes (*Skin, Shadow and Bone*); Elizabeth Corley (*Fatal Legacy*); Kate Ellis (*The Funeral Boat*); Patricia Hall (*Skeleton at the Feast*); Paul Johnson (*The Blood Tree*); Frank Lean (*Boiling Point*); Phil Lovesey (*When Ashes Burn*); Jim Lusby (*Crazy Man Michael*); Barry Maitland (*Silvermeadow*); Veronica Stallwood (*Oxford Shadows*); Margaret Murphy (*Dying Embers*). Notable newcomers included Stephen Booth (*Black Dog*); Joolz Denby (*Stone Baby*); Stephen Humphreys (*Sleeping Partner*); Mary Scott (*Murder on Wheels*); David Aitken (*Sleeping with Jane Austen*); and Sarah Diamond (*The Beach Road*).

In the promises-confirmed department, many young writers demonstrated that their raved-over early steps were not flukes and are on the fast track for stardom; they include Martyn Bedford (*Black Cat*, an impressive follow-up to the haunting *The Houdini Girl*); Nicholas Royle (*The Director's Cut*); Patrick Redmond (*The Puppet Show*); Lauren Henderson (*Chained*, featuring the indomitable Sam Jones), who was also a founder and chief troublemaker of the Tart Noir group (and Web site) of politically incorrect female writers with attitude, which also enlisted Sparkle Hayter, Katy Munger, and Stella Duffy; Laura Wilson (*Dying*

*Voices*); John Williams (*Cardiff Dead*); Jane Adams (*Angels Gateway*); and Denise Mina (*Exile*, which might still win her a third award in three years!).

Three distinct niches in crime and mystery writing have always proven particularly suited to the British and in all three subgenres, they again excelled. Fueled by ever-increasingly popularity, the historical mystery continues to thrive and among the year's offerings were Lindsey Davis (*Ode to a Banker*); Alys Clare (*Ashes of the Elements; Tavern in the Morning*); Judith Cook (*School of the Night*); Paul Doherty, prolific as ever (*The Treason of the Ghosts*, featuring Hugh Corbett, and *The Anubis Slayings*, set in Ancient Egypt); Susanna Gregory (*Masterly Murder*); Philip Gooden (*Sleep of Death*); Michael Jecks (*The Traitor of St. Giles, The Boy Bishop's Glovemaker*); Bernard Knight (*An Awful Secret*); Hannah Marsh— alias Tim Godwin (*Distraction of the Blood; Death Be My Theme*); Iain Pears (the long-awaited *Immaculate Deception*); Kate Sedley (*St. John's Fern*); Peter Tremayne (with a double dose of Sister Fidelma, a collection of stories *Hemlock at Vespers* and a novel, *Our Lady of Darkness*); Sylvan Hamilton (*The Bone Peddlar*); Deryn Lake (*Death at the Apothecary's Hall*); Edward Marston (*The Amorous Nightingale, The Elephants of Norwich*); Barbara Nadel (*A Chemical Prison*); Michael Pearce (*A Cold Touch of Ice*); Marilyn Todd (*The Black Salamander*); Gillian Linscott (*Perfect Daughter*); and David Wishart (*Old Bones*). On similar form were the exponents of comic crime, including Christopher Brookmyre (*Boiling a Frog*); Marc Blake (*24 Carat Schmooze*); Peter Guttridge (*The Once and Future Con*); and Charles Spencer (*Under the Influence*).

The end of the cold war hasn't slowed British thriller writers down, and they continue to find murky territory to explore. Pride of place naturally goes to John Le Carré for *The Constant Gardener*, a major return to form, but one must also mention Raymond Benson's latest James Bond adventure *Double or Death*; Colin Forbes (*Sinister Tide*); Clive Egelton (*The Honey Trap*); Ken Follett (*Code to Zero*); Robert Goddard (*Sea Change*); Michael Ridpath (*Final Venture*); Brian Freemantle (a Charlie Muffin caper, *Dead Men Living*); Donald James (*Vadim*, the third and maybe final volume in his brilliant near-future post–civil-war Russia police procedural series); and Peter May (*The Killing Room*). Over the past decade, a strong individual strain of distinctly British noir writing, both influenced and distanced from its American model, has established itself and echoes of it can be seen in many of the books and authors mentioned above in various categories. Some writers, however, stand on their own, and are at the vanguard of this movement. Many also published new books in 2000, and they include John Connolly (*Dark Hollow*); Mike Phillips (*A Shadow of Myself*); Jerry Raine (*Slaphead Chameleon*); Martyn Waites (*Candleland*); Mark Timlin (*All the Empty Places*); Maxim Jakubowski (*On Tenderness Express*); Boris Starling (*Storm*); Rob Ryan (*Nine Mil*); and the Tokyo-based David Peace, who offered the second volume of his searing Yorkshire quartet *1977*, confirming the promise of his debut *1974*.

Possibly affected by the number of magazines currently hosting a platform for short stories, only three anthologies appeared this year. Martin Edwards edited a final CWA volume *Scenes of the Crime*, while the undersigned published the third, and also final volume, in his series of historical mystery collections initially set up in homage to the late Ellis Peters. *Murder Through the Ages* featured many of the usual suspects from British, U.S., and European shores. I also managed to showcase various mystery writers (including Val McDermid, Nicholas Blincoe,

Stella Duffy, Denise Danks, and Manda Scott) in a collection of stories inspired by the Internet *The New English Library Book of Internet Stories.*

Lest the reader think I have indulged in sheer list-making above, I'm pleased to point out that the titles and writers mentioned in the course of this retrospective only cover a quarter of so of the books by British authors published in the U.K. in 2000. An indication, if one were needed, of the health of the genre on these shores. Long may it continue.

# World Mystery Report: Australia

## David Honeybone and Lucy Sussex

The Ned Kelly Awards for Australian Crime Writing were revived in 2000 after a hiatus of several years, and were presented at the Night Cat Bar, Fitzroy, on August 31, to coincide with the Melbourne Writer's Festival. Apart from the awards, the highlight of the evening was a spirited debate between a motley bunch of crime writers, journalists, and lawyers on the subject of "Is truth stronger than fiction?" On the Truth side were crime writers Carolyn Morwood, Shane Maloney, Peter Temple, and Liz Gaynor, QC (Queen's Counsel); on the Fiction side were author Barry Dickens, crime journalist John Silvester, and QCs John Smallwood (married to Gaynor), and Doug Salek. U.S. author Laurie King was also in attendance, and had the Australian idioms translated for her by Sue Turnbull. For the first time, true-crime writing was included in the Nonfiction category.

The winners of the Ned Kelly Awards were as follows:

Best Novel: *Shooting Star* by Peter Temple (Bantam)

Best First Novel: *The Wooden Leg of Inspector Anders* by Marshall Browne (Duffy & Snellgrove)

Best True Crime: *Huckstepp* by John Dale (Allen & Unwin); *Rule and Silvester*, Underbelly 3 (Sly Ink)

Perhaps the most controversy of the year was produced by Inez Baranay's article for the *Australian Author* (May 2000) "Oz Cri-Fi in the Gun," a cover story with the subheading "Has Australian gumshow gone off the boil?" She took the position that crime writing in Australia was in a sorry state, languishing unread, with writers not delivering fiction suited to the local market's needs—although Baranay did quote various authors and publishers who strongly disagreed. In any case, the healthy amount of local crime publishing during the year, despite the imposition of a 10 percent goods and services tax on books, which raised their retail prices, would seem to belie Baranay's article.

The last quarter of the year saw new books from established writers including: Peter Temple's third Jack Irish book, *Dead Point*, (Bantam); and Andrew Masterson's sacrilegious and highly amusing *The Second Coming* (HarperCollins), featuring messiah turned P. I. Joe Panther. Shane Maloney's fourth Murray Whelan book, *The Big Ask* (Text), was launched at Readings Bookshop in Melbourne by Opposition Leader Kim Beazley, with various state and federal Labor party politicians rubbing shoulders with the crime fans. Peter Doyle has written a prequel to his award-winning books *Get Rich Quick* and *Amaze Your Friends* set in Sydney in the 1950s. *The Devil's Jump* (Arrow) features a young Billy Glasheen and charts his early apprenticeship as a "lurk" merchant at the end of the war. Shamus winner Marele Day made a brief but welcome to the crime fold, by collecting her Mavis Levack short detective stories (an Australian Miss Marple) as

*Mavis Levack, P. I.* (Allen and Unwin), in which her main series detective Claudia Valentine also makes an appearance.

Janis Spehr won the Scarlet Stiletto Award for the second year running with her story "Dead Woman in the Water." Sydney crime writer Gabrielle Lord presented the awards in Melbourne.

It was also quite a good year for exhibitions devoted to the subject of crime fiction. The Baillieu Library, University of Melbourne, included much crime in its "Sensational Tales: Australian Popular Publishing 1890s–1990s" exhibit. In Sydney, the Justice and Police Museum was host to "Hardboiled: the Detective in Popular Fiction," which ran every weekend until October 2001. A continuing exhibition at the State Library of Victoria is "Cover Girl Cries Murder: Australian Pulp Fiction of the 1950s," largely showcasing the library's important recent acquisition of work by Marc Brody (Melbourne journalist W. H. Williams), a collection of seventy-two novels that were the author's own copies. Other pulp fictions on display were by "Carter Brown," "Larry Kent," and rare items by "K. T. McCall," once billed as "crime fiction's best-selling female author." Text also reprinted a blast from Australian crime fiction's past with *The Murder of Madeleine Brown*, originally published in 1887 by the socialist poet Francis Adams. The introduction, marred only by a lack of references, was by Shane Maloney.

The Australian crime-film sensation of the year was *Chopper*, the true story of criminal Mark Read, which won A.F.I. awards for best direction, best actor, and supporting actor. It was also featured at Sundance Film Festival. The film version of Dorothy Porter's award-winning detective novel-poem, *The Monkey's Mask*, was released in March 2001, along with a tie-in edition of the book from Pan-Macmillan. Paul Thomas has had his character Tito Ihaka transferred to the television. New Zealander Thomas, who won the inaugural Ned Kelly Award for *Inside Dope*, wrote the screenplay for "Ihaka Blunt Instrument" which was screened by Channel Ten. The tough Maori cop visits Sydney, ostensibly on a training exercise, only to find himself solving a long-closed case with the help of a female federal officer.

*Crime Factory* is a new Australian crime magazine. The first issue was published in February 2001. Predominantly concerned with crime fiction, it also includes a section devoted to true crime. The first issue has interviews with prolific Melbourne writer Kerry Greenwood, Tami Hoag, Edna Buchanan, and Edward Bunker. For further information see www.crimefactory.net.

# World Mystery Report: Canada

*Edo van Belkom*

Although most lovers of mystery and crime fiction might not consider it a work that's truly in genre, the most talked about and celebrated Canadian crime novel of 2000 is probably Margaret Atwood's *The Blind Assassin*. Atwood's tenth novel is a family drama that delves into the seedy underworld of the 1930s, replete with references to pulp fiction gin joints and the rest of the period's staples. The book won the coveted 2000 Booker Prize and is a top contender for all of the usual Canadian literary honors, such as the Governor General's Award. A more traditional crime novel that garnered plenty of attention within the genre is *Deadly Decisions*, the third novel by forensic anthropologist and best-selling author Kathy Reichs.

As crime novelists, Atwood and Reichs are as dissimilar as two writers can be (one is a "literary writer" and the other is a scientist moonlighting as a mystery author), but in a somewhat roundabout way they are both in the same boat and indicative of the sort of thing that goes on in all Canadian literary genres.

Canadians are eager to embrace someone like Atwood as a crime novelist because her inclusion validates the genre as a whole. Atwood was the subject of a similar inclusion when her novel *The Handmaid's Tale* was pronounced to be science fiction, a label she rejected at every opportunity. And Reichs, while only spending six months of the year working for the Quebec government—the other half is spent in North Carolina where she works in the office of the chief medical examiner and is a professor at the University of North Carolina—is still considered Canadian by her Canadian publisher, Canadian booksellers, and Canadian awards administrators.

The truth is that there are many great crime and mystery novels published each year by Canadians living year-round in that country and publishing all of their works in the genre. The year 2000 saw the publication of new novels by John Ballem (*Machineel*); Gail Bowen (*Burying Ariel*); Laurence Gough (*Funny Money*); Lyn Hamilton (*The Celtic Riddle*); Kenneth Oppel (*The Devil's Cure*); Caroline Roe—a.k.a. Medora Sale (*Solace For a Sinner*); and Eric Wright (*The Kidnapping Of Rosie Dawn*). Other notable books included *Hangman* by Michael Slade, a pseudonym, this time for Vancouver lawyer Jay Clarke and his daughter Rebecca; and *Evil Never Sleeps*, written by real-life police detective K. G. E. Konkel. Also, Peter Robinson published a new Inspector Banks novel called *Cold Is the Grave*. Robinson, a transplanted Brit, enjoys dual literary citizenship—much like Reichs—and is Canadian while in Canada but claimed by the British whenever he lands in the U.K., which is a couple of times a year.

A couple of short-fiction publications of note were a pair of anthologies associated with the Crime Writers of Canada. First is the *Arthur Ellis Awards* anthology, edited by Peter Sellers, and published by Quarry Press (P.O. Box 1061,

Kingston, Ontario, K7L 4Y5). The book features a history of the CWC, the first twelve winners of the Best Mystery Short Story from 1988 to 1999, a complete list of Ellis Award nominees during that period, and a list of international award–winning works by Canadians. All royalties from the book go to the CWC to help pay for the ongoing administration of the awards. The second anthology is *Over the Edge*, a reprint anthology featuring works by members of the CWC, edited by Peter Sellers and Robert J. Sawyer, and published by Pottersfield Press (83 Leslie Rd. East Lawrencetown, N.S., B3Z 1P8).

Toronto played host to the seventeenth annual Arthur Ellis Awards banquet in May with a satellite awards dinner held simultaneously on the West Coast in an RCMP officers' mess. Winners of this year's hangman's trophy were:

Best Novel: *The Feast of Stephen*, Rosemary Aubert

Best True Crime: *Cowboys and Indians*, Gordon Sinclair Jr.

Best First Crime Novel: *Lost Girls*, Andrew Pyper

Best Short Story: "One More Kill" (from *Blue Murder Magazine*), Matt Hughes

Best Juvenile Novel: *How Can a Brilliant Detective Shine in the Dark?* Linda Bailey

Best Novel (French): *Louna*, Lionel Noel.

In addition the CWC honored four volunteers who had served the organization over the past sixteen years with the Derrick Murdoch Award: Eddie Barber, Rick Blechta, John North, and David Skene-Melvin.

Finally, no year-end roundup would be complete without a mention of Bloody Words. In its second year, Bloody Words (www.bloodywords.com) is Canada's only annual mystery conference, taking place in Toronto each June. This year's guest of honor was L. R. Wright, while special guests were Howard Engel and Caroline Roe (Medora Sale) and McClelland and Stewart editor Dinah Forbes.

# World Mystery Report: Germany

*Thomas Woertche*

The year 2000 saw a radical change concerning the German mystery market that affected most German authors of the genre. The German crime-fiction/suspense market is strongly dominated by foreign authors, especially Americans. But that is true for all of Europe; even the British complain about "U.S. steamrolling." Compared to Britain, however, Germany has always suffered an enormous contradiction (due to the nearly complete lack of crime-fiction tradition) between quantity and quality, i.e., the large number of crime writers and their books and the tiny number of those among them who have international reputations.

What happened last year, thanks to the general and international "concentration on the book market," is that most of the big publishing companies closed down their traditional and established crime lines. Classics like rororo Thriller (Rowohlt Publishers' famous "black line") vanished as well as the not-less-famous Gelbe Reihe ("yellow line") of Ullstein Publishers, the Goldmann Krimis, the Heyne Krimis (of, respectively, Goldmann, a division of Bertelsmann, and Heyne Publishers). That means that a lot of authors of solidly woven "pret-a-porter" novels lost their publishing grounds. They had to seek asylum with either print-on-demand alternatives—and that kind of publisher, like Verlag der Criminale, popped up almost immediately—or with small publishing houses. Some of the latter, like Grafit Verlag in Dortmund or the rather recently founded Militzke Verlag in Leipzig, did have some reputation before, mostly as a forum for regional to national literature. For them it was, of course, also a chance to broaden their programs. Edition Trèves in Trier got more sophisticated, and Emons Verlag in Cologne even includes fashionable period pieces now, from medieval times to eighteenth-century backgrounds.

With big companies closing down crime-fiction lines, the readers and aficionados of crime fiction of course do not vanish. And the big publishers do indeed take care of them by displaying global blockbusters such as Tom Clancy, Patricia Cornwell, Mary Higgins Clark, Elizabeth George et al. Again, this is true for Europe as a whole, but there are differences. Swedish best-seller Henning Mankell for example is top-selling in Germany too, whereas American Donna Leon, with her Venice-based novels, is a German top-seller only.

The most interesting side effect stemming from the big companies genre-list shutdown has been mostly ignored in public debate. Mystery novels, suspense, crime fiction, these subgenres of fiction, are no longer labeled as such in the big companies' catalogs. It's "integrated," and that means "lost," in their mainstream lines. The label now is simply "novel." The result: the term "genre" is back where it used to be until two decades ago—equal to bad, low stuff.

However, there are promising counterwaves. The small Distel-Verlag in Heilbronn, for instance, recently started a completely new line, specializing in classic and new French writers, cooperating with the famous "Serie noir" of Paris publisher Gallimard. Unionsverlag in Zürich, Switzerland, started its "UT metro" line in spring 2000, presenting suspense fiction not from the usual sources—Anglo-Saxon fields like the U.S. or the U.K.—but from literally all over the world: Asia, Africa, Latin America, Australia, and Europe (including Turkey).

The consequences of these changes are enormous for most of the German-writing and German-speaking authors. Last decade's "scene kings and queens"—made not primarily by broad audiences but by opinion leaders of the very scene itself—like Ingrid Noll, Doris Gercke, Sabine Deitmer, Peter Zeindler (Swiss), Jürgen Alberts, Regula Venske, et al. are remarkably silent. It seems as though the readers (and buyers) are tired of all the middle-class cozies and "diaper mysteries."

The situation is well reflected in the 2000 awards for crime fiction. The Glauser, an annual award of German-language crime-writers club Syndikat was given to Uta-Maria Heim for her novel *Engelchens Ende*. Syndikat represents a large number of authors, but actually very few of even national importance. Uta-Maria Heim is a good writer and *not* part of that network, and so it's a little sensation that someone from "outside" got last year's Glauser.

Even more significant for the change is the German Mystery Award (Deutscher Krimipreis) for 2000. While the Glauser comes with DM 10,000 (about $4,500), the Deutscher Krimipreis does not include money. But it is the award with the highest prestige—it cannot be manipulated. It has a national (meaning German-language) and an international category. The national winner for 2000 was Ulrich Ritzel's *Schwemmholz* (published by a tiny Swiss publisher, Libelle Verlag). In second place was Ann Chaplet's *Nichts als die Wahrheit* (by Verlag Antje Kunstmann, Munich, an independent mainstream publisher), and coming in third was Sam Jaun's *Fliegender Sommer* (by another tiny Swiss publisher, Cosmos Verlag).

Ritzel's novel is his second. He used to be a courtroom and police reporter in a small southern German town. Sam Jaun is Swiss, living partly in Berlin, who comes up with a new Swiss-countryside mystery about every seven years.

Many other authors who have been acclaimed and accepted by the readers during the last year are either complete outsiders or newcomers, like Horst Eckert, Jürg Juretzka, or Heinrich Steinfeld and Wolf Haas (both of Vienna, Austria). Munich writer Friedrich Ani's fine novel *German Angst* had a likewise fine success and Tobias O. Meissner published the season's most interesting novel, *Todestag* (by Eichborn Verlag), about a fatal assault on Chancellor Schröder. *Todestag*, unlike most of the present German-language fiction in general, is serious and even thrilling literature.

In short, the borderline between "genre" and "mainstream" seems to be blurred not only by the big companies' politics but also by the fact that it looks as if authors and their representatives are submitting to this trend. That *could* be a positive signal—but I doubt that optimism makes sense here. German mainstream literature—i.e., "high" literature—is famous (and notorious) for its general refusal to narrate reality. But that's exactly crime fiction's finest tradition—and Germany's reality offers material galore for writers to return to the pure, raw storytelling of the genre. Some of them have never lost that strain and likewise never renounced literary quality. Pieke Biermann, for instance, who brought acknowledgment of crime fiction to the literary pages with her series of novels about a Berlin homicide squad, is now working on a street-cop novel. For, in the slightly modified words of the wonderful Bob Truluck, "All in all, street level is where crime fiction belongs."

# The 2000 Short Story Edgar Awards

*Camille Minichino*
*Chair, Edgar Short Story Committee, 2000*

Here's an image I can't shake: a nervous ex-con thrusts a five-inch blade into the pulsating throat of a cow, slitting it from ear to ear, and retches as blood pours out like shiny red glass, the stench of manure in the background. Clark Howard's "The Killing Floor" puts you in a slaughterhouse and keeps you there long after you've finished the story. A standout in a year of more than 500 short stories.

At first my new assignment was exciting—day after day, padded envelopes from UPS, priority U.S. mail cartons, chunky FedEx packages, all filled with FREE books and magazines, delivered to my door!

The Edgar Short Story submissions.

Then I realized I had to read them all—every issue of *Ellery Queen Mystery Magazine, Alfred Hitchcock Mystery Magazine, Futures, Blue Murder,* and assorted e-zines. Anthologies like *Deadly Dozen, Crime Through Time III, Malice Domestic, Unholy Orders.* Not only that, I had to *handle* them. Create a database, log in authors, from Abbott, Jeff in *Magnolias and Mayhem,* to Zackel, Frederick in *Carvezine.*

Some people think there are already enough Edgars; that the Awards Banquet goes on far too long. Not me. In fact, since not every story has everything the reader is looking for, I'd add a few categories. Best Female Character, for one. For this I'd pick the overweight Patricia—sweating and straining against the pedals of a stationary bike, planning revenge on her condescending aerobics instructor ("Spinning," by Kristine Kathryn Rusch, *EQMM,* July).

Why not a Best Title Award—maybe "Taking Out Mr. Garbage" (Judith Kelman, *Murder Among Friends*) or "Jesus Kicks Some" (Bruce F. Murphy, *Blue Murder Magazine,* October/November). For Best Weapon, I'd choose the leg of lamb ("Copycat," Joan Myers, *Deadly Dozen*). And I'd love to create a Best Pet-Free Story Award (the excellence of "Twelve of the Little Buggers" by Mat Coward in *EQMM,* for January notwithstanding). I'd give the Far Out Award to the ingenious story featuring quantum teleportation (it's not just for photons anymore) from Michael Burstein ("The Quantum Teleporter," *Analog* magazine, February), or to the talking doll in "Chatty Patty" (Taylor McCafferty, *Magnolias and Mayhem*). A Cliché Award might balance all the positives—this year: *like a deer in the headlights* (you know who you are).

In the complaint department: too many stories fell short of true mystery, better labeled "best-kept secret stories." A sample of unsatisfying denouements: the bride was really not his grandchild; third-party confessions such as I-saw-your-mother-murder-your-father (or vice versa); and one story where I, the cop, killed my partner's daughter—all delivered in a *telling* fashion. And, of course, there were the too-cute endings, like "he" was really the dog (or cat), not the husband.

For me, "Missing in Action" (Peter Robinson, *EQMM*, November) had it all. Imagine weaving a story about a missing child around his mother's speech impediment.

The whole truth: it's awesome to have almost the entire body of short stories of the year 2000 in front of me, in an overflowing maroon crate.

To all of you who wrote these stories, thanks. Really. Be sure we were honored to consider your work and to give every submission careful attention.

Edgar Awards 2000—Short Story Honorable Mentions:

Doug Allyn, "The Christmas Mitzvah," *Ellery Queen's Mystery Magazine*, December; Denise Barton, "The Ticket," *Futures*, February–March; Beverly "Booger" Brackett, *Handheld Crime*; Michael Burstein, "The Quantum Teleporter," *Analog*, September; Hal Charles, "Slave Wall," *EQMM*, February; Terrence Faherty, "The Third Manny," *EQMM*, February; John M. Floyd, "Blue Wolf," *Alfred Hitchcock's Mystery Magazine*, February; Ed Gorman, "Anna and the Players," *EQMM*, November; Tony Hickie, "Decimation," *AHMM*, March; Edward D. Hoch, "The Fading Woman," *EQMM*, April; Clark Howard, "The Killing Floor," Crippen & Landru; Rob Kantner, "My Best Fred McMurray," *AHMM*, October; Rochelle Krich, "Widow's Peak," *Unholy Orders*; Taylor McCafferty, "Chatty Patty," *Magnolias and Mayhem*; Sharyn McCrumb, "Lark in the Morning," *Crime Through Time III*; Joan Myers, "Copycat," *Deadly Dozen*; Tom Tolnay, "The Stealing Progression," *EQMM*, August; Alison White, "The Bluebird," *EQMM*, February; William Sanders, "Smoke," *Crime Through Time III*; Walter Satterthwaite, "Missolongi," *AHMM*, October; Lisa Seidman, "Over My Shoulder," *Deadly Dozen*; Serita Stevens, "The Unborn," *Nefarious*; Steven Saylor, "The Consul's Wife," *Crime Through Time III*; Peter Straub, "Porkpie Hat," *Magic Terror*.

# The Year 2000 in Mystery Fandom

*George A. Easter*

The American public buys and reads millions of mysteries every week. Most lovers of the mystery genre are content simply with the enjoyment of reading good crime novels. But there are several thousand who are so interested in the genre that they require more. These are the mystery fans who make up mystery fandom.

Mystery fans form and attend local mystery reading groups; they collect paperback and/or hardcover first editions; they go online and contribute to such sites as Dorothy L; they haunt their local mystery bookstores and attend author signings; they subscribe to mystery publications; and finally, they attend mystery conventions.

## MYSTERY CONVENTIONS 2000

The Big Kahuna of annual mystery conventions is Bouchercon, the international mystery convention named for Anthony Boucher, noted deceased mystery critic, which was held in Denver in September, 2000. (Bouchercon 2001 will be in Washington, D.C. in November, 2001.) The guest of honor was the venerable Elmore Leonard who entertained us with his crusty sense of humor. Also honored was Jane Langton, the recipient of a Lifetime Achievement Award, who mesmerized us with her wit, charm and gentility.

Earlier in the year a wonderful regional convention called Left Coast Crime (situated each year somewhere in the Western United States in February or March) was held in Tucson, Arizona. Sue Grafton was the guest of honor and Harlan Coben acted as toastmaster for the banquet. These smaller regional conventions (500–600 attendees) are more relaxed than a Bouchercon. The authors in attendance are not meeting with their agents, publishers, or publicists and so have more time to chat with the fans. Each convention has a book dealers room with lots and lots of new and used books for sale. If you plan on attending a convention, be prepared to exceed any mental budget you may set for book purchases.

Another very popular mystery convention is Malice Domestic, which is held each year in Arlington, Virginia. The purpose of this convention is to celebrate the "traditional" mystery, sometimes referred to as the "cozy" mystery (containing little or no violence, profanity or sex).

The guest of honor was the highly-entertaining Simon Brett and the toastmaster was Eileen Dryer. The fans who attended the convention voted on the Agatha Awards (see below).

## MYSTERY FAN AWARDS 2000

The major fan awards in mystery fiction are the Anthony Awards, the Agatha Awards, the Macavity Awards, and the Barry Awards. Following are the awards that were won in the year 2000, for works published in 1999.

### ANTHONY AWARDS 2000

Voted on by attendees of Bouchercon, 2000
> Best Novel: Peter Robinson, *In a Dry Season*
> Best First Novel: Donna Andrews, *Murder With Peacocks*
> Best Paperback Original: Laura Lippman, *In Big Trouble*
> Best Short Story: Margaret Chittenden, "Noir Life," *EQMM 1/99*
> Best Critical Nonfiction: Willetta Heising, *Detecting Women*, 3rd edition
> Best Series of the Century: Agatha Christie's Hercule Poirot
> Best Writer of the Century: Agatha Christie
> Best Novel of the Century: Daphne du Maurier, *Rebecca*

### AGATHA AWARDS 2000

Voted on by attendees of the Malice Domestic XII Convention
> Best Novel: Earlene Fowler, *Mariner's Compass*
> Best First Novel: Donna Andrews, *Murder with Peacocks*.
> Best Nonfiction: Daniel Stashower, *Teller of Tales: The Life of Arthur Conan Doyle*
> Best Short Story: Nancy Pickard, "Out of Africa" in *Mom, Apple Pie, and Murder*

### MACAVITY AWARDS 2000

Voted on by subscribers to *Mystery Readers International Journal*
> Best Novel: Sujata Massey, *The Flower Master*
> Best First Novel: Paula L. Woods, *Inner City Blues*
> Best Nonfiction: Tom Nolan, *Ross Macdonald*
> Best Short Story: Kate Grilley, "Maubi and the Jumbies" in *Murderous Intent*, Fall 1999

### BARRY AWARDS 2000

Voted on by subscribers of *Deadly Pleasures* magazine
> Best Novel: Peter Robinson, *In A Dry Season*
> Best First Novel: Donna Andrews, *Murder With Peacocks*
> Best British Crime Novel: Val McDermid, *A Place Of Execution*
> Best Paperback Original: Robin Burcell, *Every Move She Makes*

## MYSTERY MAGAZINES 2000

One of the most popular ways mystery fans keep up with what is going on in the field is by subscribing to one or more mystery magazines. The most popular of the current fan magazines are:

*Drood Review*, published bi-monthly for a yearly cost of $17.00. Articles and reviews in a newsletter format. 484 E. Carmel Dr., #378, Carmel, IN 46032 or order at www.droodreview.com.

*Mystery News*, published bi-monthly for a yearly cost of $20.00. Newspaper format includes cover interview, columns, articles, many reviews and a listing of current and upcoming books. Black Raven Press, PMB 152, 262 Hawthorn Village Commons, Vernon Hills, IL 60061 or order at www.blackravenpress.com.

*Mystery Readers International Journal*, published quarterly for a yearly cost of $24.00. Each issue treats a mystery theme. Calendar year 2001 will feature New England Mysteries, Partners in Crime, Oxford, and Cambridge. P.O. Box 8116, Berkeley, CA 94707 or order at www.mysteryreaders.org.

*Mystery Scene*, published five times a year for a yearly cost of $32.00. Eighty-eight pages of articles and reviews. Heavy emphasis on author contributions. 3601 Skylark Lake SE, Cedar Rapids, IA 52403.

*Deadly Pleasures*, published quarterly, for a yearly cost of $14.00. Eighty pages of articles, reviews, news, and regular columns, including the popular Reviewed to Death column. P.O. Box 969, Bountiful, UT 84011 or order at www.deadlypleasures.com.

## CHANGING OF THE MYSTERY GUARD 2000

Each year the mystery fiction genre experiences a changing of the guard. Long-time mystery fans mourn the deaths of some of the old guard and celebrate the arrival of some very talented newcomers. The year 2000 saw the passing of Sarah Caudwell, Robert W. Campbell, Duncan Kyle, Lucille Fletcher, Elizabeth Lemarchand, Patricia Moyes, Roger Longrigg (known to most by one of his three pen names, Ivor Drummond, Frank Parrish, or Domini Taylor) and Miles Tripp. And it saw the first novels published by future stars Stephen Horn, Mo Hayter, David Liss, Scott Phillips, Bob Truluck, Sheldon Siegel, Qiu Xiaolong and Glynn Marsh Alam.

# The World's
# Finest Mystery and
# Crime Stories

*Second Annual Collection*

# Kristine Kathryn Rusch

## Spinning

KRISTINE KATHRYN RUSCH has spent most of her professional life working in the fields of science fiction and fantasy. She
has also done significant editing in those fields, most notably as the
previous editor of *The Magazine of Fantasy & Science Fiction*. And
then she became a crime-fiction writer. Like that. Suddenly, suspense stories bloomed from that contraption on her desk just as
science fiction once had. And what stories they've been. Last year,
under the name Kris Nelscott, she debuted her first crime series
with the novel *A Dangerous Road*. We're pleased to present two of
the several of her stories published this year. First, "Spinning,"
which appeared in the July issue of *Ellery Queen's Mystery Magazine,* and may be her best story yet.

# Spinning

*Kristine Kathryn Rusch*

M idway through that first awful class—when the clock above the mirrors said she had only been on the stationary bike for twenty-two minutes, but her body told her she had been on it for 2.2 days, when she thought her heart was going to burst through her chest like a creature out of the movie *Alien*, when sweat poured off her in rivers, and her breath came in deep honking gasps—midway through all of that, Patricia bent her head, saw the flab on her thighs go up while her actual legs went down, and heard Tom, her instructor, call over the rock music:

"Good. Real good. Excellent. Keep going. Wonderful. Hmmm. You'll get it. Relax. Wait until it feels good. Good. Relax. . . ."

Something in the rhythm of his voice, in the involuntary nature of the sounds, told her he would sound like this in bed. He would talk, his words meaningless, an accompaniment to the beat his body had established, and the pattern would continue building, building, building, until his voice rose in a cry and everything stopped.

She focused on that, held onto that, because it felt like the only thing that made him real somehow, made him, this Greek god of a man, whose muscles were perfectly sculpted, whose eyes were warm and brown and not quite sympathetic enough, slightly less intimidating. And she needed a reason not to be intimidated.

Two hundred pounds did not fit on her delicate five-four frame. She didn't know how she had let herself go like this. Excuse after excuse, she supposed, a sense of denial, a willingness to believe, at first, that it was her clothes that were shrinking not her body that was expanding. It had taken two years of failed exercise attempts to bring her to this class, to this moment, and she had been planning to drop out of this one too until he fell into his unconscious personal rhythm and she realized that he too was human.

And then she looked up, saw those not-quite-sympathetic eyes fall on her with something like disgust. She knew how she looked. The gym had thoughtfully provided a mirror in its exercise room. She saw the five other women in the spinning class: the darling with her tight, sculpted, twenty-five-year-old body who made it clear that she had never tried this before, and who was so in shape that she managed all the motions with ease; the middle-aged housewives in the middle, looking fine to her, but complaining about that extra ten pounds they always put on in the holidays; the bartender, an older woman who looked strong and solid, who had told Patricia about the class; and the anorexic creature beside Patricia who was having just as much trouble keeping up—apparently her eating habits, like Patricia's, robbed her of the strength to exercise. But none of them looked as disgusting as she did in her sweats, her face red, her new perm damp, her body straining. Why was it that she, a woman who had to struggle to walk across the room, was being treated like the pariah, when she was the one who needed the most courage, the most strength, to be here?

It was because the others were all afraid that some day, somehow, through the same careless inattentiveness that she had shown, they would all end up looking like her.

But *he*, he had no right to look at her that way. He was supposed to be the professional, the one who helped people like her become hard bodies like him. He wasn't supposed to let her see that she disgusted him, even though she did.

It was that look, in combination with her realization about him, that gave her the determination she had lacked. As her legs went round and round, the stationary bike's resistance on its lowest setting, she realized that she now had a goal.

She had been pretty once, eighty pounds and fifteen years ago. She would be pretty again.

And when she was, he would want her. She would take him to bed, and she would find out if he really sounded like that. And if he did, she would look at him with the same disgust she had seen in his eyes only moments before. She would look at him, and she would laugh.

Meeting her goal was harder than she thought it would be. After her first spinning class, she had to go immediately to bed, and when she got up the next morning, her legs ached so badly that she could barely climb stairs. Over time, she grew used to the class, and she moved onto weights, treadmills, and aerobics.

Within six months, she had lost thirty pounds and her body had definition. The spinning classes were tedious—she had learned the pattern within a few days and knew what he would call out next—and she found herself waiting for a repetition of the moment, the moment that had inspired her. It didn't happen often, and she watched him now. He would catch himself, as if he did know how he sounded, and sometimes, he would catch her looking at him.

She always smiled. She tried to be as congenial as she could.

Fortunately, she didn't have to be congenial anywhere else. She was having trouble being pleasant. The exercise put her in a good mood for an hour or two afterward, but the exhaustion that came with it angered her. She went back to her family doctor, wondering if the exercise was hurting her (even though he claimed, up front, that it would be the best thing for her) and he had calmly, patiently explained how the human body worked.

She got a sense that he gave this explanation a lot. *You are carrying the weight of a 12-year-old girl in addition to your own body weight. It is as if you are doing these exercises for two, when everyone else in the room is doing them for one.*

She wished she could explain it to them. The looks had stopped, after her second month, except when newcomers entered the gym. Then they stared at her as if she were the freak, or the one that would fail, and eventually, they would disappear.

She remained, tenacious to the last.

It was at her job, another twenty pounds later, that she realized she was in a revenge cycle. She worked as a Web-site designer for a local Internet provider. Her brother was her boss, and he would interview the customer on tape, and she would listen to the interview, use the material, and design the Web site from there.

In the past two weeks, clients who came to the office (and there were so few of them: most of them as lonely as she was) began to compliment her on her looks. She did look better. The loss of fifty pounds had also taken ten years off her face. The exercise and all the water it forced her to drink had cleared up her skin, and the pretty girl she remembered was beginning to make appearances in her mirror.

The office was a tiny place—a three-room suite with a door opening onto a strip-mall sidewalk—that became even tinier whenever someone new came inside. The wallpaper-thin walls did not shut out any sound, so she usually heard her brother's interviews with potential Web site clients twice. Those she didn't mind, because she made notes, hearing different things on the first and second listenings. It was the casual conversations, the folks who dropped in just to update their accounts or to gossip with her brother or to see, lately, how different Patricia was looking, that got on her nerves.

She had taken to closing her presswood door and opening the window that overlooked the alley, no matter how cold it was. Sometimes, if she did that, she could focus on the whoosh of traffic on the highway, the crunch of wheels on the gravel, the occasional conversations of people entering other businesses. If she was really lucky, it all became white noise, a sort of background to the tap-tap-tap of her fingers on the keys, her mind not in Seavy Village, but inside the computer, in that vast and somewhat mysterious network of computers known as the Internet. There she could float, be someone else, anyone else, and no one seemed to care that she was different except herself.

It was in one of those moments when, on a whim, she took the quiz the local psychiatrist had asked her to put on his Web site. His self-help book, *Negative Thoughts and How to Cure Them*, had been climbing the bestseller list, and he believed he needed a way for his fans to contact him. He thought the quiz was an open door. She hadn't been too sure, but then, she hadn't been too sure about his book either, which seemed to her (when she read it) a '90s ripoff of Napoleon Hill's classic *Think and Grow Rich*. But she, like the suckers she was designing the page for, took the quiz, and as she read the paragraph summary of her answers, she saw herself in its analysis:

> You have a tendency to blame others for your problems. Instead of solving those problems, you hope that others suffer worse than you have. Sometimes you fantasize about causing the suffering yourself. This is not healthy behavior. For a solution, see page sixty-two in my book . . .

And because she had already committed herself that far, she looked up page sixty-two in the complementary copy of the book that the psychiatrist had given the office and saw the chapter heading in bold: *The Revenge Cycle: Explanations of Your Obsession and How to Cure It.*

Surprisingly, the advice made sense to her. She had focused—obsessed—on Tom, on the sound of his voice, on the revenge she would get once she had sex with him and, more important, had laughed at him. Had humiliated him with her voice and her eyes and the body she had sculpted for just that purpose.

After reading the chapter, she stood up behind her desk and ran her hands down her arms, feeling the skin beneath her cotton blouse. The skin and the muscle and the bone. She hadn't felt bone in years, the sharpness of her elbows, the two bumps on either side of her wrists. She was beginning to like this new self, beginning to accept that it, and not the woman whose thighs brushed together, was who she was.

If she ended her focus on Tom, perhaps the exercise would end too. After all, the book said that all behaviors relating to the revenge cycle had to stop in order for it to be cured.

The only behaviors she had were the good ones: the exercise, the healthy food, the grooming that she had only recently started to do again. Clothes looked good once more. Makeup made her seem older and more mysterious rather than a woman denying her encroaching middle age.

As revenge fantasies went, this was a fairly harmless one. Perhaps she might dent Tom's rather solid self-esteem. Perhaps she might even make him reconsider casual affairs. But those two things might be good for him.

They would certainly be good for her.

It felt, when she looked on that moment later, as if for one brief afternoon she surfaced from her own thoughts, had a sense of clarity, and then dove back in, like a whale coming to the surface of water to take a breath.

She didn't take another breath for a very long time.

At the end of eighteen months, she thought of spinning class as hell. But she hit her ideal weight that month, and actually came to the class in spandex that made her look athletic and not like she had squeezed her bulk into someone else's clothes. As she went through her first class at her perfect weight, she listened for the moment when Tom's voice rose, when it punctuated each word with a gasping sexual rhythm, and when it did, she looked at him and found him looking at her.

The not-quite-sympathetic expression had left his eyes a long time ago, replaced by a kind of pride. She actually overheard him talking about her to the aerobics instructor, using her as an example of how well spinning worked. She studied him as her legs worked—thighs like steel now, muscles rippling beneath hard skin—and then, slowly, she smiled.

She had been saving her smiles. They had been her best feature even when she was heavy, and she had rationed them, at least for him. She wanted to use them when she was in peak condition, knowing that he would be attracted not so much to her face as to her sculpted form. And so, as their eyes met and the smile creased her face, she saw something new. She saw his eyebrows rise briefly and knew that small movement for something she hadn't seen in years.

Flirting.

She raised her eyebrows in return, and then looked away. First salvo sent and received. Mating dance initiated. Humiliation about to begin.

She went home that night happy for the first time since she had started taking spinning classes. In her two-room apartment whose ocean view was the only thing to recommend it, she danced a small jig, and then smiled again.

Her plan would actually work.

She didn't know what would happen after she slept with him. That was the problem she was working on as she drove to the gym in her beloved 1974 Volkswagen Bug. It smelled of oil and it vibrated crazily, but she had owned that car since she bought it used in high school and it had been the one thing she had maintained through all the years.

Her job at the i.p. had begun to pay her real money and she could buy a good car for the first time in her life, but she didn't. She couldn't give up her faithful Bug. She never would. She did her best thinking in it. And as she drove up the hill to the gym, she needed a goal that would last her past her revenge on Tom. And, if she were going to be truly healthy, it had to be one that did not continue to play out her revenge fantasy.

She parked in her usual space, grabbed her gym bag, and got out, startled to see a police car parked beside the bicycle racks. In the two years she had been coming here, she had never seen a police car. But there was that one month when a paramedic tried to fit exercise into his schedule. Sometimes he parked an ambulance outside. That had unnerved her the first time as well.

She pushed her car door shut with her hip, walked around the police car, and headed down the flight of stairs to the club itself. There she saw two policemen at the front desk and the aerobics instructor, a petite thing with too much energy for a human being, sitting on a stool looking stricken. No one was on the machines, and even the hardcore gym rats who spent hours on the free weights were huddled near the Nautilus equipment. From there, any conversation at the front desk could be heard loud and clear.

Patricia opened the glass door and came inside. She walked to the desk like she always did, to sign in and pay the extra fee for her special class, when a look from one of the policemen stopped her. The aerobics instructor, whose name she had never learned, raised liquid brown eyes filled with tears.

"There's no class," she said in a shaky voice. "Tom is dead."

The words circled in her head like the wheels on the stationary bike. *Tom. Is. Dead.* He couldn't be dead. She wasn't finished yet. She hadn't had the answer to her question, she hadn't been able to look at him with not-quite-sympathy in her eyes.

The police were watching her reaction. And she looked at them, truly seeing them for the first time. The man closest to her was about her age, fifty pounds overweight and carrying it all in the danger zone around his stomach. The other man was younger, athletic, broad-shouldered. His blue eyes were sharp, his lips thin. He didn't seem to miss anything. Especially the expression that must have crossed her face. What had it looked like? Shock? Disappointment?

Fear?

For her first response, after that flash of what-about-me?, was guilt. She could have done it. She *had* done it, a thousand times, in her mind. Not killed him physically, but emotionally. Somehow she thought her contempt would destroy him.

Arrogant, of course, but arrogance was what got her through.

The younger officer stepped forward. "Did you know Tom Ansara?"

Not well enough to know his last name. Maybe not at all. "I saw him three times a week," she said. "But I didn't know him. He instructed my spinning class."

But she had a hunch about how he sounded in bed. It felt as if she had been intimate with him. It felt as if she had lost someone close.

She wanted to put her hand on the wall, on the chair, to use something for support.

Those sharp blue cop eyes watched her, seeing everything. How good an actress was she? She didn't know. Good, she hoped. Good enough.

"And you are?"

"Patricia," she said, giving her first name only, as she always did at the gym. Only after a moment, she added, "Taylor. Patricia Taylor."

With that little pause in there, her last name sounded made up, even to her. She fumbled with her purse. "I have ID."

"No need," the cop said. "Just wait with the others."

She carried her gym bag and her coat to the nearest table, littered with out-of-date health and fitness magazines. In her eighteen months at the gym, she had never sat here. She had never spent any time sitting on anything that didn't spin or move or have weights attached.

The gym seemed excessively silent. The usual loud rock-and-roll music had been turned off. Someone had muted all three television sets. A fan whirred in the corner, set to cool whoever had been on the Precor cross-training machine, but that person had been off the machine for so long that the digitized program was running on the computer screen. In the long mirror lining one wall she could see the racquetball bleachers. The Thursday night wallyball players were seated there, heads bowed, hands threaded and hanging over their knees.

No one spoke. It was as if the cops were playing Agatha Christie, waiting until all the suspects arrived before going through the list and coming up with the killer.

The other members of the spinning class threaded in: the darling, the middle-aged housewives, and the bartender. One by one they all took seats at the table, as if united in the class that no longer existed. The anorexic had given up long ago and had been replaced by the only man, an accountant with a hairy back and a tendency to take off his shirt at precisely thirty-three minutes into the session. In street clothes, he looked diminished and not at all like a man who wore a white muscle T and baggy gym shorts cut one size too small.

The aerobics instructor sobbed her line each time a class member entered, as if she were a model trying out for a play. The shock seemed similar for all of them. Only the darling asked if it was all right if she exercised while she waited. The incredulous silence that greeted her question was her answer, and even she realized that she had said something wrong.

The clock above the mirror showed that forty-five minutes had passed since Patricia arrived. On a normal night, she would be sweating through the last fifteen minutes of the routine, wondering if he would forget himself again and provide her with enough ammunition to survive another week. Instead, she was sitting as still as she possibly could in a white plastic chair, wondering if the police meant to hold them all night.

Clearly Tom's death was suspicious, and clearly it involved people from the gym. Unless he had no other life but the gym. It surprised her to realize that she knew nothing about him, not really. She hadn't even figured out which car in the parking lot was his. She had been able to tell, from the way he spoke in class, that he rode his bicycle a lot outdoors: He knew the coast highway from a rider's perspective—sometimes using actual examples for his class to imagine: *We're going to do an uphill climb. Increase the tension on the bike when I tell you. Pretend this is Cascade Head. Know how good you'll feel when you reach the top.*

She also knew that he preferred jazz to rock-and-roll, but that the darling had requested peppier music to ride to. Patricia actually missed the Al Jarreau mixed with Branford Marsalis. It had provided a great middle period to the class.

When the spinning hour was up, and all the regulars had come in, the heavyset cop told the aerobics instructor to put a Closed sign on the door and lock it. Then they took people one by one into the manager's office and asked questions.

The heavyset cop remained out front mostly, to deter conversation, Patricia supposed. He watched them all too closely too, and the mirrors didn't help. They allowed him to see everything in that large exercise area, the slightest gesture, the smallest twitch.

After people spoke to the blue-eyed cop in the office, they were allowed to leave. Exercisers were interviewed in the order in which they'd arrived. Obviously someone had kept very careful track.

What it meant was that by the time Patricia was called, the gym rats were gone, but most of the class remained. The aerobics instructor had called her boss, and he had come down to lock up. Patricia also got a sense that he wanted to speak to the police himself.

When the heavyset cop said her name, Patricia got up, legs wobbly. She almost forgot her purse and gym bag, and grabbed them as an afterthought. Then she walked past the mirrors to the office where she had only been one time: the day she had signed up. That day she had been carrying an extra eighty pounds and even though she had dressed to hide it, it had been painfully obvious in the small room.

This time, the room's contours seemed more suited to her frame. The blue-eyed cop closed the door, asked her if she minded if the conversation was recorded, and then asked her to sit.

"This is just routine," he said.

It didn't seem routine, but she didn't say that. She had promised herself out front that she would volunteer nothing, and if he spent more than five minutes asking questions—the average time he had spent with the others—she would call an attorney just on principle.

"How well did you know Tom Ansara, Ms. Taylor?" The cop sat behind the messy manager's desk and folded his hands on top of a pile of papers that clearly didn't belong to him. His blue eyes seemed even more intense in the small space.

"He was my spinning instructor."

"For how long?"

"Eighteen months."

"You know that number precisely?"

She nodded. "I started my exercise program with his class."

"Was it effective?"

"The program?"

"The class."

She shrugged. "It motivated me."

"I understand you lost a lot of weight due to Mr. Ansara."

She almost choked. She felt a flush climb up her neck, her face, and she couldn't stop it. It was as if this man, this cop, had seen into her mind, had read each secret thought, knew how Tom had inspired her.

Knew about the revenge.

"I don't know if you can blame Tom," she said at last.

Blue-eyes raised his eyebrows ever so slightly. The expression gave his face a warmth it hadn't had before. "Blame? I would think you'd be proud of the loss."

"I am," she said, and almost repeated "*I* am." But she didn't. She wasn't going to give anything.

"And Tom helped you."

"The spinning class helped me." The flush had receded from her cheeks. Now her skin was cold. She wondered if she had turned pale, and how he would read this.

"You haven't asked what happened to Tom."

"I figured you would tell me."

He studied her for a moment. "He's still in the workout room. Would you like to take a look?"

"God no!" The response came out of her mouth before she could stop it. What was this man thinking, offering her the chance to look at a dead body? Not just any dead body, but the dead body of a man she had known, and fantasized about, however inappropriately.

"How tall are you, Ms. Taylor?"

The question so startled her that she had to think before responding. "five-four." How did that relate to Tom's death? How did any of it?

She had forgotten to look at the clock, and now she was afraid to, afraid it would seem insensitive, afraid it would make her even more suspicious than she probably already was.

"All right," he said. "We're done."

She remained sitting for a moment, disoriented, as he probably wanted her to be. She opened her mouth once, then closed it.

"Although," he said, "you should probably tell me how to get ahold of you. I'm sure it's here in the gym's records, but it's easier if you tell me."

She did. She told him her work phone and her home phone, and even what hours she would be in both places. He gave her a business card with his name on it. She didn't know policemen had business cards, but apparently they did. This one had the city's symbol on it, and then "Detective David Huckleby." It was such a jokey name, a rural cop name, that in any other context, she would have smiled.

Instead she pocketed the card and stood. He stood too, came up beside her so that he could open the door.

As he reached for the knob, she said, "You still didn't tell me how Tom died."

"I didn't?" He let go of the knob. "Careless of me." When it hadn't been at all. He had wanted her to ask. He had confused her, disoriented her, and then wondered if she would remember to ask. She knew that much. It was some kind of game. Maybe she should have called a lawyer after all.

"Tom's neck was broken, Ms. Taylor," Detective Huckleby said. "We think someone wrapped an arm around his neck and snapped it."

He paused, watching her face. She felt her heart beating hard. She couldn't picture it. She couldn't picture someone grabbing Tom like that.

"You know the grip," Huckleby said. "It's the one they teach in the self-defense classes here."

She had taken one of those classes just the month before. The instructor had been from out of town, a burly man who taught self-defense all over the country. He had used her as his model victim. She had stood in front of the class, felt his fingers on her neck as he positioned her, then remained very still while his arm encircled her throat. With a sharp movement of the forearm, and a backward pull on the hair, he had said, a neck could be broken, snapped, in a heartbeat.

She hadn't known why anyone would want this information. But the class had been in self-defense. And sometimes, she knew from her television-watching experience, self-defense meant only one person got out alive.

Huckleby was watching her, waiting for her reaction. He had known she had been in the class. He had obviously seen the sign-up list.

He touched her arm, felt her biceps, the muscle clearly developed beneath a thin layer of skin. His touch was gentle and, if she hadn't been in such a state of heightened awareness, she would have thought it accidental.

"Will you miss him?" Huckleby asked.

Her mouth was dry. The feeling of guilt had grown stronger. "I'll miss his class," she said. It was the only thing she could tell him. It was the only truth she knew.

"What a sad epitaph for a man you've known for eighteen months, a man who was proud of helping you lose weight."

"I didn't know him," she said, hearing as she spoke how defensive the words sounded. "I just took a class from him."

"I hear he had a thing for pretty women."

She laughed without mirth. It was an involuntary reaction, one that had become habitual over all the years, all the weight. "That wouldn't have in-cluded me."

"It does now," Huckleby said softly.

She felt the smile, the inappropriate smile, leave her face. "I was obese when I came into his class," she said. "I couldn't even pedal the damn bike with the resistance turned off for more than thirty seconds at a stretch. Then I'd pant for five minutes and try again."

"Tenacity can be attractive."

"Maybe," she said. "But you don't forget how someone looked when you met them."

*You don't forget that not-quite-sympathetic look in the eye, the disgust when he thought no one was looking. You don't forget any of that.*

She thought those last two sentences, but had enough self-control to prevent them from coming out of her mouth.

"I don't think you know how far you've come, Ms. Taylor," Huckleby said softly.

"Oh, I do," she said. "And Tom knew it too." She glanced at the door. "Can I go now?"

His smile was gentle. If she had met him in other circumstances, she might even have thought it kind. "Sure."

She let herself out and glanced at the clock. She had been in there twenty minutes. So much for proper resolutions.

"Ms. Taylor?"

She turned. He was holding her purse and gym bag. She swallowed. "Thanks," she said, taking them from him. She bent her head and walked to the door. The gym's owner, a muscular man who looked as if he spent too much time on the bench press, let her out. She took the stairs slowly, thinking as she did so that she would never hear Tom again, never hear that odd hitch in his voice, the way it caught when he got into the rhythm of the workout, the way it soared above the music.

His body was on the floor of the exercise room, his neck tilted at an odd angle. She wondered what he looked like, if he still seemed like a Greek god, even in his death repose. And then she shuddered. She would never be able to go in that room again.

She put her bag and purse in the car, and locked it. Then she took off at a run down the parking lot, not because she was frightened but because she needed to burn off the fear she had felt.

She needed the exercise, and she had to prove to herself that she could do it without Tom.

She woke in the middle of the night with an ache in her heart and tears in her eyes. She wanted a piece of chocolate cake so badly that it hurt. Fortunately, she lived in a small town that didn't have an all-night grocery store, and she didn't keep cake mixes in her small apartment.

Comfort food. She wanted comfort food because she needed comforting.

She heard her own voice, speaking to Huckleby: *I didn't know him. I just took a class from him.*

But if it were that simple, why couldn't she sleep? Her mother hadn't been able to sleep in the first few months after her father died. Neither had she, if the truth be told. The brain was busy trying to process the loss. Too busy to sleep more than a few hours at a time.

That had been when she put on the serious weight. Chocolate cake in the middle of the night, topped with vanilla ice cream. Or Cool Whip. Or Hershey's syrup.

Her mouth watered. She needed something comforting. Now. Never deny the cravings, she knew that much. But she couldn't afford to fall back into bad habits just because her spinning-class instructor was dead.

She wondered what the local best-selling psychiatrist would say about this. Probably recommend therapy. Probably report her to the police. She could hear it now: *She had a revenge fantasy about the man. Perhaps she acted it out. Perhaps she stalked him.*

She sat down at the kitchen table she had bought at a discount furniture store and assembled herself, then put her hands in her short-cropped hair. If she were honest with herself, she knew that she could have killed him. If her revenge fantasy had taken a different, more harmful twist. If she had gotten to the acting-out stage—which she had. She had been planning to come in that night, to continue the seduction. She had heard how willing he was to date women at the club. She had known about his preference for the sleek muscular women, the clear athletes. She had planned to use that to her benefit.

And the cop had seen it. He had seen it, and something about her height made him dismiss her.

But he shouldn't have. Patricia hadn't seen the body, but she knew the room, and she knew one thing: Tom liked to sit on the floor and talk to people. She could imagine how someone like her could have killed him:

He would have been sitting cross-legged on the polished wood floor in the center of the room, holding forth on the value of good nutrition or how so many reps burn so much fat, when someone came up behind him, put him in the stranglehold, and pulled until he couldn't breathe. Then he fell back, sprawling across the floor, his neck bent at the odd angle. Simple. Easy. So simple and easy even a short person could have done it.

She wished she could mention that to Huckleby without raising suspicion, but she couldn't. All she could do was listen for the gossip, read the local papers, and pretend that Tom's death had no effect on her life.

Like a woman who had just fallen off a horse, she made herself go to the gym the following night. Getting back in the saddle, she had whispered to herself, and while that wasn't entirely accurate, it was good enough.

The owner sat behind the desk, paperwork spread in front of him. A big sign, written in black Magic Marker, announced that all classes had been canceled until further notice. He saw her stare at it, and said, "We can't have the room until the investigation's done."

She wasn't sure if that was supposed to make her feel better or worse, so she just nodded and went into the locker room to change. Another woman was standing near the row of sinks, reading a sign newly taped to the wall. The sign was computer generated and it mentioned a trust fund, set up by the gym, for Tom Ansara's daughter.

Patricia felt a jolt. "I didn't know he had a daughter."

The woman nodded. Patricia had seen her around, but had never bothered to learn her name. "Sixteen. She's being raised by the mother in Seattle. But he was here, trying to earn money for her college. Now she may never go."

Patricia almost asked what happened to scholarships, but thought that too crass. Instead she made a sympathetic noise and changed into her sweats. She went into the gym proper and used the newest StairMaster set on high for an hour, until sweat poured off her. While she worked out, she noticed that only the regulars were here. The dilettantes, the ones who showed up every January or once a month or after a particularly big meal, hadn't come at all. And that was unusual. Every night usually had one.

As she marched up and down a make-believe flight of stairs, she was conscious of the room behind her, hidden by a row of racquetball courts and bleachers, now cordoned off by the local police. The more she marched and sweated, the more she focused on that room. She wanted to see it, wanted to know, perhaps, if he were really dead.

The room had mirrors covering three walls and a row of windows covering the fourth. The windows overlooked the free-weight area. When she got off the StairMaster and grabbed her sweat towel, wrapping it around her neck, she meandered into the free-weight area as if her movement were part of her routine.

The windows showed a darkened room, lit only by the lights reflected in the mirrors. There was no chalk outline of a body on the floor—she had read somewhere that Hollywood made that up and the police never used it; she just hadn't believed it to be true—and the special spinning bikes were lined up against the back wall, just like usual, waiting for class members to wheel them toward the middle. Beside them were the pile of step mats, and next to that the boxy audio system that had threatened to ruin her hearing.

Nothing was different except the yellow police tape covering the door, and the sign attached: *Closed by Order of the Seavy Village Police*. She shuddered, wishing, somehow, that she had never heard about his death. That she had stayed away as her weight came down, and when she came back and forgot to ask about Tom, people forgot to tell her about the murder, so that she would assume he had moved away, or lost his job, or found employment that required use of his mind. But she couldn't pretend those things in retrospect, and she couldn't drop the disappointment she felt that, somehow, she had been cheated of something.

"Any clues?" A male voice behind her made her jump.

She turned. Detective Huckleby was standing so close to her that he almost pressed her against the window.

"No," she said.

"Strange," he said. "A room is always a room, even after something awful happens in it. Unless you know, the room is no different."

She had had that thought before. Apartments and hotel rooms always made her wonder, when she first arrived, if anyone had died in them. She had always thought she would be able to tell by some subtle vibration, something that had altered because of the death.

But she felt no such vibration from the gym, none from the exercise room at all, and she was surprised.

"I didn't think any of the class members would show up tonight," he said.

"I didn't just go to class," she said. "This is my routine."

"Routine." He spoke softly, as if he were musing.

Her heart had started to pound again. "I lost my weight, Detective, through exercise. I have to continue that, particularly now—"

"Now that your instructor is dead?"

She nodded.

"So he did have an influence on your weight loss."

She licked her lips. "He inspired me." That much was true.

"Who's going to inspire you now?"

She met his gaze. Electric blue. Neon blue. Like she imagined Paul Newman's eyes would be in person. "I guess I have to," she said.

"Always tough," he said. "It's always better if the motivation comes from the outside."

She wasn't sure if he was speaking of exercise now, or if he was speaking of murder. Would he be happier if the killer came from outside Seavy Village? Or outside the gym? She swallowed. She had been so focused on herself, on Tom's death, that she hadn't thought about the reality of murder. The fact that a murder victim had to have a murderer.

"Are you done with your exercise?" he asked.

"Do you want to interrogate me again?"

To her surprise, he laughed. "If you thought that was an interrogation," he said, "I don't want to put you through a real one."

She saw no humor in it. Yesterday had been a bad day, a day she did not want to repeat.

He must have seen that on her face, for his smile faded. "Sorry," he said. "You're not a suspect."

"At this time," she said.

He half shrugged. "I suppose." He looked around at the empty bleachers, the slouching owner poring over the papers behind the reception desk. "I was hoping to buy you coffee and ask a few questions about the gym."

"Me?"

He faced her, his eyes meeting hers. "Well," he said, "actually, anyone from the class who bothered to show up tonight. You're the only one."

"I thought you didn't expect any of us to show up tonight."

"I figured it would only be the exercise addicts."

It was her turn to smile, ruefully. "It is."

He nodded once. "Coffee?"

"Water or Gatorade. Coffee's a diuretic."

"Hmm," he said. "And that's bad?"

She looked at him, uncertain if that was a real joke. She supposed it was. It seemed strange to joke in front of a room where a man had been murdered.

"There's a deli and juice bar upstairs," she said, not sure why she'd agreed.

"Lead the way," he said.

"Let me change," she said. "I'll meet you there."

"I suppose you want carrot juice."

"Actually," she said, "I want bottled water. And maybe an apple."

"Done."

She pushed past him and went to the lady's locker room. Her hands were shaking and she was wondering what she was doing. He was a cop investigating a murder and he wanted to talk to her a second time, informally. She felt as if she were doing something wrong, as if she should get on the phone and ask for a lawyer or not show up or go upstairs and ask what he was charging her with. But all of that seemed melodramatic and unnecessary and a bit rude.

After a quick—very quick—shower, she put on her street clothes—a cheap cotton sweater and a pair of faded jeans. She left her tennies on, and kept her gym bag in the locker. She saw no reason to spend too much time with him.

The restaurant upstairs had gone through many formats in the eighteen months she had worked out in the gym. The first and most appalling had been the steak joint that served its meat thick and charbroiled. The next had been a vegetarian restaurant with poorly made, tasteless 1970s cuisine. Three different taverns came in after that, and now, finally, the deli, with its smoothies and juice bars. This new place was the only one that got the regulars from the gym. Sometimes they ran up the stairs, got a small sandwich and a fruit drink, and then went back down to work out some more.

She had come up more than once with a novel, usually science fiction, and had eaten alone, most often the taco deli sandwich made with fat-free refried beans. It had flavor, and it was filling, and it didn't have a lot of calories, all of which counted in its favor. The seats were comfortable, and the staff congenial, never asking her to move when she finished her meal.

Now she went up to find herself and Huckleby the only customers. The lights were out in the far section of the deli, and a single employee, an older woman whom Patricia had never seen before, cleaned behind the counter.

A bottled water and the fruit plate waited for her. Huckleby had a cup of coffee and a shortbread cookie.

"That's a lot of food."

"You looked like you could use it."

How many years had she waited for someone to say that, only to find it was someone she didn't want to impress. She slipped into the chair and opened the bottle of water.

"You had questions."

He nodded. "Tell me what you can about Tom."

"We had this conversation yesterday."

"Yesterday I knew less than I do today."

"Oh?" She took a long sip. She had been thirsty, which meant she had let herself get dehydrated. Careless of her.

"Yeah," he said.

"Like what?"

He broke the shortbread cookie in half, then broke a half into smaller pieces. "No," he said. "I get to ask the questions first."

"I already told you about Tom."

"You told me what you know. And that was official. Now I want to know what you suspect."

Suspect. Strange word. Was she supposed to tell this man that she thought Tom Ansara was self-involved and rather stupid, that he had an eye for pretty women and no real empathy for anyone who didn't look like a perfect match for him? Or should she tell him about her suspicions of Tom's performance in bed?

"I think he biked a lot," she said.

Huckleby raised an amused eyebrow. "Gee. We missed that."

She felt color rise in her cheeks. "No," she said. "I mean biked all over the city, maybe over the area."

"That's not gossip."

"You want gossip?"

"Yes."

"Talk to the aerobics instructor then. She collects it."

He leaned back and studied her. "That was harsh. You don't like her?"

"I don't know her."

"It amazes me that you could come to a gym for eighteen months and not know anyone."

"I came to work out."

"People usually make friends in places like this."

"Not with fat people."

"Why? They make friends with fat people everywhere else."

She picked up her fork and stabbed an orange slice with it, feeling a momentary victory when some of the juice shot across the table toward him. "I understand it," she said. "At least I do now. Most people who are more than twenty pounds overweight don't stay. It has nothing to do with discipline and everything to do with effort. It takes a lot of effort to move a normal weight, but add extra weight on top of it and a fat person is working twice, sometimes three times as hard as everyone else. Most can't manage it, and they leave."

"So you don't make friends with fat people at the gym either?"

"I thought we already established that I don't make friends," she said.

His gaze seemed a little too sharp for a moment, as if her admission was an admission to something else as well. "I'm sure you do in your personal life."

She had a few friends, people she talked to, but no one she confided in. She hadn't confided in anyone for a very long time. Not even her brother. They talked about casual things. She supposed that counted as friendship.

And she had a lot of acquaintances on-line. She kept a board running behind her work at all times, and answered her e-mail when it showed up. She closed out her nightly sessions in a chat room, each night a room devoted to a different subject, just to keep her mind active.

The silence between them had grown. Finally, she said, "I thought you wanted to hear about Tom."

"And I thought you didn't gossip."

She ate the orange slice. It was sour. She took a sip of water to cover the taste. "I discovered in the last twenty-four hours how little I knew about him. Like the daughter."

"There is no daughter," Huckleby said.

She set the bottle of water down very deliberately. "But the sign—"

"He told people there was a daughter, and the very kind folks in Seavy Village have started a fund. But I investigated, and I can tell you, there is no daughter. No ex-wife. No acrimonious divorce. There isn't even a Tom Ansara until he came to Seavy Village."

So there was more to this than just the gym. That relieved her somehow, made the thought of murder caused by people who frequented her safe place go away.

"All of his relationships lasted a few weeks at most," Huckleby said, "so consider yourself lucky he didn't make a pass at you."

Such a quaint old-fashioned phrase "make a pass" was. She almost smiled. But a part of her brain, the suspicious part, remained distant.

"Why are you telling me all this?"

"Because," he said, "I figured if I opened up, you would. And you look like a lady who has something to get off her chest."

She felt her eyes widen and wished she could stop them, wished she had more control than she did. Now, when she lied, he would know it. "I've told you everything I can," she said.

He stared at her for a moment. "Pity."

"I don't hold any keys," she said. "I'd tell you if I did."

"Would you?" he asked, then dropped a ten on the table and stood. By the time she got to her feet, he was gone.

All that night and as she ate her solitary bowl of cereal the next morning, she kept telling herself that it was silly to feel like she was failing Huckleby somehow. She didn't even know him, didn't know anything about him. All she knew was that he wanted information on Tom's death, and she had none.

In fact, she had even less than she had had before. She had believed the stories about Tom around the gym, had thought him a divorced man with a conventional past. Now, perhaps, he didn't have one, and he, not the murderer, had violated the safety of the gym, of Seavy Village itself.

Blaming the victim, they called it. But she knew that things were never as clear-cut as they seemed. Apparently, so did Huckleby.

When she got to work, her schedule was light: some routine maintenance of a few sites and monitoring of a few others. She opened the usual chat room where she hung out when things were slow, but couldn't concentrate.

Her brother was in his office, talking loudly on the phone. He wanted to expand their service beyond the coast, to move into the valley. It would entail hiring additional staff, getting more lines, working more computers. It would be a nightmare for her, but so far she hadn't tried to talk him out of it.

Rather than listen to him argue with another of his friends over his plans, she opened her window. The morning breeze smelled of sea salt and fish. It was cold, but she didn't mind. She needed something else to concentrate on.

But her attention kept wandering back to Huckleby's words about Tom, about his secrets, and she finally succumbed. She knew where he lived: She had followed him there once, early on, so that she could have a setting to imagine her revenge. Actually sitting in her car on that cold November night, watching him shaded against his window as he moved through his apartment, made her feel like a voyeur, a stalker, something she didn't want to be. So, even though she'd felt an urge to follow him at other times, she never had.

Still, she decided to use his name and address now to access his driver's license. Some schlub had gotten in trouble, in Oregon, for placing all the DMV records on the Internet and, even though he had removed them, Patricia had captured the file, thinking some day it would be useful.

It was. With Tom's driver's license number, she was able to get into his credit report, and that, in turn, gave her his Social Security number. It didn't belong to Tom Ansara, but to someone else, an elderly woman in Pittsburgh. Apparently he had stolen the number. But he had used it for a very long time and through it, and his credit report, she saw a life of transience, a man of many names and, as she dug, several petty crimes, mostly involving drugs, theft, and a certain roughness with women.

That last made a shudder run through her. Her revenge fantasy had been too subtle for this man. It might have turned on her. No matter how strong she was, she might not have been able to overcome his athlete's quickness. She knew that much.

It could have ended badly. For her.

At that, she rested her head on her arms and made herself breathe. How foolish she had become. How obsessed with a man she hadn't even known. She had even mourned him, in her own way, this man she had made up.

The door to her office opened, and her brother came in. She recognized him by his footsteps.

"You okay?"

She raised her head. Her brother still carried all the weight he had put on as he aged. Sometimes he eyed her new form as if it were a reproach to him. But she liked him at this weight. It gave him a cuddly warmth that he hadn't had when he was thinner.

"Yeah," she said. "Just tired."

He nodded. All he knew about Tom was what the rest of the town knew: that he had been murdered in the gym. The next day, her brother had asked her if it was safe for her to return. When she assured him it was, he had said, "I hope so," and she knew, with that terse phrase, that the conversation was closed.

He pulled up the only other chair, a folding chair she kept unfolded in the corner. It squeaked as he sat on it. "Look," he said. "If I manage to get more business, we might have to leave Seavy Village. This just isn't a good place to do business, not if we start focusing on the valley."

Her heart was pounding. She didn't want to leave. She loved it here. "I won't go," she said.

"I know. I was thinking, maybe you could be in charge of our coastal lines."

That meant customer relations. It meant working alone. "Let's wait," she said. "Talk about this when the changes become real."

"It's getting closer every day, Patty," he said. Her brother was the only person who could call her Patty and get away with it.

"I know," she said. "I just don't want to think about it now."

And she didn't, not until she was on the silly StairMaster for the second night in a row. Sweat was dripping between her breasts, and the back of her neck was damp. The club's televisions were all tuned to a football game, and their sound was on, as well as the latest Rod Stewart CD at full blast. She was surprised she could hear herself think. But the noise blurred, and she found her mind wandering, going over her brother's words, trying to see if there was any reality in the changes he was discussing for his business.

Then it hit her, what he had said. *Seavy Village isn't a good place to do business.* And it wasn't. The town was small, many of its residents unskilled workers with low-paying jobs or retirees who lived on a fixed income. The tourists were seasonal: summers, mostly, with a few spikes around the holidays. Yet Tom had been here for eighteen months, maybe more. He hadn't had a single arrest, which, considering his record before he arrived, was spectacular, and she remembered nothing that made him seem as if he had been on drugs. What had he found that kept him here? It certainly hadn't been the spinning class. And whatever it had been, someone had considered it worth killing for.

*Pretend this is Cascade Head,* he would say. *Know how good you'll feel when you reach the top.*

And all the other sites on the coast route. He would mention them, use them in his class. But he always came back to Cascade Head, as if it were important, to them, and to him.

For one long stretch of her workout, she considered buying a bike and exploring the places he had mentioned, searching. But for what, she didn't know. And she had never searched for anything. She had no idea how to go about it.

She had to talk to Huckleby. She wondered if he would think she was crazy, all the work she had done on this. He was going to want to know why and the answer she had was really no answer at all, just a truth she was beginning to discover:

That obsession, once begun, did not end easily. That losing it felt a lot like losing love.

The police station, tucked in a back road behind the post office, was a 1960s building, all metal and sand-colored brick. Its gray tile floors were spotless, and the walls had recently been painted white. She felt oddly betrayed by its cleanliness. Somehow she had expected the grit she had seen portrayed on TV.

When she asked for Huckleby, the woman at the desk—statuesque, her uniform accenting rather than hiding her figure—nodded toward the only man sitting in a sea of desks. Patricia wasn't sure how she missed him, except that she hadn't expected this place to be this way, and somehow hadn't expected him to look so lost and all alone, bathed in the fog-gray light filtering in from the cross-hatched windows.

The smell, she noted as she walked toward him, was strong: burned coffee and stale sweat, the kind of smell that a person never got used to. It wasn't until she was standing over him that he looked up, and from the movement of his lips, she guessed he had been planning to make a comment to someone else when he edited himself for her.

"I didn't expect to see you again," he said, and kicked a green metal desk chair in her direction. She sat gingerly on it, half expecting it to squeal as her folding chair did when her brother sat on it.

His comment was strange given the size of the town they lived in. They would see each other from time to time, probably had already and just hadn't known it, until now.

She licked her lips. "I did some digging."

"Oh?" He was giving her his full attention. The file before him was closed and pushed aside, his hands threaded on the desk like a man patiently waiting to hear something he didn't already know.

"The name Ansara is unusual," she said, knowing that this was an inane way to start. "There was a movie star in the late sixties and early seventies named Michael Ansara. He looked something like Tom."

"Yeah," Huckleby said, his tone dry. "I can't decide if Tom's favorite movie was *Sometimes a Great Notion* or that awful television remake of *Dracula*."

In spite of herself, she smiled. She ducked her head so that he wouldn't see how amused she was. This was serious, after all.

"But I did even more digging. I found out about his record."

His eyebrows went up. "You're good," he said. "Care to share with me how you did that?"

She had thought this through before she came, and now she told him the story she had planned: It was the entire truth minus the driver's license records. Even though anyone could get DMV records simply by writing to the division, she felt almost criminal using them, even more criminal for storing them. Still, if he asked, she would tell him. She only hoped he wouldn't ask.

He didn't, but he was leaning forward now, looking at her with a mixture of puzzlement and respect.

"I would have left it at that," she said, "except I got to wondering, what would a man like that be doing in Seavy Village for so long?"

"Staying clean?" Huckleby said. Clearly he'd thought of that too.

"Maybe," she said. "But when he did spinning class, he outlined bike routes, something we could imagine while our feet were hopelessly circling." She took a piece of paper out of her battered purse. "Here are the places he mentioned, and the way he mentioned them. Cascade Head was the one he focused on, but I always thought that was because it was so high. But he could have used the Van Duzer Corridor for the same thing, or maybe something in the Cascades, and he didn't. He just kept coming back to this one, over and over, like his mind was stuck."

Huckleby glanced at the paper. "You're quite specific. How do you remember what he said?"

She flushed. "I was in his class for a long time. It got boring after a while. You did anything you could to concentrate. I focused on his words. He repeated himself a lot."

He tapped the paper against his hand. "Nice work," he said. "I knew you'd remember something if you tried hard enough."

"Is it important?" she asked.

"Important?" He kept a grip on the paper while he reached for the phone. "It's the missing piece."

She didn't hear anything for three days. Every time she thought of calling the station, she made herself do something else. The danger with obsession, the Web site told her, was that once one went away, another sometimes arose in its place. Too many, and a person needed therapy. A single one, and perhaps the person needed more to do with her life.

More than computers, exercise, and solitary meals. More than ducking her head to avoid conversations every time she went to the gym.

She joined the aerobics class and made a point, that night, of learning everyone's name. She told her brother that she thought his expansion a bad idea at this stage in their business, and he was so pleased that she used the word "their" that he didn't even try to argue with her. He asked her what she thought the business needed, and she told him all the things she had never said. To her surprise, he made a list and walked out of her office, studying it, ready, he said, to make changes.

On the third day, the local 5:15 newscast announced that a suspect was being held in the murder of Tom Ansara. A man, with a name Patricia didn't recognize, an out-of-towner, as the announcer called him with obvious relief, who had business with Ansara that predated his arrival in Seavy Village.

She was surprised she hadn't heard from Huckleby. She would have thought that, as a courtesy, he would have told her first.

And then she wondered where that assumption came from. She had provided a small bit of information in an ongoing investigation.

He owed her nothing. She owed him nothing. And that's where things would always stand.

The details came out bit by bit, not in the local paper, which saw itself as a promoter of tourism on the coast and as such tried to cover up the seamier stuff, but in the *Oregonian*, which followed the entire case with an interest unusual in their non-Portland coverage.

Tom Ansara's real name was Andrew Thomas. He had arrests in several states for drug crimes, most of which were minor possession violations. But two states had more serious charges against him, one in an unlikely connection with a group of art thieves operating in Los Angeles. Ansara fled the area after some Mirós, Picassos, a Jackson Pollack, and an original Dali were stolen from a house in Brentwood. He came to Oregon, took a new name, and hid, careful to stay away from Seavy Village's minor drug trade, and managing, somehow, to break off his relations with women before things became too serious.

He hadn't had anything to do with the art heists, had merely stumbled on them in the course of his other shady dealings, and knew, somehow, who was involved. Police assumed he dated one of the thieves, hearing the plans for the Brentwood theft from her. But the heat on that was high, and someone threatened him. When he came to Oregon, he made notes of all he knew and buried them on Cascade Head.

He had mailed a letter to himself the day he died—obviously he had been worried; perhaps he had seen his killer, a man named Will Garetson. In the letter, Tom explained that he had hidden a box, and how far it was from Highway 101, and he gave a detailed description of the unusual tree and rock formation near the burial site. Unfortunately, he had left out what part of 101 he was talking about. When Patricia—"a private citizen" as the papers called her—had come forward, she had provided the missing piece of information: where exactly the box was. The police looked on Cascade Head at the correct distance from 101, found the distinctive tree and rock formation, and proceeded to dig.

They found the box, and in it, the names of the people involved in the heist, a tape recording with their voices on it planning that heist, and a list of the items that they had hoped to take. Also in the box was a note about the reasons Tom had hidden in Oregon: It wasn't because his conscience had finally gotten to him about the heist or because he had been discovered by the thieves. It was because, on the two jobs the thieves performed before his disappearance, they had killed security guards, and Tom was beginning to fear that killing for sport was becoming the reason behind the heists, not the theft itself.

So he vanished, and it took them a long time to trace him. He made two mistakes: He took a regular job, and he kept the old Social Security number. Eventually Garetson found him. In fact, the article said, the man who killed Tom had been the self-defense instructor at the gym a few weeks before Tom's death. Because instructors were rarely in the building at the same time, Tom hadn't seen him. Garetson had discovered Tom's routine, where he lived, and who he had offended in Seavy Village, and had apparently decided the best way to kill the man was to do it at the gym, where all the women he slept with would then become suspects.

It would have worked if it weren't for that letter, and Detective Huckleby, who felt there was something wrong with this case from the beginning.

Patricia read the articles with avid interest, worried when she learned how easy it had been for a killer to infiltrate her small town and target a man, calmer when she realized one of the reasons the man had been targeted was because of his own behavior.

It took a week for the *Oregonian* to print all the articles, but when it was done, and Garetson was in jail awaiting trial, she felt as if it was over. Or at least part of it. She could still remember the touch of Garetson's hands on her neck as he held her in place, using her to demonstrate to the rest of the self-defense class how to do the chokehold. When his arm had wrapped around her throat, she had thought how easy it would be for him to squeeze and how easy it would be for her to die.

Apparently, he had killed Tom with no struggle. She had been right. It had been easy, after all.

So she went back to her life, changed as it was. Her brother gave her more responsibility at the i.p. and she found a jogging partner, a woman whom she had spoken to a few times at the gym and felt an affinity for. They were developing a friendship composed of short conversations followed by a mile or more of gasping silence. She found that she liked talking with someone. She actually looked forward to it.

By the end of the second week, she made it through two days without thinking of Tom. Then Huckleby walked into her office. He leaned against the door, smiled at her, and let his blue eyes draw her in.

"Do you do lunch?" he asked.

"Only on every other Thursday," she said, and was surprised at the tartness of her own reply.

His smile widened into a grin. "I'm buying."

She went with him to the health-food restaurant next door. He ordered the only meal with beef in it—a shredded beef taco concoction made with cream cheese instead of sour cream—and she had their homemade tomato soup and fresh sourdough bread.

"You never followed up on the case," he said after the food was served.

"You didn't keep me informed."

He took a bite from the taco and half the cream cheese fell out. He set the food down. "I was a little busy."

"But you got him," she said.

"We got him. It's up to the L.A. cops to get the rest." He sounded relieved at that.

"More excitement than Seavy Village is used to," she said.

"More than we want," he replied. Then he put an elbow on the table and watched her. She had never had anyone watch her eat before.

"You know," he said, "in all the times we talked, you never did tell me how you felt about him."

"About Tom?" she asked, stalling. She put her soup spoon down and picked up the bread, shredding it.

"Yes."

She shrugged. "He was my spinning instructor."

"And?"

There was no harm in telling him now. No harm in saying anything. She felt herself flush. She had to look away. "And I hated him."

He let out a slow whistle, as if he hadn't expected it. "Because he was a drill sergeant?"

She shook her head. The soup was nearly gone. She had made a mess of the bread. There were crumbs on her side of the table. She stared at them instead of looking Huckleby in the eye.

"Because of how he looked at me, in the beginning. Like I offended him just by being in his presence."

To her surprise, Huckleby took her hand. She raised her head, saw him looking at her with empathy, not disgust. She wanted to look away, but couldn't.

"Do you know how many times you told me that fat people get treated differently?"

"They do," she said.

"You're no longer fat," he said.

"I always will be." With her free hand she tapped her chest. "Inside. I'll always remember how it feels. Like an alcoholic. I'll always be a fat person crammed into a skinny shell."

"If you want to be," he said. "No one sees you that way anymore. No one treats you that way. The loathing I hear when I'm around you comes from you."

He said the words softly, gently, to lessen their sting. But they still hurt. She blinked, startled. No one had ever talked that way to her before. But then, she hadn't let anyone talk to her, really talk to her, for years.

"I don't want to treat anyone else that way," she said.

"But you do," he said. "You assume all the rest of us will look at you with that same disgust that Ansara had, and you hate us in advance."

"I don't hate you," she said.

He smiled and squeezed her hand. "It's a start, at least."

"Of what?" she asked.

He shrugged. "I don't know. Friendship, maybe something more. If you're willing."

She had never fantasized about him, not in this way, never imagined what he would sound like in bed, never allowed herself to think a man like this one would even be interested. He was a person to her, not a Greek god who looked down on the less-than-perfect with complete disdain, like Tom had been. Only Tom hadn't been. He had been as imperfect as she was. It just hadn't been apparent from the way he looked, the way he dressed, the way he spoke. Only his eyes had showed it, and only if someone paid attention.

She felt a little floaty hit of adrenaline, like she used to get in her early spinning classes after she had been on the bike awhile. Just when she thought she would be ready to quit, something in her body would adjust and she would feel slightly dizzy, slightly high. A little afraid and a bit proud of herself at the same time.

Friendship. Something more. If she was willing.

"All right," she said, and squeezed Huckleby's hand.

There was no longer a need for fantasy. The fantasy had made her blind to the realities around her. Some of those realities could have harmed her—the arm around her neck, the same arm that had crushed Tom's throat—and others could have helped her, allowed her to see that things were different now, that she was different and, perhaps, always would be.

She was no longer spinning her wheels on a stationary bike. She had been moving forward for a long time; and she had finally noticed.

# Brendan DuBois

## The Summer People

BRENDAN DUBOIS first came to prominence as a short story writer, becoming so deft that his crime stories now frequently appear in *Playboy*. He combines a tight, sometimes lyrical style with some truly original storylines, as in his first story in this year's annual, the masterful "The Summer People," which appeared in the November issue of *EQMM*. He has written several novels, the most recent of which, *Resurrection Day,* won the Sidewise Award, which is bestowed on the best alternate-history novel of the year, an intriguing what-if about the Cuban missile crisis turning into World War III, and the effects thereafter.

# The Summer People

*Brendan DuBois*

The drive north from Massachusetts had taken the better part of three hours, and the first half-hour of the journey was still with Roy Toland as a dull ache continued between his shoulder blades. Those thirty minutes had been spent in bumper-to-bumper traffic, snarling along Storrow Drive in Boston, the air conditioner in their Jeep Cherokee struggling valiantly to keep things cool and comfortable in the hundred-degree weather. Twice people had cut him off—one in a Volvo that had a bumper sticker that said VISUAL WORLD PEACE—and since he and his wife were officially on vacation, Roy let both drivers live.

Now, bouncing down a dirt road towards Morrill Lake in northern New Hampshire, his wife Nicky was rubbing the sore spot on his back, saying, "Only a few minutes more, Roy. Just a few minutes more."

"Oh, I know," he said, passing a point in the road where a signpost listed about a dozen names of people owning summer cottages on this part of the lake. "But before you know it, our week will be up and it'll be time to head south."

Her hand rose up a bit to tug at his hair. "That's seven days away, love. Let's just enjoy the time and not worry about the trip back."

Then he rounded a slight bend in the road and smiled. There it was, the summer cottage they rented the first week of every August, and just the sight of it was enough to finally undo that knot between his shoulder blades. It was simple—one-story with light red paint on the clapboards. The place had a solid concrete foundation (important for keeping out four-legged pests such as field mice and chipmunks) and a screened-in porch that was about fifty feet away from the cold blue waters of Morrill Lake.

A blue canoe was chained to an oak tree, and about the cottage were tall pines that gently creaked as the wind from the lake passed over them. Roy walked with Nicky down to the water's edge. Before them were the wide waters of the lake, and to the north, the outlying peaks of the White Mountains. The only sound was that of the wind and the gentle slap of the waves, and the far-off murmuring growl of a powerboat.

Nicky slipped her arm through his. She had on khaki shorts and a white polo shirt, and her muscular arms and legs were quite tanned. Her sunglasses were pushed back on her short blond hair, and she said, "I've been thinking of this view for the past couple of hours, and it's still better than what I remember. Smell that air? Smell anything unusual?"

"Just the trees, that's all," he said, smiling at her enthusiasm.

"Right," she replied. "No diesel, no gasoline, no exhaust. Nothing."

"Well," he said, gently pulling his arm free. "If you want to smell some steaks barbecuing, we'd better get unpacked and dig out the cooler. Hungry?"

"Starved." He walked with her back to the cottage. To the left of the cottage was a grove of trees and underbrush that blocked their view of the other cottages on the road. To the right was a larger home, two-story and painted white, which belonged to the Pelletiers, who owned the rental cottage. Henry Pelletier—a retired papermill worker from Berlin—was outside, raking. He waved a hand and they both waved back. "Welcome back to Morrill Lake, you two," he called out.

"Thanks, Henry," Roy said. "How's Mrs. Pelletier doing?"

"Oh, she's on the mend," he said. "Doctor says the stitches will be coming out soon. I'm sure she'll be glad to see you when she's feelin' a bit stronger."

"Glad to hear that, Henry," Roy said. "Oh, I'll be over later to pay the other half of the rent."

"Jesus," Henry said, smiling and going back to work with the rake. "Don't be in such a hurry. Get yourselves unpacked 'fore you have to worry about that."

As Roy unlocked the front door with the key that Henry had earlier mailed to them, Nicky said, "We've been here five minutes, and already I feel like we're in a real home. You know, back in Boston we still don't know our upstairs neighbors?"

"I know that they like Gilbert & Sullivan and that their bed squeaks," Roy said, switching on the lights. "That's all I need to know."

During the next half-hour they unloaded the Jeep, and one of the first things Roy took out was Nicky's computer, which she set up on a table in the porch. There was no phone in the cottage, but there was a phone line that Nicky used so she could have Internet access, and that was that. There was no television and only a small radio that picked up the local stations. She sat down at the computer and sighed. "Work. Wish I didn't have to do this when I'm up here."

"It'll be fine," Roy said. "Just as long as you leave enough time for other things. Like canoeing."

She raised an eyebrow as she smiled. "And maybe checking how squeaky our bed is, if you're lucky."

He laughed and felt warm and cuddly towards his woman, despite her work, and resumed unpacking. One of the last things Roy took out were two black zippered duffel bags, which had been placed behind the spare tire. He knew that another reason his back ached was the content of the two bags, which he now placed behind a sliding piece of paneling in the bedroom's closet. If a state trooper or local cop had pulled him over this day and had discovered the content of the two bags, well, Roy wouldn't have had to worry about coming back to this summer place next year, or the next decade, for that matter.

Back out in the porch, he kissed his wife's neck. "Feel like dinner?"

"Only if you cook it."

"Deal," he said, and he went outside, where he got the grill going. Like every summer before, the Pelletiers had filled up the gas tank. It was nice to be back, back among people who liked having them around.

. . .

Later that night they were cuddled up in the porch on a couch, a light blanket over the two of them, the lights off, listening to the cries of the loons out on the lake. Roy felt all the worries and stresses of driving up here melt away, like snow from a late March storm. Nicky had first brought him up here a couple of years back, and he was amazed at how much he looked forward each summer to returning to the lake. They had lived for a while in California and in Washington, but there had never been a place in those two states that gave him such a sense of contentment, of belonging.

Nicky was in Roy's arms and sighed as another call came from a loon. She said, "Tell me again why we can't stay up here longer."

"First, we can't afford it," he said. "Second, the place belongs to the Pelletiers, and they've got other renters lined up for the summer. We can't hog the place for the whole summer, as much as we'd like to."

She shifted in Roy's arms, rubbed her nose against his. "Can't you figure something out?"

"I'll try."

She smiled and let her hands wander over him. "Goodie, little boy. Then come to bed and I'll reward you."

Nicky made breakfast the next morning—simple stuff, scrambled eggs and toast—and she said, "All right if I get an hour or so online?"

"Sure, go right ahead," Roy said. "It'll give me a chance to pay Henry and to see what's new on the lake."

He went outside, blinked from the bright sky. There were just a few clouds off to the south; the small peaks made their green, jagged marks against the light blue sky. The water was fairly still, with only a couple of powerboats out in the distance, so far out that he couldn't even hear them.

Henry Pelletier was at work in his yard, dressed in green chino work pants and shirt, and Roy went over to see him. The old man was sawing off chunks of white birch log—each piece about eighteen inches long—using a handsaw.

Roy said, "A chainsaw would go faster."

"Unh-hunh," Henry said, moving a length of tree in the saw stand. "It surely would. But it would make a heck of a racket and would smell up the yard, and during the year I'd have to oil the damn thing, sharpen the chain, and then winterize it when I hang it up in the cellar when the snows come. Or I can use this little handsaw my daddy gave me years ago, get a little exercise, and still get the job done."

Roy smiled and passed over the check for the rent. Henry stuck it in his shirt pocket without even looking at it, and Roy was suddenly filled with affection for the old man. Anyplace else Roy had been, this kind of transaction would have required two forms of identification, a credit check, and a signed contract. But not here. Here, a man trusted his neighbor, trusted him to do the right thing. It was a way of life Roy thought had gone forever, and it warmed him to see it still alive.

He said, "Give you a hand, Henry?"

"Sure," he said. "See that twine over there? Bundle these logs up, three at a crack. Make a handle from the twine, too. Thing is, I sell 'em at Corder's Farmstand down the road. Five dollars a bundle. Damn flatland tourists buy 'em and put 'em in their fireplace. Usually they don't even burn 'em. Look awfully pretty, don't they?"

He started separating out the logs, enjoying the feel of the rough bark against his hands. "They sure do, Henry."

Henry laughed. "Funny thing is, they do look pretty, but they don't burn worth shit. Good dried oak or maple would burn ten times better, but they don't look as nice in a fireplace in a half-million-dollar home. So who am I to educate those touristy folks?"

Roy laughed with Henry, pleased that the old man talked as if Roy himself was not a flatlander, was part of the lake, even though he and his wife were just renters, known as summer people. It was good to work with his hands, and when he had started the fourth bundle, a loud-pitched whining noise cut through the stillness of the morning, causing Henry to stop sawing and say, "Jesus suffering Christ, look at that, will you."

He stood up and looked to where Henry was pointing. Three jet skis were out on the lake, setting up plumes of spray as their operators whooped and hollered, swaying and setting up waves from their wake. A canoe almost tipped over from the moving water, but if the jet skiers noticed, they didn't let on. Henry muttered something else and then looked up at the house. "I suppose that's going to wake Muriel from her morning nap."

"How's she doing?"

Henry shrugged. "Oh, better and better, but she still tires easily. She really needs the peace and quiet but those young bucks—" he pointed out to the jet skiers "—aren't helping matters at all."

"I thought jet skis were banned on this lake," Roy said, watching the jet skiers now move in a circle, as if they were trying to create a giant whirlpool.

"They sure are," Henry said, putting his saw back in place. "But they're smart fellows, they are. They're renting a place over on Marie's Cove for a month, and they know by the time anybody calls the Marine Patrol, they can be back there and moored up, not moving a bit. You see, Marine Patrol has to cover the entire county, and it can take a half-day or longer for someone to come by. So they have their fun and laugh at all of us while swamping canoeists, running down loons or drowning their nests, and making my Muriel lose her naptime during the day."

"Somebody should do something about it," Roy said, watching the jet skis leap up and down in the water, the high-pitched whinning seeming to throb against his head.

"Yes," Henry said, "somebody should."

After dinner that night, Nicky was stretched out on the porch couch, her long legs propped up on a spare chair. Her laptop was balanced on her lap and she worked into the night while he sat across from her in an old easy chair held together by duct tape and old stitches. The chair looked like hell but was more comfortable than anything he and Nicky had back at their Boston condo. As Nicky worked, Roy read through a few days' worth of the Morrill *Sun,* a free daily newspaper that ran some fun stories, including tales of lost cats, record-size fish caught, and a retiree with too much time on his hands who thought overhead aircraft were spraying the air with experimental chemicals. A much more fun newspaper than either the *Boston Globe* or the *Boston Herald.*

Nicky looked up and said, "Well, hon, something's pulled through. A business appointment, tomorrow night."

"Where?" he said, putting the newspaper down for a moment.

"In Maine, about an hour away."

He frowned and said, "You know I don't like it when you bring work along on our vacation."

"I know, babe, honest I do," she said. "But the money's good and it won't take long."

He sighed, listening to the faint thumping noises as moths and other flying bugs battered themselves to death against the screen windows of the porch. Nicky was right; she was always right when it came to her work, and she knew that without his support, the whole thing wouldn't work. Still, it was vacation . . .

He had a thought. "All right. But tonight, I need to do something on my own."

"Oh?" she said, arching an eyebrow. "Going to rendezvous with some lake honey that you keep up here?"

He smiled at her. God, how he loved this woman. "No, nothing like that. But it's a favor for Henry."

"Really? Do you need any help?"

"Nope, but you know what? Maybe tomorrow you could take Muriel for a ride into town. A couple of her sisters are getting together for lunch. Henry mentioned something earlier about how she wants to get out of the house, but Henry doesn't trust his truck to take her into town and back. Says there's not enough room and the ride'd be too bumpy."

"Oh, I'd love to help Muriel out," she said, hands still on the laptop's keyboard. "But what about tonight? What are you doing for Henry?"

He opened up the newspaper. "I'll tell you tomorrow."

She put a whining tone in her voice. "But I want to know now . . ."

Roy grinned at her, turned the page. "If I tell you, I'll have to kill you."

She smirked back at him, returned to her laptop. "Promises, promises."

It was now three A.M. and Roy was in the canoe that came with the cottage, paddling as silently as he could through Marie's Cove. It was a still night and, luckily, there was no moon. The stars were as bright overhead as he could ever remember them, and the lights around the lake were so few that he could easily make out the misty veil of the Milky Way stretching overhead.

The cottages along the shoreline were quiet, with just a few lights showing. The water was still and silent, and he enjoyed the feel of the paddle slicing through the water. At his feet were a sealed water bag and a black inflatable life vest. Now that he'd been out on the water for a while, his night vision was good, and it only took a few minutes to spot the dock where the three jet skis were moored. The cottage at the other end of the dock was quiet, save for a single porch light.

He paddled some more into the cove, until he came to a small point of land where an evergreen was growing out over the water. In another minute he had tied off the canoe, and then took off his T-shirt and put on the life vest, which he quickly inflated with a few puffs of air into the tube valve. Then, waterbag in his hand, he quickly slid into the lake.

The water surprised him. He was expecting it to be teeth-chatteringly cold, but instead, it felt warm. He smiled in the darkness. This could be fun. He paddled slowly, the water bag floating in front of him, listening to the patient sound of the frogs. When he was near the first jet ski, there came a mournful wail from the south end of the lake, a noise that made the back of his neck prickle. A loon, calling out to its mate somewhere in the darkness of the lake waters.

He got to work on the jet skis, and when he was done he froze, holding onto a dock piling. A male voice was above him, saying, "What the hell?"

Roy hugged himself against the rough wood, waiting. Another voice joined the first, a female: "What's wrong?"

"This friggin' beer," he said. "It's empty."

"Shhh, come on back in, I'll get you another."

Some low murmurs and giggles, and then Roy swam back out on the lake. Halfway to the canoe he took a few minutes for fun and just rolled on his back, looking up at the night sky. In the space of just a few minutes, he saw two shooting stars and three satellites pass overhead. It felt good to be alive.

The next day Roy was helping Henry rake out pine needles, pine cones, and other sludge that had washed up on the tiny sandy beach. The water was fairly shallow on this part of the lake, and Henry liked to keep the bottom clean, especially for his visiting grandnieces and nephews.

It was good, solid work, pulling a garden rake across the lake bottom, and then walking over to the shore to drop off the debris. Henry would later rake it into a big pile to be burned in the fall. They both wore knee-high boots, but while Roy had on just a bathing suit, Henry had on his summer work uniform of green chino pants and shirt. Nicky had gone out as well, taking Muriel to town, and Roy had promised a little story about what he had done the previous night when they both had the time.

He and Henry didn't talk much during the work, which was fine, so Roy was surprised when Henry paused, leaning against his rake, and said, "Can you spare me a couple of minutes, Roy?"

"Sure," he said. "What's up?"

Henry wrapped both gnarled hands around the worn wood handle of the rake. "Oh, something, that's for sure. You know about my two boys, don't you? Alex and Andrew."

"Sure. Andrew's out in Detroit, working for Ford. And Alex is at the papermill in Berlin."

Henry nodded, looking pleased, as if Roy had just passed an oral exam. He said, "Both are good boys, but . . . well, Muriel and me, we wonder sometimes about what's inside of 'em."

"How's that?"

Henry took a hand off the rake and motioned up to the house. "When they was younger, they loved this place, they really did. They'd come in after Memorial Day and spend the whole summer here, and then they'd cry after Labor Day, wishing they didn't have to leave."

Roy rubbed at his chin. "Let me guess. They got older, things changed."

"Yap," and in that one syllable, Roy sensed years of disappointment. "I can't remember the last time Andrew's been here, and Alex, well, to get him and his family here for a weekend takes weeks of planning. All those soccer games, baseball practice, and everything they have to work around. And last year, at Thanksgiving, I mentioned something about leaving this place to the both of 'em after Muriel and I passed on. And you know what I found out?"

Roy had an excellent idea of what he had found out, but wanted to hear it from Henry directly. "No, I don't."

Henry leaned into the rake again. "The boys were talking in the kitchen afterwards, like they was twelve or thirteen again. They thought I had been sleeping on the couch, after all that turkey, and they were so excited about this place. But they weren't excited about keeping it, nossir. They were trying to figure out how much money they could make selling it, and how much they would split between the two of them. This house here, which I helped build with my father and his father. Sold, just for money."

Henry turned away and Roy was sure that the man's eyes were tearing up, so he gave him a few seconds as he raked the sand in the water a few times. Henry spoke up again, his voice softer. "So Muriel and I were thinking. We plan to go to town this week, change our will. We want to leave this place to someone who'll appreciate it, someone who loves it as much as we do. Roy, me and the missus want to leave this place to you and Nicky when we pass on."

Roy almost dropped the rake. "Henry, please, you can't—"

The old man turned, his face a frown. "By God, Roy, I've been an adult for most of this century, so don't you tell me what I can or can't do. You and your wife, you're not gettin' this place this summer, or even the summer after that. But you will get it, because we want you to have it. We know you'll love it as much as we do. You are both good people, real good people. And that's final. You start raising a fuss, then maybe my two boys, they'll think that Muriel and I have lost our minds, and they'll start fighting the will right now. But that won't be right. So you just stay quiet there and say yes, and we'll get back to raking this place. All right?"

He couldn't help himself, he just started smiling. "Damn it, Henry, yes. That's our answer. And don't be offended, but I hope it's many summers before we end up owning this place."

"Nope," Henry said, "I won't be insulted."

Then the noise started again, that grating, whining noise that set his teeth on edge. Roy looked up and the three jet skis were heading out to the lake, the young men whooping it up as they dodged among each other, racing over each other's wakes. Henry murmured something and Roy just watched, seeing the brightly colored watercraft bounce up and down. The noise seemed to be getting louder and louder.

Even though he was expecting it, Roy flinched when the explosions ripped out, one after another, *bam! bam! bam!* Henry swore, and they looked on as three plumes of smoke rose up and then quickly dissipated in the lake breeze. All three jet skis had turned turtle, oily wisps of smoke rising up, and Roy noted three lifejackets in the lake, arms waving, some shouts. It looked like all three young men had survived. Oh well.

"Well," Henry said, looking intently at Roy, "ain't that something?"

"Sure is," Roy said.

Henry slogged toward the shore, rake in his hands. "Guess I should do the neighborly thing, call the Marine Patrol. Funny thing is, this'll probably be the first time those boys will be happy to see them. What do you think?"

Roy sighed with contentment at the scene. "I think you're right, Henry."

Lunch was chicken and goat-cheese sandwiches, and Nicky looked over and said, "Hon, you're the best. Honest to God, you are."

"What do you mean?" he asked, pouring her a Sam Adams beer.

"What you did for Henry, that's what," she said.

He shrugged. "I just did the right thing, helping him rake out the shoreline like that."

She reached over the table and kissed him. "I wasn't talking about the raking, you silly man. I was talking about the jet skis."

Roy tried not to smile and failed. "I have no idea what you mean."

She kissed him again. "You do many things well, but lying to me isn't one of them."

Later that night, after an hour of driving, he and his wife were near the Maine town of Lovell. Nicky had on a pair of black spandex pants, black high-heeled shoes, a white top that exposed her bare midriff, and a short black jacket that seemed to emphasize her chest. He pulled up at the end of the long driveway, noting the large house up on the hill. Lights were on in the farmer's porch, and on little driveway lamps leading all the way up to the entrance. "You're sure this is the place?" he asked.

"Yep," she said, voice cheery. "The directions were perfect."

"I guess they were," he said. Roy had on a dirty pair of jeans, worn through at the knees, a Harley-Davidson T-shirt, and a black leather vest. He had slicked back his hair and looked over at his wife, loving her deeply yet hating the fact that she was working on their vacation. It was as if she sensed what was going through his mind and she leaned over and kissed him.

"It'll be fine, dearest, honest," she said. "I won't be long, and we sure can use the money."

"You just be careful," Roy said.

She opened the door, grabbed a small purse. "I always am, lover. I always am."

She slammed the door and then started walking gracefully up the long driveway, hips swaying, and he watched her until she got up to the porch. Then he started up the Jeep and drove down the road, pulled over, and waited. It was going to be a busy night. He had decided earlier not to tell her about Henry's amazing offer—he wanted to make sure she was focused on her job—but he knew he would tell her later tonight, when things were wrapped up.

From underneath his seat he pulled out a small flask of Jim Beam, and took a couple of swallows. The strong taste burned at him. He then rolled down the window of the Jeep and lit a cigarette, took a couple of puffs, and then tossed the cigarette out onto the asphalt. From the woods came the sound of an owl, *hoo-hoo-hoo*, out on a night hunt.

How appropriate. He reached under the driver's seat again, pulled out a 9mm Smith & Wesson, placed it in his lap. Then he started up the Jeep and made a careful U-turn, and returned to the house.

Roy sped up the driveway, headlights on high. He slammed the brakes to skid to a stop, making enough noise to be heard in the next county. He got out of the Jeep, strode up to the porch, bottle of Jim Beam in one hand, the pistol in the other. He plowed through the door in a matter of seconds and yelled out, "Wife! You damn whore, where the hell are you?"

Before him was a wide stairway, and off to the left was a room that looked like it would be called a formal dining room. Big polished table, lots of stiff-looking chairs. From upstairs came some noises, and he took the stairs, two steps at a time, and went to the left down a hallway that had paintings hanging on the walls. The murmuring voices got louder. The door at the end of the hallway was nearly closed. He smashed it open with a kick.

He took in the scene with a practiced eye. The bedroom was about the size of his first apartment after getting out of the army all those years ago. Heavy-looking bureaus on both sides, floor-to-ceiling mirrors, a bed the size of a Buick in the center, with four posts rising toward a chandeliered ceiling. His wife was kneeling on the bed, her eyes wide with shock. She had taken off her pants and top, and had on a skimpy black lace bra and even skimpier panties. A tube of oil was in her hands. Candles had been lit and placed on the nightstands, and in the bed with his wife was an overweight man, maybe late twenties, holding a sheet up to his pink and chubby chest.

"Oh, babe, please don't overreact, it's not what it looks like," she said, starting to get off the bed.

In the space of a few quick steps he reached her and slapped at her face, tumbling her to the floor, her long legs tangled in the sheets. She cried out and he yelled, "I know exactly what it looks like, you whore!"

Then the rage started deep inside of him, at seeing his woman, his wife, the center of his affection and love, almost naked in bed with another man, a complete stranger. He threw the bottle of bourbon at one of the mirrors, cracking it and sending a brown spray of liquid against the wallpapered wall. He jumped on the bed as the fat man tried to scurry away, grabbed at his hair, and pointed the pistol at the smooth forehead.

On the floor, his wife was weeping, but he stared at the trembling face of the younger man. "How much?" Roy demanded.

The man stammered. "Wha—wha—what do you mean?"

Roy popped the end of the pistol barrel against the man's forehead a few times. "How much were you going to pay her, you fat bastard?"

"One . . . one thousand dollars . . ." he said. "Look, I didn't know she was married, honest to God, I just met her over the Internet, it was a straight deal, nothing more, mister, honest, you gotta believe me . . ."

Roy turned, his voice still raised in anger. "Is that true, a thousand dollars? Do you have it?"

She raised her head, the tears making long mascara trails down her cheeks. "Yeah, babe, I got the money, and I—"

"Shut up," he said. "If I want to know more, I'll ask you." He turned his attention back to the man in the bed, sniffed the air. Jesus, did he ever bathe? He rapped the pistol against the forehead again. "I should shoot you, right here and now. No court in the county would convict me, a man sleeping with another man's wife. You don't think I'd get away with it?"

The man seemed to rally a bit. "Murder? You think you can kill me for something like this?"

Roy laughed hard. "Who said anything about murder? How about this?" Roy slapped the man's face and then grabbed his hand and pulled his arm out. The man yelped, and as Nicky started shrieking, Roy placed the muzzle end of the pistol against the man's right elbow.

"One squeeze of the trigger, man, one quick squeeze of the trigger and I'll shatter this elbow," Roy snarled. "I don't care how good the hospitals are around here, it'll never be the same. The rest of your life, every time you see the scar and feel the stiffness, every time you try to pick up something and your elbow aches, you'll remember me. You'll remember trying to sleep with another man's wife. You'll always remember."

Roy snapped back the hammer, the sound loud in the bedroom. "And maybe I'll do one of your knees, just to balance everything out."

The man started blubbering and Nicky stood up, sheet held against her body. "Wait, babe, wait!"

"Did I say you could talk? Did I?"

"No, please," she said, holding a hand out. "Maybe we can work out a deal. Something to make it right. I mean, I was being paid, all right? Maybe if you get compensated, too, promise not to hurt Clarence here, then we can just end it here tonight."

The man called Clarence said, "Yes, yes, that sounds good. Honest, look, let's see if we can work something out."

Roy took a relaxed breath, slowly pulled the trigger with one hand and lowered the hammer with the other. His fury and anger seemed to seep away from him, just like every time before—except for that one time each in California and Washington when things didn't go well and they had to move away—

"All right," he said. "Start talking."

In the Jeep Cherokee he was exhausted. The drive back to Morrill Lake seemed to take forever, and since they had both gotten inside and driven away from Lovell, not one word had been said for a long while.

Finally, Nicky cleared her throat and said, "Well."

"You okay?" he asked.

"Yep."

He coughed, hating the taste of the tobacco and bourbon in his mouth. "Did I get you back there, when I took a swipe at you? I thought for sure my hand caught the edge of your chin."

She laughed and he saw her hand move against her face. "Yeah, I think you did. Don't worry. I'll put an icepack on it tonight."

He reached over, squeezed her leg. "Sorry about that."

"Not to worry, not to worry."

"And who was Clarence?" Roy asked.

He could sense her smile next to him. "Some rich boy whose daddy left him a lot of money, and not a lot of social skills. A nice little boy with some very odd desires."

Another mile went by. "So," Roy said. "What's the haul tonight?"

Nicky reached up, turned on the overhead light, and then began rummaging through a brown paper grocery bag, like a housewife checking her day's shopping. "Let's see. Five thousand in cash. Five gold Krugerrands. A couple of gold bracelets. One diamond pinky ring—and if I ever see you in a pinky ring, I'll slap you silly, hon—and one of those PalmPilot computers. A good night's work, don't you think?"

He remembered seeing her almost naked in bed with that man, that rich, lonely fat man who probably thought he had gotten the date of his life through the Internet. He remembered the other times as well, where the script had been followed, and the two times when it hadn't. Once, in California, where a rich Silicon Valley guy started laughing at him, egging him on. And once, as well, in Washington, where the guy had started right in and had pinned Nicky down on a couch in the living room, tearing at her as if he thought since he was paying for her he could do anything he wanted.

Both times, things went wrong. Both times that fury inside of him had just blown out, like a rocket engine, and he had emptied his pistol in both of those guys, wiping away their grins, wiping away their hungers. After each time, they had moved away and had started up again: Such was their way of life.

He glanced over at her, smiling. "Yes, it was a good night's work."

After they got back to the cottage and had put away their tools and their rewards, they went to bed and performed the traditional after-work celebration, which was always fun, and which was always a good way of reaffirming their love and commitment to each other. Then they took a shower together, so that Roy could get the grease out of his hair, and Nicky could get the scent of another man's bedroom off her body.

The night was quite warm and they went out to the porch, still unclothed, glasses of Remy Martin in their hands. Roy slowly caressed the naked back of his wife as they stretched out on the couch, a single sheet over the both of them. Nicky went on for a while about Muriel next door, how the old woman appreciated the drive into town to meet her sisters, and Nicky said she was planning to take her grocery shopping later the next day. Then, Roy smiled and told her of Henry's offer.

Nicky sat up so quick that she almost spilled his glass of cognac. "You're not teasing me, are you? This is the God's honest truth?"

He sipped at the cognac, glad to finally wash out the taste of tobacco and bourbon from his mouth. "The honest truth, hon. Once Henry and Muriel die, we get the house and this cottage. We can live up here year round, if you'd like, and get a little income from renting out the cottage. Maybe cut back on your work schedule."

She hugged him tight. "Oh, Roy, that sounds wonderful . . . My God, it's a dream come true, it really is. Imagine being up here for the whole summer, not having to move out when the next renters come by. Imagine what it'll be like in the fall, when the leaves change. Or when the lake freezes over. We can snowshoe and ski and you can take up ice fishing and—"

He started laughing, kissing at her neck. "Slow down, hon, slow down. It's going to happen, but probably not right away. We're going to be in their wills. We're not getting everything tomorrow."

"Oh, I know, but still . . . oh, Roy, it's going to be great."

They lay there for a few more minutes, each sipping at their cognac, and then a loon call started, and then another, and then a third. The yodeling and calling echoed among the trees and bills of the lake, and Nicky snuggled in close to Roy and said, "Darling?"

"Yes?"

"Henry and Muriel . . . how old are they?"

"Don't know," he said. "Probably their late seventies."

"What do you think their life expectancy is?"

"Don't rightly know," Roy said. "They could both pass on this winter. But they're both hardy New Englanders. They could last another decade."

"Oh." The loon noise continued and Roy thought that he was the luckiest man in the world to be in such a place and to have such a woman at his side.

She spoke up again. "Do you think . . . well, do you think you could figure out a way to . . . well, you know . . . speed things up. I mean, well, I hate to think of us waiting for another ten or fifteen years, you know?"

He knew exactly what was going on in her mind, and he reached down and kissed the top of her head. "That's some thought, dear, but no. We're not going to do anything to them."

"Why?" she asked.

Roy recalled something Henry had said yesterday. "Because we're good people, that's why. Even Henry said that to me. And not killing your neighbors is what good people do."

Nicky laughed and snuggled in under his arm. "Thanks for reminding me."

He kissed her again. "You're welcome."

# Nancy Pickard

## Afraid of the Dark

NANCY PICKARD (along with other writers such as Carolyn
Hart and Joan Hess) has turned the cozy form inside out. She's
managed to keep its spunk while imbuing it with greater depth
and relevance to reflect the lives of contemporary women. This is
so true, in fact, that many of her so-called "cozies" offer the reader
much truer portraits of our time than many so-called "serious"
suspense novels. Here is one of Nancy's best stories, "Afraid of the
Dark," which first appeared in the anthology *The Night Awakens*.

# Afraid of the Dark

*Nancy Pickard*

*Friday, September 19*

She thought she'd already used up all of her courage.

Simply by stepping into the doorway of the abandoned tunnel underneath the Kansas prairie, Amelia felt as if she'd called upon every ounce of nerve she possessed. She had just enough left, maybe, to help her walk farther into the underground rooms. And after that? Then her entire lifetime's supply of bravery would be depleted, Amelia felt quite sure.

Yes, there was a bare electric light bulb hanging from the deteriorating ceiling. Yes, it glared forth a naked illumination, powered perhaps by some old generator left behind to rot. And, yes, it lighted the underground room for the first few yards that Amelia could see, as she held her breath and tried to work up enough gumption to get her legs to move forward. But she couldn't see beyond the light.

An improbable scene lay before her.

An antique barber shop. Underground. Chairs and all.

It was all revealed for the first time in who knew how many decades, by the bare light, to her astonished eyes.

The walls of the barber shop in the tunnel had been plastered, once upon a time, but she wouldn't want to touch the slime that glistened on them now. Amelia couldn't tell what color they might have been painted when the underground chambers were constructed seventy-five years ago. Fifty years before she was even born. She knew there wasn't merely this tiny barber shop but also a mercantile store, a church, and a town hall. Amelia felt there was no way she could work up the nerve to explore all of it, not now, not ever.

The decaying wood floor revealed earth beneath her feet.

It had all been a clever idea, a cool commercial and civic venue dreamed up by the citizens of Spale, Kansas, population 956 men, women, and children in the year 1922. *It's still as cool as a grave*, Amelia thought as she stood shivering in the doorway. *Just emptier.* Unless she counted herself, which in that context she didn't want to. The decrepit roads and buildings above her head were a ghost town now, with all the former residents fled to cemeteries or to other destinies.

In seventy-five years, everything made by the hand of man in Spale had changed. Not much in nature had, Amelia guessed. She imagined that the heavy heat of Indian summer hung as heavily on this day as it had all those many days ago. The humidity was probably just as high as it had ever been, and the falling leaves were no doubt just as golden as they used to be. They had escaped the heat and mosquitoes of their Kansas summers by coming down here to do their business and say their communal prayers, and they'd used it to escape cyclones and bitter winter days, as well. Thirty-two couples were married in the underground chapel. Countless whiskers were shaved in the barber shop.

Amelia knew all those facts and more.

What she didn't know was what lay in the darkness ahead of her.

At least there was light. She believed she could stand almost anything as long as there was even a glimmer of light. It was total darkness she feared more than anything on earth.

Amelia stepped reluctantly forward, until she could rest her left hand on the filigreed silver arm of the closest barber's chair. There was a badly cracked and distorted mirror behind it. She looked and saw herself. As if she were a distant observer, Amelia took in her own widened brown eyes, the disarray of her short brown, curly hair, the sweat stains on her red T-shirt, and the streaks of dirt on her jeans, and she thought, *I look scared.* Unnerved by the visual evidence of her fear, Amelia glanced away and down into the further darkness at the other end of the shop. As dim shapes revealed themselves, she realized there was a third barber chair and that someone was seated in it.

"Oh, there you are!" she exclaimed.

Several events seemed to happen at once.

Close enough now to the last chair to see who was in it, Amelia suddenly felt a deep, deep coldness. The man in the chair was dead. At the sight of his wide-eyed face, she was pierced by such unexpected sorrow that it temporarily submerged her shock.

Briefly lifting her gaze to a mirror behind the third chair, she then saw another man's face appear in the doorway behind her, and she—gratefully—recognized that man, too.

"Look!" she cried, whirling to face him. "Oh, look at what's happened—"

But instead of walking into the room to join her, he reached in with one hand. He jerked with fierce quickness on the chain attached to the light fixture. The chain broke off as the light went out.

"No! Oh, please, no!"

Pitched into total darkness, underneath the town of Spale, Amelia couldn't see the door close. But she could hear it slam with a dirt-muffled thud, and she heard the awful sound of the long wooden bar being thrown across it.

And she could hear her own screaming.

My God, what a fool she'd been.

*Tuesday, September 16*

"Ghost towns of *Kansas?*"

In New York City, in the office of the managing editor of *American Times,*

Amelia Blaney had slapped the palm of her left hand against the side of her head, as if to clear her ears. The spontaneous gesture was meant to indicate, humorously, that—surely—she had misunderstood her boss. It was not possible, her facial expression suggested, that she had heard him correctly.

One side of Dan Hale's thin mouth lifted in wry acknowledgment of her humor, but he didn't say, "Just kidding." Instead, he inquired, bitingly, "Is it the word *ghost, town,* or *Kansas* that gives you trouble, Amelia?"

She was merely young, not stupid. She knew that Dan himself was originally from the state. Maybe he hated it; maybe he loved it. Already regretting her comic miming, Amelia trod carefully with her next words.

"No doubt," she said tactfully, "Kansas is beautiful in September. All that golden . . . wheat."

"It's not a wheat state."

"It's not? Corn, then."

"Corn is green in the fields."

Amelia grasped the edge of her chair to keep from throwing up her hands. *Okay!* she thought in exasperated surrender. *Whatever!* She decided to skip over Kansas altogether and cut to the truth.

"I'm afraid of the dark," she admitted.

She said it lightly, not really expecting her boss to believe her, much less to feel sympathy and to change his mind. But it was embarrassingly true. Ever since she was a small child, Amelia had been nearly pathologically afraid of the dark. As much as a claustrophobic hates closets, as much as an agoraphobic is terrified of open spaces, Amelia was scared of the dark. She felt panicky and sick on the rare occasions when she got caught without sunlight, nightlight, flashlight, or head-light. She didn't know why, hadn't even been able to tell a shrink what it was— exactly—that she was scared was going to "get" her in the dark. She only knew the fear was excruciatingly real, and only as far away as the next sunset.

Sure enough, the characteristic little curve appeared at the side of Dan Hale's mouth again. She could see that he thought she was joking. Nearly everybody did, including her last boyfriend, who had finally walked out, angrily accusing her of ignoring his needs because he couldn't sleep with a light on in the bedroom. She couldn't sleep without it. She had cried when he left, but the truth was that she was less afraid of being alone than she was of the dark.

In one scathing word, Dan summed up his reaction: "So?"

Amelia tried one last time, though she knew that no reporter with only six months of job experience between this moment and journalism school could afford to reject an assignment, no matter if it turned her knees to custard and made her feel queasy. Dan Hale could have told her to interview a serial killer, and she might not have trembled, but this—this hit her where she knew she had a gaping hole in her courage.

"So," she explained, "that's where ghosts live. In the dark."

Amelia smiled tentatively at her boss, knowing it must look more like a gri-mace. A skeleton's grin.

He didn't appear to notice. In fact, he next uttered what at first sounded to Amelia like a total non sequitur.

"You're an animal nut, right?"

Startled at the change of subject from ghosts to animals and taken aback at his phrasing, Amelia replied with a cautious, "Yes?" She was surprised that Dan knew of her passion for animals. She supposed it must show on her college transcript that she had had a brief flirtation with veterinary medicine, before switching to J school. The transcript would not, she hoped, betray how disastrous and tragic the outcome of that flirtation had been. Amelia had ghosts of her own that she would have hated for any reporter, such as herself, to investigate.

"I thought so," Dan said. His voice was brisk now, and she knew it was a done deal. She was going to Kansas. He said, "That's why I've made reservations for you at the Serengeti Bed and Breakfast."

Amelia nearly whacked the side of her head again. Incredulously, she said, "The *what?*"

"It's a bed-and-breakfast inn on the grounds of an exotic animal farm," he told her, which only increased her astonishment. "Camels, llamas, giraffes. Ostriches, elks, kangaroos. It's all owned by a vet."

"Now, *there's* a story," she murmured, then flushed with embarrassment because she'd said it loud enough for him to hear. But good grief! She couldn't keep herself from reacting. An exotic animal farm? In Kansas? Could such a thing be true? And if so, would she get to see these animals, maybe even touch them? As unlikely as it seemed, Amelia began to feel excited about the assignment.

"No." Her boss's tone was annoyed, sarcastic. "That's *not* the story. Ghost towns are your story, remember that."

His blunt words slapped her back to earth, and to her fears.

The dark honestly frightened Amelia, down in a deep, shadowy cave in her soul. But the man seated across from her scared her in a more immediate and direct place: her pocketbook. She had student loans to pay off. She was only a beginner. She couldn't afford to beg off just because an assignment unnerved her. Amelia didn't have to look at the crowded walls of Dan's office to recall how pivotal this man's opinion could be, to her, to the city, to the world.

Those walls held awards and photographs, personally and admiringly autographed, of Dan Hale with so many heads of state that Amelia was hard pressed to identify all of them by name and country. He might be only thirty-six years old, but already he was managing editor of one of the four most influential weekly newsmagazines in the world. He was a man whose opinion, it was rumored, could end a war or start one.

Amelia was, in the old-fashioned parlance of her adopted trade, only a cub reporter. She doubted she would even get to compose any of the eventual story; more likely, she would type up her notes and turn it all over to a senior writer. Dan was sending her out as a researcher, that was all. But it was really something, to receive an assignment personally from the man himself.

*If I'm a cub,* she said to herself, as all these thoughts flashed through her mind, *then he's a bear.* It was an animal he resembled: tall, overweight, with a small-eyed, jowly face and a deceptive shambling gait that disguised a legendary ability to attack fools, in print and in the newsroom, viciously and without warning.

She felt flattered, even honored, by his interest in her.

There was nothing remotely romantic or sexual about it, Amelia felt sure. Dan Hale gave no sign that he even noticed Amelia in that way, and that was a relief to her. She liked very much meeting "brain to brain," as it were, editor to reporter. Amelia had been so saddened by her last failed love that she still tensed when a man showed any attraction to her. Compliments made her feel uncomfortable. She didn't want love, she had decided, it was work she needed, only work.

Thank God, she thought, that this interview between her and the legend was strictly professional. For some reason, this feared and respected journalist seemed to think that Amelia Blaney was worth his personal mentoring. Amelia sat up straighter and tried to swallow her doubts about the assignment. She concentrated instead on pleasing this difficult boss and reminded herself of how much she loved animals. He was doing her many favors with this assignment. She would try to appreciate it and live up to it.

Even if it meant ghost towns in Kansas.

He handed her airplane tickets and a highway map of Kansas, with certain town names circled in red ink. Then he impatiently dismissed her from his office. Only when she was standing outside his office, feeling rather breathless, did Amelia realize that he hadn't given her a single clue to *why* this assignment was made or what in the world she was supposed to be looking for.

She turned around, intending to barge back in and ask him.

But he was already on the phone, his back turned toward his window.

When she asked an older reporter about it, the woman advised her, "Don't expect explanations. Sometimes he never says why he wants you to do a story. That might prejudice your investigations. You're supposed to dig up the facts and figure out for yourself what the real story is." The older reporter grinned at Amelia. "And heaven help you if it doesn't turn out to be what he knew it was all along."

*Oh, God!* thought Amelia, feeling a terror that had nothing to do with the dark.

### Wednesday, September 17

On the connecting flight between Kansas City, Missouri, and Wichita, Kansas, the next day, Amelia studied the map Dan had given her. She decided the order in which she would drive to the abandoned, or nearly deserted, towns of Spale, Bloomberg, Wheaten, McDermott, Flaschoen, Parlance, and Stan. She loved the name of the last one. A town named Stan. It sounded friendly and, well, small-townish. Bemused, she wondered if New York City could ever have become the center of the universe (as she considered it to be) if the founders had named it Stan. On the plane, she laughed to herself.

While she was in an organizing mood, Amelia read over the bits of research she had pulled out of the library as well as from the magazine's files (which were a veritable library themselves) and the Internet. What she found was intriguing and went a long way toward explaining why her worldly-wise editor had considered the topic newsworthy in the first place. It was going to be a story of a changing America, she predicted to herself, of rural residents leaving for the cities, and of the towns they abandoned turning back into prairie dust.

These ghosts wouldn't scare her, she felt sure.

They might be sad, but they wouldn't be frightening, at least not to her personally. And, with any luck, she could do all of her research by daylight and retire every evening to the well-lighted security of her hotel room. *B&B*, she reminded herself as the outskirts of a small city appeared below the plane. Amelia had never stayed at a bed-and-breakfast lodging before. She wondered what they would serve her to eat at an exotic animal farm. Oats? Hay? *It's all cereal to me.* She laughed to herself as they landed.

She was beginning to appreciate just how deliciously bizarre this assignment could turn out to be. Giraffes and ghosts. In Kansas. Oh, my. Why, she could dine out on this story for weeks back home. Her New York friends would laugh till they begged her to stop.

Although she put away her paperwork, Amelia left the reading light on overhead. They were flying through a cloud cover that had darkened the cabin. Amelia wasn't particularly afraid of the storm or of a bumpy landing. She just liked the way the little lamp cast a circle of security around her in the passenger cabin.

Her first clue that she was nearing her destination was a camel hanging its head over a fence. Behind the camel—dromedary, she corrected herself when she saw only one hump—there were several zebras, including an adorable colt running circles around its elders. In her rental car, Amelia drove past another pasture, where huge ostriches lifted their beautiful wings and fluttered them over their backs. She was tempted to think, like Dorothy in *The Wizard of Oz,* that she "wasn't in Kansas anymore." But a large sign spelled out, "Welcome to the Serengeti." Below that: "Bed & Breakfast Inn." And farther down, stating the obvious in graceful script: "Exotic Animals." Visitors were advised: "No Tours without Permission."

Amelia turned onto a gravel lane.

Along a fence line, she stopped to stare back at the ostriches which ambled over to stare at her. As they batted their white eyelids at her, she shocked herself by nearly bursting into tears. Once, at a time that now seemed long ago, she had dreamed of being an animal doctor. And not just for any dogs and cats, either. A large-animal vet was what she'd wanted to be. "You," Amelia told the ostriches in a thick voice, "are certainly big enough, but I didn't quite have you in mind!"

Horses, cows, even sheep.

A practice in upper New York state, where she had spent summers with her grandparents. Farm country. Dairy land.

But it had all come to an ignominious, horrifying end. And she had slunk off to journalism school, not really caring anymore what degree she earned or what job she landed or even what her future held. She had, in fact, lost any grasp of the concept of future. Time became divided into then and now, and there was no tomorrow.

Suddenly impatient with herself (Amelia's grandmother had never tolerated what she called the "pig wallow of self-pity"), Amelia sniffed, blinked, and hurried on toward a white ranch-style house that waited at the end of the drive. She saw an ordinary-looking long, white motel structure to the right and metal pens and gates and a series of connected wooden barns. Nearly everything was painted white with red trim. It looked like a perfectly ordinary, well-maintained ranch. Except for the inn. And the zebras.

In a pasture beyond the barns, Amelia spotted a giraffe.

She wasn't quite sure she was going to approve of this place, this zoo on the prairie, because why weren't these wild creatures back in Africa, where most of them belonged? Still, she couldn't help but grin at the sight of the giraffe, and as she parked her car, she wondered if she ought to keep an eye out for wandering lions.

At first, it seemed as if the farm itself might be her first ghost town. "Nobody around but us chickens," she observed to a beautiful, glossy brown rooster that had walked up to the front door with her. "Are you the guard bird around here?"

When nobody answered the doorbell or her knock, she obeyed the sign that said, "Come in," and walked into a living room that had been transformed into an office. There were two desks with bulletin boards behind them. The walls were covered with photographs of people posing with animals, tear sheets from newspapers and magazines, and cute letters of appreciation from schoolchildren.

To pass the time until somebody showed up to sign her in, Amelia walked around the room, looking at all of the pictures and reading everything, feeling as if she were searching for the "real story" that Dan had sent her on. *Was* it about the economics of the heartland? Or was it about the traffic in exotic animals? How did these animals get here, anyway? Were they treated decently? Did they include endangered species that were illegal to own? Maybe, instead of researching ghost towns, she should have looked up references on the international wild animal trade—

Of late, Amelia had begun to get the sinking feeling that she was just not cut out to be a journalist. In truth, she didn't enjoy being suspicious of people, and she wasn't even particularly nosy. Curious, yes, in a courteous and scientific kind of way, but not nosy in the way of natural-born gossips. Or, she often thought wryly, journalists. She hated to ask rude questions. She much preferred to give people the benefit of the doubt rather than to suspect them. She'd drifted into feature writing, because investigative reporting was absolutely impossible for her; she always felt bad for the families of people whose lives were exposed. She stared, unseeing, down at one of the desks and thought, *And here I am, looking for a story, and I don't even know what it is!*

She had lost track of what she was reading and now discovered it wasn't about wild animals at all. *What?* she asked herself, confused by what she was seeing. Having worked her way around the room, she was now standing behind one of the desks, looking at the newspaper clippings tacked up there.

The word *murder* was in the headlines.

It was a set of clippings from local newspapers, dating back almost seventeen years. They were all about a long-ago murder. Of a girl named Brenda Rogers. Seventeen years old. A senior at Spale High School. Honor student. Valedictorian. Homecoming queen. Voted Most Likely to Succeed. Winner of a full scholarship to the University of Kansas in Lawrence. Oldest child of a couple who farmed outside town. The photos showed a smiling, pretty blond girl who appeared to enjoy having her picture taken.

A terrible crime and loss revealed itself to Amelia, and she felt sadness for the girl, the families, the town where, it was reported, "nothing so heinous has ever occurred before."

The killer's name was Thomas Rogers.

"Same as hers," Amelia murmured, transfixed by what she was reading. Also seventeen. Her brother? "My God, her *husband?*" Not only that but the father of—

"Her *child?*"

To Amelia, it seemed an unlikely combination of facts for a small town in the Midwest around 1980. But what was it that was so improbable, really? An early pregnancy? Or the fact that the boy married her? No. It was the continued high achievements of the young mother, and the scholarship, the full four-year scholarship going to a seventeen-year-old with a baby. To Amelia's mind, it all suggested an extraordinary young woman, a generous-hearted high school, a forgiving town, a trusting scholarship committee, and—more than likely—a wonderful, supportive family. Her glance passed quickly over the obituary that named the survivors.

*My Lord*, she thought sadly, *what an awful blow to all of them.*

And the boy? The husband/killer?

Also a senior. Also a straight-A student. A football, basketball, baseball star. Almost as outstanding as she was, and honorable to boot, in marrying her. Honorable, that is, except for the appalling fact that he killed her. Amelia read how her body was found in an old tunnel under the town, that it was discovered she had been strangled and dumped there. She read of Thomas's confession, conviction as an adult, sentencing to a federal penitentiary, the town's stunned grief over the fate of these young people.

He never said why he did it, she read, only that he did.

She realized that Spale was one of the ghost towns circled in red on her map, which meant that the town had emptied in the time between the murder and now.

And then she turned over one more clipping and saw, to her regret, that this was the story she was looking for and that she was going to have to go after it. The final clipping, and the most current, reported that Thomas Rogers, having served his time for the murder of his wife, Brenda, was getting out of prison at last. This week. He was quoted as saying that he would return home to live in Spale, "because there's nobody left to hate me."

Amelia knew what to do now: call Dan Hale in New York and get his approval. He would tell her to locate the released killer, alone in his ghost town, and interview him. *So tell me, Tom, how does it feel, coming back to the scene of the crime? Did you love her? Why did you kill her? Our millions of subscribers want to know!* Amelia felt frightened and sick at the idea of what she was going to have to do. Track down the girl's remaining family, her high school friends, some teachers, get them to relive a horrible time in their lives.

*I don't want to,* Amelia thought, but her practical brain inquired: *Do you prefer to be unemployed?* No, she did not. She'd do it. Maybe it wouldn't be so bad, maybe she was making too much of the whole thing. Maybe Dan wouldn't even like the story idea. That thought cheered her up, and she smiled to herself.

The front door opened, admitting a breeze and a tall man.

"You always find murder amusing?"

"What? No, I—"

"That's my desk you're—"

"I was reading all of your—"

"Yeah. Are you checking in?"

She was tempted to say, "No way," and stomp out. But giving him her usual benefit of the doubt, Amelia realized that his first sight of her could have annoyed anybody. She softened her voice and said, "I'm sorry. I've been looking at all of your photographs and mementos, and it led me around back here. When you came in, I was thinking of something else. Not the murder of that poor child. And yes, my name is Amelia Blaney, and I think there's a reservation in my name."

He stared at her for a moment, giving her enough time to realize that he was an extremely attractive man. Possibly near thirty. Tanned face with wonderful dark eyes, thick dark brown hair that curled down around the top of his shirt collar. The wide shoulders of a man who had tossed a good many hay bales. He wore dirt-streaked blue jeans over cowboy boots and a red and white plaid wool jacket over a denim work shirt. He was a big presence in the room. Amelia stepped quickly around to the front of his desk and then stood off to the side of it.

"I'm the sorry one," he said, shaking his head. "No excuses. Jim Kopecki. Welcome to our zoo. I'm the head jackass."

They both grinned, and suddenly the air was cleared between them.

*"Dr. Kopecki?"* she inquired.

"Yeah. The locals call me Dr. Doolittle behind my back."

"I'll bet they do. How'd you end up in the Wild Kingdom?"

"I've always been here," he said easily. "Inherited the farm. And the animals, too, in a way. First, it was just a few llamas out of a local rancher's estate. Nobody else wanted them; they weren't a cash crop at the time." His tone was wry. Somewhat to her dismay, Amelia felt herself being attracted not only to the story but also to the man. "Then it was a couple of abandoned ostriches from a wild animal show, and then people took to bringing me orphaned mule deers, that sort of thing. Then I read about a mistreated giraffe, and I went and got him." The young vet grinned. "You should have seen that, driving down the interstate with a hole cut in the top of an eighteen-wheeler and a half-grown giraffe sticking out of the top."

Amelia laughed. She was delighted with the story, and she was feeling warmed by Jim Kopecki's obvious feeling for animals.

"And," he concluded, "things just pretty much got completely out of hand from that point on." He made a comically rueful face and laughed along with her. "I figured that a lot of wild species are being born now in this country, and somebody's got to take care of them. When I was a kid, I dreamed of owning my own kangaroo, so maybe this falls in the category of 'Be careful what you wish for.'"

"I envy you," Amelia blurted. "I wanted my own elephant."

He shook his head and looked sincerely regretful. "Sorry, I don't have one of those yet. You might not envy me if you could see me trying to pull a calf out of a water buffalo when it's freezing cold and the middle of the night."

*Yes, I would,* Amelia thought.

He cocked his handsome head at her, and she easily read the interest that showed in his beautiful dark eyes. "So what do you do?"

"I'm a reporter," she told him, feeling like a fraud as she said it. "For *American Times* magazine."

Later, she would decide she had never seen a human face shut down so fast. All of the good humor and warmth drained out of his expression. Briefly, there was a look of shock, then disappointment. And then he returned to the cold-looking man who had first opened the door and caught her smiling beside the homicide stories.

He looked down at his desk, saying in clipped tones, "Would you like the Giraffe Room, the Zebra Suite, the Kangaroo Single, the Elk Double, the—"

Astonished by the alteration in his behavior, she managed to reply, "A single will be fine," but what she wanted to say was *What did I say? What happened? What's the matter?*

In fact, she opened her mouth to ask that very question but only got as far as "What—" when he ruthlessly interrupted her.

"You get a full breakfast with your room and a tour of the animals."

He shoved a reservation card over to her, and when she had finished filling it out, he pushed it aside without even looking at it and grabbed a key from a box on his desk. "I'll carry your bags."

"You don't have to—"

"It's my job."

Without another word, he carried her luggage into one of the motel rooms, leaving Amelia to follow along behind. But when he unlocked the door and let her in, Amelia exclaimed with surprise and pleasure. There were beautifully rendered giraffes painted right onto the walls, a thatched-roof canopy over the double bed, a lovely quilt with images of giraffes printed into it, a grass cloth carpet, and many artifacts that looked straight out of Africa. It was charmingly, whimsically designed to look like a room in a safari lodge.

"This is wonderful."

"My niece designed the rooms. Let us know if you need anything," he said formally, and then he was gone, out the door with a firm click of the lock.

Feeling offended and angry, Amelia changed into jeans, a long-sleeved shirt, socks, boots, jacket, and cap and hurried back outside, wanting to visit some animals before it got dark. As she headed toward the giraffe pasture, she saw Kopecki standing beside a beat-up, old white truck. She could have sworn that he saw her and then practically jumped into his vehicle and started it up and drove off as if a demon were chasing him.

What was it, she wondered, about the word *reporter* that scared him? Most people didn't run like that unless they had something to hide. She felt a lump of disappointment in her chest as she trudged over to the giraffe pasture.

It didn't take long for the sight of them to lift her spirits.

She propped herself against the gray metal fence to stare.

"Excuse me? Are you the new guest? Ms. Blaney?"

Amelia turned, frowning, to find a teenage girl standing close to the fence, her hands shoved down in her pants pockets. The tallest giraffe started slouching toward her, and several of the smaller giraffes pricked up their ears at the sound of her voice. When Amelia answered, "Yes," and remembered to erase her frown, the girl looked relieved. One of her hands emerged to offer itself to Amelia to shake.

"Hi, I'm Sandy Rogers. Uncle Jim said I should show you around."

Amelia heard the girl say her last name and had to work hard to keep from visibly reacting to it. *Rogers? Wasn't that the name of the girl who was killed and the boy who killed her?*

"You want to see the 'roos first, or you want to start with the giraffes?"

She looked about sixteen, Amelia thought. She had a fresh, pretty face and a sturdy little body that looked at home in the red flannel shirt, tight black jeans, and cowboy boots she wore. She had twisted her dark blond hair into a French braid, from which tendrils were escaping charmingly. Luckily, since Amelia couldn't find the right words to say, the tallest giraffe had reached them by then. He stood behind Sandy Rogers and bent his neck low, until his long-lashed, gentle face was cheek to jowl with her.

"Hey, Malcolm," she murmured affectionately. She blew gently into his nostril, and he shook his head a bit and lifted one great hoof and set it back down again. "This is one great guy, but he doesn't like to be touched, do you, Mal? The giraffes don't much, but they're sweeties, and curious as hell." She looked into the great, black, liquid eye so close to her. "Aren't you, big guy?"

Amelia stared at the two of them together—huge animal and petite girl—and felt such a painful longing that she brought her hands up and pressed them against her heart. She managed to say, "It looks as if Malcolm thinks we ought to start here. Kopecki's your uncle?"

"Yeah. Okay, Malcolm, let's tell her all about you and the ladies. Correct me if I get anything wrong, okay, big guy?" By then, two of the shorter giraffes had also loped over. Sandy bent down and picked up a clear plastic bucket from the ground. Amelia saw that it contained sliced carrots and apples. Without waiting to be invited, she reached in and picked out a slice of carrot and offered it to Malcolm. An amazingly long gray tongue curled out of his mouth and twisted itself around the vegetable, lifting it gently out of her grasp.

"Believe it or not, giraffes have only seven vertebras in their neck, just like us, but their blood pressure is twice as high as ours—"

While the girl talked, telling facts Amelia already knew—facts she felt she had been born knowing—Amelia continued to feed the giraffes until the carrots were gone.

"Want to see the 'roos now?" asked Sandy.

"Oh, yes." As they walked together toward the big kangaroo pen, she asked the girl, "How'd your uncle get wild animal training?" She couldn't think of a single vet school that offered it.

"Oh, he just makes it up as he goes along," was the airy reply. "He calls it the school of oh-hell-what-do-we-do-now veterinary medicine." She giggled, and Amelia found herself laughing, too. It was sympathetic laughter on her part, because she well knew that while some wild animal species might resemble domestic ones in some ways, on the inside a zebra was not a horse, and a gnu was not a cow. And animals as odd as giraffes and kangaroos had special needs that no amount of training in cats and dogs could teach a young vet.

They entered the 'roo pen, with Sandy telling her, "A group of kangaroos is called a mob. Adult males are called boomers." Amelia smiled to herself, remembering the joke in vet school: If an adult male kangaroo is a boomer, does that make a young male kangaroo a baby boomer?

A young joey hopped over and stuck its dainty, fingered paws into Amelia's hands to steal the slices of apple she had hidden there. She stroked the soft back and remembered that this was what it felt like to be happy.

By the time she returned to her room, a bright half-moon was rising. Amelia heard a donkey braying in the barn, answered by the trumpeting of an elk, sounding for all the world like an elephant.

She turned on all of the lights and was, for a few more moments, content. She knew she still had to drive out for dinner, in a rural setting with no street-lights. But that's what headlights were for, Amelia figured, to cut a reassuring path for her after dark.

As there were no telephones in the motel rooms, she went searching for a pay phone, which she found in the unlocked office. She was relieved to find Jim Kopecki gone, so that she had his office to herself again.

The first thing she did was to check the names of the survivors of Brenda Rogers. She read that Brenda had left her parents, Alfred and Betty Kopecki, a twelve-year-old brother, James, and an infant daughter, Sandra Gay. This time, the obituary was a shock. Amelia had half expected Sandy to be related to the victim and her uncle to be distantly connected. Instead, it was as close as it could be: Sandy was the daughter of the victim and the killer. Dr. Jim Kopecki was the victim's brother.

Amelia wanted to give him credit for providing a home for his niece, but what kind of home could it be for her with such a nasty uncle?

She walked over to the pay phone to do her next duty.

Amelia felt naive and nervous, calling her boss long-distance. Three times, she coughed and cleared her throat. When he picked up the receiver and barked, "Hale," into it, Amelia blurted out the whole story—of an old murder and of a killer returning to a ghost town—almost in a single breath. It was proof of Dan Hale's quick mind, she thought later, that he didn't have to ask her to slow down or to repeat herself.

"Do it," he said.

That was it, and he hung up. No advice. No caveats. Nothing but "Do it." She only wished that she wanted to! He had hung up too fast even to hear her say, "Thanks, Dan."

But Dr. Jim Kopecki did hear her, having walked in the front door at just that moment. He nodded at her curtly, a look of distaste on his face, transforming him, in Amelia's eyes, from a handsome man to an ugly one. He crossed to his desk without a word to her.

Appalled by his behavior, Amelia lost her own natural sense of courtesy. "Don't you think it's cruel," she asked him, "to keep those articles up there? Aren't they constant reminders to your niece of what her father did to her mother?"

He looked up, his face thunderous. In a voice as cold as the winter winds that blew across her grandparents' farm, he said, "I wondered when you were going to get around to asking your first question. Here's your answer: sleep in our bed, eat our food, pet our animals, pay your bill, and leave my niece and me alone."

Stunned, she could only stare back at him.

"Got it?" he asked her.

Amelia's reply was to walk out the door with as much dignity as she could summon. In truth, she was shaking. The man was nuts, clearly. He was a crazy man, with a farm full of wild animals and one young girl, all totally dependent on him. And all those articles pinned to the wall? They looked like vengeance to Amelia. They looked like a constant reminder: *remember, remember.* And just what was this vengeful, unpredictable man planning to do, now that his sister's killer was coming home? And how would it all affect that sweet girl?

Amelia wasn't hungry anymore.

She returned to her room, locked her door, and remained there throughout a mostly sleepless night, until the light of the morning.

*Thursday, September 18*

When she saw that it was Sandy fixing breakfast in the cookhouse and not the lunatic uncle, Amelia decided it was safe to eat there. Within a few minutes, she was delighted with her decision. The home-cooked buffet included scrambled eggs, sausage, biscuits, whipped butter, local jelly and honey, cinnamon rolls, cereal, coffee, and juice. None of the farm's other guests was present, so she ate alone while gazing at the camels and zebras lining up to eat at their troughs.

"Heaven," she said gratefully to Sandy when she carried her own dishes back into the kitchen. "Thank you so much."

"You're welcome. Sleep well?"

"Great," Amelia lied. The girl seemed so friendly that Amelia could only suppose the crazy uncle hadn't yet poisoned his niece's mind against her. "You do all this work and go to school, too?"

"Only 'cause I love it."

*And your uncle forces you to,* Amelia suspected. *How can I get you to tell me the truth about what goes on around here and about what these years have been like for you?* There wasn't an opportunity, because the girl was pulling off her apron and hurrying to grab a backpack from the floor.

"See ya!" she called gaily.

Too gaily, Amelia thought, for a girl facing a week in which a father she did not know was getting out of prison and returning to the town—only a few miles away—where he had made her a veritable, if not literal, orphan.

Amelia's heart ached for her.

And suddenly, she had all the desire she needed in order to pursue her story. Maybe by publicizing this child's plight, she could liberate her from the monomaniacal control of the vicious uncle.

Overnight, the weather had changed into Indian summer.

Amelia put away her jacket and donned a short-sleeved white silk blouse and summer-weight gray wool slacks with gray silk socks and black loafers. She wished it were shorts, a T-shirt, sandals, and a baseball cap, like Sandy had been wearing when she hurried off to school.

In her rented car, with the air conditioning on, Amelia drove back into Wichita, where she spent the rest of the morning in the main library. She found out that years of a depressed economy had emptied Spale. Between the lines, she intuited that the incomprehensible murder of their brightest girl by their brightest boy had wounded Spale to its heart, perhaps dealing the final blow. What an interesting town it once had been, she thought, with its amazing system of tunnels and underground shops.

While she was at the computer, she researched the status of imported wild animal species. When she located no condemnatory information about Jim

Kopecki's farm, she didn't know whether to feel disappointed or relieved. She settled on relieved, but only for the sake of the animals, she told herself.

She avoided the local newspaper, acting on a competitive instinct she didn't know she had. Maybe they'd be helpful, but maybe they'd want to keep the story for themselves.

She did, however, place a call to the federal penitentiary where Thomas Rogers was incarcerated to find out exactly when he was due to arrive back in Spale.

"Should be there by now," was the clipped reply.

She attempted to hold the prison officer on the phone by asking, "What kind of prisoner was he?"

"Model," was the answer, followed by a string of accolades that made Rogers sound more like the honor student he used to be than the murderer he was. "Perfect record. Early release. Earned three college degrees. BA, MFA, PhD. Created convict tutoring program. Taught prison classes in reading and math, plus led a creative writing class. Started a prayer/meditation group. Anything else you want to know?" Amelia said no, but she was thinking, *Yeah, where's the eagle scout badge?*

Feeling as cynical as a veteran, world-weary journalist, she got back into her rental car and drove to Spale. All the way, she felt fueled by righteous fury aimed at the man she was planning to interview.

"Don't you *dare* try to give me any of that born-again crap," she fumed aloud, as if speaking to Thomas Rogers himself. "I've met the daughter you betrayed so horribly!"

Amelia had not realized how many other journalists might also consider the return of a murderer to a ghost town to be a juicy story. When she got within sight of Spale, she saw that it was, in one of the clichés she was trained to avoid, a media circus.

As it turned out, there was only one thing missing among the television vans and the other rental cars: Tom Rogers, the ex-convict himself.

"He arrived," a writer from *Newsweek* told her, leaning against her car. "That we know, because we saw him dropped off at that building." He pointed to a falling-down storefront on the former Main Street. "But he must have sneaked out the back. Maybe he had another car waiting. I don't know. We've been in there, and there's nobody there. We're packing up and going home. He'll surface again someplace. But who the hell cares now? It's not a story now. Killers walking the streets of cities are a dime a dozen. But one of them living alone in his own private town full of ghosts? That was going to be good, damn it. You find any decent place to eat around here?"

She didn't tell him about the Serengeti Bed and Breakfast.

And she didn't tell him where Thomas Rogers probably was, either, although Amelia was pretty sure she knew: in the old forgotten tunnels, beneath the town. Where he had dumped his young wife's body. And where he now had a perfect place to hide for the rest of his life, if that's what he wanted to do.

Amelia was regretfully willing to give him what he wanted, because there was no way she was going into the darkness underneath the ground in order to search for a man who had already killed at least one woman.

No way.

"No," she said to her boss, back at the pay phone in the Serengeti office. "I'm sorry, Dan, but I won't do it. It would be stupid and dangerous for me to go down there alone."

She was surprised at how calm she felt saying that, almost as if she was relieved that she was about to be fired. Finally, she could admit to herself and to the rest of the world that she had never been meant to be a journalist. She didn't have a clue what she *was* going to be once she was out of a job and a salary, but now she knew that reporting wasn't it.

"Why the hell do you think I want you to do anything that idiotic?" Dan Hale demanded, to her surprise. "I only ask war correspondents to do stupid things that could get them killed. For God's sake, this story isn't as important as Bosnia. But I still like it, so here's what I'm going to do—" He was going to fly a more experienced reporter down to join her, he informed Amelia, and she was going to meet him at ten in the morning in the town of Spale.

Although she still wanted very much to help Thomas Rogers's daughter, Amelia found herself wishing that Dan Hale had just gone ahead and fired her. The only good thing about the exchange, from her point of view, was that Dr. Jim Kopecki hadn't walked in during the middle of it. She hadn't, in fact, seen him or his niece all that day.

She couldn't do any more that day, so she spent the remainder of it typing up her notes and observations, then wandering around the farm, communing with the animals. And composing, in her head, the right questions to ask a killer.

### Friday, September 19

Amelia awoke suddenly that night and stumbled to a window, pulled by the sound of an engine running. The bedside clock displayed the time: one-thirty.

The headlights of a white truck dimly illuminated a scene: the veterinarian and his niece outside at the edge of a pasture, pulling something dark and heavy from the truck bed, dumping the object into a depression in the ground, then shoveling—dirt?—on top.

"Oh, God," Amelia whispered. "What are you doing?"

What were they burying? Should she try to call local law enforcement? But how? From Kopecki's office, where she might get caught? And if she ran to her car, he'd hear her leave . . .

Amelia had a terrible feeling that she would not find Thomas Rogers in the tunnels. If she didn't, she would advise the local police to dig up the fresh hole—grave?—in the pasture.

And then what would happen to the girl?

"Oh, God," Amelia whispered again, but this time it was a prayer.

For a second night, she hardly slept. By the time the sun rose, she was exhausted and badly frightened by her own vivid imagination. The hours alone in the bedroom, surrounded by the darkness outside, took a heavy toll on her heart.

"I can't do this," she told her image in the mirror.

It didn't try to argue the point with her.

When she walked out after breakfast, pretending to take a casual stroll, she saw dirt covering what appeared to be a fresh hole in the ground. Amelia ran back to her room, grabbed her packed bags, and got quickly into her car. Let New York take care of paying her bill, she thought, *I just want out of here.* Her brain said it never wanted her to return to the Serengeti, but her heart felt bereft at the sight of the zebras fading from view in her car mirrors.

It was still early when she arrived in Spale.

Amelia parked at the edge of town to wait for her reinforcement to arrive. She wasn't quite so terrified anymore about going down into the tunnels, because she no longer expected to find anybody alive down there.

When the backup reporter's rental car pulled up next to hers and the driver got out, Amelia reacted with shock.

It was the man himself, Dan Hale.

His mouth wore its characteristic one-sided smile when she hurried out to greet him.

"Surprised, Amelia? You shouldn't be. Don't you remember where I'm from?"

"Kansas, but—"

"Spale, Kansas." His tone implied that she ought to have known, and Amelia felt instantly humiliated. She also felt resentful, because how was she supposed to have known something that she had never heard or seen mentioned before? In fact, she specifically recalled hearing that he was from Kansas City. She was rebelliously tempted to answer his contempt with her own sarcastic, *So?*

"I didn't know," she said instead. "But still, why—"

"Because I knew them. Brenda and Tom. We were best friends."

Her eyes widened. "Oh, Dan! Gosh, I'm—"

"Sorry? So will he be, when we're finished with him. He's going to wish he'd stayed in prison."

"But Dan, Thomas Rogers may not be here," she said, and felt a petty satisfaction that this time she had managed to shock him. "He may not even be alive." Amelia told her boss what she had witnessed from her window.

Hale looked confused, disturbed. He said, "That's impossible."

Amelia didn't see why. It seemed horribly possible, even probable, to her.

"Stay here," he commanded her. "I'm going down into the tunnels to find him."

He left Amelia standing by herself at the edge of town, sweating in the warm prairie wind that was blowing dust from one side of the abandoned town to the other and then back again. She waited for more than half an hour, coughing now and then and thinking, *Well, at least there's one good thing about Dan showing up. He knows how to get in and out of the tunnels.* But when forty-five minutes had passed, she began to worry about him and to fear that she was going to have to go down to look for him.

Still, she waited, hot, exhausted, frightened of many things.

*What if something fell on him?* she thought. *What if he's been injured?*

But he emerged from a decrepit storefront—different from the one he had entered—and walked toward her. For once, Dan Hale was smiling fully.

"He's down there, all right," he told her.

"He *is?*"

"Go on down and interview him, Amelia. He's waiting for you. Don't worry. He's harmless now. You don't have anything to fear from Tom Rogers."

When she hesitated, he grasped her elbow and pulled her along, saying reassuringly, "Don't worry! I'll be right behind you."

"But the dark—"

"It's not dark. He's got an old generator up and running, so there's even electric light."

Amelia thought that if Dan told her one more time, "Don't worry," she would hit him. Reluctantly, unhappily, she let herself be led into one of the old buildings, through a door in the floor, and down a wooden ladder into a cool, earthen chamber. He had told the truth; it was lighted, if dimly.

Amelia relaxed a little.

She could stand anything, she thought, if there was light.

"Dan?" she asked in a low voice. "How'd you ever get out of Spale?"

Behind her, he answered in a normal voice, as if he didn't care what Thomas Rogers heard them saying. "I got her scholarship. Brenda's. They couldn't very well give it to Tom." His chuckle was a warm breath on her neck. "I never looked back."

They reached an open door with a sign still visible beside it: "Barber Shop."

"Go on," he urged her. "Tom's in the last chair. He'll tell you the whole story." Hale thrust something warm into her hands: a trim black gun. "Here. If it helps you feel safer."

Amelia stepped inside the barber shop.

Amelia recognized the dead man in the chair from his recent photograph in the local newspaper: Thomas Rogers.

Feeling overwhelmed by the tragedy of all of their lives, she had turned and also recognized the face of the man in the doorway: Dan Hale. He broke the light chain, slammed the bar across the door, and left her there in the utter darkness with a corpse. Before the light went out, she saw that Tom Rogers had been shot several times. As she screamed and screamed, the warm gun in Amelia's hands slid to the floor.

The darkness felt eternal.

She knew she would lose her mind before she died.

Amelia's brain played those two messages over and over, and it seemed an eternity, indeed, before another thought could fight its way past the terror: Dan had gone in one store and come out another.

Two tunnel exits. At least two, maybe more.

In the nightmare that had become her life, Amelia found the slimy walls and felt her way entirely around her burial chamber. There was no other exit, no other way out. By feel, she located one of the other old barber chairs and sank into it. She thought about the endless time that lay ahead of her. And then she remembered the gun, and she realized that she could kill herself now and foreshorten her own suffering. Frantically, she found her way to the floor and felt around until metal touched her fingers.

The end of the gun barrel was resting inside her right ear when she changed her mind.

Slowly, in the dark, Amelia brought the gun down and placed it gently, lovingly, in her lap.

In case there was even the slightest chance that she would be found, she must stay alive to clear the innocent name of Sandy's father, to give the girl the final peace of knowing that her father had not killed her mother. It seemed clear to Amelia that Dan Hale had killed them both. The one for a scholarship that was his exit to a grander world. The other for his silence. She couldn't imagine why Tom Rogers had never told the truth, if that was it.

Amelia wept and cursed her own conscience.

What good would it do to stay alive if she was out of her mind with horror when they found her—if they ever did? She started screaming again. *Please, somebody, hear me!*

A sound awakened her.

A rat? A ghost?

Amelia screamed again.

Someone yelled back at her. And soon she heard a thud, and then the door opened, and Brenda Rogers's little brother stood there in the doorway, holding a huge flashlight. The beam paused on her face, and he said, "Thank God!" Then it passed over onto the face of the dead man, and the little brother . . . the young brother-in-law . . . the grown-up veterinarian . . . came over to Amelia, collapsed to his knees, dropped his head in her lap, and began to cry.

"Dan Hale killed sis for the scholarship."

Amelia, Jim, and Sandy were huddled on hay bales in a corner of the barn, while two young black llamas sniffed around their feet and knees. Jim was explaining to Amelia, while he kept an arm wrapped around his pale, sad niece. "Then he threatened Sandy's life. He told Tom that he had to confess to the crime. Dan said that he'd kill Tom's baby girl unless Tom took the rap for him. And Tom was young and scared and didn't know what else to do."

"How'd you find out all this?"

"Tom wrote to me from prison and told me to take care of Sandy for him. And he told me the truth, and also why we couldn't reveal it, not even to my parents. They raised Sandy, and when they died, I asked her to stay on the farm with me. Dan still could have killed her, at any time, and he was very powerful by then."

"You believed him?"

"Oh, yes. I knew them both very well. I knew what they were capable of. I'd never liked or trusted Dan Hale, and I'd always loved Tom." He smiled wryly. "Little brothers know these things. What broke everybody's heart was that Brenda died, and also that we couldn't believe Tom would do that. And yet he claimed steadfastly that he did. If you knew what it did to his parents . . ." Jim Kopecki closed his mouth and shook his head. After a moment, he continued, "When he told me the truth, I knew it *was* true."

"You saved all those articles—"

"So we wouldn't forget him. I told Sandy the truth, when she was old enough to contain it. I wanted her to be able to love her father."

Amelia reached out to grasp one of the girl's hands.

Over Sandy's bowed head, the adults looked at each other.

Sandy whispered, "I was so excited to meet him. We fixed up a room here, for him to live. He was going to hide out in Spale until the publicity went away, and then we were going to try to sneak him onto the farm and make like he was just a hired hand so he could be with us."

"It might not have worked," Jim admitted.

"Because of Dan Hale?" Amelia asked, and he nodded. She didn't say so, but it sounded to her as if Tom Rogers might have had a miserable existence if he had lived, although at least he would have had the comfort of the love of his daughter and his brother-in-law. What she did say, to Jim, was, "No wonder you hated me."

"Not you. Dan Hale."

"He was using me as bait."

"Yeah."

"If anybody ever found me, they'd say that Tom Rogers had trapped me in the tunnels, probably attacked me, I'd shot him in self-defense, and then killed myself when I found I couldn't get out."

Jim looked horrified at the idea of it. "Amelia, would you have—"

"I don't know. Maybe, eventually. Wouldn't you?"

He thought a moment, then sighed. "Yes."

Later, when it was just the two of them, she told Jim about how desperately she had wanted to be a vet herself. About her straight A's and about the woman-hating professor who had blamed a stable fire on her.

"Three calves died. The professor had been smoking in there, but he said it was me, and who was I against his word?"

"But now you love being a journalist."

"I hate it!"

He laughed in surprise.

She whispered, "Tell you a secret? I'm a rotten reporter. I hate to hurt people's feelings!"

Impulsively, Jim hugged her, and impulsively she returned it, and suddenly it became an embrace that turned into a kiss, which lasted and lasted and then repeated itself again and again.

Much later, Amelia sighed. "I wonder what I'm going to do for a job now."

"Stay here, of course."

She stared at him, holding her breath.

"Room and board," he said, smiling at her hopefully, "and a small salary, and all the hay you can lift. Do you want to, Amelia?"

She read between the lines, looking into his eyes, and said, "I do."

"I do, too," Dr. James Kopecki told his new stable hand and future wife.

# Gillian Linscott

## For All the Saints

GILLIAN LINSCOTT'S story we've chosen for inclusion, "For All the Saints," which first appeared in the anthology *Crimes Through Time III*, was short-listed for the Crime Writer's Association Golden Dagger Award. Her first mystery series was about Birdie Linnet, an ex-cop turned fitness trainer. The scene was contemporary England. The second series, about the wonderfully named Nell Bray, a British suffragist, gives us a look at the London of early in the last century. If you haven't picked up the Bray series yet, you're missing one of the best mystery stylists writing today. Adept at any historical period, from the medieval to the modern day, her voice keeps gaining distinction and poise with each amazing new short story and novel.

# For All the Saints

*Gillian Linscott*

Saint Catherine was late. Ten o'clock was when Trillow had told her to get there, so as not to waste any of the March morning light. Ella was kneeling to put knobs of coal on the back of the fire in the studio because the saints needed warmth. Trillow had taken the hearth brush and was using it on an old broken-spoked cart wheel he'd borrowed from the coalman and propped up against the *chaise-longue* on the model's dais. Coal dust and flakes of black paint were scattered around it, sheets of screwed up drawing paper and charcoal sticks that had got broken and trodden into the boards.

"Ella, come over here, would you."

She stood up at once. Trillow always talked to her like a brother to a younger sister. There were three of them in the household: Trillow the artist, his friend Ned, the engraver, and Ned's sister Ella. It wasn't a conventional arrangement, but Ned and Ella's mother had died three years ago, when Ella was thirteen, and it had either been move in with Ned and Trillow or go into service among strangers. They'd taken three rooms together in a tall house in Pimlico. Trillow had his studio on the first floor, Ned his print-making room upstairs, next to the kitchen where they ate, and Ella attended to the housekeeping and slept in a cupboard-bed alongside the fire. She was almost entirely happy. There was very little money to spare, but she knew all the saints watched over them. The saints paid the coal bills, kept bread on the table, provided Trillow's sticks of best quality charcoal and Ned's plates of shining copper and cakes of yellow beeswax. She put down the fire tongs and went obediently up to the dais. Trillow signed to her to stand alongside the coal-cart wheel, took her arm and draped it over the rim. She stood ecstatic, not moving a muscle, as he went over to his board and started drawing with quick strokes. Ella knew Saint Catherine had been martyred on a wheel, although she wasn't entirely sure how. When she was much younger she'd imagined her going slowly around and around on the wheel of the grocer's cart, gold hair trailing in the mud, and assumed she'd died from humiliation and dizziness. But the how didn't matter. Saints in Triumph were what Ned and Trillow depicted, like Saint Catherine after martyrdom, radiant in virgin white, one arm resting on the transcended wheel, the other hand holding a palm frond. Children were given them as certificates for regular attendance at Sunday school. It was her dream that Trillow would ask her to model for one of the saints.

A knock on the front door one floor below, the confident knock of some-body who didn't expect to be kept waiting. Trillow sighed with relief and threw down his charcoal.

"Her at last. Go down and let her in, Ella."

On her way out, she glanced at his drawing board. Only a hand on a wheel, that was all. She'd half hoped—more than half hoped—that a miracle would have happened and Trillow would have bestowed sainthood on her. As she went down-stairs, the segs of her boots tapping on the uncarpeted boards, she tried to crush down her disappointment. Her face was too angular, body too thin, hair too ordi-narily brown to make her a saint. Saints Triumphant had smooth faces, rounded bodies under their white draperies, swathes of black or golden hair.

Saint Catherine was waiting impatiently on the step. She was wearing a black velvet jacket over a skirt of yellow and black tartan, draggled with mud at the hem. A red shawl covered her head and the fringe that frizzed out of it at the front was as gold as fried egg yolk. She pushed past Ella without saying anything and went upstairs trailing a smell behind her. It was a warm, sourish smell, the sort you got when you knelt down to watch the mother cat feeding her kittens on the old blanket in the corner of the kitchen. As soon as Saint Catherine set foot on the landing the door to Trillow's studio opened. She went inside. The door shut.

"Come along, Kate dear, give a little more."

"Me knee's stiff."

"Rub it then. Ah, that's good. Keep your hand there like that. Don't move."

"Thought you said I could rub it."

"Shhh. Keep still."

"Rub somewhere else if you want."

"Only ten bob extra. Yes, I know."

"So what's ten bob to you?"

"A lot of money. Now try lifting your petticoat up and holding it there on your knee. Knees apart for goodness sake."

"Ten bob's not a lot when you're selling them for five guineas."

"Who says we're selling them for five guineas?"

"Urse knows a man."

"Ursula talks too much. Stop fidgeting."

"Me titties are getting cold. I'll get goose pimples."

"It's not cold in here."

" 'Ow would you know? You've got a jacket on.

"Alright, five minutes' break if you must."

"Something to warm me up?"

"Help yourself. I only hope it puts you in a better mood."

"Ten bob'd put me in a better mood."

"Pity, because you're not getting it. We have a lot of expenses to cover."

"Like bribing policemen to look the other way."

"Just get your drink and sit down."

"Only bribes don't always work, do they? You know Dutch Joe was raided last week? Took all 'is pictures and plates away and 'e's had to do a bunk."

"Are you threatening me?"

"Ten bob."

"I'll have to ask Ned."

The door of Trillow's studio stayed closed. Ella and Ned lunched in the kitchen off tea, bread and cold mutton. His long hands were flecked with acid burns and a distinctive smell clung to him; of ammonia, linseed oil and resin, overlaid with the strong tobacco he smoked when he wasn't working to drive the chemical fumes out of his lungs. Ned had to sleep in his workroom. Through the winter his thin face had turned yellowish and there was a boil on his neck that wouldn't go away. When Ella had cleared up the lunch things, she went through to his room to help. There was a new batch of copper plates to be prepared, first cleaned with ammonia and whiting, then heated over a burner and spread with a fine film of wax. Ned had taught her the business as if she were a proper apprentice and she did all the preparation work and clearing up.

Ned stood at his big table by the window with a drawing Trillow had made the day before spread out in front of him, copying it onto a waxed copper plate with a sharp engraving tool. Ella left her first plate drying and went over to watch. The picture was of Saint Ursula and her eleven thousand virgins, a snaking line of them with their palm branches, stretching to infinity in correct perspective. Ursula was tall and stately, with dark hair stretching down nearly to her feet. Ella thought of Trillow's long charcoal strokes drawing it and felt as if her own hair were being stroked into sleekness by his hand. A little shiver went through her.

"She's beautiful, isn't she?"

Ned didn't answer. He'd seemed preoccupied over the past few days. She noticed that he kept passing his hand over his eyes.

"Eyes tired?"

"A little."

"You're working too hard."

She heard him from her cupboard bed next door working late into the night, coughing from the fumes of nitric acid.

"We have to work while the market's there."

"Surely people always need saints."

He laughed and it turned into a cough. "Wouldn't you like to live in a house, Ella, with bedrooms and meals on a proper table and a skivvy to make up the fires?"

"I suppose so."

"I suppose so too."

"And Trillow?"

"Oh, I don't know what Trillow wants."

The possibility that there might be a future without Trillow sent a different sort of shiver through her.

She said, diffidently, "Trillow works too hard as well. He's out every night."

Evenings were a good time to sell, Trillow said. It surprised her a little that Sunday school people should be doing business in the evenings. She waxed another plate and tidied the workroom. Artists like Trillow could work in confusion, but engravers had to be orderly: the sharp tools in racks on the walls, sheets of dampened paper piled between plates of glass ready for printing, bottle of lin-

seed oil for mixing the ink, bottle of nitric acid for biting the design into the copper plates. Damping the paper, keeping the tools clean and the bottles topped up
were part of Ella's work. At about half past three they heard feet stamping down
the stairs and the front door slamming. Soon afterward heavier feet tramped
upstairs and Trillow came in, carrying a sheet of paper.

"That bloody woman . . ."

Ned gave him a warning look and glanced at Ella. Trillow went over to the
work table and dumped his paper on top of the picture that Ned was copying.

"One Saint Catherine, as per specification."

Ned looked at it, frowning.

"More of a sketch, isn't it?"

"The light was going. You can put in the detail when you're copying."

"It's not that easy."

"For heaven's sake, I have to deal with these women. It's all very well for
you to sit up here and—"

"Ella dear, would you go and make us a pot of tea?"

She went obediently and, from the kitchen, was aware of low voices rumbling next door. She couldn't hear what they were saying, but knew it was an
argument. It hurt her that the two people who meant most to her should argue.

"So I told her I'd ask you."

"You decide."

"No. You're not putting it all on me. Equal profits, equal risks."

"It seems a lot of money. But then if she's a good model . . ."

"If you catch her quick between the third and fourth glass of gin she's not so
bad. I'll bring the other ones up later, when Ella's out of the way."

"So you mean, you think she's worth it?"

"Nothing to do with it. It's not a model fee she's asking, it's blackmail."

Ned put down his engraver's point and stared.

"She wouldn't, would she?"

"She dropped a hint about Dutch Joe."

"Oh God, don't you think we ought to leave off for a while?"

"No! With Joe out, we can take over his market. Every porter at every gentleman's club in London knew Joe. They'll need somebody to send their people
to now he's gone."

"We shouldn't get in so deep. Just a few months of it, we agreed."

"Oh yes, enough for the rent on a little house in Barnes for you and your sister, then puppy dogs and prayer book markers for the rest of your life. Ned, there
are thousands of pounds, tens of thousands in this—town house, flunkeys and carriage."

"Is that what you want?"

"I certainly don't want to spend the rest of my life in a scrubby studio getting whores drunk."

"Shhh."

"Oh for goodness sakè, your sister must have some notion of what's going on."

"Of course she hasn't, and she's not going to."

Trillow shrugged. "So?"

"So?"

"Do we pay Kate's ten bob or don't we?"

"I don't know."

The raid came three days later at around four in the morning while it was still dark. Ella, closed into her cupboard, heard the knock at the front door like something at the back of a dream, then woke as noises of outrage rose through the house, with tenants poking heads out of doors to ask what was happening, and heavy steps clacking on the stairs, strange voices. While she was sitting up and blinking, trying to separate reality from dream, she heard the door open and steps coming into the kitchen, soft steps, not like the ones on their way upstairs. The fire was out and the room quite dark.

"Ned? Ned, what's happening?"

Somebody pulled the cupboard doors open and stood close to her in the dark. Not Ned. Not Ned's smell.

"Ella, take these. Keep them in there with you and stay where you are."

Trillow. He pushed something at her, something that dug against her ribs. Her hands closed around it and she knew at once what it was. Parcels of copper plates were as familiar to her as bread and cheese. Then the cupboard doors closed on her and Trillow was gone. She heard his voice out on the landing, louder and grander than usual.

"There's a sick girl in there. If you must go in, show some humanity."

Then Ned's voice from the doorway, not all loud or grand.

"Ella dear, I'm afraid there are some people coming in."

Through a gap where the doors didn't quite meet she saw oil lanterns beaming over the kitchen, making ordinary chairs and bowls look sinister. Then steps toward her cupboard and Ned's voice, "No, my sister . . ."

Trillow's voice, full of contempt, "If they insist on violating a poor girl's sick bed, let's get it over and done with."

The doors flapped back. She shrank against the wall from the lamplight, pulling the blanket up to her chin. The parcel of plates was pressed between her spine and the wall at the back of the cupboard. The light beamed at her for several heartbeats, making her screw up her eyes until a rough voice murmured, "Sorry, miss," and the doors shut on her.

She heard Trillow asking, "Are you quite satisfied now?" in a voice as sharp as any engraving tool. Then the feet went clacking away downstairs.

Much later, when the house was quiet again, Ned came to her. She heard his apologetic whisper through the doors.

"Ella, are you awake?"

She sat up and opened the doors. He was carrying a candle in an enamel holder. His face in the light reminded her of a severed head in an engraving of a cannibal feast.

"What happened?"

He pulled a chair over and sat down.

"Ella, my dear somebody . . . oh, so much malice . . ."

"It was the police?"

"Yes. You see, when you're in trade, when other people see you doing well, you make enemies . . ."

"What did they want?"

"Our plates . . . you see, somebody who wanted to do us harm had told them we were . . . doing things we shouldn't. So they've taken the plates and . . ."

"Not all of them."

She pulled the parcel of plates out from under the blanket. The candle wavered in his hand, sending shadows rocking across the room.

"How did they get there?"

"Trillow brought them."

He turned away. "I'll . . ." She waited, but he didn't say anything else, only put down the candle, grabbed the package from her and stumbled out.

Three days later, with casual apologies, a police constable returned fourteen engraved and etched copper plates of Saints in Triumph.

"We're safer now the police have made fools of themselves."

Trillow leaned back on the *chaise-longue*, brandy glass in hand. Ned stood by the table, compulsively sorting sticks of charcoal into a neat length-graded row. His face was yellower than ever in the lamplight, the boil on the back of his neck more vivid.

"If they'd found the other plates . . ."

"Luckily, one of us didn't panic."

"But to hide them in her bed . . . I don't see how you could think of it."

"It was either that or harder beds for all of us—her included."

"Not Ella, no."

"She helps you, doesn't she?"

"Not with those."

"Would the police believe that?"

Ned came up the step to the dais and stood at the end of the *chaise-longue*, hands clenched together.

"I'm getting out. Now. I want my share of the money and I'm getting out now."

"Where to, Ned? And how long will a couple of hundred pounds last you? Give it a few more weeks with the plates we've got and an open field and I'll guarantee you ten times that."

"What if the police come back?"

"Unlikely."

"And Kate?"

"I'll speak to her."

The next day at six o'clock it was getting dark and Ned was out buying ink powder. Ella was on her own in the kitchen, grating suet onto a plate ready for tomorrow's steak and kidney pudding. She was alarmed by her brother's nerviness and loss of weight and had decided that more red meat might counteract the overwork and the acid fumes. Every night shut into her rectangle of darkness, she fell asleep to the creaking of his printing press. Sometimes she woke as the first gray light was coming in through the crack between the doors and heard him still moving about next door. He was getting through their supplies at an unprecedented rate. Every morning the stacks of dampened paper were used up, the linseed oil bottle empty, the floor scattered with bits of ink-stained muslin. Every morning Ella tidied up, refilled bottles, damped more paper. The stacks of finished prints under weights on the drying bench were twice as high as usual. She thought about it as white flakes of suet piled into a pyramid, and imagined their saints being seen and possessed from Land's End to the Hebrides or even further afield, going with the missionaries along the steaming rivers of Africa or across the plains of China. Then the kitchen door opened and Trillow walked in, pouring blood.

Most of it came from a torn ear, though she didn't realize that at the time. She saw the odd way he was walking, hunched forward with his head sunk into his shoulders and a hand clapped over his left ear. Blood was seeping through his fingers, running down inside his coat sleeve and soaking the cuff of his shirt. He came lurching across the room and, without speaking, leaned his elbows on the table where she'd been working, his head down. She gasped and dropped the grater, scattering suet. It mingled with the drops of blood coming through his fingers onto the table. He asked in a terrible flat voice where Ned was. She gasped, "Out."

"Water. In a bowl."

Shaking, she filled a soup tureen with water from the bucket in the corner, slopping it over the floor. He pulled a chair up to the table, grabbed the pudding cloth, soaked it in the water and held it to his ear. When she took a proper look at his face she gave a little scream. His left eye was closed, the flesh around it swollen and purple-red. His lip was split and a line of congealed blood ran down his chin. The pudding cloth was already turning red.

"More cloth."

She ran into her brother's printing room and came back with a roll of muslin, used the kitchen knife to hack pieces off it. She passed piece after piece to him. As each one was soaked he let it drop to the floor and grabbed another. Gradually the flood slowed until the pieces were only stained pink. He took a long shuddering breath.

"Brandy. Down in the studio."

It took her a long time to find it. When she got back he took the bottle and drank from it, shivering as the brandy went down. His ear had stopped bleeding but the swollen eye looked worse.

"Should I put some steak on it?"

He nodded. She went to the meat safe and took out the sliver of rump steak on its chipped plate, feeling a pang of regret for her brother's dinner, but mostly relief that she had anything to offer Trillow. He scooped it off the plate and clapped it over his eye.

"What . . . what happened?"

She hardly dared ask and thought for a long time he wasn't going to answer. Then he said, wincing from the split lip, "There was a ruffian mistreating a woman."

"Oh." She felt as if somebody had punched her in the chest. "You fought him?"

"What else could I do?"

"Wasn't there anybody else there? Nobody to help?"

He started shaking his head, then stopped because it was dislodging the steak.

"Nobody. Just me."

"And she?"

"She's alright."

Ella stood looking at him, so full of love that she thought it would burst her whole body apart. Love and envy, because she knew that she'd have given or done anything, suffered any of the torments the saints did before they triumphed, if she could have been the woman he'd rescued.

Much later, with Ella upstairs, Ned and Trillow talked in low voices in the studio. Trillow was on the *chaise-longue*, Ned hunched on the floor beside it.

"Her young man, that's what Kate called him. Protector's what she means."

"Did you hit him back?"

"If you think you can stop a fourteen-stone costermonger with a slug of lead in his fist, you go and discuss it with them next time."

"Next time?"

"They won't go away, Ned. She's decided she wants a quarter share and she says she's going to get it. She's coming here tomorrow and wants an answer."

"Here?"

"To pose as usual, damn her. She says now she's going to be a shareholder she wants to be sure the profits keep up."

When Ella went into Ned's workroom at breakfast time she expected to find him asleep as usual, on his camp bed beside the printing press. Instead there was a note on the table in his handwriting saying he'd gone out and wouldn't be back till the afternoon. Later, Trillow came up for his tea and toast, fully dressed with his working smock over his shirt. In spite of the steak his eye was still half closed and the bruise around it was glowing greenish-purple, like a puffed-out pigeon's breast. He hardly seemed to notice Ella, beyond saying that Catherine would be coming at ten and he'd let her in himself.

Ella stayed in the kitchen, tidying up and ironing. She heard the knock on the door just after ten, one pair of feet going downstairs, two pairs coming up to the landing below and the studio door closing. The house was quiet, apart from the occasional cart rumbling past. Then, when she was on the last of Ned's shirts, there was an interruption. Quick feet came tapping up the stairs from the floor below and a woman's voice outside the door called, "Anybody there?" She opened the door and there was Catherine in the long green wrap that Trillow kept for his models, yellow hair cascading over her shoulders and down to her waist. Ella stood with the shirt over her arm, dumbfounded. She was always uneasy in the presence of the saints, awed by whatever quality it was that they possessed and she didn't. None of them had come up to her kitchen before.

"Got a glass, ducky? 'E's gone and broken the one downstairs."

She ran to the cupboard, took out one of their thick drinking tumblers and handed it over. Then, still tongue-tied, she shut the door and heard the feet going back downstairs. Only a few minutes after that the scream came ripping up through the floorboards, a terrible bubbling scream like a curlew's cry only longer and louder, feet pounding upstairs and Trillow's discolored face at the door, saying something she didn't understand until he grabbed her by the shoulder and said it again. She must run to the doctor around the corner and tell him to come at once, because Catherine had drunk acid.

She had to tell the coroner about it, and the ten men on the jury who sat staring at her in a way that made her feel she'd done something wrong. She told them how quickly she'd run, not even stopping to put on hat or coat. It wasn't her fault that the doctor was away on a confinement and she had had to run again to a house three streets away, dodging carts and carriages, slipping in gutters. It wasn't her fault that by the time she'd got back, with the doctor running alongside, Catherine was beyond speaking, almost beyond breathing, beyond anything except terrible harsh yelping noises that Ella heard through the closed door out on the landing, with the landlady and the other tenants crowding round, whispering, staring. Then Ned had arrived.

It turned out, much later, that he'd been out looking for other lodgings for himself and Ella. He'd collapsed there on the landing and had to be carried upstairs. The coroner wanted to know about Ella's last sight of Catherine. Had she appeared distressed or agitated? Ella shook her head and had to be reminded to speak up. No. Had Ella seen or heard her go into the workroom next to the kitchen where the bottle of nitric acid was kept? No. She'd been back in the kitchen, door closed. When Ella was allowed to step down, Trillow followed her into the witness box, tall and grave in his black top hat. It was the first time Ella had seen him since the day Catherine died. He'd left the house that same evening, after a conversation with Ned that she didn't hear. She'd asked Ned where he was lodging but he'd said he didn't know.

Now, as he gave his evidence, her eyes didn't stray from his face. She noticed that his lip was healed and there was only a faint yellow tinge around his eye. He answered the questions put to him in a calm and grave voice. Catherine Bell was an artist's model and had sat for him many times for religious pictures. She suffered from moods in which she would make threats against both herself and other people for bringing her to her low state in life. Yes sir, she had on occasions spoken of wishing to end it all. How he wished he could have guessed that on that occasion she really meant it. Yes, he'd believed it was gin she had in the glass. Yes sir, Miss Bell was accustomed to drink gin in the mornings.

The verdict was suicide, without the rider "while of unsound mind." When the three of them met on the steps outside, Trillow raised his hat to Ella, stared Ned blankly in the face and walked away.

Ned and Ella went home in silence to pack. They were moving out of London, down to the coast. The next morning a cart would come for the printing press, the plates and bottles, their few household goods. Ned thought there might be a market for seaside pictures, piers and so on.

"Peers?" Ella had questioned, her distraught mind picturing men in ermine and coronets on the sands.

"Piers and promenades. Not too many people, except in the middle distance with sunshades."

As long as he didn't have to do detailed figures, he could manage both drawing and engraving himself. They'd live. Still in silence they wrapped unused copper plates in bits of clean sheet, stowed inks, instruments and bottles in baskets. As the orange light of the setting sun was coming through the window they knelt on the bare floor, cording up the last package. With her finger on the half-made knot to hold it while her brother tightened the string, Ella spoke at last.

"He killed her, didn't he?"

The string went slack. She glanced sideways and saw Ned kneeling, head down.

"How did you know?"

"The bottle. It was empty when I looked in the morning, before she came upstairs. I know because I thought how quickly it was going."

His head went lower. She knew she was hurting him, but there were things that must be said and she could only say them in this gap, when the old life had finished and a new one not yet started.

"And now I know why he killed her. I understood this morning at the inquest—what sort of woman she was."

"Ella, it's not right for you . . ."

"No, listen. It's because of what you and Trillow were doing."

He groaned "I never wanted to. I swear on our mother's grave I never wanted to."

"The saints. Your lovely saints, and everybody all over the world seeing them. They were so beautiful, especially Catherine. He'd made her a saint and then, somehow, he found out that she wasn't worthy of it and . . ."

Ned was trembling and crying, great drops falling and spreading over the wooden floorboards.

"Ned, don't judge him harshly. I know it was wicked of him but he was so pure . . . so pure, you see." She was crying now too. She felt Ned's shaking arm around her shoulders. "I'm right, aren't I, that's why he did it? Because she wasn't worthy."

"Yes, yes. Don't cry now. Oh, don't cry."

Later, packing up the things in the kitchen when Ned was downstairs, she found an engraved copper plate under the mattress in her bed cupboard. She knew it must have slipped out from the parcel that Trillow had given her the night the police came. Curious, she took it over to the lamplight and looked at the grooves in the bright copper. She'd learned to see the picture on a plate as clearly as if it were printed on paper. It was one of the saints, an ecstatic smile on her face and long hair flowing, spreadeagled and ready for a kind of martyrdom that she couldn't imagine and was clearly too terrible to be in any of the books. She stared at it for a while but when she heard her brother coming upstairs she pushed it back into the bed cupboard, where it would stay when they left so that there was nothing to remind him.

# Lawrence Block

## Let's Get Lost

LAWRENCE BLOCK got famous the hard way. Took him well into his third decade of professional writing to do it, but there he was in the spotlight—equally lauded for his comic Bernie Rhodenbarr mysteries and for his dark novels about private investigator Matt Scudder. Along the way, Block wrote just about every form of commercial fiction there is, and did all of it with his usual style and grace. Authors don't get much more readable than Larry Block, who has been feted with the Mystery Writers of America's highest honor, the Grand Master Award. After a sentence or two of "Let's Get Lost," which was first published in the September/October issue of *Ellery Queen's Mystery Magazine*, we guarantee you'll be hooked.

# Let's Get Lost

*Lawrence Block*

When the phone call came I was parked in front of the television set in the front room, nursing a glass of bourbon and watching the Yankees. It's funny what you remember and what you don't. I remember that Thurman Munson had just hit a long foul that missed being a home run by no more than a foot, but I don't remember who they were playing, or even what kind of a season they had that year.

I remember that the bourbon was J. W. Dant, and that I was drinking it on the rocks, but of course I would remember that. I always remembered what I was drinking, though I didn't always remember why.

The boys had stayed up to watch the opening innings with me, but tomorrow was a school day, and Anita took them upstairs and tucked them in while I freshened my drink and sat down again. The ice was mostly melted by the time Munson hit his long foul, and I was still shaking my head at that when the phone rang. I let it ring, and Anita answered it and came in to tell me it was for me. Somebody's secretary, she said.

I picked up the phone, and a woman's voice, crisply professional, said, "Mr. Scudder, I'm calling for Mr. Alan Herdig of Herdig and Crowell."

"I see," I said, and listened while she elaborated, and estimated just how much time it would take me to get to their offices. I hung up and made a face.

"You have to go in?"

I nodded. "It's about time we had a break in this one," I said. "I don't expect to get much sleep tonight, and I've got a court appearance tomorrow morning."

"I'll get you a clean shirt. Sit down. You've got time to finish your drink, don't you?"

I always had time for that.

Years ago, this was. Nixon was president, a couple of years into his first term. I was a detective with the NYPD, attached to the sixth precinct in Greenwich Village. I had a house on Long Island with two cars in the garage, a Ford wagon for Anita and a beat-up Plymouth Valiant for me.

Traffic was light on the LIE, and I didn't pay much attention to the speed limit. I didn't know many cops who did. Nobody ever ticketed a brother officer. I made good time, and it must have been somewhere around a quarter to ten when I left the car at a bus stop on First Avenue. I had a card on the dashboard that would keep me safe from tickets and tow trucks.

The best thing about enforcing the laws is that you don't have to pay a lot of attention to them yourself.

Her doorman rang upstairs to announce me, and she met me at the door with a drink. I don't remember what she was wearing, but I'm sure she looked good in it. She always did.

She said, "I would never call you at home. But it's business."

"Yours or mine?"

"Maybe both. I got a call from a client. A Madison Avenue guy, maybe an agency vice president. Suits from Tripler's, season tickets for the Rangers, house in Connecticut."

"And?"

"And didn't I say something about knowing a cop? Because he and some friends were having a friendly card game and something happened to one of them."

"Something happened? Something happens to a friend of yours, you take him to a hospital. Or was it too late for that?"

"He didn't say, but that's what I heard. It sounds to me as though somebody had an accident and they need somebody to make it disappear."

"And you thought of me."

"Well," she said.

She'd thought of me before, in a similar connection. Another client of hers, a Wall Street warrior, had had a heart attack in her bed one afternoon. Most men will tell you that's how they want to go, and perhaps it's as good a way as any, but it's not all that convenient for the people who have to clean up after them, especially when the bed in question belongs to some working girl.

When the equivalent happens in the heroin trade, it's good PR. One junkie checks out with an overdose and the first thing all his buddies want to know is where did he get the stuff and how can they cop some themselves. Because, hey, it must be good, right? A hooker, on the other hand, has less to gain from being listed as cause of death. And I suppose she felt a professional responsibility, if you want to call it that, to spare the guy and his family embarrassment. So I made him disappear, and left him fully dressed in an alley down in the financial district. I called it in anonymously and went back to her apartment to claim my reward.

"I've got the address," she said now. "Do you want to have a look? Or should I tell them I couldn't reach you?"

I kissed her, and we clung to each other for a long moment. When I came up for air I said, "It'd be a lie."

"I beg your pardon?"

"Telling them you couldn't reach me. You can always reach me."

"You're a sweetie."

"You better give me that address," I said.

I retrieved my car from the bus stop and left it in another one a dozen or so blocks uptown. The address I was looking for was a brownstone in the East Sixties. A shop with handbags and briefcases in the window occupied the storefront, flanked by a travel agent and a men's clothier. There were four doorbells in the vestibule, and I rang the third one and heard the intercom activated, but didn't hear anyone say anything. I was reaching to ring a second time when the buzzer sounded. I pushed the door open and walked up three flights of carpeted stairs.

Out of habit, I stood to the side when I knocked. I didn't really expect a bullet, and what came through the door was a voice, pitched low, asking who was there.

"Police," I said. "I understand you've got a situation here."

There was a pause. Then a voice—maybe the same one, maybe not—said, "I don't understand. Has there been a complaint, officer?"

They wanted a cop, but not just any cop. "My name's Scudder," I said. "Elaine Mardell said you could use some help."

The lock turned and the door opened. Two men were standing there, dressed for the office in dark suits and white shirts and ties. I looked past them and saw two more men, one in a suit, the other in gray slacks and a blue blazer. They looked to be in their early to mid forties, which made them ten to fifteen years older than me.

I was what, thirty-two that year? Something like that.

"Come on in," one of them said. "Careful."

I didn't know what I was supposed to be careful of, but found out when I gave the door a shove and it stopped after a few inches. There was a body on the floor, a man, curled on his side. One arm was flung up over his head, the other bent at his side, the hand inches from the handle of the knife. It was an easy-open stiletto and it was buried hilt-deep in his chest.

I pushed the door shut and knelt down for a close look at him, and heard the bolt turn as one of them locked the door.

The dead man was around their age, and had been similarly dressed until he took off his suit jacket and loosened his tie. His hair was a little longer than theirs, perhaps because he was losing hair on the crown and wanted to conceal the bald spot. Everyone tries that, and it never works.

I didn't feel for a pulse. A touch of his forehead established that he was too cold to have one. And I hadn't really needed to touch him to know that he was dead. Hell, I knew that much before I parked the car.

Still, I took some time looking him over. Without looking up, I asked what had happened. There was a pause while they decided who would reply, and then the same man who'd questioned me through the closed door said, "We don't really know."

"You came home and found him here?"

"Hardly that. We were playing a few hands of poker, the five of us. Then the doorbell rang and Phil went to see who it was."

I nodded at the dead man. "That's Phil there?"

Someone said it was. "He'd folded already," the man in the blazer added.

"And the rest of you fellows were still in the middle of a hand."

"That's right."

"So he—Phil?"

"Yes, Phil."

"Phil went to the door while you finished the hand."

"Yes."

"And?"

"And we didn't really see what happened," one of the suits said.

"We were in the middle of a hand," another explained, "and you can't really see much from where we were sitting."

"At the card table," I said.

"That's right."

The table was set up at the far end of the living room. It was a poker table, with a green baize top and wells for chips and glasses. I walked over and looked at it.

"Seats eight," I said.

"Yes."

"But there were only the five of you. Or were there other players as well?"

"No, just the five of us."

"The four of you and Phil."

"Yes."

"And Phil was clear across the room answering the door, and one or two of you would have had your backs to it, and all four of you would have been more interested in the way the hand was going than who was at the door." They nodded along, pleased at my ability to grasp all this. "But you must have heard something that made you look up."

"Yes," the blazer said. "Phil cried out."

"What did he say?"

" 'No!' or 'Stop!' or something like that. That got our attention, and we got out of our chairs and looked over there, but I don't think any of us got a look at the guy."

"The guy who . . ."

"Stabbed Phil."

"He must have been out the door before you had a chance to look at him."

"Yes."

"And pulled the door shut after him."

"Or Phil pushed it shut while he was falling."

I said, "Stuck out a hand to break his fall . . ."

"Right."

"And the door swung shut, and he went right on falling."

"Right."

I retraced my steps to the spot where the body lay. It was a nice apartment, I noted, spacious and comfortably furnished. It felt like a bachelor's full-time residence, not a married commuter's *pied-à-terre*. There were books on the bookshelves, framed prints on the walls, logs in the fireplace. Opposite the fireplace, a two-by-three throw rug looked out of place atop a large Oriental carpet. I had a hunch I knew what it was doing there.

But I walked past it and knelt down next to the corpse. "Stabbed in the heart," I noted. "Death must have been instantaneous, or the next thing to it. I don't suppose he had any last words."

"No."

"He crumpled up and hit the floor and never moved."

"That's right."

I got to my feet. "Must have been a shock."

"A terrible shock."

"How come you didn't call it in?"

"Call it in?"

"Call the police," I said. "Or an ambulance, get him to a hospital."

"A hospital couldn't do him any good," the blazer said. "I mean, you could tell he was dead."

"No pulse, no breathing."

"Right."

"Still, you must have known you're supposed to call the cops when something like this happens."

"Yes, of course."

"But you didn't."

They looked at each other. It might have been interesting to see what they came up with, but I made it easy for them.

"You must have been scared," I said.

"Well, of course."

"Guy goes to answer the door and the next thing you know he's dead on the floor. That's got to be an upsetting experience, especially taking into account that you don't know who killed him or why. Or do you have an idea?"

They didn't.

"I don't suppose this is Phil's apartment."

"No."

Of course not. If it was, they'd have long since gone their separate ways.

"Must be yours," I told the blazer, and enjoyed it when his eyes widened. He allowed that it was, and asked how I knew. I didn't tell him he was the one man in the room without a wedding ring, or that I figured he'd changed from a business suit to slightly more casual clothes on his return home, while the others were still wearing what they'd worn to the office that morning. I just muttered something about policemen developing certain instincts, and let him think I was a genius.

I asked if any of them had known Phil very well, and wasn't surprised to learn that they hadn't. He was a friend of a friend of a friend, someone said, and did something on Wall Street.

"So he wasn't a regular at the table."

"No."

"This wasn't his first time, was it?"

"His second," somebody said.

"First time was last week?"

"No, two weeks ago. He didn't play last week."

"Two weeks ago. How'd he do?"

Elaborate shrugs. The consensus seemed to be that he might have won a few dollars, but nobody had paid much attention.

"And this evening?"

"I think he was about even. If he was ahead it couldn't have been more than a few dollars."

"What kind of stakes do you play for?"

"It's a friendly game. One-two-five in stud games. In draw, it's two dollars before the draw, five after."

"So you can win or lose what, a couple of hundred?"

"That would be a big loss."

"Or a big win," I said.

"Well, yes. Either way."

I knelt down next to the corpse and patted him down. Cards in his wallet identified him as Philip I. Ryman, with an address in Teaneck.

"Lived in Jersey," I said. "And you say he worked on Wall Street?"

"Somewhere downtown."

I picked up his left hand. His watch was Rolex, and I suppose it must have been a real one; this was before the profusion of fakes. He had what looked like a wedding band on the appropriate finger, but I saw that it was in fact a large silver or white-gold ring that had gotten turned around, so that the large part was on the palm side of his hand. It looked like an unfinished signet ring, waiting for an initial to be carved into its gleaming surface.

I straightened up. "Well," I said, "I'd say it's a good thing you called me."

"There are a couple of problems," I told them. "A couple of things that could pop up like a red flag for a responding officer or a medical examiner."

"Like . . ."

"Like the knife," I said. "Phil opened the door and the killer stabbed him once and left, was out the door and down the stairs before the body hit the carpet."

"Maybe not that fast," one of them said, "but it was pretty quick. Before we knew what had happened, certainly."

"I appreciate that," I said, "but the thing is, it's an unusual MO. The killer didn't take time to make sure his victim was dead, and you can't take that for granted when you stick a knife in someone. And he left the knife in the wound."

"He wouldn't do that?"

"Well, it might be traced to him. All he has to do to avoid that chance is take it away with him. Besides, it's a weapon. Suppose someone comes chasing after him? He might need that knife again."

"Maybe he panicked."

"Maybe he did," I agreed. "There's another thing, and a medical examiner would notice this if a reporting officer didn't. The body's been moved."

Interesting the way their eyes jumped all over the place. They looked at each other, they looked at me, they looked at Phil on the floor.

"Blood pools in a corpse," I said. "Lividity's the word they use for it. It looks to me as though Phil fell forward and wound up face downward. He probably fell against the door as it was closing, and slid down and wound up on his face. So you couldn't get the door open, and you needed to, so eventually you moved him."

Eyes darted. The host, the one in the blazer, said, "We knew you'd have to come in."

"Right."

"And we couldn't have him lying against the door."

"Of course not," I agreed. "But all of that's going to be hard to explain. You didn't call the cops right away, and you did move the body. They'll have some questions for you."

"Maybe you could give us an idea what questions to expect."

"I might be able to do better than that," I said. "It's irregular, and I probably shouldn't, but I'm going to suggest an action we can take."

"Oh?"

"I'm going to suggest we stage something," I said. "As it stands, Phil was stabbed to death by an unknown person who escaped without anybody getting a look at him. He may never turn up, and if he doesn't, the cops are going to look hard at the four of you."

"Jesus," somebody said.

"It would be a lot easier on everybody," I said, "if Phil's death was an accident."

"An accident?"

"I don't know if Phil has a sheet or not," I said. "He looks vaguely familiar to me, but lots of people do. He's got a gambler's face, even in death, the kind of face you expect to see in an OTB parlor. He may have worked on Wall Street, it's possible, because cheating at cards isn't necessarily a full-time job."

"Cheating at cards?"

"That would be my guess. His ring's a mirror; turned around, it gives him a peek at what's coming off the bottom of the deck. It's just one way to cheat, and he probably had thirty or forty others. You think of this as a social event, a once-a-week friendly game, a five-dollar limit and, what, three raises maximum? The wins and losses pretty much average out over the course of a year, and nobody ever gets hurt too bad. Is that about right?"

"Yes."

"So you wouldn't expect to attract a mechanic, a card cheat, but he's not looking for the high rollers, he's looking for a game just like yours, where it's all good friends and nobody's got reason to get suspicious, and he can pick up two or three hundred dollars in a couple of hours without running any risks. I'm sure you're all decent poker players, but would you think to look for bottom dealing or a cold deck? Would you know if somebody was dealing seconds, even if you saw it in slow motion?"

"Probably not."

"Phil was probably doing a little cheating," I went on, "and that's probably what he did two weeks ago, and nobody spotted him. But he evidently crossed someone else somewhere along the line. Maybe he pulled the same tricks in a bigger game, or maybe he was just sleeping in the wrong bed, but someone knew he was coming here, turned up after the game was going, and rang the bell. He would have come in and called Phil out, but he didn't have to, because Phil answered the door."

"And the guy had a knife."

"Right," I said. "That's how it was, but it's another way an investigating officer might get confused. How did the guy know Phil was going to come to the door? Most times the host opens the door, and the rest of the time it's only one chance in five it'll be Phil. Would the guy be ready, knife in hand? And would Phil just open up without making sure who it was?"

I held up a hand. "I know, that's how it happened. But I think it might be worth your while to stage a more plausible scenario, something a lot easier for the cops to come to terms with. Suppose we forget the intruder. Suppose the story we tell is that Phil was cheating at cards and someone called him on it. Maybe some strong words were said and threats were exchanged. Phil went into his pocket and came out with a knife."

"That's . . ."

"You're going to say it's farfetched," I said, "but he'd probably have some sort of weapon on him, something to intimidate anyone who did catch him cheating. He pulls the knife and you react. Say you turn the table over on him. The whole thing goes crashing to the floor and he winds up sticking his own knife in his chest."

I walked across the room. "We'll have to move the table," I went on. "There's not really room for that sort of struggle where you've got it set up, but suppose it was right in the middle of the room, under the light fixture? Actually that would be a logical place for it." I bent down, picked up the throw rug, tossed it aside. "You'd move the rug if you had the table here." I bent down, poked at a stain. "Looks like somebody had a nosebleed, and fairly recently, or you'd have had the carpet cleaned by now. That can fit right in, come to think of it. Phil wouldn't have bled much from a stab wound to the heart, but there'd have been a little blood loss, and I didn't spot any blood at all where the body's lying now. If we put him in the right spot, they'll most likely assume it's his blood, and it might even turn out to be the same blood type. I mean, there are only so many blood types, right?"

I looked at them one by one. "I think it'll work," I said. "To sweeten it, we'll tell them you're friends of mine. I play in this game now and then, although I wasn't here when Phil was. And when the accident happened the first thing you thought of was to call me, and that's why there was a delay reporting the incident. You'd reported it to me, and I was on my way here, and you figured that was enough." I stopped for breath, took a moment to look each of them in the eye. "We'll want things arranged just right," I went on, "and it'll be a good idea to spread a little cash around. But I think this one'll go into the books as accidental death."

"They must have thought you were a genius," Elaine said.

"Or an idiot savant," I said. "Here I was, telling them to fake exactly what had in fact happened. At the beginning I think they may have thought I was blundering into an unwitting reconstruction of the incident, but by the end they probably figured out that I knew where I was going."

"But you never spelled it out."

"No, we maintained the fiction that some intruder stuck the knife in Ryman, and we were tampering with the evidence."

"When actually you were restoring it. What tipped you off?"

"The body blocking the door. The lividity pattern was wrong, but I was suspicious even before I confirmed that. It's just too cute, a body positioned where it'll keep a door from opening. And the table was in the wrong place, and the little rug had to be covering something, or why else would it be where it was? So I pictured the room the right way, and then everything sort of filled in. But it didn't take a genius. Any cop would have seen some wrong things, and he'd have asked a few hard questions, and the four of them would have caved in."

"And then what? Murder indictments?"

"Most likely, but they're respectable businessmen and the deceased was a scumbag, so they'd have been up on manslaughter charges and probably would have pleaded to a lesser charge. Still, a verdict of accidental death saves them a lot of aggravation."

"And that's what really happened?"

"I can't see any of those men packing a switch knife, or pulling it at a card table. Nor does it seem likely they could have taken it away from Ryman and killed him with it. I think he went ass over teakettle with the table coming down on top of him and maybe one or two of the guys falling on top of the table. And he was still holding the knife, and he stuck it in his own chest."

"And the cops who responded—"

"Well, I called it in for them, so I more or less selected the responding officers. I picked guys you can work with."

"And worked with them."

"Everybody came out okay," I said. "I collected a few dollars from the four players, and I laid off some of it where it would do the most good."

"Just to smooth things out."

"That's right."

"But you didn't lay off all of it."

"No," I said, "not quite all of it. Give me your hand. Here."

"What's this?"

"A finder's fee."

"Three hundred dollars?"

"Ten percent," I said.

"Gee," she said. "I didn't expect anything."

"What do you do when somebody gives you money?"

"I say thank you," she said, "and I put it someplace safe. This is great. You get them to tell the truth, and everybody gets paid. Do you have to go back to Syosset right away? Because Chet Baker's at Mikell's tonight."

"We could go hear him," I said, "and then we could come back here. I told Anita I'd probably have to stay over."

"Oh, goodie," she said. "Do you suppose he'll sing 'Let's Get Lost?' "

"I wouldn't be surprised," I said. "Not if you ask him nice."

I don't remember if he sang it or not, but I heard it again just the other day on the radio. He'd ended abruptly, that aging boy with the sweet voice and sweeter horn. He went out a hotel-room window somewhere in Europe, and most people figured he'd had help. He'd crossed up a lot of people along the way and always got away with it, but then that's usually the way it works. You dodge all the bullets but the last one.

"Let's Get Lost." I heard the song, and not twenty-four hours later I picked up the *Times* and read an obit for a commodities trader named P. Gordon Fawcett, who'd succumbed to prostate cancer. The name rang a bell, but it took me hours to place it. He was the guy in the blazer, the man in whose apartment Phil Ryman stabbed himself.

Funny how things work out. It wasn't too long after that poker game that another incident precipitated my departure from the NYPD, and from my marriage. Elaine and I lost track of each other, and caught up with each other some years down the line, by which time I'd found a way to live without drinking. So we get lost and found—and now we're married. Who'd have guessed?

My life's vastly different these days, but I can imagine being called in on just that sort of emergency—a man dead on the carpet, a knife in his chest, in the company of four poker players who only wish he'd disappear. As I said, my life's different, and I suppose I'm different myself. So I'd almost certainly handle it differently now, and what I'd probably do is call it in immediately and let the cops deal with it.

Still, I always liked the way that one worked out. I walked in on a cover-up, and what I did was cover up the cover-up. And in the process I wound up with the truth. Or an approximation of it, at least, and isn't that as much as you can expect to get? Isn't that enough?

# Clark Howard

## Under Suspicion

CLARK HOWARD, Edgar winner, novelist, screenwriter, is best known for his short stories, which number among the finest ever written in the crime-fiction genre. Howard is unique in examining the lives of people at the bottom of the social ladder. He finds in them, on many occasions, beauty, dignity, meaning, sometimes even charm. "Under Suspicion," which first appeared in the March issue of *Ellery Queen's Mystery Magazine,* is one of his finest stories.

# Under Suspicion

*Clark Howard*

Frank Dell walked into the Three Corners Club shortly after five, as he usually did every day, and took a seat at the end of the bar. The bartender, seeing him, put together, without being told, a double Tanqueray over two ice cubes with two large olives, and set it in front of him on a cork coaster. Down at the middle of the bar, Dell saw two minor stickup men he remembered from somewhere and began staring at them without touching his drink. Frank Dell's stare was glacial and unblinking. After three disconcerting minutes of it, the two stickup men paid for their drinks and left. Only then did Dell lift his own glass.

Tim Callan, the club owner, came over and sat opposite Dell. "Well, I see you just cost me a couple more customers, Frankie," he said wryly.

"Hoodlums," Dell replied. "I'm just helping you keep the place respectable, Timmy."

"Bring some of your policemen buddies in to drink," Callan suggested. "That'll keep me respectable *and* profitable."

"You're not hurting for profits," Dell said. "Not with that after-hours poker game you run in the apartment upstairs."

Callan laughed. "Ah, Frankie, Frankie. Been quick with the answers all your life. You should've been a lawyer. Even my old dad, rest his soul, used to say that."

"I'm not crooked enough to be a lawyer," Dell said, sipping his drink.

"Not crooked *enough!* Hell, you're not crooked at all, Frankie. You're probably the straightest cop in Chicago." Callan leaned forward on one elbow. "How long we known each other, Frank?"

"What's on your mind, Tim?" Dell asked knowingly. Reminiscing, he had learned, frequently led to other things.

"We go back thirty years, do you realize that, Frank?" Callan replied, ignoring Dell's suspicion. "First grade at St. Mel's school out on the West Side."

"What's on your mind, Tim?" Dell's expression hardened just a hint. He hated asking the same question twice.

"Remember my baby sister, Francie?" Callan asked, lowering his voice.

"Sure. Cute little kid. Carrot-red hair. Freckles. Eight or ten years younger than us."

"Nine. She's twenty-seven now. She married this Guinea a few years ago, name of Nicky Santore. They moved up to Milwaukee where the guy's uncle got him a job in a brewery. Well, they started having problems. You know the grease-balls, they're all Don Juans, chasing broads all the time—"

"Get to the point, Tim," said Dell. He hated embellishment.

"Okay. Francie left him and came back to live with my brother, Dennis—you know him, the fireman. Anyhow, after she got back, she found out she's expecting. Then Nicky finds out, and he comes back too. Guy begs Francie to take him back, and she does. Now, the only job he can get down here is pumping gas at a Texaco station, which only pays minimum wage. He's worried about doctor bills and everything with the baby coming, so he agrees, for a cut, to let a cousin of his use the station storeroom to stash hot goods. It works okay for a while, but then the cousin gets busted and leads the cops to the station. They find a load of laptop computers. Nick gets charged with receiving stolen property. He comes up for a preliminary hearing in three weeks."

"Tough break," Dell allowed, sipping again. "But he should get probation if he's got no priors."

"He's got a prior," Callan said, looking down at the bar.

"What is it?"

"Burglary. Him and that same cousin robbed some hotel rooms down at the Hilton when they was working as bellmen. Years ago. Both of them got probation on that."

"Then he's looking at one-to-four on this fall," Dell said.

Callan swallowed. "Can you help me out on this, Frankie?"

Dell gave him the stare. "You don't mean help you, Tim. You mean help Nicky Santore. What do you think I can do?"

"Give your personal voucher for him."

"Are you serious? You want me to go to an assistant state's attorney handling an RSP case and personally vouch for some Guinea with a prior that I don't even know?"

"Frank, it's for Francie—"

"No, it isn't. If Francie was charged, I'd get her off in a heartbeat. But it's not Francie; it's some two-bit loser she married."

"Frank, please, listen—"

"No. Forget it."

There was a soft buzzing signal from the pager clipped to Dell's belt. Reaching under his coat, he got it out and looked at it. It was a 911 page from the Lakeside station house out on the South Side, where he was assigned.

"I have to answer this," he told Callan. Taking a cellular phone from his coat pocket, he opened it and dialed one of the station house's unlisted numbers. When someone answered, he said, "This is Dell. I got a nine-one-one page."

"Yeah, it's from Captain Larne. Hold on."

A moment later, an older, huskier voice spoke. "Dell? Mike Larne. Where's Dan?" He was asking about Dan Malone, Dell's partner, a widower in his fifties.

"Probably at home," Dell told the captain. "I dropped him off there less than an hour ago. What's up, Cap?"

"Edie Malone was found dead in her apartment a little while ago. It looks like she's been strangled."

Dell said nothing. He froze, absolutely still, the little phone at his ear. Edie was Dan's only child.

"Dell? Did you hear me?"

"Yessir, I heard you. Captain, I can't tell him—"

"You won't have to. The department chaplain and Dan's parish priest get that dirty job. What I want you to do is help me keep Dan from going off the deep end over this. You know how he is. We can't have him going wild thinking he'll solve this himself."

"What do you want me to do?"

"I'm going to assign you temporary duty to the homicide team working the case. If Dan knows you're on it, he might stay calm. Understand where I'm coming from?"

"Yessir." Dell was still frozen, motionless.

"Take down this address," Larne said. Dell animated, taking a small spiral notebook and ballpoint from his shirt pocket. He wrote down the address Larne gave him. "The homicide boys have only been there a little while. Kenmare and Garvan. Know them?"

"Yeah, Kenmare, slightly. They know I'm coming?"

"Absolutely. This has all been cleared with headquarters." Larne paused a beat, then said, "You knew the girl, did you?"

"Yessir."

"Well," Larne sighed heavily, "I hate to do this to you, Frank—"

"It's all right, Cap. I understand."

"Call me at home later."

"Right."

Dell closed the phone and slipped it back into his pocket. He walked away from the bar and out of the club without another word to Tim Callan.

Edie Malone's address was one of the trendy new apartment buildings remodeled from old commercial high-rises on the near North Side. The sixth floor had been cordoned off to permit only residents of that floor to exit the elevator, and they were required to go directly to their apartments. Edie Malone's apartment was posted as a crime scene. In addition to homicide detectives Kenmare and Garvan, there were half a dozen uniformed officers guarding the hallways and stairwells, personnel from the city crime lab in the apartment itself, and a deputy coroner and Cook County morgue attendants waiting to transport the victim to the county hospital complex for autopsy.

When Frank Dell arrived, Kenmare and Garvan took him into the bedroom to view the body. Edie Malone was wearing a white cotton sweatshirt with MONICA FOR PRESIDENT lettered on it, and a pair of cutoff denim shorts. Barefoot, she was lying on her back, elbows bent, hands a few inches from her ears, feet apart as if she were resting, with her long, dark red hair splayed out on the white shag carpet like spilled paint. Her eyes were wide open in a bloated face, the neck below it ringed with ugly purplish bruises. Looking at her, Dell had to blink back tears.

"I guess you knew her, your partner's daughter and all," said Kenmare. Dell nodded.

"Who found her?"

"Building super," said Garvan. "She didn't show up for work today and didn't answer the phone when her boss called. Then a coworker got nervous about it and told the boss that the victim had just broken up with a guy who she was afraid was going to rough her up over it. They finally came over and convinced the super to take a look in the apartment. The boss and the coworker were down in his office when we got here. We questioned them briefly, then sent them home. They've been instructed not to talk about it until after we see them tomorrow."

The three detectives went into the kitchen and sat at Edie's table, where the two from homicide continued to share their notes with Dell.

"Coroner guy says she looks like she's been dead sixteen, eighteen hours, which would mean sometime late last night, early this morning," said Garvan.

"She worked for Able, Bennett, and Crain Advertising Agency in the Loop," said Kenmare, then paused, adding, "Maybe you know some of this stuff already, from your partner."

Dell shook his head. "Dan and his daughter hadn't been close for a while. He didn't approve of Edie's lifestyle. He and his wife had saved for years to send her to the University of Chicago so she could become a teacher, but then Dan's wife died, and a little while after that Edie quit school and moved out to be on her own. Dan didn't talk much about her after that."

"But Captain Larne still thinks Dan might jump ranks and try to work the case himself?"

"Sure." Dell shrugged. "She was still his daughter, his only kid."

"Okay," Kenmare said, "we'll give you everything, then. Her boss was a Ronald Deever, one of the ad agency execs. The coworker who tipped him about the ex-boyfriend is a copywriter named Sally Simms."

"Did she know the guy's name?" Dell asked.

"Yeah." Kenmare flipped a page in his notebook. "Bob Pilcher. He's some kind of redneck. Works as a bouncer at one of those line-dancing clubs over in Hee-Haw town. The Simms woman met him a couple times on double dates with the victim." He closed his notebook. "That's it so far."

"Where do we go from here?" Dell asked.

Kenmare and Garvan exchanged glances. "We haven't figured that out yet," said the former. "You've been assigned by a district captain, with headquarters approval and a nod from our own commander, and the victim is the daughter of a veteran cop who's your senior partner. We'll be honest, Dell: We're not sure what your agenda is here."

Dell shook his head. "No agenda," he said. "I'm here to make it look good to Dan Malone so he'll get through this thing as calmly as possible. But it's your case. You two tell me what I can do to help and I'll do it. Or I'll just stand around and watch, if that's how you want it. Your call."

Kenmare and Garvan looked at each other for a moment, then both nodded. "Okay," said Kenmare, "we can live with that. We'll work together on it." The two homicide detectives shook hands with Dell, the first time they had done so. Then Kenmare, who was the senior officer, said, "Let's line it up. First thing is to toss the bedroom as soon as the body is out and the crime lab guys are done. Maybe we'll get lucky, find a diary, love letters, stuff like that. You do the bedroom, Frank. You knew her; you might tumble to something that we might not think was important. While you're doing that, we'll work this floor, the one above, and the one below, canvassing the neighbors. We'll have uniforms working the other floors. Then we'll regroup."

With that agreed to, the detectives split up.

It was after ten when they got back together.

"Bedroom?" asked Kenmare. Dell handed him a small red address book.

"Just this. Looks like it might be old. Lot of neighborhood names where Dan still lives. None of the new telephone exchanges in it."

"That's it?"

"Everything else looks normal to me." Dell nodded. "Clothes, makeup, couple of paperback novels, Valium and birth-control pills in the medicine cabinet, that kind of stuff. But I'd feel better if one of you guys would do a follow-up toss."

"Good idea." Kenmare motioned to Garvan, who went into the bedroom.

"Neighbors?" Dell asked.

"Zilch," said Kenmare.

Kenmare and Dell cruised the living room and small kitchen, studying everything again, until Garvan came back out of the bedroom and announced, "It's clean." Then the men sat back down at the kitchen table.

"Let's line up tomorrow," Kenmare said. "Dell, you and I will work together, and I'll have Garvan sit in on the autopsy; he can also work some of the names in the address book by phone before and after. You and I will go see Ronald Deever and Sally Simms at the ad agency, maybe interview some of the other employees there also. We need to track down this guy Pilcher, too. Let's meet at seven for breakfast and see if there's anything we need to do before that. Frank, there's a little diner called Wally's just off Thirteenth and State. We can eat, then walk over to headquarters and set up a temporary desk for you in our bullpen."

"Sounds good," Dell said.

Kenmare left a uniformed officer at the door to Edie Malone's apartment, one at each end of the sixth-floor hallway, one at the elevator, and two in the lobby. When the detectives parted outside, Dell drove back to the South Side, where he lived. When he got into his own apartment, a little after midnight, he called Mike Larne at home.

"It's Dell, Captain," he said when Larne answered sleepily.

"How's it look?" Larne asked.

"Not good," Dell told him. "Only one possible lead so far: an ex-boyfriend who threatened to slap her around. We'll start doing some deeper work on it tomorrow."

"Was she raped?"

"Didn't look like it."

"Thank God for that much."

"I'll let you know for sure after the autopsy."

"All right. How's it setting with Kenmare and Garvan? You getting any resistance?"

"No, it's fine. They're okay. They're giving me a temp desk downtown tomorrow. What's the word on Dan?"

"The poor man is completely undone. The chaplain and the parish priest managed to get him drunk and put him to bed. Jim Keenan and some of the other boys are staying at the house until Dan's sisters arrive from Florida. Listen, you get some sleep. I'll talk to you tomorrow."

"Okay, Cap."

Dell hung up and went directly to the cabinet where he kept his bottle of gin.

At the Able, Bennett, and Crain advertising agency the next day, on the fortieth floor of a Loop building, Kenmare sat in Ronald Deever's private office to interview him while Dell talked with Sally Simms in a corner of the firm's coffee room. Sally was a pert blonde who wrote copy for a dental-products account. She told Dell that Edie Malone had been employed by the agency for about eight months as a receptionist and was well liked by everyone she worked with. Sally had double-dated with her half a dozen times, twice with the man named Bob Pilcher.

"He's from North Carolina, a heavy smoker," she said. "That was the main reason Edie quit going out with him; she didn't like smokers. Said kissing them was like licking an ashtray."

"What's the name of the club where he works?" Dell asked.

"It's called Memphis City Limits. Kind of a hillbilly joint. Over on Fullerton near Halsted."

"What made you tell your boss that you were afraid Pilcher might rough Edie up?"

"That's what Edie told me. She said Bob told her he wasn't used to women dumping him, and maybe she just needed a little slapping around to get her act together. Edie wasn't sure he meant it, but I was. I mean, this is one of those guys that doesn't just walk, he *struts*. And he wears those real tight Wranglers to show off his package. Got real wavy hair with one little curl always down on his forehead. Ask me, he's definitely the kind would slap a woman around. I told Edie she was better off sticking with guys like Bart Mason."

"Who's he?" Dell asked.

"Bart? He's a nice young exec works for the home office of an insurance company down on twenty-two. They dated for a while, then broke up when Edie started seeing someone else."

"Who did she start seeing?"

Sally shrugged. "I don't know. She went out a lot."

"Have you told Bart Mason that Edie's dead?"

"Why, no. That detective in Ron Deever's office told both of us not to mention it."

"We appreciate that you didn't," Dell said. "Besides this Bart Mason, do you know of any other men in the building that Edie went out with?"

"No," Sally said, shaking her head.

Just then, Kenmare came into the room. He said nothing, not wishing to interrupt the flow of Dell's interview. But Dell rose, saying, "Okay, thanks very much, Miss Simms. We'll be in touch if we need anything else."

"Do I still have to not talk about it?" Sally asked.

"No, you can talk about it now. It'll be in the afternoon papers anyway. But don't call Bart Mason yet. We want to talk to him first." When Sally left the room, Dell said to Kenmare, "Bart Mason, guy works for an insurance company down on twenty-two, used to date Edie. Supposedly doesn't know she's dead yet."

"Let's see," said Kenmare.

Going down in the elevator, Dell asked, "Anything with Deever?"

"Nothing interesting."

The insurance company occupied the entire twenty-second floor, and the detectives had a receptionist show them to Bart Mason's office without announcing them. Once there, Kenmare thanked her and closed the door behind them. They identified themselves and Kenmare said, "Mr. Mason, do you know a woman named Edie Malone?"

"Sure. She works for an ad agency up on forty," Mason said. "We used to date." He was a pleasant looking young man, neat as a drill instructor. "Why, what's the matter?"

"She was found murdered in her apartment."

*"Edie?"* The color drained from Bart Mason's face, and his eyes widened almost to bulging. "I don't believe it—"

"Can you tell us your whereabouts for the last forty-eight hours, Mr. Mason?"

Mason was staring incredulously at them. "Edie—murdered—?"

"We need to know where you've been for the last couple of days," Kenmare said.

"What? Oh, sure—" Mason picked up his phone and dialed a three-number extension. When his call was answered, he said, "Jenny, will you come over to my office right away? It's important."

"Who's that?" Dell asked when Mason hung up.

"My fiancée. Jenny Paula. She works over in claims. We live together. We're together all the time: eat breakfast together, come to work together, eat lunch, go home, eat dinner, sleep together. We haven't been apart since a week ago Sunday when Jen went to spend the day with her mother." He took a deep breath. "My God, Edie—"

A pretty young woman, Italian-looking, came into the office. She looked curiously at the two detectives. Mason introduced them.

"They need to know my whereabouts for the last few days," he said.

"But why?" she asked.

"Just tell them where I've been, hon."

Jenny shrugged. "With me."

"All the time?" asked Kenmare.

"Yes, all the time."

"Like I said, we do everything together," Mason reiterated. "We work together, shop for groceries together, stay in or go out together, we even shower together."

"Bart!" Jenny Paula said, chagrined. "What's this all about anyway?"

"I'll explain later. Can she go now, Officers?"

"Sure," said Kenmare. "Thank you, Miss Paula." She left, somewhat piqued, and Kenmare said to Mason, "We may need to talk to her again, in a little more depth."

"We're both available anytime," Mason assured him.

"How long did you date Edie Malone?" Dell asked.

"About six months, I guess."

"Were you intimate?"

"Sure." Mason shrugged.

"When did you break up?"

"Late last summer sometime. Around Labor Day, I think."

"What caused you to break up?"

"Edie began seeing someone else. I didn't like it. So I split with her."

"Do you know who she started seeing?"

"Yeah. Ron Deever, her boss upstairs at the ad agency."

Dell and Kenmare exchanged quick glances. They continued to question Mason for several more minutes, then got his apartment address and left.

On the way back up to the fortieth floor, an annoyed Kenmare, referring to Ron Deever, said, "That son of a bitch. He never mentioned once that he went out with her. I think I'll haul his ass in and take a formal statement."

"He'll lawyer up on you," Dell predicted.

"Let him."

When they got back to Able, Bennett, and Crain, Kenmare went into Ron Deever's office again while Dell took Sally Simms back into the coffee room.

"Did you know that Edie Malone had dated Ron Deever?" he asked bluntly. Sally lowered her eyes.

"Yes."

"I asked you if you knew of any other men in the building that Edie had gone out with and you said no. Why did you lie?"

"I'm sorry," she said, her hands beginning to tremble. "Look, this guy is my boss. I'm a single parent with a little boy in day care. I didn't want to take a chance of losing my job." She started tearing up. "First thing he asked me after you left was whether I told you about him and Edie."

"Why was he so concerned?"

"He's married."

"Did Edie know that when she was seeing him?"

"Sure. It was no big thing for her."

Dell sighed quietly. Reaching out, he patted the young woman's trembling hands. "Okay. Relax. I'll make sure Deever knows it wasn't you who told us. But if I have to question you again, don't lie to me about anything. Understand?"

"Sure." Sally dabbed at her eyes with a paper napkin. "Listen, thanks."

Dell sent her back to work and went into Deever's office, where Kenmare was reading the riot act to him.

"What the hell do you think this is, a TV show? This is a *homicide* investigation, mister! When you withhold relevant information, you're obstructing justice!" He turned to Dell. "He's married. That's why he didn't come clean."

"I just chewed out Miss Simms, too," Dell said. "Told her how much trouble she could get into covering for him."

"All right," said Kenmare, "we're going to start all over, Mr. Deever, and I want the full and complete truth this time."

A shaky Ron Deever nodded compliance.

When they got back to the squad room, Garvan was waiting for them and a spare desk had been set up for Dell.

"She wasn't raped or otherwise sexually assaulted," he reported. "Cause of death was strangulation—from behind. Coroner fixed time of death at between

146 | C L A R K  H O W A R D

nine at night and one in the morning. Best bet: between eleven and midnight."
He tossed Edie's address book onto the desk. "You were right about this, Dell: It's
old. Some of these people haven't seen or heard from her in three or four years.
The ones who have couldn't tell me anything about her personal life. You guys
make out?"

"Not really," said Kenmare. "We've got one guy who could have slipped out
while his fiancée was asleep and gone over and done it—but it's not likely.
Another guy, married, was at his son's basketball game earlier in the evening, then
at home with his family out in Arlington Heights the rest of the night. One of us
will have to go out and interview his wife on that this afternoon."

"I'll do it," Garvan said. "I need the fresh air after that autopsy. Oh, I almost
forgot." He tossed five telephone messages to Dell. "These were forwarded from
Lakeside. Three are from your partner, two from your captain."

"If you need some privacy to return the calls," Kenmare said, "Garvan and I
can go for coffee."

Dell shook his head. "Nothing I can't say in front of you guys. You both
know the situation." He could tell by their expressions, as he dialed Mike Larne's
number first, that they were pleased at not being excluded. "It's Dell, Captain,"
he said when Larne answered. "I told you I'd check in when I had the autopsy
results. Edie wasn't raped or anything like that. Somebody strangled her from
behind, between nine Tuesday night and one on Wednesday morning." He listened for a moment, then said, "Couple of soft leads, is all. Very soft." Then:
"Yeah, he's called me three times. I guess I better get back to him."

When he finished his call to Larne, Dell dialed Dan Malone's home. The
phone was answered on the third ring. "Hello."

"Yeah, who's this?" Dell asked.

"Who are *you?*" the voice asked back.

"Frank Dell. Is that you, Keenan?"

"Oh, Frank. Yeah, it's me. Sorry, I didn't recognize your voice. How's it
going?"

"Very slow. Dan's been calling me, I guess. How is he?"

"Thrashed, inside and out. But the boys and me have him under control.
And his two sisters are here with him. He's sleeping right now. It means a lot to
him that you're working the case, Frank. He's got a couple of names that he wants
checked: old boyfriends of Edie's that he didn't like. Wasn't for you being on the
case, he'd probably be out doing it hisself. Pistol-whipping them, maybe."

"You have the names?"

"Yeah, he wrote them down here by the phone."

Dell took down the names and told Keenan to tell Dan that he'd see him
tomorrow with a full report of the case's progress. After he hung up, he handed
the names to Kenmare. "Old boyfriends," he said.

Kenmare gave them to Garvan. "Start a check on them before you go out to
interview Deever's wife. Frank and I are going out to that line-dancing joint—it's
called Memphis City Limits—to interview Bob Pilcher. We'll meet back here at
end of shift."

Memphis City Limits did not have live music until after seven, but even in
midafternoon there was jukebox country-western playing and a few people on

the dance floor around which the club was laid out. It was a big barn of a building that had once been a wholesale furniture outlet, then remained vacant for several years until some entrepreneurial mind decided there might be a profit in a club catering to the area's large influx of Southerners come north to find work.

Dell and Kenmare found Bob Pilcher drinking beer at a table with two cowgirl types and a beefy man in a lumberjack shirt. Identifying themselves, Kenmare asked if they could speak with Pilcher in private to ask him a few questions. Pilcher shook his head.

"Anything you want to ask me about Edie Malone, do it right here in front of witnesses."

"What makes you think it's about Edie Malone?" Kenmare asked.

"No other reason for you to be talking to me. Story's been on TV news all morning about her being murdered." Pilcher spoke with a heavily accented drawl that sounded purposely exaggerated.

"When did you see her last?" Dell asked.

" 'Bout a week ago." He winked at Dell. "She was alive, too."

"Can you account for your time during the past seventy-two hours?" Kenmare wanted to know, expanding the time period more than he had to because of Pilcher's attitude.

"Most of it, I reckon," Pilcher replied. "I'm here ever' day 'cept Sundays from no later than six of an evening to closing time at two A.M. Usually I'm here an hour or two *before* six, as you can see today. As for the rest of my time, you'd have to give me specific times and I'd see what I could come up with." His expression hardened a little. "Tell you one thing, though, boys, you wasting good po-lice time on me. I didn't off the gal."

"We have reason to believe you slapped her around now and then," Dell tried.

"So what if I did?" Pilcher challenged. "You can't arrest me for that: She's *dead*, fellers, hell!" He took a long swallow of beer. "Anyways, one of the reasons women like me is that I treat 'em rough. That one wasn't no different."

"So you did slap her around?"

"Yeah, I did," Pilcher defied him, lighting a cigarette. "Go on and do something about it if you can."

"Where can we find your employer," Kenmare asked, "to verify that you've been here the last three nights?"

Pilcher smiled what was really a nasty half-smirk. "So she was offed at night, huh? For sure you'll have to pin it on somebody else." He nodded across the club. "Manager's office is that door to the right of the bar."

Pilcher blew smoke rings at the two detectives as they left him at the table with his friends and sought out the club manager. He confirmed that Pilcher had indeed been on duty from at least six until two every night since the club had been closed the previous Sunday.

"Brother, would I like to nail that hillbilly for this," Kenmare groused as they walked back to their car. "I'd plant evidence to get that son of a bitch."

"So would I," Dell admitted. "Only there's no evidence to plant. Anyway, the time line doesn't jibe. A second-year law student could get him off."

When they got back to the squad room, Garvan had already returned. "Struck out," he announced. "Deever's wife puts him at home from about ten-thirty, after their son's basketball game, until the next morning about eight when he left for work." He turned to Dell. "And those two boyfriends your partner didn't like: One of them's in the navy stationed on Okinawa; the other's married, lives in Oregon, hasn't been out of that state since last July. You guys?"

"Pilcher's a scumbag, but his alibi's tight," Kenmare said. He looked at his watch. "Let's call it a day. Thursday's a big night for my wife and me," he told Dell. "We get a sitter, go out for Chinese, and see a movie."

Dell just nodded, but Garvan said, "Go see a good cop picture tonight. Something with Bruce Willis in it. Maybe you can pick up some tips on how to be a detective."

"Up yours, you perennial rookie," Kenmare said, and left.

Garvan turned to Dell. "Buy you a drink, Lakeside?"

"Why not?" said Dell. "Lead the way, Homicide."

At two o'clock the next morning, Dell was in his car, parked at the alley entrance to the rear parking lot of the Memphis City Limits club. He was wearing dark trousers and a black windbreaker, and had black Nikes on his feet. Both hands were gloved, and he wore a wool navy watch cap low on his forehead, and a dark scarf around his neck. The fuse for the interior lights on his car had been removed.

He had been there for half an hour, watching as the last patrons of the night exited the club, got into their vehicles, and left. By ten past two, there were only a few cars left, belonging to club employees who were straggling out to go home. The lot was not particularly well lit, but the rear door to the club was, so it was easy for Dell to distinguish people as they left.

It was a quarter past two when Bob Pilcher came out and swaggered across the parking lot toward a Dodge Ram pickup. Dell got out of his car without the light going on and, in his Nikes, walked briskly, silently toward him from the left rear, tying the scarf over his lower face as he went. When he was within arm's length of Pilcher, he said, "Hey, stud."

Pilcher turned, a half-smile starting, and Dell cracked him across the face with a leather-covered lead sap. He heard part of Pilcher's face crack. Catching him before he dropped to the ground, Dell dragged the unconscious man around the truck, out of sight of the club's back door. Dropping him, he rolled him over, facedown. Pulling both arms above his head, he pressed each of Pilcher's palms, in turn, against the asphalt, held each down at the wrist, and with the sap used short, snapping blows to systematically break the top four finger knuckles and top thumb knuckle of each hand. Then he walked quickly back to the alley, got into his car, and drove away. The whole thing had taken less than two minutes.

Be a long time before you slap another woman around, he thought grimly as he left. Or even hold a toothbrush.

Then he thought: That was for you, Edie.

The next day, Dell went to be with Dan Malone when he came to the funeral parlor to see Edie in her casket for the first time. The undertaker had picked up her body when the coroner was through with it, and one of Edie's aunts and two cousins had gone to Marshall Field's and bought her a simple mauve dress to be laid out in.

There were a number of aunts, uncles, cousins, and other collateral family members in attendance when the slumber room was opened, and groups of neighbors gathered outside, easily outnumbered by groups of police officers, in uniform and out, who had known Dan Malone for all or part of his thirty-two years on the force and had come from half the police districts in the city to offer their condolences.

Dell was shocked by the sight of Dan when the grieving man arrived. He looked as if he had aged ten years in the three days since Dell had seen him. A couple of male relatives helped him out of the car and were assisting him in an unsteady walk toward the entrance when Dan's eyes fell on Dell and he pulled away, insisting on a moment with his partner. Dell hurried to him, the two men embraced, then stepped up close to the building where people cleared a space for them to speak privately.

"Did you find those two bastards Keenan gave you the names of?" Dan asked hoarsely.

"Yeah, Dan, but they're clean," Dell told him. "They're not even around anymore."

"Are you sure? I never liked either one of 'em."

"They're clean, Dan. I promise you. Listen," Dell said to placate him, speaking close to his ear, "I did find one guy. He's clean for the killing, but he'd slapped Edie around a couple of times."

"The son of a bitch. Who is he?" The older man's teary eyes became fiery with rage.

"It's okay, Dan. I already took care of it."

"You did? What'd you do?"

"Fixed his hands. With a sap."

"Good, good." Malone wet his dry, whiskey-puffed lips. "I knew I could count on you, Frankie. Listen, come on inside and see my little girl."

"You go in with your family, Dan. I've already seen her," Dell lied. He had no intention of looking at Edie Malone's body again.

Dell gestured and several relatives hurried over to get Dan. Then Dell returned to a group of policemen that included Mike Larne, a couple of lieutenants, Keenan and other cronies of Dan's, and a deputy commissioner. Larne put an arm around Dell's shoulders.

"Whatever you said to him, Frank, it seemed to help."

"I hope so," Dell said. "Listen, Captain, I'm going to get back down to Homicide."

"By all means," said Larne. "Back to work, lad. Find the bastard who caused this heartache."

In the days immediately following the funeral and burial of Edie Malone, the three detectives on the case worked and reworked the old leads, as well as a few new ones. A deputy state's attorney, Ray Millard, was assigned to analyze and evaluate the evidence as they progressed. Disappointingly, there was little of a positive nature to analyze.

"It's too soft," Millard told them in their first meeting. He was a precise, intense young lawyer. "First, you've got the guy she worked for: older man, married, concealed the relationship when first questioned. Solid alibi for the hours just before, during, and after his son's basketball game which he attended on the night of the murder. Decent alibi for the rest of the night: a statement by his wife that he was at home. He *could* have slipped out of his suburban home when everyone was asleep, driven into the city, and committed the crime—but *why* would he have done that, and who's going to believe it?

"Second, you've got the good-guy ex-boyfriend. He's well set up with a new girlfriend, and the two of them are practically joined at the hip: live together, work together, play together. Again, he *could* have slipped out of their apartment around midnight when his fiancée was asleep, gone to the Malone woman's apartment, a relatively short distance away, and killed her. But again, *why?* Let's remember that *he* dumped *her*, not the other way around. Soft, very soft.

"Third, bad-guy ex-boyfriend. The hillbilly bouncer." Millard paused. "Incidentally, I understand that the night after you guys interviewed him, somebody jumped him outside the club and broke his nose, one cheekbone, and both hands. You guys heard anything about that?"

The detectives shrugged in unison, as if choreographed. "Doesn't surprise me," Kenmare said.

"Me either," Dell agreed. "Scumbags like that always have people who don't like them."

"Well, anyway," the young lawyer continued, "bad-guy boyfriend would be a beaut to get in court. I could try him in front of a jury of his *relatives* and probably get a death sentence—except for one thing: He's got a home-free alibi on his job. No way he could have been away from the club long enough to go do it without his absence being noticed. He's the bouncer; he's got to be visible all the time." Millard sat back and drummed his fingers. "Anything else cooking?"

Kenmare shook his head. "We're back canvassing the neighbors again, but nothing so far. We had one little piece of excitement day before yesterday when a little old retired lady in the victim's building said she'd heard that the building super had been fired from his last job for making lewd suggestions to female tenants. We checked it out and there was nothing to it. Turned out she was just ticked off at him for reporting her dog making a mess in the hallway a couple times."

"Too bad," Millard said. "The super would've made a good defendant. Had a key to her apartment, found the body, whole ball of wax. He alibied tight?"

"Very. Lives with his wife on two. They went to a movie, got home around eleven, went right to bed. He's got a good rep—except for the little old lady with the dog."

"Had to be somebody she knew," Millard said. "No forced entry, no lock picked. No rape, no robbery. This was a personal crime. She let the guy in." He tossed the file across the desk to Kenmare. "Find me that guy and we'll stick the needle in his arm."

The three detectives took off early and went to a small Loop bar where they settled in a back booth. Dell could sense some tension but did not broach the subject. He knew Kenmare would get around to whatever it was.

"We've enjoyed having you work with us, Frank," the senior detective finally said. "We had our doubts about your assignment, but it's turned out okay."

"Yeah, we had our doubts," Garvan confirmed, "but it worked out fine."

"I tried not to get in the way," Dell said.

"Hey, you've been a lot of help," Garvan assured him. "Got me away from this nag for a while," he bobbed his chin at Kenmare.

"Listen to him," the older man said. "Wasn't for me, he'd be directing traffic at some school crossing."

"What's on your mind, boys?" Dell asked, deciding not to wait.

Kenmare sighed. "It's a bit delicate, Frank."

"I'm a big boy. Shoot."

They both leaned toward him to emphasize confidentiality. "That first night in the apartment, you commented that Dan Malone and his daughter hadn't been close for a while," Kenmare recalled.

Garvan nodded. "You said he didn't approve of her lifestyle."

"You said he didn't talk much about her after she quit college and went out on her own."

Dell's expression tightened and locked. "You're getting very close to stepping over the wrong line," he said evenly.

"I'm sorry you feel that way, Frank," said Kenmare. "It's a step that has to be taken." He sat back. "You know as well as I do that if he wasn't one of our own, he'd have been on the spot from day one. As soon as we decided there was no forced entry, no rape, no robbery, we would have included an estranged father in our investigation. But Garvan and me, we kept hoping that evidence would lead us to somebody else. Unfortunately, it hasn't."

"Look, Frank," Garvan said in a placating tone, "it doesn't have to be a complicated thing. It can be, like, informal."

"Of course," Kenmare agreed, his own voice also becoming appeasing. "Drop in on him. Have a drink. Engage him in casual conversation. And find out where he was during the critical hours, that's all."

"Sure," said Garvan, "that's all."

Dell grunted quietly. Like it would be a walk in the park to handle a thirty-two-year veteran cop like that. He took a long swallow of his drink. His eyes shifted from Kenmare to Garvan and back again, then looked down at the table, where the fingers of one hand drummed silently. He did not speak for what seemed like a very long time. Finally Kenmare broke the silence.

"It's either that way or it'll have to be us, Frank. But it's got to be done."

With a sigh that came from deep inside of him, Dell nodded. "All right."

The tension that permeated the booth should have dissipated with that, but it did not. Dell once again became, as he had been at the very beginning of the investigation, an outsider.

Dan Malone smiled when he opened the door and saw Dell.

"Ah, Frank. Come in, come in. Good to see you, partner. I've missed you."

"Missed you too, Dan."

They embraced briefly, and, Dell sensed, a little stiffly.

"I was just having a beer after supper," said Dan. "You want one?"

"Sure."

"Sit down there on the couch. I'll get you one." He turned off a network hockey game, picked up a plastic tray on which were the remains of a TV dinner, and went into the kitchen with it. In a moment, he returned with an open bottle of Budweiser. "So," he said, handing Dell the beer and sitting in his recliner, "how's it going?"

"It's not going, Dan. Not going anywhere," Dell replied quietly, almost dejectedly.

"Well, I figured as much. Else you'd have been in closer touch. Not getting anywhere on the case?"

"No. I've been meaning to drop by and talk to you about it, but I thought you probably still had family staying with you."

"My two sisters were here for a week," Dan said. "And there've been nieces and nephews running in and out like mice. Finally I had enough and ran them all off. Then my phone started ringing off the hook all day, so I finally unplugged that just to get some peace and quiet. I guess they all think I'm suicidal or something."

"Are you?" Dell asked.

Dan gave him a long look. "No. Any reason I should be?"

Dell shrugged. "Sometimes things like this are hard to get over. Some people want to do it quickly."

"That's not the case with me," the older man assured him. "I lost Edie a long time ago, Frank. I think I probably started losing her when she slept with her first man. Then every man after that, I lost her a little more. Until finally she was gone completely."

"Were there that many men?"

"You're working the case; you ought to know."

"We've only found three."

Malone grunted cynically. "You must not have gone back very far." He stared into space. "I used to follow her sometimes. She'd go into a bar and come out an hour later with a man. Night after night. Different bars, different men. It was like some kind of sickness with her."

They both fell silent and sat drinking for several minutes. Dell, who had always been so comfortable with his partner, felt peculiarly ill at ease, as if he had now become an outsider with Dan Malone as he had with the two homicide detectives. Finally he decided not to prolong the visit any more than necessary.

"How long have we known each other, Dan?" he asked.

"What's on your mind, Frank?" the older policeman asked knowingly.

It had been he who taught Dell that reminiscing frequently led to other things.

"The night of Edie's murder."

"What about it?"

"I need to know where you were."

Malone nodded understandingly. "I wondered when they'd get around to it." He smiled a slight, cold smile. "Suppose I tell you I was right here at home, alone, all night. What then?"

"Tell me what you did all night."

"Watched the fights on television. Drank too much. Passed out here in my chair."

"Who was fighting in the main event?"

Malone shrugged. "Some Puerto Rican against some black guy, I think. I was sleepy by the time the main go came on; I don't remember their names."

"Neither do I," said Dell.

"What?" Dan Malone frowned.

"I don't remember their names either. But you weren't alone that night. That was the night I dropped over. We both drank too much. I fell asleep on the couch. Didn't wake up until after one o'clock. Then I put you to bed and went home. That was the night, wasn't it, Dan?"

The older man's frown faded and his face seemed to go slack. "Yes," he said quietly. "Yes, I do believe that was the night."

There was silence between them again. Neither of them seemed to know what to say next, and they could not look at each other. Malone stared into space, as he had done earlier; Dell stared at the television, as if it had not been turned off. Only after several minutes did Dell drink the rest of his beer and put the bottle down. He rose.

"I'll be going now. You won't be coming back to work, will you, Dan?"

Malone looked thoughtfully at him. "No," he replied. "I'm thinking of putting in for retirement. My sisters in Florida want me to move down there."

"Good idea. You'd probably enjoy yourself. Lots of retired cops in Florida." Dell walked to the door. "Goodnight, Dan."

"Goodnight, Frank."

Only when he got out into the night air did Dell realize how much he was sweating.

The next morning, Dell typed up a summary of Dan Malone's statement, along with his own corroboration of the alibi. After signing it, he handed the report to Kenmare. The lead homicide detective read it, then passed it to Garvan to read.

"You've thought this through, I guess," Kenmare said.

"Backwards and forward," Dell told him.

Garvan raised his eyebrows but said nothing as he handed the report back to Kenmare.

"I don't think the brass will buy this," Kenmare offered.

"What are they going to do?" Dell asked. "Suspend Dan *and* me? Open an internal investigation? On what evidence? And how would it look on the evening news?"

"The higher-ups might feel it was worth it," said Garvan.

"Worth it why?" pressed Dell. "What's the gain? The department's getting rid of Dan anyway; he'll be retiring."

"But you won't," Garvan pointed out.

"So? What have I done that the department would want to get rid of me?"

"Helped him get away with it, that's what," said Kenmare.

"*If* he did it," Dell challenged. "And we don't know that he did. All we know is that we can't find anybody else right now who *did* do it." He decided to throw down the gauntlet right then. "You guys going to let this report pass, or are you going to make an issue of it?"

"You didn't mention this alibi last night when we were talking," Kenmare accused.

"Maybe I had my days mixed up." Dell shrugged. "Maybe I thought it had been Monday night I had dropped in; maybe Dan had to remind me it was Tuesday."

"Maybe," Kenmare said. He looked inquiringly at his partner.

"Yeah, maybe," Garvan agreed.

"You're sure Malone's retiring?" Kenmare asked.

"Positive," Dell guaranteed.

Kenmare pulled open a desk drawer and filed the report. "See you around, Dell," he said.

"Yeah," said Garvan. "Take it easy, Dell."

Dell walked out of the squad room without looking back.

That night, when Dell came into the Three Corners Club and took his regular seat at the end of the bar, it was the owner, Tim Callan, who poured his drink and served him.

"I've missed you, Frankie," he said congenially. "How've you been?"

"I've seen better days," Dell allowed.

"Ah, haven't we all," Callan sympathized. He lowered his voice. "I'm really sorry about the young lady. Edie, was that her name?"

"Yeah, Edie." Dell felt the back of his neck go warm.

"I seen her picture in the paper and on the news. Took me a few looks to place her. Then I says to myself, 'why, that's the young lady Frankie used to bring in here. Always wanted the booth 'way in the back for privacy.' " Callan smiled artificially. "I remember that every time I loaned you the key to use the apartment upstairs, I had to make you promise to be out by midnight so's I could get the poker game started. And you never let me down, Frank. Not once. 'Course, we go back a long ways, you and me." Now Callan's expression saddened, genuinely so. "I'm really sorry, Frank, that things didn't work out between you and Edie."

"Thank you, Tim. So am I." Dell's heart hurt when he said it.

"They still don't know who did it?"

Dell looked hard at him. "No."

They locked eyes for a long moment, two old friends, each of whom could read the other like scripture.

"What was the name of that brother-in-law of yours charged with receiving stolen property?" Dell finally asked.

"Nick Santore," said Callan. "Funny you should ask. His preliminary hearing's day after tomorrow."

"I'll talk to the assistant state's attorney," Dell said. "I'll tell him the guy's going to be a snitch for me, that I need him on the street. I'll get him to recommend probation."

"Ah, Frankie, you're a prince," Callan praised, clasping one of Dell's hands with both of his own. "I owe you, big time."

"No," Frank Dell said, "we're even, Timmy."

Both men knew it was so.

# S. J. Rozan

## Childhood

S. J. ROZAN is the acclaimed Shamus and Anthony winning author of the Lydia Chin and Bill Smith series. She combines the serious purpose of the literary ethnic novels of the forties and fifties with the penetrating style and wit of the contemporary urban crime novel. With each book, her audience increases. She is already a major figure on the suspense scene; it's just that some people have yet to get the message. "Childhood" first appeared as part of the electronic anthology *Compulsion*.

# Childhood

*S. J. Rozan*

I haunted the Maine coast that year as summer turned to fall, a restless ghost too real, footsteps too heavy on the wet, sinking sand, shape too solid moving through the fog. Long after it was over, I stood on the cliff, listening for cries long since silenced, searching the rocks and the tugging surf for floating, broken forms forever gone. I never told Ben, but over and over, maybe after dinner, maybe before breakfast, I found myself locking up my place, getting out the car. I made the long drive, six hours of highway and then the smaller roads, always knowing I had to go, always knowing I could do no good.

Those times, after, I turned straight for the shore; but that first time, when it started, I drove into town, parked in the sheriff's lot, went in to see Ben.

It was a long way to come, six states distant, but Ben and I went way back. We'd been in the navy together, both of us joining up at seventeen, both of us coming from Brooklyn, though I'd lived there not two years and Ben all his life. We met the first week in basic training and it turned out we served the whole three years together; same base, same ships. Ben was as rock steady as I was explosive, those years; any trouble I managed to stay out of, it was because Ben was there, holding me back. The difference between us: Ben liked the navy, I hated it. After discharge, we both went back to New York, me to college and Ben to the NYPD, but Ben didn't stay long. The sea was part of him now, the way it was always changing and always the same, and after a few years he headed up to Maine. In the small coastal town of Phillip's Point he found an opening in the county sheriff's office. Now, twenty years later, Ben was sheriff.

When he'd called, I wasn't surprised. That was how it went with us, a call every six, eight months from the big wooden house with the porches and gardens to my apartment in New York where the trucks rumbled over the streets outside and the stars were invisible in the night-lit sky. We'd talk, saying nothing, and sometimes he'd invite me up and if I could I'd go, spend a weekend doing nothing in Maine. The only times I'd been on a boat and liked it since the day I left the navy were times in Phillip's Point with Ben.

"Damn tourists in the summer," he'd say when you asked how life was up there. "Damn rain in winter. Damn redneck hicks in this two-bit burg." Ben loved his town and he loved his job.

But what he'd said on the phone that night, the call that started it, was, "I need help."

I leaned back in my chair with the beer I'd opened before the phone had rung. "Guy climbs onto ten feet of fiberglass, gets sunburned and soaked, catches two fish and calls it fun? Damn right you need help."

"No," Ben said, "real help. I need you to come up here."

This was different, his voice, his tone.

"What's wrong? Are you okay? Alice, the kids?"

"Yeah, they're fine. But I got a situation up here. I need someone from outside."

"You want me to come do a job?"

"Something like that, yeah."

I shook a cigarette from the pack. "I'm not licensed up there, Ben."

"I'll put in a word for you," he grunted. "With the sheriff."

That was late at night; early the next morning I was on the road, Joe Williams in the tape deck as the tired trees of late summer slipped past me on the interstate. I pulled into Phillip's Point midafternoon, parked on Main Street. Inside the blue-shuttered, whitewashed county hall, I introduced myself to the young deputy behind the desk.

The kid jumped up from his chair, all muscles and brush-cut helpfulness. "Yes, sir, Sheriff Martin's expecting you. Let me see if he's free." He stuck his head into the office behind him, said something, and came out with a smile, visibly relieved that he had no bad news for me.

Ben came to greet me, took me behind the desk. "I told him not to ask," he grumbled, closing the door on the sheriff's private office. "I told him, just bring you in." He pointed me to a worn leather armchair. Sun streamed in the open windows. "You must've flown pretty low," Ben said. "Or gotten up with the chickens." He pressed a speaker-phone button. "Hey, Richie, see if you can scare up some coffee."

"Yes, sir!" Richie's voice crackled, attentive and efficient. Ben rolled his eyes.

"Chickens in my neighborhood sleep until noon," I said. "I told the Highway Patrol I was on a mission for the sheriff of Phillips County. They were impressed as all hell and waved me through."

Ben snorted. Richie came in, two steaming mugs in one hand, a quart of milk and half a dozen sugar packets in the other. The coffee in one mug was pale, the other black. "You want milk, sugar, anything?" Richie asked me, giving Ben the light coffee, waving his offerings in my direction.

"No," I said. "Thanks." I took the mug he handed me. Phillips County coffee was the only good-tasting cop coffee I'd ever had.

Ben sipped from his mug, made a face.

"Oh, shit," said Richie. "Too sweet, huh? I'll get you another one."

"No, Richie, it's okay," Ben said.

"No, I can—"

"It's okay, Richie."

Richie stood for a moment, shifting from one foot to the other.

"Thanks, Richie," Ben said.

Richie grinned, lifted the milk at me again in case I'd changed my mind. When I shook my head he shrugged, turned, and left.

Ben sipped his coffee. "Three years a deputy," he said. "And every time that kid brings me coffee, it's too sweet." His chair creaked as he settled into it. Ben had put on some weight over the years, a comfortable guy in a comfortable place. "Listen, I wouldn't have called you—"

"—if you could've found someone who knew what he was doing, but you couldn't, up here in the middle of nowhere. I count on that to make a living. What's up?"

Ben drank his coffee, looked off over my shoulder for the words he wanted. "No," he said. "Really. When you hear . . . but I've got to do something here."

The two big windows in his office framed Main Street; beyond it, distant, the shore and the sea. Tourists in Jeep Cherokees and locals in rusted pickups rolled along; people walked the sidewalks in and out of the shade of the awnings at the hardware store, the beauty parlor.

"Little over a week ago, we had a kid killed," Ben said, sipping coffee, watching me. "Eight years old. Tom Rogers' son."

The cry of a gull floated in through the windows, answered by another, then a third. I shifted my gaze to the sky, tried to find them. This was what he'd meant, then, that he wouldn't have called me. In the long years since the navy, Ben and I had both married, and both had children. Ben and Alice's youngest son still lived with them in the big wooden house; their other two were grown and gone. My marriage had been wrong, and short, and the only good to come of it, our daughter, Annie, had died in a car crash when she was nine.

I lit a cigarette, shook out the match. I watched the sky a little longer, but it was empty. Ben knew about Annie. I didn't know what he wanted, but whatever it was, he wouldn't have called me if he'd thought he had another choice. "Killed?" I asked. "Killed how?"

"Drowned," Ben said steadily, eyes on me. I met his look. He went on. "Down at Gray's Cove. All the local kids hang out there. Looked like an accident at first." He drank his too-sweet coffee. "Still may have been. He was alive when we pulled him out of the water, died a few hours later. They did an autopsy, routine, because it's procedure in accidental death, not because we thought we'd find anything."

"But you did."

Ben nodded. "Sexual molestation." He pushed each syllable out of his mouth, drank some coffee afterward to clear the taste. "Recent."

I pulled on my cigarette. "The two could still be unrelated, Ben."

"I know. Just because someone messes with a kid, doesn't mean the kid doesn't go fishing, fall in the water. But it also could be someone threw him in, keep him quiet."

"It could."

"Tom Rogers thinks it does." Ben clunked his coffee mug onto his desk. "Never much of a father, Tom. He and Agnes drink. Their four kids raised themselves. This kid, Frankie, was their youngest." Outside, the sun glinted off the windows of a truck. Ben glanced that way. "Nice kid, Frankie. Always looking for someone to say a good word to him, that's all. Father's an asshole, doesn't mean the kid deserves—" Ben broke off, maybe worried about what he'd said. But what he'd said was true.

"He have an alibi?"

"Who, Tom? Listen, Tom's always been an asshole, but not like that. But," Ben shrugged, "I've always been a cop. So yeah, I checked. He went straight to Grogan's after work. Agnes was already there. They were still there at midnight when I went looking, to tell them about Frankie." Ben picked up his coffee, but he didn't drink. "Tom said I was a lying s.o.b., just trying to scare him into going home. When I said I wasn't he stared at me, sort of froze. Then he had another drink. Like he always does, anything happens. Like it ever works."

The truck pulled away. I watched a tourist couple stroll through the sunlight and shadows. "I still don't see why I'm here."

Ben nodded. "The problem's this. We got a guy here, out by the county line. Bob Hurst. Been living here three, four months. Did seven years in Maine State Correctional for sodomy and solicitation. We don't have a law here, these guys don't have to register, but I got a heads-up from the state when he got out."

"Underage victim?"

"Eight-year-old boy."

I picked up my coffee again.

Ben said, "And that's the conviction, Smith. Families of four other boys swearing out complaints, but the prosecutor didn't try to make those cases. And God knows how many others they never heard from."

"Sodomy and solicitation," I said. "Five complainants, none for assault, no other violence?"

"No," Ben said, reluctance in his voice. "But now Hurst's spent seven years in state, because some kid testified. Could be he doesn't want to go back."

"You talk to him? Hurst?" But of course he had; Ben knew his job.

"Three times. No idea what I'm talking about. Never saw the kid. He's through with all that. Rehabilitated. Has a job, reports to his parole officer, lives a quiet life."

"You believe him?"

Ben's eyes held mine. "I swear as I'm sitting here, Smith, he killed that boy."

The scent of the sea drifted back in on a changing breeze. Cars stopped for each other, moved again along Main Street.

"How do you see it?" I asked.

"Hurst works at Ralph's Auto Repair out on Route Three. We got a park out there across the road from Ralph's. Peewee League softball plays there. Frankie would have been out there two, three times a week all summer."

"Anyone see him and Hurst together?"

"No. But the thing about Frankie, Tom and Agnes could never be bothered to take him out there, pick him up, anything like that. Sometimes he'd hitch a ride with some other kid's mom, but mostly he rode his bike."

"And you're thinking a guy like Hurst would notice that."

"All summer, Smith. Game's over, this kid's alone. All summer."

I pushed out my cigarette. "Alibi?"

"The day this happened, Hurst told Ralph he had some business to take care of, left work early."

"How early?"

"Before the ballgame ended. He stopped for a drink at the Trap, his usual hole, like he told us, but later, at his usual time. He's got about an hour and a half unaccounted for."

"What does he say?"

"Went to the outlet mall on Twenty-seven and to Home Depot. We checked, but no one remembers him."

"Places like that, they don't remember anyone."

Ben nodded. "And if I wanted a bullshit alibi, that's a good one."

"What does he say he was buying?"

"Roofing nails, roll roofing, Tyvek. Get his place ready for winter."

"You see any of that stuff at his place?"

Ben nodded. "But nothing to say when it was bought. Says he didn't know he was going to need the damn receipts to show some damn cop."

"Okay. Anything else?"

"I got a witness saw a blue car like Hurst's at Gray's Cove, but she can't swear it was Hurst's. I got someone saw a blond kid on a bike there, but he can't swear it was Frankie."

Ben took out a blue bandanna, wiped sweat from his face. The day was hot, but with an openness to it, not the stifling heat of the city.

"One other thing, one reason I called you. I got a nut lives up there, Gray's Cove, name of Larry Crandall. Lost a son to that water, years back. Last time anyone drowned, up here." Ben paused. He could have been thinking of that time, or of the quiet years between. "Larry never got over it."

"Blames himself?"

Ben looked at me, maybe knowing why I asked that. "Shit, no. Everyone else."

"Everyone, who?"

"Well, me, for one. Thinks I didn't respond fast enough, when the call came in. And Richie, out there? He was a kid himself, twelve, thirteen. Swam out, pulled Larry's boy from the water, but too late. Everyone called him a big hero, but he wouldn't hear it. Said a hero would've saved the kid. That's why he joined the department. Still trying to make up for that, be that hero."

The same as everyone, I thought wearily. Trying to be that hero, now, too late.

"Anyway," Ben said, "Larry agrees. Thinks someone, Richie, me, the guy on the ambulance, someone should have saved that kid. What's really going on, he was supposed to be watching the kid and he wasn't. Nine years later, he still won't talk to us."

"Won't talk?"

"Larry was never the sharpest knife in the drawer, even before. Now, anyone in a uniform talks to him, even hello-how's-the-weather, he just stares through you, like he doesn't see you. Calls up here every now and then, though."

"Calls up? Why?"

"To remind us his boy is dead and it's our fault."

"Christ."

Ben shrugged. "It's hardest on Richie. Larry knows when it's him on the phone."

"What does he say? Richie?"

"Nothing. Rule is, don't talk, put Larry through to me. I just tell him I'm sorry. What else can I do?"

"God, Ben."

Ben looked into his coffee.

I asked, "You think he could have seen something?"

"He lives up there. Spends a lot of time on the beach, just sitting. Watching, I guess."

"And he might talk to me?"

"The state offered to send someone, but to Larry, a cop's a cop."

I looked beyond Main Street to the cliffs and the sea. "Who found him?" I asked.

"Frankie? We got a call. Man, wouldn't give his name, said there was a kid in the water at Gray's Cove. Richie and me were there in three minutes, pulled him out. Like I said, seemed he might live. Richie broke down and cried when he died."

Ben got up, looked at something out the window. He drank his coffee. I didn't ask him what he'd done when Frankie died.

"You get anything off the nine-one-one tape?"

"No. Could be just some tourist, doesn't want to screw up his vacation by getting involved." He turned, sat heavily again in the sheriff's chair. "I got nothing, Smith. But I'll tell you what I got: I got a guy who did this before, and if I can't stop him, he'll do it again, some other kid, some other time." He looked out the window again, to the street, the shore, the sea. "And I got a town, they find out who this guy is, someone's going to go out there and take care of the problem himself."

"They don't know?"

"I been hearing whispers around town lately, but I think no one knows for sure. I told my guys, keep it quiet."

"Why?"

"We got some hotheads out here. I guess I was more afraid of what they might do than what he might do. I thought . . ." He looked at me. I recognized the look in his eyes; I'd seen it in the mirror more than once. "It's a quiet town, Smith. It's been quiet, all these years."

To that I didn't say anything. What came to mind was, *It's not your fault*, but Ben didn't need that from me.

"What can I do?" I asked.

"I can't get a search warrant. I can't get anything. I need something, Smith."

"You want me to get you something that connects Hurst to the kid?"

He nodded. "And soon."

"How?"

"Drink with him. Break into his place. Hold a gun to his head. I don't care."

"You're kidding."

"You know me better. Shit, if I could do it myself, I would. If I could send Richie, one of the other guys, I would. But anything like that, we do it, it fucks up any case we make." He sighed. "And shit, Smith, I'm the law around here. Some of these kids"—he gestured to the door, to the rest of the building beyond the sheriff's private office—"they have enough trouble finding the line. It can't be me pushes them over it."

I shifted my eyes to the window, looked over Ben's town myself. "Talking to your guy Crandall's one thing. Hurst, if I break into his place or beat the crap out of him, what I get may not be admissible."

"You bring me something, I'll find a way to make it admissible. Don't doubt it."

I didn't.

"If I get caught?"

Ben grinned, for the first time. "By who? Me? Richie? One of my other guys? 'Gave us the slip, Your Honor. Don't know who he was, but he was slick. Must have been some big-city dude.' "

"But he left behind this silver bullet."

Ben's face grew quiet, calm like the surface of a night sea. "Bring me that bullet, Smith. Bring me that."

Ben gave me his incident report to look over, and Richie's. He handed me a photo of Frankie Rogers, a yellow-haired, shy-faced kid. He showed me a picture of Larry Crandall, and Bob Hurst's mug shot, gave me directions to Hurst's place at the far side of the county and to the place he worked. I gave Ben my cell phone number, and what reassurance I could. On the way back through the outer office I stopped to talk to Richie.

"I understand you were the first on the scene when Frankie Rogers died," I said to him.

"Yes, sir," Richie answered. His eager smile faded. His eyes looked at something I couldn't see. "Me and the sheriff."

"Can you tell me what happened?"

"I gave him CPR." Still looking away, swallowing. "I did everything you're supposed to do. I thought he'd be okay."

"I'm sure you did. What I want to know, did you see anyone else, anything odd, anything that sticks in your mind?"

"No, sir. Just Frankie . . . in the water . . . it's all in my report."

"Nothing you thought was maybe too dumb, too meaningless to put in the report, to tell the sheriff about?"

"No, sir." He looked up at me, suddenly. "Was there—did I miss something? Should I have done something else?"

"No," I said.

Richie nodded, unconvinced. There was nothing else I could say to him; I turned to go.

"The other time," I heard, and turned back to see him looking away again, speaking softly and not to me, "I was just a kid the other time. I'm a cop now, I've been trained, I should've been able . . ."

"No," I said again.

He raised his head, as though surprised to find himself not alone. Our eyes met, Richie waiting to hear what I had to say. But there was nothing. *Christ, Smith,* I thought. *You really have something to tell this kid about being a hero?*

I couldn't help him. I turned and left.

I drove out first to the repair shop on Route 3, Hurst's job. His shift ran until six; I just wanted a look at him, make sure he hadn't left early. A picture's one thing, but when you're going to break into a guy's house you want to size him up, if you can.

I stopped the car at the park where kids played softball. I sat and looked across the street, at the repair yard. Half a dozen guys were hard at work there, erasing the scars of things that had happened. The yard rang with the pounding of metal on metal. A circular saw screamed its way through a steel sheet. I spotted Hurst, a big guy, brown hair, a little thick in the waist. His jaw set, he gripped a wrench in both hands, fought with a bolt that wouldn't budge. The wrench slipped. Hurst's knuckles scraped, drawing blood. He shook the pain out, set the wrench on the bolt again. Sweat ran down his face; his T-shirt was black-streaked and damp.

I watched, then drove away. Hurst, nothing in his world right then but the solid refusal of the rusted bolt, never saw me.

It took me forty-five minutes to get out to the place Hurst lived, a squat wood cabin on the landlocked side of the county. The neighbors on each side were far enough and the scrubby trees between big enough that I figured I was okay. I parked off the road about fifty yards beyond Hurst's driveway; he wouldn't see the car, coming home after work, if I was still there. I made my way back to the house and around it: the back door's always a better bet than the front, hidden, usually a weaker lock. I went to work, for ten minutes moving nothing but my fingers, concentrating as hard on the thin steel picks as he had on the five-pound wrench clenched in his fists. The lock finally gave. I wondered if the rusted bolt had.

The cabin wasn't much, and there wasn't much there. Old shabby furniture, battered pots and pans. The back door opened into the kitchen, and the kitchen, with a change of flooring, became the living room; a bedroom, shades still pulled, was off beyond the living room to the left, bathroom beyond that, and no more.

I moved through the place, opening closets and drawers. It was clean enough but with a stale, closed-up air: people up here left their windows wide in heat like this, home or not, but Hurst's were closed and locked. In prison nothing you have is your own. Some guys, when they get out, build a fortress.

The magazines and books weren't hard to find, just hard to look through: kids, doing things they would never get over. Like anyone else, people who went in for this had preferences and favorites. Hurst's was young boys, not infants, not teens: around eight years old, and blond. I wondered, briefly, what Hurst had looked like when he was eight.

I went through the stack and left them in the bottom of the bedroom closet where I'd found them. I dumped the trash can looking for mailing wrappers. Possession of this stuff was legal, but getting it through the mail wasn't. If I could show Hurst had done that it would be a parole violation, and Ben could pick him up.

But the trash held nothing. I did the rest of the place, hope fading with the lowering sun. No photos, no kid's clothing, no letters, no diary. If Ben had been able to get a search warrant it would have gotten him nowhere.

All right. I put a cigarette in my mouth but didn't light it, stood in the middle of the floor, looking around. This had been an unlikely route to a payoff, but it had to be tried. There were a couple of other things I could do. One was talk to Hurst, but for that I needed to sound convincing. I let myself out the back door. A breeze rustled branches. I stood for a moment, letting it brush across my face, breathing air that was moving, that had come from somewhere clean.

I drove to the shore. Near Gray's Cove I parked on the shoulder of the road. Small stones rolled down the path under my feet as I worked my way to the water. The sun was almost gone from the land by now and the sea was in darkness.

A small sand beach curved like a new moon, backing onto the cliff I'd come down. Where it narrowed to nothing, waves crashed on piles of boulders, jetties stretching away into the water. I walked along the beach just beyond the reach of the lapping waves, smelling the salt, feeling the spray, listening to the roar, the murmur, the roar again, of the endless sea.

The towering cliff was black now, and I stopped to look, to learn its contours. I took the measure of the beach, estimated the jetties. I listened to the waves and counted their rhythm. I was going to lie to Hurst, and I was going to be good.

I reached the boulders that marked the end of the beach. For a while I stood and looked out over the sea. The lights of boats on the surface of the water gleamed through a thin mist that, above me, hid the stars. I turned and started to walk back, heading along the beach to the rocks at the other end.

I got near and realized I wasn't alone. A figure sat on the rocks, arms wrapped around knees, unmoving in the blowing spray.

My feet slipped along the wet stones as I climbed to where he was. I came to stand next to him and he turned, then turned his face back to the sea.

"Larry Crandall?" I asked. I raised my voice above the crashing of the surf.

He didn't look at me this time. He took a while to answer, and when he did it was only to say, "Be careful how you step."

"I'm Bill Smith," I told him. I squatted beside him on the rocks. He didn't move; it was as if I wasn't there. I looked where he was looking, watched the waves rear back, break over the rocks.

"Someone should do something," I said. "When it's a kid, someone should do something."

Waves rolled in and broke, slipped out again. White foam flew, briefly airborne, but could not keep the height. It fell and was taken back by the sea.

Crandall finally spoke. "No one will."

"I will, if I can."

"They say they want to." He wasn't speaking to me now, but to the sea, or to the past. "Sorry, Larry, we tried. They say."

"I'm not them."

"Another chance. It was the same." He turned his head to me, his eyes and voice suddenly full of the ferocity of the waves. "He should have saved my boy. Ah, but he's only a kid himself, Ben says. He did what he could. And Frankie? He's a man now. What about Frankie?"

At first I didn't understand. A man now? A shift of the wind covered us in salt spray. Then I thought: *Richie, Ben's deputy. He didn't save Crandall's son, and he and Ben didn't save Frankie.* Crandall's eyes blazed; then all the fury faded, like a wild surf subsiding. He turned back to the water.

Carefully, I asked, "Did you see Frankie here, that day?"

In a voice as dull as fog, he said, "Frankie rode his bike on the cliff."

"That day?"

Crandall shrugged. "Frankie rode his bike on the cliff."

"Did you see anyone with him?"

"No one will help."

"Was anyone with Frankie?" *Calm, Smith,* I told myself, *stay with the rhythm of the sea.*

Crandall answered, "I don't know him."

I kept my voice even. "Who?"

"They had ice cream cones. But I don't know him."

"Would you recognize him?"

Crandall turned his head from the crashing surf to stare at the black cliff rising like a stone wave above us. "There," he said. Then, "No."

I scanned the cliff top. It was far, and in late afternoon the sun would have been behind anyone up there. And Larry Crandall's word might not be good for much, in court. But someone had been with Frankie Rogers at Gray's Cove that day.

"I'm going to do something," I said. "About Frankie."

Crandall looked at me as though what I'd said meant nothing, was in a language he didn't speak and didn't care about. His face was flat and dull, but tear tracks glistened on it like the water left behind by a pulling tide.

I straightened, standing over him now. "Thank you."

He didn't answer. I turned and left, picking my way along the boulders to the beach, careful how I stepped.

I drove back to Hurst's place, working out what I would say, the lies most likely to work. By the time I got there the darkness was complete, lying heavily on the cabin and the spindly trees. The cabin's windows were dark and no car was parked nearby. I hadn't locked the back door when I left and I let myself in it now. In the closet with the magazines, earlier, I'd spotted Hurst's Winchester; it was empty when I found it, but a half dozen shell boxes were piled on the closet floor. I broke it open, loaded it, and, setting it across my lap, sat down in the dark to wait.

I don't know how long the wait was; it was however long it takes to smoke three cigarettes, and to let the need between them build up hard. I don't know what I thought about, either, in the heat, in the dark, in that closed-up house, but I was ready when headlights swung into the driveway and a moment later a car door slammed.

When Hurst switched on the light inside the front door I was still in the chair, facing him squarely, the rifle raised. The bag he held dropped to the floor in a thud.

"Close it, Bob," I said.

"What—"

"Close the door."

I moved the rifle. He closed the door.

"Who the hell are you?" His voice was ragged. Fear widened his eyes.

"I want to talk to you."

"Get out," he tried, because he had to, though the game was obviously mine.

"Frankie Rogers," I said. "The little boy you raped and killed up at Gray's Cove."

Hurst flinched. "I never saw that kid. Who the hell are you?"

"State police," I said. "Out of uniform, but that doesn't mean I won't shoot you. I was out of uniform the night you killed Frankie Rogers, too."

"I never saw that kid."

"Bullshit."

"What kind of—?"

"I saw you."

Hurst stood, mouth half open. He took a step toward me.

"No," I said, moving the rifle again.

He stopped. I could smell the cup of coffee that had smashed on the floor in the bag he'd dropped. Other things had been in there, too, eggs, milk. A pool grew slowly at Hurst's feet, reaching toward me.

"You saw me what?" Hurst said. "What the hell does that mean?"

"With the kid. Up on the cliff, late afternoon. You bought him ice cream. That where you raped him, Bob?"

His faced reddened. Good; it was that word. I used it again. "After you raped him you killed him, right? So he wouldn't tell. So he wouldn't tell anyone you're a monster."

"It wasn't like that!" he shouted. Eyes wide, he stopped, clamping his mouth shut.

I waited. Then, "It wasn't like what?" I asked softly. Hurst said nothing, jaw clenched, eyes blazing.

"I know it wasn't, Bob." I kept my voice low, gentle. "That's why I'm here."

A pause; then, "What the hell are you talking about?" His voice was a whisper.

"I told you: I saw you. You cared about that kid, Bob. I saw that. I'll bet you cared about them all."

I watched Hurst, one thing in his eyes, another in the line of his still-clenched jaw.

"And this kid, the Rogers kid, he liked you, too, didn't he, Bob? You were nice to him. That's all he wanted, someone to be nice to him. You cared about all of them, you were nice to them. That's why this is so unfair."

"What . . ." Hurst's shoulders slumped. He looked around the room, his place, his closed-up fortress. He brought his eyes back to mine, saying nothing.

"It's like this," I went on. "I saw you with the kid. I'm a cop and I have to report that. But I wanted to talk to you first, give you a chance. Because I know how it is. Because it isn't like they say."

Everything in the cabin was still, no sound, no movement. Just the smell of coffee from the puddle on the floor.

"He was a good kid," I said. "He liked you. They say you killed him, Bob."

For a long time, nothing.

"If you don't tell me," I said, "I have to report it just like I saw it. But I wanted to talk to you, Bob."

Slowly, Hurst shook his head. "I want to sit down," he said.

I nodded, gestured with the rifle to the couch in front of the living room window. He settled tentatively on it, as though it was not something he knew.

"I never wanted to hurt that kid," he said, hands on his knees.

"I know, Bob. But they're saying you did."

"No one cared about him," Hurst said. "Frankie. Someone needed to care about him."

"And that was you."

A long silence. Finally, "No one else cared about him."

"He played baseball out by your job, didn't he?" I said.

Hurst nodded. "He liked baseball. After a game he'd come looking for me. After a game. He knew."

"Knew what?"

"He knew I cared."

I slipped a cigarette into my mouth, lit it. "So tell me what happened, Bob. At Gray's Cove."

But something more important was on his mind. He looked up at me. "You said 'rape.' That's wrong."

"Wrong, Bob?"

"Just, I cared about him. I wanted to show him. *He* wanted to show *me*."

"Tell me what happened."

"I never meant to hurt him."

"Then tell me."

Hurst slowly shook his head, a man overwhelmed by the unfairness, the arbitrariness, of life. "He wanted me to see how good he was, climbing on the rocks. Like a little mountain goat." He smiled, but the smile faded. "He was happy. But he was so happy he wouldn't go home."

"What did he want to do?"

"Come home with me. I said he couldn't, but he said if I made him go home he'd tell about me."

I waited. Then I said, "You couldn't let him do that, could you?"

"I tried to tell him. I tried to talk to him. He ran away, over the rocks." Hurst looked up at me with desperate eyes. "He fell."

"Just like that? He fell?"

He looked away. "He slipped. He fell off the rocks into the water."

"You chased him and he fell. Did you catch him? Did you talk to him?"

"I couldn't let him tell anyone! And then . . . he fell."

I wondered if Hurst thought I believed him. I wondered if he believed himself. I asked, "What did you do?"

Hurst jerked his head up to look at me. "What the hell could I do? Jump in? I don't swim that good. And anyone finds out I was with him . . . I ran like hell to the car, drove to a pay phone, called nine-one-one. Kid in the water, Gray's Cove, I said. Best I could do. Best I could do."

I met his eyes, said nothing. That part, the call, squared with what Ben had told me. The rest, I wasn't sure. Maybe it had happened that way, a slip, a small mistake, and the world changed. Or maybe Hurst had decided there was only one way to avoid going back to prison for caring about a kid in ways the rest of us didn't understand. And then maybe he'd found that was where his own line was, the one he hadn't meant to cross, after he'd done it.

In any case, I had enough now for Ben, and I could take Hurst in, let Ben take over. I stood, and Hurst's face clouded; he knew what was coming. But before I could say anything the cell phone in my pocket started to vibrate. It had to be Ben. My eyes and the rifle still on Hurst, I took the phone out.

"Smith."

Ben's voice, rapid and loud. "You anywhere near Bob Hurst?"

"At his place."

"He there?"

"Yes."

"Grab him and get out."

"Why?"

"We've got another one."

"Another what?"

"Kid. Gray's Cove. A tourist's kid."

"What—"

"I don't know. But Tom Rogers and two carloads of drunks are on their way out there. So am I, and I called the state, but Tom's way ahead of us."

"Okay," I said, then, "Shit!" as headlights flooded the room and brakes squealed. "They're here, Ben. I'm armed. I'll do what I can."

"Shit!" he echoed. "Try not to kill anyone. Try not to get killed."

"Thanks," I said. "Advice always welcome." I flipped the phone shut. In a stride I reached the switch, killed the light.

"What the—"

"The other kid, Bob." I crouched at the living room window, took a look outside. Two cars, doors hanging wide, headlights glaring; dark forms, shifting, moving, vague behind the glare.

"What kid? Who's out there?" He started to rise from the couch, turn to the window.

"Get down!" I shoved him back.

From the shapes in the yard, a shout: "Hurst! You fucker, get out here!"

Hurst turned wild eyes to me.

"The tourist's kid, tonight," I said. "That why you're home so late, Bob? You go back to Gray's Cove? You care about that kid, too?"

"What are you talking about?"

"Shut the fuck up, Bob. These guys came out here to kill you and it's not a bad idea."

"I told you! I told you about Frankie. He fell!"

"And the kid tonight?"

"What kid tonight?"

I said nothing, watching the dark forms.

"I was at work!" Hurst grabbed my arm. I shook him off. "Ralph needed someone to stay. He pays time-and-a-half! I was done, I came here. Stopped at the 7-Eleven. You could ask the girl, you could ask Ralph! What the hell are you talking about, a kid tonight?"

I felt a coldness slip up my spine. That kind of story made a bad lie, too easy to check. Maybe Hurst was so scared he couldn't think of anything better; or maybe he hadn't been out at Gray's Cove tonight.

One of the shadows in the yard made a fast, jerky movement, and I ducked just before the window broke, showering glass into the room like ocean spray.

Showtime.

"On the floor," I ordered Hurst. "They're probably out back, too, so don't think about leaving."

Hurst dropped to the floor, huddled against the couch. I could see him trembling.

Actually, I didn't think they were out back. None of the shapes had peeled off, as far as I could see, and this wasn't a military operation, it was a mob. They needed each other for the courage to do what they didn't really want to do.

Yanking open the front door, I stood in the blaze of headlights, the shouldered rifle pointed into the dark forms. "State police!" I shouted, thinking if I said it again I'd believe it myself. "The sheriff's on his way, more state cops behind him. Get out of here before I see your faces."

"We want Hurst!" a voice yelled. A rumble started, others echoing.

"He's secured," I said. By his own fear, but I didn't add that.

"He killed my boy!"

Silence, then a growl, and the shadows surged forward.

I lifted the rifle, fired into the air. The shot's thunder made a barrier between us; as though they'd hit it, the men faltered, stopped.

"Tom Rogers!" I shouted. "I know that's you. Let the sheriff handle this."

"He hasn't done a damn thing yet!"

Another shout: "How many more kids?"

"He had nothing to go on," I said. "He has now." I said nothing in answer to the second voice, the question.

Someone yelled something else, a curse; more men muttered, growled, but no one moved, not me, not them. Then the wind shift brought the scream of a siren. The men before me heard it too: all voices silenced, and then the siren howled loud and close, and tires scattered pebbles as a new set of headlights swept into the yard.

Red and blue light pulsed from the roof of the new car, the sheriff's car. Before it stopped the passenger door flew open and I heard Ben yell, "All right, you guys! Back off! Back off!"

He came forward, gun still holstered. After the slightest hesitation the young deputy who climbed out from behind the wheel did the same, just followed Ben's example, waded into the mob. Ben moved through, speaking calmly, calling the men by name, and so did the deputy, and the wildness subsided, the mob became a crowd. I lowered the rifle as Ben came to stand beside me.

From the doorway, lit by the glaring headlights, Ben looked over the men in the yard. "Go home," he said.

Some muttering, some movement. Ben and the deputy just stood, looking, and I did too. Ben spoke quietly to the deputy: "Move the car, Andy."

The dark forms moved aside for Andy as he crossed the yard to the sheriff's car. He started it up, and pulled it forward, out of the driveway, close against the trees. When he shut the engine silence was everywhere, and for a few long moments the night stayed like that, nothing changing at all. Then another engine growled to life. Men moved, car doors slammed. Trees, grass, the sheriff's car were lit and then dark in the jumpy headlights as the cars backed down the driveway. We heard the shift as tires scratching gravel became tires brushing asphalt, and then we heard nothing.

"Shit," Ben said, letting out a long breath. Coming up beside him, the deputy gave a shaky grin. Ben put his hand on the deputy's shoulder, then turned and walked through the doorway into the cabin. I flicked on the light. Ben stepped over the puddle seeping from the broken paper bag to where Hurst still huddled against the couch, surrounded by shards and splinters of glass.

"Come on," he said.

From the floor Hurst looked up. "I didn't mean to hurt that kid."

"Get up."

"Ask him. He knows," Hurst said, nodding toward me. Slowly, he got up.

Ben glanced at me.

"You can take him in," I said.

"I cared about him," Hurst said again.

"Okay," Ben said, cuffing Hurst's wrists. "Take him to the car, Andy. Read him his rights."

The young deputy clamped his hand on Hurst's arm, walked him out the door. Hurst threw one glance back at me, but didn't say anything else.

"He was there," I said to Ben, when we were alone in Hurst's cabin. "With Frankie. He'll tell you, I think. He molested him up there and I think he'll tell you that too. And your man Crandall might be able to identify him. Hurst's the one who called nine-one-one. He says the kid fell."

Ben gave me a long look. "Fell? You believe him?"

"No. He's trying to tell himself that's what happened, but no."

Ben nodded. "And the second one? The kid tonight?"

"He says he worked late, stopped at the 7-Eleven, came straight here."

Ben frowned. "That's easy to check."

"I know."

A siren wailed, came closer. Another set of headlights poured into the room. A corner of Ben's mouth tugged up. "The fucking state." He stepped out the front door as the siren cut off abruptly. "Gleason?" he called to one of the figures piling out of the cruiser. "That you?"

"Yeah. Everything all right?"

"No thanks to you. How come you heroes never make it on time?" Ben crossed the yard, talked with the state cops while an idea I didn't like formed in my mind.

The cops got back in the cruiser, K-turned in the yard and were gone. "Useless," Ben said as I went down to stand with him.

"What's the story on the kid tonight?" I asked.

"Six years old," Ben told me, still watching the car. "Family's camping out at the point. Kid wandered away, no one saw him again until they found him dead on the beach. Could be an accident," he said, sounding unconvinced. "Set Tom and the guys off, but it could be an accident."

"Yeah," I said. "Is Andy okay taking Hurst in alone?"

Ben met my eyes. "Sure. Level-headed kid, Andy. Always been that way."

Andy, with Hurst, headed back toward town in the sheriff's car. In my car Ben and I drove to the shore. As we got closer the fog thickened. I asked, "Who found him? The kid tonight."

"Older sister. They had a search party going, other campers, local volunteers. I was off duty. They called the department but no one thought to call me. I'd have been all over Hurst."

"Who responded?"

"When she found him? State was closest—not Gleason, some other car they had near there. Too late, kid was dead when they got there, but they did all the things you're supposed to do. They're not bad guys, really." He looked over at me, to make sure I hadn't gotten the wrong idea about state cops.

"What about your guys?" I asked.

"The deputy who's on tonight with Andy, Mike Lane, he got down there a few minutes after the state. So did Fred Reilly—he's off duty, but he had his radio on. Shit, I wish I'd had the damn radio on. When they called for a search party." He turned to watch out the window at the dark trees, the starless sky. "There'll be an autopsy, see if anyone messed with the kid. But if Hurst was at Ralph's . . ."

"I don't think you'll find it," I said. "I don't think that's what happened."

"What do you think?"

I told him.

"No," he said. He stared at me. "Oh, no. That's got to be crazy."

I said nothing.

"No," he said again.

"I don't know," I said. "Maybe I'm wrong."

Neither of us said anything more until we reached Gray's Cove, except that Ben used my cell phone to call the 911 dispatcher. She patched him through to Mike Lane, the deputy on night duty in his office. Ben told him to call all units, have them call my cell number, didn't say why. Andy, by then almost in town with Hurst, responded quickly. So did Fred Reilly, and a guy named Tod, on his way home from the movies with his girlfriend. That was it.

The trees thinned but the fog didn't as we approached the shore. Ben directed me to the dirt road where Larry Crandall's small frame house stood, but it was dark and empty, so we went down to the water.

From the top of the cliff we saw the waves break and fall. We saw dark masses of rock, and patchy gray fog on the sea. No lights on the water, and no stars.

"There," Ben said.

I looked where he pointed. A figure stood on the boulders below, watching the waves.

Ben and I climbed down the cliff together; then Ben hung back and I worked my way along the rocks. The sea was wilder than before, the waves larger. Cold spray soaked my clothes. The figure didn't move as I approached. Maybe, over the sound of the sea, he didn't hear me coming, or maybe he didn't care.

I came up to stand next to him. "Larry," I said.

Nothing, just the waves and the spray.

"What happened, Larry?" I asked.

Without turning he said, "You don't care what happened."

"You're wrong."

He didn't answer.

"Frankie Rogers," I said. "The sheriff arrested the man who was with Frankie."

"Frankie's dead."

"But the man's in jail. He won't hurt anyone else."

Again no answer.

"I told you I'd help, and I did," I said. "Now you have to help me."

The words came: "No one can help," but they came from a different voice, the voice I'd been waiting for, hoping not to hear.

That voice was behind me, in a shadow in the rocks. I turned that way. A dark shape, muscular, stepped toward me.

"Tell me what happened, Richie," I said.

"I don't know." Richie's voice was ragged. His eyes searched mine the way Crandall's searched the sea.

"The little boy," I said. "Was he in the water, Richie? When you got here?"

Richie was silent.

Crandall said, "No."

As quietly as the waves would let me, I said to Richie, "You wanted to save that kid."

Crandall said, "He was out here. On the rocks out here."

Richie said nothing, his eyes not leaving mine.

"You heard he was lost," I said, still speaking to Richie. "That they needed a search party." Behind Richie I saw Ben approaching slowly, stepping carefully among the boulders. "You came right down."

"I wanted to find him," Richie said. He looked away from me, at the water.

"Larry Crandall's boy, and Frankie Rogers," I said. "You couldn't save them. You couldn't be the hero they needed. This was another chance. This kid needed a hero, too."

Richie spoke. His eyes, like Crandall's, were on the sea. "I wanted to help. I wanted to save him. I came down here."

"Looking for him."

Richie nodded.

"And he was here."

He pointed to the end of the jetty. "Way out there, on the rocks. Just sitting."

"So you went out there, where he was."

Richie's arm dropped to his side. He didn't answer.

"Did he fall in the water, Richie?" I asked.

Richie said, "Fall?"

Behind him, Ben moved closer. Looking to the sea, Richie watched a wave rise, then break.

Larry Crandall said, "No."

Slowly, very slowly, Richie shook his head. He also said, "No."

Richie looked back at me, sudden bright hope in his eyes. "I jumped in," he said. "Right after I—right after he went in. I pulled him to shore."

"To be his hero."

"Yes."

"But you couldn't save him."

Eyes turned away again, the bright hope gone, a whisper: "No."

"And he didn't fall."

Richie stared at the sea, the waves pounding, rising and falling, always changing, always the same. "No."

Ben stood with us now. Softly he said, "Richie."

Richie turned his head, looked at Ben. "I'm sorry," he said. His voice was rough; tears mixed with the salt spray that dampened his face. "I thought I could make it be different, this time. But I couldn't save him, Ben."

"Come on." Ben put a hand on Richie's arm; his voice was hoarse, too.

Richie gave Ben a long look, as though he didn't understand. Or maybe he was looking through him, didn't see him, didn't know he was there.

Richie broke away from Ben. He dashed along the rocks. We ran after him, Ben and I, but on the wet rocks footing was bad. At the end of the jetty, where the boulders reached into the sea, Richie stood for a moment watching the waves. I shouted, "No!" but I couldn't stop him. He leaped high off the rocks. For a moment he was suspended in air; but unable to keep the height, he fell and was taken back by the sea.

# Donald E. Westlake

## Art & Craft

DONALD E. WESTLAKE has long been known as one the crime field's true and enduring stars. And this holds sway whether he's writing comic capers, the brooding Richard Stark hardboiled novels, or the serious mainstream novels, such as his recent (and perhaps most affecting work), *The Hook.* He is a Mystery Writers of America Grand Master, an Academy Award nominee for his script for *The Grifters,* and a sometimes droll reviewer for *the New York Times.* "Art & Craft," first published in the August issue of *Playboy,* is an apt title for a master storyteller like Westlake.

# Art & Craft

*Donald E. Westlake*

The voice on the telephone at John Dortmunder's ear didn't so much ring a distant bell as sound a distant siren. "John," it rasped, "how ya doin'?"

Better before this phone call, Dortmunder thought. Somebody I was in prison with, he figured, but who? He'd been in prison with so many people, back before he had learned how to fade into the shadows at crucial moments, like when the SWAT team arrives. And of all those cellmates, blockmates, tankmates, there hadn't been one of them who wasn't there for some very good reason. DNA would never stumble over innocence in that crowd; the best DNA could do for those guys was find their fathers, if that's what they wanted.

This wasn't a group that went in for reunions, so why this phone call, in the middle of the day, in the middle of the week, in the middle of October? "I'm doin' OK," Dortmunder answered, meaning, I got enough cash for me but not enough for you.

"That makes two of us," the voice said. "In case you don't recognize me, this is Three Finger."

"Oh," Dortmunder said.

Three Finger Gillie possessed the usual 10 fingers but got his name because of a certain fighting technique. Fights in prison tend to be up close and personal, and also brief; Three Finger had a move with three fingers of his right hand guaranteed to make the other guy rethink his point of view in a hurry. Dortmunder had always stayed more than an arm's reach from Three Finger and saw no reason to change that policy. "I guess you're out, huh?" he said.

Sounding surprised, Three Finger said, "You didn't read about me in the paper?"

"Oh, too bad," Dortmunder said, because in their world the worst thing that could happen was to find your name in the paper. Indictment was bad enough, but to be indicted for something newsworthy was the worst.

But Three Finger said, "Naw, John, this is good. This is what we call ink."

"Ink."

"You still got last Sunday's *Times*?" he asked.

Astonished, Dortmunder said, "*The New York Times*?"

"Sure, what else? 'Arts and Leisure,' page 14, check it out, and then we'll make a meet. How about tomorrow, four o'clock?"

"A meet. You got something on?"

"Believe it. You know Portobello?"

"What is that, a town?"

"Well, it's a mushroom, but it's also a terrific little cafe on Mercer Street. You ought to know it, John."

"OK," Dortmunder said.

"Four o'clock tomorrow."

Keeping one's distance from Three Finger Gillie was always a good idea, but on the other hand he had Dortmunder's phone number, so he probably had his address as well, and he was known to be a guy who held a grudge. Squeezed it, in fact. "See you there," Dortmunder promised, and went away to see if he knew anybody who might own a last Sunday's *New York Times*.

The dry cleaner on Third Avenue had a copy.

> Life is very different for Martin Gillie these days. "A big improvement," he says in his gravelly voice, and laughs as he picks up his mocha cappuccino.
>
> And indeed life is much improved for this longtime state prison inmate with a history of violence. For years, Gillie was considered beyond any hope of rehabilitation, but then the nearly impossible came to pass. "Other guys find religion in the joint," he explains, "but I found art."
>
> It was a period of solitary confinement brought about by his assault on a fellow inmate that led Gillie to try his hand at drawing, first with stubs of pencils on magazine pages, then with crayons on typewriter paper, and, finally, when his work drew the appreciative attention of prison authorities, with oil on canvas.
>
> These last artworks, allegorical treatments of imaginary cityscapes, led to Gillie's appearance in several group shows. They also led to his parole (his having been turned down three previous times), and now his first solo show, in Soho's Waspail Gallery.

Dortmunder read through to the end, disbelieving but forced to believe. *The New York Times*; the newspaper with a record, right? So it had to be true.

"Thanks," he told the dry cleaner, and walked away, shaking his head.

Among the nymphs and ferns of Portobello, Three Finger Gillie looked like the creature that gives fairy tales their tension. A burly man with thick black hair that curled low on his forehead and lapped over his ears and collar, he also featured a single, wide block of black eyebrow like a weight holding his eyes down. These eyes were pale blue and squinty and not warm, and they peered suspiciously out from both sides of a bumpy nose shaped like a baseball left out in the rain. The mouth, what there was of it, was thin and straight and without color. Dortmunder had never before seen this head above anything but prison denim, so it was a surprise to see it chunked down on top of a black cashmere turtleneck sweater and a maroon vinyl jacket with the zipper open. Dressed like this, Gillie mostly gave the impression he'd stolen his body from an off-duty cop.

Looking at him, seated there, with a fancy coffee cup in front of him—mocha cappuccino?—Dortmunder remembered that other surprise, from the newspaper, that Three Finger had another front name. Martin. Crossing the half-empty restaurant, weighing the alternatives, he came to the conclusion no. Not a Martin. This was still a Three Finger.

He didn't rise as Dortmunder approached, but patted his palm on the white marble table as if to say siddown. Dortmunder pulled out the delicate black wrought-iron chair, said, "You look the same, Three Finger," and sat.

"And yet," Three Finger said, "on the inside I'm all changed. You're the same as ever outside and in, aren't you?"

"Probably," Dortmunder agreed. "I read that thing in the paper."

"Ink," Three Finger reminded him, and smiled, showing the same old hard, gray, uneven teeth. "It's publicity, John," he said, "that runs the art world. It don't matter, you could be a genius, you could be Da Vinci, you don't know how to publicize yourself, forget it."

"I guess you must know, then," Dortmunder said.

"Well, not enough," Three Finger admitted. "The show's been open since last Thursday, a whole week. I'm only up three weeks, we got two red dots."

Dortmunder said, "Do that again," and here came the willowy waitress, wafting over with a menu that turned out to be eight pages of coffee. When Dortmunder found regular American, with cream and sugar—page five—she went away and Three Finger said, "Up, when I say I'm only up three weeks, I mean that's how long my show is, then they take my stuff down off the walls and put somebody else up. And when I say two red dots, the way they work it, when somebody buys a picture, they don't get to take it home right away, not till the show's over, so the gallery puts a red dot next to the name on the wall, everybody knows it's sold. In a week, I got two red dots."

"And that's not so good, huh?"

"I got 43 canvases up there, John." Three Finger said. "This racket is supposed to keep me out of jewelry stores after hours. I gotta have more than two red dots."

"Gee, I wish you well," Dortmunder said.

"Well, you can do better than that," Three Finger told him. "That's why I called you."

Here it comes, Dortmunder thought. He wants me to buy a painting. I never thought anybody I knew in the whole world would ever want me to buy a painting. How do I get out of this?

But what Three Finger said next was another surprise: "What you can do for me, you can rip me off."

"Ha-ha," Dortmunder said.

"No, listen to me, John," Three Finger said. Leaning close over the marble table, dangerously within arm's reach, lowering his voice and peering intensely out of those icy eyes, he said, "This world we're in, John, this is a world of irony."

Dortmunder had been lost since yesterday, when he'd read the piece in the newspaper, and nothing that was happening today was making him any more found. "Oh, yeah?" he said.

Three Finger lifted both hands above his head—Dortmunder flinched, but only a little—and made quotation signs. "Everything's in quotes," he said. "Everybody's taking a step back, looking the situation over, being cool."

"Uh-huh," Dortmunder said.

"Now, I got some ink," Three Finger went on. "I already got some, but it isn't enough. The ex-con is an artist, this has some ironic interest in it, but what we got here, we got a situation where everybody's got some ironic interest in them, everybody's got some edge, some attitude. I gotta call attention to myself. More ironic than thou, you see what I mean?"

"Sure," Dortmunder lied.

"So, what if the ex-con artist gets robbed?" Three Finger wanted to know. "The gallery gets burgled, you see what I mean?"

"Not entirely," Dortmunder admitted.

"A burglary doesn't get into the papers," Three Finger pointed out. "A burglary isn't news. A burglary is just another fact of life, like a fender bender."

"Sure."

"But if you give it that ironic edge," Three Finger said, low and passionate, "then it's the edge that gets in the paper, gets on TV. That's what gets me on the talk shows. Not the ex-con turned artist, that isn't enough. Not some penny-ante burglary, nobody cares. But the ex-con turned artist gets ripped off, his old life returns to bite him on the ass, what he used to be rises up and slaps him on the face. Now you've got your irony. Now I can get this sheepish kinda grin on my face, and I can say, 'Gee, Oprah, I guess in a funny way this is the dues I'm paying,' and I got *43* red dots on the wall, you see what I mean?"

"Maybe," Dortmunder allowed, but it was hard to think this way. Publicity was to him pretty much what fire was to the Scarecrow in Oz. There was no way that he could possibly look on public exposure as a good thing. But if that's where Three Finger was right now, reversing a lifetime of ingrained behavior, shifting from a skulk to a strut, fine.

However, that left one question, so Dortmunder asked it: "What's in it for me?"

Three Finger looked surprised. "The insurance money," he said.

"What, you get it and you split it with me?"

"No, no, art theft doesn't work like that." Three Finger reached into the inside pocket of his jacket—Dortmunder flinched, but barely—and brought out a business card. Sliding it across the marble table, he said, "This is the agent for the gallery's insurance company. The way it works, you go in, you grab as many as you want—leave the red dot ones alone, that's all I ask—then you call the agent, you dicker a fee to return the stuff. Somewhere between maybe 10 and 25 percent."

"And I just walk back in with these paintings," Dortmunder said, "and nobody arrests me."

"You don't walk back in," Three Finger told him. "Come on, John, you're a pro, that's why I called you. It's like a kidnapping, you do it the same way. You can figure that part out. The insurance company wants to pay you because they'd have to pay the gallery a whole lot more."

Dortmunder said, "And what's the split?"

"Nothing, John," Three Finger said. "The money's all yours. Don't worry, I'll make out. You hit that gallery in the next week, I get ink. Believe me, where I am now, ink is better than money."

"Then you're in some funny place," Dortmunder told him.

"It's a lot better than where I used to be, John," Three Finger said.

Dortmunder picked up the business card and looked at it, and the willowy waitress brought him coffee in a round mauve cup the size of Elmira, so he put the card in his pocket. When she went away, he said, "I'll think about it." Because what else would he do?

"You could go there today," Three Finger said. "Not with me, you know."

"Sure."

"You case the joint, if it looks good, you do it. The place closes at seven, you do it between eight and midnight, any night at all. I'm guaranteed to be with a crowd, so nobody thinks I ripped myself off for the publicity stunt."

Three Finger reached into his jacket again—Dortmunder did not flinch a bit—and brought out a postcard with a shiny picture on one side. Sliding it across the table, he said, "This is like my calling card these days. The gallery address is on the other side."

It was a reproduction of a painting, one of Three Finger's, had to be. Dortmunder picked it up by the edges because the picture covered the whole area, and looked at a nighttime street scene. A side street, with a bar and some brick tenements and parked cars. It wasn't dark, but the light was a little weird, streetlights and bar lights and lights in windows, all a little too green or a little too blue. No people showed anywhere along the street or in the windows, but you just had a feeling there were people there, barely out of sight, hiding maybe in a doorway, behind a car. It wasn't a neighborhood you'd want to stay in.

"Keep it," Three Finger said. "I got a stack of 'em."

Dortmunder pocketed the card, thinking he'd show it to his faithful companion this evening and she'd tell him what to think about it. "I'll give the place the double-O," he promised.

"I can't ask more," Three Finger assured him.

The neighborhood had been full of lofts and warehouses and light manufacturing. Then commerce left, went over to New Jersey or out to the island, and the artists moved in, for the large spaces at low rents. But the artists made it trendy, so the real estate people moved in, changed the name to Soho, which in London does not mean South of Houston Street, and the rents went through the roof. The artists had to move out, but they left their paintings behind, in the new galleries. Parts of Soho still look pretty much like before, but some of it has been touristed up so much it doesn't look like New York City at all. It looks like Charlotte Amalie, on a dimmer.

The Waspail Gallery was in a little cluster that had been touristed. In the first place, it came with its own parking lot. In New York?

A U of buildings, half a block's worth, had been taken over for a series of shops and cafes. The most beat-up of the original buildings had been knocked down to make access to the former backyards, which were blacktopped into a parking area, plus selling and eating space. The shops and cafes faced out onto the three streets surrounding the U, and they all also had entrances in back, from the parking lot.

The Waspail Gallery was midway down the left arm of the U. The original of the postcard in Dortmunder's pocket stood on an easel in the big front window, looking even more menacing at life size. Inside, a stainless-steel girl in black presided at a little cherrywood desk, while three browsers browsed in the background. The girl gave Dortmunder one appraising look, glanced outside to see if it was raining, decided there was no telling and went back to her *Interview*.

All the pictures were early evening or night scenes of city streets, never with any people, always with that sense of hidden menace. Some were bigger, some were smaller, all had weirdness in the lighting. Dortmunder found the two with red dots—*Scheme* and *Before the Rain*—and they were the same as all the others. How could you tell you wanted this one and not that one over there?

Dortmunder browsed among the browsers, but mostly he was browsing for security. He saw the alarm system over the front door, a make and model he'd amused himself with in the past, and he smiled it a hello. He saw the locks on the doors at front and back, he saw the solid sheet metal-articulated gate that would ratchet down over the front window at night to protect the glass and to keep passersby from seeing any burglar who might happen to be inside, and eventually he saw the thick iron mesh on the small window in the unisex bathroom.

What he didn't see was the surveillance camera. A joint with this alarm and those locks and that gate would usually have a surveillance camera, either to videotape with a motion sensor or to take still pictures every minute or so. So where was it?

There. Tucked away inside an apparent heating system grid high on the right wall. Dortmunder caught a glimpse of light reflecting off the lens, and it wasn't until the next time he browsed by that he could figure out which way it pointed—diagonally toward the front entrance. So a person coming in from the back could avoid it without a problem.

He went out the back way, past the tourists snacking at tables on the asphalt, and home.

He didn't like it. He wasn't sure what it was, but something was wrong. He would have gone in and lifted a few pictures that first night, if he'd felt comfortable about it, but he didn't. Something was wrong.

Was it just that this was connected with Three Finger Gillie, from whom nothing good had ever flowed? Or was there something else that he just couldn't put his finger on?

It wasn't the money. Gillie didn't plan to rip off Dortmunder later on, or he'd have agreed to share the pie from the get-go. It was the publicity he wanted. And Dortmunder didn't believe Gillie meant to double-cross him, turn him in to get himself some extra publicity, because it would be too easy to show they used to know each other in the old days and Gillie's being the inside man in the boost would be obvious.

No, it wasn't Gillie himself, at least not directly. It was something else that didn't feel right, something having to do with that gallery.

Of course, he could just forget the whole thing, take a walk. He didn't owe Three Finger Gillie any favors. But if there was something wrong, was it a smart idea to walk away without at least finding out what was what?

The third day, Dortmunder decided to go back to the gallery one more time, see if he could figure out what was bugging him.

This time, he thought he'd walk in the parking entrance and go into the gallery from that side, to see what it felt like. The first thing he saw, at an outdoor cafe across the half-empty lot from the gallery, was Jim O'Hara, drinking a Diet Pepsi. At least, the cup was a Diet Pepsi cup.

Jim O'Hara. A coincidence?

O'Hara was a guy Dortmunder had worked with here and there, around and about, from time to time. They'd done some things together. However, they didn't travel in the same circles on a regular basis, so how did it happen that Jim O'Hara was here, and not looking at the rear entrance to the Waspail Gallery?

Dortmunder walked down the left side of the parking area, past the gallery (without looking at it), and when he was sure he'd caught O'Hara's attention, he stopped, nodded as though he'd just decided on something, turned around and walked back out to the street.

The remaining parts of the original Soho neighborhood included some bars. Dortmunder found one after a three-block walk, purchased a draft beer, took it to a booth and had sipped twice before O'Hara joined him, having traded his Diet Pepsi for a draft of his own. For greeting, he said, "He talked to you, too, huh?"

"Three days ago," Dortmunder said. "When'd he talk to you?"

"Forty minutes ago. He'll talk until somebody does it, I guess. How come you didn't?"

"Smelled wrong," Dortmunder said.

O'Hara nodded. "Me, too. That's why I was sitting there, trying to figure it out."

Dortmunder said, "Who knows how many people he's telling the story to."

"So we walk away from it."

"No, we can't," Dortmunder told him. "That's what I finally realized when I saw you sitting over there."

O'Hara drank beer, and frowned. "Why can't we just forget it?"

"The whole thing hangs together," Dortmunder said. "What got to me, in that gallery there, and now I know it, and it's the answer to what's wrong with this picture, is the security camera."

"What security camera?" O'Hara asked, and then said, "You're right, there should have been one, and there wasn't."

"Well, there was," Dortmunder told him. "Tucked away in a vent thing on the wall. But the thing about a security camera, it's always right out there, mounted under the ceiling, out where you can see it. That's part of the security, that you're supposed to know it's there."

"Why, that son of a bitch," O'Hara said.

"Oops, wait a minute, I know that fella," O'Hara said the next night, back in the gallery-facing parking lot. "Be right back."

"I'll be here," Dortmunder said as O'Hara rose to intercept an almost invisible guy approaching the gallery across the way, a skinny slinking guy in dark gray jacket, dark gray pants, black sneakers and black baseball cap worn frontward.

Dortmunder watched the two not quite meet and then leave the parking area not quite together, and then for a while he watched tourists yawn at the tables around him until O'Hara and the other guy walked back together. They came to the table and O'Hara said, "Pete, John. John, Pete."

"Harya."

"That Three Finger's something, isn't he?" Pete said, and sat with them. Then he smiled up at the actor turned waiter who materialized beside him like a genie out of the bottle. "Nothing for me, thanks, pal," Pete said. "I'm up to here in Chicken McNuggets."

The actor shrugged and vanished, while Dortmunder decided not to ask for a definition of Chicken McNuggets. Instead, he said, "It was today he talked to you?"

"Yeah, and I was gonna do it, that's how bright I am," Pete said. "Like the fella says, I get along with a little help from my friends, without whom I'd be asking for my old cell back.

O'Hara said, "Happy to oblige." To Dortmunder he said, "Pete agrees with us."

Pete said, "And it's tonight, am I right?"

"Before he recruits an entire platoon," Dortmunder said.

O'Hara said, "Or before somebody actually does it."

For a second, it looked as though Pete might offer to shake hands all around. But he quelled that impulse, grinned at them instead and said, "Like the fella says, all for one and one for all and a sharp stick in the eye for Three Finger."

"Hear, hear," O'Hara said.

Three-fifteen in the morning. While O'Hara and Dortmunder waited in the car they'd borrowed out in Queens earlier this evening, Pete slithered along the storefronts toward the parking area entrance at the far end of the block. Halfway there, he disappeared into the shifting shadows of the night.

"He moves nice," Dortmunder said in approval.

"Uh-huh," O'Hara said. "Pete's never paid to see a movie in his life."

They waited about five minutes, and then Pete appeared again, having to come almost all the way back to the car before he could catch their attention. In that time, a couple of cruising cabs had gone by on the wider cross-streets ahead and behind, but nothing at all had moved on this block.

"Here's Pete now," O'Hara said, and they got out of the car and followed him back down to the parking area's gates, which were kept locked at night, except for now. Along the way, speaking in a gray murmur, O'Hara asked, "Any trouble?"

"Easy," Pete murmured back. "Not as easy as if I could bust things up, but easy."

Pete had not, in fact, busted anything up. The gates looked as solidly locked as ever, completely untampered with, but when Pete gave a small push they swung right out of the way. The trio stepped through, Pete closed the gates again and here they were.

Dortmunder looked around, and at night, with nobody here, this parking area surrounded by shut shops looked just like Three Finger's paintings. Even the security lights in the stores were a little strange, a little too white or a little too pink. It was spooky.

They'd agreed that Dortmunder, as the one who'd caught on to the scam, had his choice of jobs here tonight, and he'd picked the art gallery. It would be more work than the other stuff, more delicate, but it would also be more personal and therefore more satisfying. So the three split up, and Dortmunder approached the gallery, first putting on a pair of thin rubber gloves, then taking a roll of keys from his pocket. The other two, meantime, who were also now gloved, were taking pry bars and chisels from their pockets as they neared a pair of other shops.

Dortmunder worked slowly and painstakingly. He wasn't worried about the locks or the alarm system; they were nothing to get into a sweat over. But the point here was to do the job without leaving any traces, the way Pete had done the gate.

The other two didn't have such problems. Breaking into stores, the only thing they had to be careful about was making too much noise, since there were apartments on the upper floors here, among the chiropractors and psychic readers. But within that limitation, they made no attempt at all to be neat or discreet. Every shop door was mangled. Inside the shops, they peeled the faces off safes, they gouged open cash register tills and they left interior doors sagging from their hinges.

Every shop in the compound was hit, the costume jewelry store and the souvenir shop and the movie memorabilia place and both antique shops and the fine-leather store and both cafes and the other art gallery. They didn't get a lot from any one of these places, but they got something from each.

Dortmunder meanwhile had gained access to the Waspail Gallery. Taking the stainless-steel girl's chair from the cherrywood table, he carried it over to the grid in the wall concealing the security camera, climbed up on the chair and carefully unscrewed the grid, being sure not to leave any scratches. The grid was hinged at the bottom; he lowered it to the wall, looked inside, and the camera looked back at him. A motion sensor machine, it had sensed motion and was now humming quietly to itself as it took Dortmunder's picture.

That's OK, Dortmunder thought, enjoy yourself. While you can.

The space was a small oblong box built into the wall, larger than a shoebox but smaller than a liquor store carton. An electric outlet was built into its right side, with the camera plugged into it. Dortmunder reached past the lens, pulled the plug and the camera stopped humming. Then he figured out how to move this widget forward on the right side of the mounting—*tick*—and the camera lifted right off.

He brought the camera down and placed it on the floor, then climbed back up on the chair to put the grid in its original place. Certain he'd left no marks on it, he climbed down, put the chair where it belonged and wiped its seat with his sleeve.

Next, the tapes. There would be tapes from this camera, probably two a day. Where would they be?

The cherrywood table's drawer was locked, and that took a while, leaving no marks, and then the tapes weren't there. A closet was also locked and also took a little while, and turned out to be full of brooms and toilet paper and a bunch of things like that. A storeroom was locked, which by now Dortmunder found irritating, and inside it were some folding chairs and a folding table and general party supplies and a ladder, and stuff like that, and a tall metal locker, and that was locked.

All right, all right, it's all good practice. And inside the metal locker were 12 tapes. At last. Dortmunder brought out from one of his many jacket pockets a plastic bag from the supermarket, into which went the tapes. Then he locked his way back out of the locker and the storeroom, and added the camera to the plastic bag. Then he locked his way out of the gallery, and there were O'Hara and Pete, in a pool of shadow, carrying their own full plastic bags, waiting for him.

"Took you a while," O'Hara said.

Dortmunder didn't like to be criticized. "I had to find the tapes," he said.

"As the fella says, time well spent," Pete assured him.

Dortmunder's faithful companion, May, came home from her cashier's job at the supermarket the next evening to say, "That fellow you told me about, that Martin Gillie, he's in the newspaper." By which, of course, she meant the *Daily News*.

"That's called ink," Dortmunder informed her.

"I don't think so," she said, and handed him the paper. "This time, I think it's called felony arrest."

Dortmunder smiled at the glowering face of Three Finger Gillie on page five of the *News*. He didn't have to read the story, he knew what it had to say.

May watched him. "John? Did you have something to do with that?"

"A little," he said. "See, May, when he told me that all he wanted was publicity, it was the truth. It was a stretch for Three Finger to tell the truth, but he pulled it off. But his idea was, every day he talks another ex-con into walking through that gallery, looking it over for maybe a burglary. He's going to do that every day until one of those guys actually robs the place. Then he's going to show what a reformed character he is by volunteering to look at the surveillance tapes. 'Oh, there's a guy I used to know!' he'll say, feigning surprise. 'And there's another one. They must of all been in it together.' Then the cops roust us all, and one of us actually does have the stolen paintings, so we're all accomplices, so we all go upstate forever, and there's steady publicity for Three Finger, all through the trials and the appeals, and he's this poster boy for rehabilitation, and he's got ink, he's on television day and night, he's famous, he's successful, and we probably deserved to go upstate anyway."

"What a rat," May said.

"You know it," Dortmunder agreed. "So we couldn't just walk away, because we're on those tapes, and we don't know when somebody else is gonna pull the job. So if we have to go in, get the tapes, we might as well make some profit out of it. And give a little zing to Three Finger while we're at it."

"They decided it was him pretty fast," she said.

"His place was the only one not hit," Dortmunder pointed out to May. "So it looks like the rehabilitation didn't take after all, that he just couldn't resist temptation."

"I suppose," she said.

"Also," he said, "you remember that little postcard with his painting that I showed you but I wouldn't let you touch?"

"Sure. So?"

"Myself," Dortmunder said, "I only held it by the edges, just in case. The last thing we did last night, I dropped that postcard on the floor in front of the cash register in the leather store. With his fingerprints all over it. His calling card, he said it was."

# Peter Crowther

## The Allotment

PETER CROWTHER didn't begin writing until he was into his forties. Since then, his work—novels, short stories, television plays—has been seen and appreciated around the world. He is a quiet writer of great range and skill, at home in the darkest suspense as well as mainstream crime fiction. "The Allotment," which first appeared in the June issue of *Ellery Queen's Mystery Magazine*, shows him to be at the top of his form.

# The Allotment

*Peter Crowther*

Perhaps the only person in Luddersedge who *hadn't* known that Maureen Walker was fed up to the back teeth of her husband Stanley was Stan himself. But then there were many things that life, in its infinite and capricious wisdom, blew past Stan's eyes and even right under his nose . . . just like the tick-tock, tell-the-time dandelion seeds forever airborne around the hummocks and holes of Stan's beloved allotment.

It wouldn't be fair to say that Stan didn't *care* for Maureen, although to suggest that he actually loved her possibly stretched the truth a jot. He cared for her in his very own special way, even though she wasn't the be-all and end-all of his life (she did turn out to be *one* of those, but that's jumping the gun a little).

The truth was that the two things which probably came closest to earning Stan Walker's affection—aside from his allotment—were (a) watching football on the TV and (b) the Black Sheep brewery up in Masham, to whose continued financial success and security Stan had contributed more than his share over the years.

Stan's only other weakness was a seemingly endless stream of ideas for how he and Maureen could get rich quick, such as the specialist sweet shop in Todmorden or the mobile dating agency he set up in Rochdale: Stan was always promising his wife that the next one would be The Big One—that once-in-a-lifetime golden opportunity to make money—but each scheme had come and gone with little to show for its passing but another hole in their meagre savings.

All of these were thorns in Maureen's side but, in aggravation terms, it was the allotment that took the biscuit.

The allotment—one of six in a stand-alone patch of land on Honeydew Lane, edging onto the lane itself as well as onto Smithfield Road, Carholme Place, and Carholme Drive—was an eighty-square-yards rectangle of vegetable-festooned soil interspersed with narrow grassy "tending" paths. The allotment's main border, Honeydew Lane, one of the town's primary vehicular arteries and site of the notorious Bentley's Tannery, was an area blighted by such permanently pungent fumes that, or so local legend had it, the infamous Hounds of Luddersedge—an itinerant canine pack of all shapes and sizes (though mostly of a common variety: Heinz 57) given to defecating on the pavements of the town—were drawn to the

locality, frequently depositing turds of varying consistency in and around the carefully and even lovingly cultivated plants and produce.

It was here that Stan spent increasing amounts of his time. Since his retirement (aged 52, now some four years ago) from the buses (a mobile and carefree
life wandering the lanes between Rochdale and Burnley and Halifax), he had
spent the hours and days and weeks (not to mention months, seasons, and years)
dreaming of The Big One—the idea that would make them, their millions (or at
least a few thousands)—and tending his prided potato crop.

There had been a time, in the late fifties, when the streets of Luddersedge
had been an olfactory grotto of the smells of Yorkshire-pudding mix and quietly
cooking joints of meat and pans of vegetables on a Sunday morning, and the allotments had been well tended and picturesque. The young Stan had gone there to
help his father every week. But those were the old days. Now, two of the other
five allotments had gone to weed and a third one, Maureen had noticed one day
when she walked down to the shops, was already showing signs of neglect. Stan
would regularly come home looking glum because he'd found half-squashed
empty beer cans jammed in amongst his sweetpeas . . . and, on one occasion, a
used condom beside a flattened section of potato plants.

"Some folk'll do it anywhere," Stan announced on his return from that particular Sunday visit to the allotment, wafting straight to the sports pages of *The
News of the World* as he sat waiting for his dinner. "I don't know what's happening to the world, I really don't."

Serving the mashed potatoes out onto her best blue-flowered plates using an
ice cream scoop bought for her at the massive Ikea warehouse on an all-too-
infrequent outing to Leeds by Stan for her birthday, Maureen quietly but fervently
wished that her husband might introduce a similar element of adventure and
spontaneity into their own love life. At fifty-three, and still in the prime of her life
(as she delighted in telling anyone who would listen), Maureen Walker craved
some excitement. The truth was, she craved anything at all that would break the
humdrum of the life she had somehow drifted into without even seeing it coming towards her. But such was not to be the case.

Stan Walker was not an adventurous man. Nor was he spontaneous, affectionate, interesting, learned, amusing, successful, or even (much as Maureen didn't
even like to think it) handsome. And while her husband had probably never been
any of these things even when he was running around the streets and lanes of
Luddersedge in his short trousers, playing hide-and-seek or looking for conkers in
the cool autumns of the Calder Valley, Maureen firmly placed the blame for her
current situation at but one door: the allotment.

As far as Maureen Walker was concerned, it was the allotment that was the
villain of the piece . . . and so it was, on one of those lonely, empty summer
mornings when Stan had already left the house, that the arrival of an official-
looking letter from the local council provided her with what she considered to be
a neat solution to her problem.

In those days when the pair used to go out together of an evening—usually
down to the Conservative Club on Eldershot Road but more often to The Three
Pennies public house on Penny-pot Drive, where Stan could get his fix of Black
Sheep—Maureen used to joke, though somewhat without humour even then,

that Stan's "other woman" was a piece of ground filled with cabbages and carrot tops. It used to get a laugh for a time, from whoever might be sitting with them . . . and even from Maureen herself, though Stan would never respond. He would simply throw an occasional nod into the conversation, a distant half-smile on his face that suggested he had been drugged or was pulling out of a long coma into a world that he neither recognized nor cherished. And all the while he would repeatedly lift the ever-present pint glass of Masham's finest for a series of life-renewing slurps.

Unable to get much out of her husband, Maureen took to laying it on the line as far as her home life went with anyone who would take the time to listen—and as far as Luddersedge went, that was a lot of people.

Maureen would bemoan her lot to Joan Cardew and Miriam Barrett—of numbers 10 and 14 respectively—over the rickety fence that separated her and Stan's house from Joan's and Eddie's and the shock of privet that formed an unkempt but effective barrier with the widowed Mrs. Barrett's threadbare patch of grass.

With clothes hung freshly out to dry in the wind blowing through the Calder valley—predominantly Stan's voluminous Y-fronts and Maureen's no-longer-very-lacy bras and panties from Marks and Sparks—Maureen would, at one time, in the early days, tell either Joan or Miriam that she was nearing the end of her tether. That if he didn't leave her then she would take the bull by the horns and leave *him*.

She would tell the same thing to lisping Bert Green at the greengrocer's on the High Street, as Bert watched her pressing the sides of his avocados with undisguised annoyance; and to young Kylie Bickershaw with the bitten-down fingernails who worked the checkout at the Netto's behind the station car park and seemed to make a habit of shortchanging everyone; and even to Billy Roberts, the quiffed and always-tanned would-be gigolo who carved a mean rack of chops in his father's butcher's shop at the corner of Lemon Road and Coronation Drive.

Sometimes, when Maureen was watching young Billy—some thirty years her junior—carve a joint or pound beefsteak, it was all she could do to keep from openly drooling . . . watching those biceps work, and those thighs balloon out to fill his tight black trousers. One time, when he caught her and saw the naked desire on her face, Billy said, "Looks to me you could pop it into your mouth right here, Mrs. Walker," and Maureen readily agreed, blushing faintly at the idea that Billy might well have read her thoughts . . . not one of which had anything to do with meat (at least, none of the stuff being turned around on Billy's slab). Needless to say, Billy knew that just as well as Maureen did.

And so it was that word spread around Luddersedge the way it will spread around any small town, sometimes reaching the far end before the person who set it off even gets there. Not that Maureen actually wanted everyone to know her business—she didn't.

It was simply a release valve and, anyway, subconsciously, she considered service people and neighbours to be the souls of discretion—but, of course, things don't always work out the way we intend them. And when a release valve becomes blocked, the pressure has to escape somewhere.

"I hear things aren't so good with you and your Stan," Mary Connaught said to Maureen one day, groaning with relief as she switched the straining net carrier bag from her welt-disfigured left hand into the right. "Is it that you're get-ting sick of waiting for The Big One?"

Maureen decided to ignore the remark about Stan's schemes—"treat it with the contemp it dizzerbs," her mother would have said in her characteristic pidgin-English dialect. "Whoever told you that?" she asked, feigning surprise and even a dose of healthy indignation, one hand lifted to fiddle with the cameo brooch that Maureen's Auntie Lillian had bequeathed to her the previous year and the other laid spread-fingered on her hip.

Mary Connaught shrugged. "A little bird," she said.

The confidant in question was neither a bird nor was it little. It was, in fact, Jim Fairclough, with whom Mary had been having something of a hot-and-sweaty flirtation since the departure of Mary's husband Thomas—Thomas having fled the family nest not only with the contents of his and Mary's joint account at the building society over in Hebden Bridge (amounting to some £16,000 when interest had been added) but with the cashier who served him to boot. The pair were said to be now living in Ibiza—where Thomas and Mary had spent their summer holidays for their entire married life of eight-getting-on-nine years (". . . adding insult to injury," was how Miriam Barrett had summed it up . . . an opin-ion undoubtedly echoed by Mary)—and, for a time, Mary had considered trying to track them down. But then she started the relationship with Jim and all other things just kind of got pushed to the back of her mind.

Jim Fairclough's brother, Martin, was a regular feature wherever Billy Roberts appeared—there were some about town who said the two of them were like one person and that person's shadow, though who was which was a debatable point—and so Mary had heard all about Maureen's looks and the perspiration that always appeared on her top lip while Billy was pounding his meat. She heard about them on Jim's now frequent visits to her house—always under cover of darkness . . . though that did not matter a jot to Harriet Williams, the eagle-eyed sentinel of number 41 (Mary's house was number 43) who, in turn, was spreading the news to any who would stop and listen.

The conversation drifted to other things—a move started with Maureen's wide-eyed and innocent enquiry as to whether Mary had heard anything from her errant husband—and then pulled to a close with both women suddenly remembering other places they had arranged to be.

As Maureen watched Mary Connaught walk purposefully across the road, pausing only to give a wave to Pete Dickinson in his customised Cortina (Pete was the mechanic at Tony Manderson's garage over on Eldershot Road), she realised just how incestuous Luddersedge really was. It shouldn't really have taken her so long: After all, Miriam Barrett had said once that you couldn't break wind in Luddersedge without folks stopping you in the street to ask if you were having tummy problems. But you rarely saw the whole picture when you were only one of the characters painted into the scene.

However, there were other things that the momentous encounter with Mary Connaught brought to the fore: The main one of these was that Maureen could go on no longer talking behind Stan's back. She frowned at this thought. *And why is that?* a small voice enquired from the deep recesses of her head.

Yes, why *was* that?

Maureen looked up at the stone buildings that hemmed her in, imagining the roads that lay beyond them—roads that led to other towns, other cities, even other countries—and she suddenly yearned for them and for the freedom to travel them, with the wind in her hair and not a care on her shoulders.

Mary Connaught reached the pavement at the other side of the road and looked determinedly in the Oxfam shop window.

And why couldn't she *do* that? Maureen wondered to herself—fully knowing the answer even before it came. Why *couldn't* she drift along the great Highway of Life with carefree abandon? Just one reason: Stan.

*Exactly!* said the small voice.

So why did she need to keep her own counsel after so many years of simply telling things the way they were?

Because, the small voice whispered (with Maureen suddenly realising that it was her own innermost thoughts given a kind of vocal substance), if she were going to get rid of him, she needed to appear in harmony with her husband in order to avoid attracting undue attention.

She was momentarily shocked. And then, slowly, a smile pulled at her mouth. The phrase "get rid of" was somehow exciting . . . as if Stan was no more than a troublesome rash that needed only a spot of Clearasil to banish forever— and Maureen nodded to herself, watching Mary Connaught reach the double frontage of Luddersedge Bakery and turn to give her a glance. Maureen waved, gave a big smile, and turned around, her back feeling straighter than it had done for some time.

A decision had been made . . . or, more accurately, acknowledged: It had actually been *made* a thousand trips to the allotment ago; a million snores ago; and a hundred unexciting and demeaning sessions of her husband's clammy and clumsy explorations of her body ago.

The truth was, indeed, out there: Stanley had to go.

And if he wasn't going to go of his own accord—which he clearly wasn't— well . . . then she would have to give him a helping hand.

Deciding to kill her husband after years of unconscious vacillation was like the sudden arrival last autumn at a decision to shift the sofa from against the back wall of the drawing room—where it had languished for as long as she could remember—over to beneath the window.

Complacency and a lack of adventure were the prime offenders and, just like it had been with the sofa, Maureen now saw lots of reasons why this was the obvious thing to do. More than that, it provided her with a frisson of excitement that had been missing from her life more or less since she and Stan had married in 1967.

The newspapers had called it the "summer of love"—either that year or the one before or after: Maureen couldn't exactly recall which—but for the newly-wed Walkers it had been the year of *"business pretty much as usual."* In other words, the spectacle of the panting, groaning figure of her husband (slimmer then, it had to be said, but still carrying a stone or so too much flesh) climbing on board the good ship Maureen for a quick launch before rolling over into a sleep promoted by Black Sheep and interspersed with raucous snoring.

The snoring had sometimes grown so loud that Maureen had taken to pinching her husband's buttocks between her fingernails to interrupt his slumber.

It proved to be highly effective and—Maureen now realised in the flush of her decision to do away with her resident market-gardener (who now carried some four stones more than was ideal for his age and height)—it was strangely enjoyable in a kind of sadistic way.

So, there was the snoring: that would end; and there were the monosyllabic conversations in the Conservative Club or The Three Pennies—those would stop. And all the half-baked get-rich-quick schemes and the long-promised Big One that would keep them in clothes-pegs and manure for the rest of their empty lives. Not to mention, of course, the daily intake of Black Sheep, the constant loamy smell of earth and outdoors that Stan wafted in front of her when he deigned to return home for his food, and—worst of all, she now realised—Stanley's occasional need to remove his striped pyjama bottoms and claim his conjugal rights while Maureen stared over his thrusting shoulders at the bedroom curtain blowing in the breeze from the open window . . . imagining, lying there with her legs spread wide, she was Tinkerbell in the Peter Pan story, preparing to fly off into the night and over the spires and sooty roofs of Luddersedge into a new and distant morning somewhere far away. Somewhere better.

Yes, it would be just like moving the sofa.

But how to do it was the question.

Eventually, having discounted garroting and knifing (she didn't have a gun, so shooting was a nonstarter), Maureen had almost lost hope—already starting to convince herself that the whole thing had been a pipe dream . . . the naive whimsy of a bored housewife, like something out of a macabre version of Mills & Boon—when BBC2 ran a film about a hit man hired to murder the wife of a wealthy industrialist.

The film was complex—all the more so because Stan spent the entire duration of it slouched in the easy chair by her side snoring so loudly that she kept missing pieces of dialogue—but it was the basic principle that attracted her. For the first time in a long time, she felt randy—really randy: not the dull ache she got watching Billy Roberts but something almost primal . . . accentuated by the fact that Stan was right by her side, oblivious to the drama unfolding before his closed eyes.

"I'm going to do this to you," Maureen whispered, nodding toward the TV, her face bathed in the flickering glow of the screen on which a man stealthily crept around the outside of a house that, in Luddersedge, would have been a stately home. "I'm going to hire a hit man. What do you say to that?"

Stan snuffled and moved his head to one side before resuming his cacophonous drone.

The following day, with Stan already gone for a full session at the allotment, his pack-up of tuna-and-mayonnaise sandwiches in his little Tupperware container, Maureen did the dishes while she stared out of the window and wondered where she should go to hire someone to kill her husband.

Somehow, the prospect seemed daunting.

What went on in America—a fabled land that Maureen had never visited—seemed hard to translate in English terms. And even harder to translate in terms of Luddersedge.

It was like pop music, she mused, placing her favourite floral-designed plate lovingly in the back of the draining rack beside the sink. Like "Twenty-four Hours From Tulsa" (she had always loved Gene Pitney)—you could never imagine it being "Twenty-Four Hours From . . .": from where? Tottenham? It had to begin with a "T" to preserve the alliteration (that wasn't how she thought of it, not knowing alliteration from an adverb, but she did recognise the need for a *tuh* sound to balance the one in "*tuh*wenty-four"). Torquay?

She sang the first line over the sound of Terry Wogan, while he rambled on about the DG in Auntie Beeb. "Own-lee twenty-four hours from Tor-quay . . . own-lee one day away from your harms . . ." She chuckled and dropped cereal spoons and a butter knife into the holder, trailing suds across the crockery already drying.

It was comical but it was serious, too. It was serious because it was impossible . . . ridiculous and impossible. Where on earth could she find a hit man around Luddersedge . . . or even in the comparative metropolises of Halifax and Burnley and Bradford? The watery autumn sunshine through the kitchen windows was already making the whole idea seem a nonsense, the idle dream of a woman too long in one place and far too long in one relationship; a relationship which had spawned nothing but familiarity and indifference.

The answer came, as answers so often do, when Maureen was quietly but firmly prepared to abandon the problem that had called for it.

It came with the clatter of the post-box in the front door and the dull plop of something landing in the hallway, resounding so emphatically over the sound of the radio that Maureen half expected Terry Wogan to comment: *Well, listeners, let's find out what's in the "Big Goody" that the postie's just dropped through the post-box of Luddersedge's very own Maureen Walker!*

The Big Goody in question was neither big nor good: It was only an update catalogue from Empire Stores. It lay on the mat with two letters at its base, looking briefly, for all the world, like a skull and crossbones. One of the letters, Maureen saw even as she stooped to pick them up, was a window envelope containing the gas bill. The other, a franked brown job, had Stan's name carefully typed in bold.

It was accepted in the Walker household that all post could be opened by whoever picked it off the mat in front of the door, no matter who it was addressed to. Thus it was that Maureen opened the official-looking letter that turned out to be from the local council.

The letter, from a clerk (of unknown gender and indecipherable signature) who went by the unlikely multisyllabic name of S. Willingtonton (surely a typo), said in formal tones which oozed insincere regret that, as had been "previously intimated," the "allotment facility" in which Stan "heretofore owned a one-sixth portion" was to be "compulsorily withdrawn" and sold to a "local consortium" for "extensive redevelopment" by their (unnamed) client. Stan would be, S. Willnigtonton continued, "duly recompensed." It closed with (a) a request for Stan to contact the council offices as soon as possible and (b) the assurance that the author remained—"sincerely," no less—Stan's.

She clutched the single sheet of paper in a quivering hand and smiled up at the ceiling.

Her husband's beloved allotment was soon to be no more and he was about to become depressed. *Very* depressed. Moreover, though he did not yet know it, he was about to become suicidal.

Maureen had her hit man—it was Stanley himself.

The next day was a maelstrom of activity for the soon-to-be-widowed Maureen Walker, but then speed was essential.

Clearly, Stan could not be allowed to see the letter. Even a man as docile as Stanley Walker would be spurred to frenetic activity by the prospect of losing all that he held dear in life. Telephone calls would be made and, perhaps (God forbid), in the face of organised resistance on the part of the gardeners affected, the council might even reconsider its decision.

The letter therefore duly disappeared into the labyrinthine recesses of Maureen's handbag, a shadowy and even hostile (being overtly feminine) terrain of mirrors and lipsticks and thick bandages with flyaway wings that Maureen inserted into her pants for a few days every month. It was a domain into which Stan seldom ventured unless pressed.

However, if Stan were to be rendered so uncharacteristically distraught, Maureen reasoned that the letter from S. Willingtonton—effectively her husband's suicide note—would not realistically be sat upon for too long. For the scenario she had concocted to work, he must receive it and he must take action immediately, while the balance of his mind was on the blink (or whatever they usually said in such cases).

Poison was the answer. And, with Stan's allotment shed undoubtedly containing all manner of suitable candidates for the job—slug pellets, greenfly sprays, and other assorted insecticides—Maureen recognised an almost comical irony in the situation: An enemy for so long, the allotment was proving to be the means of her very salvation.

How to administer the answer to her prayers, however, posed something of a problem . . . but not for long. The solution, when it came, brought with it a pleasantly appropriate subtext: It would be in a healthy glass of Masham's finest. Stan would be put to rights by a Black Sheep.

*Who* done it? Maureen mused to herself as she sat in bed on the night of the fateful letter's arrival, with her husband happily snoring by her side, oblivious to the trip he was about to make out of her life forever. *Ewe* done it!

It was all she could do to keep from laughing out loud. But she didn't think that would be either appropriate or fair: After all, letting him sleep undisturbed, even without the usual pinching of the fleshy pads masquerading as Stan's buttocks, was tantamount to a last meal. Let him enjoy it.

The small puzzle as to how Maureen might gain access to Stan's allotment shed without Stan being there was also neatly and unexpectedly solved the next morning when Stan announced over his breakfast that he wouldn't be needing his customary pack-up because he had to go into Leeds. Maureen didn't ask what the reason for this expedition might be: She didn't believe in looking a gift horse in the mouth and, anyway, Stan occasionally made the trip to Leeds when something was needed for his allotment. (They had shops there that actually catered for the devoted gardener, their shelves replete with all manner of equipment and tools . . . not to mention a healthy supply of poisonous substances: Maureen hoped that Stan already had plenty of these in his shed.)

"Will you be coming straight back?" she asked, hardly daring to hope too much for the response she wanted. "I mean, do you want me to make you some sandwiches for later in the afternoon?"

Stan shook his head silently and spooned sugar into his pot of tea. Without even looking up from his *Sun* newspaper, Stan explained that he would get something in Leeds.

Maureen felt like doing a little dance but managed to maintain her self-control and, instead, put two more pieces of bread into the toaster by means of celebration. "Getting something in Leeds" meant that Stan would call in at one of the pubs that served Black Sheep—he knew them all—but, more importantly as far as Maureen was concerned, it meant that his palate would, she hoped, already be so suitably fogged by the time she presented him with her "special" bottle that he might not notice any unusual additional ingredients . . . or, at least, not until it was too late.

Stan left the house for the ten o'clock Rochdale-to-Halifax bus (he would change for the Leeds bus in Halifax) and Maureen watched him walk along the path with something that might almost—almost—have been sadness, short-lived though it was.

The rain started as she finished the washing-up, further evidence—if any were needed, she thought—that the gods favoured her plans: The rain meant that any other would-be market gardeners would think twice before spending time in their allotment, so there shouldn't be too many (if any) witnesses to her visit. Even Stan was reluctant to venture out of the house in the rain and, for a moment, Maureen became concerned that the change in the weather might dissuade him from the trip to Leeds.

She sat on the bed watching out of the window until the bus came. She could see the top of it through the gardens across the street, though she couldn't see if anyone was standing at the stop. But the bus stopped—so there must have been someone there—and then, just to make sure, she waited a few minutes to see if Stan returned before setting out, her hands encased in a pair of light blue Marigold gloves and the shed key tucked safely in her coat pocket, on the first part of her mission.

By the time she reached Honeydew Lane, the rain had grown heavier and the skies across Luddersedge—and across the entire valley, Maureen reasoned, looking over to the horizon in each direction—were slate grey and menacing.

Maureen slipped through the metal gate, cringing at the sound of hinges in desperate need of a drop or two of oil, and made her way to Stan's section.

She passed the two other neat sections, with rows of trimmed plant-tops (whose identity Maureen neither knew nor cared) that appeared clonelike in their similarity, and felt a wave of animosity towards them. It seemed as though, as she passed them, they sniggered at her in the wind and she felt like running amongst them, kicking at them with her shoes and swinging with her bag, tearing them out of their loamy houses with a vicious strangulating hold inflicted by her light blue Marigolds. If she had not been so preoccupied with these thoughts of garden-murder, she might have wondered why the three plots across from these three neat ones were so comparatively uncared for.

But she didn't.

As she reached Stan's shed door and inserted the key into the old lock, Maureen felt her pulse quicken. When she was inside, amidst the sudden silence and the smell of creosote and earth, under the accusative eyes of hoes and rakes and spades, she felt even worse: She suddenly felt her bowels loosen. Must be nerves, she thought to herself, scanning the carefully lined-up bottles and cans on the shelf at the back of the shed. After all, weren't there lots of stories about crooks leaving a mess on the carpet of the homes they burgled? Maureen now had some sympathy for their situation.

She read the various labels, taking care to remind herself mentally every few minutes that under no circumstances must she remove the Marigolds, until she found what she wanted: EXTERMINATE!, an old, tall can whose title appeared on four separate lines—EXT, ERM, IN and ATE!. The label carried numerous warnings printed in bold red capital letters (DANGER!, CARE!, and CAUTION!) and the top around the cap had rusted. Trying to loosen the cap, Maureen doubted that this product was still being made, and she hoped (assuming she would eventually get inside) that the contents were still in good working order.

When the top finally succumbed to pressure, Maureen removed it fully and peered inside. There seemed to be plenty there for her purpose and, even better, EXTERMINATE! had no noticeable smell. Of course, there was always a possibility that Stan was simply using the can to store some other potion—possibly one with few or no harmful effects to humans—but a quick glance across the shelf showed that Stan always used Sellotaped labels denoting the contents when those contents were different from the can containing them.

She replaced the cap, tightly, to make sure there could be no leakage into her pocket (even though she intended first wrapping the container in an old Netto's plastic bag) and checked around to make sure there was no evidence of her visit. Once satisfied, she pushed the shed door open slightly and peered out: The coast seemed clear—no doubt thanks to the continued rain—and, without further ado, she slipped out, closed and locked the door, and went on her way.

This time, the plants in the allotment rows did not snigger. This time they were still (though it was probably just that the wind had dropped) and altogether more respectful. "You're *all* going to die," she whispered into the rain, thinking of the council letter. "Every one of you."

Once she was safely back on Honeydew Lane, Maureen removed the Marigolds and walked down the hill to the Threshers on Eldershot Drive, where she bought three bottles of Black Sheep bitter. Then, pleased that she had not seen anyone that she knew (another vote of thanks for the rain!), she made her way back home.

The stage seemed to be pretty well set: Now all she needed was the star performer to return from his jaunt.

Maureen's star performer arrived back in the house at a little after four o'clock. Allowing for time spent each way on the bus and an hour or an hour and a half in the pub, he had been in Leeds for more than four hours. You could buy a lot of tools in four hours, Maureen thought. And so wasn't it a little surprising that he arrived back without so much as a single bag? Maybe so. But by this time, Maureen was concerned only with the job in hand.

Thinking ahead, she had realised that leaving the addition of EXTERMI-NATE! until the actual pouring of the beer itself left room for all kinds of unpleasant developments. Thus, with considerable dexterity, she had opened the bottle—carefully, without bending the cap too much out of shape—poured out a little of the beer, and topped it up with the special brew retrieved from Stan's shed. She had considered repeating the exercise with a second bottle (it could only be two at the most because she needed one "untreated" bottle for another purpose) but felt that one should be enough. Anyway, she had ensured a generous dose.

The cap had then been carefully replaced and tapped down with a small claw hammer Stan kept in the bureau drawer in the hall for when Maureen wanted pictures moved around.

Trying to think of all the things she needed to do had caused her head to ache, so Maureen had written them down on one of the sheets of paper by the phone—itemised thus:

★ add poison to bottle and replace cap
★ put bottles in pantry
(Stan hated his beer to be too cold, so the fridge was out of bounds.)
★ give Stan a drink!

(After this particular item, Maureen assumed Stan would be dead although she refrained from any additional note to that effect but opted instead for the exclamation mark.)

★ put bottle in dustbin
★ pour out the contents of the spare bottle and leave it by the glass

(Maureen was particularly pleased with this point. Although she stood by her decision to add the poison to the bottle itself and not to the glass, she knew there would have to be a bottle alongside the dead man and she also knew that, although it was hoped that the whole thing would be an open-and-shut case, traces of the poison in the bottle—when the "victim" had drunk from a glass—would cause unnecessary suspicion.)

★ make sure Stan's fingerprints are on the EXTERMINATE (She omitted the exclamation mark on this.) and leave the can beside the bottle and the glass
★ leave the council letter by the bottle, can, and glass

Stan's first port of call on arriving home—with little more than a grunted acknowledgement of Maureen's presence—was the toilet. Interrupting the Niagra-like cacophony of his flow as it resounded through the house, Maureen shouted up to see if her husband would like a beer. The answer was an emphatic "Great!" followed by another stream of water (no doubt caused by excitement at the prospect of more beer or the need to make more room for same). The toilet flushed as Maureen took the treated bottle of Black Sheep from the pantry. She was opening it when Stan arrived in the kitchen behind her, an arrival announced by two things: the slurring noise of his feet and Stan's voice saying, "What's this?"

When Maureen turned around, Stan was frowning at her list of things to do . . . albeit, she was delighted to note, the wrong side.

"It's someone's telepho—"

"Sheila Hilton," Maureen said, springing across the room and doing her best to get the paper back without appearing to snatch it. She stuffed it into her pinny pocket and turned back to the table where Stan's final drink was already half poured. "I saw Jackie Cartwright the other day at the market in Tod—getting black pudding," she added, filling the lurking silence with unnecessary information that she knew would blank out Stan's concentration (and, more importantly, his curiosity). "And she said she'd call me with Sheila's number. Haven't seen her in years," she added, pouring the final drops from the bottle and squinting down at the now-full glass for any telltale signs.

Stan grunted, apparently satisfied with the explanation.

"Do you want a few crisps?" Maureen asked. "Or some nuts?" Considering the imminence of the condemned man's execution, nuts and crisps was as close as she could get to the obligatory "hearty meal."

Stan shook his head and plonked himself down at the table.

Maureen watched as he reached for the glass.

Stan looked at her as he raised the glass to his mouth.

Maureen knew that this was the moment beyond which there was no return: If she were to save her husband, now was the time to knock the glass from his hands. But by the time she had thought up an excuse for such a strange action (telling Stan that she had seen a wasp on the rim of the glass seemed like the favourite explanation), Stan had drunk half of the contents. He sat the glass on the table, looked at it for a moment, and then reached for it again, frowning.

"Something up with it?" she asked, hoping he could hear her voice above the drumming thunder of her pulse.

Stan didn't respond. He lifted the glass again and sniffed.

"Is it off?" Maureen enquired, keeping her voice calm.

Stan did one of his usual facial shrugs—a strange lifting of the nose and eyebrows—and put the glass to his mouth. He was halfway through the remaining beer when the glass dropped from his hands and he doubled over on the chair.

Maureen backed away against the cabinet where she kept her best blue-flowered crockery, wincing at the sound of the delicately positioned piles shifting as she hit the cupboard with her bottom.

Stan hit the floor jackknifed, his big hands anxiously kneading his stomach all the way and even when he was flat out.

The sound that Stan emitted was a long drawn-out groan, but not the kind of sleepy groan he gave when the alarm clock went off (always an alarm clock, even though the only place he ever had to go since leaving the buses was his damned allotment). This groan was the collective sigh of all the souls in hell bemoaning their eternal torment. It was the sound of organs deflating and dying, being seared into immediate submission by a concoction of age-old poison and bottled beer.

"I'll get the doctor," Maureen said, rushing out into the hall, keen to avoid the spectacle of her partner for these past three decades and more melting into the checked and threadbare kitchen linoleum.

She lifted the phone and pretended to hit the buttons, staring at Stan as he writhed around. He called out again a couple of times—words and phrases that Maureen could not recognize—and then he began to howl. Maureen thought about switching on the radio to drown out the noise, so that Stan didn't attract attention from the neighbours, and then he went quiet. She ran back to the kitchen and knelt down beside him, thinking he might be gone, but when she rested a hand on his shoulder she could feel it shuddering deep down inside her husband's body, as though Stan were a road-digger. "Doctor's on his way, love," she said softly against his ear.

Stan nodded and gave a low whine.

He opened his eyes slowly and the shuddering stopped.

His stare moved slowly until it rested on Maureen's face. She raised her eyebrows, expecting him to say something . . . to maybe get to his feet and say, *Well, nice try old love: Now it's my turn!* . . . stretching his meaty hands out to her throat . . .

But none of that happened.

What did happen was that Stan's eyes locked on Maureen's and in that split instant she knew that he knew what she had done. Then, without another movement, he went. His eyes were still wide and still in the same position but the life just went from them . . . fell away from the body like a mist banished by the sun and captured on fast film for one of the nature programmes on the TV.

Maureen got to her feet and thought about doing something about the high-pitched hum she could hear . . . until she realised that she herself was making it. She clenched her teeth tightly and swallowed.

She got out her piece of paper and read the notes.

The bad bottle went into the peddle bin until she thought better of that and retrieved it to put it into the dustbin outside (along with the light blue Marigolds: a sudden afterthought, just to be on the safe side), beneath all the other stuff they'd thrown away over the past few days.

The contents of a second bottle went down the sink, flushed away by a long run of the cold tap, and the bottle went onto the table. (The third bottle, spared for a while, would languish in the fridge for a few weeks before being consigned, untouched and unused, to the bin long before its sell-by date.)

The letter from the council also went on the table.

She left the glass on the floor.

The poison (duly fingerprinted by Stan's limp right hand) went on the table next to the letter.

Then she went and looked out of the windows. Nobody was around.

Maureen went into the hall and phoned the police.

The interview with the police seemed to go well, as far as Maureen could judge these things. She felt she had displayed a suitable mixture of hysteria and disbelief, both of which, she was a little surprised to note, were fairly genuine.

All she kept saying was that she had no idea why her husband should do such a thing . . . explaining that she had left everything just as she had found it.

She tried to feel unconcerned when one of the officers carefully removed the glass, bottle, and EXTERMINATE!, placing them into polythene bags and labelling them.

It seemed to be an open-and-shut case, the detective explained, his voice dripping with regret. Her husband's allotment was his whole life—"No disrespect intended, Mrs. Walker," he had added, to which Maureen had first frowned and then nodded, with a dismissive wave of the hand—and the prospect of losing it had been too much to bear. Stan had brought a can of poison from his shed, mixed it with a glass of beer, and . . . "Bob's your uncle," he said. (Actually, none of Maureen's uncles was called Bob, but she didn't think that that mattered too much.)

The good thing, the detective (a very nice man with a very nice smile, Maureen thought with a slight colouring to her cheeks) assured her, was that Stan wouldn't have suffered . . . he was sure. He may well have been a nice man with a nice smile, Maureen thought, but he didn't know very much at all about drinking EXTERMINATE!

Would she be all right in the house overnight? (It was now after six o'clock and growing dark outside.) Maureen said that she would and, a little before seven, she was alone. Alone the way she would always be.

That night, she slept soundly.


The next morning, Maureen dressed as sombrely as she felt was appropriate and as frivolously as she felt she dare (considering her "unhappy" situation).

After a quick breakfast of Alpen and toast, Maureen left the house early and got the bus to Bradford, where she spent the day wandering around the shops and practicing how she would respond to all the expressions of condolence she would have to endure.

Where the time went, she didn't know.

For lunch, she had egg and chips, bread and butter, two pots of tea, and a jam doughnut from a cafe in the market—it was greasy, a little on the tasteless side, and the doughnut was rock-hard, but to Maureen Walker (newly-made widow of the parish) it was a banquet fit for a queen . . . and all for less than two pounds.

More shop-wandering (and practising) in the afternoon and then a visit to the cinema—alone: She felt *so daring!*—to see a film called *Dark City* that she thought might be a thriller, but she couldn't understand it: All it seemed to be was a load of buildings growing up out of the ground and then shrinking down into it again, and the ending showed them all out in outer space. Things had come a long way since the likes of Cary Grant and Alan Ladd and, in Maureen's opinion, the trip hadn't been worth the effort.

On the bus going home, Maureen realised that tomorrow she would have to make all the necessary arrangements. Staring out of the windows onto the black countryside, she tried to make a list in her head of how many people she would need to cater for . . . wondering whether to have a go at making the sandwiches herself or buying them in.

Letting herself into the house, she felt tired and, suddenly, just a little lost. It would pass: It was just the excitement of the past couple of days. She made sure the doors were well locked—going back to them twice to double-check—and made a cup of camomile tea to go to bed with. No sooner had she drained the last dregs, watching her foot stray under the covers into the cool of Stan's side of the bed, than she settled down and drifted off into a deep sleep in which she dreamt of buildings growing up all around her and hemming her in.

The next day, her second morning of freedom, Maureen slept in.

It was after nine o'clock when she was disturbed by a noise downstairs.

She opened her eyes wide and listened.

What had that been? Had it been the stealthy sound of a slippered foot on the stairs . . . the sound of her husband, returned from the morgue in Halifax

General (a journey that had taken Stan a full day and a night to make), slurring along the lonely lanes to Luddersedge to arrive with the—

The postman! That was what it had been.

Maureen got out of bed, slipped into her slippers, and pulled on her dressing gown.

On the way downstairs, she could see the single letter on the doormat. Another brown job.

Maureen lifted it up.

Somewhere nearby, a car engine sounded . . . growing louder.

The letter wasn't even addressed to them but to *Luddersedge Development, Ltd.* . . . in a swirling, italicised script, at their address for some reason. That disappointed Maureen. Here she was on the first day of the rest of her life and the whole thing had been kicked off with a mistake.

She shuffled the letter inside the envelope until another line appeared above Luddersedge Development Ltd. The line read: *Stanley Walker Esq., Chairman.*

Maureen frowned.

She stretched and turned the envelope over, slitting it open with her finger and removing the single sheet.

As she scanned the letter, she noted that the car engine had stopped. It had stopped somewhere nearby.

Maureen read, "Good to meet you yesterday after so many conversations on the telephone," the letter began. It was from a firm of solicitors in Park Place, Leeds . . . someone called K. Broadhurst.

Maureen felt the first stirrings of anxiety.

The letter went on to congratulate Stanley and the three fellow members of his (*his! Stanley's?*) consortium on their acquisition of the allotment plots on Honeydew Lane. "As I pointed out yesterday, the proceeds of the eventual transaction" (K. Broadhurst continued) "will be considerable" and (he/she was delighted to inform Stan) the purchaser was now prepared to consider "a high-end six-figure sum, but one which was not expected to exceed £800,000." When payment to the council had been made—and their own fees deducted, K. Broadhurst seemed keen to point out—the resulting sum should be in the region of £550,000.

Maureen's eyes grew wider and wider as she finished the letter (the signature looked like it might be Kenneth Broadhurst, although the two words were little more than elongated squiggles) and then read it again.

It was The Big One: He had done it. Stanley had brought it off.

When the doorbell rang, Maureen had stopped wondering whether clinching The Big One could ever really be considered a sensible reason to drink a tipple of Black Sheep mixed with EXTERMINATE!

As she made her way to the front door she was worrying that perhaps she should have disposed of the bottle in someone else's dustbin. Or whether any EXTERMINATE! traces had rubbed off on her light-blue Marigolds.

Or even—Maureen thought almost idly as she fast-forwarded all the events of that fateful day—what the police might make of a man who was able to open a can of poison one-handed.

When she opened the door, Maureen was not surprised at all to see that the nice detective wasn't smiling today.

# Mat Coward

## Twelve of the Little Buggers

MAT COWARD'S stories and novels have become one of Great Britain's most delightful exports. Coward writes with a tart tongue and pitiless eye, and yet there is a pleasing tomfoolery in much of his work, a tone of forgiveness for our foibles missing in so much crime fiction today. Our first selection by him, "Twelve of the Little Buggers," was first published in the January 2000 issue of *Ellery Queen's Mystery Magazine*.

# Twelve of the Little Buggers

*Mat Coward*

Middle of September, one of my editors rang—would I like to do a jokey piece on cats?

"Cats?" I said.

"Right," said Jenni. "Like, we were talking it over in the office, and we thought, you know—robins, turkeys, reindeer, et cetera et cetera, puddings . . ."

I couldn't immediately see the connection. "Puddings?" I said.

"Right," said Jenni. "I mean, only three more planning months to Christmas, right?"

"Oh," I said. "The Christmas number. Gotcha."

"Right," said Jenni. "So we thought—no: Let's do cats. Not very Christmas-y, but, you know, different. Cute. Nice big puddy-tat on the cover. Lots of interior pics, lots of colour. Kittens peeking playfully out of Christmas stockings. Lovely tabby mummy-cats posing proudly on Yuletide logs. Sweet old toms dozing amid the prezzies, 'neath the glittering tree. And then, seasonal cat stories. Tragic tales of cats given as gifts, but with, like, happy endings. A hundred and one things you can buy your kitty for Christmas. Recipes—"

"Instead of turkey?"

She laughed one of those editorial laughs; the very short sort, because even if editors had a sense of humour they certainly wouldn't have time to indulge it with only three planning months left before Christmas.

I've only met Jenni once in the flesh—what there is of it. She really doesn't have anything much but teeth; that and a slight lisp, which is, in fact, so slight that I tend to doubt its authenticity. First time she commissioned me, she took me to lunch at a reasonably fashionable West End Italian place. I drank imported beer; she ordered mineral water. She asked the waiter for a yogurt—a main-course yogurt, right?—and seemed pretty surprised when he told her they didn't have any. So she just ate bread sticks instead.

I ordered the whole menu.

I could tell now, by listening to her on the phone, that she had that habit of twisting her professionally frazzled hair around her fingers while she spoke; not from coquetry, though, but from repressed, generalized irritation.

"Special celebration recipes. What to feed Tiddles while the family's enjoying the mince pies."

"Yes, I get it," I said, in case she thought I was still confused.

"And, of course, humour."

"Of course," I said. That's what I do: I write humour for humourless magazines. Been doing it all my life. I could have done something else, I suppose. Could have become a mercenary, for instance, but I didn't fancy the training.

"So we thought, you know, Jim Potter. Jim's our man for a spot of cat humour."

"I'm flattered." I wasn't.

"Well," said Jenni, "you're the best, Jim." I wasn't. "We were thinking, you know, urban cats. An A through Z feature, maybe. Or a 'Twenty Crazy Things You Never Knew About.' Or whatever you like."

"Fine," I said. "How many words you want?"

"Well, we were thinking, you know, you could go to twelve, maybe. Or eight, with a big photo."

"I'll do eight," I said. Jenni's magazine pays a flat rate, not according to word count. "When do you need the copy?"

"Ummm . . . how about yesterday?" she asked playfully.

"Tricky," I replied, coyly.

"Okay. Week tomorrow?"

"No prob."

"By the way, Jim, I ought to check—you have got a cat yourself? Only if you haven't, you know, sorry, I should have said . . ."

"Oh yeah," I said.

"Oh, really? That's great! I thought you must have. We've got this survey in the Christmas issue, says that men in their thirties living alone are almost always cat persons."

"Oh yeah," I said. "Matter of fact, I've got twelve of the little buggers."

"Twelve!" she squealed. "That's great! You must really love cats!"

The girl's a genius.

I wrote the piece the next day—"Urban Cats: An Unreliable History"—then waited a week until the deadline was up, and faxed it through. Jenni rang to say she loved it. Then she rang again ten minutes later and said my "stuff" was so fabulous, she was putting it on the cover. More money, obviously. Quite a lot more, you know, *money*. Actually.

"And then we were talking about it, and we thought—you know, let's get some pics."

"Great," I said.

"You know," she said, "of your cats. All twelve of them. Wouldn't that be great?"

"Oh yeah," I said.

"Great! So, listen, no time to waste, I'll send a photographer round this afternoon, okay? About five, five-thirty?"

"Oh yeah," I said. "Great."

Then we rang off, and I thought: Jesus-in-a-manger—where am I supposed to get twelve cats from, by five o'clock this afternoon?

The woman at the cat rescue centre wasn't all that helpful. "You want to provide a new home for *twelve* cats?"

"No, hell, that's the last thing I want to do, I don't even like cats. I just want to borrow them for a couple of hours. Really, they'll be back here before anyone notices they've gone."

"You want to *borrow* twelve cats?"

"Listen, don't get hung up on the number. Half a dozen'd probably do. I could say they'd eaten the others."

"You want to borrow *six* cats?"

"Yeah. One thing; do you deliver? I'm a bit tied up this afternoon, that would really be a great help."

"I don't know if this is some kind of joke, or what, but I think you don't understand what we do here. This isn't Feline Express. We don't keep a fleet of moonlighting students on mopeds, biking Cats-With-Everything direct to your door, thirty minutes max or your money back. We don't—what I'm trying to say is—we don't *lend* cats. Okay? This isn't the National Whiskers Library."

I thought that over for a moment. "Look, if it's a matter of money, I'd be more than happy to put a couple of quid in the collecting tin. Or in your own private collecting tin, if that'd be better."

And then, while she was telling me that she hoped we might meet one day, because she knew a vet who could be relied upon to keep his scissors open and his mouth shut, I suddenly remembered the allotments.

I don't do gardening myself (as you'll know if you've ever read my column, "How Not To Do Gardening," in *Gardener's Week Magazine*), but the quickest route from my house to the pub is via a footpath that runs alongside a little river, right past the allotments—and even I know what an allotment site is: a patch of wasteland divided up into strips, which the local council rents out to residents, mostly old people and food faddists, so that they can grow their own fruit and veg there. Though why anyone should want to bother, when they're lucky enough to live in a country with perfectly good burger bars conveniently situated on every street corner, is far beyond my powers of explanation.

The point is, however, this: What did I often see on those allotments, on my way to and from the boozerama? Cats. I saw cats. Loads of them. Stray cats, presumably. Well, either that, or gardening cats.

Never having had a cat, I didn't know what kind of gear you needed to catch them. So I just grabbed everything I could think of: a big sack, a length of wood, a tin of date-expired treacle, a box of candles, and a whistle.

Took me two hours. Partly, that was because I kept losing count. It's not easy—and if you ever have anything to do with cats yourself, you might want to remember this—it's not easy to count cats in a big sack. Eventually, I had a brainwave: What did it matter if I got too many cats? I mean, if there were thirteen of them, I could just tell the photographer that one of the little buggers had had a baby, right?

Don't ask me to describe the cats. They were various colours. I don't know what you call cat colours. Some were sort of splodgy, some sort of spotty, some sort of stripy. And some were sort of splodgy and spotty and stripy all at once. They were various sizes.

They were cats, anyway, so I took them home.

I just about reached the gate when all of a sudden there was a man standing in front of me holding his arms out like a recently demoted traffic cop. I didn't like the look of him: a long, cruel face, a superior scowl. Fair enough, though—he obviously didn't like the look of me, either.

"What have you got in that sack?"

"In the sack?"

"What's moving about in your sack?"

"Oh, yeah. Tortoises," I explained.

*"Tortoises?"* Like he didn't believe me.

"Certainly," I said. "Just picked 'em up in those woods back there."

Trying to edge round me, trying to get a good squeeze at my cat-sack, he said: "There are no *tortoises* in those woods, for heaven's sake."

"Of course there aren't," I said, "I got them all in this sack."

"What for?" he sneered.

"For? Why, for my three kids, naturally. They love tortoises, but the way they get through them, I can't afford to keep buying them. Kids, huh? So I thought: Hey, do it yourself!"

He sneered on in silence.

"So I'm taking them home for . . . for little Gerald," I said. "And . . ." The man waited. "And for little Geraldine."

"That's only two children," he said, unpleasantly.

"Well, not really," I said, "because you see, the third one's also called Geraldine, due to, like, y'know, a mix-up at the hospital."

He started to say something that apparently began with *"You—"* but then he stopped, and I realised he was staring over my shoulder. Turning round, I saw in the distance, back by the entrance to the woods, a scruffy young guy in a combat jacket, striding towards us.

"You just stay away from those cats. Got it?" And with that the interrogation was broken off, as the long-faced vigilante disappeared through a gap in the bushes.

Weird behaviour. But then, once people let cats into their lives, they do strange things. That's a medical fact.

Home safe, with about thirty minutes to spare, I unleashed the cats. Then I poured a gigantic vodka, lit a small cigar, and relaxed.

Carl, the pointlessly enthusiastic, ponytailed lensman—bright orange shirt, collar size XXL—was pretty impressed with my cats. "Great cats!" he said. "They're so—I dunno, they're so wild, aren't they?"

"Oh yeah," I said. "They really are."

"They just never keep still for a moment, do they? Rushing around like crazy things!"

"Oh yeah," I said. "Thing is, they're not really used to company."

"No?"

"Not really. I tend to ignore them, myself."

"Okay! Look, do you think you could get them, sort of, all together in one place? You know, so I can do the old clickety-click?"

"Well," I said. "It's like you said yourself: They're pretty wild cats."

"Maybe if you fed them?"

"Brilliant!" I said. "That's a brilliant idea. Um . . . you got any mice or anything?"

The photographer laughed—rather meaninglessly, I thought. "Might be easier if you just, you know, opened a can or something."

"Oh yeah," I said. "Good thinking." So I opened a few cans, emptied the contents into a plastic washing-up bowl, and put the bowl on the kitchen floor. Sure enough, the cats came running.

"That is amazing," said Carl.

"Must've been hungry," I said.

"Yeah, but—chili con carne? I never knew cats ate chili con carne."

"Oh yeah," I explained. "Your cat, you see, your average cat is a big meat-eater."

He laughed again and started setting up his lights. "Well, they obviously love it. And I can see you love your cats, too. That tinned chili costs a lot more than cat food."

*Cat food*, I thought. *Damn.*

An hour later, he'd gone ("Listen, if you ever decide you've got too many cats," he said on the doorstep, "my little girl . . ."—"Don't worry," I said, "you'll be the first to hear") and it was over. Just call me Mr. Resourceful.

It wasn't over.

Once the photographer's car had disappeared around the corner, I loaded up the old sack again, and set off once more for the allotments. I whistled as I walked, light of heart though heavily burdened.

I didn't meet anyone on my short journey, except a comedian in a milkman's tunic, who told me: "You want to change your butcher, pal. That meat's wriggling."

Back amongst the beans and squashes, I shook out the sack, and out tumbled the cats. They sat there on the ground, looking at me, but they didn't look for long. They couldn't, because I wasn't there for long.

Late that night, a crashing sound woke me. By the time I got downstairs, there were three cats sitting in my hallway, making cat noises. Even as I stood there, another two appeared through a small, flapped hole in the door (which I'd previously supposed was there for the benefit of short-sighted postmen).

I hastily gathered up a couple of cats and opened the door. That was a mistake. The cats in my arms screeched, scratched, and then leapt back into the house. A cat which had been in the process of using the hole when I opened the door, and which was now swinging there like a magician's assistant interrupted in the middle of a sawing-the-lady-in-half trick, just screeched. And all the cats outside, who had been queuing patiently for the hole, dashed past me with the odd chirrup of appreciation at my good manners.

*Right*, I thought. *Deep breaths. Go about this logically.*

I found a bit of stiff cardboard and sellotaped it over the hole. I retrieved my trusty sack and carried it up to my bedroom. There I found three cats: one under the bed, one already asleep inside the bed, and another squatting vulgarly on top of the wardrobe. Not without some difficulty, and a few minor wounds, I achieved their ensackment.

Then I left the bedroom, shutting the door firmly behind me, and emptied the captured cats out onto the street. There was no way I was visiting the allotments at this time of night, dressed only in boxer shorts and a pair of mock-leather slippers.

I repeated this operation in each room, methodically, and then, exhausted and slightly bleeding, went back to my bedroom.

Which now contained four cats.

It was a hot night, and I'd left most of the windows in the house open. Not open enough for burglars, but evidently open enough for cats.

I started over.

I have a vague memory of myself, at some stage in that eternal furry night, standing in the hall with a bottle of vodka in one hand and a box of Elastoplast in the other, singing, "Close the doors, they're coming in the windows! Close the windows, they're coming in the doors!"

I don't know if you've ever been in one of those situations where you're trying to shove a number of small jellies up a wide drain-pipe? I know I haven't. I don't suppose anybody ever has, actually, but if by some extraordinarily unlikely chance you know what I'm talking about, then you'll know exactly how I felt.

Late morning, crusty on the sofa, I awoke to discover I still had the vodka, I still had the sticking plaster, and I still had a house full of cats. Twelve of the little buggers.

Obviously, clearing them out one by one, or even sack by sack, wasn't going to do it. They'd probably just hang around the front door, and I'd never be able to go outside again for fear of inviting reinfestation. No; what I needed here was a permanent solution.

So I called my Aunty Cissie.

Aunty Cissie is eighty-seven, and to my certain knowledge she's been dead three years. I should know: I was at her funeral.

"Jim, my dear! You good boy, you've just rung up to see how I am."

"Now then, Aunty. You know I only ring when I want something." Incapable of hearing harsh truth without disbelieving it, my Aunty Cissie; podgy, breathless, sagging, permanently on the homeward leg of a return trip to doolally-land. Or do I mean a jolly, rotund, chuckle-faced, happy-go-lucky senior citizen? No, I don't.

"Do you know, I haven't seen you for three years?" she said, as delightedly as she said everything. "Not since your Great-Uncle Norman's funeral."

"Oh, right," I said. Now I come to think of it, it might not have been her funeral. Might have been somebody else's. I don't remember; I didn't stay long. "So you're still alive, then?"

She chuckled. "Just about, dear. You are sweet. I know how you worry about me."

"Mmm-mmm," I said. I don't like to commit myself too strongly over the phone; you never know who's listening. "Look, Aunty. You know about cats. You ever heard of cats . . . adopting people?"

"Oh yes, they'll do that, dear. If their old owners have got a new baby, or a new kitten, or a new computer game. Cats demand attention, and they won't tolerate rivals. Or if they've been mistreated, or living rough, or they're not getting the kind of food they like. I had a cat once that wouldn't eat anything but Chinese stir-fried mushrooms."

"How about twelve at once? Mass defection—you ever hear of a case like that?"

"Oh, dear! Is that what you've got? Twelve of the little buggers! Well, I'm not surprised. You always were a gentle boy. They must all be in love with you!"

*Just my luck*, I thought. *In a world full of seventeen-year-old nymphos . . .*

"Still," said Aunty Cissie. "They're company, aren't they? And we all need company, don't we, now and then?"

*Oh, God . . .*

"Which reminds me, dear. When are you coming to see me? How about next week?"

"No, sorry, I'm pretty busy next week. And the week after. But you're right, we must make a definite date. Tell you what, I'll come round one day next year."

"Oh, that is kind of you, dear. I shall count the hours! Oh, but Jim?" she added as I began the long process of hanging up. "Don't make it a Thursday."

"Not a Thursday, Aunty. Right you are."

"No, dear. You see, Thursday's my night for going to the lavatory."

So, there you are. Cat psychology is pretty simple really, once you know what you're doing. And what I did was this: I didn't feed them, and I removed the cardboard from the hole. And after twenty-four hours of involuntary hunger-striking, they forgot the taste of chili con carne, began to wonder what they were doing here, and one by one slipped off back to the allotments—having first peed on every available surface and in every imaginable crevice. I could have rented out the house as a rehabilitation centre for the nasally-disadvantaged.

Anyway, it was over.

Until Jenni rang again.

"Jim—the pics are totally fabulous! What we thought was, we'd like to blow one of your cats up."

"Blow them all up if you like," I said, pleased to hear so sensible a suggestion from so unexpected a source.

"For the cover," she said. "That gingery one with the kinky tail—you know which one I mean?"

Was there a gingery one? "Oh yeah," I said.

"Great! So, like, what do you call her?"

"Stinking rat," I said.

"Stinking *what?*"

"Er—no, no. Not stinking. Slinking. Slinking Cat."

"Oh, that's *sweet.*"

"Slinky for short."

"Oh, that is so sweet!"

"Oh yeah," I said. "Well, she's a sweet cat. Glad you like her."

*"Love her,"* said Jenni. "In fact, what we were thinking was, you know, why don't we send Carl over again, get him to do some more pics? Just of Slinky, you know, make a bit of a feature of her."

"Great," I said. "Some more pics. Great idea."

"Well, you know, we're talking about maybe even a calendar. You know, like a spin-off. She's really a special little puss. My publisher's own personal idea, actually. First one he's had for ages! Whoops, no, he's, you know, smashing, actually. Anyway, if it works out, we could actually pay you some, you know, truly decent money for once. I mean, the publisher's just given me this cheque with, like, a signature at the bottom and nothing else! So, what do you think, Jim?"

"Oh yeah," I said. "Totally fabulous."

A flashlight. A writer on the edge of madness. The allotments by night.

"Slinky . . . Slinky . . . C'mere, Slinky . . ."

What the hell was I calling her *Slinky* for, for God's sake?

Yup, that was Slinky all right. Sitting on my bed, eating chili con carne from a plastic washing-up bowl. I could tell by comparing her with the big photo Jenni had faxed me. Good old Slinky, my sweet little, special little golden goose.

There was a knock on the door.

The man now standing in my hall was angry. He was also fiftyish, well-dressed, greyly bald, and the same boney bloke who'd doubted my tortoises on the allotments the other day. But mostly he was angry.

"It's *my* cat, Mr. Potter. You have stolen my cat, and I demand its return. Without any further argument. Understand?"

"Must be some mistake, Dr. Lane. My little Slinky and me, we—"

"Look! I saw you take the damn cat. From the allotments. I was down there looking for her—because she was missing, right? And I saw you take her, and I followed you home. Now hand her over, please."

"Ah," I said. "I think I can solve this misunderstanding." I dragged a crumpled twenty-pound note from my back pocket. "I'll keep Slinky, my beloved pet of long-standing, and you take this and get another cat."

"Twenty pounds?" he yelled.

"Hey, if you're proud, I can respect that. We'll go halves. A tenner each."

Sounded fair to me, but what I hadn't counted on was that the phrase *get another cat* turned out to mean "Why don't you stick this in your ear and twist it?" in Dr. Lane-language. Must have done, I reckoned, because Lane was really horrified.

"Get another cat?" he gasped.

I don't know if you've ever been to one of those weddings where everybody keeps throwing up on the bride's mother? But if you have, then picture in your mind the expression the bride's mother was wearing by the end of a long day, and you'll know just how much disgust one face can be made to contain.

"You obviously know nothing of cats, Mr. Potter, or you would realise that when one loses one's cat one doesn't just go out and buy another one."

"Sure," I said. "I can understand that. I'll tell you what, how about a *dozen* cats? Hey, think about it: If dry-cleaners took compensation that seriously, they'd all go out of business, right?"

He looked at me as if I'd just escaped the noose on an insanity plea, and marched out of the house, down the street, without another word.

"Seriously, Dr. Lane," I called after him. "I'm not kidding! I know where I can lay my hands on more cats than a faith-healer in a violin factory!"

So, okay: When I got home from the pub two days later to find one of my ground-floor windows broken open, and the house doing a neat imitation of a Slinky-Free Zone, it wasn't exactly a three-pipe puzzle.

But, honestly. All that fuss over a cat? After all, Lane didn't know how much Slinky was worth.

I had about three hours before Carl arrived to take the portfolio which, with any luck, would keep me in sunshine holidays for the next three winters.

"Should've called you Lucky," I told Slinky, as I stuffed her back into the sack which, by now, was becoming like her second home. "I never thought nasty old Dr. Lane would be idiotic enough to let you out to play on the allotments so soon."

Which was when Dr. Lane, approaching unobserved from the rear, slammed his fist into my spine, shouting: "You moron! You've no idea what you're interfering with here!"

What I had no idea of was why a grown doctor should be willing to assault a virtual stranger just to keep possession of a gingery cat with a kinky tail. What I did have an idea of, however, was that Lane had a big stick in his hand, and was just about mad enough to use it on me as I lay sprawled at his feet. His grey face was red now.

On an impulse, I swung the sack, Slinky and all, right into his belly. The cat screamed; he didn't. He just tripped, fell, and landed with a splash in the shallow river. A splash and a thud, the latter caused by the sudden connection of his head with a rock.

I stared at him for about a minute. He didn't move.

I was still a little shaky when Carl arrived, but the vodka was helping.

"Where're all the other cats?" he asked, as I should have guessed he would.

"Who knows where staff go on their afternoons off?" I replied, haughtily. "To the pictures, I expect."

Carl laughed (which used up about ten minutes of the day, right off), took his photos, and eventually left. Slinky had chili for dinner. I had vodka.

When a noise in the hall woke me the next morning, I thought for a moment it was one of Slinky's old mates discovering how to enter a house through the letter box. But it was the local paper, with a stop-press item announcing the suspicious death of Dr. Reginald Lane, 54, research scientist, at his home in River Walk.

At his home?

Police were said to be unable to explain why, when found dead sitting in a sun-lounger on his veranda, Dr. Lane (who had been shot twice in the lower body at short range) was wearing wet clothing and had a crude, apparently self-applied, freshly blood-stained bandage on his head.

The mystery—for me—only lasted until the lunchtime TV news, which reported that an animal-rights activist had confessed to the "justified execution of a mass-murderer." Lane had been right; I'd had no idea what I was interfering with.

Far from being an aggrieved pet lover, the doctor was actually what that Sunday's tabloids called a vivisectionist. Slinky—and all the other cats on the allotments—had been part of an experiment, a deeply illegal experiment, it transpired, designed to develop a rapidly contagious but easily contained feline disease.

Quite who was sponsoring Lane's alfresco laboratory has never been established, but speculation centered on the government, on the property developers, on all the usual suspects. At any rate, some people, it seems, do not value urban feral-cat populations in quite the way that I have come to value them.

And I certainly do value Slinky. I do. The calendar—*Slinky's Big Year* (text by J. Potter)—will be, Jenni's marketing colleagues assure me, the biggest-selling gift item nationwide next Christmas. There is talk of an animated television series. Two book publishers are bidding for the rights to Slinky's autobiography, which I am to ghostwrite (well, yeah, *obviously*). I'll have to make up some amusing adventures for her. The truth, I think, would not do at all.

Which brings me to why I'm writing this strictly private memoir.

The remaining allotment cats were rounded up by the council's vet and taken away for tests "as a precaution." There was really no cause for concern, the authorities insisted, but just to be on the safe side . . .

(I bet they ended up on some health farm, all chili con carne and Ping-Pong and free booze, and all at the public's expense. While your average humourist has to virtually kill himself just to meet the mortgage. Ask me, the welfare state saps enterprise. Look at Slinky: She got herself a career, she didn't sit around waiting for handouts.)

I don't know if you've ever lived in close proximity to a cat which may or may not be carrying an unidentified bug, which may or may not be transferable to humans, and which may or may not kill you at some time in the future. But if you have, then you'll know that it's something that tends to worry you a little.

But really, most of the time I'm too busy worrying about what it's going to be like entering the super-tax bracket.

Still, "just to be on the safe side . . ."

If I should predecease my Aunty Cissie, I would like her to inherit my copyrights and royalties. And please, whoever reads this, tell her I'm terribly sorry I never visited her.

I'm not, in fact, but what I always say is: Being nice doesn't cost anything, does it?

At least, it doesn't when it doesn't cost anything.

# Peter Robinson

## Missing in Action

PETER ROBINSON is one of the finest writers to come out of the cold northern lands of Canada in recent years, with numerous appearances in *Ellery Queen's Mystery Magazine*, in other anthologies, and writing some of the best mystery novels of the past decade. Like many others in our collection, his name and fame are growing with each new story or book. "Missing in Action," first published in *Ellery Queen's Mystery Magazine* in November of 2000, has it all, his wry voice, a spot-on sense of history, and a keep-you-reading-until-the-last-page whodunit plot.

# Missing in Action

*Peter Robinson*

People go missing all the time in war, of course, but not usually nine-year-old boys. Besides, the war had hardly begun. It was only the twentieth of September, 1939, when Mary Critchley came hammering on my door at about three o'clock, interrupting my afternoon nap.

It was a Wednesday, and normally I would have been teaching the fifth-formers Shakespeare at Silverhill Grammar School (a thankless task if ever there was one), but the Ministry had just got around to constructing air-raid shelters there, so the school was closed for the week. We didn't even know if it was going to reopen, because the idea was to evacuate all the children to safer areas in the countryside. Now, I would be among the first to admit that a teacher's highest aspiration is a school without pupils, but in the meantime the government, in its eternal wisdom, put us redundant teachers to such complex, intellectual tasks as preparing ration cards for the Ministry of Food. (After all, *they* knew what was coming.)

All this was just a small part of the chaos that seemed to reign at that time. Not the chaos of war, the kind I remembered from the trenches at Ypres in 1917, but the chaos of government bureaucracies trying to organize the country for war.

Anyway, I was fortunate enough to become Special Constable, which is a rather grandiose title for a sort of part-time dogsbody, and that was why Mary Critchley came running to me. That and what little reputation I had for solving people's problems.

"Mr. Bashcombe! Mr. Bashcombe!" she cried. "It's our Johnny. He's gone missing. You must help."

My name is actually *Bascombe*, Frank Bascombe, but Mary Critchley has a slight speech impediment, so I forgave her the mispronunciation. Still, with half the city's children running wild in the streets and the other half standing on crowded station platforms clutching their Mickey Mouse gas masks in little cardboard boxes, ready to be herded into trains bound for such nearby country havens as Graythorpe, Kilsden, and Acksham, I thought perhaps she was overreacting a tad, and I can't say I welcomed her arrival after only about twenty of my allotted forty winks.

"He's probably out playing with his mates," I told her.

"Not my Johnny," she said, wiping the tears from her eyes. "Not since . . . you know . . ."

I knew. Mr. Critchley, Ted to his friends, had been a Royal Navy man since well before the war. He had also been unfortunate enough to serve on the fleet carrier *Courageous*, which had been sunk by a German U-boat off the southwest coast of Ireland just three days ago. Over 500 men had been lost, including Ted Critchley. Of course, no body had been found, and probably never would be, so he was only officially "missing in action."

I also knew young Johnny Critchley, and thought him to be a serious boy, a bit too imaginative and innocent for his own good. (Well, many are at that age, aren't they, before the world grabs them by the balls and shakes some reality into them.) Johnny trusted everyone, even strangers.

"Johnny's not been in much of a mood for playing with his mates since we got the news about Ted's ship," Mary Critchley went on.

I could understand that well enough—young Johnny was an only child, and he always did worship his father—but I still didn't see what I could do about it. "Have you asked around?"

"What do you think I've been doing since he didn't come home at twelve o'clock like he was supposed to? I've asked everyone in the street. Last time he was seen he was down by the canal at about eleven o'clock. Maurice Richards saw him. What can I do, Mr. Bashcombe? First Ted, and now . . . now my Johnny!" She burst into tears.

After I had managed to calm her down, I sighed and told her I would look for Johnny myself. There certainly wasn't much hope of my getting the other twenty winks now.

It was a glorious day, so warm and sunny you would hardly believe there was a war on. The late afternoon sunshine made even our narrow streets of cramped brick terrace houses look attractive. As the shadows lengthened, the light turned to molten gold. First, I scoured the local rec where the children played cricket and football, and the dogs ran wild. Some soldiers were busy digging trenches for air-raid shelters. Just the sight of those long, dark grooves in the earth gave me the shivers. Behind the trenches, barrage balloons pulled at their moorings on the breeze like playful porpoises, orange and pink in the sun. I asked the soldiers, but they hadn't seen Johnny. Nor had any of the other lads.

After the rec I headed for the derelict houses on Gallipoli Street. The landlord had let them go to rack and ruin two years ago, and they were quite uninhabitable, not even fit for billeting soldiers. They were also dangerous and should have been pulled down, but I think the old skinflint was hoping a bomb would hit them so he could claim insurance or compensation from the government. The doors and windows had been boarded up, but children are resourceful, and it wasn't difficult even for me to remove a couple of loose sheets of plywood and make my way inside. I wished I had my torch, but I had to make do with what little light slipped through the holes. Every time I moved, my feet stirred up clouds of dust, which did my poor lungs no good at all.

I thought Johnny might have fallen or got trapped in one of the houses. The staircases were rotten, and more than one lad had fallen through on his way up.

The floors weren't much better, either, and one of the fourth-formers at Silverhill had needed more than fifteen stitches a couple of weeks ago when one of his legs went right through the rotten wood and the splinters gouged his flesh.

I searched as best I could in the poor light, and I called out Johnny's name, but no answer came. Before I left, I stood silently and listened for any traces of harsh breathing or whimpering.

Nothing.

After three hours of searching the neighbourhood, I'd had no luck at all. Blackout time was 7:45 P.M., so I still had about an hour and a half left, but if Johnny wasn't in any of the local children's usual haunts, I was at a loss as to where to look. I talked to the other boys I met here and there, but none of his friends had seen him since the family got the news of Ted's death. Little Johnny Critchley, it seemed, had vanished into thin air.

At half-past six, I called on Maurice Richards, grateful for his offer of a cup of tea and the chance to rest my aching feet. Maurice and I went back a long time. We had both survived the first war, Maurice with the loss of an arm and me with permanent facial scarring and a wracking cough that comes and goes, thanks to the mustard gas leaking through my mask at the Third Battle of Ypres. We never talked about the war, but it was there, we both knew, an invisible bond tying us close together while at the same time excluding us from so much other, normal human intercourse. Not many had seen the things we had, and thank God for that.

Maurice lit up a Passing Cloud one-handed, then he poured the tea. The seven o'clock news came on the radio, some such rot about us vowing to keep fighting until we'd vanquished the foe. It was still very much a war of words at that time, and the more rhetorical the language sounded, the better the politicians thought they were doing. There had been a couple of minor air skirmishes, and the sinking of the *Courageous*, of course, but all the action was taking place in Poland, which seemed as remote as the moon to most people. Some clever buggers had already started calling it the "Bore War."

"Did you hear Tommy Handley last night, Frank?" Maurice asked.

I shook my head. There'd been a lot of hoopla about Tommy Handley's new radio programme, "It's That Man Again," or "ITMA," as people called it. I was never a fan. Call me a snob, but when evening falls I'm far happier curling up with a good book or an interesting talk on the radio than listening to Tommy Handley.

"Talk about a laugh," said Maurice. "They had this one sketch about the Ministry of Aggravation and the Office of Twerps. I nearly died."

I smiled. "Not far from the truth," I said. There were now so many of these obscure ministries, boards, and departments involved in so many absurd pursuits—all for the common good, of course—that I had been thinking of writing a dystopian satire. I proposed to set it in the near future, which would merely be a thinly disguised version of the present. So far, all I had was a great idea for the title: I would reverse the last two numbers in the current year, so instead of 1939, I'd call it *1993*. (Well, *I* thought it was a good idea!) "Look, Maurice," I said, "it's about young Johnny Critchley. His mother tells me you were the last person to see him."

"Oh, aye," Maurice said. "She were round asking about him not long ago. Still not turned up?"

"No."

"Cause for concern, then."

"I'm beginning to think so. What was he doing when you saw him?"

"Just walking down by the canal, by old Woodruff's scrap yard."

"That's all?"

"Yes."

"Was he alone?"

Maurice nodded.

"Did he say anything."

"No."

"You didn't say anything to him?"

"No cause to. He seemed preoccupied, just staring in the water, like, hands in his pockets. I've heard what happened to his dad. A lad has to do his grieving."

"Too true. Did you see anyone else? Anything suspicious?"

"No, nothing. Just a minute, though . . ."

"What?"

"Oh, it's probably nothing, but just after I saw Johnny, when I was crossing the bridge, I bumped into Colin Gormond, you know, that chap who's a bit . . . you know."

*Colin Gormond.* I knew him all right. And that wasn't good news; it wasn't good news at all.

Of all the policemen they could have sent, they had to send Detective bloody Sergeant Longbottom, a big, brutish-looking fellow with a pronounced limp and a Cro-Magnon brow. Longbottom was thick as two short planks. I doubt he could have found his own arse even if someone nailed a sign on it, or detect his way out of an Anderson shelter if it were in his own backyard. But that's the calibre of men this wretched war has left us with at home. Along with good ones like me, of course.

DS Longbottom wore a shiny brown suit and a Silverhill Grammar School tie. I wondered where he'd got it from; he probably stole it from some schoolboy he caught nicking sweets from the corner shop. He kept tugging at his collar with his pink sausage fingers as we talked in Mary Critchley's living room. His face was flushed with the heat, and sweat gathered on his thick eyebrows and trickled down the sides of his neck.

"So he's been missing since lunchtime, has he?" DS Longbottom repeated.

Mary Critchley nodded. "He went out at about half-past ten, just for a walk, like. Said he'd be back at twelve. When it got to three . . . well, I went to see Mr. Bashcombe here."

DS Longbottom curled his lip at me and grunted. "Mr. Bascombe. *Special* Constable. I suppose you realize that gives you no real police powers, don't you?"

"As a matter of fact," I said, "I thought it made me your superior. After all, you're not a *special* sergeant, are you?"

He looked at me as if he wanted to hit me. Perhaps he would have done if Mary Critchley hadn't been in the room. "Enough of your lip. Just answer my questions."

"Yes, sir."

"You say you looked all over for this lad?"

"All his usual haunts."

"And you found no trace of him?"

"If I had, do you think we'd have sent for you?"

"I warned you. Cut the lip and answer the questions. This, what's his name, Maurice Richards, was he the last person to see the lad?"

"Johnny's his name. And yes is the answer, as far as we know." I paused. He'd have to know eventually, and if I didn't tell him, Maurice would. The longer we delayed, the worse it would be in the long run. "There was someone else in the area at the time. A man called Colin Gormond."

Mary Critchley gave a sharp gasp. DS Longbottom frowned, licked the tip of his pencil, and scribbled something in his notebook. "I'll have to have a word with him," he said. Then he turned to her. "Recognize the name, do you, ma'am?"

"I know Colin," I answered, perhaps a bit too quickly.

DS Longbottom stared at Mary Critchley, whose lower lip started quivering, then turned slowly back to me. "Tell me about him."

I sighed. Colin Gormond was an oddball. Some people said he was a bit slow, but I'd never seen any real evidence of that. He lived alone and he didn't have much to do with the locals; that was enough evidence against him for some people.

And then there were the children.

For some reason, Colin preferred the company of the local lads to that of the rest of us adults. To be quite honest, I can't say I blame him, but in a situation like this it's bound to look suspicious. Especially if the investigating officer is someone with the sensitivity and understanding of a DS Longbottom.

Colin would take them train-spotting on the hill overlooking the main line, for example, or he'd play cricket with them on the rec or hand out conkers when the season came. He sometimes bought them sweets and ice creams, even gave them books, marbles, and comics.

To my knowledge, Colin Gormond had never once put a foot out of line, never laid so much as a finger on any of the lads, either in anger or in friendship. There had, however, been one or two mutterings from some parents—most notably from Jack Blackwell, father of one of Johnny's pals, Nick—that it somehow *wasn't right*, that it was *unnatural* for a man who must be in his late thirties or early forties to spend so much time playing with young children. There must be something not quite right in his head, he must be up to *something*, Jack Blackwell hinted, and as usual when someone starts a vicious rumour, there is no shortage of willing believers. Such a reaction was only to be expected from someone, of course, but I knew it wouldn't go down well with DS Longbottom. I don't know why, but I felt a strange need to *protect* Colin.

"Colin's a local," I explained. "Lived around here for years. He plays with the lads a bit. Most of them like him. He seems a harmless sort of fellow."

"How old is he?"

I shrugged. "Hard to say. About forty, perhaps."

DS Longbottom raised a thick eyebrow. "About forty, and he plays with the kiddies, you say?"

"Sometimes. Like a schoolteacher, or a youth-club leader."

"Is he a schoolteacher?"

"No."

"Is he a youth-club leader?"

"No. Look, what I meant—"

"I know exactly what you meant, Mr. Bascombe. Now you just listen to what *I* mean. What we've got here is an older man who's known to hang around with young children, and he's been placed near the scene where a young child has gone missing. Now, don't you think that's just a wee bit suspicious?"

Mary Critchley let out a great wail and started crying again. DS Longbottom ignored her. Instead, he concentrated all his venom on me, the softie, the liberal, the defender of child molesters. "What do you have to say about *that*, Mr. Special Constable Bascombe?"

"Only that Colin was a friend to the children and that he had no reason to harm anyone."

"*Friend,*" DS Longbottom sneered, struggling to his feet. "We can only be thankful you're not regular police, Mr. Bascombe," he said, nodding to himself in acknowledgement of his own wisdom. "That we can."

"So what are you going to do?" I asked.

DS Longbottom looked at his watch and frowned. Either he was trying to work out what it meant when the little hand and the big hand were in the positions they were in, or he was squinting because of poor eyesight. "I'll have a word with this here Colin Gormond. Other than that, there's not much more we can do tonight. First thing tomorrow morning, we'll drag the canal." He got to the door, turned, pointed to the windows, and said, "And don't forget to put up your blackout curtains, ma'am, or you'll have the ARP man to answer to."

Mary Critchley burst into floods of tears again.

Even the soft dawn light could do nothing for the canal. It oozed through the city like an open sewer, oil slicks shimmering like rainbows in the sun, brown water dotted with industrial scum and suds, bits of driftwood and paper wrappings floating along with them. On one side was Ezekiel Woodruff's scrap yard. Old Woodruff was a bit of an eccentric. He used to come around the streets with his horse and cart yelling, "Any old iron," but now the government had other uses for scrap metal—supposedly to be used in aircraft manufacture—poor old Woodruff didn't have any way to make his living anymore. He'd already sent old Nell the carthorse to the knacker's yard, where she was probably doing her bit for the war effort by helping to make the glue to stick the aircraft together. Old mangles and bits of broken furniture stuck up from the ruins of the scrap yard like shattered artillery after a battle.

On the other side, the bank rose steeply towards the backs of the houses on Canal Road, and the people who lived there seemed to regard it as their personal tip. Flies and wasps buzzed around old Hessian sacks and paper bags full of God knew what. A couple of buckled bicycle tires and a wheelless pram completed the picture.

I stood and watched as Longbottom supervised the dragging, a slow and laborious process that seemed to be sucking all manner of unwholesome objects to the surface—except Johnny Critchley's body.

I felt tense. At any moment I half expected the cry to come from one of the policemen in the boats that they had found him, half expected to see the small, pathetic bundle bob above the water's surface. I didn't think Colin Gormond had done anything to Johnny—nor Maurice, though DS Longbottom had seemed suspicious of him, too, but I did think that, given how upset he was, Johnny might just have jumped in. He never struck me as the suicidal type, but I have no idea whether suicide enters the minds of nine-year-olds. All I knew was that he *was* upset about his father, and he *was* last seen skulking by the canal.

So I stood around with DS Longbottom and the rest as the day grew warmer, and there was still no sign of Johnny. After about three hours, the police gave up and went for bacon and eggs at Betty's Cafe over on Chadwick Road. They didn't invite me, and I was grateful to be spared both the unpleasant food and company. I stood and stared into the greasy water a while longer, unsure whether it was a good sign or not that Johnny wasn't in the canal, then I decided to go and have a chat with Colin Gormond.

"What is it, Colin?" I asked him gently. "Come on. You can tell me."

But Colin continued to stand with his back turned to me in the dark corner of his cramped living room, hands to his face, making eerie snuffling sounds, shaking his head. It was bright daylight outside, but the blackout curtains were still drawn tightly, and not a chink of light crept between their edges. I had already tried the light switch, but either Colin had removed the bulb or he didn't have one.

"Come on, Colin. This is silly. You know me. I'm Mr. Bascombe. I won't hurt you. Tell me what happened."

Finally, Colin turned silently and moved out of his corner with his funny, shuffling way of walking. Someone said he had a clubfoot, and someone else said he'd had a lot of operations on his feet when he was a young lad, but nobody knew for certain why he walked the way he did. When he sat down and lit a cigarette, the match light illuminated his large nose, shiny forehead, and watery blue eyes. He used the same match to light a candle on the table beside him, and then I saw them: the black eye, the bruise on his left cheek. DS Longbottom. The bastard.

"Did you say anything to him?" I asked, anxious that DS Longbottom might have beaten a confession out of Colin, without even thinking that Colin probably wouldn't still be at home if that were the case.

He shook his head mournfully. "Nothing, Mr. Bascombe. Honest. There was nothing I *could* tell him."

"Did you see Johnny Critchley yesterday, Colin?"

"Aye."

"Where?"

"Down by the canal."

"What was he doing?"

"Just standing there chucking stones in the water."

"Did you talk to him?"

Colin paused and turned away before answering, "No."

I had a brief coughing spell, his cigarette smoke working on my gassed lungs. When it cleared up, I said, "Colin, there's something you're not telling me, isn't there? You'd better tell me. You know I won't hurt you, and I just might be the only person who can help you."

He looked at me, pale eyes imploring. "I only called out to him, from the bridge, like, didn't I?"

"What happened next?"

"Nothing. I swear it."

"Did he answer?"

"No. He just looked my way and shook his head. I could tell then that he didn't want to play. He seemed sad."

"He'd just heard his dad's been killed."

Colin's already watery eyes brimmed with tears. "Poor lad."

I nodded. For all I knew, Colin might have been thinking about *his* dad, too. Not many knew it, but Mr. Gormond senior had been killed in the same bloody war that left me with my bad lungs and scarred face. "What happened next, Colin?"

Colin shook his head and wiped his eyes with the back of his hand. "Nothing," he said. "It was such a lovely day, I just went on walking. I went to the park and watched the soldiers digging trenches, then I went for my cigarettes and came home to listen to the wireless."

"And after that?"

"I stayed in."

"All evening?"

"That's right. Sometimes I go down to the White Rose, but . . ."

"But what, Colin?"

"Well, Mr. Smedley, you know, the Air-Raid Precautions man?"

I nodded. "I know him."

"He said my blackout cloth wasn't good enough and he'd fine me if I didn't get some proper stuff by yesterday."

"I understand, Colin." Good-quality, thick, impenetrable blackout cloth had become both scarce and expensive, which was no doubt why Colin had been cheated in the first place.

"Anyway, what with that and the cigarettes . . ."

I reached into my pocket and slipped out a few bob for him. Colin looked away, ashamed, but I put it on the table and he didn't tell me to take it back. I knew how it must hurt his pride to accept charity, but I had no idea how much money he made, or how he made it. I'd never seen him beg, but I had a feeling he survived on odd jobs and lived very much from hand to mouth.

I stood up. "All right, Colin," I said. "Thanks very much." I paused at the door, uncertain how to say what had just entered my mind. Finally, I blundered ahead. "It might be better if you kept a low profile till they find him, Colin. You know what some of the people around here are like."

"What do you mean, Mr. Bascombe?"

"Just be careful, Colin, that's all I mean. Just be careful."

He nodded gormlessly, and I left.

As I was leaving Colin's house, I noticed Jack Blackwell standing on his doorstep, arms folded, a small crowd of locals around him, their shadows intersecting on the cobbled street. They kept glancing towards Colin's house, and when they saw me come out, they all shuffled off except Jack himself, who gave me a grim stare before going inside and slamming his door. I felt a shiver go up my spine, as if a goose had stepped on my grave, as my dear mother used to say, bless her soul, and when I got home I couldn't concentrate on my book one little bit.

By the following morning, when Johnny had been missing over thirty-six hours, the mood in the street had started to turn ugly. In my experience, when you get right down to it, there's no sorrier spectacle, nothing much worse or more dangerous, than the human mob mentality. After all, armies are nothing more than mobs, really, even when they are organized to a greater or lesser degree. I'd been at Ypres, as you know, and there wasn't a hell of a lot you could tell me about military organization. So when I heard the muttered words on doorsteps, saw the little knots of people here and there, Jack Blackwell flitting from door to door like a political canvasser, I had to do something, and I could hardly count on any help from DS Longbottom.

One thing I had learned both as a soldier and as a schoolteacher was that, if you had a chance, your best bet was to take out the ringleader. That meant Jack Blackwell. Jack was the nasty type, and he and I had had more than one run-in over his son Nick's bullying and poor performance in class. In my opinion, young Nick was the sort of walking dead loss who should probably have been drowned at birth, a waste of skin, sinew, tissue, and bone, and it wasn't hard to see where he got it from. Nick's older brother, Dave, was already doing a long stretch in the Scrubs for beating a night watchman senseless during a robbery, and even the army couldn't find an excuse to spring him and enlist his service in killing Germans. Mrs. Blackwell had been seen more than once walking with difficulty, with bruises on her cheek. The sooner Jack Blackwell got his call-up papers, the better things would be all around.

I intercepted Jack between the Deakins' and the Kellys' houses, and it was clear from his gruff, "What do you want?" that he didn't want to talk to me.

But I was adamant.

"Morning, Jack," I greeted him. "Lovely day for a walk, isn't it?"

"What's it to you?"

"Just being polite. What are you up to, Jack? What's going on?"

"None of your business."

"Up to your old tricks? Spreading poison?"

"I don't know what you're talking about." He made to walk away, but I grabbed his arm. He glared at me but didn't do anything. Just as well. At my age, and with my lungs, I'd hardly last ten seconds in a fight. "Jack," I said, "don't you think you'd all be best off using your time to look for the poor lad?"

"Look for him! That's a laugh. You know as well as I do where that young lad is."

"Where? Where is he, Jack?"

"You know."

"No, I don't. Tell me."

"He's dead and buried, that's what."

"Where, Jack?"

"I don't know the exact spot. If he's not in the canal, then he's buried somewhere not far away."

"Maybe he is. But you don't *know* that. Not for certain. And even if you believe that, you don't know who put him there."

Jack wrenched his arm out of my weakening grip and sneered. "I've got a damn sight better idea than you have, Frank Bascombe. With all your *book* learning!" Then he turned and marched off.

Somehow, I got the feeling that I had just made things worse.

After my brief fracas with Jack Blackwell, I was at a loose end. I knew the police would still be looking for Johnny, asking questions, searching areas of waste ground, so there wasn't much I could do to help them. Feeling impotent, I went down to the canal, near Woodruff's scrap yard. Old Ezekiel Woodruff himself was poking around in the ruins of his business, so I decided to talk to him. I kept my distance, though, for even on a hot day such as this, Woodruff was wearing his greatcoat and black wool gloves with the fingers cut off. He wasn't known for his personal hygiene, so I made sure I didn't stand downwind of him. Not that there was much of a wind, but then it didn't take much.

"Morning, Ezekiel," I said. "I understand young Johnny Critchley was down around here yesterday."

"So they say," muttered Ezekiel.

"See him, did you?"

"I weren't here."

"So you didn't see him?"

"Police have already been asking questions."

"And what did you tell them?"

He pointed to the other side of the canal, the back of the housing estate. "I were over there," he said. "Sometimes people chuck out summat of value, even these days."

"But you did see Johnny?"

He paused, then said, "Aye."

"On this side of the canal?"

Woodruff nodded.

"What time was this?"

"I don't have a watch, but it weren't long after that daft bloke had gone by."

"Do you mean Colin Gormond?"

"Aye, that's the one."

So Johnny was still alone by the canal *after* Colin had passed by. DS Longbottom had probably known this, but he had beaten Colin anyway. One day I'd find a way to get even with him. The breeze shifted a little and I got a whiff of stale sweat and worse. "What was Johnny doing?"

"Doing? Nowt special. He were just walking."

"Walking? Where?"

Woodruff pointed. "That way. Towards the city centre."

"Alone?"

"Aye."

"And nobody approached him?"

"Nope. Not while I were watching."

I didn't think there was anything further to be got from Ezekiel Woodruff, so I bade him good morning. I can't say the suspicion didn't enter my head that *he* might have had something to do with Johnny's disappearance, though I'd been hard pushed to say exactly why or what. Odd though old Woodruff might be, there had never been any rumour or suspicion of his being overly interested in young boys, and I didn't want to jump to conclusions the way Jack Blackwell had. Still, I filed away my suspicions for later.

A fighter droned overhead. I watched it dip and spin through the blue air and wished I could be up there. I'd always regretted not being a pilot in the war. A barge full of soldiers drifted by, and I moved aside on the towpath to let the horse that was pulling it pass by. For my troubles I got a full blast of sweaty horseflesh and a pile of steaming manure at my feet. That had even Ezekiel Woodruff beat.

Aimlessly, I followed the direction Ezekiel had told me Johnny had walked in—towards the city centre. As I walked, Jack Blackwell's scornful words about my inability to find Johnny echoed in my mind. *Book learning.* That was exactly the kind of cheap insult you would expect from a moron like Jack Blackwell, but it hurt nonetheless. No sense telling him I'd been buried in the mud under the bodies of my comrades for two days. No sense telling him about the young German soldier I'd surprised and bayonetted to death, twisting the blade until it snapped and broke off inside him. Jack Blackwell was too young to have seen action in the last war, but if there was any justice in the world, he'd damn well see it in *this* one.

The canal ran by the back of the train station, where I crossed the narrow bridge and walked through the crowds of evacuees out front of City Square. Mary Critchley's anguish reverberated in my mind, too: "*Mr. Bashcombe! Mr. Bashcombe!*" I heard her call.

Then, all of a sudden, as I looked at the black facade of the post office and the statue of the Black Prince in the centre of City Square, it hit me. I thought I knew what had happened to Johnny Critchley, but first I had to go back to his street and ask just one important question.

It was late morning. The station smelt of damp soot and warm oil. Crowds of children thronged around trying to find out where they were supposed to go. They wore name tags and carried little cardboard boxes. Adults with clipboards, for the most part temporarily unemployed schoolteachers and local volunteers, directed them to the right queue, and their names were ticked off as they boarded the carriages.

Despite being neither an evacuated child nor a supervisor, I managed to buy a ticket and ended up sharing a compartment with a rather severe-looking woman in a brown uniform I didn't recognize, and a male civilian with a brush moustache and a lot of Brylcreem on his hair. They seemed to be in charge of several young children, also in the compartment, who couldn't sit still. I could hardly blame them. They were going to the alien countryside, to live with strangers, far away from their parents, for only God knew how long, and the idea scared them half to death.

The buttoned cushions were warm and the air in the carriage still and close, despite the open window. When we finally set off, the motion stirred up a bit of a breeze, which helped a little. On the wall opposite me was a poster of the Scarborough seafront, and I spent most of the journey remembering the carefree childhood holidays I had enjoyed there with my parents in the early years of the century: another world, another time. The rest of the trip, I glanced out of the window, beyond the scum-scabbed canal, and saw the urban industrial landscape drift by: back gardens, where some people had put in Anderson shelters, half-covered with earth to grow vegetables on; the dark mass of the town-hall clock tower behind the city-centre buildings; a factory yard, where several men were loading heavy crates onto a lorry, flushed and sweating in the heat.

Then we were in the countryside, where the smells of grass, hay, and manure displaced the reek of the city. I saw small, squat farms, drystone walls, sheep and cattle grazing. Soon, train tracks and canal diverged. We went under a long noisy tunnel, and the children whimpered. Later, I was surprised to see so many army convoys winding along the narrow roads, and the one big aerodrome we passed seemed buzzing with activity.

All in all, the journey took a little over two hours. Only about ten or eleven children were shepherded off at the small country station, and I followed as they were met and taken to the village hall, where the men and women who were to care for them waited. It was more civilized than some of the evacuation systems I'd heard about, which sounded more like the slave markets of old, where farmers waited on the platforms to pick out the strong lads, and local dignitaries whisked away the nicely dressed boys and girls.

I went up to the volunteer in charge, an attractive young country-woman in a simple blue frock with a white lace collar and a belt around her slim waist, and asked her if she had any record of an evacuee called John, or Johnny, Critchley. She checked her records, then shook her head, as I knew she would. If I were right, Johnny wouldn't be here under his own name. I explained my problem to the woman, who told me her name was Phyllis Rigby. She had a yellow ribbon in her long wavy hair and smelled of fresh apples. "I don't see how anything like that could have happened," Phyllis said. "We've been very meticulous. But there again, things *have* been a little chaotic." She frowned in thought for a moment, then she delegated her present duties to another volunteer.

"Come on," she said, "I'll help you go from house to house. There weren't that many evacuees, you know. Far fewer than we expected."

I nodded. I'd heard how a lot of parents weren't bothering to evacuate their children. "They can't see anything happening yet," I said. "Just you wait. After the first air raid you'll have so many you won't have room for them all."

Phyllis smiled. "The poor things. It must be such an upheaval for them."

"Indeed."

I took deep, welcome breaths of country air as Phyllis and I set out from the village hall to visit the families listed on her clipboard. There were perhaps a couple of hundred houses, and less than fifty percent had received evacuees. Even so, we worked up quite a sweat calling at them all. Or I did, rather, as sweating didn't seem to be in Phyllis's nature. We chatted as we went, me telling her about my school-teaching, and her telling me about her husband, Thomas, training as a fighter pilot in the RAF. After an hour or so with no luck, we stopped in at her cottage for a refreshing cup of tea, then we were off again.

At last, late in the afternoon, we struck gold.

Mr. and Mrs. Douglas, who were billeting Johnny Critchley, seemed a very pleas-ant couple, and they were sad to hear that they would not get to keep him with them for a while longer. I explained everything to them and assured them that they would get someone else as soon as we got the whole business sorted out.

"He's *not* here," Johnny said as we walked with Phyllis to the station. "I've looked everywhere, but I couldn't find him."

I shook my head. "Sorry, Johnny. You know your mum's got a speech impediment. That was why I had to go back and ask her exactly what she said to you before I came here. She said she told you your father was missing in action, which, the way it came out, sounded like missing in *Acksham*, didn't it? That's why you came here, isn't it, to look for your father?"

Young Johnny nodded, tears in his eyes. "I'm sorry," he said. "I couldn't understand why she didn't come and look for him. She must be really vexed with me."

I patted his shoulder. "I don't think so. More like she'll be glad to see you. How did you manage to sneak in with the real evacuees, by the way?"

Johnny wiped his eyes with his grubby sleeve. "At the station. There were so many people standing around, at first I didn't know . . . Then I saw a boy I knew from playing cricket on the rec."

"Oliver Bradley," I said. The boy whose name Johnny was registered under.

"Yes. He goes to Broad Hill."

I nodded. Though I had never heard of Oliver Bradley, I knew the school; it was just across the valley from us. "Go on."

"I asked him where he was going, and he said he was being sent to Acksham. It was perfect."

"But how did you get him to change places with you?"

"He didn't want to. Not at first."

"How did you persuade him?"

Johnny looked down at the road and scraped at some gravel with the scuffed tip of his shoe. "It cost me a complete set of 'Great Cricketers' cigarette cards. Ones my dad gave me before he went away."

I smiled. It would have to be something like that.

"And I made him promise not to tell anyone, just to go home and say there wasn't room for him and he'd have to try again in a few days. I just needed enough time to find Dad . . . you know."

"I know."

We arrived at the station, where Johnny sat on the bench and Phyllis and I chatted in the late afternoon sunlight, our shadows lengthening across the tracks. In addition to the birds singing in the trees and hedgerows, I could hear grasshoppers chirruping, a sound you rarely heard in the city. I had often thought how much I would like to live in the country, and perhaps when I retired from teaching a few years in the future I would be able to do so.

We didn't have long to wait for our train. I thanked Phyllis for all her help, told her I wished her husband well, and she waved to us as the old banger chugged out of the station.

It was past blackout when I finally walked into our street holding Johnny's hand. He was tired after his adventure and had spent most of the train journey with his head on my shoulder. Once or twice, from the depths of a dream, he had called his father's name.

I could sense that something was wrong as soon as I turned the corner. It was nothing specific, just a sudden chill at the back of my neck. Because of the blackout, I couldn't see anything clearly, but I got a strong impression of a knot of shifting shadows, just a little bit darker than the night itself, milling around outside Colin Gormond's house.

I quickened my step, and as I got nearer I heard a whisper pass through the crowd when they saw Johnny. Then the shadows began to disperse, slinking and sidling away, disappearing like smoke into the air. From somewhere, Mary Critchley lurched forward with a cry and took young Johnny in her arms. I let him go. I could hear her thanking me between sobs, but I couldn't stop walking.

The first thing I noticed when I approached Colin's house was that the window was broken and half the blackout curtain had been ripped away. Next, I saw that the door was slightly ajar. I was worried that Colin might be hurt, but out of courtesy I knocked and called out his name.

Nothing.

I pushed the door open and walked inside. It was pitch dark. I didn't have a torch with me, and I knew that Colin's light didn't work, but I remembered the matches and the candle on the table. I lit it and held it up before me as I walked forward.

I didn't have far to look. If I hadn't had the candle, I might have bumped right into him. First I saw his face, about level with mine. His froth-specked lips had turned blue, and a trickle of dried blood ran from his left nostril. The blackout cloth was knotted around his neck in a makeshift noose, attached to a hook screwed into the lintel over the kitchen door. As I stood back and examined the scene further, I saw that his downturned toes were about three inches from the floor, and there was no sign of an upset chair or stool.

Harmless Colin Gormond, friend to the local children. Dead.

I felt the anger well up in me, along with the guilt. It was my fault. I shouldn't have gone dashing off to Acksham like that in search of Johnny, or I should at least have taken Colin with me. I knew the danger he was in; I had talked to Jack Blackwell before I left. How could I have been so stupid, so careless as to leave Colin to his fate with only a warning he didn't understand?

Maybe Colin *had* managed to hang himself somehow, without standing on a stool, though I doubted it. But whether or not Jack Blackwell or the rest had actually laid a finger on him, they were all guilty of driving him to it in my book. Besides, if Jack or anyone else from the street *had* strung Colin up, there would be evidence—fibres, fingerprints, footprints, whatever—and even DS bloody Longbottom wouldn't be able to ignore that.

I stumbled outside and made my way towards the telephone box on the corner. Not a soul stirred now, but as I went I heard one door—Jack Blackwell's door—close softly this time, as if he thought that too much noise might wake the dead, and the dead might have a tale or two to tell.

# Edward D. Hoch

## The Haggard Society

EDWARD D. HOCH is having one of his more memorable years. In addition to writing his usual monthly story for "Ellery Queen," he is also receiving two of the most prestigious awards in crime fiction: The Mystery Writers of America Grand Master Award and the Bouchercon's Life Achievement Award, Bouchercon being the annual convention that gathers writers and readers from around the world. And as if that weren't enough, just a few months ago he received another important award, The Eye, for Lifetime Achievement citation from the Private Eye Writers of America. After reading "The Haggard Society," first published in the anthology *The Night Awakens*, you'll see why he deserves all these accolades.

# The Haggard Society

*Edward D. Hoch*

The first time Jean Forsyth heard of the Haggard Society, she was at her desk at the radio station, checking the advertising log for the previous night, trying to establish whether they needed to schedule make-goods on any of the thirty-second spots that were supposed to run during the baseball game. As always, a loudspeaker carried the station's current programming to every office in the building, and though it could be turned off if necessary, none of the people in the billing department was ever brave enough to do it.

So Jean heard the brief public service announcement along with everyone else: "Tonight's monthly meeting of the Haggard Society has been rescheduled for tomorrow evening at eight o'clock at Fenley Hall. The guest speaker will be Eugene Forsyth."

Jean turned to the young woman in the next cubicle. "Marge, what's the Haggard Society?"

"Beats me. I never heard of them before. Maybe one of those self-help programs. Why the sudden interest?"

"Their guest speaker is my brother. I haven't seen him in two years. I didn't even know he was back in town."

"Maybe it's just someone else with the same name."

"Maybe," Jean agreed. But there couldn't be that many Eugene Forsyths around these days. Her brother was three years older than she, and all through their growing-up years he'd resisted using "Gene" as a nickname because it would be confused with her name, something that had never occurred to their parents when they were christened. Eugene had gone off to college in Ohio when he was eighteen, then dropped out after a couple of years. He told them if he worked a year and established residence there, he could attend Ohio State at a lower tuition. But he never went back, and his letters home became less frequent.

Two years ago, Jean had gone out to Cleveland where he was living. Their parents had moved to Florida, and it was a summer when she was feeling especially lonesome. She wanted to see Eugene, to establish the old ties that had withered since he left home. He had an apartment in an older part of the city, an area that had once been middle-class but was now on the fringes of poverty. From his window, Jean could see drugs being sold openly on the street corner.

Eugene professed to have a job as a camp counselor, but it was the middle of

July, and he didn't seem to be working at all. She didn't ask him too much about it. After three days, she cut short her visit and returned home. She hadn't seen him since, and her trip to Cleveland didn't even prompt a Christmas card.

Now, if this was really him, he was speaking to something called the Haggard Society. Jean thought about that, wondering if it might be an organization of sickly folk. Might her brother have AIDS? She considered phoning their mother in Florida but decided that would accomplish nothing. First, she should go to the meeting and see for herself if it was really him.

Fenley Hall had been known originally as the Labor Lyceum, a meeting place for union members during the 1930s and the postwar years. The neighborhood had changed during the '60s, and it became less expensive for unions to rent a party house when they needed to hold a rally or take a vote. The Labor Lyceum became simply Fenley Hall, named after some forgotten politician. It was rented now for wedding receptions, political rallies, and various lecture series.

When Jean Forsyth arrived shortly before eight o'clock, the first thing she saw was her brother's picture out front on a sign advertising the event: "The Haggard Society presents a talk by Eugene Forsyth followed by an open discussion. Admission free!" He looked older with glasses and a mustache, but it was clearly Eugene. The hall itself was about half full, with more than a hundred people seated on the folding chairs provided for the occasion. One or two appeared to be street people merely looking for a place to sleep, but most were young or middle-aged and middle-class. Some walked to the front of the hall, where a slender black-haired woman was accepting books that they returned. Jean almost asked a man seated ahead of her what the purpose of the society was but decided she might appear either flirtatious or stupid. Besides, she would know soon enough.

Promptly at eight o'clock, the black-haired woman walked onto the stage and lit a single candle by the rostrum. She was quite slim, and her makeup seemed too severe for the occasion, whatever that might be. "Good evening, ladies and gentlemen, and welcome to the July meeting of the Haggard Society. I am Antonia Grist. As most of you know, we gather here monthly to discuss our mutual interests. We were hoping tonight to hear from one of the newer members of our group, Eugene Forsyth, but he is indisposed. We plan to reschedule his talk very shortly. Instead, may I present my husband and president of the Haggard Society, Martin Grist."

The audience applauded politely, and Jean half rose from her seat, ready to leave. Then she abruptly changed her mind. Since she'd come this far, she might as well learn the nature of the group and possibly something of her brother's involvement.

Grist was slender, like his wife, with a lined middle-aged face and thinning hairline. He crossed to the microphone with a purposeful stride. "Thank you, Antonia," he said in a surprisingly deep voice. "I am hardly a replacement for Mr. Forsyth, whom we hope to have with us at a future meeting, but I'll do the best I can. I apologize in advance to those of you who have already heard my views on this subject."

He paused for a drink of water and then continued. "She Who Must Be Obeyed is H. Rider Haggard's greatest creation, a woman at once beautiful, erotic, headstrong, and selfish, cruel to her enemies yet tender to her lovers. Ever since her first appearance in Haggard's 1886 novel *She*, readers have found her as irresistible as she is deadly. I first came upon Haggard's writings when I stumbled onto a well-thumbed copy of *King Solomon's Mines* in my high school library . . ."

Jean could hardly believe her ears. It was a literary society devoted to the writings of a British author from the last century! And her brother, who'd hardly finished a book in his life, had been scheduled to speak there. She began to think there was some mistake. Surely, this was a different Eugene Forsyth, despite the picture out front.

Martin Grist droned on for some thirty-five minutes, covering H. Rider Haggard's life and works in the most general way. Jean, who'd read a couple of the books during her teens, remembered them as being more exciting than the talk, which Grist finished by recalling the novel's most vivid image. "It is fire," he told his audience, "the Flame of Life that is supposed to bring immortality but instead brings only a withering, terrible death."

There was polite applause as Grist concluded his talk and asked for questions. One man inquired about the possible value of a first edition of *She*. "There was a misprint in the first issue of the first British edition," Grist explained. "Line thirty-eight, page 269, has 'Godness me' instead of 'Goodness me.' That version is valued at around six hundred dollars. The corrected version is worth only half as much."

A woman asked about Haggard's early adult years in Africa and the long-rumored affairs with native women. Grist seemed a bit taken aback by the question. "We don't go into those matters here," he replied. "This is strictly a literary society."

It was the answer rather than the question that caused Jean to turn in her seat and look at the woman, seated three rows behind her. She was in her twenties, brown-haired and wearing pink-rimmed eyeglasses. She'd stood up to ask her question. Unsatisfied with Grist's response, she continued standing and said, "I have one more question."

Martin Grist seemed momentarily taken aback, and his wife suddenly appeared onstage. But before she could reach the microphone, the young woman asked, "Why wasn't Eugene Forsyth allowed to speak tonight?"

"Mr. Forsyth was taken ill," Grist answered.

His wife grabbed the microphone and said quickly, "That concludes our program for this evening. Because of the shortened nature of tonight's meeting, we will try to schedule another program shortly. If you wish to be notified of it, please leave your name and address on the pad by the door. As usual, we also have some hardcover editions of Haggard's novels for those who would like to borrow them till the next meeting."

There was an immediate hum of conversation from the crowd, and Jean sensed that the abrupt ending was most unusual. A dozen or so people came forward to accept the proffered books, doled out by Mrs. Grist from two piles, while the rest of the audience filed out. Jean hurried to the front of the hall and requested a copy of *She*. "Excuse me," she said to Grist's wife. "I'm Eugene Forsyth's sister. I came to hear his talk. Where is he?"

That stopped her momentarily. "I know nothing of your brother," she said. "He was taken ill minutes before his talk and left the hall."

"You must have his address."

Her husband had gone on ahead, but now he returned to grip her arm. "Come, Antonia."

She looked into Jean's eyes and said simply, "I can't help you." Then they were gone.

Jean looked around with a feeling of helplessness. Most of the audience was gone, but the young woman in the pink-rimmed glasses was still there, watching her. Perhaps she had overheard part of the conversation. Jean strode across the hall to join her. "You're the one who asked the question about Eugene," she said. "I think he's my brother."

The woman put a hand to her mouth. "I'm worried about him."

"What's the matter? Where is he? What's happened to him?"

She glanced around nervously. "Look, I can't talk here. Meet me at the coffee bar on the corner in ten minutes. Turn left, and cross the street."

"All right," Jean said. The young woman hurried away without giving her name.

Jean left a moment later, lingering along the dark street to gaze casually into lighted shop windows. She was almost to the corner when she heard a woman's scream and the thump of metal against flesh. Someone yelled, and two or three people nearby turned and ran. Jean reached the corner and saw them standing by a fallen figure on the pavement.

"What happened?" she asked a man.

"Car hit her. I just caught a glimpse of it. He didn't even stop."

"Did anyone get his license number?" somebody else asked, but no one answered.

Jean saw the pink-framed glasses on the street by the body. "Is she—?"

"Someone call nine-one-one, but I don't think it'll do much good."

She didn't wait for the ambulance and police to arrive but hurried away from there. Whatever was happening, whatever it meant, was a threat to her. More especially, it seemed to be a threat to her brother Eugene. Something had happened to him, but she couldn't bring herself to think about that. The young woman in the pink-framed glasses had suspected as much, or she wouldn't have asked that question at the close of the meeting.

Jean hurried home to her apartment, parking the car in its usual place and ducking in the side door. The accident she'd almost witnessed had unnerved her, possibly because it might not have been an accident. A car had hit the woman and then sped off in the night. Did such things happen as a rule? Wasn't it far more likely that an innocent motorist would have stopped and tried to help the victim?

On the eleven o'clock television news, a report of the fatal accident was in the second spot, right after a fire in a pizza parlor across town. Police were seeking the driver of the vehicle, and the victim's name was being withheld pending notification of next of kin. She read the following morning's paper at work over coffee, as was her custom. The dead woman was now identified as Amanda Burke, an unmarried librarian employed at the main library downtown. That might explain her interest in H. Rider Haggard, but it didn't explain her connection with Jean's brother, if there was one.

On her lunch hour, she walked the few blocks across town from the radio station to the main library, dodging fire engines on the way. It was a new four-story building with a glass-topped atrium that flooded the place with subdued sunlight. Amanda Burke had worked in the literature division, and Jean headed there at once. She identified herself to the librarian at the desk and said, "I met Amanda Burke last evening shortly before her terrible accident. I wonder if you could tell me something about her."

The woman stared at Jean as if she were from another planet. "You're a radio reporter, did you say?"

"No, no, I just work at the station. I—it's very important for me to learn what I can about Amanda. I believe she was a friend of my missing brother."

The woman hesitated and then said, "Mark Jessup knew her. He might be able to tell you something."

She rang him on the phone, and after a few moments, a tall, angular young man joined them at the desk. "Hi, I'm Mark Jessup. Can I help you?"

"I wanted to ask you about Amanda Burke."

He led her over to some chairs near the window. "Amanda was a wonderful young woman. We're all still in shock over the accident."

"I almost saw it happen," Jean explained. "I'd just met her, and she wanted to talk further about my brother."

"What's his name?"

"Eugene Forsyth."

He nodded. "She's mentioned someone named Eugene. I kidded her about having a boyfriend, and she didn't deny it."

"I'm afraid something bad has happened to my brother, but I don't know what." She gave a little laugh. "I know it's crazy to be concerned, when I don't even know where he's been for the past two years."

"Have you seen him lately?"

She shook her head. "Just his picture at a meeting of the Haggard Society."

"That's where you met Amanda?" Jessup asked.

Jean nodded. "My brother was supposed to speak there, and I went to hear him. They said he'd been taken ill, but Amanda questioned that from the floor. The people running the meeting, Martin Grist and his wife, abruptly ended it."

"Strange."

"What do you know about the Haggard Society?"

"Not a great deal. Grist's wife brings flyers around to leave at our information desk downstairs whenever they're having a meeting."

"Did Amanda have a family?"

"In New York, I think. They've been notified."

She looked into his face and decided he was a man she could trust. "Could you let me know if anything turns up among her possessions here at the library? Especially anything about my brother? Here, I'll write down my home phone number."

He took it from her with a smile. "I'm sure he'll turn up, but if I hear anything, I'll let you know."

In the days that followed, it was as if the events involving the Haggard Society had never taken place. Jean thought about it constantly, her mind dwelling on the picture of her brother every time she picked up the borrowed copy of *She* and read a few pages. There was no listing for the society in the phone book, and when she dialed a number for the only Martin Grist listed, there was never an answer.

One day she found herself back at the library, and Mark Jessup helped her search through the computer database for some mention of the Haggard group. "Not a thing except the dates of their meetings," Jessup told her, swinging the computer screen around so she could view the listings for herself.

"What about Fenley Hall?" she suggested. "Somebody must own it. They must rent it for their meetings."

"Good idea," he said, smiling at her. "I'll check on it."

But the following day, when she came again on her lunch hour, the news was gloomy. "The owner of Fenley Hall is in New York," Mark told her. "They know nothing about the society except that it's a literary group. They rent the hall for the third Wednesday of every month and pay in advance. Occasionally, someone calls to arrange an additional meeting."

She was discouraged by the news, another dead end, and perhaps that was why he invited her out to dinner that night. The idea cheered her, and it was not until they were starting dessert at a small Italian restaurant near the library that she suddenly blurted out, "This is like a date!"

Mark grinned at her across the table. "Sure. What's wrong with that?"

For the first time, she really looked at him. He wore his sandy hair a bit long, and when he smiled, he had tiny dimples in his cheeks. She guessed him to be in his late twenties, about her own age. He was of medium build, tall but hardly athletic. "How did you happen to become a librarian?" she asked, trying to steer the conversation away from dating.

"I was recruited by Longyear Corporation just out of college. They had quite a corporate library and wanted me to run it. I always liked books, so I let them pay for my librarian's degree. Right after I got it, the company downsized, and I was out on the street. I was a librarian without a library, so I went to work for the city."

"That's where you met Amanda?"

He nodded. "A swell girl. If she was deliberately killed—"

"What about my brother? You said she mentioned his name, but you never met him."

"I think he brought in flyers for patrons to pick up, the way Mrs. Grist does. That's how Amanda met him."

After dinner, Mark walked her the few blocks to her apartment but declined an invitation to come up. Later, when she was alone, she thought about the evening and decided she liked him. When he phoned her at the radio station the following day, she was almost pleased. "How's business at the library today?" she asked.

"Fine. I have some news for you. I thought you'd want to know Mrs. Grist stopped by with another stack of announcements. The Haggard Society is holding a special meeting on Thursday, and your brother is listed as the speaker."

"My God! I have to go!"

"That's not all. I was on the information desk when she came in, and I told her we had new regulations. Anyone leaving material for distribution at the library had to give us the address of the organization. She grumbled a bit, but she gave it to me. They're out on Willow Terrace."

"That's a residential street."

"It must be where she and her husband are living now."

"I'm going there after work," Jean decided.

"Not alone! Remember what happened to Amanda."

"I'll be all right."

"Let me drive you out. They won't try anything with me along."

She had to agree it might be safer. "All right. I get finished here at five."

Promptly at five o'clock, Mark was waiting in the parking lot. "I managed to get out a bit early," he said, passing her the Haggard Society announcement on pink paper.

"You have the Grists' address?" she asked grimly.

"Right here." He showed her the slip of paper.

"Let's go talk to them."

The house was a modern colonial with a wide driveway and two-car garage. Mark Jessup parked in front of it just as Grist himself emerged to check the mailbox. He seemed none too happy to see them, but Mark had already called out his name before he could retreat inside the house. "What is it?" he asked. "I'm a busy man."

"I know Mrs. Grist from the library," Mark quickly explained. "My friend here, Jean Forsyth, wants to ask you about her brother."

Martin Grist peered at her, squinting as if the sun bothered his eyes. "You're Eugene's sister? Weren't you at our last meeting?"

"That's right. I haven't seen him in some time, and I'm anxious about him."

"He'll be speaking again on Thursday night. You can see him then." He turned back toward the door.

"But—"

"I'm sorry. I have no time now."

Jean was not to be put off so easily. She followed him up to the door and might have continued inside, but suddenly the entry was blocked by Mrs. Grist. "Go away!" she commanded. "We don't want you here. My husband and I are very busy."

Mark hurried up to Jean's side. "Come on. We can't learn anything here."

Reluctantly, she allowed herself to be led back to the car. Both the Grists had disappeared into the house and closed the door. "That was a waste of time," she grumbled.

They drove back to the station parking lot where she'd left her car. She felt somehow she should repay him for the time he'd spent going out there with her. "I've got some pasta at home if you'd like to join me for a light supper. It's not much, but—"

"I love all sorts of pasta," he insisted.

"Then come along. Follow me in your car. You know where I live."

It proved to be the most pleasant evening Jean had spent in some time, enough to make her forget the growing concern for her brother. More than that, Mark was a perfect gentleman, ending the evening with a chaste good-night kiss as he left the apartment. She watched at the window as he drove away, against a night sky lit by a distant fire, perhaps in a warehouse across town.

Rather than face the dirty dishes in the morning, Jean tackled them right away, bundling up the rest of the rubbish to drop down the incinerator chute in the hallway. By the time she'd finished and was walking back along the darkened hall to her apartment, she decided she was ready for bed. Glancing at her watch, she saw it was already a few minutes after midnight.

That was when a hand darted out from the shadows and closed over her mouth as another pinned her arms. "Don't scream," a voice whispered in her ear.

She felt a rush of terror and then a soothing recognition.

It was her brother Eugene.

"You've changed," she said when they were back in her apartment with the door safely shut. She'd poured them each a glass of wine. "You're looking a bit like our father these days."

The young man seated opposite her, barely past thirty, wore dark-framed eyeglasses and a neat mustache that combined to make him seem older. "I hope not," he said with a smile. For just an instant, he was the brother she remembered and loved from her youth, and then the vision faded, and he was this stranger who had entered her life.

"Where have you been, Eugene? I haven't heard from you in two years."

"I've been working here and there," he answered with a shrug. "Sometimes it was difficult to keep in touch."

"I never would have found you if I hadn't heard about your lecture. Are you living in town?"

"I'm here for a while," he said, keeping it vague.

"That woman Amanda, the one who was killed by the car—"

"What about her?"

"She seemed worried about you. At the end of Martin Grist's talk, she asked why you hadn't been allowed to speak."

"That was a misunderstanding. I was taken ill at the last minute."

Suddenly, Jean doubted his words. "Did you cancel because you saw me in the audience?"

"No, no. I never looked at the audience. I just felt I couldn't go on."

"When did you develop this sudden interest in Haggard's books? I can't remember you being much of a reader."

"Dad didn't exactly encourage it, did he?"

She realized that his attitude hadn't really changed with the years. "He was a fireman, for God's sake! He was out earning the bread for our table. And it killed him in the end. Do you resent that, too?"

Eugene shrugged. "They gave him a nice funeral."

"Do you ever talk to Mom in Florida?"

"I don't have her address or phone number."

"I can give you both of them."

He sighed. "What am I supposed to say to her after all these years?"

"More than you're saying to me, I hope. Eugene, you come back into my life after two years, and you don't ring my bell or knock on my door. You grab me in the hallway and scare me half to death!"

"I'm sorry about that, sis."

"What about Amanda Burke?" she asked. "You knew her, didn't you?"

"Yes," he admitted. "We'd been dating a bit."

"Living together?"

"Not formally."

"Was she murdered?"

He turned his eyes away. "I don't know what happened out there. Anything's possible."

"Is that why you sneaked into my building, so you wouldn't be seen?"

He took a sip of wine and said, "Look, sis, you've been asking too many questions. You were out to the Grists' house today, and I saw you come up here with that fellow who worked with Amanda."

"You know Mark?"

"I saw him a couple of times at the library." For a moment, his face took on an anxious expression. "This isn't about him, it's about you. I don't want anything to happen to you."

"Like what happened to Amanda Burke?"

"This is serious business. Stay away from the meeting on Thursday."

"Do you really expect that of me? You're my brother, for God's sake! If you're in trouble, I want to help you."

"There's nothing you can do." He finished his wine and stood up.

"Eugene—"

"Good night, sis. Be careful crossing streets."

As he was at the door, she said, "I'll be there Thursday night. There's no keeping me away."

"I suppose not."

"Tell me one thing. What is the Haggard Society?"

He hesitated and then said, "Ask me that question at the meeting on Thursday."

Jean didn't mention her brother's visit when she met Mark Jessup for lunch the following day. She especially didn't want to tell him about Eugene's grabbing her in the hallway of her building. It made him sound a bit weird, and maybe he was. Maybe that's why he'd stayed away from her so long. Mark had the evening shift at the library that day, so she wouldn't be seeing him after work. Following a bit of casual banter, he asked, "Are you going to that meeting tomorrow night?"

"Of course. I have to see Eugene."

"I'm worried about you, Jean, after what happened to Amanda."

"I'll be careful crossing the street," she said with a smile, remembering her brother's warning.

"It's no joking matter. From what you've told me, I think her death is connected with your brother in some manner. You said she asked a question about him before she died, and now you've been asking questions about him. I'd feel better if I came with you tomorrow."

"All right," she agreed readily. She trusted Mark, and she was beginning to wonder about her brother.

"We can get something to eat after I finish work and then walk over to Fenley Hall together."

That night, when she arrived home from the station, Jean was careful to glance up and down her street, paying particular attention to parked cars. But they all seemed to be empty, and no one was lurking in doorways. She went upstairs to put a frozen dinner in the microwave.

Thursday was drizzly with rain, the sort of day Jean would rather have stayed in bed. Her clock radio was always tuned to the station for which she worked, and the first sounds she usually heard in the morning were the jovial banter of their weatherman and the news anchor at seven o'clock. This day was no different. The weather always came first in the morning, because they figured that was what people most wanted to know about at the beginning of the new day. Then there was the traffic report and finally the morning's top story, an overnight fire in a suburban strip mall. Jean slipped out from between the sheets and padded into the bathroom.

While she was brushing her teeth, she suddenly remembered Eugene and the meeting of the Haggard Society that evening. Because she was meeting Mark for dinner first, she wore one of her better dresses, prompting Heather at the desk next to her to speculate, "Heavy date tonight?"

"I'm going to hear my brother speak at a literary society."

Heather groaned. "Sounds dull. What is it, the Jane Austen Society?"

"H. Rider Haggard."

"Does anyone still read the old boy?" she asked.

"Apparently. They loan out copies of his novels at each meeting."

Heather grunted. "What was that one where the woman burned to death at the end?"

"You probably mean *She*, but the flames simply withered her, destroying her immortality. I know because I just read it again."

She gave Jean a pitying look. "Well, enjoy yourself."

When she and Mark arrived at Fenley Hall around a quarter to eight, the place was already half full. Mrs. Grist was up front wearing a long black dress with wide, full sleeves. She was doing some early book collecting, and Jean returned her copy without comment. Some readers were continuing with the story, she noticed, borrowing copies of *Ayesha*, the first sequel to *She*. There was no sign of Eugene anywhere, and she settled down to wait.

This time, it was Martin Grist who strode to the podium promptly at eight o'clock. "Ladies and gentlemen, welcome to this special meeting of the Haggard Society. Those of you who still have books to return or exchange can bring them up to my wife after our program. We're very pleased this evening to offer the delayed talk by Haggard expert Eugene Forsyth. Mr. Forsyth established the first Haggard site on the Internet. He'll tell us about that experience, as well as the joys and sorrows of reading and collecting the works of H. Rider Haggard. Please give a warm greeting to Eugene Forsyth."

For the occasion, Eugene had dressed in an open khaki jacket such as Haggard's hero Alan Quatermain might have worn while searching for King Solomon's mines. "Is that your brother?" Mark whispered beside her.

"That's him." Until this moment, she hadn't really expected him to appear. Now he seemed like a different person as he stood behind the lectern speaking of those century-old books.

". . . Those of you who know Alan Quatermain only from *King Solomon's Mines* and its sequels may be surprised to learn that Haggard brought his two most famous creations together in the 1920 novel entitled *She and Alan*. This book is set shortly before the events recounted in *She*. . . ." As he spoke, her mind flew back to childhood days, to the shock of their father's death. Perhaps he'd changed after that, but how? One of the great mysteries of recent years had been her inability to come to grips with the truth about Eugene. That, she supposed, was why he'd remained so distant from her. ". . . If Haggard was never truly a great novelist, he was certainly a great storyteller, making up for weak characterizations and an occasionally irritating style with authentic backgrounds and an exciting imagination. . . ."

He told about his Haggard site on the Internet, which had brought him in contact with Martin and Antonia Grist. Then he concluded by saying, "I can take questions for fifteen or twenty minutes, if you care to ask any."

A man on the other side of the hall raised his hand and asked, "Is it true that Haggard was knighted in England for his adventure novels?"

Eugene smiled. "If only it were so! He received his knighthood for his studies of British agriculture and land utilization."

Jean raised her hand, but he called on someone else first. "What are you going to ask?" Mark whispered.

"You'll see."

This time, Eugene pointed to her. "The young lady there."

She stood up, making eye contact with him for the first time since he began his talk. "What is the Haggard Society?" she asked in a clear voice.

Eugene leaned both hands on the podium and smiled. It was as if he'd been waiting a long time for this moment. "The Haggard Society is a criminal conspiracy to provide arson for hire, using anonymous agents to carry out contracts arranged by Martin Grist and his wife."

Antonia Grist's hand appeared from the wide sleeve of her dress, holding a small automatic pistol. She raised it toward Eugene, but suddenly two men from the front row were upon her. Someone blew a police whistle, and all at once the Haggard Society was in the hands of its enemies.

It was a long night after that. When Eugene finally joined Jean and Mark at police headquarters, she almost sobbed with relief. "I thought—"

"I'm sorry to have made it all so mysterious, sis," he said as he hugged her. "It was important to get those people, especially after they killed Amanda. She thought they'd done something to me when I didn't speak at the last meeting. When she asked that question, it made Grist's wife nervous. As they were leaving in their car, they saw Amanda crossing the nearly deserted street, and Antonia ran her down. They claim it wasn't premeditated, but everything else they did was."

"You're with the police?" she asked.

Her brother nodded. "More or less. I'm an undercover arson investigator. It all started in Ohio when I took that year off from college. The Haggard Society was operating there at the time, and the police needed someone young to infiltrate them. I established the Haggard Internet site and tried to make myself visible enough so they'd contact me. It didn't work at first, because they were frightened off and moved here. Pretty soon, this city had a marked increase in arson fires, and the police asked me to keep up the Haggard business on the Internet. I finally managed to get a rise out of Grist. I came to see him, and the Ohio police loaned me out to the department here. At first, I still couldn't figure out exactly what was happening, except that a large number of fires were being triggered by identical incendiary devices."

"So the interest in Haggard was all a cover?" Mark asked.

"On their part and mine, too. I met Amanda one day while I was doing Haggard research at the library. I never thought I'd be putting her in any sort of danger. They must have started to suspect me, or they never would have killed her like that."

"But how was the society linked with the arsons?" Jean asked.

"They recruited a number of people willing to take part in the conspiracy. Most of them were arrested tonight. They attended the meetings, and if they were willing to earn money for starting a fire, they came up before or after the program and accepted a book from Mrs. Grist. Strangers got real books, conspirators received hollowed-out volumes containing an incendiary device, the address of the target, the best time for the job, and the necessary payment."

"They were paid before they did the job?"

"Oh, they went through with it, if they ever wanted another job. It was a perfect setup, really. The property owners, or whoever was paying for the arson, arranged for an alibi. They never knew who did it, and the actual arsonist didn't know who'd ordered the job. You know it was successful when you think about the number of fires this city's been having lately."

Jean remembered the television reports and the red skies in the nighttime. She even remembered Mrs. Grist lighting a candle before each meeting. It was all about fire, like the flame that destroyed She Who Must Be Obeyed. "Why did you cancel your talk two weeks ago?"

"I was going to use the talk to spring a trap on the conspirators, as I did tonight, catching as many as possible with the hollowed-out books. At the last minute, some lab work wasn't ready, and we weren't ready to make an arrest. Rather than give the speech, I postponed it a couple of weeks so we could follow through with the original plan. We had a dozen men scattered through the audience, with uniformed officers outside."

He walked outside with them and lingered for a moment with Jean. "Mark seems like a nice guy."

"He is." There was something else she had to ask Eugene. "This undercover work—it was all because of what happened to our father, wasn't it?"

"I suppose so. I didn't much like him, growing up, but he died in a fire. To me, fire has always been the enemy."

"It was the Grists who were the enemy." She gave him a hug. "It's good to have you back."

# Stuart M. Kaminsky

## Scorpion's Kiss

STUART M. KAMINSKY has juggled several series over the course of his long career, and juggled them well. From his dark, intense mysteries starring Porfiry Rostnikov, the Moscow police inspector who always solves the impossible cases assigned to him by his superiors, to his funny-melancholy chase-mysteries with Toby Peters, a Hollywood P.I. in the 1940s, to his wry-solemn Abe Lieberman books about a Jewish detective in modern-day Chicago . . . all his series have one thing in common: the deft touch of a master craftsman. In "Scorpion's Kiss," first published in the German anthology *Aszendent Mord*, he proves once again that he's just as good at shorter lengths.

# Scorpion's Kiss

*Stuart M. Kaminsky*

Ringerman was almost finished shaving when the doorbell rang. No one had rung his bell or come to his door in the three months he had lived here, but he wasn't surprised by this announcement of his first visitor.

He looked in the mirror. He had been through much in forty-six years. His face still looked youthful and smooth and there was no more than a little gray in his hair.

The doorbell rang again.

He had stepped out of the shower only minutes ago. He wanted to be ready for what he had to do this afternoon. Now he stood barefooted, shirtless. He wiped away the soap and washed his face with cold water. Then he dried.

Ringerman had not worked out with weights for more than four months but his body was still firm and he did do a half hour of push-ups and sit-ups every morning and at night.

The doorbell rang.

He examined himself once more, brushed back his hair with his hands and went through the door. He had one more thing to do in his bedroom and living room.

The doorbell rang.

Finished with what he had to do, he moved across the wooden floor to the heavy, metal-reinforced door he had installed when he moved in. One of his conditions, which the landlord of the building accepted because he was having difficulty renting in this rapidly declining district, was that Ringerman could put on a new door and install bars on the windows.

Since the apartment was on the fifth floor, the tired-looking landlord in the crumpled suit, head balding, tinged with sweat, agreed. He had nothing to lose. When Ringerman left, the landlord, whose name was Gentry, would use the bars and reinforced door as inducements for a possible tenant.

The doorbell was ringing again as Ringerman opened it after looking through the peephole. On the wall across from his door in the corridor, Ringerman had installed two mirrors three feet apart at angles. The mirrors were small, unobtrusive and allowed him to see to the end of the corridor both right and left. There was no one outside but a woman looking back at him.

He opened the door.

"Robert Miles Ringerman?" she asked.

She was as tall as he, dark of face as he was, and definitely pretty. Her hair was short and blond. Her dress was dark and fashionably expensive. She looked as if she were no more than thirty-five. He was certain she was older, close to his age. She was holding something in her hand.

"Yes," he said standing in the doorway.

"Here."

She handed the wallet to him.

"You dropped it in the Jewel, near the deli counter."

He took the wallet.

"Thanks," he said.

"You're welcome. You going to count the money, check the credit cards?"

Her smile showed perfect white teeth.

"No, I'm not going to count the money or check the credit cards."

"Then it's all right?" she said.

"Yes, thank you. It's fine."

"Then I'll go."

"Can I offer you? . . ."

"No," she said with a smile. "I . . . no, but thank you."

"Please come in. Just for a minute. Let me get you something to drink or . . ."

She looked at the thin gold watch on her left wrist and puckered her full lips in thought.

"A minute," she said.

He stepped back and she entered. Ringerman closed the door behind her. It clicked shut, metallic, firm. He threw the dead bolt.

She looked at the door, unafraid.

"You're careful," she said.

"Paranoid," he said. "If you're afraid . . ."

He reached over to open the door again.

"No, no."

He nodded and said, "Coffee. Can I offer you coffee?"

"Coffee would be nice. Black."

She smiled nervously, looking around the room.

Ringerman didn't smile.

"I'll have it ready in a minute or two," he said. "Have a seat, please."

She nodded and gave a careful smile.

He went through a door to his right and out of sight.

She looked around the room, glanced at the barred windows. It was late afternoon. The sun was still shining. She looked at the furniture and the polished wood floor. When he moved in, Ringerman had pulled up the dirty carpets and found good oak underneath. He had polished it into respectability. The furniture was simple, consignment, two armchairs, a sofa. They were a rough fabric, gray with a series of black stripes. A small television stood on an oak cabinet against the wall near the door he had gone through. There were three floor lamps and a handmade bookcase about three feet wide and reaching to the ceiling. The shelves were filled with neatly lined-up books.

But what really drew her were the paintings, twenty of them, all in simple black frames, some horizontal, some vertical, all of them the same size, about two feet by two and a half feet.

She heard him moving around the kitchen as she moved to the wall, drawn by the paintings. The paint was thick on the first ones to her left, thick, heavy, dark standing out in three dimensions like irregular mountain ridges. She thought she felt anger in what she saw. As she moved down the line, the paint was laid on less thickly. The colors were brighter. They moved from left to right from abstraction and darkness to sunlight and portraits of men, women, children.

The first six paintings of darkness were of the same room, a room without windows and no people, just furniture. The furniture was simple. There were different angles of the room.

The next set of paintings was less dark but more abstract. The one that held her longest was of a simple balance scale, grayish white against a background of blue. The scale was tipped to the right because the left plate of the scale was empty and the one on the right held a red scorpion, its tail raised, ready to strike.

She moved quickly past the rest of the paintings of people, mostly men, tired men, smiling men, and finally to the portraits of women, four of them, all beautiful, all, she could now see, were of the same woman. The woman's hair was short and blond in one painting, long and dark in another, piled dark and red in the third, and hanging in an almost white ponytail over her right shoulder. She was smiling in all of the pictures. These were followed by another set of four children, each different, ages from perhaps five to twelve.

He was still moving around the kitchen. She moved to the bookcase, pausing to examine the scorpion on the scale for a moment. The painting held her till she forced herself to look away and step toward the high bookcase.

There was no pattern to the books. There was a book on Inuit art, a history of Peru, a thin book on learning to play the banjo, a book on diplomatic relations with India, biographies of movie stars, authors, soldiers, a book on clocks and clock repair, and novels, Mickey Spillane, Tolstoy, Joyce Carol Oates, James Fenimore Cooper, Hans Helmut Kirst, Albert Camus, Roald Dahl, Louis Lamour, Borges, Marjorie Kinnan Rawlings.

She was holding a book on astrological signs in her hand when she sensed him in the kitchen doorway across the room. She turned slowly, book in hand.

"You read all of these?" she asked looking at the rows of books.

He stood with two mugs, identical, blue, in his hands. He was wearing a long-sleeved button-down denim shirt now.

"Yes," he said.

She carefully returned the book to the shelf and moved toward him to take the warm cup. Their fingers touched.

"Your taste is certainly . . ."

"Eclectic," he said. "I read whatever comes to me."

"Have you ever seen *The Manchurian Candidate*?"

"Sinatra? Yes."

"After he's been brainwashed he reads everything, anything, book after book, piled up all over. He meets Janet Leigh and he stops the manic reading."

"I remember," he said. "Saw it a long time ago on television. Guy is brainwashed into killing some friends. Then he kills his girlfriend and her father and then his stepfather and mother."

"You're right. Does he kill any brothers or sisters?"

"He didn't have any," Ringerman said.

"And you?"

"Brothers or sisters?"

"Yes," she said. "Wife, children, mother? father?"

"Mother and father are dead," he said. "I have one sister, a twin. I'm not married."

"Are you close? I mean you and your sister?"

"Very," he said. "You?"

"Yes," she said stepping back to sit on the sofa. She held the mug in both hands. Her long red fingernails formed a jagged pattern. "I have a husband, a fourteen-year-old son, and a brother."

"Are you close?" he asked.

"With my husband and son? Yes. With my brother, not really. I'd say 'no'. These paintings. Yours?"

"Yes," he said, still standing, looking toward the paintings.

"You've done more?"

"Yes."

"Many more?" she asked.

"About eighty more. Some of them went to friends. I've got other ones stored."

Something clattered outside, maybe a truck. They could hear it far away through the closed and barred windows and down five floors. Ringerman and the woman paused.

"That one," she said pointing toward the wall when the clatter had stopped. "The one with the scale and the scorpion. Before you put your shirt on I saw . . ."

"Scars," he said.

"Yes," she answered. "Scars and what looked like that scale tattooed on your left arm, right by the muscle."

"Libra," he said. "I'm a Libra."

"Your only tattoo?"

She sipped her coffee.

"Yes," he said.

"Coincidence," she said.

"What? You're a Libra?"

"No," she said, "Scorpio."

She put her mug down on a *Time* magazine on the table in front of her and kicked off her left shoe, looking up at him as she did it. She turned her foot so he could see the very small tattoo just below her ankle bone.

"It's a scorpion," she said. "I'm a Scorpio."

"Your only tattoo?"

"Yes," she said kicking off her other shoe. "That's a scorpion on the scale in the painting."

"Yes," he said looking at the painting.

"You know a Scorpio?"

"I'm not really into astrology," he said. "That was done a long time ago. A roommate of mine was a Scorpio."

"A roommate. That room in the paintings," she said. "You were in jail, weren't you? It's none of my business, but it looks like a cell."

"Prison," he said. "I was in prison. That's where I got the tattoo. When I first went in. If I flex the muscle, it tips the scale."

"Which way?" she asked with a smile.

"Whichever way I want it to go. You want to leave?"

"No," she said. "No. I haven't finished my coffee. You want to get rid of me?"

He looked directly at her.

"No," he said.

"I've never known an ex-convict," she said. "I got married young, moved to Wilmette with my husband, an accountant. Got a college degree in not much of anything, joined groups. Not a very interesting biography. Your life?"

He still stood looking at her. He stood for a long, slow thirty seconds before he spoke.

"Lived with my mother in Wisconsin," he said. "Small house, right on Lake Michigan, just below the Michigan border. Lots of land. No money. My father died when my sister and I were babies. I wasn't much of a student in school. I wasn't much of a son. I wasn't any kind of a brother. Loner, quiet. Started with small crimes, stealing cars. There was a chop shop in Madison my friend and I used to drive them to. His name was Charlie. He wasn't much of a friend. Spent his money getting drunk . . . and on women. We were kids. Sure you want to hear this?"

"I'm sure," she said curling her legs under her.

Ringerman could see that she had good, long legs.

"I split with Charlie when we were both twenty-five," he said leaning back against the wall, not drinking his coffee. "Went on my own. Safer."

"Your mother?"

"She didn't know. I told her I was driving a truck. She worked in a shop that rented uniforms till her legs gave out. She got disability, read, watched television, mostly game shows. *Wheel of Fortune* was her passion. She actually said that. I just remembered. "*Wheel of Fortune* is my passion." I'd drive days away, as far as Duluth or outside Chicago or Fort Wayne, put something, cheap mask, stocking, over my face, point a gun in the face of a department store manager or a jewelry store owner, take the cash and get out of town. I'd wear gloves, do all the right things and never go near the same town twice. I'd always use a cheap stolen car, a car I stole from somewhere about twenty miles from the place I'd hit. After, I'd drive the car back to where I'd parked my car out of sight, wipe it down. Did all right. Then . . ."

"Then," she said looking up at him intently.

"Got greedy, getting older, almost thirty-five, and getting greedy. I was doing fine, but not big fine. I decided to go for a bank. Not inside where they have the alarms you can't stop and people ready to be heroes. Or maybe someone gets scared and runs even with a shotgun leveled at them. I decided to take the armored car at the end of a pickup day. Come at the guard, stick the shotgun in his face, grab what he had in both hands, cut the truck tires, back the guard up to my stolen car to keep the armored car driver from helping and get away fast. It was all worked out. I checked the bank out for a week eating at a McDonald's across the street, sitting in the parking lot of the mall where the bank was, reading a book. Had it all worked out."

"But?" she asked.

"But," he repeated. "Everything went down perfectly. Truck, tires, guard, gun, bags. A few people were watching, but I didn't care. None of them moved. You never know. When I was backing up with the guard, a little kid, a boy no more than five or six, got away from his mother who was watching. She screamed. The kid ran at me, grabbed my leg and wouldn't let go. I tried to shake him loose, but I had the shotgun at the guard's neck, two heavy bags in the other hand and my eyes on the doors of the armored car. The kid bit me."

"Too much television," she said.

"He wanted to be a superhero," Ringerman said pushing away from the wall and moving to the chair across from her. "I told the guard to get the kid off of me but my time was running out. The whole thing had broken down. The guard made a halfhearted move to get the kid loose, but the kid's mother was running fast at me and only a few yards away."

"And you got caught?"

"Gave up," he said after taking a long drink of coffee. "If I believed in astrology I'd have said the stars and planets were against me. The kid was a hero. They said I would have gotten away with two hundred thousand and change. Instead I wound up with fourteen years and change, the change being three months. They tied me to some of the other smaller jobs I'd done. I did ten years with good behavior. Could have been worse, much worse. More coffee?"

"I don't think so," she said.

"My mother was seventy-nine and ailing," he said. "She died a few months after I went in. Since the job had been done in Illinois, I did my time in Stateville."

"How long have you been out?" she asked.

"Three months, four days," he said. "Three months, four days."

"And now?"

"I'm on parole. I drive a bus up and down Western Avenue, report to a parole officer, mind my business."

Ringerman smiled.

"Am I missing a joke?"

"I don't know. Just kind of funny that I wear a uniform now instead of looking at other people wearing them."

"And you built your own prison cell," she said looking at the barred window and then at the bolted, reinforced door.

"What did you study in college, psychology?"

"A little of lots of things," she said. "Nothing to make a living with. I think I should be going."

She stood, barefoot, and handed the empty mug to Ringerman, who stood to take it. Then she just stood there looking at him. He looked back.

"Have you . . . it's none of my business, but have you been with a woman since you've gotten out?"

"Yes, twice," he said. "Paid for it."

"You're a good-looking man," she said. "I wouldn't think you'd have to pay."

"That's the way I wanted it," he said.

"This is crazy," she said with a laugh, shaking her head, looking up at the ceiling and then back at him. "Would you like, do you want? I mean with me?"

Ringerman clinked the two empty mugs together.

"You mean? . . ."

"Yes," she said. "Before I change my mind. I've never done anything like this before, not even remotely like this. We're strangers. We'll never see each other again. One time. No more. Never again."

He stood looking at her and she looked at him.

"Not your type?" she asked.

"My type covers a lot of possibilities," he said. "You're a very beautiful woman."

"Thanks, but?"

"No 'but'," he said.

"You have protection. I mean . . ."

"I have," he said. "You sure you want this?"

"I'm sure," she said. "I'm very sure."

She moved in front of him, reached for the top button of his denim shirt, paused and then leaned forward to kiss him. They were about the same height. After a few seconds, he put his arms around her and kissed her, feeling her breasts against his chest.

"I feel you," she said pulling her face a few inches back.

He saw her full lips, her white, even teeth. He nodded his head.

"Before I panic, before I change my mind, before . . ." She paused. "The bedroom?"

He turned his head toward the closed door next to the bookcase.

"You want to know my name?" she asked.

"Make one up," he said.

"Emma," she said. "Emma Bovary."

"Emma Bovary," he repeated.

"I'll go in first," she said. "Please. I need a minute, just a half minute. This is crazy . . . I need a minute. Please, wait till I call you."

"I'll wait," he said.

She hurried into the bedroom and began to take off her clothes. She did it carefully, laying each item out on a chair, not taking time to look at the paintings on the bedroom wall. The bed was narrow. A single. She and her husband had a king-size. When she was naked, she looked around for a mirror to examine herself in. There wasn't one. She got into the bed and called, "Ringerman."

He appeared in the doorway, stripped down to his undershorts. She knew he was freshly showered and she knew his body was strong and hard. She searched for the tattoo. He moved to the bed, sat beside her and touched her breast.

"Oh, God," she said sitting up. "I forgot something in my purse. I'll be right back."

Ringerman sat, back straight, looking at one of the ten paintings in the room. It was of his mother's house, now supposed to be his house, at least as he had remembered it. If it were still standing, it was probably smaller, probably in worse shape than he recalled. Probably not quite so close to the massive cold lake of dead, dark black and blue.

He could hear her go into her purse.

When she came back into the room, he was still looking at the painting. He did not turn his head toward her.

"That was our house," he said.

"I know," he heard her voice, soft, not at all confident.

Then he turned his head.

She stood there with a small gun in her hand. She was quite beautiful. He knew how old she was but her body was young, straight. Her breasts were high, not large.

"I'm going to kill you," she said.

He nodded, unsurprised. His lack of surprise or fear made her shake slightly, but she was determined.

"You're not afraid," she said.

"No," he answered.

"I want you to be afraid," she said.

"I'm sorry," he said. "I'm not much of an actor."

"Don't you want to know why I'm going to kill you? You think I'm just some crazy robber?"

"No," he said.

"I've been having you watched for weeks," she said. "Since you got out. I've been having you watched."

"By a little man, neat, not much hair," he said.

"Ye-Yes."

He nodded.

"I wanted to know where you lived, what you did, where you shopped. When I knew, I paid him and ended his services. He told me you were a very careful man."

Ringerman looked at the painting again.

"You learn to be careful in prison," he said. "Still you get scars. If you survive, you have scars."

There was another rumble beyond the room. The windows in here were also barred. The rumble this time was distant thunder. The sun was still shining.

"When you dropped your wallet, I saw my chance. Are you interested in this?"

"Yes," he said.

"Then look at me. Look at me."

There was a distinct edge to her voice now. Ringerman turned his head to look at her.

"Do you know who I am?"

"You're not Emma Bovary anymore," he said.

"I never was."

"No."

"My name is Charlotte Brenner. The name doesn't mean anything to you?"

"No."

"Before I married, it was Charlotte Dianne Glicken, a name given to me by my adoptive parents, and before that for a few days it was Charlotte Ringerman," she said. "I'm your sister, your twin sister. The Scorpio born less than an hour after your sign, Libra, had ended and mine had begun."

She looked at him for a reaction. There was none.

"I was the one they chose to give up for adoption," she went on. "You were the one they chose to keep. The boy. The boy who became an armed robber and went to jail."

"Prison."

"Prison," she repeated.

"So you're going to shoot me because our parents gave you up for adoption and you blame me? You've been holding this inside and now because our parents are dead you hold me responsible?"

"Yes."

"No," he said shaking his head. "It doesn't make sense. Resentment, maybe, but hate? No, unless you're crazy. I've known people in prison and out who killed for crazy reasons. There was a kid named Ramirez two cells down from me, in for drug dealing. Low-level stuff but he got caught and the Dade County attorney wanted numbers. Ramirez was a number. He was twenty-four when he took his sharpened spoon in the yard and started stabbing everyone he could reach who had a wife and kids. He went right by the single guys, young, old, black, Mexicans, me. Just started stabbing. Killed five, hurt the hell out of two more. One of them, Ian Plickwell, lost his voice box. Ramirez went for a guard. Guard was shaking, pissed in his pants. Guards weren't armed in the yard. Ramirez went down and out with two shots from a tower guard."

Ringerman lay back on the bed and flexed the muscle of his left arm. The scale moved first one way then the other. He reached down and ran his finger along a raised pink scar about four inches long, the memory of a prison gang fight he hadn't wanted to be in.

"You're the crazy one," she said, now holding the gun in both hands to try to keep the weapon steady.

"Maybe," he said. "I've thought about it. I mean whether or not I'm crazy. I don't think so, but maybe. I don't think you're crazy either. A year before I got out I had a friend who got out the year before check on Mom's property. A resort had built up around it. Choice lakefront property. Worth close to a million, maybe more. My friend, Alan, poked around. He was good at it. Con man. Knew how to find out things and use them. Alan found out I had a sister. I had him find you. Not hard. When did you find out you had a brother?"

She had stepped forward now, nearly frantic.

"It doesn't matter."

"Does to me," he said looking at his arm. "Does to me. You're going to shoot me dead. Least you could do is answer and be honest."

"I got a letter from a lawyer," she said. "He was trying to find out who owned the land. I don't know how he tracked me down. He said something about adoption records. That's when I found out about you, about me."

"And you told him you were the only heir?"

"Yes."

"You told him your brother was dead and he believed you? Stopped at that?"

"Yes. He wanted to believe me."

"But you had someone find out I was alive and in prison. I wonder why they couldn't find me. The lawyer. I wasn't that hard to find. But I've known men who've been lost in the system for years. Records lost, misplaced. People mistaken for other people. A guy named Pope released from a twenty-year sentence for tearing a woman's arm out and then raping her. He got out in two years. The Pope who was supposed to get out spent five extra years locked up. Of course, the second Pope was simpleminded. I doubt he knew till another con . . ."

"Stop it," she screamed. "Stop it. Stop it."

"You got the money," he said.

"I needed it," she said. "We owed almost three hundred thousand. My husband's business went bankrupt."

"It wasn't yours," he said.

"Half of it should have been mine," she said moving closer, but not close enough so he could come off the bed.

"Half of it should have been yours," he agreed. "You got one million two hundred and fifty thousand. You give me six hundred and twenty-five thousand and we'll be even. Law says it's all mine, but I figure half is yours."

"It's gone," she said, removing one hand from the gun to brush back her short hair, which needed no brushing back. "It's spent. We paid off the debt, bought a new house, invested. There's only a little more than than two hundred thousand in the bank."

Ringerman put his hands behind his head and looked at the barred window. She could see the tattooed scale on his bicep quivering, undecided about which way to tip. She remembered that the painting in the other room had the scorpion on the right side of the scale. She watched, sobbing without hearing herself sob, unable to take her eyes from the scale which moved first one way than the other.

"I have to kill you," she said. "I knew you'd get out, that you'd find out what I'd done, that you'd come for your money, put me in jail, humiliate me. I deserved something."

"Half," he said. "You deserved half. I'll take the two hundred thousand. I'll forget the rest, forgive the rest."

"No," she said. "I can't trust you. I've got a life that . . . I can't trust you."

"Don't pull the trigger, Charlotte," he said still looking out the window.

"I have to. I have to. Oh, God, I have to."

He heard the click of the trigger as she pulled it back. He heard the tripping sound. Nothing happened. She was crying now, crying and firing.

When Ringerman turned his head toward her, she was crying and moaning, the gun at her side, her shoulders sagging. Ringerman got off the bed slowly and went to his closet. He took out a white terrycloth robe and moved toward her. She saw him coming, let out a whimper like a dog expecting a beating, and backed away. He handed her the robe and took the gun from her hand.

"Put it on," he said quietly.

She obeyed.

"You've had your man watching me," he said. "I had my friend Alan watching you. I came to Chicago to serve out my parole so you'd be able to find me. Alan said you'd try to have me killed. I didn't want to believe it, but I've been wrong lots of times. You can see some of the scars. I knew you were watching me at the supermarket. I dropped the wallet so you'd pick it up."

He threw the gun on the bed and turned her around gently guiding her back into the living room.

"I took the bullets out before I came into the bedroom," he said.

She had stopped crying. He sat her down on the sofa, near her shoes. She slumped forward. Her mouth was open. Her face was white and she looked almost her age and his.

"Coffee?" he asked.

"What?"

"You want some coffee?" he asked again.

"You're going to kill me," she said.

"My only sister? No. Took me too long to find you. You want coffee, water, tea?"

"Tea," she said.

"Stay right there," he said gently, "You won't be able to work the locks on the door and you can't get through the windows. Just sit. I'll get the tea."

She sat. Her eyes moved to the paintings on the wall, the dark cell, the portraits and the scale and scorpion. She stared at the scale and scorpion. Somewhere inside she registered the sound of water from the tap in the kitchen, the sound of a humming microwave oven. No time seemed to pass.

Ringerman stepped back in the room, still clad only in his underpants. He handed her the tea and sat next to her.

"What do you . . . what are you going to do?" she asked.

"Two hundred thousand even," he said. "Talk to your husband, draw it out, cash. I meet you. You give it to me and you don't see me again unless you ride the Western Avenue bus, which I don't see much chance of. I owe Alan fifty thousand for his help. The rest goes to . . . I haven't really thought too much about it. The money. You get the money tomorrow. Talk to your husband if you like, but I get it tomorrow or I go to the police. I don't like going to the police. It'll get complicated. You might get by but I don't think so, and a good lawyer'll take the money and your house."

"All right," she said.

"I'd like to see my nephew once, maybe," he said. "You have a photograph?"

She gulped back some tea, put the cup down and reached for her purse, the purse in which she had carried the gun she had planned to use to kill the man who sat next to her gently asking about her son. She took out her wallet and handed it to him. Ringerman opened it and looked at the photographs: Charlotte and her husband, a smiling man with a tanned face and white teeth that looked false; Charlotte alone, a candid of her smiling over her shoulder at the camera in front of a tree; three photographs of a boy, one when he was no more than three, another when he was about seven or eight sitting on a white fence and waving his hand, and the last, a tall boy wearing a suit and tie.

"Looks like me." Ringerman said.

"Yes, a little," she agreed.

He removed all the photographs except the one of Charlotte and her husband and placed them on the table in front of him, side by side.

"I'll keep these," he said.

"Why?"

"The only family I've got. I've got one of our mother and father when they were young. I can get you a copy."

"No, thank you," she said, a touch of her earlier anger returning. "No, no, thank you. They didn't want me. I don't want them."

"Suit yourself," he said. "You can get dressed and go. I'll meet you at the bank at ten in the morning."

"How do you know which bank?" she asked getting up.

"I know."

"Your friend Al?" she asked.

He nodded.

"You can take the gun," he said.

It was her turn to nod.

"Don't think about coming back with new bullets," he said. "I had tape recorders running from the second you came through my front door. I'm putting the tapes in an envelope and mailing them to Al right after you leave. You shoot me and . . . well you understand."

"I won't shoot you," she said. "I'll get your money.'

She moved to the bedroom and dressed while Ringerman sat waiting. When she was ready, he watched her take a mirror from her purse and reapply her makeup.

"I . . . you want to hear something crazy?" she said. "Very crazy?"

"I've heard enough crazy in the last hour to last me the rest of my days," he said.

"Maybe . . . I mean maybe we could be . . . you know, see each other. You could meet my husband, your nephew."

"I'll pick my time to see the boy," he said. "He won't know. I won't bother him. If you hadn't pulled the trigger in the bedroom, I might have considered your offer, but not now. Not now."

He got out of the chair. She watched him walk to the wall and take down the painting of the scorpion on the scale.

"It's yours," he said holding it out to his sister.

She slung her purse over her arm and took the painting.

"The woman in the other paintings," she said turning her head toward them. "Who is she?"

"No one," he said looking at the paintings with her. "I made her up."

Ringerman walked to the front door, threw open the heavy bolt and turned the other locks. He opened the door.

She stepped into the corridor.

"Tomorrow morning at the bank, ten sharp," he said.

"Thank you for the painting. I wish . . ."

He was shaking his head 'no', not sure of what she might wish, but certain that he would have no part in making it come true.

"Emma Bovary," he said softly. She didn't seem to hear.

She walked slowly down the hall, painting held out in front of her. Ringerman closed the door and bolted it. The envelope was ready, addressed and stamped. He got the tapes from the two recorders and dropped them into the envelope.

In a few minutes, he would get dressed, go down and drop the envelope in the mailbox a block away. Now he sat in front of the table in his living room and looked at the photographs he had spread out.

They would go in his wallet along with the old snapshot of his parents and if anyone ever asked him about his family, he would show them his collection.

He looked at the photograph of Charlotte for about a minute and said aloud, "We don't look like either of our parents. Not even a little."

He would take the bars off the windows now. He would remove the bolt lock from his front door. He would not keep himself locked in or keep others locked out.

Ringerman touched the image of his sister, got up and moved to the bedroom to get dressed.

# Bob Mendes

## Noble Causes

BOB MENDES was a chartered accountant until 1989, when he became a full-time writer. His lyrical power and style catapulted him to the front ranks of the European authors. He has twice won the Golden Noose, Belgium's highest mystery award, in 1993 for his novel *Vengeance*, and in 1997 for *The Power of Fire*. His novels have been translated into French, German, Spanish, and Czech. "Noble Causes," which first appeared in the magazine *De Standaard*, showcases all of his strengths in one tightly woven story.

# Noble Causes

*Bob Mendes*

It was Friday afternoon and pouring with rain. Walter Goldwasser was the last person to leave the Diamonds International building at precisely two o'clock. He left through a reinforced side door leading to the executive car park. Eighteen seconds after he pulled the door closed behind him, the second phase of the newly installed security system was automatically activated.

His Mercedes SL 600 was parked ten meters away. With his Delvaux calfskin attaché case in one hand and a man's pocketbook and his car keys in the other, he risked the plunge through the rain. Halfway between the door and his car, he pushed the remote control button to unlock the car doors. No satisfying click, no flashing car lights: the remote wasn't working. Of course, the car was in a puddle so he couldn't even put his attaché case down. In order to free one hand, he put his pocketbook on the roof of the car. With his thumb he slid the flat emergency key out of the remote and put it in the lock.

As he tried to open the car door, he saw Fanny Galinda, the newly appointed secretary, on the sidewalk behind the fence. She was trying to find her way among the puddles, holding a newspaper over her head. She was wearing a white blouse and red pullover, on a black leather miniskirt riding up even farther because of her raised arms, so that he could admire the flawless shape of her thighs and calves in the black leggings even more.

Fanny was a Romanian refugee who had been hired a week ago because of her knowledge of Russian and other Slavic languages, in view of the constant expansion of trade with the East. Only this morning she had told him in a confidential mood that she had no friends in Antwerp. The least he could do in this weather was offer her a ride.

He called her name, but she was too busy trying to keep her hairdo and legs dry. She didn't hear him.

Goldwasser hastily slid behind the wheel and started the engine. Heat sensors and TV cameras recorded the changing situation. Now he had to punch in the code number for the security system on his mobile or radiotelephone within thirty seconds otherwise he would set off the alarm. He made a mistake the first time and had to start over. At last the gate opened. He drove through it. Relieved, he saw Fanny standing thirty meters up the road, under the awning of a jewelry store admiring the window display. He turned on the CD player and took his time choosing an appropriate piece of music.

The steel gate closed automatically behind the car; the security system went into its third and final phase.

When Goldwasser pulled up abreast of Fanny, he slowed down and smiled invitingly. It was all the encouragement she needed. Pleasantly surprised she ran round the car and sank into the empty seat beside him with a contented sigh. "You have just saved my life," she cooed happily.

The mighty twelve-cylinder engine accelerated. Goldwasser was happy to listen to her telling him how lucky she was, working for a company like Diamonds International and people like Mr. Goldwasser. He thought that the weekend ahead might turn out quite nicely. His wife was on holiday in Marbella and he didn't expect her back before Monday.

Not for one moment did he remember his pocketbook and other valuables still on the roof.

Pier was preparing breakfast and Rosa was calculating how much extra income they had earned this month, on an old copy of a regional paper. "Almost three hundred and sixty euros," she said. "If we do all right today, we could deposit two hundred euros for the Damian fund at the end of the week." She made a quick calculation. "They can buy medicine for seven lepers with that." Pier and Rosa both lived on social security and since Pier had moved in with her, they could make ends meet fairly well. They earned extra income by putting advertising pamphlets in mailboxes for Rosa's brother, in the city's difficult districts. Her brother gave her half of what he got from the Belgian Distribution Service, the company with the monopoly on door-to-door advertising. He spent the other half in 't Heilig Huiske café on Klooster Street. The advantage was that Pier and Rosa got their money under the counter. That's why they thought it no more than fair to donate part of these earnings to a charitable institution every month. This way none of it would get stuck to anyone's fingers, and they were left with a clean conscience.

Pier put the bacon and eggs on the Formica kitchen table. He knew she'd already explained to him once but he'd forgotten. "What is a euro again?" he asked.

"The euro replaces the former franc but it's worth forty times as much. And you can use it in almost all European countries."

Pier put a rasher of bacon between two slices of bread and sank his teeth in. "It's going to rain today," he said, chewing. "We'd better put on our raincoats."

Rosa nodded. "There. Now you see how lucky we are. When I was a child we didn't have raincoats. We were so poor that we wore the same clothes year-round. Rain or shine." She spread margarine on her bread and jabbed her fork into the pan. "What areas are we doing today?" she asked.

"The Diamond district and the Jewish district." Pier answered. "From Vesting Street to the Charlottealei. A regional, two DIY leaflets, and three supermarket flyers. Everything is folded and ready. We'll have to come back twice to get more." He knew exactly how many houses and how many mailboxes there were on each street.

They continued eating and Rosa was talking about her childhood again, about how there had been ten of them at her house and how sometimes they had to share two or three eggs among them. "See how lucky we are?" she repeated as she scraped the last bits of egg from the pan with a slice of bread, broke it in two and gave half to Pier.

The downpour had turned into a dull rain that left dirty tracks on the windshield of the SL 600. Fanny wasn't only good at languages but she'd also studied art history for a while and when Goldwasser told her he had a collection of rare Chagall prints at home, she showed great interest. A gift from heaven to Goldwasser. He'd been trying to find an excuse to take her with him to his impressive house on the Kastanjelaan, near Nachtegalen Park. They drove down Quinten Matsijslei, with the city park on their right. At the intersection of Plantin and Moretuslei and the Loosplaats the traffic lights changed to red. Goldwasser took his foot off the accelerator and cleared his throat. "Maybe we could go to my place first . . ."

Fanny pointed through the windshield. "Look at those tramps. They look like a couple from the silent movie era."

At the intersection, a strange-looking couple was pushing across a rickety old pram, laden with door-to-door advertisements. They had prepared themselves for a long period in the rain by wearing two raincoats, a short one on top of a long one. Little hats with sun cream ads printed on them perched on their heads. The pram's wheels were wobbly so their progress was slow. They stopped on the first traffic island and stared at the approaching SL 600. The man was scratching his beard and saying something to the woman.

Goldwasser stopped in front of the pedestrian crossing. The man pointed at the car and said something about getting wet. Fanny giggled. "I think they're asking for a ride. They're getting wet."

The diamond merchant ignored them. He was used to people looking at his car or making remarks about it. The man stepped into the gutter and tapped on the car roof. This was going too far. Goldwasser wanted to grab the radiotelephone to alert the police if necessary, when the light changed to green. He accelerated and sped away. The tramp jumped backward. "Hey, watch it!" he yelled. "There's a pocketbook on your roof."

But Goldwasser didn't hear him. Fanny had turned the music down a bit and cuddled up against him. "Why don't you show me your collection before you drop me off at my place, Mr. Goldwasser? Or don't you like showing me your best stuff?"

His thoughts raced ahead. He glanced quickly in the rearview mirror and saw the tramp standing in the middle of the intersection and picking something off the street. Fools! Risking their lives for a cigarette butt. The man was waving something at the disappearing car, but Goldwasser wasn't the least bit interested. Fanny put a hand on his knee and kept it there.

Rosa and Pier were sitting on the roofed terrace of the park café. A cup of coffee with a filter in front of them and the empty pram beside their table. They had finished their round through the Jewish district first. The pocketbook was lying on the table. They were discussing what to do with it. From where they were sitting, they had a view of the beautiful four-story, turn-of-the-century brick building in which the city-center police station was housed.

"Shall I hand it in over there?" he suggested. "Tuur Dommelaar's daughter works there. Nice girl."

Rosa emptied the small, silver cream jug into her coffee. She never wasted anything. She was thinking. "We'd better see who it belongs to first," she said, as she stirred her coffee "Because of the reward."

"Reward for what?" Pier asked.

"Our finders fee. But that means we'll have to take the pocketbook back to the owner personally. If we hand it in at the police station, he'll get it anyway, with a little delay, but that won't help anyone."

"You mean the police will keep the reward for themselves."

"No, silly, they're not allowed to accept money. We are, because we'll donate it to charity. I'm thinking of Starving Africa. What do you think?"

As always, Pier agreed with her.

He opened the pocketbook and spread the contents out across the table. A wallet, a mobile no bigger than a credit card, a cigarette holder and a gold lighter.

Rosa inspected the wallet. She found an ID card in a plastic cover, belonging to a Walter Goldwasser, born in Vienna on December 25, 1958. A Christmas baby. His address was Kastanjelaan 32A, Antwerp. The picture showed a man with a round, puffy face, heavy eyebrows and a hint of baldness.

She also found a few blank checks belonging to the Diamonds International office in the Hoveniersstraat, five hundred euros in bills, two bank cards, an American Express Gold Card and a couple of tissue paper envelopes. She opened one of them. At the same time the sun broke through the clouds. About ten polished diamonds of the highest quality lay sparkling in the sunlight. She closed the envelope.

"Do you know where the Kastanjelaan is?" she asked.

Pier nodded. "Near the Acacialaan and the Berkenlaan. South of Nachtegalen Park. The most expensive neighborhood in the city. The people who live there are mainly very rich diamond merchants, Israelis, Indians, Pakistanis. Only a hundred and eight mailboxes."

Rosa put the cookie she had been given with her coffee next to Pier's filter. She knew he had a sweet-tooth and he deserved to have the extra one. "We'll go home now, to pick up the rest of the leaflets," she said. "And then I'll finish the round. You ride your bike to the Kastanjelaan to reassure Mr. Goldwasser that we've found his pocketbook. But in order to give him a chance to think about some reward or other you tell him . . ." She leaned forward and lowered her voice.

Pier listened respectfully. Rosa always had these brilliant ideas.

Fanny had put a CD with music by French chansonniers into the CD player. She zapped through the songs until she heard Jane Birkin and Serge Gainsbourg's voices singing *"Je t'aime, moi non plus."* It sounded very suggestive. And when Fanny started tapping the rhythm on Goldwasser's knee with her fingers, he had great difficulty in keeping his mind on his driving.

"Is your wife going to mind you showing me your Chagall collection?" she asked when the song had ended.

"My wife doesn't care for art. When the weather here is like this, she feels better on the Costa del Sol. We own a little pied-à-terre there. She won't be back until next week. If she likes the weather there, that is."

"Good for her."

They reached Kastanjelaan 32A, a large villa in a spacious garden, surrounded by a 2.5-meter-high gate guarded with cameras. He stopped the car in front of the entrance and punched in a code on the radiotelephone. The gate swung open and he drove through. The gate closed behind them and at the same time the garage door opened automatically. Inside, he switched off the engine. He waited until the gate was closed before getting out of the car.

"The security in your home is just as good as at the company," Fanny remarked. "Not just for the Chagall prints, is it?"

"You can't be too careful these days." Goldwasser answered. "Carjacking, burglary, robbery in broad daylight. It happens all the time. You have to be especially careful when you arrive home. The criminals lie in wait and just slip inside with you. But there's no chance of that here. Here no one enters unless I say so. You can sleep soundly." He led her through a kind of lockage into a spacious hall. "I just hope that you have no intention of doing so," he joked.

"Do what, Mr. Goldwasser?"

"Sleep soundly."

"Naughty, naughty." Fanny shook an admonishing finger. "But don't worry, I'm much too curious about seeing your Chagall collection."

They walked down the hall together. He showed her the Chagall prints, the Dali, original drawings and the Picassos. With a certain pride, he also showed her how the camera system and the infrared and volumetric sensors worked. At the first sign of trouble they alerted the central office in town, staffed round-the-clock, on a special wavelength. If necessary, they'll warn the police.

They finished the tour in a living room with luxurious couches and a mahogany bar. Goldwasser flipped a switch beside the door. The curtains closed and the lights went on. Hidden speakers emitted mood music. Fanny walked past the paintings on the wall and studied the signatures. She saw a discreet security control panel. She pointed at it. "Isn't that a bit over the top?" she asked. "It's like a fortress in here. What if you're just having some friends over? How do they get in without upsetting the entire neighborhood?"

"You check the monitor first to see if it's really your friends and then you push the welcome button. Look. The rest is automatic." He rested his hand on her hip as if by accident. "What would you say to a glass of Champagne before we look at the real works of art?"

Fanny giggled. "And I was afraid this was going to be a dull day."

Goldwasser walked to the bar with a spring in his step and fetched a bottle of Dom Perignon from the fridge. He got two glasses. "Here we go," he said cheerfully and popped the cork.

At the same time Fanny pushed the welcome button.

Her tinkling laughter and the bubbling Champagne drowned out the control panel's warning beep.

When a short but heavy downpour broke, Pier bowed his head over the bicycle's handlebar. He peddled as fast as he could. Riding a bicycle in Antwerp was very dangerous, not just because there were hardly any bike paths but also because of the rude disdain with which Antwerp drivers claimed the right of way and were never given a ticket for disregarding all the traffic rules. But he wasn't intimidated. In his boxing days he hadn't been afraid of anything either. He'd had thirty professional bouts, of which he'd won seven by knockout. Too bad he'd taken that nasty fall in the last one. It had meant the end of his career, especially because he sometimes had problems concentrating since then.

For instance, he'd been wondering for a while now why he hadn't taken the pocketbook and its contents with him straight away. He even considered turning back to ask Rosa again but he didn't want her to think he wasn't playing with a full deck. He rode on, trusting that he would remember in time.

He reached the Kastanjelaan in no time at all. He leaned his bike on the gate to number 32A. There was a sticker over the mailbox: No commercial leaflets, please. Typical rich people. He rang the bell and stared at the perforated ornamental plating, which he suspected hid a microphone. Nothing happened. Only the cameras over the gate made a zooming noise. He rang again. Suddenly a red light went on in the door panel. A voice with a strange accent asked: *"Qu'est-ce que vous voulez?"*

Suddenly he remembered. "I came for the reward." he said.

Walter Goldwasser held his glass by the stem and raised it. "Here's to a happy ending."

Fanny stirred the Champagne with her pinky and was admiring the rising bubbles. "I have a better plan," she said. "Let's drink to the jackpot we're about to take with us."

Goldwasser suddenly looked dubious. "What jackpot?"

"I think it's about one million euros." She put her pinky in her mouth and sucked the liquor off. "That's what the contents of the vault at Diamonds International are worth at the moment, isn't it?"

The provocatively pouted lips and the words she spoke somehow didn't match. Goldwasser didn't understand at all. "What are you talking about?" he asked, frowning. "What do the contents of the vault? . . ."

Fanny listened with her head tilted. She smiled. "Maybe you'd better get two more glasses out." She pointed behind her with her thumb. "We're going to have company."

Goldwasser looked over her shoulder at the door. He was shocked to the core. Two men dressed in dark blue jeans and anoraks were standing in the doorway. They looked like Slavs and had dark, mean-looking eyes and they looked as alike as two drops of water. Like a perfect hostess Fanny was doing the honors. "May I introduce these gentlemen to you? The man who is slightly cross-eyed is Kosta. His twin brother, recognizable by the small lump on the left side of his nose, calls himself Stako. Both are specialists at obtaining information, especially from people who would rather remain silent. They refined their interrogation techniques while working for the KGB, but since Russia has introduced a free market economy, they have been offering their services to the highest bidder."

Goldwasser was so angry he could hardly listen. "Get the hell out of here. All three of you!" He made a move towards the control panel but stopped dead in his tracks when Kosta and Stako simultaneously pulled out dangerous-looking guns. He was still more angry than frightened. The fact that he had allowed a floozy like Fanny to trick him like that bothered him most of all. All things considered, she wasn't even attractive. "Who are you?" He snapped. "What do you want from me?"

"Compliments from Igor Fedojev. You know him, don't you?"

"No."

"Oh, come on, Walter. You worked for him once."

"Me? Never! I have heard of him, that's true. I know he controls a large part of the gold and diamond trade in Moscow, but I've never had business dealings with him and I have no intention of doing so now. His reputation is not too good in the West."

"That'll change very quickly now that he's about to take over Diamonds International."

"That's what you think. My company isn't for sale. I'm far too young to quit."

"More to the point, you're too young to die."

Goldwasser now understood he'd better pull in his head. "Now, listen here, Fanny, uh . . . Ms. Galinda. You'd better run along now, while you still can." As he spoke he moved backward, until he reached a pedestal with a painted plaster sculpture of a hamadryas baboon in attack position on it. His hand was only centimeters away from the alarm button built into the pedestal when Kosta without taking aim, pulled the trigger and shot the baboon's head into smithereens. One of the shards drilled straight through Goldwasser's cheek. Tasting blood he was convinced that he'd been hit by the bullet itself. He put a hand against his cheek and backed away. "Okay," he moaned. "If it's money you're after." He gestured at the Floris Jespers painting. "Behind there is a small safe. Some of my wife's jewelry is in there and some cash. At least two hundred thousand euros. Take it."

"Empty it."

Goldwasser hastened to comply. He spread the money and jewels out on a table and looked at them beseechingly. "Is this okay?"

"Take your clothes off." Stako ordered.

Goldwasser swallowed some blood. "What's that?"

Stako leveled his gun at Goldwasser's crotch. "Take them off, now!"

"He means it, Walter. If you don't hurry you'll never be able to show anyone your collection again."

Goldwasser didn't doubt that Stako would carry out his threat. With trembling hands he took off his clothes. When he was down to just his underpants he gave Fanny a beseeching look. "Please, Miss Galinda."

Fanny looked at his potbelly and shrugged her shoulders.

Moments later Goldwasser was sitting on a chair in just his underpants. He'd been bound to the chair hand and foot, with plastic handcuffs.

Kosta and Stako stuck their guns in their belts.

With growing fear Goldwasser saw how they pulled up a low table on which they put all sorts of instruments which they got from the pockets of their anoraks: a straight razor, two detonators, a transmitter, a syringe, and a few ampoules. But what frightened him most was the extension cord with a plug attached, alligator clips, and a voltage regulator.

Fanny pulled up a chair and made herself comfortable. "Shall we start by clearing up a few things?" She didn't wait for an answer, "As we know, your real name isn't Walter Goldwasser, but Salomon Slepak. And you're a Russian Jew. As Slepak you worked as a diamond sampler for the Department of Mineralogy in Siberia until the Soviet Union fell apart. After the wall came down, you went to Moscow to work for Igor Fedojev, an ex-KGB colonel who had started privately exporting Russian industrial diamonds."

Goldwasser shuffled his backside across the chair. "You have mistaken me for someone else, Miss Galinda. I was born in Vienna and lived there until I moved to Antwerp six years ago, to establish Diamonds International. I can prove it."

Fanny picked up the razor and opened it. "As Slepak you became Fedojev's confidant. Six years ago you brought a diamond valued at half a million dollars to London on a business plane owned by Fedojev. Once over the Channel the plane sent out a mayday. It crashed. Some time later the coastguard found the wreck. It was partly submerged, lying on a sandbank. The pilot's body and Slepak's had been washed away. The diamonds had disappeared as well." With a quick movement she put the razor on Goldwasser's hairy upper leg and scraped off some of the hair. A drop of blood welled up from a small nick and trickled down his shin. "I'd better shave all of it off to conduct the electricity better. Too bad for you my hand isn't very steady."

Goldwasser was shivering with fear. He understood that it made no sense to deny it. "The entire diamond trade in Russia was in the hands of the mob, Miss Galinda, headed by Fedojev. He forced me to work for him, but I wanted to lead an honest life, free from blackmail, murder, and manslaughter."

"Nobody leaves Fedojev, except feet first, Slepak. And anyone who crosses him signs his own death warrant. As his former lieutenant you should be aware of this." The razor slid across his chest in the direction of his navel and left fresh, bleeding cuts. Goldwasser's eyes nearly popped out with fear. "I haven't sold Fedojev short. I gave him the case with the diamonds back later, saying that it had just been found."

"You shouldn't have done that, Slepak, it made Fedojev think. Honesty doesn't always pay." The blade swiped downward.

Goldwasser couldn't take any more. "Stop, please." he begged. "Tell me how to make it up to you!"

"You can start by signing a document to the effect that Diamonds International will only trade in goods and money from Fedojev Trading."

That meant that his company would be used to launder Fedojev's money. He didn't care. Anything was better than this. "Okay!" Goldwasser moaned. "Untie me. I'll sign."

"Afterwards we'll drive to the Hovenierstraat together to empty the vault. A million euros is the least you owe Fedojev for your disloyalty."

"That can't be done until Monday morning at nine o'clock," Goldwasser said. "The vault is on a timer. Until then the security in and around that building is so good that a fly couldn't land in the parking lot without alerting the entire diamond district."

"I know," Fanny said. "But I also know that you have a secret code with which you can bypass the timer."

"That's right. But if anyone uses that number to open the vault, an automatic alarm signal is sent to the central office. They then send a patrol car to see what's going on. Even if I tell them over the phone that everything is all right, they will come and see whether I'm acting under duress."

"We've taken that into consideration." Fanny smiled. "As I officially work for you, nobody is going to think it strange that I'm in the building with you. And, to prevent your tongue from slipping when the police come to check, we'll put one of these small detonators in your underpants. It's remote controlled and the explosive power is just big enough to damage certain parts of the body permanently."

Goldwasser turned pale just at the thought. "It won't have to come to that," he said. "The code number is the arithmetical complement of the number on my ID card. It's very simple. For every digit you take the difference with nine, for the last digit, the difference with ten. My ID card is in my wallet."

Fanny stood up. "All right. But remember. We'll also detonate the device if you gave us the wrong number. Where's your wallet?"

"In my pocketbook." Suddenly his eyes opened wide. His breathing was so fast that Fanny thought for a moment he was having a heart attack.

"What is it?" she asked suspiciously.

"God help me. The pocketbook. I left it on the roof of the car . . . drove off . . . forgot. It's gone."

"That's not my problem. All I need is the code."

He shook his head violently. "That's just it. I don't know it by heart. Without my ID card we can't get in."

Fanny brought her face close to his. "You don't think you can trick me that easily, do you?"

The sweat was now pouring off him. "I swear to you, Miss Galinda. We'll have to wait until Monday morning. There's no other way."

Fanny straightened. "That's what you think. Kosta and Stako won't need more than ten minutes to help you refresh your memory." She snapped her fingers. "Go ahead, boys."

Kosta and Stako quickly went into action. Kosta unrolled the wire and plugged it in. Stako poured the Champagne over Goldwasser's head because he would conduct electricity better when wet. With a practiced move he clamped one of the alligator clips to the struggling Goldwasser's right nipple, and the other on the small toe of his left foot. Meanwhile, Kosta had the voltage regulator ready. "We work with a scale from one to ten," he declared with an evil grin. "We'll start you on four to warm you up. Until now we've never had to go higher than seven. Brace yourself."

Goldwasser bent his back in anticipation and screeched with fear.

But before Kosta could flip the switch, the doorbell's little melody rang through the house.

For seconds nobody moved. Then Fanny bent over Goldwasser and pushed the razor under his nose. "Are you expecting anyone?"

Goldwasser hardly dared move his mouth to answer. "No one."

Fanny increased the pressure. "A silent alarm maybe?"

"No way," Goldwasser whispered. "Check the monitor."

Fanny was beside the control panel in two steps and studied the screen. "Blast!" she said. "It's that bum with the two raincoats. What's he doing here?"

The doorbell rang a second time.

In a flash, Goldwasser remembered the tramp standing in the middle of the intersection waving a dark object. He thanked God for his mercy. "Let him in," he sighed, relieved. "The good fellow has found my pocketbook."

Fanny waited for Pier at the door. He recognized her by the red top. In his Antwerp Seefhoek dialect he asked her whether he could speak to Mr. Goldwasser. Fanny tried, first in French and then in English, to make him understand that he had better hand over the pocketbook straight away and then get lost. Because he didn't understand her, she lost patience with him. She pulled him inside, slammed the door shut, and took him upstairs.

Pier looked dumbfounded at the naked man in the chair, whom he recognized as the driver of the Mercedes. Rosa had told him that rich people played strange games sometimes and hurt each other for fun, but this seemed to be a little over the top to him. The woman in the miniskirt spoke to the two men in Russian. He'd boxed against a Russian once and he had sworn at Pier in that incomprehensible language during the whole bout until Pier had silenced him with a direct left. The man in the chair asked him about the pocketbook in Dutch and when he told him that it was still at Rosa's he went berserk. He alternated between begging for the pocketbook and cursing Pier for not bringing it. Pier got so upset that he didn't react immediately when the two men brought his hands together behind his back and cuffed him. Not until they pushed him roughly into a chair did it register that he was in trouble. "Stop that right now!" he protested. "If you think I'm going to play along with your dirty games, you're mistaken."

"It's not a game," Goldwasser moaned, beads of sweat on his forehead. "They are robbing me, those two men are vicious gangsters and if you don't give them my pocketbook and the wallet immediately, I wouldn't give a dime for our lives."

"Rosa has the pocketbook," Pier said with sudden clarity of mind. "She didn't want me carrying all that money across town and we didn't want to hand it in at the police station because of the reward we are going to send to Starving Africa."

"Rest assured, my good man. Give me back my wallet and I will reward you handsomely. Where does Rosa live?"

Pier shook his head. "I'm not supposed to tell anyone." No one was allowed to know they were living together, otherwise they would lose part of their social security.

"What's the moron saying?" Fanny asked impatiently.

Goldwasser translated, and Pier just couldn't understand why his refusal to give Rosa's address caused such a commotion. The angrier they got, the tighter he shut his mouth. They tore clumps of hair from his beard and used his head for a punching bag, but he had learned to take it and even when they threatened to cut off his left ear—the deaf one—but they didn't know that, he didn't even flinch. And just as the gong had saved him from a knockout in many of his fights, so the doorbell saved him now. It rang just as the man with the razor was about to carry out his threat.

Rosa had quit after only thirty mailboxes and returned home. She should have known better than to send Pier out on his own and with an unusual assignment.

He was all right as long as he was in a familiar environment and stuck to his daily routine. Essentially he was a good man with a heart of gold who only wanted to do household chores for her or to take care of her when she had one of her attacks. They complemented each other perfectly. She had the brains, he the brawn.

She got to the house, put the pocketbook and its contents into a backpack, and got on the bike. Pier had a twenty-minute jump on her. The only way to overtake him now was in a taxi. As soon as she'd thought of it, she rejected the possibility. A taxi would cost bits of people, the money could be better spent. Pier would understand. In their mania for noble causes too, they were on the same wavelength.

In the Jan van Rijswijcklaan the wind was behind her so she could increase her tempo a little. She thought about her first meeting with Pier, a good seven years ago.

She'd been on her way home from the post office where she'd collected her monthly social security. Just fifty meters from her house she'd had one of her epileptic fits. She had severe muscle spasms and fell on the sidewalk against the front of her house. All the passersby walked around her and even when three young hoods took the opportunity to grab her handbag, no one intervened. Except Pier. He had seen what happened, collared one of the thieves and shook him. The other two had gone for Pier with knives. With a few well-aimed upper cuts, he knocked them off their feet. He had taken the stolen handbag from them and concerned himself with Rosa. The fit was over but now she had the blinding headache and confused feeling that always followed an attack. Pier had taken her in his arms and carried her up to her apartment on the third floor. He had stayed with her until she was able to take care of herself again. A few days later a pressure group had filed charges against Pier because he was an ex-boxer and had handled the young thieves too roughly. He was penalized and had had to pay their medical expenses. Ever since then, Rosa and Pier had kept each other going. She made sure he didn't get involved in any other incidents because Pier clearly didn't know his own strength. And he took care of her when she had one of her attacks.

She reached the Kastanjelaan and to her relief, saw his bicycle parked against the gate. She didn't hesitate for a moment. She put her thumb on the bell and kept it there.

There was no language barrier between Fanny and Rosa and Fanny was at her best. "He's upstairs," she answered sweetly to Rosa's inquiry after Pier. "Follow me."

Upstairs, Rosa saw what was going on with one glance. Tears came to her eyes when she saw what they had done to Pier. He was lying in the chair barely conscious. One eye was beaten shut and blood was running from his nose and mouth. She walked toward him and tried to help him up. Then she saw that his hands were tied behind his back. "Monsters," she screamed. "Untie him at once!"

"You hand over Slepak's wallet, now!" Fanny barked at her. "Or would you prefer us to cut your pimp to ribbons?"

Rosa was standing in front of Pier to protect him. "I don't have any Slepak's wallet," she said. "Only a Goldwasser's."

Kosta's patience had run out. He took the razor from Stako's hand and pushed Rosa aside. He'd show her they weren't playing games. But before he had a chance to use it, Rosa attacked him. She scratched him with her nails and bloody stripes appeared on both sides of Kosta's nasty face. His reaction was brutal. With his free hand he punched her in the face so hard she fell over backward and stayed down, dazed.

Pier was back in his corner in the ring. He knew he'd lost the bout, but that was all right. Rosa didn't want him to fight back. It would only make things worse, she always said.

The sound of Rosa being hit in the face registered in his numbed brain like the sound of the gong announcing the final round in a title fight. He sprang up. Mustering every ounce of strength his aging body still possessed, he launched his attack. Hands bound behind his back but head forward, he rammed Kosta in the stomach. Kosta never knew what hit him. He was out cold before he hit the floor.

Pier turned to face Stako. He was once again the mighty young street fighter from the Seefhoek district. Stako panicked. Russian bullies aren't used to their victims fighting back. He aimed his gun and pulled the trigger but had forgotten to take the safety off. Before he could correct the mistake, Pier was on top of him. With a head butt he broke Stako's nose, and a merciless knee in the groin finished him off.

Pier now turned his attention to Fanny, who backed away in fear. There was no stopping him now. In the Seefhoek you never gave an enemy a second chance. But before he could attack her, Rosa said: "That's enough, Pier. We're going home. We still have our paper round to finish."

Pier relaxed immediately. He smiled.

"Yes, Rosa." he said.

Pier was putting food onto their plates. The menu was mashed potatoes and cabbage with fried sausage. Rosa sat at the kitchen table, with a pile of banknotes in front of her, which she was counting and then dividing into equal piles. A note was on each pile with the address of the charity it was going to and a simple signature: "Rosa and Pier," no further explanation.

Pier was not completely happy with it though. "Are you sure there'll be no trouble over this?" he asked.

"Very sure." Rosa answered. "Goldwasser was scared to death we were going to involve the police. I think that may have had something to do with that other name of his, Slepak. If you ask me, Goldwasser wasn't completely innocent either."

"But didn't you blackmail him a little to get him to give us the money that was lying there as a reward?"

"Maybe," Rosa said. "But I had a noble cause."

Pier put the plates on the table.

They started eating and stared at the piles of brand-new bills.

"A lot of money," Pier said after a while.

"Yes," Rosa said. "Two hundred thousand euros."

Pier put a piece of sausage in his mouth and chewed. He thought for a while. Then he said: "I wanted to ask you something, Rosa but you mustn't get angry."

She shook her finger at him. "If you're thinking of keeping part of the money, the answer is no."

He looked indignant. "Of course not."

"That's all right, then," she said satisfied. "What did you want to ask me?"

He cut off a piece of sausage. "I was just wondering what happened to all this European money, francs, marks, and guilders we used to have?"

# Gary Phillips

## The Sleeping Detective

GARY PHILLIPS grew up in South Central Los Angeles, and much of his fine, brave work reflects that fact. With such novels as *Bad Night Is Falling* and *Jook*, Phillips takes his readers to places they probably haven't been before. For all the rough turf, however, there's a gentle, even melancholy aspect to his work and a strong, redemptive sense of humor. He is one of those enviable writers who grows stronger with each book. "The Sleeping Detective," published in *The Shamus Game*, features his series detective Ivan Monk doing what he does best.

# The Sleeping Detective

*Gary Phillips*

Monk wasn't quite himself. His arms swung loose at his sides as the heels of his brown wing tips echoed in the long hallway. The corridor stretched underneath Los Angeles International Airport. It was the last old part of the sprawling facility, constructed in 1961 and still connecting the TWA terminal with the outside. Wait, he asked himself, what year is this anyway?

His heels clacked a rhythmic pattern as Monk—no, it was McGill, yeah, his name was McGill, and it was 1967—strode confidently along the tiled passageway. The walls were also covered in tile, done in multicolored linear designs.

McGill cared nothing of style or theories of architecture. He cared nothing that he'd been double-crossed and left for dead in a windblown shack in the Tehatchapis. He projected little about what willful fate had spared him the grave after being shot twice, point-blank. No, the only thing McGill cared about was getting back the $67,000 owed to him. And if he had to do it over the bodies of his best friend Veese and his wife, Jill, so be it.

McGill's tie herked and jerked as his tall, fluid frame pounded toward the end of the corridor. His face was as empty of emotion as the hallway was devoid of other passengers. His close-cropped, prematurely gray hair complemented his crisp Brooks Brothers suit. The muscles in his legs flawlessly propelled him toward the end of the passageway, and closer to his goal.

S'funny, but he didn't ache from the wounds, the holes his dear darling lovingly put in him. This while her boyfriend, Veese, the guy he'd saved once on a job gone wrong, looked on, licking his lips. If McGill was the chatty sort, and he wasn't, he'd be vague on the details of how he got out of that below-freezing cabin at night and got himself healed up.

Suddenly he was no longer in the airport. The echo of his shoes blended in with the sounds of midday traffic. The sun was bright and glinted off the windshield of the new Biscayne he'd stolen as he parked on the rise. He removed the hand shading his eyes. Up there past that wall and shrubs was the door to their love nest. If he could still remember how to smile, he would have.

Now he was moving across the threshold, the .357 Magnum in his right hand. His left hand was in Jill's face, pushing her back and out of his way. She'd been so shocked upon seeing him, all she could do was whisper his name over and over. Not that it mattered to him if she called out Veese's name. He wanted him to step into the cross hairs.

Everything—his motion, her falling, the door banging back—happened in slow motion, defying logic and the laws of gravity. He kicked in the door to the bedroom, aiming and firing in the same heartbeat that thudded in his throat. The recoil of the pistol made his arm twitch. It wasn't his .45, and absently he wondered why he'd traded that for this bruiser. He emptied the gun's six bullets into the unmade, and unattended, bed. He whirled as real time jumped back on track.

"A ghost, an avenging specter." Jill had a hand to her forehead as if she were fevered. "McGill, I—" She couldn't finish, didn't dare to offer an excuse.

He stood there, spent, close on her, and despite himself that familiar feeling flooded over him, if only momentarily. He pointed the gun barrel at the bed. "Where?"

"Gone."

"How long?"

"Months. He stops by every so often. Sends money by courier each month."

"When?"

"Today, later."

He glanced back at the bed. Behind the headboard was a floor-to-ceiling mirror so Veese could watch himself as they made love. On the nightstand was a box. It was open, and on its side read CONTINENTAL DONUTS.

He turned back to her as they sat on the couch. For some reason his eyes were closed and he couldn't get the lids to lift. . . .

"Ivan," she said, kissing his ear. "Ivan, when did you get in, baby?"

He yawned, his arms encircling the pillow. "Ummm," he drooled, "after five." He lay half awake, the details of the dream fleeing his conscious mind.

Jill Kodama got off the bed, rubbing the back of his head. "I didn't hear you get in. You must have driven straight from New Mexico after I talked to you yesterday."

"Wanted to get home, sleep."

She leaned over and kissed his cheek. She smelled like flowers. "Aren't you a bit perfumed up for a judge?"

"You want me to smell like cigars and Old Spice like you do?" She slapped his butt under the blanket. "I'll call you later, see if you want to come downtown for dinner. Let's try Ciudad. The Veese case I'm trying is about wrapped up."

"Is he guilty?"

"That's for a jury to decide, citizen Monk."

He opened an eye, a kraken awakening from the depths. "Is he guilty?"

She was at the door to their bedroom. "I'd say he has blood on his hands. Call you." She left, and he tried to get back to sleep. After some effort, as his body wound down again, the phone rang, and rang, and rang.

"Boss, somebody's been puttin' the nab on our doughnuts."

It was Elrod, the manager of Continental Donuts, the small business he owned in the Crenshaw District. Elrod's bass was an indication of the size of a man who'd give Jesse Ventura palpitations.

"You mean, some cat broke in and took our doughnuts but not cash?" he breathed into the handset. Why wouldn't they let him sleep?

"No," the manager boomed, irritated. "For the last week, glazes, fancy twists, maple and chocolate crullers and jelly-filled have been gettin' filched while the shop's been open. Sixty-seven, I counted. Sixty-seven doughnuts have been taken."

Monk was going to question just how the big man could be so exact in his count, but he didn't want to encourage a long discussion. He coughed, clearing his throat and rolling onto his back. "You have suspects?" He scratched himself.

"Well," Elrod rumbled on the other end, "I hate to say it, but it has to be one of the staff. The inventory has been gettin' filched off the racks as the goods cool in the back."

"You mean the new guy, Moises, right?"

"Aw, see, I don't want to say that for sure." Elrod, like Monk, had been born and raised in the 'hood. Unlike Monk, he was also an ex-con, and was sensitive to the notion he should disparage someone trying to be responsible.

The new guy was a young man from the area where the shop was located. For the last two months since he'd begun, there had been no suggestion of problems with him. If anything, Monk had noticed the young man had looked more harried and thinner the last week or so as he'd been diligently working with Elrod in learning how to perfect his doughnut making.

"It ain't mutant rats, is it?"

Elrod didn't deign to answer such a ridiculous remark.

"Okay, how about you see if you can correlate the times you've noticed doughnuts missing with Moises' shifts. If the times are the same, then I'll have a talk with him. You haven't said anything to him yet, have you?"

"No, you're the private detective. I was kinda figuring you'd want to take over this investigation."

"Carry on, my swarthy cohort."

"I'll let you know."

Monk hung up and lay on his stomach. Of course, now the missing doughnuts intrigued him, and he had to concentrate to stop himself from thinking about them. He put on the radio, the volume low. If nothing else, he'd get filled in on a few current events, and hopefully the drone of voices would be an electronic lullaby to put him back to slumber land.

He switched from FM and National Public Radio to AM and KNX, the all-news station. He settled under the covers once more, tamping down deep whatever angst he might be developing about missing doughnuts. There was a report about a tie-up on the 101 in both directions. Monk smiled inwardly, feeling superior that he didn't have to be out there with those poor bastards today.

Tom Hatten, the entertainment reporter, came on after a commercial. "I'm saddened to report today the passing of Jack Denning, one-time fifties and sixties leading man of such neoclassic tough-guy films as *Prison Cell 99* and *Desperation Alley*. Younger listeners attuned to TV Land reruns will no doubt remember Mr. Denning in later years as the mysterious reclusive millionaire Raxton Gault in the cult seventies TV show *The Midas Memorandum*."

Monk began to drift off, an image of Denning in snap brim hat and trench coat punching out some crook slipping past his eyelids. Hatten went on, his voice seeming to come to him as if though thick glass. "And, of course, the older crowd out there, like yours truly, have fond memories of Jack Denning as half of that sleuthing man-and-wife team the Easterlys, a late fifties, early sixties TV show that . . ."

Alex Easterly was walking Sergei, the silver-tan Afghan hound, through the park. The grass in the park was awfully green, more like carpet than real blades, it occurred to him. There were places where the grass bulged, and it was as if it wasn't somehow lying flat upon the earth. And the park bench where the man waited for him, what of those bushes behind him? Wasn't that glint a jiggling wire leading from the greenery, shaking the limbs as if there was a slight wind?

"Mr. Easterly?" The man looked off, past Easterly's shoulder. He stood and they shook hands.

"Yes, he said, sitting next to him. Sergei rested on his haunches, his head regally erect. What kind of dog didn't pant? "You said over the phone there was a matter you could only talk to me in person about, Mr. Jones. Or should I say, Mr. Masters." He took out a cigarette case inlaid with whitish jade tinged with green. When the hell had he started smoking those? "Care for one?" he said, snapping the case open as if he'd done it a thousand times before.

Nolan Masters declined, showing the flat of his hand. "I guess you're as sharp as they say you are."

"You're not exactly unknown, Mr. Masters." He lit the cigarette and placed it in his mouth. In doing so, his fingers brushed against his chin—where was his goatee? But damned if that cigarette wasn't smooth as he didn't know what. "I peruse a number of publications, Mr. Masters, including *Business Today*."

"Yes, well," the other man began, uncrossing his legs. "It's my business that I need help with, unfortunately. Someone has been stealing some of our, well, let's call them plans, shall we? This is hush-hush stuff we've been keeping under wraps until the right moment to introduce them on the market, you see."

He was about to reply but turned his head at a sound. Was that someone watching them over there, beyond the ring of light from the street lamp next to the bench? "You know I'm retired now, Mr. Masters?" The damned dog hadn't looked their way once. He just stared off in the direction he heard the sound coming from. "Any of this have to do with the space race, Mr. Masters?"

Flustered, he blurted, "How—why did you ask that? My company makes tubes and transistors for radios and TVs."

"As I said"—he dropped the cigarette—"I read various publications." He ground out the butt, a black area appearing in the supposed grass beneath his toe. "Our new President Kennedy in his last speech made it clear we need to be doing more to reach the stars for the U.S.A. This Sputnik satellite the Russians put up caught a lot of us sleeping." He winked at the man, but he wasn't sure why.

"And your company has done work for the State Department before." Finally the dog looked at him, panting. There was the snap of a finger and the dog stopped, then resumed his previous rigid stance.

Masters leaned forward as if a great weight were upon him. He stared at the ground, his hands pressed together. "As per your reputation, Mr. Easterly, I knew you to be the man for the job."

He then stared intently at Easterly. Oddly, he seemed to be suppressing a smile as he did so. "An experienced sleuth, and someone from outside who could easily go undercover in my company to ferret out what may be spies in my organization. Because of the press to get our work done, I've made several new hires. And Mr. Easterly, in under three days—sixty-seven hours, to be precise—I need to deliver a top-secret device to the government. I must know if I've been compromised or not. Of course, you can name your price."

"This is for my country, sir." Yeah, but didn't he have a mortgage he had to help pay? "How will you introduce me?"

"As the new accountant."

"What happened to the previous one?"

"He was murdered."

Kettle drums suddenly boomed, and a guitar and horn joined in. Easterly frowned as the camera came in tight on his face. Things went black, and when the lights came up again, he was dancing with his wife, Jill Easterly, in their posh living room. Now a swinging jazz number played on the stereo unit: a lot of vibes and strings. Ice melted in two tumblers amid amber liquid on the wet bar.

She murmured in his ear. "I thought you said walking Sergei was excitement enough, Alex?"

"I'm just helping out an old friend, dear. Nolan and I were in the army together. And he's asked me to look into how to better the security at his company, that's all." He spun her around. She was a gorgeous woman.

"Uh-huh, how come you've never mentioned him before?" She came back into his arms. She smelled like flowers.

"I don't talk about everybody from my past." They danced real slow, his face near hers. He turned to kiss her.

Her lips were on his. "This wouldn't have anything to do with the fact Masters Electronics is rumored to be aiding our space effort, does it, darling?"

Alex Easterly frowned, pulling his face back from hers. "Yes, well, that's so, only—"

She put her arms around his neck. "Do you think I while away my days reading Jane Austen and getting my hair done? Not that you noticed my new hairstyle." She lightly touched the ends of her coiffured locks.

Alex Easterly suddenly didn't feel like romancing his wife. As if someone were reading his mind, the music abruptly ceased too. But he was so flustered, he didn't notice that it had happened. "It's not that, dear, really. It's simply I didn't want you to be concerned, that's all."

She walked to the bar and shook a cigarette loose from his pack of Lucky Strikes lying there. She shook two loose and lit one, inserting the thing in his mouth. "Don't you think I might want to know if my husband is facing danger, going up against what may be a spy ring?" She'd lit the other cigarette for herself, talking over it as it dangled from her lipsticked mouth.

Jill Easterly then sipped from her drink. "Did you think I'd sit home and weep and be hysterical?"

"No, I know you're an independent woman." He felt as if he was in the dock and she was cross-examining him. This must come from reading that new magazine *Cosmopolitan* and what not.

"And didn't you think I might be of some help in this matter, considering some of my investments have been made in Masters Electronics?"

"I didn't know that," he reluctantly admitted.

"Of course you didn't, honey." She blew smoke at the ceiling and belted down more alcohol. "You seem to believe that because I inherited money, I just trot down to the bank now and then and draw out some and not think about where it comes from."

She sat down and crossed her legs, her foot bobbing up and down. "I admit, when Daddy died, I was befuddled as to the whys and wherefores of his steel and shipping empire. Of course, his law firm was very solicitous, helping the little woman figure out all those complex contracts and business relationships." She fluttered her eyes dramatically.

Alex Easterly sagged against the bar, his hand blindly seeking his own drink. "It's as if I'm seeing you for the first time," he muttered. He drank deeply.

"Sweetie," she said, "I haven't been hiding anything from you. But you work so hard solving cases—the gaunt woman matter as a good example—and trying to keep me from helping you, you haven't noticed that I've focused my inquisitiveness on other things too."

Easterly came over to his wife. "And how was it that Masters came to call on me?"

Jill Easterly inclined her head and puckered her lips. "A word to a friend of a friend. That's how business is done, you know that."

He had to smile. He sank to one knee beside her chair. "I may be getting long in the tooth, but maybe I can learn a few new tricks, huh, partner?"

Her fingers played with the nape of his neck. "Yes, that is so, Mr. Easterly." She kissed him tenderly. Then, "I think your going undercover is a good idea. While that takes place, I'll use my entré from the financial end to investigate some of the board members."

"Any particular suspects?"

"Oh, not exactly the fellow travelers you and Nolan might be thinking about, my love. There's this Shockman on the board who is brilliant in electronics but dreary in human understanding. In fact, during the war years he was a youth member of the German-American Volksbund. And I have it on solid background he's maintained his crypto-fascist ties. The East may be red, but there are plenty of those with brown shirts still in their closets."

"You're full of surprises, Mrs. Easterly."

"Ain't I, though?"

He rose to fill their drinks. In doing so, he happened to catch their reflections in the mirror on the wall. Absently, he noted the gray in his temples that seemed to have increased since breakfast. At the bar he had to look around again, a troubling notion gnawing at him.

"What is it dear?"

"Ah, ruminating on our next steps." In the mirror he blinked at the middle-aged Negro, or was it colored now? He was dressed impeccably: monogrammed sleeves and creased pants. This fellow's arm lifted when Easterly lifted his arm. By George, he was this fellow, and he was mixing drinks for himself and the woman in the chair. And damned if he hadn't paid attention before, but she was Oriental. That was his wife, right?

"Alex, are you okay? You look distracted."

"The case, the enormity of it, I guess." As if he were an automaton, he brought her the drink.

"Umm," she said, taking her glass. She put it on the floor beside the chair and stood. The mellow jazz score started again.

Hearing the signal, Easterly put his drink down too and began dancing with her again. "He said we had sixty-seven hours," he whispered in her ear.

"As I said, love," she began, "the answer might not be what you think. The missing doughnuts may be missing because the thief is looking for something else."

He looked hard at her as a knock sounded at their door. The knock persisted as the fire alarm also went off. Easterly seemed to be moving through hot tar to reach the door. The bell's ringing drowned out all other sound. . . .

"Elrod," Monk slurred into the receiver.

"Oh, you're still sleeping," he asked innocently. "I called over to the office, and Delilah said you'd probably be taking the day off. I guess she said why, but I guess I wasn't listening. This doughnut thing's got me worked up."

"The times that Moises has been at work don't jibe with the times you've counted doughnuts missing, do they?"

Elrod was quiet on the other end for several moments. "Damn, that was pretty good, chief."

"Then it doesn't look like he's our man," Monk amplified. "He doesn't have a key, right?"

"No, and he couldn't have had a duplicate made either."

"Then when the probable has been eliminated, my dear colleague, all we have left is the improbable. Or words to that effect."

"Meaning what?"

"Has to be one of the regulars." He yawned.

"Yeah, I was afraid of that."

Through the walls Monk could hear a power motor starting up. He was doomed. "Who's been around?"

"Let's see," the big man rumbled, "Abe Carson, Peter Worthman, and Karen Oh." He snapped his fingers. "And Willie, Willie Brant stopped by too."

Oh was a defense attorney whom Monk had done some work for. "She's not a regular," he pointed out.

"No, but I remember her 'cause she asked about you. This was yesterday and you were still out of town." He got quiet again. "You just drove back this morning, didn't you?"

"Don't sweat it, El D. You've got me curious about the missing doughnuts too."

"Aw, man, I'm sorry, I should have realized," he apologized.

"The game is afoot. Okay, from your list the one that doesn't fit is Karen, but she only showed up yesterday. Yet the doughnuts were gone before she showed up."

"That's right," the big man said on the other end of the line. "She didn't tell me what she wanted, but said she'd try to get a hold of you today."

"That leaves us with the—hey, what the hell did Willie want? He hardly ever comes by the doughnut shop. I always see him at Kelvin's." Monk was referring to the Abyssinia Barber Shop and Shine Parlor on Broadway in South Central Los Angeles he and Willie, a retired postman, frequented.

Elrod said, "You know, now that we're talking about it, I'm not sure, but I think Willie was here more than once in the last couple of days."

"Just to hang out?" Monk wondered aloud.

"The first time he came in after Abe showed up. They just seemed to be shootin' the shit and all. Willie broke down with his cheap ass and bought a small coffee and then complained about having to pay for a second refill. And," he added ominously, "that was the night I first noticed some chocolate twists had been taken."

Another power motor joined the first—must be gardener day in Silverlake, he glumly concluded. "Why would Willie steal our goodies, Elrod? He can't be selling them on the side."

"He might. Should I question him on the sly, like?"

He didn't have to activate much of his imagination to see how that might go. "Hold off, all right? How could he be sneaking the doughnuts out? If you're not there, Josette or Donnie or Moises is around, right?"

"Unless one of them is in on it with him." Elrod sounded like Jack Webb drawing in his dragnet.

"I tell you what, before you start hauling everybody in and putting them under the hot lights, let's sleep on this, dig? Let me catch a few hours of Z's, then I'll come over and we can formulate a plan."

"A plan is good," the other man concurred.

Monk, despite his interest in the doughnut caper, could feel the lead weights pulling his eyelids down. "We'll figure it out, Elrod, you'll see."

"Okay. Get some rest."

The line went fuzzy, and Monk stretched and scratched himself like a domesticated bear. The mowers were still going, but their engines were like a motorized melody to his overtired body. He lay still, curled up under the covers again. The world went about its business outside the bedroom, and no doubt bad actors were out there doing bad, bad things. And apparently one of them was a reprobate scarfing down his ill-gotten doughnuts. And he was probably washing down Monk's meager profit margins from the shop with cups of exquisite coffee.

The answers, he reminded himself, would have to wait until he joined the waking again. Although, he advised himself, a cup of coffee would be just the right nectar of nourishment right now. And for him, he could drink the stuff day or night and go right to sleep. He got up and traipsed into the kitchen. Kodama had left the coffeemaker on, and he poured a cup. He walked back to the bedroom carrying the morning *L.A. Times*.

Propped against the headboard, he leafed through the paper. In the Calendar section he saw a piece about a new film version being made from Ferguson Cooper's last book, *Platinum Jade*. This novel was the final in the series of sardonic and surreal tales Cooper had written about two South Side Chicago cops called Tombstone Graves and Hammerhead Smith. Cooper, a black writer who would later reinvent himself with "mainstream" novels about race and class in the seventies and early eighties, would subsequently disavow the hard-boiled books as merely ways to meet the rent while living in Kenya and Cuba.

But toward the end of his life, Cooper admitted he'd had a lot of fun writing about Graves and Smith, and thus published *Platinum Jade* in 1983. The book was both running commentary on the coopting of the civil rights movement, women's lib and the Reagan-led backlash against social safety nets, as well as a pretty solid mystery. Monk sipped some coffee and put the paper and cup aside. He stretched and soon his head sagged against the headboard, blissfully sleepy.

"Carson is a carpenter. Honest Abe they call him. Ain't that sweet?" Hammerhead Smith snickered in his basso profundo voice and tossed aside the bio and photo of the man printed on card stock. He pushed the aged bowler back on his large head, crossing his size-seventeen Stacy Adams on the desk where he'd propped them up. His hand, as large as a car engine's fan, held up the next Criminal Investigations Division print off the desk.

"Peter Worthman, longtime labor organizer and general rabble-rouser," Smith's partner, Tombstone Graves, illuminated upon eyeballing the photo. "He's operated in some interesting circles over the years: backroom deal making with pols, getting thousands of workers to strike and stay united on the picket line, and been married to more brainy, good-looking women than I can shake your dick at."

"You the one the chicks go for, man," Smith said, not without a touch of jealousy. "Here I am, all six feet eight big dark burnished inches of me, and with thumbs that are, shall we say, longish." He winked, chomping on the smoldering cigar in his mouth. "But no, you with your Savile Row and St. Laurent suits, alligator and ostrich skin ankle boots . . ."

The dig was coming, but Graves didn't mind, so much now anyway. It was his gruff partner's way of saying he liked him. "But to top it all off"—Smith flapped the file card in the air—"that bullet-scarred mug of yours seems to actually turn the ladies on. They love to feel your scars, Je-sus."

"Back to the case," Graves said, hiding his ego boost. "Worthman can be ruthless, so we can't rule him out."

Smith unlimbered his brogans from the table and straightened in his chair. "He's no pie-card union fat cat sitting on his can collecting his worker's cut from their dues check-offs,"

"Spoken like the son of a city hall clerk that you are," Graves said, adjusting his gold chain-mail cuff link.

"My point, fashion plate, is why in the hell would Worthman—hell, any of these supposed suspects—be involved in the theft of sixty-seven assorted doughnuts? In fact, why the hell did the Captain assign this goofball penny-ante misdemeanor to us anyway?"

"Because there's more to it than what's apparent, Sergeant." The new voice belonged to Captain Mitchum. Phones rang, perps and cops bustled and argued, yet there was a quality to his baritone that cut through the institutional din. He was standing near their desks, his lidded eyes at once giving nothing away yet taking in everything. He shoved his hands in the box-style coat he always favored. His barrel chest strained against the coat's buttons.

"Word just hit the streets that the shop owner where those doughnuts were swiped is offering sixty-seven grand for their return."

"A thousand dollars a doughnut?" Graves asked rhetorically, gazing at his partner.

"It would seem," Mitchum confirmed. "Could be there's more missing than icing and jelly."

"Like something hidden in the doughnuts." Smith shoved the bowler even farther back on his broad forehead.

"And, ah"—Mitchum moved the file cards around on the desk—"don't forget that our good counselor Oh also legally goes by the name Kodama." He tapped the woman's card for emphasis.

Smith was staring at the photos, then suddenly clapped his mammoth hands together. "And she defended Willie Brant."

"How do you know that?" Graves asked.

"I was down at the courthouse last week on that Veese matter. So I'm strolling down the hall, and who do I see all huddled up on the bench outside one of the courtrooms but Oh and Brant? Me and her nod at each other and I keep going. But I recognize Brant from his picture here."

"We got to get out and circulate," Graves said.

"Keep me posted." In that particular gait of his, Mitchum stepped back into his office, whistling a tune.

The next thing Graves knew, he and Smith were tooling along Quincy in their big, beat-to-hell-looking Ford. Underneath the hood, the gas-guzzling 425-cubic-inch V8 performed like a champ. It was nighttime, but Graves couldn't remember what he'd done after the conversation in the squad room. Presumably, he reasoned, he and his partner had been busy working the case.

Smith guided the car along several rain-slick streets. Lit neon announcing everything from cocktail lounges to twenty-four-hour shoe repair was reflected in the shallow puddles. Odd too, Graves reflected, he didn't recall any rain storm either. Must be working too hard. The car pulled to a halt across the street from an office building that must have been constructed during the Warren G. Harding administration. From the upper floor the chiseled eyes of stone gargoyles looked down from their perches.

"She's in," Smith stated, glaring up at a lit window on a particular floor. He blew white cigar smoke into the ebon sky.

As he extricated himself from the passenger seat, Graves said, "Let's see what our beautiful defense attorney has to say about missing doughnuts."

The two men made for an imposing pair as they crossed the narrow thoroughfare, cars of various eras cruising by. The hem of each man's rumpled top coat came to mid-shin, and flailed behind him like dusters worn on the plains a century ago. Smith towered over most civilians, but people tended to forget that Graves, too, was large, six feet two and built like an aging linebacker. Together, the duo reached the vestibule of the building.

"How long we been doing this, partner?" Smith flicked the butt of his cigar into the street. As it bounced, it gave off orange and yellow sparks.

"You thinking of retiring?" Graves replied. He didn't know how long they'd been chasing criminals. It seemed to him this occupation of theirs, if that was the right term, had been a forever job.

"Just making small talk," Smith deflected. His pale grin gave away his true feelings, but he didn't pursue the matter further as the night watchman let them in. Their flat cop feet slapped against the marble floor of the lobby, the sound bouncing everywhere in the cavernous area.

In the elevator, Smith said, "I was wondering, that's all, Tombstone. I've been trying to figure out what it all means, ya know?" He adjusted his bowler, shading his deep-set eyes.

Tombstone Graves said, slumped against the far wall, "Our lives of absurdity, you mean?"

The elevator stopped, and the doors opened on an opulently appointed reception area. "Exactly, my man, exactly."

"Gentlemen," Karen Oh, a.k.a. Jill Kodama, greeted them from a doorway to their right. She was a handsome woman of average height and a build belying her fortysomething years. Her hair was of a moderate length with auburn highlights. She wore a dark blue power suit and a magenta blouse underneath. Her look told them she was formulating several moves ahead of their questions even before they spoke.

"Come on in." She made a gesture with a sheaf of papers she held toward her inner office. They hung their top coats up.

"About these missing doughnuts," she said after everyone was settled. She grinned and lit a thin cigar after offering the two of them one from her humidor. "I can be unequivocal in that my client, Mr. Brant, had nothing whatsoever to do with these items being eaten."

"How do you know they were eaten?" Smith jabbed. His bowler rested on the mound of his knee.

"Why else would a hungry person take food?" She looked from the big man to his partner. Her eyes stayed on him for more than a beat.

"We think there may have been something hidden in one or more of the doughnuts," Graves put in. "We know that the doughnut shop owner has been involved in some questionable activities in the past."

"Allegations, not convictions," she averred.

"And we find it interesting that your other client happened to come to the doughnut shop at or around the time the doughnuts went bye-bye." Smith worked his tongue on the gristle stuck between his teeth from the pastrami sandwiches they'd scarfed down for dinner.

"What's your point, Detective?" Again, she did a sideways glance at Graves. As she did so, she repeatedly touched a ring on her finger. A particular kind of ring Graves had seen before.

"Of course," Tombstone Graves suddenly blurted out.

"What?" Smith glared at him.

"Of course," his partner repeated, snapping his fingers. Kodama, too, was standing, and he felt an irresistible urge to kiss her. So he did. And to his pleasure, she kissed him back. "You're terrific," he told her.

"So are you, big boy. I knew you could do it."

"You two mind telling me what the hell's going on?" Smith now dressed in a chef's apron with streaks of flour on it. He adjusted his chef's hat as he sank doughnut dough into the industrial deep fryer.

The oil crackled and popped to a beat that hummed in Graves's head. He and the attorney slow-danced to Nat King Cole singing "It's Only a Paper Moon." The fish in her aquarium sang the melody. As the great crooner went on, the sound of the doughnuts frying replaced his voice, and Monk woke with a start.

He rubbed a hand over his face and looked at the time: a few minutes past eleven in the morning. Scratching his side, he dialed Elrod. Idly, he considered mentioning to the big man how he looked in a bowler in his dream.

"I know why the doughnuts have been missing," he announced after pleasantries. "And why Moises did it."

"You talked to him?"

"Nope." He didn't explain further. "I'll be there around three, Elrod. See you then." With that he hung up and finally slept soundly.

Moises had been destroying doughnuts because the one material thing in his life, his high school ring, had disappeared. He was sure it had somehow been sucked off his thin finger by the sticky doughnut dough. He was also replacing the doughnuts as he learned how to make them by working with Elrod. His accomplices in this deed were the other employees Josette and Lonnie, whom he'd enlisted, swearing them to silence. He didn't want to seem like a flake to Elrod, his immediate boss.

Moises had figured once he knew how to make the various styles of doughnuts, he could sneak in and replace all of them.

As it turned out, the ring had been left on the shelf above the washbasin in the back. The young man had taken it off one time cleaning up and had forgotten it was there. Subsequently, a can of cleanser had been placed in front of the ring, and it was therefore out of sight.

Monk had recalled on a subconscious level the last time he'd seen Moises, the ring had been absent from his finger. While days before that, he'd observed the kid was very keen on keeping the ring clean. The private eye had seen him use a cloth to rub it after he'd laid down the chocolate on a rack of french crullers.

Karen Oh finally caught up with Monk. She wanted him to look into a matter for a client of hers. It seems this Nolan Masters was plagued by industrial thefts from his high-tech electronics firm.

And Monk soon tired of the regulars at his doughnut shop calling him the sleeping detective.

# Stanley Cohen

## A Night in the Manchester Store

STANLEY COHEN'S novel *Taking Gary Feldman* was perhaps the first original twist on the kidnap story since "The Ransom of Red Chief." And it wasn't a gimmick story, either, but a fully fleshed, poignant look at the troubled lives of a little rich boy and one of his kidnappers. Since then, Cohen has written other novels, most notably *Angel Face*, and continues to write excellent short stories as well. In "A Night in the Manchester Store," first published in the anthology *Murder Among Friends*, what starts as an unusual night out takes a decisive turn for the worse.

# A Night in the Manchester Store

*Stanley Cohen*

It all started one night as we were driving home from La Guardia. Wally said to me, "Whaddaya say we go to The Manchester Store on our way."

Out of the clear blue sky? I said, "Wally, are you serious? Now? What the hell for?"

"I want to check on something."

"Check on what?"

"Something. I might even buy it, tonight."

Or steal it, maybe? "Wally, it's almost nine now. And we're a good fifteen minutes away from there. Don't they close at nine?"

"Nine-thirty."

"Well, that still doesn't leave us much time. Can't it wait? Because I'd really like to get home. We've been away for three days. Is this something important?"

"Yes, it is, or I wouldn't have brought it up. And you'll be glad we stopped. You're going to have a great time. Count on it."

I'll have a *great* time watching him shop? Or I'll just have a *great* time? What the hell did that mean? . . .

What was he up to? Was this going to be another one of his crazy-ass things? . . . It'd been a lot of years since the last one. A long time. Was there going to be some element of risk involved, this time? . . . I decided not to bother responding to his comment about the "great time." Just sweat it out and hope for the best. So we'd be a few minutes later getting home. And he *was* the boss.

And since *he* didn't say anything further about it, we just lapsed into a period of quiet as he continued driving. He loved to drive, usually very fast. He thrived on doing reckless things, taking chances of all kinds, challenging fate, it always seemed to me, and I don't recall his ever failing, or getting caught, at anything he'd decided to do. He simply never got caught . . .

Wally Hunter and I go back a long way. We'd worked together at the national lab in Oak Ridge. He was a brilliant engineer, and he did his expected work, more or less, but he was also a cynic, always spouting sardonic humor about everything around us, knowing, as I guess I also did, that the project to which we were assigned was never going to produce anything. An aircraft engine powered by a nuclear reactor was not a realistic objective and was never going to fly.

And so we joked and laughed a lot about it. And we attended the regularly scheduled progress meetings, listened to all of the optimistic feasibility reports, carried out our assigned tests and experiments, compiled our data, and wrote up our results. It was, as they say, a living.

But that was only part of what made life with Wally Hunter in Oak Ridge so fascinating. I never thought of him as a close friend. He really wasn't that likable. And he wasn't someone I ever saw or even expected to see socially. I never met his wife. I thought of him instead as a very intriguing fellow worker, a sort of "what will this nut come up with next?" kind of guy.

And what made my association with him so unforgettable was that he occasionally sucked me into some wacko thing to do, either on or off the job, but mostly off. A Saturday-morning adventure for two engineers with weekends free. I was always a little nervous about what he'd get me into, but somehow I was drawn to him, and I seldom resisted the opportunity to spend time joining him in one of the far from routine things he came up with, despite some element of risk or danger that was always involved.

Like the cave. He was, among a myriad of other things, a spelunker, someone who loved to explore caves, and he'd found one that contained this unique chamber he said I just had to see, so one Saturday morning we drove to it, parked the car, and with his waterproof flashlight, which he'd probably stolen somewhere, we plunged ahead, into the depths of the cave.

We came to a passage he'd known about, of course, but never mentioned, where we had to crawl through an opening no larger than our bodies, and which had water, very cold water, running through it. But it was summer, and our clothes would dry, so what was the problem? He went first and snaked right through the hole. Then it was my turn.

I started through and got stuck! I couldn't move in either direction! Although he was at first amused by this, I was in a state of panic, and despite having my belly in cold water, I began to sweat profusely. *I absolutely couldn't move!* Stuck in a hole in a cave? Who needed this? What kind of crazy business was this for a nice Jewish boy? Better I should have been in the synagogue, attending services with my wife! . . . Not that we went that often, frankly. But at that terrifying moment, wedged tightly in that hole in solid rock, blocking the passage of the freezing water, which was beginning to deepen under my chest and approach my face, my brain was also alive with poisonous snakes, water moccasins with dripping fangs, and all sorts of other fearful creatures, and with visions of being stuck there for who knew how long, wondering if I'd ever get out alive.

After he'd enjoyed his moment of amusement at my panicked state, he finally began reaching under me, cleaning out the small stones and gravel, and then he grabbed me by the hands, told me to exhale, and pulled me through the opening, leaving my poor chest and belly, and a couple of spots on my back, rubbed raw.

He led me to the subterranean chamber he'd brought me to see, and I guess it was everything he'd promised it would be, but all I could think about at the time was the return trip through that hole to get back to the outside world. And to this day, I still shudder at the thought of having been stuck there.

And then there was the abandoned quarry, just a stone's throw off one of the main roads inside the government-restricted area. On another Saturday morning we went there with his .22 rifle and his .22 target pistol and all the bottles and cans we could scrounge up, and we set up our collection of targets on a rock, down in the quarry, and climbed up to the rim, sat there, and had a little target practice.

It was great fun but it was also very illegal. We were fooling around with firearms inside the government-restricted area and definitely had no business being there. We could have easily found ourselves trying to deal with the rotten local gendarmes, redneck deputy-sheriff types who were allowed access to the roads. Or maybe government security types, connected to the plants. But of course we didn't . . .

. . . And I still wonder where some of those shots might have gone as they ricocheted off that rock. What goes up must come down at virtually the same velocity it went up, it seems to me. Gravity is gravity. What if . . . ? But that was years ago.

And Wally was a master thief. He simply loved to steal. He was constantly taking things home from the lab. Tools, expensive instruments, electronic stuff, whatever . . . At times he could hardly lift his briefcase when he left work and walked through guard stations to the parking lot. And of course he never got caught. The same was true when he visited the various stores in town, satisfying his love for thievery. He never got caught. I was with him one afternoon in a small downtown department store, and when he began lifting things, I didn't quite know what to say or do. All I wanted was to get the hell out of there.

And being as smart as he was, he spent most of his time at the lab, on company time, writing for several technical magazines, articles totally unrelated to his job at the laboratory, and he was getting paid good money for them. And he was never questioned, even when he got our company secretary to type them. Because he never got caught at anything.

He left the job in Oak Ridge several years before I did, and I never expected to see him again. Finally, years later, when my wife and I decided we'd spent enough of our life in that unique community, we, too, decided it was time to leave. I went to an employment clearinghouse at a convention, got several offers, and took one which brought us to Connecticut. Senior engineer at Metals and Materials Technology, Inc.

On my first day on the new job, the personnel director said to me, "I understand you already know the section chief you'll report to."

"I do?"

And in walked Wally Hunter. "Welcome to 'Met'n'Mat Tech,' " he said with a wide grin. And he was wearing a suit and tie. All those years in Oak Ridge he'd worn nothing but jeans or suntans and sport shirts, while most of the other professionals around him, including me, "dressed for business" and wore jackets and neckties to work.

He led me to his spacious office, and after we'd gabbed a few minutes about whether things had changed much in Oak Ridge since he'd left, he advised me that he'd been able to get me a separate office, and with a window, no less. "I refused to let them toss you into the bullpen where most of the fresh meat gets thrown," he said.

Then he added, "And the salary offer they made you? The one that you accepted? I insisted on having it increased a hundred a month. They don't do that too often, around here, once they've gotten an acceptance, but I told them you had special skills that our section needed badly, and I didn't want to take any chances on losing you." Listening to all of that, I was rapidly getting over the shock of running into him again and discovering that he was my new boss. I was even beginning to feel a little pleased about it.

The first year of working with him went by fast. He was still the same old Wally Hunter in most respects, entertaining to be around for his total cynicism, but a little more scary than I remembered. He'd become much more intense in his attitudes toward the world around us, and the fact that it owed us a living. His cynicism could at times become almost incendiary.

Since we were no longer both living in the same small Southern town where there wasn't much to do, the "Saturday-morning adventures" were ancient history. All of that small-town stuff was behind us. We were out of the sticks and into upscale areas in the civilized world, living in widely separated Connecticut towns within commuting distance of the plant.

But, occasionally, when on the road together, we'd do things I considered a little strange. One night in Chicago he insisted we go to a notorious gay bar and have a couple of drinks so we could observe how "that other ten percent" lives. In offhand comments about his own sexuality once, he'd suggested that he was into "limited," or "mild," sadomasochism, from the sado side, of course. I'd still never met his wife.

At the end of my first year at Met'n'Mat Tech, he called me into his office one day for my "annual review," and rather sternly asked me, as an opening remark, how much salary increase I felt I deserved. I was hesitant. "Whatever you can get me, Wally. Seven, eight percent, hopefully something over five. I'd feel very good about ten."

He broke into a broad grin and said, "I got you fifteen."

And that was the end of our so-called annual review, a type of corporate activity he considered to be total bullshit. One of his favorite forms of larceny was getting me, and I suppose others in our small section, as much money from the corporation as he could manage. He signed my expense accounts, and when we traveled together, he'd often say, "You lie and I'll swear to it." It was these attitudes toward company funds which probably explain the strong sense of loyalty we all had to him . . .

. . . When we arrived in front of the Manchester Store, he didn't pull into the store's private lot, but parked instead on the street, around the corner from the store's main entrance. I asked him why.

"I like this better," he said in a familiar tone of voice he used once in a while when he didn't want to be questioned further about something. We got along well, but on the occasions he used this tone, I'd learned to just cool it.

Before getting out of the car, he opened his briefcase and took out his cell phone, dropping it into his jacket pocket.

"Just curious, Wally, what do you need with that?"

"Why not take it with us? The company pays for it. If I decide I want to make a call, I'll have it handy. I don't want to have to use a public phone or go through the store's switchboard."

Knowing Wally, that somehow had a little bit of a scary sound to it. What call would we want to make some fifteen minutes before the store was closing? Why were we even going in there when all the clerks would be anxious to leave? But what the hell? This was Wally.

The Manchester Store was unique. It was large and complete, with huge, tasteful spreads of just about everything a department store could offer. In addition to extensive, major-name-brand departments for clothing and footwear, and of course, perfumes and cosmetics, it also specialized in furniture, appliances, fine jewelry, toys, and sporting goods of every description, including a widely respected department of everything needed for hunting and fishing, and finally, a rather nice restaurant.

But it wasn't its size and completeness that made the Manchester Store unusual. It was its style and character. The Manchester Store was an old, long-established family business, and the Manchester family was dedicated to preserving the store's venerability, maintaining the special charm and ambience of earlier years. Only recently had its management made such radical changes as installing escalators, while still maintaining those ornate old elevators with the filigreed silverish doors. The store had even finally started accepting credit cards other than those issued exclusively for use in the store. The Manchester Store, an ageless example of period architecture among other things, stood alone in all respects, including location. It was a very popular alternative to the fancy New York chain department stores and the gigantic malls where they were usually found.

We walked around the first floor for a minute or two, among other customers still milling around, and then went to the fancy jewelry department, where Wally shopped for an expensive string of cultured pearls, presumably for his wife. A very proper elderly lady waited on us, unlocking the glass case and taking out the one he pointed to, and it became quite clear that he knew more about pearls than she. But this didn't surprise me. He knew more about most things than most people.

As he discussed them with her, I glanced at my watch and saw the store was to be closing in a matter of minutes. The saleslady was growing impatient. He asked her about gift cases and she hurriedly pulled one out of a drawer and showed it to him.

Finally, he told her he'd think about it, and led me away. "Let's go up to the fifth floor, to furniture," he said.

"Wally, the store's closing in a couple of minutes."

"Come on."

"For what?"

"Because I want to go up there. And I'm driving. Come on. We'll have a ball."

A ball, now? What the hell kind of a ball? It was no use. It had been a long time, but once again, I sensed that I was being sucked into one of Wally's things. And this time I had no idea what the hell it was. But this one clearly smelled of trouble, serious trouble, and I was beginning to feel more than a little damp around the collar.

We took the escalator to the top floor, strode toward the furniture and bedding area, and as we arrived there, the earsplitting bell rang for some twenty to thirty seconds, announcing that the store was officially closed. We looked around and there wasn't a salesperson in sight.

"Wally, they're closed. We've got to get the hell out of here, now, or we're going to get in trouble."

"Relax, for Christ's sake. Follow me. There's a men's room right over here, and I've got to go bad."

"Can't we just leave? Can't you wait until you get home?"

"No way. Come on!"

I followed him. We went into the men's room and I stood there while he calmly pulled a paperback from his jacket pocket, went into a stall, hung up his jacket, dropped his pants, and sat down. The paperback was a spy novel he'd been reading on the plane. He consumed paperback spy stuff. But was this the time to be doing it? I looked at my watch. Minutes were ticking away and I was sweating heavily. What the hell was this? The reading hour?

When he finally came out, he asked, "Don't you have to piss or anything?"

I wasn't sure I wasn't too nervous to perform any bodily functions, and I was getting worse by the minute. But I figured it was probably a good idea, because I had no idea what was going to happen next, so I fronted up to a urinal and, with considerable concentration, managed to get it done. "Wally, you want to tell me what the hell's going on, here?"

"I thought we'd spend the night here in the store. Do a little easy unhurried shopping."

Had I heard him right? "Wally, did I hear you right?"

"Relax, man. I've done it before. We'll have a ball."

He was serious! I felt a little dizzy. This topped anything from the Oak Ridge days by a couple of quantum leaps. "Wally, we've got to get the hell out of here! Now! Before they shut the place down and turn on their security setup! If we don't, we're going to be in a lot of trouble."

"Will you relax? I told you, I've done this before."

And he *was* relaxed. Completely. I couldn't believe it. "Well, look," I said, "I want to get on home. I told my wife I'd be home around ten, ten-thirty, and that's what I want to do. I don't want her worrying."

He pulled the cell phone from his jacket pocket and handed it to me. "Here. Give her a call. Tell her we missed our flight and she'll see you tomorrow."

"What if I just leave now and I'll go look for a cab home? You can stay if you want. I can get my suitcase from you tomorrow."

He looked at his watch. "You're too late, pal. The front door's already shut. Nobody's down there. And if you start looking around for somebody to let you out, you're going to run into some rather tedious problems . . . Why don't you relax? We'll have a great time here, tonight. I told you before, this is not my first time doing this."

"What do you do?" I asked, partly as a joke, "sleep in the furniture department?"

"Of course," he answered with his usual cynical grin, "and then be the first person in the coffee shop for a great bacon-and-eggs breakfast in the morning." Then he handed me his phone. "Call your wife and tell her you'll see her tomorrow."

"I don't believe you. I don't think you've ever done this before. You can't walk around this store at night. They must have some kind of fancy electronic security system, motion detectors, closed-circuit TV, some damn thing, that'll pick us up and start ringing bells and have police coming in here like gangbusters. What I do think is, you've gotten me in a lot of trouble, and I have to tell you, Wally, I'm sweating bullets. How in hell are we going to get out of here?"

"Will you take it easy? First of all, they *don't* have any fancy electronic stuff here. In the Manchester Store? Never. It wouldn't be in keeping with the store's image. What they do have is a night watchman who walks the store once an hour, on the hour, and sticks his key in one of those old time clocks on every floor, and then returns to his little office in the basement, where he does have closed-circuit TV monitors covering all the outside doors to the building."

Then Wally looked at his watch. "Keep an eye on that middle aisle of the floor. He'll go walking down it in about five minutes to go to the time clock on the back wall, back there in appliances. We'll stay down, out of sight, but I'll bet he doesn't even look in this direction."

"Well, when he shows up, I hope you don't mind, but I'm going to tell him I accidentally got caught in here after the doors closed, and ask him to let me out. And I'll look for a taxi to take me home."

"A taxi ride from around here to where you live, even if you could get one, which I doubt, could cost you a couple hundred bucks. Have you got that kind of cash with you, hotshot? I doubt it. And taxis don't take credit cards. And even if you do have cash, you can't put *that* on your expense account. Whether I sign it or not, it won't fly."

"I don't care. Wally, I'm a nervous wreck. What I want to do is leave."

"Well, you can't. If you do, he'll call the cops to come and investigate, and the cops'll write it up. And you don't want that. Do you hear what I'm saying? Why can't you just relax and have some fun doing a little *shopping*? It's great not having a bunch of stupid clerks trying to wait on you."

My shirt was getting damper by the minute and clinging to my body. "Wally, I'm scared out of my head being in here like this, now."

"Jesus, I thought you'd love it." He looked at his watch. "It's just about time for the night watchman to come traipsing through. Let's sit here on this sofa and keep our heads down and we can watch for him. You can call home after he's gone."

I did as I was told. I had no idea what else I could do. And I was shaking. What if the guard decided to come walking over to the furniture department to browse? He could. He could be in the market for a sofa. Maybe even the one on which we were slumped, watching for him. "Tell me, gentlemen," he could say, when he came strolling over, "how does this sofa sit? Nice? Comfortable? And try to keep your dirty shoes off of it. I may want this particular one. And by the way, you're under arrest."

And just as Wally had said, we heard elevator doors open, followed by footsteps, and finally, there he was. The area had been darkened from what it had been during sales hours, but from our crouched position, peering over the back of the sofa, we could still see him clearly. Wally had picked us a spot where we could watch through a maze of lamps and stick furniture, and easily go unnoticed. The guard was a big man, middle-aged, burly, tough looking despite a potbelly.

He walked slowly along the middle aisle of the floor, glancing in all directions. He moved out of our view as he reached the back of the floor, in appliances, and, in the quiet, we heard the small mechanical sound of his key being inserted into the time clock. He then walked back toward the elevators, and we kept our heads down until we heard the elevator door open and close.

"That's a different watchman from the one I saw the last time I was here," Wally said.

"It is?"

"This one's a *big 'un*. The last time I was here, the guy was so old and puny he looked like a good strong fart would knock him down."

"Wally, you're not making me feel any better."

"Oh, for Christ's sake, relax. We're not going to be seeing him up close. We'll be seeing him just like we did, then. From a distance. Every hour on the hour. And in between his hourly visits, we'll do a little shopping."

"He thinks he's alone in this store, Wally. What makes you so damn sure he won't do something different?"

"Because that's his job. He's gotta hit every one of those clocks at a specific time, and he spends the rest of his time sitting on his ass in that office in the basement. They provide him with a television to keep himself occupied."

"How do you know that?"

"I've been down there. I talked to the other guy down there one night, just before closing. I started picking his brain and he was more than happy to spill his guts. He told me everything about his job. They provide him with a TV to watch while he's keeping an eye on all those closed-circuit screens monitoring the outside doors."

I was impressed, as usual, with Wally's research. Almost as much as with his nerve. He was a crazy man. But he never got caught at anything. Never.

"Here," he said, "take the phone and call your wife."

I couldn't think of an immediate alternative. I told her the flight had been canceled because of mechanical problems, and I'd be home the following day. Then I returned the phone to him. "I guess you can call *your* wife now."

"She'll see me when she sees me." He stuffed the small phone into his jacket pocket. Then he said, "Let's go do a little shopping. We've got a good forty-five minutes before he gets off his ass again."

"How about if I wait here for you?"

"Are you kidding? Come on. I'm going to help you with your Hanukkah shopping. Make a real hero out of you. Let's go."

I reluctantly got to my feet and went with him. I guess it was out of a long-established habit of letting him talk me into doing things that I was absolutely sure I'd regret doing. This was crazy. This was no cave exploring or deserted-quarry target practice. This was big doings. Felony-sized . . . So what else was new?

We walked to the escalator, which was silent and unmoving, turned off for the night. Then it was cautiously down the steps, tiptoeing just far enough to be able to survey the next floor before continuing down into it. I followed behind him, gradually becoming a little more relaxed. I had to marvel at the fact that he really seemed to know what he was doing. He'd never gotten caught at anything. Despite his almost deranged driving habits, he'd never to my knowledge even gotten so much as a ticket.

We approached the first floor, and after surveying it longer than any of the others, we moved toward the fine jewelry area. Despite the subdued lighting, visibility was still adequate. Wally stepped behind the counter where he'd seen the fancy pearls, and it was at this moment that I knew for sure he'd been planning this. He reached into a pocket and pulled out thin, plastic-film gloves! As he slipped his hands into them, he whispered, "You keep *your* hands in your pockets."

I understood perfectly. He and I had come to Oak Ridge during a time when all new employees were fingerprinted on being hired, and those prints were still on file somewhere. I was more than glad to do that. I had no desire to touch anything. I wanted no part of the whole business. But I did have a question: how was he going to get into those jewelry showcases? They were all locked.

And as quickly as I wondered about the question, I got my answer. He poked his hand into his pocket and came out with a bunch of those little metal things that locksmiths use to open locks.

"I'll bet you were wondering how I'd get into this showcase without breaking any glass," he said with his cynical smile.

"As a matter of fact, yes, I was."

"You think I want to smash the place up? That wouldn't be any fun. I'm not here to rob the store. The challenge is just to do a little shopping without their help. And if they do notice that something's missing, which I doubt will even happen, they'll maybe ask a few questions and then write it off to employee pilferage and get the loss reimbursed by insurance."

"And those lock picks? Where'd you get those?"

"I've got a buddy who's a key-and-lock guy, and he's been checking me out on this particular skill. These little locks on the jewelry showcases? Shit! These are kid stuff."

Another of my firmest beliefs shattered. Locksmiths sell absolute security. It's their stock-in-trade. So it goes. "And The Manchester Store is your favorite store," I said. "Right?"

"A fine old store. Everything is of highest quality." And with a flourish, a smile, a wave of his hands, and a softly whispered musical "ta-da," he opened the display cabinet.

He reached inside and from an extensive array of pearl necklaces, he carefully lifted out a necklace, a double strand of large cultured pearls, priced at thirty-five hundred dollars. It was not the same one he'd looked at before. That had been a single strand, and much cheaper. He avoided disrupting the arrangement of necklaces in the black velvet tray, pushing the others together just enough to eliminate the gap left by the missing one.

He next opened the drawer in a side cabinet, the drawer opened by the saleslady earlier, and took out one of the black gift cases. He laid the necklace into it and smiled. Then he began opening other drawers until he found a small box made to contain the gift case. He put the case into this box and slid it into his jacket pocket. Then he looked at me. "Which one would you like?"

"What?"

"Pick out one. Come on. We haven't got all night."

"Uh, no. Really. No thanks."

"Come on, pal. Don't be a schmuck. We're standing here. Pick something."

"No. Really, Wally. Forget it. It's not necessary. Actually, to tell you the truth, my wife's not much into jewelry." And what a whopper of a lie that was. But I'd made up my mind.

"Shit! For Chrissakes, will you pick out something? This is last call."

"Nothing for me, Wally, but thanks." I backed away a few feet from the showcase. He was hot, but somehow, I just couldn't make myself be a party to it.

"Schmuck!" Wally snapped. "What the hell's the matter with you? That's why I brought you here." He relocked the showcase. "Come on, then. Let's get back upstairs."

We made our way back up the escalator steps to the fifth floor, and furniture. I still couldn't believe what was happening. Did he really think I was going to be able to sleep through the night up there? But it was still early.

We just sat and stared at our watches until eleven o'clock approached, and then we began to anticipate the next pass by the guard. And he appeared, as expected, just as Wally had assured me he would. He walked the length of the floor, this time, hardly looking around, until he entered the appliances area, where he disappeared. He looked even larger this time than I'd remembered from his first pass. We heard the sound of his key in the time clock and then he reappeared as he made his way back to the elevators.

After we heard the elevator door open and close, Wally said, "How about that? Everything right on schedule." There was still a trace of annoyance in his voice, but he was cooling down.

I asked, "And he just sits down there in an office and watches the tube for an hour, and then repeats his rounds?"

"If he doesn't key those clocks on schedule, *he's* in a lot of trouble. Maybe one of these days, during store hours, I'll take you down there and show you around. There's a lot of stuff going on down there." Wally smiled. "If he's there, we'll get him to give us a tour."

"And are we supposed to just go to sleep now, and wait for morning?"

"First, I've got one more little item to shop for, as soon as he's had time to get back to his office, and after that we can think about getting a little rest. Matter of fact, I could use some sleep. It's been a long day. We got up early in Chicago this morning, did a day's work, drove to O'Hare, and flew home. And we were up late last night, running around . . ." Then he looked at me and grinned one of his familiar teasing grins. "How about you, hotshot? Think you'll be able to get to sleep after all this excitement here tonight?"

He'd read my mind. I felt a little weak at the knees every time I remembered just where the hell we were . . . But I had to hand it to him. He was right at home. How many times *had* he done this, before?

Then he said, with his playful smile, fully aware of my state of unrest, "Okay, let's go. One more little purchase and then we can turn in." He chuckled. "I'm a pretty good customer here, you know? My wife loves this store. She spends a fortune here. She'll love getting this gift, knowing it came from the Manchester Store. She doesn't much like all the New York stores they have around, up this way."

"What floor this time?" I asked.

"The fourth."

"What department?"

"Sporting goods."

"Oh? Whaddaya need?"

He glanced briefly in my direction and gave me one of his special, wait-and-see smiles. "Be surprised."

As soon as we entered the sporting-goods area, he walked directly to a large, glass-topped showcase filled with handguns.

"A gun, Wally?"

"I've been thinking that I need a good handgun for protection at home."

"Don't you already have handguns? I remember that day in Oak Ridge when we went out shooting, you had a handgun. I remember shooting it."

"That was a twenty-two target pistol. They're strictly for recreation. You'd have to hit a man right in the eye to stop him with that. If it was on the line, I wouldn't want my life depending on the protection I'd get from that." Before touching anything, he once again slipped on his plastic-film gloves and then brought out his lock picks. It took him a matter of seconds to open the cabinet.

He looked through the glass top of the cabinet at the array of guns inside and the first thing he lifted out was an ornately engraved, oversized revolver with a very long barrel, probably the kind of thing only a collector would think of buying. He broke it open to see that there were no cartridges in it, then snapped it shut again, aimed it at the middle of my chest, and clicked it a couple of times. "How do you like this cannon?" he said. "Shit, I'd be Wyatt Earp with this thing. Hit a guy in the chest with a slug from this baby and you could send him right through a window." He put it back and continued studying the selection.

While I was nervous just being there, I was fascinated with what he was doing. I didn't own a gun of any kind. Not even a rifle. He wanted to be prepared to win a shoot-out involving heavy artillery right in his own home. I couldn't imagine such a thing. But watching him was like watching a movie. "Well?" I said. "See the one you want?"

"You bet your ass." He picked up a heavy-looking handgun that appeared to be like one of the new guns cops carry these days. He played with it for a moment, getting the feel of it, aiming it, examining it . . . He pressed something on it, allowing the clip to drop out of the handle, into his hand. "Nice," he breathed. "Very nice." He was a baby with a new toy. He snapped the clip back into place. Then, without warning, he abruptly tossed it at me. "Here, hold this in your hand and see how you like it."

I clumsily managed to catch it and then took it and played around with it for a moment as he had done. It was kind of a kick. But I couldn't possibly imagine owning something like it. "This is a pretty high-caliber weapon, isn't it, Wally?" What did I know about such things?

"Yes, it is."

"Wouldn't it have a lot of recoil when you shoot it?"

He nodded. "Quite a bit. It'd tear a big-ass hole right through you, too."

"I'll bet it would." I handed it back to him. And then the thought occurred to me that my fingerprints were on it. But if that was the one he kept? . . .

He surveyed a glass-doored cabinet behind the counter that was filled with boxes of cartridges and finally located the match for his new toy. He pulled on the knob and this cabinet was also locked. But that posed no problem. He took out his little picks and had it open in seconds.

He lifted out a box of the shells, dropped the gun's clip, and began loading it.

"You're loading it now?"

"What good's a gun if it's not loaded?"

What? . . . But I decided not to ask any further questions. No point in sounding any more naive to him than I already did. What the hell? He wasn't planning to shoot *me*. At least I didn't think so.

"You want to pick something out for yourself?" he asked. "How about it? While we're standing here with the showcase open. I'll help you pick out something if you want."

"No thanks, but thanks for offering."

"How about just a twenty-two target pistol? You had a great time that day at the quarry back at the Ridge. You did pretty good with it, as I remember."

"I'd shot twenty-twos years ago, Wally, when I was just a kid at camp."

"This is last call, pal."

"I don't want anything, Wally. But as I said, thanks anyway."

"Listen, nobody should be without some kind of protection in their home in today's world."

I didn't respond.

He was amused at my skittishness. I could see it in his eyes. But this was nothing new in our relationship, which had existed over a lot of years, and after the scene an hour earlier in jewelry, I guess he decided it wasn't worth the trouble of knocking himself out trying to do me a favor.

He moved the guns around in the showcase until it no longer looked as if one was missing, and relocked it. Then he locked the cabinet behind the counter. *And then*, he stuck the gun into his belt, just like he was one of the "wiseguys," and stuffed the box of shells into a jacket pocket. "What say we go turn in?"

I was dead asleep when I felt the hand shaking my shoulder. I hadn't expected to be able to sleep, but after we dropped ourselves onto beds in the furniture department, I disappeared into a world of dreamless slumber with remarkable swiftness. It *had* been a long day. Driving from our hotel to our customer's offices in Chicago, making our pitch, taking them to lunch, with drinks, getting to O'Hare, flying to La Guardia, driving to Connecticut, and then, a late evening of "shopping" at the Manchester Store. A full day.

And as I began to wake up, I felt I had slept long and well. I felt rested, but still a little groggy. It was apparently time to get up and get moving. Wally had set the alarm on his fancy-schmancy watch, which he'd probably stolen somewhere, so we could get up at the exact right moment to swing into action, Wally-style. But why was he shaking me so damn hard?

"What in the name of holy hell are you guys doing in here?"

That voice! I looked up at . . . It *wasn't* Wally! . . . He looked like he was nine feet tall, standing over me! It was the night watchman! With his huge shoulders and arms, and his slight paunch, he looked like he weighed three hundred pounds. He had a handlebar mustache and a bulbous nose, and graying, light hair. He gripped my upper arm in his ham hand and he was still shaking me, shaking my entire body, in fact, like I weighed nothing.

I got up on one elbow and looked around. Wally was lying there, apparently still asleep. I sat up, rubbed my eyes, and asked, "What time is it?"

"It's six in the morning," the man answered, "and I want to know what in hell you two are doing here."

As I hesitated, trying to think of something intelligible to say, Wally stirred, rolled over, and sat up, dropping his legs over the side of his bed, and I wondered what *he* was going to do at this point. Would the man see the gun in his belt? I muttered, "Uh, what happened was . . ."

"What happened was . . . ?" the watchman snapped, mocking me. He was hot! And I could see that he was a man who could rightly be called one big, tough, mean, son of a bitch! I glanced at Wally again, and he had buttoned his jacket. The gun was hidden. "Uh, what happened was . . . what happened was . . . uh . . . we were in the men's room, up here on this floor, when the bell sounded, and by the time we got down to the main floor, all the doors were locked, and nobody was around, and we couldn't get out."

"That must have been one hell of a leak you took, because the bell rings at nine-thirty and the main door doesn't get locked and left until at least nine-fifty, nine fifty-five."

"Well, that's what happened." I tried to look as straight at him as I could. "I have this intestinal problem, which—"

"I don't need the bullshit! I don't know what you two are doing here now, but it ain't kosher, and it'll have to be written up. We'll have to get the police in here on this."

"Oh, come on," I pleaded, "it was nothing. Really. I promise you." Then I looked at Wally, and he had the gun out, leveled at the watchman. I suddenly felt dizzy.

Seeing my expression, the watchman turned to Wally, and shock registered on his face. "Where'd you get the gun?"

"Downstairs in your gun department."

"Is it loaded?"

"Of course it's loaded. What good is a gun if it's not loaded?"

The watchman knew he was in trouble. He held out his hand. "Look," he said, "if you'll just give me the gun, I'll let you guys leave outta here, no questions asked, no police, no nothing. We got a deal?"

"Sorry," Wally answered flatly.

"All right, then," the watchman said, "keep the gun. Just put it away. And I'll let you two out, and you can go on about your business, no questions asked, no police, no nothing. We got a deal now?"

"I don't think so."

"Why not?"

"Because we have no way of knowing what you'll do after we walk out the door."

"I'll do whatever you tell me to do."

"But after we leave, how will I know that?"

"Look. You tell me whatever it is you want me to do. I'll go along with whatever you say. Okay?"

"You can say that, but I'll have no control over it."

I was listening to Wally's mind working, his very sharp, analytical mind. And if I'd felt stricken when I first saw that he'd drawn the gun, I was suddenly feeling lightheaded.

The watchman saw it coming, too. "Then what do you want me to do?" he asked.

"Nothing," Wally answered.

I looked at Wally's hand and saw his grip tightening. "*No, Wally! Please God. No!*"

"Sorry," Wally said, to the man, almost in a whisper. "Nothing personal." He fired twice, point-blank, into the man's chest. The shots were deafening and echoed around the huge display floor. The man's body jerked from the impact of the slugs, one of which exited from his back, splashing out a little blood and stuff with it as it shattered the base of a table lamp across the area. The man crumpled to the floor, ending up in a contorted heap, his eyes still open and glazed.

"Wally?" I gasped, looking back and forth between him and the dead man on the floor.

"It was the only way we were going to walk out of here, completely clean," he answered quietly. "Think about it."

His analytical mind.

Wally squatted next to the watchman's body and disconnected the man's loaded key ring from his belt loop. "One of these'll open one of the doors to the street. It's early. There won't be any traffic outside. We'll go to the diner near the plant and spend a couple of hours having some breakfast and then go into the office. If anybody asks, just say we caught the five A.M. out of O'Hare. That works out about right."

Shortly after leaving the vicinity of the store, we drove onto a bridge over a river. There was no traffic at that moment. Wally slowed down, lowered his window, and tossed, first, the man's keys, and then the gun, into the water.

I don't know how I got through that day at the office. I could still hear those two shots ringing in my ears. I felt sure everyone could see in my face that I was beyond just a little disturbed about something, but, bless them, nobody inquired. I avoided spending time with Wally the rest of the day.

I took off a little early and drove home in my own car, which I'd left in the company's parking garage. And of course, I heard all about it on a local radio station as I drove. The watchman had a wife and four children.

I was sure I'd find two men in suits, two of our small town's detective squad, waiting for me when I arrived home, to lead me away in handcuffs. But when I got home, they weren't there. And they didn't come the next day or the day after that, or the day after that. And the thing I wondered was, if they finally did come, would they believe *my* story? Would anybody? Ever?

But the two men haven't come looking for me . . . And it's been quite a while . . .

. . . And neither Wally nor I has ever again mentioned our night at the Manchester Store.

# Dorothy Cannell

## What Mr. McGregor Saw

DOROTHY CANNELL is a transplanted Brit who still manages to spend a good deal of time in England. Her novels about Ellie and Ben Haskell, interior decorator and writer-chef respectively, have been fashionable and popular since they first began appearing in 1984. She added to her laurels recently by winning an Agatha Award for her short story "The Family Jewels." The story chosen for this year's volume, "What Mr. McGregor Saw," first published in the anthology *Malice Domestic 9,* shows her at her witty and wry best.

# What Mr. McGregor Saw

*Dorothy Cannell*

Y ou can talk all you want but I don't believe in them," said the young woman with hazel eyes. She was wearing a brown felt hat and standing in a drizzling rain outside the Sea View Guesthouse.

"Believe in what, Eileen?" Her companion, a fair-haired man in his late twenties, more pleasant faced than good looking, retrieved the suitcase deposited by the taxi driver on the curb and drew her gently toward the white-washed steps leading up to the door framed by Victorian stained-glass panels.

"In miracles. That's what you've been hoping for, isn't it? You think that by my coming back here and facing up to what happened I'll be struck by some burst of heavenly light and find peace at last."

"Well, I wouldn't go that far." A lace curtain at the bay window parted an inch and a blurred face peered out at them. "All I'm hoping, darling, is that reliving the memories of the week you spent here will help you to open up to me. Darling, I'm your husband. We've been married six whole months and you've never given me more than the bare bones of the story. Stuff I could have read about in the papers."

"I know, I know." Eileen stumbled on the last step and caught hold of his arm. "You've been so wonderful, Andrew; most men would have run a mile before hooking up with a girl with my history. I can't blame your parents for being scared stiff and threatening to ship you off to India. After all, who's to say that one day I might not go completely off my rocker and . . ." Before she could finish the door opened and they were ushered into a small vestibule with a mosaic tile floor and an aspidistra standing guard in the corner.

"Come on in," a friendly voice welcomed them. "I'm Vera Gardener and I was watching for you. Didn't want you standing out in the wet a moment longer than necessary. A nasty night if ever there was one, but like as not it'll be sunshine tomorrow. We get some lovely days even this late in September." Talking away, Mrs. Gardener, who had run the Sea View for the past couple of years, led them into a narrow hall with a mustard and red carpet runner that accentuated rather than relieved the gloom of brown varnish. But fortunately Mrs. Gardner did much to offset the impression that any of the other guesthouses on Neptune's Walk might have been preferable to this one. She was a soft-spoken grey-haired body who was seldom out of sorts and always greeted arrivals with a warm smile, but as she urged this young couple to hang their damp coats on the hall tree on the staircase wall, she felt just the least bit unsettled. For a moment she couldn't think why. And then it came to her. The girl's face was vaguely, disturbingly familiar. A photo in one of the newspapers—not recently, more like years ago. Those haunted eyes. Mrs. Gardener remembered thinking she'd never forget the look of them, and in a child's face too, poor Godforsaken little mite! Even so, it took another few seconds for the whole thing to fit into place. Such a horrible tragedy! But here she was, back at the scene of the crime, so speak.

"Mr. and Mrs. Shelby. I've got that right, have I?" she said, hoping her voice wouldn't let on that her thoughts were all of a whirl. "If you'd like to sign the guest book, I'll take you up to your room. Unless, that is, you'd like a nice cup of tea first?"

"No." Eileen picked up the pencil from the hall table and fiddled with it before handing it to Andrew. "We'd rather get settled in right away. It is the room directly at the top of the stairs, isn't it? I particularly asked for it when I telephoned. The person I spoke to said it still had the wallpaper with the red roses on it. I—" again she looked at Andrew, "my husband and I—we were quite definite about wanting that one."

"Oh, absolutely," he agreed quickly. "The person who suggested we stay here made a point of saying we should ask for that room. Wonderful view of the sea and all that."

"Well, I must say it is a nice comfortable room. One of the nicest we've got," Mrs. Gardener responded a little too brightly. "A lot of people ask for it specially." This wasn't strictly true. In fact, she'd had guests who made a point of asking not to be put in that room because of its particular associations. To hide her confusion she bent to pick up the suitcase that the young gentleman had put down on signing the guest book, and upon his insisting that he carry it himself, she led the way up the stairs to cross a narrow landing and opened the door directly opposite.

"Well, here we are!" Switching on the light. "Plenty of red roses on the wallpaper." She was not usually a woman to flutter, but after needlessly twitching the rose sateen eiderdown into shape she adjusted a toiletry dish on the dressing table. Meanwhile, the young lady stood two feet away from her like an additional bedpost, so that when she spoke it seemed natural that she should do so in a small wooden voice.

"Our friends, the people who suggested we come to the Sea View, said the place was run by a Mr. and Mrs. Rossiter. But of course it was years ago that they stayed here. At least ten, isn't that what they said, Andrew?" Without giving him a chance to answer, Eileen hurried on. "So would you have been here at that time?"

"No, dear." Mrs. Gardener stooped to turn on the gas fire. "When my husband died and our only son went out to Australia, wanting to make a life for himself as was only right, I fancied I'd like to move to the seaside and bought this place from the Rossiters. That was two years ago last month."

"You must find it rather a lot at times." Andrew had wandered over to the window and now returned to stand by the bed.

"Not too bad really. We've only got the six bedrooms. And I like to keep busy. Keeps me from growing old. Besides, I've got my niece and her husband working for me. And when the season slows down as it does around about this time of year I get to rest up a bit." Mrs. Gardener, very conscious of sounding too bright and breezy, stood with her hand on the doorknob. "Now I'd better leave you nice people to unpack, hadn't I? The bathroom's two doors down to your left. We serve dinner between seven and eight. But don't you worry. We can always heat you up something if you don't want to rush. We often do that for guests coming in late after a day's sightseeing or a hike across the downs. Like the clergyman we've got staying with us now. He always comes this same week. Every September, has done for years, long before I took over from the Rossiters. Set in his ways, I suppose, but as gentle and kind an old gentleman as you could ever wish to meet."

"That's nice," said Eileen.

Feeling more and more at a loss, Mrs. Gardener mentioned that the bathroom was two doors down to the left. Then she retreated downstairs to the kitchen to restore herself with a cup of tea and explain the situation to her niece, who was mashing potatoes in a big saucepan on the draining board.

"You mean this Mrs. Shelby is the little girl—the daughter in the VanCleeve murder?" Nellie, a big, red-faced woman, wasn't often put off her stroke, but she did pause before adding a dollop of butter and a splash of milk to the potatoes. "How old would she have been at the time, Auntie Vera, do you think?"

"From what I remember," Mrs. Gardener sat at the scrubbed wood table brooding over her cup, "about twelve or thirteen. The worst time, if there could be one, to go through something like that. You know how emotional girls can be at that age, worse than boys some of them, even in normal circumstances."

"I suppose," said Nellie. "But what's she like now?"

"Not bad looking, pretty you might say, in a pale, sad-eyed sort of way. But nothing like the beauty her mother was said to be."

"That's not what I was asking." Nellie returned to mashing the potatoes. "I meant does she look loony? It would only be expected, wouldn't it? Coming from homicidal stock. And it certainly doesn't sound normal to me her wanting to spend even one night in that room. You know the Rossiters said they had people say they felt a presence up there—a darkness even when the lights were on. And we've had some of the same talk ourselves."

"A lot of nonsense. It's not like the murder took place there," responded Mrs. Gardener practically. "But if you want to know, I have tried to figure out the mother. What was her name? Evangeline? Something fancy and sort of French sounding. No, I've got it," looking at the pots of geraniums on the window sill. "It was Genevieve. Anyway, fancy bringing the child with her when she made her get-away! Holing up here, waiting to be found out. I'd have had to phone the police."

"Throw themselves on their mercy so to speak?" Nellie looked dubious. "I can't say I've ever gone around thinking of coppers as a bunch of bleeding hearts. But then I've not got money and a posh-sounding name."

"I just couldn't have had it hanging over my head. But we all are made different I suppose." Mrs. Gardener got up to pour herself another cup of tea. "I couldn't have pretended to my daughter that we were off on a seaside holiday when I was looking at those cuts on my hands, remembering my husband grabbing the knife away from me before I hit him over the head with a candlestick."

She shook her head. "No one's ever called me a nervous Nellie. But I tell you I'm worried about that girl. She looks so lost, even with that husband of hers standing beside her. What if she waits until he's asleep and turns on the gas?"

"So we can all wake up dead." Nellie tossed a couple of sprigs of mint into a saucepan of peas. "You know Ed's opinion." Ed was her husband, who was currently in the dining room serving up a steamed fish meal to two spinsters of undetermined age but definite ideas on eating delicate fare at an early hour. "He said we should have changed those gas fires for electric ones, just for the sort of reason we're talking about."

"I wonder," Mrs. Gardener stirred a second teaspoon of sugar into her tea, "if the murder would have been splashed all over the papers if Genevieve Van-Cleeve hadn't been debutante of the year, always being photographed in *The Tattler* and those other high-society magazines. And the husband . . ."

"Gerald, wasn't it?" Nellie took a peek at the Lancashire hotpot in the oven, eyeing with undiminished satisfaction the rich gravy bubbling up through the thinly sliced crust of golden brown potatoes.

"Yes, well, what I was saying," her aunt sat back down at the table, "is that it was bound to make it all the more of a story with him being a highly decorated officer in the war. A real hero from the accounts of it. Badly wounded—losing the sight in one eye and afterwards always being in a lot of pain from other injuries. It's a terrible thing when a man does his duty to his country and ends up the way he did."

"What did the Rossiters think of them?" Nellie closed the oven door and concentrated on the peas. "The mother and daughter, I mean."

"They said they would never have guessed a thing was wrong from how Mrs. VanCleeve behaved the week she was here. The only thing that could have tipped them off something was fishy was that she was a cut above the sort that usually comes. More the type you'd expect to take her holidays on the French Riviera. Nothing flashy about her, just skirts and jumpers, but that look about her that comes from having gone to the very best schools and mixing with the upper crust. They said she was soft-spoken and always very appreciative, told them how much she enjoyed the meals, that sort of thing. The Rossiters weren't much taken with the girl. Said she was a right little madam, but she didn't look like one this evening." Mrs. Gardener closed her eyes and tried to picture what was happening in the bedroom with the red roses on the wallpaper. She hoped that young man with the kind face had his arms around his wife and was telling her that they should take their suitcase and leave. But she had the sinking feeling that the evening was not going to turn out that simply.

Eileen was, in fact, standing in the same spot where Mrs. Gardener had left her. She took off her hat almost in slow motion and let it drop to the floor. She had silky nutmeg brown hair, cut in a bob—not because it was fashionable, but because she never had to do anything to it. Any more than she thought about clothes in general, or in particular the grey wool frock she had put on that morning. She never wore makeup. Not even lipstick. It wasn't indifference. She had made a conscious decision that the world—and that included Andrew—could take her as she was. Someone no one would ever call beautiful, perhaps adding, "Well, you only have to remember her mother and where her looks got her. What girl in her right mind would want to follow in those footsteps?"

Andrew sat on the bed watching her, loving her so dearly, and feeling as he so often did, unable to reach any part of her. It was a mistake, he decided, to have pushed her into coming here. She wasn't going to open up to him. More likely she would shut down even more completely. He was sure that she wasn't even aware that he was in the room. And he was right. Eileen didn't see him. She could hear her own childish voice denouncing the Sea View guesthouse as the horridest place in the world. She saw her mother bending over a suitcase on the bed, lifting out a teddy bear with an arm and a leg missing and propping him against the pillows.

"I don't know why you brought that old thing," she petulantly replied. "I don't sleep with him anymore."

"But I thought you might like to, because of being in a strange place." Her mother's voice came back to her on a breath of salt wind. The window wasn't open now, but it had been on that day long ago. "And I don't want to sleep in the same bed with you, Mummy."

"Eileen, they didn't have a room with two single beds. We'll have to make do. It's something everyone has to do from time to time."

"The wallpaper's horrible. But I don't suppose you mind. You adore red roses."

"Perhaps not this many. But it could be worse. Cousin Aggie has a bedroom with girls on swings on the wallpaper. She said it looked so lively and cheerful in the sample, but after it went up she felt dizzy every time she went into that room. Eileen, dear, I think you would really love cousin Aggie. I spent a lot of time with her on long holidays when I was growing up. And it's a pity I haven't taken you to see her, but Daddy said he would find the journey too much. She lives in Northumbria, which is a trek from London. But she has the most beautiful garden with a wonderful plum tree. And always at least three dogs and a cat. You know how you've always wanted a pet. But Aunt Mary, of course, wouldn't hear of it. And with Hawthorn Lodge being as much her house as Daddy's, her feelings have always had to be considered."

"I don't know why you had to drag me here. You didn't even let me say goodbye to Daddy."

"Dearest, you know it's not a good idea to disturb him early in the morning." Her mother's voice was fainter now; but her own echoed shrilly, accusingly in her ears.

"That's not the reason. Why do you always have to upset Daddy? It was about that Mr. Connors, wasn't it? He's in love with you. Don't deny it, Mummy. And you feel the same way about him. Aunt Mary said you were flirting with him when he came for lunch last Saturday."

"Aunt Mary sometimes gets things wrong. She's not a very happy person. Mr. Connors is Daddy's friend. And he's very sad because his wife was killed in a motor accident only two months ago."

"Leaving the two of you free to run away together."

"Is that what Aunt Mary said?"

"I've got ears, haven't I? I heard you and Daddy arguing. I heard him say that he wouldn't give you a divorce, not ever! And that if you thought that living with Mr. Connors would be all romance and flowers you ought to remember that the rotten cad hasn't a bean to his name."

Suddenly there were no more voices inside Eileen's head. Andrew's concerned face swam into view. Then she saw her mother clearly. It was as if walking out of the past were no more than walking down a hallway between one room and the next. Now she was sitting on the bed peeling off her silk stockings. Now she was picking up the old teddy bear from the floor where he had been tossed and gazing at him for a long moment before putting him in a drawer. Now she was seated on the dressing table stool brushing her waist-length hair. And with every movement there were lightning red flashes of the slash marks on her hands and wrists. Outside the room she kept her sleeves well pulled down and whenever possible wore gloves. But you couldn't wear gloves when eating. And Eileen remembered the elderly man. What was his name? Something Scottish. He had been the only person in the dining room on the first morning that she and her mother went down for breakfast. Eileen remembered the smell of kippers from his table. She could see the crack in the flowered teapot sitting next to the pot of marmalade on their table. And she could see the man's thin face, silver hair, and grey cardigan. He appeared to be reading from a little black book, but Eileen had been sure that he was looking at her mother. But not in the same way that she had seen other men do. And she had been seized by the absolute certainty that he was a policeman pretending to be on holiday.

The clock on the mantelpiece began to strike and Andrew's voice became woven into the silvery chimes, saying that it was seven o'clock and wouldn't it be a good idea if they went down for dinner.

"Darling; you need to eat, you hardly took a bite at lunch."

"You're right." She managed a smile for him, before she went quickly out the door and down the stairs. Away from the blood red roses on the wallpaper and the dressing table mirror in which her mother's face hovered as if trapped in moonlight. Or had it been her own? The same hazel eyes, the same gloss of brown hair, the same fine features and pale clear skin. What made the difference between great beauty and what was merely pretty at best? It wasn't the lack of makeup or the ability to wear the right clothes in the right way. Eileen knew with a tightening of her throat that she couldn't go on telling herself that was all there was to it.

The two spinster ladies came out of the dining room as she and Andrew reached the bottom of the stairs. They were dressed in black and looked like women who existed on a diet of boiled fish and kept a rigid time schedule.

"Good evening," Andrew greeted them with his usual kindly courtesy, to which they responded with the most meager of nods before retreating into the sitting room across the hall. There had been a pair very much like them on that other stay at the Sea View. Eileen remembered saying unimaginatively that they looked like a couple of crows.

"Yes, poor old things," her mother had answered with faint smile, "but perhaps they've never had the chance to do more than peck away at life. That could make anyone look sour."

"I hate it, Mummy, when you do that," the petulant childish voice answered.

"Do what?"

"Sound so horribly smug."

"I don't mean to. Blame it on my childhood, Eileen—growing up in a vicarage with parents who knew how to be happy. And then there was dear cousin Aggie quite content to be a bit odd in her purple trousers and enormous sun hats."

"But you don't have the right."

"What right?"

"To pretend to be such a goody-goody. Not with the way you carry on. Making Daddy so unhappy. Do you want to know what Aunt Mary calls you?"

"No."

"Well, you're going to hear it. She says you're a tart. She says you were never good enough for him to begin with. That your father was just a country vicar and your mother was only good for making jam."

"Aunt Mary is a very disappointed woman, but that's no excuse for you talking about your grandparents that way. I wish they could have lived so they could have known you. They would have loved you so much."

"Yes, like you do, when you're not too busy being nice to Mr. Connors. I wonder if he really was sad that his wife died in that accident? I wonder if it really was an accident . . ."

"Eileen!"

It was Andrew's voice speaking to her now. And she came back to her surroundings to find herself seated across from him at a round table in a corner of the dining room. It was the same table where she had always sat with her mother. It was all the same. The bottle green wallpaper with the burgundy frieze. The mantelpiece crammed with Victorian vases and jugs, barely giving the heavily ornate bronze clock room to breathe, let alone tick. The same swagged and fringed velveteen curtains framed the lace at the window. The only difference Eileen could see was the small vases on all the tables, each containing sprigs of flowers or a couple of roses. There were red roses at their table. One was still fresh. The other was beginning to droop.

There was no one else in the room but them. "Eileen," Andrew said again. "Look at me! Please, darling, take your hands away from your ears."

"I didn't realize." She blinked and let her arms fall to her sides. "I must have been trying to shut out the voices."

"Talk to me instead."

"I can't." She spoke to the roses and somehow her lips kept moving. "I hated her, you see. You can say I was a child but that doesn't change anything, does it?"

"But you must have loved her once."

"Oh, yes I did! We had such wonderful times together when I was little. She would take me for picnics and bicycle rides and make up stories to tell me at night. It was only about a year before the . . . end that I became so angry with her. Everything she did seemed wrong to me."

"Lots of girls that age feel that way." Andrew reached for her hand, then changed his mind. She was like a bird ready to fly away at the least movement.

"I was at that really plain stage. Gawky, spotty faced. And knew people were thinking, even saying, she'll never be a beauty like her mother. Aunt Mary said I should be glad of that, and the way she kept saying it made me begin to notice things that I never had before. All those letters Mummy got. The flowers that came that she didn't want Daddy to know about—she let him think she had bought them herself. The times she went out for lunch and came back looking the way I felt when I got home late from school for no proper reason."

"It's a pity your Aunt Mary didn't move out and make a life for herself."

"She couldn't. Daddy needed her. He wasn't an invalid exactly. But there were times when he was in pain from his injuries and she was wonderful with him. She would sit with him and put cool cloths on his head and they would talk for hours with the curtains closed about the days when they were children."

"And your mother."

"He didn't want her there at those times. That's what he told me. He said he didn't want her cooped up looking after him. But I began to think she couldn't be bothered to be with him during the bad times. Because she was too selfish. Too eager to be out enjoying herself as Aunt Mary said, with the likes of Mr. Connors. And those women friends of hers who weren't up to any good either. So much for the vicar's daughter, fooling the gullible into thinking she was all sweetness and light."

Now that Eileen had started talking she had trouble stopping. But she did break off when Mrs. Gardener came in and crossed the room to close the heavy curtains before coming over to their table. The proprietress had told Nellie's husband Ed that she would get the young couple's dinner to them, if he'd be so kind as to start washing up some of the saucepans. She had wanted to see if Mrs. Shelby looked any less haunted than on her arrival. Looking at her now she didn't know whether to be reassured or not. There was a little more color in her cheeks but her eyes had a look to them that she couldn't read.

"I was wondering whether you'd like a fruit salad or soup to start off with." Mrs. Gardener felt as though she was trying to jolly along a couple of kiddies who didn't want to eat their dinner.

"Fruit salad, please." Andrew responded without looking at his wife. "But there's no hurry if it's all right with you. We're enjoying sitting here in all this solitude. Have the other guests eaten all ready?"

"Only the Misses Phillips. The other two couples are dining out this evening. And that nice old clergyman I was telling you about earlier said he probably wouldn't be back till after eight.

"Then," Andrew smiled up at her, "if we're not troubling you . . ."

"Not a bit of it. You go on having a nice chat. The Lancashire hotpot will keep just fine in the oven. Even better for letting the gravy have a nice simmer."

Mrs. Gardener returned to the kitchen to inform Nellie that she wished one or other of them was a mind reader.

"That's one of the happy memories I have of when Mummy and I stayed here," Eileen heard herself tell Andrew.

"What is, darling?"

"She said that she couldn't make jam like her mother did, or nurse Daddy half as well as Aunt Mary could when he had one of his bad times, but that being a vicar's daughter she could always tell a clergyman even when he wasn't wearing a clerical collar. I remember she made it sound like a talent for acrobatics or something else terribly clever and we both laughed."

"And were there other good moments?"

"Some. Going for walks and down onto the sand to paddle. It was much too cold to swim. And I liked hearing her talk about her parents and cousin Aggie and what fun it had been collecting eggs from the hen house when she spent holidays with her. But there were always the other thoughts that I couldn't push away. Especially when she spoke about Daddy and how I needed to understand that he got upset and went into rages sometimes because the injury to his head that had caused him to go blind in one eye had affected his mind. She said that he imagined all sorts of things that weren't true. And that he was even jealous of her friends, anyone she was fond of—even cousin Aggie, which was why she had never been able to take me to see her. But that his doctor wouldn't put him in hospital because he had known Daddy for years and Aunt Mary had persuaded him that she could take perfectly good care of her brother at home."

"You didn't believe her?" Andrew asked gently.

"No! I told her if Daddy got angry sometimes it was because of the disgusting way she was carrying on with Mr. Connors. And probably lots of other men besides."

"You loved your father very much?"

"How could I help it? He was so dear and kind to me. We would sit and do jigsaw puzzles together. We both loved them. And he liked me to play the piano for him. Chopin was his favorite composer. Daddy said the music helped soothe his headaches."

"So he did have them?"

"They were the price he paid for being a hero. I told Mummy she made them worse. And nothing she could say made me sympathize with her one bit. I lay awake at night in that bedroom upstairs with the red roses on the wallpaper. In the darkness everything became so clear. Aunt Mary was away the night before we left home. She had gone to stay with an old school friend for a couple of days. Something she did once a year. And our cook and the maid were away also; Mummy had said that they needed a break too and that it would be fun for her and me to take care of the house together. We could even have a try at making jam. But thinking it over, the pieces all began to fit together just like one of Daddy's and my jigsaw puzzles."

Eileen fell silent, to sit as if she were indeed in a dark room in the middle of the night. But Andrew did not speak. He sat waiting until she took up the thread of memory again.

"She planned it all. Taken advantage of Aunt Mary's absence, got the help out of the way so that she could have a clear field to pack up what she needed to take with her when she ran off with Mr. Connors. He was free. His wife had been conveniently killed in that car crash. But that still left Daddy, who had refused to give her a divorce. Maybe she tried to talk him into giving her one, hoping he would do so without Aunt Mary to back him up; that was somewhat more bearable to think than that my own mother had killed my father in cold blood. I'm not sure how many nights it took for me to face up to the certainty that he was dead. But there was no getting around those cuts on her wrists that she refused to explain. There was the fact that she hadn't let me say goodbye to Daddy and the rush about leaving the house, all the while telling me that we were just going off on a surprise holiday so she and I could get close again. To this sort of guesthouse! The four of us—my parents, Aunt Mary, and myself—had always stayed in hotels before, fashionable ones, where we would always meet people we knew. And then there was the man in the grey cardigan."

"What man, Eileen?"

"An elderly man, with thoughtful, knowing eyes. He was Scottish, with a name like McDougal—no, McGregor. I remember it made me think of Peter

Rabbit. He was eating breakfast—kippers—the first morning we came down to this room. He was sitting over at that table in front of the window. I saw him looking at Mummy not just that time, but on other occasions when we happened to be eating at the same time. It grew upon me with a sort of creeping horror that he was a policeman, a detective on holiday, and because of what he was, he knew what she had done. I could see it, the look that revealed he saw right through to her soul. I was sure she sensed it, because I saw her talking to him one day by the staircase, with her head bent close to his. I wondered what lies she was telling him to charm away his suspicions. And it reached the point that I couldn't bear it anymore—the waiting, the awful waiting for it all to be brought out into the open. That my mother had murdered my father and perhaps even conspired in arranging the accident that killed Mr. Connors's wife. I pictured her being taken away to be tried and hanged. And there was nothing I could do to stop it. I didn't know that I wanted to—I just knew that I wanted it to be over, so I did the one thing she had begged me not to do. I slipped away while she was having a rest one afternoon and went down to the telephone box at the corner of the road. I meant to speak to Aunt Mary, but . . ."

"It was your father who answered the phone." Andrew was suddenly aware of how cold the room had grown.

"Yes," Eileen's voice did not wave. "He said he had been worried about Mummy and me because we hadn't been in touch and he had misplaced the address of where we were staying that she had written down for him. But that otherwise he was perfectly well. And he didn't want me to say anything to Mummy about my ringing up, because they'd had a small quarrel and he understood she needed time away to sort out her feelings. So it would be best not to put a spoke in the wheel, just let things take their course and we would soon be back together, just like we were meant to be. It was such a relief, Andrew."

"Of course."

"How could I know?" Eileen asked in the voice of a twelve-year-old girl. "How could I know what I had done? It never crossed my mind that I had become my father's accomplice in killing my mother. But he was there when she and I went for a walk on the downs the next afternoon. He had found out from one of the other people staying here that we always went out around that time. When I saw him, saw the look on his face—the terrible maniacal rage when Mummy walked toward him—I screamed at him to stay away, even before I saw him lift the knife and bring it slashing down on her. She screamed at me to run, but I couldn't move. I just stood there and listened to him shouting that she had got away from him once. But never again. And as I watched her die I kept repeating over and over again inside my head, 'He's ill, he's ill, he can't help it. You're the one who killed her.' "

"He was ill," Andrew reached out and gripped her hands tight, "too ill to be found fit to be tried for murder. He went into hospital, where he should have been all along. And he died. It was the war that killed him, but you did not kill your mother. You were a child doing what you thought was right."

"I was jealous of her. I was willing to believe everything bad that Aunt Mary had to say about her."

"Eileen, you couldn't have stopped what happened."

"He's right." The speaker was a silver-haired man wearing a grey cardigan over a clerical collar. Neither of them had seen or heard him come into the room. "My name's McGregor. Ian McGregor. You probably don't remember me, but I was staying in this house that week you spent here with your mother. And I have returned every year at the same time, hoping perhaps that you would feel called to return and that I would be granted the opportunity of a few words with you."

"I do remember you." Eileen struggled to stand up but needed Andrew's help to guide her out of her chair. "I thought you were a policeman."

"No, my dear, I am as you see." Mr. McGregor tapped at his collar. "A clergyman. Your mother recognized me as such even though I was out of uniform on that occasion. It was at a point in my life when I was feeling somewhat adrift from my life's work. I came here feeling a need that week to escape from the world, and myself."

"And you sensed that Eileen's mother was also escaping," Andrew said.

"Not that." Mr. McGregor shook his head. "I saw in her face a look I had witnessed on the faces of some of the men and women with whom I had talked and prayed in my work as a prison cleric. People on whom the sentence of death had been passed, and who had found within themselves the peace that passes all understanding. Your mother, Eileen—if I may call you such—had fully accepted the inevitability of what lay in store for her. She wasn't afraid to die. What she feared was that her young daughter wouldn't learn to live. I made several attempts to see you, but I found it impossible even with my connections to be apprised of your whereabouts."

"I went to live with a cousin, Agatha, and she guarded me like a dragon until I married Andrew."

"But somehow I was always certain that I would see you again. I believe that your mother intended I should." Mr. McGregor smiled, looked upward, and bade them goodnight. "Perhaps I will see both you young people at breakfast," he said before exiting the room.

"I thought he was going to say in church. A nice man," said Andrew.

"Yes." Eileen plucked the two roses from the vase on their table. "Would you mind if we took a walk? I know it's dark, but there's a sliver of moon and I'd like to go out to where it happened on the downs."

Andrew took her hand. They were unpegging their coats from the hall tree when Mrs. Gardener came out of the kitchen.

"Going out for a breath of fresh air?"

"Yes," they replied.

"Well, don't get wet. It looks like it might come on to rain again."

"It doesn't matter," said Eileen.

"No, I don't suppose it does." Mrs. Gardener stood in the doorway watching what she had come, in the space of a couple of hours, to think of as her young couple walk arm-in-arm down the road. Then she closed the door and went back to the kitchen to tell Nellie that things were going to be all right. She could feel it in her bones.

"I still don't believe in them—miracles, I mean. But I wish," Eileen looked up at Andrew, "that I had that man's pure unclouded faith."

"It would be a good thing to have," he agreed. The Sea View receded behind them into the mist, so that if they had looked back all they would have seen was a glimmer of light shining through a chink in the curtains of an upstairs window.

"But I believe in you, Andrew. I believe in us. That's a beginning, isn't it?"

"Yes." He smiled down at her, tucking her arm more securely into his. "It most certainly is."

# Noreen Ayres

## Delta Double-Deal

NOREEN AYRES'S Smokey Brandon is one of the more unique characters in modern crime fiction. You don't often meet—in real life or in fiction—a former cop who was also an exotic dancer. Noreen's fiction straddles the fences of good strong commercial fiction and literary fiction, a balancing act that's hard to ignore. Or put down, for that matter. She brings real depth to her work. And her sentences, my, do they shine. "Delta Double-Deal," first published in *The Night Awakens*, reveals her talents in a completely different kind of mystery story.

# Delta Double-Deal

*Noreen Ayres*

Minnie Chaundelle was a beautiful big woman with waved hair swept close to her head like raked copper. The color was by way of her stylist boyfriend, and a front tooth rimmed with gold came courtesy the neighborhood dentist. The dentist never charged Minnie and Minnie never charged him, so it was a nice arrangement that kept Minnie in a wholesome smile.

How I met Minnie Chaundelle Bazile was a phone call. She wanted her brother found.

I always ask to see my clients first time face-to-face. She said she wasn't about to truck all over town no matter how nice a man I was.

"What makes you think I'm a nice man?" I asked.

"The word get around," she said.

Gross Street, offa Dallas. There's a Corrections for boys on one side of Dallas and a school for the retarded. On the other side's a cemetery. No one comes there anymore, she said, not even to die. If I took the right road past the cemetery I'd see her on her porch. If I took the wrong road I wouldn't.

It was the first day after a hard rain and the sun was boomin' hot already. When I turned my key to lock up, the mosquitoes were spraddle-legged up against the siding of my house, stunned by the heat themselves.

I stay in Neartown, about a mile from the heart of Houston. Gangstas and old-time politicians call it Fourth Ward. Despite a few bad apples, I like it here. From my office on the second floor I can see trees green as broccoli, and skyscrapers the color of turquoise, rust, chalk, and shined silver against a clean blue sky. At night I watch the moon play games between the towers, and when it's wet, their edges go soft in the rain-smoke.

And from my perch I watch old men black as roof paper cross the road to talk to each other, hands in their pockets like they're countin' change. Or a kid on a bicycle hoppin' holes. I could afford better but I'd have to work harder, and then I'd own more things and things lock up your freedom.

I came in off Clay near a condo complex walled off like a fortress for folks who make more money than God. An old black dog with his tail drooped under ambled across the road, fixin' his eyes the color of pennies on me.

Down the way were four wood-frame houses with plants spillin' off the porches. One porch had a line strung between its pillars holding cinnamon-colored work jackets pinned upside down, the arms danglin' like dead men hung up for show.

I drove my old brown complainin' Plymouth easy over chuckholes worse than on my street. At the end was a lot filled with patches of water and weeds. Opposite were six tiny houses sunk down in the tall grass and so far gone of paint you could see right through to air. A baby carrier leaned against a tree stump in one yard, and in the next were so many rusted gadgets it made you want to come up and browse. There, at the next house, sat a woman on a porch swing, just as she said she'd be. I parked and got out and crossed a drainage ditch laid over with crunchy dirt.

When I got a good look at Minnie Chaundelle, without hardly realizing it I sucked my stomach in before she got a good look at me. She was talkin' into a blue cell phone and wore a purple dress lit with orange embroidery, the skirt spread from one end of the bench to the other. On her feet were gold wove slippers Japanese ladies wear.

"Miz Bazile?"

"Catch ya latuh, Asyllene," she said, and punched off, then slipped the phone between her thigh and the side of the swing. From her heft and manner you could take her for thirty-five, but I knew from a source she'd just made thirty.

I put my hand out. "Cisroe Perkins."

"Minnie Chaundelle," she said and took it. Her skin was moist from the heat and had a glow like dark honey. She motioned me to sit on a barrel with a red cushion on top, and we talked there among her fern and trailing begonias. The air was thick with a sweet familiar scent. It mixed with that of a jasmine bush so happy by the side of the house it long ago turned itself into a tree.

"My brother's name is Verlyn Venable," she said. "He's twenty-four years ol' and still don' know enough to hold his diapers offa his knees."

I took out a notepad and made my face like I knew all things.

"He had hisself a good job," she said. "*Good* job. I got it for him, fr'en o' mine. He was doin' perfect. Then he ups and ghostifies. They owe him a pay check, but they cain't trace him down. I call ovah his place, call and call. What kinda man don' know enough to catch gold nickels fallin' out the sky?"

She was sayin' all these worryin' words, but her voice could calm a bobcat in a pepper field.

"His boss been out to his place, been out there and back to Egypt. They *took* to him, like I say. But you cain't count on patience to live overlong."

I asked when was the last time she saw her brother.

Her thumb rubbed a finger like she was about to start a fire. "He drop ovah here las' week and tol' me hold sumpin' for him. I say, 'How long,' and he go, 'Oh a day or two.' Six days now I don't hear nothin'. Three days he ain' showed at work."

Minnie flicked a dark thing off the armrest. It hit hard against the wall and landed in a white plastic U.S. Post Office bin people take home full after they've been on vacation a long time. Inside was what I made out as pecan shells. Then it come to me what comprised the strip of red dirt I walked on out front and what I smelled in the air: shells, and nutmeats maybe in a pie.

I asked did she file a Missing Persons. She cocked her head and grinned like to say, What planet you from, boy?

The button in the center of the cushion was biting into my bony behind. I shifted away from it and asked, "What was it your brother lef' off?"

"Hode on. I need to know how long you think it take to find him befoh I know I can afford you."

"I charge twenty-five a hour," I said, resting my arms on my knees. "If there's long-distance, faxes, fees for records, well, that's additional."

"I be cookin' up a *buncha* nuts for that kine money. How many hours, you think?"

"Sometimes I find people in a hour. Sometimes never. I'll give you a runnin' report of my time weekly or bi-weekly as you choose. You tell me to cease and desist anytime you want. Bi-weekly—that's twice a week."

"I may be beautiful, Mr. Perkins, but I ain' dumb."

We smiled at each other as if there was more to the words than what hung in the air. My mind was wanderin' where it shouldn't. "I just like to clarify," I said.

"Clarify all you want, Mr. Perkins. You a educated man, I c'n see that."

"Cisroe."

"Mr. Cisroe," she said, with that cat smile.

"I had a couple years after the army, but I wouldn't say I'm educated, Miz Bazile." But I don't think she heard me.

She put her elbow on the armrest and framed the side of her face with a thumb and a finger. The swing was carrying her toward me, then away.

"Come to think on it, it's not gon' take all that long to fin' that boy. He either pokin' his nose where he oughtn'ta, hangin' in Slick Willie's Billiards down Sugahland, or . . ."

I waited, one hand clasped on the other, notebook danglin'. That woman made the hairs on my chest snap and crackle. I was listenin', listenin' hard, but I was seein' her inside her house, invitin' me in for tea.

"Or swimmin' with the mocs in the bayou," she said, and squeezed and unsqueezed the rope fixed to the porch swing. "He just a dumb baby, Mr. Cisroe. He think he Eddie Murphy. What I'm worried about: his hard head."

Minnie Chaundelle went inside to get what her brother gave her. She turned back and asked me did I want some tea. Just like that, did I want some tea. But it wasn't the time for me to offer a different tone, and I said yes with a right and decent attitude.

I sat on there on the porch and ruminated on what I already knew about Minnie Chaundelle. I had placed a call to Stinger Gazway. Stinger drifts all over Fourth and Fifth Wards. If anyone knows anything about anybody, he does. He told me Minnie married a man named Sparrel Bazile six years ago, then laid him in the grave a year later. Sparrel was comin' home from work on the Katy at two A.M., same time a drunk was comin' home from a party.

While I waited on Minnie's porch, the clouds were forming a dark blanket from the south. The air was thick enough to punch. I pulled the collar of my shirt away from my neck. Two white women with mismatched clothes walked by holdin' hands, their glasses half-down their noses and their hair cut straight across, and I could see they were short a few cards, maybe come from the school for the retarded down the way.

Minnie returned bringin' two iced teas on a tray with a high lip on it and sugar, lemon, spoons, and napkins from Whataburger. She nodded at a book with a marbleized cardboard cover like you buy for notes at school and said, "Here," and I took it off the edge of the tray.

The label on front said *Brickner Deposit* at top, and on the bottom was the company name and an address on West Loop. I turned the pages and saw typing and charts and plot diagrams. Soon I figured out it had somethin' to do with a drilling operation off the Gulf's Terrebonne Bay.

Minnie Chaundelle set the tray across the top of the postal bin and commenced asking me my tea preferences, then mixed and stirred. "That mus' mean sumpin' to some freak a nature," she said, glancing at the book. "But not t' me."

"Uh-huh," I said, making myself out to be a thoughtful man. I took the glass of tea and swallowed deep but didn't drain it, not wantin' to inconvenience her. I asked if she showed the notebook to anyone, say, that friend of hers who gave her brother the job in the first place.

"Verlyn tol' me don' show it to nobody, so I dint. Till you."

"Sounds like maybe you don't trust your friend hired your brother."

She glanced down like she was sorry for a sick puppy hid behind a chair. "It shunt be that way in this world, but I guess sometimes it is." Then she met my eyes and said, "Oh, well now, don't take me wrong. I just be steppin' on my own toes sometimes. Then again, you never know. Verlyn say, 'Anything happen t' me, you turn this ovah the *po*-lice.' I say, 'What you talkin' about?', but he don' ansah dat. Jes get in his car and go." She flapped the edge of her dress as if it got out of position, then moved inside it till she got comfortable. "He don' see me with no stickum sticker say 'Back the Blues.' Oh, cops ain' all bad. But enough o' them is." The swing went into motion lazy as a boat on a sea but Minnie's brow was scrunched up tight.

"You don't go out to where he stays?"

"One, I don' drive. Two, my fr'ens could take me, but time marches by and here it is, and you come highly recommended."

She slid down me with her eyes. I slid up her the same way.

I'd already decided Verlyn Venable was goin' to be found for about a hundred dollars.

The cemetery behind Minnie's house was dense and shadowed thick with pin oaks and two pecan trees Minnie said she took a rake to, then paid a little Mexican boy down the street a quarter a bucket to pick up the nuts. She candied pecans for people to sell in beauty parlors and gun shows at $7.50 per two paper-cones' worth. That, plus what she gets from the state for a bad back, is what she'd be payin' me from, she said. Bad back from bein' too much on it maybe—Stinger's the one told me this. But I don't judge what a woman with looks does to get by.

I didn't much want to hit the freeway down to Sugarland to check out Verlyn Venable at four-thirty when traffic's all hinky. Instead, I swung over east a couple blocks to Kroger's grocery down on Montrose, thinking I might run into Stinger.

He was sittin' in a booth by the side of the bakery, smearing mustard on a

soft pretzel with a coffee stirrer. I asked if Minnie's brother was the type to mess
with trouble. "Not that boy," Stinger said. "It don't fit, 'less he got mixed up with
drugs down the way. He play Little League when my own boy was livin' here
with his mama. Used ta, I'd see him drivin' Minnie Chaundelle the doctah when
she had breathin' difficulties. They parents die young but dem two kep' they nose
clean, I say dat. 'Course there's Minnie with her fellas. But hell, she give it away
for free you real down and out. Used ta, anyways."

Across the room in a Formica booth a man the color of summer grizzly was
sittin' silent with his knees out into the walkway, his blond girlfriend opposite.
She had a cut under one eye and on her cheek, surrounded in green and yellow.
"Ain't that a damn shame," I said, nodding in that direction.

Stinger looked over while he bit into the pretzel, leavin' mustard in his
goatee. "Some women go outta they way to find somebody ta whack 'em," he
said with his mouth full. He swallowed and said, "Ever'body got a choice wever
to walk in dry socks or piss in they boots and whine about it."

Stinger wasn't a low man but he was one to take serious.

"Verlyn got a lady by Buffalo Speedway," he said. "I cain't tell you the *add*-
ress, but I c'n show you."

Stinger went to his pickup truck and unlocked the door, glancing right and left,
then reached behind the seat where there's space enough for his paste bucket. He
hunched his shoulders then, and I knew he'd slipped his .38 into his waistband
under his loose shirt. He glanced around again, shut the pickup door, and headed
my way. His top half was a sandy-colored shirt and a Rockets cap. His bottom half
was brown pants and red sandals, and he moved like all his tendons had been
stretched too long on the rack.

How he came by the gun was one time he was drivin' home after a wallpaper job when a man was yellin' and wavin' a gun in the street with his own children lookin' on. Stinger pulls over, walks up to the goon and says, "I know you
want to get rid of that piece, man." A woman who saw it said he held out his palm
"like he ain't got no normal skin a bullet go through."

While we drove to the street Stinger pointed out, the air was heavy and
worthless from a storm comin' in off the Gulf. Lightning flickered like dyin' neon
and low thunder rumbled, making promise the sky would rip open and relieve
itself so we could breathe again.

Halfway down the street we saw a girl in gray shorts and a black halter-top
come runnin' barefoot toward us, wavin' her hands. "Uh-oh," I said, and slowed
the car.

"Tha's her," Stinger said. "Tha's Verlyn's stuff."

Her hair was dark and curly and she had a light, fleshy look to her limbs
when she came jammin' up to my window. A blue-rose tattoo showed on the rise
of her left breast when she leaned in. "There's a guy with a knife! He's attacking
someone!" she said.

I told Stinger to get in the back so she could get in the front, and she hung
onto the dash, pointing backwards as I smoked tires up to the outside pay phone
at Popeye's Chicken. She hopped out and dialed, rocking foot to foot. Stinger
said, "She get done, le's go take us a look." She came back, fear still in her face,
and I told her to wait in Popeye's, where there's light.

We found the apartments no sweat, and saw through a wire fence trailed in vine two lean men with no shirts standing by the pool smokin' cigarettes. The Cauc was wearin' black trousers. The other one had long beige shorts on and somethin' white wrapped around his shoulder and under his armpit with the pattern like a big red rose coming through. Stinger said, "Well, he's alahve but he's nicked."

All the while we talked, Verlyn smoked his cigarette and kept an eye on the breezeway. He could've been a golden panther, what with his hard jaw and yellow eyes.

I told him I was a friend of his sister's. She was worried about him. He nodded but kept his counsel.

There was a quiet but alert resolve about him, like he was just goin' to catch his breath before he took care of business. I'm like that myself sometimes. I once in a while get criticized over it, like by the woman who left me a few months ago. She took a bunch of things I called mine, but I didn't go after her when she very well knew I could hunt a whisper in a big wind. By the time I got through mulling it all over, she was askin' to come back, but my head was in a different place. It takes this cement a while to set, but when it does it's what it's going to be for a long, long time.

The Anglo did all the talkin'. His hair was buzzed close so you could see the metal studs embedded in his scalp down to an arrow's point. I'm not squeamish but that did catch my attention.

He said, "Me and Verlyn and Bitsy was kickin' it, watchin' the game, like that, this hype comes outta my room. Lucky he ain't stone dead, man." He laid off a bunch of rowdy names on the culprit while Verlyn stood there offering no contradiction, his eyes held steady on somethin' the rest of us couldn't see. I thought then that the only thing missin' in that young man's face was a young man's youth. Stinger and I bend the polar ends of forty, but the kid seemed worn ragged at the cuffs.

I gave out my card and said if they have any more problems to give me a call. Then I told Verlyn he might ring up his sister, too. A change came into his eyes at his sister's name. Softer. Younger.

He said, "Keep this under your hat, okay?"

"I got no problem with that," I said.

Stinger and I left out the opposite side of the courtyard when we saw the baby-blue cars of Houston's finest because we'd as soon not waste everybody's time.

When we pulled back into the lot at Kroger's the clouds opened at last. I could feel the difference in the air already.

"Thanks, man," I told Stinger.

"No problem, baby," he said, and pinched a wad of Bandits into his cheek before he opened the door. As he hurried to his truck, big drops pelted the back of his shirt like loads off a fully choked shotgun. He ducked like he thought if he was shorter the rain wouldn't hit so hard.

I drove away, thinking Minnie Chaundelle would sure be grateful to know her baby kin was still healthy. Maybe she'd give me some pecans in a paper cone, or bake me a pie.

It was comin' on to six o'clock and the rain was drummin' so hard I thought the ark would have to be broke out. Lookin' through my windshield was like lookin' through seven sheets of waxed paper. But when I got to Gross Street and parked, like magic, the rain sucked back in a heavenly tide.

I was about to get out when I saw a tall man in a light suit emerge from a car and cross the culvert to Minnie's. Up on the porch he closed his umbrella and tugged at his jacket before he knocked. The front door opened and the screen door right after, and Minnie beckoned him in with a big sweet smile. She was framed in the golden light and I imagined I smelled candied pecans cooking on the stove.

I drove on by.

Seven the next morning my phone rang. I reached for a glass of water on my low-boy and slugged some before I answered.

The voice said, "This is Verlyn. Could I talk to you?"

I met him at Starbuck's off West Gray. He was wearin' olive-green pants and a pale green polo, butterscotch loafers with no socks. In one ear was a gold ear-ring and on his hand a class ring from U.T. We got our orders and sat outside in the pleasant morning. He drank juice and took a bite out of a dry croissant I knew was dry because I had one too. I asked him did he call his sister. He said he woke her up and apologized for bein' absent without leave, told her this before she had it together to yell at him too much. Once in a while he'd flex his shoul-der a little and wince. Each car pulling in he gave a long stare.

I said, "You ready to tell me who's the snook got a grudge against you?"

"Somebody don't like what I know, okay? Somebody thinkin' to scare me." He pressed his middle finger to the fallen powdered sugar on the paper and put it to his tongue.

"And did he do a proper job on that?"

Verlyn leveled his eyes at me. "A bee don't flee."

"Say again?"

"You swat him, he bite," he said in an old man's mimic.

"Thataway you can get a buncha trouble comin' at you, brother."

"Not if you go after the head nacho, right?" He blew on his coffee, took a sip, then said, "I need to go pick up a computer I left at the office. I could use some company."

Am I workin' for you now?, is what I wanted to say, not a complete damn fool, the man's got money to spend. But what I did ask was, "Cain't your friend there, Toolhead, what's his name, come with you?"

"William? Not the right one."

"I charge twenty-five an hour," I said.

"I'm down with that," he said, causing me to ponder just how much he made on his job. He said, "It may already be takin' up window space at E-Z Pawn," he said. "Cheapskates. Making me bring in my own computer."

"So far, not a capital offense, far as I can see."

"Well, there's stuff going on . . . ," he said, leaning closer to the table so his chest hit the edge. "Some of these wildcat drillin' outfits will do any damn thing to get money for the next hole. They take on more investors than they can han-dle. And they get away with it because they tell people they're drillin' in a 'prohibitive frontier,' kinda like drillin' on the moon, so nobody should be all that fried when it comes up dry."

"Makes some kind of sense," I said.

"But the thing is, good people invest in these things, people like my rich aunties, if I had any. And too many times they get the hot yanked right out of their fire."

"I don't quite get the scam here."

He took a bite of his pastry and chewed awhile and got a look of a man still plannin' what his next step would be. I let off the pressure a bit and asked him a side-question. "So why didn't you show up for work three days?"

Verlyn sat back and crossed his legs. "Disgusted," he said, and turned in his chair and crossed his legs the other way. "There's this one temp agency I been with for more than five years. They had a rush job, so I filled in. Hey, I know it's not stand-up to do Mitchell Corporation that way. But what they pull is worse. I'm serious. I got names. I could hurt 'em."

"Most people would just shut their eyes and go to lunch."

"Most would, I give you that. You met my sister? She raised me right. Tomorrow I go to the D.A."

"That's one you might want to think over."

"A bright man don't chew on something that's eating him."

"I'd just hate to answer to Minnie Chaundelle over you."

"That's something I'd hate myself," he said, managing a grin.

We went to a high-rise off the West Loop and rode a glass elevator lookin' down on Buffalo Bayou, where a dozen gray shapes cut the green water—turtles with their long necks out, or baby 'gators.

Verlyn's lip was beaded with sweat.

"Nobody gonna shoot you here, boy," I said.

He rolled that shoulder but smiled and said, "Can't be a hundred percent on that, now, can we?"

Verlyn went to an office along one wall of a roomful of cubicles. He said to stand by, and I did, leanin' against a wall and cleanin' my fingernails with my pocket knife. Before long I heard a raised voice say, "You leave me high and dry like this? Thank you very much." Someone down a lane poked a head out a cubicle, then pulled back in. I moved so I could see into the office where Verlyn was and got a look at a short man with a lot of scalp edged with white hair, over a fall of red face. When the man saw me he stared, then flipped his hand at Verlyn, like Go on, get out of here.

In the car Verlyn unzipped his laptop case and fired up to look at his files. What files? The machine was wiped clean. He cursed and hit the door with the side of his fist, but then seemed to resign himself.

"How about we go get the book you left with Minnie Chaundelle?"

He said maybe later, he had to grab some sleep. I caught him in a smile again. He said, "My girl likes a wounded man."

Back home, I phoned Minnie and told her her brother might be along, maybe with me, except I had a job to do early in the evening so I didn't know.

"Oh honey, that is a great relief," she said. "Anytime you want to drop on by, I sure be happy to pay you what I owe." I wondered if she was sittin' on her porch swing talkin' to me.

When I hung up, I checked my closet to see what shirts I had clean, fried up some okra and sausage with red bell peppers and leftover noodles, then took a nap and dreamed of a bayou I lived on as a child, and how a yellow butterfly used to land on a bush outside, and the smell of jasmine and apples and pine.

That afternoon I did a records check on the drilling company. Mitchell Corporation had racked up litigation against them draggin' on for years. On a hunch I ran a criminal history on the president, the V.P., and the operations manager, Guy Grundfest. The president had a domestic on him two years ago. The V.P. was clean. Grundfest had two assault convictions, one in El Paso, one in Houston, and a theft-by-check out of Huntsville. What rang a bell, though, was the name of the company CEO, Ray Wayne Wooley. I'd seen that name before but didn't know where. It gave me a funny feeling. The more I wanted to shake it off, the more it hung on.

In an hour I'd have to get ready for my evening job, the one I mentioned to Minnie Chaundelle.

I called Stinger. "Who you know named Wooley? Ray Wayne Wooley."

"Not a single sinnin' soul."

"Don't sound familiar, nothin'?"

"Nope."

"Okay, what do you know about drilling outfits? That Bazile boy's workin' for a company might be doin' some fishy stuff, but it seems like he's not quite ready to lay it all out."

"Sonny's maybe got to boil in his own oil a while," Stinger said.

"I'd like to see what I can do to avoid that."

"You'd like to see what Minnie Chaundelle's sugah tase like."

"That too. But in the meantime I don't want to see no jacko playin' slice-'n'-dice with that boy again neither."

"Lemme ask around. You up the car lot this evenin'?"

"That's right. I'll have my cell phone with me, you need to call."

"I don't know, maybe I need a new car. Maybe I'll see ya around."

I rang up a reporter I met at a legal investigator's conference one time, nerdy guy named Jobar Wilson, liked to go by Buck. Once you saw him you knew how bad he needed to, but it was hard for me to remember to say that name. He was rackin' on a story about the blues bands playin' for the Juneteenth festival. That's the three-day annual celebration marking the about-date when word reached Texas the slaves were freed. Buck supported what Verlyn told me about wildcatters sometimes overselling a well. "An investor might put up the million it takes to drill a hole, okay?, but then the wildcatters get greedy. Say they meet a guy at the Petroleum Club's got another million to toss around. They take him on, don't happen to mention they already got their million to start the drill. That way they're sure to have enough money in case they run into problems. Or, they're lookin' ahead to the next hole. Say, then, their kid's buddy has a daddy with money to invest. Okay, they take him on too. Problem: Now the well comes in productive. Oops. They got too many people to pay, 'cause it's not going to be *that* productive. Ass-is-grass time."

"So they go bankrupt," I said. "Happens every day."

"Wrong deal." He waited like an actor thinking he invented timing. "Nuh-uh. What they do, *they plug the hole*. Plug the hole and *say* it's dry."

I said, "And they go unplug it later."

"No. What do they care if the poor schmucks don't get a return? They're not in the production/refining business, they're in the drilling business."

"Hey now," I said. "Grifters everywhere."

I was letting him go when I got him back and asked, "Jobar, does the name Ray Wayne Wooley mean anything to you?"

There was a pause and I wondered if he was playin' me, till he said, "Might be, Cisroe. But I'd sure rather you call me Buck."

"Sorry, man. Buck." I could hear him clacking on a keyboard.

"Ray Wayne Wooley," he said. "He's the brother of Brant Wooley. D. A. down the courts building. Saw that name in the Society page the other day."

I rang up Verlyn several times. He either didn't have a machine or it was turned off. If Verlyn knew the connection between Mitchell Corp.'s CEO and the chief district attorney for the city, that boy owned more sap than I'd given him credit for. Maybe more stupid, too. Maybe that's what his sister meant.

At six I had to give it up and get to my evening job. It was for a rich brother bought a fancy pre-owned car and suspected the dealer fooled with the odometer. Asked me would I pose as a salesman to see if I could sniff out their practice—didn't matter what-all it would cost him, it was the principle. I said I'd do it for a week but how'd I know I could even get hired? He laughed. His voice sounded like a nail coming out of hard wood. "You Sneaky Petes just another kind of con man. Tell me different and I'll show you a hog can dance."

This business, you do a lot of things for a dollar.

So I was up on the auto corridor on North Shepherd, standing outside in a shirt with too much starch in it and listening to a blues station over headphones hooked up to a radio clipped to my belt. Now and then I'd roll down the sound and take out my cell phone and try Verlyn's number again.

Two couples came in, took my time, walked away. I was going for a bathroom break when I saw Stinger's faded tan truck. He got out and put on his shades against the lot lights. When he reached me, he said, "You might want ta come with me, Cisroe. They got your boy."

Verlyn Vincent Venable, twenty-four years old. Ideals, character, history, brains, beauty. All that, ready . . . for what? To be put in the ground for worm feed. Officials said he didn't make one of the curves up on Allen Parkway, the tree-lined drive that streams along in sync with the bayou.

Stinger guessed better, and so did I.

But it wasn't till the next morning at four A.M. that I knew for sure. Buck Wilson reported the findings to me after I gave him a call and he reached a contact at the morgue down on Old Spanish Trail. A single .40-caliber round sent parts of Verlyn's skull zinging over the black bayou waters that carried a full moon on its back. Rage and sorrow filled my soul. I shattered a pane in my bedroom window when my loose shoe went through.

My heart cinched down for Minnie, that big lovely woman struck with grief, and I was going to go over her place, when Stinger said he already called and a friend of hers answered, and he could hear some awful wailing in the background, and what women need at a time like this was other women.

By the book, I had no more to do for Minnie Chaundelle. I'd found her brother briefly, and that's all I was paid for. But it made me sick thinkin' I could've maybe done somethin' to prevent him being given over to evil.

I stayed away from Minnie's but I thought of her and that poor boy in and out all that day. After a while, I played back what Stinger said about pissin' in your boots and whinin' about it, and about Verlyn himself saying spit or swallow. I decided I wanted to have a second look at that book he left at Minnie's.

Around five I was leavin' my house to get dinner when Stinger came by. I stood talkin' to him outside his pickup.

Across the street, men were handling pieces of tin for a new roof. The sun was a gray, sharp light through the clouds, and the brilliance it gave off struck Stinger's face in a way that made him look hard and mean.

"We gon' get him," he said.

"Which one? We got no idea—"

"The hail we don't."

I said, "It could be Grundfest, sure. He's got assaults. It could be a high muckety like Wooley. Or it could be a low-ass snake-clambake like the one cut the boy in the shoulder. How you gon' pick which one?"

"Young brother down, Cisroe. Could've done good in this world."

"I know that. But there are ways to handle it."

"Sure there *are*."

"Legal ways."

"Bullshit," he said, and yanked the far window handle in circles till the glass got down low enough he could spit. Then he pulled out a white sock he carried in his pocket and wiped his mouth with it. "Who gon' tell Minnie Chaundelle that? You?"

After dinner we drove to Minnie's. A woman named Ardath Mae was there. She had silver in her hair and a church look about her that I guessed made Stinger all of a sudden shy. Ardath Mae said Minnie went with another friend to make Verlyn's funeral arrangements. "That child *all* broken up," Ardath Mae said. "Don't know how she gon' come out thothah side."

I asked if it would be all right if I checked Minnie's bedroom for something Verlyn might've left there.

Ardath looked at Stinger before giving me a nod. As I was leaving to the back, I heard her say, "Whatchu been up to, Mistah G.? Been a long time, ain't it, now?"

Minnie's room was full of picture frames and vases glued with beads and nutshells, and more hanging in strands in front of the closet like something out of the hippie days. It took me all of a minute to find Verlyn's book under a shoebox on the closet shelf. When I came out, Stinger and Ardath Mae were standing kind of close together. I showed her what I was going to make off with and told her to tell Minnie. She frowned but said okay, and then I saw her hand slip out of Stinger's, which was hiding behind a fold of her skirt.

Back at my place, I set a bottle of JW Black on the table, got glasses, the ice tray, hot peppers and pretzels, and commenced to read Stinger the list of investors in Mitchell Mining and Drilling Corp. He'd nod at each one, sip his whiskey, and let the sounds roll by while his lids were half-closed. There were eleven names, with sums from a quarter million to a cool eight zeroes posted. When I got to name number nine, Stinger's eyes came open. He said read that one to me again.

Houston is rich in gentlemen's clubs—Centerfolds and Baby Dolls, La Nude and Peter's Wildlife; Rick's and a dozen others. The one we were headed for you had to know was there to know was there. It was a sandstone stucco box with soft-lit arches guarded by two palm trees and had no sign out front, but I knew the place from when it did, remembered it when Stinger said to read that name to him again—Barsekian's Lounge.

We found a place to park at the back of the lot. In the shadows off to the side a security cop in a black uniform sat still as cardboard in his golf cart. The white wafers of his eyeglasses drew him into a cartoon.

Inside, I asked of a man with bleached hair and a face like a chunk of chipped concrete for Mr. Barsekian. He gave us the twice-over, asked our names, then left off through the crowd.

Armen Barsekian used to be one of the biggest bookmakers on the Third Coast, but he retired at the behest of the *federales*. Maybe he was trying to go legit now, run with the bulls down the slick streets of Oil and Gas. If he was the same A. Barsekian listed as an investor in Verlyn's notebook, maybe he'd just like to stimulate an accounting of the Brickner Deposit operation. Only thing was, if this was the hood I thought he was, he also used to be the kind you don't mess with unless you have a fondness for medical personnel of the emergency kind.

Glamour-boy came back and said Stinger could see Mr. B. I'd have to wait at the bar. I started to object but thought maybe Stinger, with his lighter skin, thinner build, and grayer hair, wouldn't be so terrifying as Cisroe Perkins to an old, beat white man.

I went up to the bar and ordered a stout from a woman whose outfit left little to the imagination. She looked about ready to blow and shower us all with beer fuzz. She wore a skirt that could make a man holler and not even know he did.

The crowd was mixed, but not very. I thought I recognized a cop smiling pretty at a dancer and figured you take your pleasure where you can. The music wasn't over-loud, but it was that kind of music anyway, and before long I felt a pulling need for someone with heat and perfume and a great, kind heart.

When Stinger came back I was on my second. He swiped at his goatee, then tipped his head back toward the office door, and said, "It's done, man. It's in the right hands."

Armen Barsekian was an influential man. I didn't much like what I might have guessed about the various businesses he was in nor how he conducted them, but sometimes, I thought, you have to let water cut the channels it is born to cut.

Minnie's baby brother Verlyn Vincent Venable had died on a Wednesday night. The Friday following, way out the Katy, a hunting dog learning to retrieve on a swamp-lake by a shooting range found Guy Grundfest, operations manager at Mitchell Corp., in a dive to its muddy depths. And Ray Wayne Wooley suffered an unfortunate mishap that broke both his legs at the knees, jet-skiing, he said, on Lake Houston on Saturday midnight when he knew he'd had too much too drink.

Monday I took a trip to Chicago, work-related. I was gone four days. When I came back I had other things to attend to, so I didn't make it by Minnie Chaundelle's till the Saturday following.

When I drove down Gross Street, the sun was bright enough to score diamonds. The radio reported ninety-five degrees and about the same dewpoint and I thought it would be all right on this sticky day if it turned out Minnie Chaundelle wasn't there. She didn't answer the door. But then I walked around back and looked through the thick stand of glowering green oak in the cemetery and saw that lovely full-figured woman who from here seemed tiny as a child as she stood by a gravestone.

I walked through the high weeds, watchful for snakes. Walked by headstones broken and stacked in piles and others whole but overturned as though a tractor had plowed them down. I took my time, glancing at the stones, wanting Minnie Chaundelle to see me and get used to the intrusion. Some of the graves had sunken so the names barely showed above the soft earth, and I thought what a shame it was: Gone, then double-gone.

As I got closer I saw the clean mounded earth Minnie stood by. At its head was a shiny black stone with Verlyn's name and dates on it. Minnie turned eyes on me deep as the River Sorrow. No words could cover a time like this, so I didn't try. I just poked out a finger in the direction of her slack hand, and she took it and held it hard as if she were slipping in quicksand.

She said, "This here ain' the real stone. They'll be more on it latuh."

"I know it will be nice," I said. "The best it can be."

She nodded and clamped her lips and leaned into me, wiping her left eye with the ball of her palm. "It's gon' say, 'A ray of sun would be enough. But there was you.'"

"That's real nice, Minnie Chaundelle."

"Ain' it evah?"

The wind took a path alongside us and blew Minnie's skirt forward and tunneled through the brush and leaves ahead as if showing a new way. We stood there, Minnie Chaundelle and me, head touching head, arms about each other, like old lovers locked in memories too hard to name. After a while, I walked back with her to her house, where I comforted her some more.

Later that night, I left my desk to go to the window where the moonlight painted the sill blue and powdered the tops of trees and houses in the same cool shade. I felt sorry for those men caught in the wash of greed, and for the weak ones who open the gates, and for those women held blameless who somewhere wait for both.

And as I unbuttoned my shirt to prepare for bed and smelled the sweet scent of Minnie Chaundelle still upon me, a single tear fell beside my foot on the hardwood floor. I wondered what was becoming of me, letting other men take care of my work so that I could not in honesty lie next to a grieving woman and tell her Cisroe Perkins looked after justice the way he best knows how.

I resolved to do better next time.

# Mat Coward

## Three Nil

THIS SECOND of Mat Coward's stories that we're featuring in the volume is just as entertaining as "Twelve of the Little Buggers," but in a rather different vein. It was first published in the November issue of *Ellery Queen's Mystery Magazine*.

# Three Nil

## Mat Coward

Along with two billion other people, I was watching the biggest sporting event in TV history, the final match of the 1998 FIFA World Cup. France had just scored their second goal against Brazil (the defending champions, red-hot favourites, and the world's greatest soccer-playing nation), when my doorbell rang.

Of course, not all two billion were watching the match in my microscopic north London flat. I don't know where the rest of them were—here and there about the globe, I'd guess—but at my place there were just three of us, and two of them were ostentatiously not responding to the summons of the bell.

So: Not only was it my flat, my TV, my beer, and my crisps—looked like it was my turn to answer the door, too.

"Don't let anyone score while I'm away," I told my guests, and went to discover what sort of person rings your doorbell while two billion other people are watching the biggest sporting event in TV history. A rugby fan? A North American? A North American rugby fan?

Good guess, as it transpired. At least, I couldn't instantly intuit the level of her devotion to rugby, but the woman standing on my step was clearly North American. Even if I hadn't heard her accent before I'd finished opening the door, her huge white teeth would have given her away.

"Are you Charlie?" she said. "The cat detective?"

I admitted it. I trade under the name *Charlie WFYC*—Will Find Your Cat. That's what I do for a living: I find lost cats, in the suburbs north of London, for money. It's what you could call a niche market. Or it's what you could call a desperate way to pay the rent, depending on how you feel about euphemisms.

"I am Charlie," I said. "I am the finder of cats. But at the moment I'm watching the football, along with two billion other people, so perhaps—"

"Right," she said. "Follow me." And with that she turned and began ascending the stone steps that lead from my dilapidated basement bedsit to the dilapidated street on which it rots. She didn't look back.

Well, I stopped taking direct orders from women when I was fifteen, and then again when I was thirty, so I didn't follow her. I went back into my room to drink some more beer and continue enjoying the rare spectacle of Brazil getting stuffed at footie by a nation of cyclists. But I left the front door open in case she chose to return. I hadn't had a paying client all month. I couldn't afford to appear too unwelcoming.

The game finished three-nil, with Brazil taking the nil part, and Paris erupted into what was, according to the newsmen, a bigger street party than that which marked the end of World War Two. You don't see something like that every day of the week, and I pitied the big-toothed American woman for having missed it. What would she tell her grandchildren in years to come, when they asked "Where were you the day Brazil got done over by France, Granny?"

Well, yes, possibly she'd tell them, *"I was trying to get some help finding my cat from a guy who advertised his services as a cat finder, honey. Only he didn't want to know, the cold-hearted bastard."*

Well, yes, possibly.

"I've got to pop out," I told my guests—who by now were starting to act more like lodgers. "Make yourselves a nice cup of tea, if you fancy one." That got a few laughs, at least.

I wasn't really looking for the woman. I needed fresh air, some cigarette papers, and some pizza, anyway, so I thought while I was out I might as well have a quick butcher's up and down the street, round the block, and in the nearest pub. Just in case.

First thing I did when I came out of the door was trip over a large rockery stone, apparently laid upon my step for that precise purpose. I wasn't as upset as I might have been, though, because the stone was acting as a paperweight for a fifty-pound note. You ever seen a fifty-pound note? Nice design. I especially like the part where it says "Fifty Pounds."

Written along the edge of the banknote, in red felt-tip, was the message: "Want more? Find me. Where? You're the detective."

I walked up as far as the main road, keeping my eyes open for an American female, my sort of age, large teeth, expensive sunglasses, dyed red hair, slim (by British standards, I mean; by American standards, downright skeletal), carrying a black leather attaché case. I didn't see her. I had a quick look in the pub, and a squint through the window of the cafe. She wasn't there. I picked up my smokes and my pizza, and walked home by a different route. Still didn't spot her.

Fifty pounds, and the promise of more. I decided to go and fetch my car, extend the area of the search. She wanted to be found, after all: She had to be somewhere.

I got back to my place and there she was, sitting next to the money-stone, right there on my step.

She was quite good-looking, if you go for the all teeth and bones look, and, frankly, it's a long time since I could afford to be fussy. Even so, she was beginning to irritate me. I sat down next to her, got my notebook out of my pocket, and said, "Let's start with a description of the missing cat."

"No, let's start with you giving me my fifty pounds back."

*Now* I was irritated. "Why should I give you the money back?"

"Because it was an advance on your fee for finding me. You didn't find me. I was here all the time." She pointed towards a tumble-down, roofless wooden shack which hid the communal dustbins (from sight, though rarely from smell). "I was right over there."

"Then you hired me under false pretences," I said. But I gave her the money anyway. I suppose I'd known all along that that fifty-quid note had "Too Good to Be True" written all over it, in red felt-tip.

She put the money in her rear jeans pocket, then stood up and brushed the brick dust off her backside. "My name's Marie," she said. "Can we talk in your office?"

I lit a cigarette. "We are doing," I said.

"Oh, I see. Classy operation, huh?" Marie chuckled. From the sound her throat made I guessed she was a smoker, but if she wanted a smoke now, she could have one of her own. "Okay," she said, still standing. I stood up too, because it seemed like the polite thing to do. And because my bum had gone to sleep on the stone. It's not as young as it used to be, that bum of mine.

Marie reached round to her back pocket and brought out the (by now legendary) fifty-pound note. Then she dug in one of her front pockets and came up with its twin. She held them both out to me. I just about stopped myself from kissing them. "This is a retainer, okay?" said Marie.

I tucked the hundred away, somewhere deep within the folds of my poverty. "Okay. So what's the cat's name?"

"Venus Arisen."

"Venus Arisen?" I wrote it down. "That's a pity."

For the first time since we'd met, Marie looked a little unsure. "A pity? Why?"

One of the worst parts of this job is having to be polite to annoying people. Since it's one of the worst parts, I rarely bother with it. "A pity to give a cat such a bloody stupid name," I explained. "How long's she been missing?"

"*He*. I don't believe in gender-restricted names. And he's *not* missing." She showed me an unpleasantly, if appropriately, feline smile, designed to prove that she was back in control of the conversation after a brief derailment.

What she didn't know was—well, she didn't know me. She didn't know that, with one hundred pounds of her money in my pocket, I really couldn't care less what silly games she wanted to play. "So you know where the cat is?"

"I know where the cat is."

"And you want me to get it back for you?"

"Nope."

"You don't want me to get the cat back for you?"

She shook her head loosely from side to side. Frankly, it was not what I would consider a very grown-up gesture. "What I want you to do is, I want you to find out where the cat is."

Oh, *right*. A loony. No problem. Far as I'm concerned, you can be as loony as you like, just as long as you're paying. Like, in advance. "Well," I said, cheerfully, "that should be simple enough."

"Oh yes?"

"Sure. I'll ask you where the cat is. You tell me. Then I'll tell you, and you can pay me. Yes, that ought to work. Though it leaves unresolved the question of what I'm going to do with my evenings now the World Cup's over."

She burst into tears. I mean, she *exploded* into tears, like an Iraqi water-cooler hit by an underachieving smart bomb. "You're not taking this seriously!"

Now, that hurt. How could she say such a thing about me? This woman had given me one hundred pounds and implied that there was more to come. And she thought I wasn't taking her seriously?

"Madam," I informed her, "I can assure you I take this matter most seriously and will endeavour to deliver complete satisfaction in whatever mission with which you see fit with which to charge me with. How many withs was that?"

She dabbed at her tears with her sleeve. "I don't know. I lost count."

"The thing is, I need to get all the facts straight in my head." Even if they're not straight in *your* screwy nut, I could have added. But didn't, obviously. "So, tell me the whole story, will you?"

"Okay." She sniffed up the last of the tears. "My ex-partner, that is, my ex-boyfriend, he has the cat."

"Ah-ha. Now we're getting to the heart of the doughnut."

"You're really not very good at that, you know?"

"At what?"

"That wisecracking banter stuff. It's not your forte."

"Listen," I said, impatience beginning to win out over greed once again, which has always been one of my most perilous failings. "I find cats, like it says on my card. You want banter, you should . . ."

She waited. I dot-dot-dotted. Eventually she said, "I should what?"

"Hire a banter specialist," I mumbled.

"See what I mean? Not your forte. Lim has the cat. It's my cat, I've had it for years, ever since I came to this country, but he won't give it back. Now, for reasons I don't choose to share with you, so don't bother asking, I don't wish Lim to know that I know that he has the cat. Okay? So I want you to 'find' the cat, report back to me, then I can confront Lim with your report and demand return of my property. Namely, one cat."

Reasons she didn't choose to share—that'd be female pride, I reckoned. "I don't usually do custody battles," I said. "Too messy"

Marie shook her head. "It's nothing like that. Lim has no claim on the cat, believe me."

"All right," I said. "But I come back to my earlier point—you tell me where the cat is, and I'll—"

"No way!" She reacted as if I'd made an indecent suggestion. "I'm from the States, pal. The land of the proactive consumer. You think I'm going to pay you for doing nothing, you think again."

Counting slowly to ten, and then even more slowly to twenty, I rolled, lit, and smoked a cigarette. It was important that I ignored the loonier aspects of this case and focused on the essentials. That's right—the money. If she wanted to pay me to locate a non-missing cat, that was fine. No one has ever accused me of putting job satisfaction or professional dignity ahead of paying the bills.

"You understand that I charge a daily rate?"

She nodded.

"All right, then. Will you at least tell me where the cat went missing from?"

Marie took an envelope out of her attaché case. "In here, you'll find a photo of the cat, the address of the apartment where the cat was stolen from, and the keys to that apartment."

I took the envelope and rattled it. "Can I contact you at this address?"

"No, I'm not there anymore. And before you ask, I don't choose to tell you my current address."

Another slow ten, another slow twenty. A prayer of thanks for nicotine. "That's going to make it hard for me to contact you, Marie."

"I'll contact you," she said.

I'd had enough arguing with foreign maniacs for one day, so all I said was: "Right. Gotcha. You're the boss."

The flat was a two-bedroom place in a moderately prosperous dormitory street near Kentish Town tube station, and although it was fully furnished, right down to a box of tea bags in the kitchen, the unmistakable aroma of human occupation was entirely absent.

This was, undoubtedly, rented accommodation resting between tenants. I knew the type: In my younger days, I'd squatted plenty such, armed only with a paperback guide to property laws, a portable record player, and a couple of Stones LPs. Of course, this was back before I never got married, when I was a young man, before I became a bachelor.

I sat on the naked mattress in the main bedroom, its pillows and blankets piled at one end, and looked down at my unnecessarily soft midriff, and past that to my almost pretentiously scuffed brown shoes, and I thought about how far I hadn't come in thirty years. I still lived in the same kind of places now—difference was, these days I paid rent, like any other mug.

Not to mention that, to my own daily astonishment, I'd turned out to be not a legendary bluesman but a cat finder.

I lifted my gaze off the floor with the kind of effort an Olympian weightlifter uses when he feels the chalk on his palms begin to sludge in the sweat, and let it rest instead on what was clearly Kitty Korner. A piece of plastic sheeting lay across a square yard of carpet, and upon it stood a food bowl, a water bowl, a dirt tray, a poop-scoop, a box of dry food, and—

And it was all brand new. Unused. Just to make sure, I went over and sniffed the tray. Definitely: Not the faintest whiff of mog. This flat wasn't a cat's previous address. This was a cat's *next* address.

I picked my knees up off the floor and carried them back over to the bed. I sat down, rolled up a roll-up, and while I smoked it I thought.

Mine is generally a pretty simple line of work, not involving too many brilliant feats of detection. What usually happens is, people's cats wander a bit beyond their territory, get lost, panic, and go feral. They rarely run far, and I've yet to encounter one that has bothered with false documents or reconstructive facial surgery. The only truly essential talents required of a cat finder are, in reverse order of importance, low cunning, a high boredom threshold, and exceptional bladder control.

But this . . . this was clearly something a little odd. Weird, even. And so was my client, Mad Marie.

As I've already implied, I have no particular objection to taking money off mad people. Not wishing to sound cynical (whilst at the same time not giving a damn whether I do or not), I have to make a living. Everyone has to make a living, after all, except archbishops, members of the House of Lords, and whoever's in charge of quality control on the privatised railways. Besides, loopy Americans have just as much right to the services of a cat finder as does anyone else. It would be discriminatory of me to refuse Marie's dosh.

That wasn't my problem. My problem was that despite, on all the evidence, being as crazy as a wasp in a jar full of glue fumes, Marie was solidly in control of this daft game—or whatever it was. That made me uncomfortable.

It wasn't until I was at home in bed that night, failing to sleep, that the very obvious solution finally entered my non-detective's head. Don't follow an invisible cat; follow the client. Brilliant! Obvious, but brilliant.

(The reason I couldn't sleep, by the way, was that every time my eyelids began to droop, I would spring back awake, thinking: *I sniff cat trays. For a living. Meanwhile, Howlin' Wolf doesn't even know I exist.*)

"Ah Marie, I'm glad you phoned. I have what is known in the argot of the detecting racket as a Hot Lead."

"Oh, you do?"

"Oh, I do."

"Oh." There was a pause, during which I could hear her tongue clicking thoughtfully against her big, shiny gnashers. "Okay. Great. You want to tell me what it is?"

"Not over the phone."

"I see. You are what is known in the argot of the psychiatric racket as A Touch Paranoid."

"Quite possibly. Either way, I'd like to deliver my report face-to-teeth."

"I beg your pardon?"

I shook the telephone and made sizzling noises into the mouthpiece. "Face," I said. "Face-to-face. There's a pub in Harrow called the Load of Hay. Will you meet me there tonight at eight-thirty?"

Another pause, more clicking. "Well . . . yeah, I guess."

"Great. I'll wear a carnation so you'll recognise me."

"Huh? We've already met."

"Badinage, Marie. Mere banter."

There was a Country and Western night happening at the pub. People have to make their own entertainment in the suburbs, I understand that, it's just a pity that most of them are so bad at it. I have nothing against Country and Western music, provided I don't have to listen to it, but there is something about the sight of middle-aged British suburban folk wearing cowboy clothes and calling each other "Pardner" that I find mildly irritating. If I were ever to visit Montana and discover the pubs there full of middle-aged American suburban folk dressed as Morris Dancers and calling each other "Mate," I would probably react with precisely the same degree of nose-wrinkling distaste.

Or else wet myself laughing, one or the other.

I did a quick tour of the pub, weaving between the bogus cow persons, who were getting outside some beer in preparation for an evening spent steppin' out to the down-home sounds of Willie Wyoming and His Western Wildmen. I'd arrived early for our rendezvous, and I wanted to make sure that Marie hadn't arrived even earlier. It was pretty packed, I wasn't as slim as my elusive client, and as I squeezed past a corner table my hip caught a pint of lager, sloshing its contents onto the lap of a man wearing cowboy clothes several sizes too small for him. He was big and round. Rounder than a pig with a pig inside it. When he spoke it was with a deep, rough Glasgow accent.

"You got a problem, pal?"

"Yeah," I said. "My best friend done run off with my dawg."

To my great relief he laughed at that, slapped me on the back, and said "Yee-haw." I returned the salutation, and returned to my car, parked a few yards away, with a clear view of the pub car park.

She arrived soon after, in a maroon Escort even more clapped-out than my own ancient chariot. She drove it as if it was on fire.

I gave her a moment to get settled, then I phoned the pub on my mobile. It took awhile to make the barman understand my request over the noise of the fiddles and the banjos, but eventually Marie came to the phone.

"Yee-haw, Charlie," she said, her tone weary.

I almost yee-hawed her back, then remembered that I wasn't supposed to know what was going on at the pub. "Hi, Marie. Look, I'm sorry about this, but I can't meet you after all. This red-hot lead? It's suddenly gone critical. I have to chase it before it burns out. Ring me tomorrow, okay? I should have more news for you then?"

I hung up before she could ask any questions. I think that annoyed her: She came out of the pub immediately, muttering to herself, probably about the unreliability of men in general and cat finders in particular. Her tyres sprayed gravel over late-arriving cowpersons as she exited the car park at speed. I followed, a little more sedately.

We ended up in Wembley, where she pulled up outside a small, seriously grotty bungalow, in a street that was more ghostly than quiet. I parked my tin can behind a big van and watched as she fished around in her attaché case for the door key.

She went in. I sat in the car, smoking and telling myself that I still had the bladder control of a man twenty years my junior. By way of distraction, I took out the photo she'd given me of the non-missing cat, a fluffy, all-white youngster, and looked at it properly for the first time. Then, for no particular reason beyond boredom, I turned the photo over and read the processing date stamped on the back.

Well now, I thought. That's curious.

Marie came out, got back in her car, and zoomed off again. I let her go. Somewhere in that house, I hoped, I would find the address of Lim, the ex-boyfriend. Looking at the tatty shack, I was confident that it wouldn't be too difficult to get into.

It wasn't. When I knocked on the door, just to make sure that nobody was at home, it turned out that somebody was at home. His teeth were smaller than Marie's but his muscles were much bigger.

"Ah," I said, "you must be the ex-boyfriend." But what was he doing at Marie's place?

"I'm Lim," he said, his accent Yorkshire. "Nothing ex about me, pal. How about you?"

I stood there, staring into space, with my mouth open. I can't help it, it's what I look like when I'm thinking. Marie had told me that she'd had the cat for years—"ever since I came to this country." But the cat in the photo wasn't more than two or three years old. And the date stamp on the reverse of the print was from last month.

Stealing pets for ransom isn't an uncommon crime these days, according to the newspapers. My guess had been that Marie and Lim were amateur catnappers who'd fallen out over the spoils.

But if Lim was still here, it didn't look like they'd fallen very far.

Lim seemed to take my silence on his doorstep as an insult. "Tell you what," he said. "I think I'll hit you."

I couldn't think of anything to defend myself with other than my business card.

"Will Find Your Cat? Jesus," he said. "The old bag hired a detective?" He laughed. "You better come in, pal."

I took a step forward, and Lim pushed me hard in the chest. While I was busy falling over, he scarpered out of the kitchen door and away over the back fence. That was fine with me. I rarely chase people, and never if they're running.

In a large cage, which dominated the cramped, underfurnished living room, I found Venus Arisen—white, young, and fluffy. See? Told you I was a cat finder.

A disc hanging from his collar was inscribed with his phone number, but before I had a chance to ring it, Marie came in, looked at me, and said, "Hell's bells."

"If you run, I won't chase you," I said. "I'll just sit here and wait until you get back."

She dropped down onto a sofa with a big *whump* and lit a cigarette. She made a big production out of not offering me one. Petty.

"Is the cat all right?"

"Don't worry," I said. "The cat's fine."

"Pity," she said, on a stream of blue smoke. "I was hoping Lim had used it to hit you with. I can't stand cats. Lim's gone, I guess?"

"You just missed him." I sat down on the smelly sofa, between her and the door. Just in case. I tried to think of a bit of banter to cheer us both up, but nothing came to mind. I settled for, "Tell me the story, Marie."

She did, in a quiet, depressingly sane voice. It took me awhile to realise she was crying, she made so little of it.

Lim and Marie wanted to get married. They got a flat sorted out—the one with the all-new litter tray which I'd visited the previous day—but then Lim lost his job, and Marie was *damned if she was going to pay for everything*, so they came up with the cat-napping plan. Simple. But no sooner had they installed Venus Arisen in his temporary quarters, when Marie met someone else.

"Someone richer," I guessed.

"What? I'm supposed to apologise for having self-worth?" She wiped her nose on her sleeve. "This country, really! The only time you see *ambition* is on a Scrabble board."

Simply walking out on Lim was, apparently, not an option. "The man is possessive. A fat old milksop of a cat finder like you, no offence intended, Charlie, could not even begin to visualise what I mean when I say that he is possessive."

"Slightly lumpy," I said. "Not fat." I might have objected to milk-sop, too, but I wasn't a hundred percent sure what it meant, and I didn't want to make a fool of myself by objecting to a compliment.

"I knew I had to shake Lim off good and proper, but I couldn't think of a way. Then I saw your stupid advert on a postcard in a launderette window."

"Can you remember which launderette? It'd be a great help for my marketing strategy."

"I convinced Lim that we shouldn't move the cat to the new flat yet, in case we were seen. And then I hired you. You thought I was crazy, didn't you? See, that's what I wanted you to think—I didn't want you taking the job too seriously."

"Yes, Marie," I said. "You give great crazy."

Her entire plan might have served as evidence of her craziness—except that it worked. She assumed that I would stake out the new flat, since it was the only address I had. She assumed this because she assumed that I was cheap, lazy, dishonest, unimaginative, and slightly lumpy, and not a proper detective. That annoyed me: I have never *claimed* to be a proper detective.

Due to my incompetence, Lim would be sure to spot me (he was over there several times a week, making sure the love nest didn't fall to squatters) and assume that I was either a cop or a private eye. Why would he assume that?

She laughed out a cough of smoke. "Let's just say that dear Lim has had his ups and downs in life. He might look like Mr. Clean—"

"He doesn't," I said.

"Well, even if he did, it would be an inaccurate image. Believe me, I know this: If he sees a cop, real or imaginary, he runs." She looked me up and down, ran her tongue over her big teeth awhile, and laughed again. "Bet he's the first person ever to run from a cat finder, though."

"From what you say, isn't he the type to come looking for you, when he thinks it's safe to return?"

"Probably. But I'd be gone."

I sat for a moment, thinking it through. "And the reason you gave me the address of the new flat, instead of this place, was you didn't want to risk me actually finding the cat. You were still planning to go ahead with the ransom, minus the inconvenience of your ex-partner."

"Well—right," she said, and I could see from her amused eyes that there was something else there, some game yet unfinished. She saw that I knew and spoke quickly to cover the moment. "I hadn't counted on you tailing me. For God's sake, you're lousy at banter, I made sure of that, and I assumed you'd be lousy at all the other detective skills, too. I mean, finding cats—how hard can that be?"

Bloody cheek! "I'd like to see you do it," I said.

"Oh, please! I went to school—finding cats, that's a career for someone who was raised by chimps."

I was still wondering what it was that she wasn't telling me. "You don't look all that happy, Marie. Seeing as you're free of Lim, which was the whole point."

She sighed. "Yeah, I got rid of Lim, all right. But the other guy . . ."

"Ah," I said. "He went back to his wife."

"Still," said Marie, suddenly all business, "you are right—you did what I hired you to do, even if it wasn't quite how I planned, and even if you didn't know you were doing it. So I owe you for your time. My money's in the car. I'll just go get it. Okay?"

She stood up, but she couldn't easily get to the door without me moving my outstretched legs. Our eyes met, and I found myself thinking, *Well, we all make mistakes*, so I decided to make one of my own.

"Sure," I said, folding my legs up. "You go and get the money. I'll wait here."

Marie nodded, smiled a little bit, and slipped away. She drove off quietly— almost like a mark of respect.

I'm no vet, but Venus Arisen didn't seem to have suffered much from his imprisonment. His white fur was white, his eyes were bright, his yowling was louder than a chain saw, and he gave me a few decent scratches as I bundled him into a carrying case.

I leant against the car, with the cat box in one hand and my mobile phone in the other, and dialled the number from Venus's identity collar. Venus carried on yowling.

"*Whitey?* Whitey—is that you?"

An elderly woman, with a posh voice, threadbare clothes, and milky eyes came tottering out of the bungalow next to Marie's. She looked in my direction but didn't seem to see me, so I walked towards her.

"You've found my cat! Oh, God bless you, you've brought my Whitey back! Please—can you bring him in? My phone's ringing."

I switched off the mobile.

"Oh," said the old woman as she reached her front door. "It seems to have stopped."

I put the mobile in my pocket, thinking: *Whitey?*

I followed the woman into her house, thinking: *Next door.* They stole the cat from their next-door neighbour. That was the bit Marie hadn't told me. That was her final game. That and the damn stupid name.

I closed the door behind me, put the cat box down, and opened it. Whitey disappeared in the direction of the kitchen.

His owner started asking me who I was, and how, and why, and where, so I gave her one of my cards. She stared at it for a while and then said, "What does it say, young man? I'm afraid my eyes . . . cataracts, you know."

For a brief mad moment, it struck me that I could tell her anything I liked. "The bearer of this card is the Prince of Wales. Please give him all your silver and a large chocolate cake."

Instead, I said, "My name's Charlie. I find lost cats."

"Charlie? Charlie WFYC? But I was going to call you! I was, my niece saw your advertisement in a newsagent's window. She wrote down the number for me, but—"

"But your eyes," I guessed. "Cataracts."

"I *didn't* hire you, did I?" she said, squinting up at me.

"No," I sighed.

"Oh dear. I can't very well pay you for bringing him back then, can I? If you weren't working for me."

"No," I sighed.

"Still, it wouldn't be right to let you go empty-handed. Wait there, please, young man."

A tip, I thought. Well, that went with the posh voice—paying tips instead of wages.

She scuttled off to the kitchen and came back a minute or so later carrying a jar of homemade gooseberry jam. I knew it was homemade, and gooseberry, because it said so on the label. "Homemade Gooseberry Jam, 1991." The cellophane cover had come loose and there was grey mould around the edge of the jar.

"There," she said, pressing it into my hands reverently. "Fair exchange is no robbery, isn't that right?"

"No," I sighed. "Or yes. Or whatever." I saw myself out.

On a lamppost next to my car there hung a rubbish bin. I put the jam into it and got into my car. As I fiddled with my seat belt, I saw in my wing mirror a flash of white fur scooting across the road and up and over a tall fence. Through the open driver's window, I heard a posh voice calling, "Oh no, he's got out again! Oh please, young man, I say—I say, don't go! Young man, could you possibly . . ."

I decided I had cataracts of the ears, closed the window, and drove home.

It was all rather sad, really, because I like jam, and I like money, and on this job I'd got no money—twice—and the only jam I'd been offered was inedible.

Life versus Charlie: three-nil to Life. I demand a rematch.

# Jan Burke

## The Man in the Civil Suit

JAN BURKE'S Irene Kelly novels are among the most critically and commercially blessed of our time. And with each book, their audience grows. There's a breathless, thrillerlike pace to Jan's books that make most mysteries seem sluggish by comparison—a quality that makes them perfect for today's thrill-seeking book buyers. Not that Jan isn't a wily observer of this particular historical moment. Each of her novels is filled with crackling observations about our little particular spin through the galaxy. "The Man in the Civil Suit," first published in *Malice Domestic 9*, shows her up to her usual high standards.

# The Man in the Civil Suit

*Jan Burke*

I have a bone to pick with the Museum of Natural History. Yes, the very museum in which the peerless Professor Pythagoras Peabody so recently met his sad, if rather spectacular, demise. I understand they are still working on restoring the mastodon. But my grievance does not pertain to prehistoric pachyderms.

If the administrators of said museum are quoted accurately in the newspapers, they have behaved in a rather unseemly manner in regard to the late Peabody. How speedily they pointed out that he was on the premises in violation of a restraining order! How hastily they added that he had similar orders placed upon him by a number of institutions, including the art museum, the zoo, and Ye Olde Medieval Restaurant & Go-Cart Track! When asked if he was the man named in the civil suit they filed three days ago, how rapidly the administrators proclaimed that Professor Peabody was no professor at all!

Oh, how quickly they forget! They behave as if the Case of the Carillean Carbuncle never occurred. A balanced account of recent events must be given, and as one who knew the man in the civil suit better than any other—save, perhaps, his sister Persephone—I have taken on the burden of seeing justice done where Pythagoras Peabody is concerned.

Although Pythag, as his closest friends—well, as I called him, because frankly, few others could tolerate his particular style of genius at close range— although Pythag never taught at a university or other institution, it is widely known that the affectionate name "Professor Peabody" was bestowed upon him by a grateful police force at the close of the Case of the Carillean Carbuncle, or as Pythag liked to call it, 300. (Some of you may need assistance understanding why—I certainly did. Pythag explained that the first letters of Case, Carillean, and Carbuncle are Cs. Three Cs, taken together, form a Roman numeral. I'm certain I need not hint you on from there, but I will say this was typical of his cleverness.)

Need I remind the museum administrators of the details of 300? This most unusual garnet was on display in their own Gems and Mineralogy Department when it was stolen by a heartless villain. True, the museum guards were in pursuit long before the ten-year-old boy left the grounds, and after several hours of chasing him through the halls, exhibits, and displays—including a dinosaur diorama, the planetarium, and the newly opened "Arctic and Antarctica: Poles Apart" exhibit—while conducting what amounted to an elaborate game of hide-and-seek, they caught their thief.

Unfortunately, the Carillean Carbuncle was no longer on his person, and he refused to give any clue as to its location. This was, apparently, a way of continuing the jollification he had enjoyed with these fellows. Not amused, the museum called the police. The boy called in his own reinforcements, and his parents, in the time-honored tradition of raisers of rogues, defended their son unequivocally and threatened all sorts of nastiness if he were not released immediately. The boy went home, and the Carillean Carbuncle remained missing.

Enter Peabody. Actually, he had already entered. It was Pythag's habit to be the first guest to walk through the museum doors in the morning, and the last to leave at closing. He made himself at home in the Natural History Museum, just as he once had in the art museum, and in the zoo. (The trouble at Ye Olde Medieval Restaurant & Go-Cart Track occurred before we were acquainted, but Pythag once hinted that it had something to do with giving the waiters' lances to the young drivers and encouraging them to "joust.")

I have said I will give a fair accounting, and I will. Pythag was a man who knew no boundaries. His was a genius, he often reminded me, that could not be confined to the paths that others were pleased to follow. I know some stiff-rumped bureaucrats will not agree, but if he were here to defend himself, Pythag would undoubtedly say, "If you don't want a gentleman born with an enviable amount of curiosity to climb into an elephants' compound, for goodness sakes, rely on more than a waist-high fence and a silly excuse for a moat to keep him out."

Likewise, he would tell you that if your art museum docent becomes rattled when a gentleman with a carrying voice follows along with a second group of unsuspecting art lovers, telling them a thing or two the docent failed to mention to his own group, well then, the docent stands in need of better training. Pythag enjoyed himself immensely on these "tour" occasions, tapping on glass cases and reading aloud from wall plaques to begin his speeches.

He soon varied from the information in these written guides, however. He often told visitors that when x-rayed, the canvases beneath the museum's most famous oil paintings were shown to be covered with little blue numbers, a number one being a red, two a blue, and so forth. This, he claimed, was how the museum's restoration department could make a perfect match when repairing a damaged work of art. He also claimed to be such an expert as to be able to see the numbers with his naked eye, which, he said, "Has quite spoiled most of these for me."

The art museum director, Pythag declared, would soon be under arrest for the murder of Elvis—the director's supposed motive for the killing being to increase the value of his secret, private collection of velvet portraits of The King. (I understand the We Tip Hotline, tiring of Pythag's relentless pursuit of this idea, blocked calls from the Peabody home number.)

I'll wager a tour with Pythag was much more interesting, if less enlightening, than one taken with the regular docents. The art museum, however, was unwilling to offer this alternative. It seemed a little harsh to tell him that he, and not the director, risked arrest if he returned. As Persephone argued when she came to fetch him home, how could anyone in his right mind fault a person for being *creative* in an *art* museum?

Please don't bother to mention Pythag's exile from the Museum of Transportation. Pythag would tell you that a velvet rope may be seen by a man with panache (and if he could have withstood one more *P* in his moniker, panache would have been Pythag's middle name) as less a barrier than an invitation to step over it and into the past. He went into the past by way of an eighteenth-century carriage, as it happened, and ever seeking the most realistic experience possible, Pythag had to bounce in it a bit. "I promise you," Pythag told the irate curator, "the King of Spain bounced when *he* rode in the dratted thing."

Perhaps you have already seen from these examples that Pythag was the perfect man to consult on the matter of the missing carbuncle. Who was more qualified to determine what a clever boy, let loose in a museum, might do? Indeed, I readily admit that for all his genius, Pythag's enthusiasm sometimes led him into rather childish behavior. I concede that he was subject to bouts of stubbornness over silly things, bouts that made him not much more than a child himself at times.

On the very afternoon the carbuncle was stolen, for example, he *insisted* on staring into the penguins' eyes in the Antarctic exhibit, convinced that each penguin retained on his retina a memory of its last moments. If he could catch the reflection of this last recollection, he decided, he could experience the thing itself—it would be, he said, "Bird's eye *deja vu*." This was one of those times when, were I not courting Persephone, I would have been tempted to leave the exhibit without him. Nothing I said would convince him that memory resides in the brain rather than the eye. He utterly rejected my claim that these were not the penguins' actual eyes, but glass reproductions, and rebuked me loudly and in horrified accents for suggesting such a thing.

But as Persephone was most appreciative of my willingness to watch over her brother and accompany him to public venues, I did my best to overlook his occasionally irritating behaviors. Persephone, brilliant and far less given to acting on impulse than her brother, told me that restraining orders were a small price for Pythag's genius, but she'd just as soon not be asked to pay any larger prices for it.

Thus I made an effort to distract him from the penguins by mentioning his beloved mastodon. (Pythag had a fondness for all things the names of which begin with the letter *P*. His attachment to the mastodon puzzled me, and I wondered if he was taking on the letter *M* as well, until I noticed that he constantly referred to it as the "proboscidean mammal.") Pretending to be struck by a sudden inspiration, I muttered something to the effect of, "an elephant's ancestors might also 'never forget,' " then asked Pythag if he thought there might be some memory retained in the eye socket of the mastodon. The ruse worked, and soon we were off to the Prehistoric Hall.

Here he was again distracted, this time by the sight of several policemen carefully searching for the carbuncle. Pythag managed, in his inimitable way, to quickly convince a detective that he was an official at the museum. He induced the fellow to follow him to the planetarium—not a bad notion, for the young thief had most certainly visited this facility during his flight.

The carbuncle being ruby in color, Pythag's theory was based on meteorology. "Red sky at night is a young rogue's delight!" he shouted as we ran after him.

He believed the boy might have been planning to alter the color of the light in the planetarium projector. With the help of the policeman, he hastily disassembled the rather costly mechanism, but alas, it was not the hiding place.

At my suggestion that they both might want to quickly take themselves as far away from the results of their work as possible, Pythag made one of his lightning-like leaps of logic, and announced that "Polaris was beckoning." We sped back to the polar exhibits.

Here Pythag had another brainstorm, saying that there was something not quite right about the Eskimos, and delved his hand into an Inuit mannequin's hide game bag. In triumph, Pythag removed the carbuncle.

On that day, you will remember, he was the museum's darling. Pythag's new policeman friend, perhaps distracting his fellows from the disassembled projector, extolled Pythag's genius in solving the mystery of the missing gem, and proclaimed him "Professor Peabody," by which address the world would know him during the brief remaining span of his lifetime.

Not many days later, tragedy struck. Having dissuaded him from climbing atop the mastodon skeleton's back, and seeing that he was again entranced by the penguins, I felt that it was reasonably safe for me to answer the call of nature at the Natural History Museum. But when I returned from the gents, Pythag was nowhere to be found.

I heard a commotion at the entrance to the exhibit, and rushed toward it, certain he would be at the center of any disturbance. But this hubbub was caused by the bright lights and cameras of a cable television crew from the Museum Channel. The crew was taping another fascinating episode of *Naturally, at the Natural.* This particular segment focused on a visit by the museum's newest patron, Mrs. Ethylene Farthington. Mrs. Farthington was possessed of all the right extremes, as far as the museum was concerned: extremely elderly, extremely wealthy, and extremely generous. Add to this the fact that she did not choose to meddle in the specifics of how her donations would be spent, and you see why the director of the museum thought her to be perfection itself.

Her progress through the polar exhibits was regally (if not dodderingly) slow, but none dared complain. For reasons that do not concern us or any other right-thinking person, Mrs. Farthington was fond of places made of ice, and her sponsorship of this exhibit was but the beginning of the largesse she was to bestow on the museum. That day, she was on her way to sign papers which would finalize her gift of a staggering sum to the museum. She would also sign a new will, supplanting the one that currently left the remainder of her enormous estate to her pet tortoise, and establishing in its stead a bequest for the museum. Apparently, there had been a falling out with the tortoise.

So taken was I by the sight of the frail Mrs. Farthington gazing at the *faux* glaciers, I nearly forgot to continue my search for Pythag. If I had not chanced to glance at the opposite display, where I saw a familiar face among the penguins, I might not have known where to look for him. The face was not Pythag's, although the clothes were those of the man who now asked me to address him as "Professor." No, the face was that of an Inuit mannequin. How careless of Pythag! Everyone knows Inuits and penguins do not belong in the same display!

I did not for a moment imagine that Pythag was cavorting about the museum in the altogether. He had decided, undoubtedly, to expand upon his experience with the hide bag, and bedeck himself in the clothing and gear of the Inuit.

I was a little frightened to realize that I knew his mind so well, even if gratified to see that there was one rather unusual member of the Inuit family represented in the display. I had no difficulty in discerning which of the still figures was Pythag, and had I never met him before that day, I doubt I would have failed to notice the one apple which seemed to have fallen rather far from the Inuit family tree. There are, undoubtedly, few blond Inuits. Besides, none of the other mannequins blinked.

Otherwise, he was remarkably doll-like, clad in all his furs, and I was unable to fight a terribly strong urge to enjoy a few moments of seeing Pythag forced to be still and silent. How many times since that day have I told myself that had I foregone this bit of pleasure, disaster might have been avoided!

When I turned to see if anyone was watching before bidding him to hurry away, I was vexed to espy Mrs. Farthington and entourage approaching the display. There was nothing for it now but to wait until the group had passed on to the next display. But as if taking a page from her tortoise's book, Mrs. Farthington was not to be hurried, and stood transfixed, perhaps on some subconscious level perceiving what Pythag had perceived so recently—that something was not quite right about the Eskimos.

Pythag was masterful. Even under this prolonged scrutiny, he—as the saying goes—kept his cool. Or would have, were it not for the television lights. The heat they generated would have made puddles of the exhibit if any of the ice and snow had been real. Instead, it made a puddle of Pythag. He began to perspire profusely.

I do believe he still might have carried it off, had not Mrs. Farthington chanced to look at him just when he felt forced to lift a finger to swipe a ticklish drop of moisture from the end of his nose.

Mrs. Farthington, startled to see a mannequin move, clutched at her bosom and fell down dead on the spot.

The tortoise inherited.

When his friends in the police department refused to pursue a criminal case against him, Pythagoras Peabody was sued by the museum.

Persephone was not pleased with me.

This last was uppermost in my mind when I strolled alone through the museum the day after the civil suit was announced, and my own suit of Persephone rejected. Had I not loved her so dearly, I might have been a little angry with Perse. Her brother was a confounded nuisance, but she blamed me for his present troubles. I should have kept a closer watch, she told me. Had *she* deigned to accompany him on his daily outings? No. Monday was the worst day of the week, as far as she was concerned. That was the day her lunatic brother stayed home. I decided to give her a little time with him, to remind her of my usefulness to her.

One would think I would have gone elsewhere, now that I had the chance to go where I pleased, but there was something comfortable about following routine at a time when my life was so topsy-turvy. So I returned to the museum.

Standing before the great mastodon, I sighed. It had been Pythag's ambition to ride the colossus. Could it be done? To give the devil his due, that was the thing about going to a place like this with Pythag—he managed, somehow, to always add a bit of excitement. I mean, one really doesn't think of a museum as a place where the unexpected might happen at any moment. Unless one visited it with Pythag.

Why should Pythag have all the fun? I overcame the hand-railing with ease.

It was not so easy to make the climb aboard the skeleton, but I managed it. I enjoyed the view from its back only briefly—let me tell you, there is no comfortable seating astride the spine of a mastodon. Knowing that Pythag would be nettled that I had achieved this summit before him, I decided that I would leave some little proof of my visit. I made a rather precarious search of my pockets and found a piece of string. Tied in a bow about a knot of wires along the spine, it did very nicely.

The skeleton swayed a bit as I got down, and the only witness, a child, was soon asking his mother if he might go for a ride, too—but in a stern, Pythag-inspired voice, I informed her that I was an official of the museum, repairing the damage done by the last little boy who climbed the mastodon, a boy whose parents could be contacted at the poor house, where they were working off payments. Although we haven't had a poor house in this city in a century, she seemed to understand the larger implications, and they quickly left the museum.

As anticipated, Persephone called the next day.

"Take him," she pleaded. "Take him anywhere, and I'll take you back."

"Persephone," I said sternly.

"I know, and I apologize, dearest. I will marry you, just as we planned, only we must wait until this suit is settled. I won't have a penny to my name, I'm afraid, but the three of us will manage somehow, won't we?"

"Three of us?"

"Well, I can't leave poor Pythagoras to fend for himself now, can I?"

And so once again, I found myself in the Museum of Natural History with Pythag at my side. He had donned a disguise—a false mustache and a dark wig. A costume not quite so warm as the Inuit garb, but no less suited to its wearer.

He began teasing me about my recent setback with Persephone. If he was an expert at devising troublesome frolics, Pythag's meanness also derived benefit from his ingenuity. When he told me that Perse would never marry me, that she had only said she would so that I would continue to take him to the museum, I felt a little downcast. When he averred that she would keep putting me off, always coming up with some new excuse, I found his Pythagorean theorem all too believable.

I had experienced such taunting before, though, and I rebuffed his attempts to hurt and annoy me by remaining calm. Outwardly, in any case. The result was that he became more agitated, more determined to upset me. At one point, he said that she would never marry me because I was dull, and lacked imagination and daring.

"Really?" I said, lifting my nose a little higher. "As it happens, *Professor*, I have done something you haven't dared to do."

His disbelief was patent.

"I've climbed the mastodon," I told him.

"Rubbish," he said.

"Conquered the proboscidean peak."

"Balderdash!"

"Not at all. There's a little piece of string, tied in a bow on his back to prove it."

It was enough to do the trick. He climbed, and it seemed to me the skeleton swayed more than it had the day before. As I watched him, and saw him come closer to my little marker, it became apparent to me that I had tied the string at a most fragile juncture of supporting wires.

It was a wonder, really, that I hadn't been killed.

The thought came to me as simply as that. One minute, Pythag was astride the spine, asking me to bring him a piece of string, so that he might tie his own knot. I imagined spending the rest of my days nearly as tied to him as I would be to his sister. All my life, protecting treasures of one sort or another from a man who thought rules were only for other people, never himself.

"You must bring my own string back to me," I said. "That is how it's done."

And that was how it was done.

I was horrified by the result, and remain so. Mastodon skeletons are, after all, devilishly hard to come by. Persephone is convinced that the experts there are actually enjoying the challenge of reassembling the great beast.

The museum, no matter what it may say to the papers, is considering dropping its civil suit, hoping to extract a promise from Persephone not to pursue a wrongful death action against them. We are mulling it over.

I say *we*, because Pythagoras was mistaken, as it turns out. His sister will marry me. I confessed all to her, of course. Persephone merely asked me what took me so long to see what needed to be done.

Persephone and I are indeed well-suited.

# Robert J. Randisi

## Black and White Memories

ROBERT J. RANDISI had a very busy year in 2000. His most recent novel was *Blood on the Arch* featuring Detective Joe Keough. *The Shamus Game*, a Private Eye Writers of America anthology edited by him, was also published in Oct. of 2000. His short story collection, *Delvecchio's Brooklyn,* was published in January 2001. Any of these novels or collections reveals his gift for superb characterization, up-to-the-minute dialogue, and a real grace for revealing how people think and act, especially when crime is involved. "Black and White Memories," published in the electronic magazine *The Mississippi Review,* reveals all this and more.

# Black and White Memories

*Robert J. Randisi*

# 1

Guilt had long since bled the color from Truxton Lewis' memory of Elizabeth Bennett. Whenever the first strains of Dusty Springfield's "You Don't Have To Say You Love Me" started playing it all came back to him, but always in black and white. He wondered for years why that was. Then it came to him. It was the guilt.

Despite the guilty sinking feeling when he remembered the one time in his forty years of marriage he had been unfaithful, he would not have given up the memories for any reason—no matter what color they came in. The song was playing on the radio as Tru Lewis pulled up in front of the house owned by Jack Langston. Since retiring from the police department ten years ago—and since the death of his wife several years earlier—Tru had been housesitting across the country in an attempt to relieve the boredom of being retired and a widower. One was bad enough, but both were too much to handle. The house was on Seven Mile Beach in Port May, New Jersey, a beautiful, Victorian town a county over from Atlantic City. It was October, which meant the tourist season was over. When Tru discovered that there was a house available in Port May he hurriedly made the call that got him the job of housesitting the place for a month. He stopped the car in front of the house, one of the largest on the beach. Apparently, Jack Langston had made a ton of money dealing in commodities, and this was his family's summer home. Tru would "sit" in it for the month and then someone else would take over. A month was Tru's personal limit.

He retrieved his suitcase from the trunk and a bag of supplies from the back seat of his car, an '89 Ford Galaxy he'd borrowed from a friend, and let himself into the house with the key the real estate office had supplied him with. There were several keys, and he'd been well schooled in their use. He had not been in the house before, but had seen a diagram and knew where the guest room—his room—was. He'd learned early on in his housesitting career that owners did not appreciate a stranger invading their master bedroom and usually insisted on an alternative.

He left the bag of supplies in the kitchen, then went directly to the guest room and dropped his suitcase on the bed, which was full-sized, and comfortable looking.

Next he took a walk through the house, checking each of the rooms to make sure it was secure and had not been violated since the owner's departure. Finding everything in order he tried to decide whether to go back to the bedroom to unpack, or to the kitchen to put away the supplies. He opted for the kitchen.

His "supplies" consisted of six bottles of his favorite beer—Michael Shea's—and a box of one hundred Tetley tea bags. It took him a moment, but because the beer was warm he decided to put it in the refrigerator and make himself a cup of tea.

Armed with the steaming cup he went to the sliding doors at the back of the house, off the livingroom, and went out onto the full deck. There was a breeze coming off the water. He stood there and enjoyed it, sipping the tea, thinking about the last time he'd been in Port May.

# 2

*Port May, New Jersey September 1966*

Tru Lewis was twenty-nine years old, had been a member of the New York City Police Force for seven years. From the beginning he seemed to be on the fast track to the top. He'd made detective after four-and-a-half years, much of that spent working undercover. However, it was that time period that was the cause of his recent problems. Suddenly, two-and-a-half years after his last undercover assignment had ended he was under investigation by the Internal Affairs Division, who suspected him of skimming off the top of three million dollars in drug money which had been confiscated by Tru and his partners. What made it even worse was that his "partners" were apparently testifying against him.

"You have to get away, Tru," his wife told him. "I know that. I can understand that. But why can't we get away together?"

He couldn't tell her why. He couldn't bring himself to tell her he was sick to death of the smell of baby powder and puke. It seemed to him that babies smelled of either one or the other, and recently those smells had attached themselves to her, as well.

"I'm not good to be around, sweetie," he told her. "Let me do this. The verdict comes down Monday. I just want to spend the weekend alone. I'll be back Monday, I promise."

She'd held tight to the front of his shirt and asked, "You're not going to do anything foolish, are you?"

"Like swallow my gun? That's not my style, hon. I'll be back. I swear."

She'd kissed him fiercely and he'd left and driven to Port May, New Jersey, where his uncle—a retired cop—had a cottage he said he could use.

"Fuck 'em, kid," his uncle had told him. "Go to my cottage and don't think about it."

Not thinking about it was easier said than done, but going to the cottage did seem like a good idea. He could get away from the suspicious stares of his "friends and neighbors," as well as the constant crying and spitting up of his new daughter.

And his wife. Suddenly the love of his life had become someone he wanted to run away from. Her solicitous behavior around him, combined with the fact that their daughter had become an appendage on her hip, served only to irritate him.

His uncle's cottage was on Seven Mile Beach. He hadn't been there since he was a kid. When he pulled up in front it looked the same. It actually looked the same as the last time he'd seen it, almost fifteen years earlier. He stood in front and studied the side of the house where his uncle had once tried to smoke out some hornets from a nest but had only succeeded in setting the house on fire.

He used the key his uncle had given him to open the door. Even the inside looked the same. The furniture worn and musty, the walls cracked and peeling. He was carrying a small duffel bag with extra clothes in it, and a paper bag with a six-pack of his favorite beer, Ballantine. He put the beer in the fridge, dumped his duffel in the smallest of the two bedrooms, and then went out back on the porch to look at the water. He left the front and back doors open to air the place out.

After twenty minutes he decided to close up the house again. He put on a windbreaker, because the salt air was cool in September, stuffed his hands into the pockets of his jeans, and started walking.

Being alone turned out to be a bad idea. All he could think about was what he would do if he was kicked off the force—or worse, kicked off and arrested. He replayed each scenario over and over again. Just when he started to think that swallowing his gun might not be such a bad idea he came to the end of the beach and saw the shack.

Not actually a shack, but a small restaurant. It almost looked like what his old man used to call a roadhouse. He decided it was more of a café than anything else.

It was getting dark and the place was lit, though not brightly. He looked around and was struck at how black and white everything seemed. The sand was white, the sides of the building were white, the water was dark, there was not a hint of color anywhere. It was as if he had stepped through a portal into an alternate dimension where color had been drained from everything. He could smell fish frying, and hunger suddenly gnawed at his belly. He realized he hadn't eaten since that morning, when his wife had tried to force breakfast on him. He'd finally agreed to eat some toast before leaving, just to shut her up.

He walked towards the little cafe and as he got closer he could hear music coming from inside. It was Dusty Springfield singing "You Don't Have To Say You Love Me." As soon as he opened the screen door and stepped inside he saw her.

The interior of the place continued to foster the colorless illusion of the moment. The floor was laid with black and white tile, the walls, tables and countertops were also white. The leather of the booths and counter stools was black. A man behind the counter wore a long white apron over a white t-shirt and black pants. What hair he had left was black, a wispy fringe around his head and a thick mat on his forearms.

And in the midst of all this she stood, a shining oasis of color in a desert of black and white.

And the color was gold.

# 3

Her skin was pale, and her waitress uniform was a white apron, a white peasant blouse and a black skirt—but her hair was golden blond, and made her stand out, although she would have done so, anyway. Her figure was Monroesque, with full, round breasts, the nipples of which were prominent, probably because the place was airconditioned to the point of freezing.

A few of the booths were occupied, and some of the tables. Since the tourist season was over Tru decided these had to be locals.

"Sit anywhere," the man behind the counter said.

Tru only saw the one waitress, so it didn't matter where he sat, she'd be waiting on him. He chose a booth with no one seated directly in front or behind him.

When she came over he saw that she was older then he'd first thought, maybe late-twenties instead of early. She had blue eyes, which he hadn't been able to notice until now. The blue of her eyes and gold of her hair were the only hints of color in the place.

"Can I get you something?" she asked, and he realized this was the second time she'd spoken. He'd been staring and hadn't heard her the first, but now he did and her voice had a smokey, throaty quality to it.

"Oh, uh, a burger," he stammered, feeling fourteen again, when being near any girl, let alone one as beautiful as this one, had made him stammer.

"How'd you like it?"

"Well done."

"Fries?"

"Sure."

"A shake?"

"Why not?"

She smiled and his stomach fluttered. That annoyed him. He wasn't fourteen anymore, and he was married, so why should he be reacting this way?

"I could just about sell you anything, couldn't I?" she asked, lowering her pad.

He nodded and said, "Just about."

"Well," she said, staring at him with a look of amusement, "why don't we just leave it at a burger, fries and shake for now?"

"Um . . ." he said, and she walked away, leaving in her wake a scent that tickled his nostrils and drove out all memory of baby smells.

She returned briefly with a glass of water and a smile and he breathed in her scent once again. He found himself waiting anxiously for his food, though his hunger had suddenly become a secondary concern. It was only because she would be bringing it.

While he waited he noticed three men come into the place and immediately seat themselves in a booth. They were all dressed similar to the way he was, jeans and windbreakers, but they all had Elvis hair and were eight or ten years younger than him. At that point the waitress started toward him with his plate of food in one hand. One of the new arrivals grabbed her free arm, halting her progress.

"Come on, Lizzie, we need some service, here."

She yanked her arm away and said, "Don't grab me like that again, Hal. I'll get to you when I finish with this guy. And don't call me Lizzie!"

"You love me," Hal called after her. "I know it."

She made a face that he couldn't see and walked to Tru's booth.

"Old boyfriend?" he asked, without stammering.

"He wishes," she said, setting his plate down. In doing so she bent over and brought her cleavage tantalizingly close to him. If her scent had teased him up to now it was suddenly heady, wafting up from between her breasts and making his head swim. "Can I get you anything else?"

"Uh, that shake."

"Oh yeah, right," she said, laughing, full, ripe lips parting to reveal perfect white teeth. "I'm sorry. What flavor?"

"Strawberry."

"Comin' up."

She had to walk past the booth with the three men and the one called Hal reached for her again. She avoided him, causing his friends to laugh at him. She went behind the counter, made Tru his shake, and started for his table again. As before Hal grabbed her free arm.

"Come on, Lizzie," he said, "don't be like that."

She tried to pull her arm away again, but he held fast this time.

"You're hurting me!" she snapped.

"Liz—"

Abruptly she overturned the shake glass and poured the contents onto his head. He shouted, released her arm and jumped up. His friends were now shedding tears, they were laughing so hard.

"Goddamn it, you bitch!" Hal swore.

Tru could see that Liz looked frightened so he got up and hurried over to the action. He got between her and Hal before the man could do anything.

Abruptly, his two friends stood up and got behind him. He started to reach for his badge before he remembered it wasn't there. They'd taken it from him pending the investigation—that and his gun. All he had left was the adrenaline rush he always got in situations like these.

"I think you boys better go and eat someplace else," Tru said.

"What's it to you?" Hal demanded.

"That was my milk shake," Tru said. "Because of you, I have to wait for another one."

The strawberry colored liquid was still dripping from Hal's chin and there was clumps of it in his hair and on his shoulders.

"That bitch had no call—"

"She asked you to stop grabbing her and you didn't listen. I think you got what you deserved, don't you?"

Hal stared at Tru, looking ridiculous and more pink than strawberry. Behind him his friends gave Tru the meanest looks they could muster, but he saw they weren't going to do anything without their leader's say so. He closed the distance between himself and Hal, invading the man's space, causing him to step back a pace before he could stop himself.

"Time to leave, Hal," Tru said, quietly.

Hal tried to match Tru's stare but in the end he couldn't, and looked away.

"Hal?" one of his friends asked.

"Let's go," Hal said. "Burgers in this place stink, anyway."

They backed away a few steps, then turned and shuffled out the door, Hal pushing them from behind.

He felt her hand on his shoulder and then he turned and faced her. She was taller than his wife, who had dark hair and dark skin and brown eyes. This girl was all pale and golden, and took his breath away.

"My hero," she said. "Thanks."

"No problem," he said. "I was kind of mad he got my shake."

"Go sit down and I'll bring you another one—on the house."

"Thanks."

He went back to his booth and started on his burger, not really tasting it. He was coming down from the rush of facing those three punks without a gun and badge, but was still high from the girl.

"Cop?"

He looked up at her standing there with another shake, smiling down at him. "What?"

"I asked, are you a cop?" She put the shake down, this time without bending over.

"Why did you ask that?"

She shrugged. "Because you act like one."

"Well," he said, "it's a long story, but yes I am—I was . . ."

"Hey," she said, waving her hands in front of her, "none of my business. I'm sorry I asked. How's the burger?"

"It's fine."

"Look," she said, "I just want to warn you about those guys . . ."

"They didn't seem so tough."

"Well, you were facing them," she said. "Just be careful, okay? And really . . ." She put her hand on his shoulder and leaned over to kiss his cheek. She was so plush that for a moment he was blinded by the paleness of her skin. "Thank you," she said. "It's been a long time since anyone stood up for me." He couldn't understand that, at all.

# 4

After the last of the customers left she came over and sat opposite him in his booth.

"Close up for me, Liz?" the boss called out.

"Don't worry, Lenny," she said. "I'll lock everything."

The boss left and she leaned forward, a move which pressed her breasts against the table so that they swelled, threatening to spill out of her blouse. And there were those blue eyes, that full, soft mouth.

"Give me a quarter," she said.

"A quarter?"

"For a song."

He reached into his pocket and handed her one. She went to the jukebox and punched in the number she wanted. Then turned and walked slowly toward him while the song started. Once again he heard Dusty Springfield's "You Don't Have To Say You Love Me."

"Dance with me?" she asked, ample hips already swaying.

He pushed away his partially eaten burger and got up. She came into his arms and pressed against him. He forgot about everything—his wife, the baby, Internal Affairs, his badge . . . everything. Nothing else existed except her in his arms. He knew he should be feeling guilty. After all, his wife was at home taking care of their new daughter, his career was on the line, and here he was dancing with a woman he'd only just met, but wished he could stay with forever.

"You're married, aren't you?" she asked. Her head was on his shoulder, her mouth near his ear.

"Yes."

"The good ones always are."

They danced until the song ended and then he didn't want to let her go. They stepped away and looked into each other's eyes.

"I know this is crazy," she said, "but would you like to come home with me tonight?"

"More than anything else in the world."

"No strings," she said. "Just tonight."

"No strings."

"I don't want to break up a marriage," she said, "but I feel like if I don't take this chance I'll always wonder . . . you know?"

He nodded. "I know."

"I'll lock up," she said, and began to scurry about, turning off burners, and lights, and locking doors, until finally they were going out the front door together.

They were on him like a pack of wild dogs.

Her arm was linked with his so that when they pulled him from the steps she went sprawling into the sand as well, away from the action. They rained down punches and kicks on him. He tried to give back as good as he got, but it was three against one and they had caught him unprepared. He had no doubt that it was the three punks from earlier in the evening. In fact, one of them still smelled sweetly of the shake Elizabeth had poured over his head.

She finally got back to her feet and decided to join the fray rather than call fruitlessly for help. She jumped on the back of one of the men and began to pummel him.

"Get her off me!" he shouted.

"Stop it!" she cried. "You're killing him!"

The other two stopped kicking Tru long enough to pry Elizabeth off the third man's back, sending her into the sand again.

"We're not gonna kill him, Lizzie" Hal said. "We're just teachin' him a lesson."

"Yeah," one of the others said, "No big city asshole better come here and mess with our women."

"What the hell are you talking about?" she demanded. "You losers don't have any women."

The three men exchanged glances, wondering how to respond to that.

"Besides," she said, before they could make up their minds, "you're really in trouble now."

"And why's that?" Hal asked.

"Because he's a cop," she said. "You three dimwits just assaulted a cop."

"A cop?" Hal said.

"Jesus," one of the others said. "We didn't know."

"A cop, Hal," the third one said. "We gotta get outta here."

"Lizzie—" Hal started.

"Just get out of here," she said, cutting him off, "and don't call me that."

"He started it," Hal said. "He stuck his nose—"

"I can keep him from reporting this if you'll just get out of here!" she said, urgently.

"Come on, Hal," one of the others said, grabbing his arm. "Let's go."

Hal gave one last look at Tru, lying in the sand, bloody and battered, and then allowed his friends to pull him away.

"Jesus," Elizabeth said, and dropped to her knees next to him. "Are you all right?"

"I—I think so," he said, spitting blood from a split lip.

"You're not dead, or anything?"

He laughed, then hissed because that split his lips even more.

"No," he said, "I'm not dead."

"Do you have a place around here?"

"Just up the beach."

"Well," she said, "I guess we better go there so I can look after you. Can you get up?"

"Yeah," he said, his head clearing somewhat. "Where did they go?"

"They ran off when I told them you were a cop." She helped him to his feet. "You don't want to go after them or anything, do you?"

"No," he said, "I just want to forget the whole thing."

"Well then, lean on me," she said. "This isn't exactly what I had in mind, but I guess I'll have to play Florence Nightingale."

"Not what I had in mind, either."

She tended to his wounds, which were more annoying than serious, and then helped him into bed. She'd kissed his forehead then his mouth and said, "You're not in shape for much more than this," which he later thought had probably been for the best.

She'd walked to the door then, turned and said to him, "I'm not leaving my number."

He nodded. "I understand."

"Too bad," she'd said, "Mr. Cop."

She left, the taste of her on his lips, and he'd never even told her his name.

*The Present . . .*

He took the tea cup back into the house and put it in the sink. Then locked all the doors, going out the back and walking down the deck steps to the sand. He started down the beach, then turned and frowned at the house. He hadn't noticed it before, but it was apparently on the same lot his Uncle's house had been on. He'd thought it a coincidence that a house on Seven Mile Beach had become available for sitting, but not this much of a coincidence. He continued down the beach as dusk came and seemed to bleach the color out of everything. The sand was white, the water was getting dark. He wondered if the small café would still be there, and if it was she couldn't possibly still be working there as a waitress, could she?

When he finally came to the end of the beach he saw it. Only one wall still stood, but it was the one with the front door in it. He walked to the steps that the three men had pulled him down from. He'd gone home the next day, hugged his wife and baby, told her that he'd come home early because he'd gotten mugged—and because he missed them. That Monday he found out that I.A.D. had cleared him and his career would continue.

He'd thought about Elizabeth over the years once in a while, especially when he heard that Dusty Springfield song. He'd recall how they talked, how their eyes met, how they'd danced in the café and what they had almost done—and would have done—if the three punks hadn't jumped him outside. He'd felt guilt all these years because of how good he'd felt just dancing with her. How bad would it had felt if he'd spent that night with her?

He'd never cheated on his wife in all the years they'd been together and had always considered the café the place where he'd come the closest. As a younger man he'd felt that even the dance had been a betrayal, but now, thinking back, he knew it hadn't been. It had simply been a cleansing time for him, a few moments respite from a life that had suddenly become filled with turmoil.

There was no harm in that.

# Robert Barnard

## Nothing to Lose

INTERNATIONALLY RECOGNIZED as one of the masters of the mystery form, Robert Barnard has worked in a wide variety of styles, voices and forms over the years. He is one of the few writers certain to survive his time. Most of his novels have the feel of true classics. One of his most compelling quotes is that he never draws directly from life because, "People can be so much nastier, can act so much meaner, than they are usually allowed to do in books." In "Nothing to Lose," he is once again at the top of his game. This fine tale first appeared in the anthology *Malice Domestic 9*.

# Nothing to Lose

*Robert Barnard*

When Emily Mortmain finally consented to go into an old people's home, her relatives predicted a spate of suicides by the other residents before her first week was over. If other possible outcomes of the move occurred to them, they did not speak of them openly.

Emily Mortmain had been a disagreeable woman all her life, and old age had intensified her cantankerousness. Her husband had volunteered for a suicide mission in World War II, and all his contemporaries in the RAF had said how heroic he was, since he was still young and had so much to live for. He had smiled heroically, and said nothing. Her daughter had emigrated with her family to Australia many years before, and had opined at the time that Australia's only drawback was that it was not far enough away. As Emily became increasingly unable to fend for herself, neighbors had tried to help, then fellow church members (for Emily was a "good" churchwoman), and then social workers. All attempts had ended in disaster—plates being thrown by or at her, screaming altercations at her back door, even an attempted throttling. When the local vicar lost his faith and left the church, the parish joke was that he had found himself unable to believe in a God who could create an Emily Mortmain.

The members of her family who came to see her off on the morning she left for the home were two nieces and a nephew. Their contact with her over the years had been sporadic, but had never dropped off entirely, for Emily had money, and it was known that her daughter had been ritually cursed by bell, book, and candle and cut out of the will. Who, if anyone, had been cut in was not known, but it was generally agreed that there was no charity with aims unpleasant enough for Emily to want to give it money.

There was no rivalry among the relatives. They knew no one could suck up to Emily Mortmain, because it was not in humankind to be pleasant to her for long enough to gain any favor. None of the three volunteered to drive her to the home, for each feared the inevitable bust-up in the car. They stood by the front gate waving cheerily as she was driven away in a taxi provided by the local social services. Then they gave a muffled cheer and went away to have a drink together and swap "Aunt Em" stories.

Emily was silent on the drive to Evening Glades. One did not talk to taxi drivers. One did not tip them either. A wheelchair was waiting for her in the driveway of Evening Glades, and the resident handyman got her into it and pushed her into the foyer. She did not thank him, and merely stared stonily ahead at Miss Protheroe the manageress when she introduced herself. She maintained her silence when she was taken up in the lift and shown her room, and preserved the same arctic chill when she was wheeled down into the communal sitting room to await lunch.

Miss Protheroe (whose only fault, if she had one, was a slight tendency to talk to the residents as if they were children) made a special effort to take her round and introduce her to her "new friends" as she called them.

"Miss Willcocks . . . Captain Freely . . . Miss Cartwright . . . Mr. Pottinger . . . Mrs. Freebody . . ."

But she needn't have bothered. Indeed, the introductions died away in her throat. Emily Mortmain had risen from her wheelchair with the aid of a stick, and placed herself in the nearest available armchair. She acknowledged neither the names, nor the tentative (or in some cases appalled) greetings of the other residents. When Miss Protheroe had finished she merely announced, "My room does not have a sea view."

Miss Protheroe, as was quite often necessary in her job, took a firm line.

"The rooms with a sea view are very highly prized here. Mrs. Freebody, Mrs. Johnstone, and Captain Freely have the sea views at the moment, as our residents of longest standing."

Emily Mortmain fixed each in turn with a look of malevolence that seemed designed to ensure that all three rooms shortly became available.

"And when—if—they should for any reason . . . become vacant," said Miss Willcocks, greatly daring, "there is a long waiting list."

Emily Mortmain's face took on an expression of relish, as if she was spoiling for a fight which she had no doubt she would win.

"Lunch in half an hour," said Miss Protheroe brightly.

It was predictable that lunch was not to Mrs. Mortmain's liking. The gravy was too thin, the beef was overdone, and the peas were tinned. She aroused in the others a vociferous and unusual enthusiasm for thin gravy, well-done beef, and tinned peas. This cut no ice with Emily Mortmain, who had all her life adopted the position that anyone who had an opinion contrary to her own on any subject whatsover was either a fool or a degenerate. When the pudding came, a rhubarb tart, she pushed it away. "I can't abide rhubarb."

As she made her way slowly, with the aid of a stick, toward the sitting room, she shouted to Miss Protheroe, "Remember, I can't abide rhubarb!"

"Funny," said Mr. Pottinger. "I'd have thought rhubarb and Mrs. Mortmain would have suited one another."

"I do *wonder* whether she's going to fit in here," said Miss Willcocks.

That was a matter on which there could be only one opinion, but it was an opinion that was bounced backwards and forwards over the rhubarb tart; it was productive of a satisfactory gloom at things not being what they used to be. This feeling was reinforced when they all trailed back to the sitting room and stood horrified in the doorway. Emily Mortmain had appropriated the armchair closest to the fire.

The comforts of Evening Glades were distributed with a rough-and-ready attempt at democracy. The possessors of the rooms with a sea view did not have the chair closest to the fire, and the person with the first rights to the *Daily Mail* in the mornings was someone else again. The armchair by the fire was Miss Will-cocks's by right.

"Tell her!" Miss Willcocks urged Captain Freely, poking him quite painfully in the ribs.

Captain Freely was only just an officer and not quite a gentleman, but he could be quite splendidly officerly and gentlemanly if the occasion called for it. He advanced with the solemnity of Black Rod on a state occasion.

"Mrs. . . . er . . . Mortmain, I'm afraid you don't yet know our little ways here . . . our customs and conventions . . . The armchair you are sitting in is—hmm—reserved for the use of Miss Willcocks here."

The evil black eyes looked at him, then moved toward Miss Willcocks, then back to Captain Freely.

"Switch on the television, will you?" she said. "It's time for *Jacaranda Avenue*."

There was an immediate twitter of protest.

"We don't watch *Jacaranda Avenue* at Evening Glades," said Captain Freely. Then, aware that they had let themselves be sidetracked, he went on, quite severely, "I don't think you quite understood what I just said about—"

"Oh, I understood. Switch on the television."

The other residents stood round aghast. It was at this point that Captain Freely's military training told. Emily Mortmain had taken hold of her stick, and clearly intended to use it to press the appropriate button on the television set. Captain Freely, with great presence of mind, wheeled the set a further two feet away.

"Here at Evening Glades," he said sententiously, "we watch *Coronation Street* and *EastEnders*. We think that that is enough soap opera without adding an Australian one."

"Northern filth and cockney filth," sniffed Emily Mortmain. "At least the Australian program is *clean*."

But Captain Freely, with the nodded support of the other residents, had turned on a wildlife program. Emily Mortmain felt at an unusual moral disadvantage from the fact that she had preferred a soap to this.

"Such a graceful bird," said Mrs. Johnstone, as they watched a flying condor. "One can almost imagine angels' wings."

Such a rubbing in of superior taste drove Emily Mortmain to a suppressed frenzy. Her instinct—for she had all the childishness of the very old—was to get up and change the channel. On the other hand she knew that one of the others—in whom childishness was certainly not absent—would nip over and take her chair. Indeed, Captain Freely had remained standing while all the rest had sunk into chairs, and he hovered near her, no doubt meditating a chivalrous dash to rescue the chair on behalf of Miss Willcocks should the opportunity arise. Emily Mortmain fumed, but sat on.

At 2:30 precisely Emily Mortmain took up her stick and pressed the bell for Carter, the man of all work.

"Take me to my room," she ordered, hobbling towards her wheelchair. "It's my time for a lie-down. Remember that. Half past two is always my time to lie down."

The other residents watched her go in dignified silence, and no one scuttled over to take her chair. Only when the lift had gone up did Miss Willcocks walk over to her rightful place with great, if wounded, presence. She sat down to a little burst of applause, and Captain Freely summed up the general feeling when he said, "We shall have to fight back."

It was generally agreed that, though they would be scrupulously polite to the new resident, it was no use at all relying on good manners or conventional decencies. If the chair by the fire was to be kept for Miss Willcocks, this would have to be done by stratagem. After various possibilities were considered, Captain Freely dragged down from the bookshelves more than a dozen bound copies of *Punch*, dating from the 1920s. He placed them near the chair and declared that at meal times, or when Miss Willcocks took her constitutional, he himself would place these on the chair, which Mrs. Mortmain, with her limited ability to move, would find exceedingly difficult to remove. "I haven't lost *all* my strength yet, thank the Lord," he declared. It was agreed that for the moment the television would remain at some distance from all the chairs, however inconvenient this was for those with poor eyesight. It was also agreed that the morning paper would be kept for Mrs. Freebody in the office until she called for it after breakfast. Thus was the strategy conceived, and the mere discussion of the measures gave the old people an agreeable sense of having taken part in a council of war.

"Just like the Home Guard," said Mr. Summerson, the oldest inhabitant, "planning what to do when Jerry landed."

But of course Jerry had not landed, and it was typical of Mrs. Mortmain that by the next day she had decided to fight on a completely different front. What had most rankled about the skirmishes of her first day had been (not that she admitted it in these terms to herself) that she had allowed herself to be put at a moral disadvantage. Her insistence on the Australian soap when the others (*apparently*, and so they *said*) preferred to watch a wildlife program was, in retrospect, unwise. It was imperative to regain the moral initiative.

The following day was warmish, and Mrs. Mortmain affected not to have seen the piled copies of *Punch* on the chair by the fire. She took an armchair over by the bookcase, the farthest from the television, and she turned it away from the despised screen. She fortunately found among the stock of books a volume of sermons which had been the comfort of a previous resident, now gathered to the bosom of the Lord. This she opened and ploughed doggedly through, whatever program was on the television. She was not spoken to by any of the residents, but if addressed by Miss Protheroe or Carter she would read aloud the passage she was at, ostensibly to mark her place.

"Would you prefer carrots or greens with your meat loaf, Mrs. Mortmain?"

" '. . . the ungodly shall perish in a sea of tormenting fire.' What precisely do you mean by 'greens'?"

This ploy was gratifying to her sense of superiority, if in the long run monotonous. For the rest, too, it was a respite, and they found that life at the Glades could go on pretty much as normal, almost as if Mrs. Mortmain had not been there. This, though, was not Emily's intention in the long term. Having regained the moral heights, she was impelled once more to assert her presence.

Sunday provided many opportunities. Breakfast was no sooner over than Emily Mortmain demanded to know when the transport would be leaving for church.

"I'm afraid there is no transport for church," said Miss Protheroe, with a tired—almost desperate—kind of brightness. "Those who can get to church, and want to go, of course . . . go. The rest of us make do with the television service. And of course, the vicar comes and gives us our own special little service once a month."

"Incredible! Quite incredible!" Emily Mortmain surveyed the other residents, who were deep in the *People*, the *News of the World*, and the *Sunday Telegraph*. "It's news to me that the Lord intended his day to be consecrated to the reading of newspapers!"

"It's news to me he ever said anything on the subject of the *News of the World*," said Captain Freely cheekily. But he felt on dubious moral ground. It was difficult to imagine a God who would approve of the *News of the World*.

Mrs. Mortmain had a taxi summoned, and was driven in solitary state to and from the nearest Anglican church. If any of the other residents had attended the service they might have noticed that she ignored on principle all the changes that had occurred in the Church of England forms of worship over the past two decades or so. Change was, to Emily Mortmain, synonymous with degeneracy. When the vicar shook her hand at the church door, she informed him that next time he came to Evening Glades, she wished to see him. "Alone," she intoned. "In private."

The vicar didn't see how he could refuse. Though thinking it over afterwards he didn't see why he should have accepted either. But Emily caught him on the hop, and he said that since she was a new resident at Evening Glades, and a new parishioner, he would come along especially to see her later in the week. Emily nodded to him curtly, and let the taxi driver wheel her away.

Mrs. Mortmain made a great thing of this approaching interview with the vicar. She said nothing about it directly to the other residents, but she communicated quite effectually through Miss Protheroe.

"The vicar will be calling to see me on Thursday," she announced on Monday at lunchtime. "Make sure that he is brought *straight* to my room."

And again on Thursday at breakfast time.

"When the vicar calls we must be *absolutely* private."

The rest of the residents, as they were meant to, wondered.

"She has the sort of obsession about secrecy that afflicts some prime ministers," said Captain Freely acutely.

The vicar, when he came, found the whole interview profoundly depressing. He was a well-meaning man, verging on the ineffectual. His depression took the form of wondering why so many deplorable people were attracted by the Christian religion. He listened to her demands that he insist on the banning of television on Sundays at Evening Glades, that the home should cease subscribing to any Sunday newspapers, that regular churchgoing by the able-bodied be a condition of acceptance, and so on and so on, and his heart sank.

Yes, he was on the governing board, he said, but no, he didn't have that sort of power. And in fact he had no wish to start dictating to a group of old people how they should spend their spare time. Did we really want the Christian religion to seem so negative and coercive? he wondered aloud.

All this was not unexpected to Emily Mortmain. She knew that Church of England vicars these days lacked fire in their bellies, had no relish for a fight. To her, religion was essentially belligerent: a fight against moral laxity, atheism, other sects, and anyone who happened to disagree with her on any matter whatsoever. Emily Mortmain would have fitted in perfectly in Northern Ireland.

But Emily was not in the least disappointed in the vicar's response, for she had not hoped for anything better. The whole business merely provided her with the opportunity for one more skirmish on this particular front, before she switched tack and tried out something completely new. It was a *casus belli*, and when it fizzled out she would find another, equally good. Certainly she had no intention of telling the truth about the interview.

At lunch the next day, when everyone was discussing the previous evening's episode of *EastEnders* and the amorous activities of Dirty Den the publican, Mrs. Mortmain announced, "At least we shall soon have an end to Sunday television. That's an abomination that will be swept away."

"I beg your pardon?" said Miss Willcocks.

"*And* Sunday newspapers. I've spoken to the vicar, and he will be pressing the governors very hard indeed on the issue. It's high time we had a more godly atmosphere in this place. And this is only a beginning."

She ended with an expression of triumph in her voice. The table gazed at her stonily, and then returned to their meals in silence. Silence was one of their weapons these days, though it seemed unfortunately to give Emily Mortmain the impression that she had won.

Only when she went up for her afternoon lie-down at 2:30 did they break out in protest.

"Well, really! What *does* she think she's doing this time? A ban on Sunday television! We might be living in the Victorian age!"

"I believe that even the Queen watches television on Sundays," said Miss Willcocks. She had in fact no information whatsoever on this point, but she was inclined to bring the Queen in to support her position, rather as Emily Mortmain brought in the Almighty.

"And a ban on Sunday newspapers!" said Mr. Pottinger. "It's only on Sundays that the papers are *any good*!"

"Let's be a bit calm about this," said Captain Freely. "Is she just trying to work us up?"

They thought for a moment.

"We do *know* most of the governing body a little," said Mrs. Johnstone. "They come here and talk to us, and they all seem quite kind. They don't appear to be religious fanatics."

"Quite," said Captain Freely.

"On the other hand," said Miss Willcocks, "Evening Glades was founded to be run on Church of England principles."

"Contradiction in terms," said Captain Freely robustly. "No, the fact is the woman's just trying to make trouble."

"I do think it's hard," exclaimed Mrs. Johnstone. "One comes to a home like this, at the end of one's life, for *peace*! 'Sleep after toil, port after stormy seas,' as somebody said. Or is that death? Anyway, you know what I mean. A quiet, orderly existence, without too much responsibility, and without *rows*. This woman seems to thrive on rows, unpleasantness, and bad feeling. I do think it's *hard*! And it will go on like this as long as she's here."

"There is one advantage in being old," said Miss Willcocks pensively, into the silence that followed.

"What's that?" asked Mr. Pottinger.

"One has very little to lose . . . If only one could hit on a plan . . ."

Emily Mortmain died in her room, some time on Sunday afternoon. After lunch she had sat with her back studiously to the television, while the rest watched a film they had all been looking forward to, which gripped their attention. At 2:30 precisely, before the film had ended, Mrs. Mortmain had rung to be taken upstairs, as was her habit. At 4:45 Miss Protheroe had taken up her tea and toast and had discovered her dead.

The doctor, from the beginning, was very unhappy indeed. Though it appeared that the body was face down into the pillow, there were clear signs, or so the doctor thought, that it had been turned over after death. Deliberate suffocation is a difficult death to prove, and he thought the best thing would be to have a word with Miss Protheroe, to discover if, for instance, there could have been an intruder.

"Quite impossible," she said. "The domestic staff were off, and the kitchen door was locked. I was working in my office off the hall, with a perfect view of the front door. No one came in or went out."

"I see." The doctor shifted from foot to foot. "I wonder what the old people were doing."

Miss Protheroe shot him a quelling look.

"I will find out, tactfully, if you really think it worthwhile. I will tell you what I learn if you would be so kind as to return tomorrow."

When he did come back she was in triumphal mood.

"It was totally satisfactory. They were all—all—watching the film until 3:15. Then four of the ladies played whist, Captain Freely and Mr. Jones played chess, and the other six played *Trivial Pursuit*—a new game with us, but very popular. They were all in the lounge, or in the conservatory just through the door, and they were there all the time, until some time after I discovered the body. No one left even for a moment."

The doctor began his shifting-from-foot-to-foot routine again.

"That would be most unusual, not to leave even for a few minutes. Old people's bladders—"

"No one left even for that." Miss Protheroe got quite commanding. "In any case, how long would this . . . what you suggest . . . take?"

"Quite some time," admitted the doctor. "There was comparatively little obstruction . . . up to ten minutes."

"You see? And how much strength would be required?"

"Oh yes, certainly it would require strength."

"You see? These are *old* people, doctor. Even Captain Freely, though active, is no longer strong. It's quite impossible."

The doctor's voice took on a wild note.

"Perhaps two of them," he suggested. "Or all of them in relays."

Miss Protheroe rose in wrath.

"Doctor, that is as disgraceful as it is absurd. A joke in extremely bad taste. To suggest that all of my residents, respectable old people, should gang up to kill a newcomer—"

The doctor was young, and saw he had gone too far.

"Yes, yes, of course. I was merely theorizing, getting too fantastical. Point taken, point taken."

And he signed the certificate.

Miss Protheroe sensed the excitement in the residents after the death of Emily Mortmain, but there was nothing unusual in that. After any death in Evening Glades there was always excitement, even a sort of exultation: I have survived, she has gone under. Always there was an attempt to disguise it too. Now Captain Freely, if he realized she was in the room, would mutter, "Terrible thing, terrible thing," and the rest would cluck their agreement. Miss Protheroe was not deceived. They were pleased and excited, and if these emotions were more intense than usual, this was not surprising, in view of Emily Mortmain's character. Even her relatives, after the funeral, had seemed cock-a-hoop.

Amongst themselves they did not talk about the death a great deal, and to outsiders, of course, it was a matter of no importance. Only Miss Willcocks mentioned it, in her weekly letter to her niece (letters which generally remained unread, or even unopened). Miss Willcocks's treatment of the matter, it must be said, was not entirely honest:

> Here we have been greatly upset by the death of Mrs. Mortmain, a new resident. Death is always upsetting, and particularly so in this case, as we had not had time to get to know her. It quite spoiled our Sunday, which up to then had been extremely enjoyable, with a quite thrilling game of Trivial Pursuit, and before that a most entertaining film on television. Did you see it? It was Murder on the Orient Express—so amusing, and with such a clever solution . . .

JOSEPH HANSEN

# Widower's Walk

JOSEPH HANSEN'S Dave Brandstetter was the first openly gay protagonist in a serious mystery series. Hansen has said that he felt gay characters were treated poorly by mystery writers and he wanted to offer a balance. The Brandstetters are among the most stylish and yet quietly realistic of all modern detective novels. Not only does Hansen give us an open look at a gay man, he gives us an equally open look at our culture in general. He is widely known as a writer's writer. "Widower's Walk," published in *The Night Awakens*, features his other series character, Bohannon, in a polished tale of mystery and murder in a small town.

# Widower's Walk

*Joseph Hansen*

The new kid has overslept and, being not much more than a teenager, could sleep till noon. Bohannon drags on Levis and boots, flaps into a shirt, steps over the windowsill onto the long porch of the ranch house, and heads for the stable building, clean, low lines against the gray background of the drowsing mountains. Horses move restlessly, rumble, and blow air through their big sinuses behind the closed doors of their box stalls. "Buck?" he says. "Seashell? Geranium?" And names the rest as he passes. His own horses and horses he boards for folk in the little town of Madrone, at the foot of this canyon, beside the ocean.

He raps knuckles on the tackroom door, white-washed planks. "Kelly? Time to get up." No reaction. He knocks again. Silence. He lifts the black metal tongue that serves as latch, swings the door inward, pokes his head inside. "Kelly? Wake up." But the steel cot looks empty. He steps inside. It's empty, all right. But slept in hard, sheets tangled, blankets half on the floor. He glances around in the weak morning light from the single window. Two of George Stubbs's horse drawings on the walls. (Shouldn't there be three?) No boots under the cot. He opens the drawers of the unpainted chest. Nothing. No clothes in the closet. He shuts his eyes and swears. Another one gone.

He walks back along the sheltered length of the stable building, opening the top doors as he goes. He doesn't turn to see, but he knows heads are poking out to watch him. Hooves move fidgety, hopefully. At the end stall, he opens the whole door and takes Buck's bridle and leads him out. He loops the reins around a post and goes inside the building and gets his saddle.

"Come on," he says, throwing blanket and saddle over Buck's broad back. "Start you and me off with a ride today." He grunts, bending to cinch up the girth. Buck grunts, too. Bohannon puts boot into stirrup and swings heavily aboard. "Nice long ride." He nudges Buck's ample sides with his heels, and they move out onto the gravel under the rustling trees. "Hell, maybe we'll just keep riding." Buck heads for the gate, which has a wooden arch over it, which holds the single name "BOHANNON" in cutout wooden letters. "Maybe we'll never come back." He leans from the saddle to unfasten the left leaf of the gate and, when they're past it, leans and drags it closed again. Habit. This morning, he wouldn't mind if somebody came and stole the place, horses and all. They'd be doing him a favor. Out on the pitted blacktop road, he reins Buck to the left up the canyon.

He can't remember how many stable hands he's lost since losing first Rivera—he'd expected that; Rivera had been training all along to be a priest— and then George Stubbs, the veteran rodeo rider who'd come to Bohannon already old, and whom arthritis at last had put into a nursing home. There'd followed drunks and itchy-footed men, green and lazy boys, even one girl, who worked hard but quit to get married. Bohannon promised himself when he hired young Kelly that he'd be the last. If Kelly walked out on him, it would be a signal to give up and sell the ranch to a land developer, the way everybody else in the canyons seemed to be doing. It was all work and no fun anymore. Why prolong the misery?

He's a couple of miles up the canyon now and no longer on the main track. Buck is paying more attention than he is to his surroundings, and Buck shies. Now, this is not the kind of shy that would unsettle any rider but the newest. Buck is, after all, no colt. He's got fifteen years on him, if not more. And he's heavy. So his shy only *almost* unseats Bohannon. For a second, the man has to fight to keep upright. At a hard-bitten fifty-two or -three, his reflexes aren't what they used to be.

"Whoa, what's the matter?"

But before the words are quite out of his mouth, he sees what's the matter. A man is lying facedown in the road, half in the road, half on the shoulder. "Easy." Bohannon turns Buck's head, and they cross the road, where Bohannon swings down and ties the reins to a tree. He gives Buck's trembling flank a couple of soothing strokes, then crosses the road to the man. He kneels and touches the man, lays fingers lightly on the man's neck below the ear. But there's no need to feel for a pulse: the man is cold. He's been dead for hours.

Bohannon was for a long time a deputy sherriff. He knows how to act in situations like this. From his crouch, he looks around him, first at the whole wide scene—canyon, trees, rocks, dry streambed below—then up the slope that climbs to his right. Next, he studies the immediate site. Close to the body. Spatters of blood. Then what's near his boot soles—dried leaves, sickle-shaped eucalyptus, curled oak, pine needles, pebbles, no bullet, no shell casing. Nothing is stuck to the soles of the man's shoes.

The man is well dressed and not for a rustic place like this but for city life. The suit is dark. There's a necktie. The shirt is white. Where it isn't blood-stained. Somebody shot this man. From the front. Bohannon knows an exit wound when he sees one, and he sees one. Right between the shoulderblades. Not much blood. The man died fast.

He doesn't touch the body again, or the clothes. It was his job once but no more. He stands, brushes grit off his hands, and looks to the right again. Some way up the slope, among trees, rocks, ferns, and brush, he thought earlier he'd glimpsed metal. He had. He climbs toward it, and his heart sinks when his guess about what it is turns out to be a fact. It is Steve Belcher's battered camper truck. Belcher is a bearded, longhaired Vietnam veteran who lives in the camper and leaves everybody else alone and wishes they would leave him alone. The best luck he has had in his four or five years here is since he took to the canyons. First he'd parked the camper different places in Madrone, and the citizens had moved him on. "On" proved to be a leaky old fishing boat he'd anchored in Short's Inlet, a body of water nobody cared about except some migrating ducks now and then but that everybody got protective about once Belcher had started to live there. Belcher was polluting, wasn't he? A beautiful natural wildfowl habitat.

So Belcher gave up after making some ugly scenes at town council meetings—he had a rough mouth on him, did Belcher—and he'd taken to the canyons with this rusty camper. He never went into town except to pick up his disability check every month and buy supplies. The rest of the time, he kept out of the way. Except for establishing his campsite once in the Mozart Bowl. Dr. Dolores Combs and the rest of the town's wealthy music lovers damn near had him hanged for that.

Bohannon's boots crunch across strewn paper and crushed cans and plastic packaging. Coyotes or raccoons have broken open a trash bag, looking for a meal. He hears a noise and looks up, and Belcher is standing, buck naked, in the camper's dented doorway, holding a Browning 9mm.

"It's me," Bohannon says. "Don't shoot."

"You woke me up," Belcher grunts. His dirty-blond hair and beard are tousled from sleep. "What do you want? You never give me no trouble. Not you." He narrows mistrustful eyes. "Not yet."

"There's something down on the trail," Bohannon says, "that shouldn't be there. Put on some clothes. I want you to take a look at it."

Belcher tilts his head. "What do you mean, 'something'?"

"A body," Bohannon says.

Belcher stares. "A dead body?"

"Shot through the chest. Middle of the night. You hear anything?"

"Nope." Belcher scratches his beard. "No."

"You want to answer me?" Bohannon says. "You want to hand me your gun to sniff at?"

Belcher jerks with surprise. He's forgotten the gun. "It ain't mine." He puts it down inside the camper. "It ain't been fired." His voice is hoarse, and he has grown pale though his skin is like tanned leather. "And I didn't hear no shot."

"Not yours? It's the kind the Army issues, Steve."

"Banged against the truck. Middle of the night. Found it there by the front wheel." He kicks into ragged jeans. "Why here?"

"It's not your lucky day," Bohannon says. "Come on. Have a look at him."

"I don't see what for," Belcher says.

"So I can see your face when you say you don't know who he is. I've always trusted you. I want to see if I still can."

Belcher grunts and comes loose-limbed down the trailer's little metal stairs. His feet are dirty. "I don't want to see no more floppies. I seen enough. I told you that. Hell, Bohannon, I killed enough. Too many. Drives me crazy dreaming about it. I'd never kill again."

"You still keep your pistol," Bohannon says.

"I would," Belcher says, "if it would kill ghosts. It's not mine, Bohannon, I told you that. I hate the goddamn things."

"Come on." Bohannon turns away and starts downhill. "You know Lieutenant Gerard is going to home in on you. You're the obvious suspect." He goes quickly. The underfoot is slippery with morning dew, and he almost falls. "He and I were partners once, and if I tell him I'm sure it wasn't you, it might help." He looks over his shoulder.

The truck's cab door slams. The starter whinnies.

Bohannon turns back, loses his footing, falls to hands and knees. "Wait. Steve—don't do this."

The truck engine roars. Belcher looks out the window. "Forget it, Bohannon. You know what Gerard will do. I'm a homicidal maniac. He's been waiting years to prove that." He lets the parking brake go, the truck rolls backward about a foot, then springs forward. "So long." With old gray tires kicking up duff, Belcher weaves the truck away fast, in and out among the trees.

Bohannon struggles to his feet. "You're only making it worse," he shouts.

But maybe not. Maybe there's no way Belcher could do that.

He sits on a stump, lights a cigarette, and waits. He can't leave the body. If instead of riding Buck up here, he'd come in the truck, he could radio the sheriff station. He's just stuck, is all there is to it. Until somebody comes along. And Rodd Canyon is not known for heavy traffic. Whole damn day could pass without a single car. Sure as hell won't any horses be coming by. Not till he gets back down to his place. It's the only rental stable around. He stands up. This is a hell of a note.

It remains that for forty minutes (he keeps checking his watch), and then he hears an engine, the loose tool rattle and spring squeak of a vehicle. It's a red pickup. Fire patrol. He steps into the road. The driver is Sorenson, whom he's known for years. Sorenson stops the truck. He stares through the windshield at the body on the road.

"What does that mean?" he asks Bohannon.

"Means you can use your two-way," Bohannon says, "to let them know down at Madrone, and they can come pick him up. Shooting victim."

"Get in." Sorenson stretches across and opens the door on the passenger side of the cab. "You know how to use the thing."

"Do it for me," Bohannon says. "And lie a little, will you? Tell T. Hodges you found him. Leave me out of it."

Sorenson, blond and sunburned, looking twenty years younger than his age, wrinkles his brow. "What for? You don't want her to know you were riding your horse up the canyon? Why not?"

"Just do it," Bohannon says.

"Hey." Sorenson half lies across the seat, craning to see up the slope. "Where's Steve Belcher? He had his camper up there."

"Did he?" Bohannon says. "Not here now."

"I wonder why?" Sorenson says. "You've protected him time and again, Hack. But for a shooting? A killing?"

"Don't drag Belcher into it," Bohannon says. "Just tell them about the body, okay?"

Sorenson takes the part of the two-way radio you talk into from its hook and puts it to his mouth. There are noises, cracklings, sandpaper voices, indistinct words. He switches those off and talks into the mike. "Sorenson, up here in Rodd Canyon, trail that drops off the main road at the stand of big old eucalyptus trees on the left? Dead body of an older man lying in the road. Shooting victim, looks like." An answer crackles, and Sorenson says, "Ten-four," and hangs up the micro-phone.

"Thanks. Really appreciate it." Bohannon is already astraddle Buck and headed back for the main road. "Got to get home. Lost my stable hand again. Work enough for three men waiting for me."

For an answer, Sorenson gives a short hoot on his siren.

"As a licensed private investigator," Gerard says, "you can't encourage a suspect to flee. You can't aid and abet—"

"Shut up, Phil," Bohannon says, grinning. "This is my house, and I don't have to listen to you rave. Not here. Sit down. Have a drink."

Red-faced, Gerard yanks a chair out from the round deal table that stands in the middle of Bohannon's big pine-plank kitchen and drops onto it. He bangs his helmet down on the table. "Naw, I'm serious, Hack. You just stood there and watched him take off. And you let us think you weren't even up there." Bohannon hands him a glass with Old Crow in it. "I can't understand you."

"Was the man shot with a nine-millimeter Browning?"

"Nine-millimeter something." Gerard takes a swallow from his glass and makes a face. "How can you drink this stuff?"

Bohannon chuckles. "I manage. You find any ID on the body?"

"Robbery," Gerard says. "That's what Belcher wanted it to look like. Any-way, no wallet. But that's a good suit, and the labels are in it. Expensive, maybe even tailor-made. We'll check the shop out tomorrow."

Bohannon grunts. He has his glasses on and papers spread out in front of him. He pushes them into a raggedy stack and pokes the stack into a manila enve-lope. This was George Stubbs's job. Bohannon can't do paperwork and drink. Hell, he hates paperwork at the best of times. And this is not the best of times. He's worn out from rubbing down horses, picking gravel out of hooves, mucking out stalls, raking gravel, hauling water, pitching hay, writing receipts, answering damn fool phone calls, trying to collect overdue board bills, walking little kid rid-ers around the railed oval he had built for that back when Rivera was here.

"There was nothing on the soles of his shoes to indicate a hike. He drove there."

Gerard studies him. "No car around. One car brought him and his killer both? And the killer drove it away afterward?"

Bohannon nods. "Which leaves out Steve Belcher."

"How?" Gerard says. "His camper was within yards of the victim. Why didn't Belcher bring him up from town for some kind of meeting? And it went sour, and Belcher lost his temper and shot him? He's got a mad dog temper, Hack. You've got to admit that."

"Maybe, but he's only a little bit crazy. He wouldn't leave the body lying there. He'd take it someplace else. Come on, Phil."

Gerard makes a skeptical sound, picks up his helmet, and gets to his feet. "We'll see what turns up in that camper."

Bohannon stares. "You've got it?"

"It's not hard to spot," Gerard says. "He hadn't got to Fresno yet when the CHP pulled him over. On our APB."

Bohannon switches on the lamp in the middle of the table. There's still some daylight outside, but the kitchen doesn't get a lot of it. The lamp is an old kerosene lantern fitted out for electricity and enameled red. Linda's idea—his wife, who is in a private mental home just over the ridge, has been for a long time and looks like being there forever. Gerard walks to the open door.

Bohannon tells his back, "You're going to find the dead man's car up the canyon someplace. What? Mercedes? BMW? Jaguar? Abandoned in a ditch. Wiped clean of fingerprints."

"I know how to do my job," Gerard says, and pushes open the screen door.

Bohannon says, "Oh, and find a kid named Kelly. Hold on a second." He walks to the sideboard and takes a slip of paper from a drawer. He puts on the damn reading glasses again and peers at it. "Kelly Larkin. Hails from San Bernardino. Jockey-size, shaved head, tattoos. He'll likely be on foot, doesn't own a car. He was my stable boy till this morning very early. Maybe about the same time the man in the expensive suit got so fatally shot."

"We've got the nut who shot that man," Gerard says, "and you know it. Steve Belcher has been a disaster waiting to happen for years now. You always took his side. Don't make that mistake this time. You're already in deep, letting him get away this morning."

"What was I supposed to do? He had a gun. I didn't. He had a car. I didn't."

"Right. So why not admit right away that you were there? Way you handled it, anybody can think anything they want."

"They'll do that anyway." Bohannon walks to the door, steps out, watches Gerard go off along the porch to his brown sheriff's patrol car. He calls after him, "Did you find the bullet up there? It went right through him."

"Not yet," Gerard calls, "but we'll find it. Don't get your hopes up." He starts the car, slams the door, and takes off.

Bohannon can't understand it. He comes from his bedroom down the hall to the kitchen, following bacon smells, coffee smells. Hair wet from the shower, he stands barefoot in jeans and T-shirt, blinking in the lamplight. It's not daylight yet. The old school-room clock on the kitchen wall reads 5:10. And beside the monster nickel and porcelain stove stands T. Hodges, the slim, dark young woman deputy who is Bohannon's prime friend. She is beating up eggs in a pottery bowl that has Indian designs on it. She throws him a smile. "Good morning."

"I'll say. What's the occasion?"

"The lieutenant told me Kelly's left you," she says. A pitcher of orange juice is on the counter. She pours him a glass and holds it out for him. He limps to her and takes it. "That you're trying to do it all here. Stubbs's work, Rivera's work, and yours."

Bohannon nods and swallows some orange juice. "True, but—"

"So, I thought at least I could fix breakfast for you," she says.

"Mighty nice. Pretty early for you to get up, though." He sets the orange juice glass on the table and goes to take the old speckled blue enamel pot off the back burner on the stove and pour himself a mug of coffee. He raises the pot to her. "Pour some for you?"

"Not yet, thanks. Go sit down and enjoy that." She examines an iron skillet, turning it in the light, finds it acceptably clean, sets it on the stove, and cuts butter into it. "There's news. The dead man's name is Lubowitz, Cedric. A stockbroker. Beverly Hills. Age sixty-five. Newly a widower."

Bohannon lights a cigarette and squints at her past the light of the table lamp. "How'd they come by all this?"

"His picture on the news," T. Hodges says. "Seems he used to appear now and then on *Wall Street Week*."

"Nobody in your department watches *Wall Street Week*."

She laughs. "Picture it if you can," she says.

"And what was he doing in Rodd Canyon? What did he want up this way at all? Only stock up this way is livestock."

"And commodities were not his line," T. Hodges says.

The coffee is hot and strong. He douses it with cream. "And Belcher. Did Belcher know him?"

"Belcher watches *Wall Street Week* even less than Gerard." She brings a plate of bacon, eggs, and hash browns and sets it in front of Bohannon. "Eat hearty."

"What about you?" he says.

"Coming up," she says, and it is. In another minute, she has taken the pressed-wood chair opposite him. Now there's a stack of toast on the table, too. She tucks in a gingham napkin, picks up her fork, then looks at him. Very seriously. "Hack, you can't let Gerard do this to Steve Belcher. He's the gentlest, sorriest creature in the world. But everybody is ready to believe the worst, you know that."

Bohannon piles guava jelly on a slab of toast. "So does Belcher. Nothing I can do about it. He'd have been better off it he just hadn't—"

"He didn't kill that man!" T. Hodges says hotly.

"I guess not," Bohannon says. "But I'm not the jury."

"You mean you're going to let it happen? Just sit back and—"

"Teresa," Bohannon says gently, "you've already told me I'm trying to do three men's work around here. It's my living. I can't play detective anymore. Even if I had the energy, I haven't got the time."

"I'll do the leg work for you," she says. "You just tell me what needs to be done, and I'll do it. Kelly. Gerard says you think Kelly might have done it. I'll find him and bring him here."

"You have a job, love," Bohannon says. "Eight hours a day and sometimes more. Anyway, Gerard wouldn't tolerate you working the case against him. Behind his back. Don't think about it." She opens her mouth to argue, and he says, "Eat your beautiful breakfast, kid, and listen to your old man. Things happen every day that are at least as unjust as what's happening to Steve Belcher. All over the world. We can't stop them, no matter how much we'd like to."

"Oh, rubbish," she says. "Honestly, Hack. 'Old man,' indeed. I repeat: You tell me where to go, what to look for, who to talk to, and I'll do it. Yes, I have a job, but I have a lot of time away from that. Besides, Gerard is sexist. He never lets me have a case. Closest I get is tracking down lost children. A case like this is man's work, right?"

"That's Phil." Bohannon grunts. "These are better hash browns than Stubbs ever made. What's your secret?"

"Don't boil the potatoes first. Grate them up raw." She gives her head an impatient shake. "Don't change the subject, damn it. Hack, Fred May says it's hopeless; he can't win without you."

May is the local public defender, those rare times when a public defender is needed around here. Fat and amiable, he devotes most of his time to his wife and kids, and to protecting the whale and the wolf and the wilderness. Bohannon has often acted as his investigator.

"Don't look at me that way," he says. "I can't do it, Teresa. I have horses to look after. They can't feed themselves and clean up after themselves. You know that. Be reasonable."

"Reasonable won't save Steve Belcher." Tears are in her eyes. "The town can't wait to get rid of him. You know that."

"And I can't stop them." Bohannon stands, picks up his plate and hers—she's hardly eaten—and carries them to the sink. He brings the coffee pot back and refills their mugs. When he sits down, it is a gesture of disgust. "What the hell was Cedric Lubowitz doing here, anyway?"

"I thought you'd want to know," a tart voice says from the doorway. Belle Hesseltine stands there, backed by the first faint light of sunrise. She is a doctor who moved up to Madrone to retire many years ago now, and instead got busier than she'd ever been before. A lean, tough old gal, she's a mainstay of hope and courage and caring for many. For Bohannon, too. "I went past the substation to tell the lieutenant, but he hasn't come in yet." She walks toward the table, pulls out a chair, seats herself, looks at T. Hodges. "You weren't there, either." She sets her shoulder bag on the floor. "So I thought the one to tell was you, Hack."

"Well, you're wrong about that," Bohannon says. "But I'm happy to see you, all the same. Coffee?"

"I'll get it," T. Hodges says, and hops up and goes away into the shadows. "You persuade him he's got to help poor Steve Belcher."

Belle Hesseltine scowls at Bohannon. "Persuade? What's that mean? You aren't going to—? But the man's doomed unless somebody intervenes. He hasn't a chance. He can't rely on himself. He can't put his thoughts together. He can't fight back. Hack, I'm shocked."

"I'm stuck, Belle. I have to run this place alone. Time a day is over, all I'm good for is to sleep."

Belle watches T. Hodges set a coffee mug down for her. "What happened to my tattooed angel?"

"Kelly? Spread his wings yesterday morning and flew away. I told Gerard, it could have been the same time Lubowitz was shot. Phil doesn't see any connection. If I know him, he won't even bother to check." It is risky, and he knows it, but he lights a cigarette anyway. The old woman glares disapproval, but this time she doesn't bawl him out. And he asks, "So . . . what's Lubowitz's connection to our little township?"

"His sister-in-law," Belle says, and tries the coffee. "Ahh!" She holds the steaming mug up for a moment, admiring it, then sets it down with a regretful shake of her head. "Why is it that everything that tastes so good is so bad for us?"

"Sister-in-law?" T. Hodges wonders.

"Mary Beth Madison." Belle Hesseltine leans toward the table's center, peering intently. "Is that some of George Stubbs's guava jelly? Hack, push that toast and butter over here. That wicked old man made the most sinfully delicious preserves." She steals Hack's knife and goes after the toast and jelly as if the world had stopped for her convenience. When her mouth is jammed and her dentures are clacking happily away, when she is licking her fingers, slurping coffee, she notices their strained faces and makes an effort to swallow so she can speak. She sets down the coffee mug. "Very good Pasadena family. It was Mary Beth's older sister, Rose, that Cedric Lubowitz married. There was a scandal and talk of disinheriting Rose for marrying a Jew, but that blew over."

A corner of the old woman's mouth twitches in a smile.

"The Lubowitzes were neighbors, after all, and their house was just as splendid. The girls and young Cedric had spent their childhoods together, very close. I also suspect some Lubowitz financial advice had helped stabilize the Madison fortune. It was shaky. Henry Madison III had not been clever with his inheritance. Among his lesser follies was buying land in Madrone and Settlers Cove. Worthless at the time. That's how it happens that Mary Beth settled here. And"—she looks at first one, then the other—"the reason I retired here. My father, the Madison family doctor, had accepted a lot up here to settle a bill when times were bad."

"And that's how you know all this dishy stuff," T. Hodges marvels. "But doesn't Miss Mary Beth Madison live with Dr. Dolores Combs? The Chamber Symphony? The Canyon Mozart Festival? The Gregorian Chant Week at the Mission?"

Belle Hesseltine nods. "And much else as well. Yes, that's Dolores. Hard to believe that as a child she was scarcely more than a foundling, isn't it?"

T. Hodges's jaw drops. "Are you serious?"

"The Madison girls took to her, brought her home from the park one summer with them, and after that she was in the Madison mansion almost constantly. The family soon accepted her. After all, what she lacked in breeding and background she made up for in brains and talent."

Bohannon says, "She cuts quite a figure these days."

Belle Hesseltine smiles. "Her people were poor, uneducated; the father drank. They had no idea they had a musical prodigy on their hands. It was the Madisons who bought her a piano, got her lessons, sent her to university."

"And so," T. Hodges says, "when it came time for Cedric Lubowitz to marry, and he chose Rose, Dolores Combs and Mary Beth Madison soldiered on alone together?"

Bohannon is laughing.

She frowns at him, startled. "What's so funny?"

"You never told me you liked love stories." He grins.

"Well—well, I don't," she protests. "But this is about a murder case, Hack. It's straight out of the training manual. The most important person in any murder case is the victim. And the most likely killer is someone the victim knew well. Right?"

"Sounds more like Agatha Christie to me," Bohannon says.

"Well—" Belle Hesseltine unfolds her tall, bony frame from the chair and picks up her shoulder bag. "I have patients to see."

"Wait," Bohannon says. "Was Cedric Lubowitz up here to visit Mary Beth? Is that what you're saying?"

"Oh, I don't suppose so, really. He owned one of those lots his father-in-law bought so long ago," the old doctor says. "He may have planned to build on it and settle down here to live out his sunset years in quiet. Hah! I could have told him a few things about that, couldn't I?" She opens the screen door and pauses to look back. At T. Hodges, really, so maybe she's teasing. "Then again, perhaps having lost dear, pretty Rose and feeling lonely, he came to renew acquaintance with Mary Beth, who is every bit as pretty. I suppose, if you like love stories, you're free to think that."

And with a bark of laughter, she marches off.

Tired as he is, he goes to see Stubbs. It's a long drive to San Luis, but he skipped last night, and it's not fair. The old man is lonesome as hell. Anyway, Bohannon misses him. If there's nothing to talk about, they play checkers or watch horse racing or bull riding on television. Tonight there is Steve Belcher to talk about, and Cedric Lubowitz. Stubbs regards Bohannon from his narrow bed with its shiny rails, where he is propped up with his wooden drawing kit and drawing pad beside him on the wash-faded quilt. When the pain isn't too bad, he can still draw.

He says reproachfully, "You ain't gonna help him?"

"Stable boy left me. No time, George."

"Oh, Kelly." Stubbs grunts. "Yeah, I know. He come by here real early yesterday. Says will I tell you. Gotta go home. Ma needs him. Runnin' her out of the mobile home park. Fightin' with the boyfriend."

"He could have left a note," Bohannon says.

"Nothin' to write with," Stubbs says. "Nothin' to write on."

"On the kitchen table," Bohannon says. "He knew that. Knew where I sleep, too. He could have wakened me and told me. He woke you."

Stubbs waves a gnarled hand. "Had to see me. Had one of my drawings. Took it down off the tackroom wall. Wanted it for his room at home. Wouldn't steal it. Offered me five bucks for it. I give it to him."

"How did he get in here so early?"

"It was warm." Stubbs nods at the window. "Come in there."

Bohannon says, "Didn't say anything about the killing, did he?"

Stubbs frowns. "How would he know about it?"

"Just asking," Bohannon says.

Stubbs squints at him, surprised. "You don't think he'd have killed this Lubo—what's his name. Why?"

"I'd like to ask him," Bohannon says.

"He'd need a gun," Stubbs says. "Where would he get it?"

"A Browning automatic. I don't know. Someone got hold of one. Threw it away after the shooting."

"And Belcher just picked it up?" Stubbs says.

"That's his story. I doubt they'll find a record of it. Bought on the street, most likely. And the tattoos suggest Kelly knows the streets."

"Ballistics report in already?" Stubbs's white, tufty eyebrows are raised. "They know it was the Browning?"

Bohannon shakes his head. "They can't find the bullet," he says. "But a paraffin test says Belcher shot the gun lately."

"Oh, hell," Stubbs says.

"He told Gerard it was to scare off a prowler," Bohannon says, "but he told me earlier it hadn't been fired."

"You see why you have to pitch in and help him?" Stubbs says. "The fool's his own worst enemy. Always has been."

"Not always," Bohannon says. "Once it was Uncle Sam."

"Just a minute." Stubbs massages his white beard stubble thoughtfully. "Could the prowler have been Kelly?"

Bohannon blinks surprise. "Well, I'll be damned," he says. "Good thinking, George. Why not?"

He swings into the ranch yard and in the headlights sees a brown sheriff's patrol car. Lights wink on top of it. Two doors stand open. Two people struggle beside it. He drives on hard toward them. One is T. Hodges, her helmet on the ground. The other is Kelly Larkin. He pushes T. Hodges backward so she falls. He turns and comes running directly at Bohannon's truck. From one wrist dangles a pair of handcuffs, glinting in the light. His shirt is torn down the back and slipping off his shoulders, showing his tattoos. Bohannon jams on the Gemmy's brakes, jumps down with a yell, and grabs the boy. Who twists and hits out with the handcuff-dangling fist. It knocks Bohannon's hat off.

"Stop it," he says. "Stand still, damn it, Kelly."

"Aw, let me go," the boy says. "I didn't do nothin'."

"Then don't fight," Bohannon says. "There. That's better." He calls to T. Hodges, whom his headlights shine on. "You all right?"

"Kelly . . ." she says in a menacing voice, and comes toward them.

"I'm sorry," the boy says, hangdog.

"I should think so." She is wiping dust off her helmet with her sleeve. "I was taking the cuffs off him. I told him I was sure I could trust him. And look what happened."

"We'll just put them back," Bohannon says, and clips the cuffs on him again. "There." He picks up his hat. "Now, let's go into the kitchen, sit down, have some coffee, and talk this over civilized. All right?"

"I don't know anything to talk about," Kelly says, stumbling along, Bohannon holding his arm. "This is crazy."

They step up onto the long covered walkway that is the ranch-house porch. Bohannon looks over Kelly's head at T. Hodges. "Is it crazy?"

"I don't think so," she says. "Not when you consider that his last name isn't Larkin—"

"It could be," Kelly says. "It was my mom's name."

Bohannon pulls open the kitchen screen door, they walk inside, and he hangs up his hat. The lamp on the table glows. "It's Belcher, right?"

Kelly stares. "How did you know?"

"Sit down," Bohannon says. He goes to the looming stove and picks up the speckled blue coffee pot. But T. Hodges comes and takes it out of his hand. "I'll do it," she says. "You talk to him."

"This is going to get you into a mess with Gerard," he says.

"We'll deal with Gerard later," she says.

Bohannon drops onto a chair at the table and, as he lights a cigarette, studies the sulking boy. "You didn't happen in on me by accident, looking for work. You found out your father was here, and you wanted to see him, talk to him."

"He left when I was four," Kelly says. "Walked out on my mom and me. Beat her up and walked out and never came back."

"Which broke your mother's heart?" Bohannon asks.

"Not exactly. She couldn't take it anymore. He was so mixed up and half out of his gourd from the war, all that killing, those nightmares, the way he'd scream and hide . . ." Tears shine in Kelly's eyes, and he drops his head and sniffles hard and wipes his nose with the back of one cuffed hand. "It wasn't his fault. I knew that. She knew it, too, but he wouldn't get help. The veterans, they're entitled to help, and he got some before they got married, but then he was happy, and it was all right for a while, but the horrors came back, you know? It started all over again. He couldn't keep a job, he started boozing all the time, throwing stuff, smashing stuff, hitting her—" The boy's voice breaks, and he shakes his head and looks at the floor.

"And you came to get him to come home?" Bohannon asks.

The boy nods, lifts his tear-shiny face. "It was years ago. And she needs him. She's always getting new men. And they're none of them any good. Highway trash. She's a waitress, works hard, they just take her money and lay around watching TV all day."

"You think he's cured now?" T. Hodges brings coffee mugs into the light and sets them down for the two men. "Kelly, he doesn't work, either. Lives off his disability check."

"Yeah." Kelly touches his coffee mug. "And hates everybody."

"You talked to him?" Bohannon says.

Kelly makes a face. "He wasn't happy to see me. It wasn't a good talk. Nothing like what I expected."

" 'Dreamed,' you mean." T. Hodges sits down with her own coffee in the circle of lamplight. "Kelly, some things just aren't meant to be."

Kelly blows steam off his coffee and gingerly tries it. "I wasn't giving up. I was going to take him back. I promised my mom. Take him back with me, and we'd be like we were in the seventies, a family. We had good times. He was okay then. Steady. Cheerful, even. A good dad. I really have missed him. Twenty years is a long time."

"Granted," Bohannon says. "So you tried talking to him again?"

"Three, four times. He ordered me off, told me to leave him the hell alone."

T. Hodges hasn't done this for a long time, but now she reaches for Bohannon's Camels on the tabletop and lights one. In the slow-moving smoke that circles the lamp, she says, "And night before last?"

"I couldn't sleep. I kept arguing with him in my head. Yeah, I went up there." Kelly doesn't look at her or at Bohannon. His voice is almost too low to be heard. "He took a shot at me."

"You sure he saw you, knew who you were?"

"Well, hell, how do I know?" Kelly says. "Think I stayed around to find out? He had a gun. You don't know how fast you can run till somebody shoots at you."

"Uh-huh," Bohannon says. "And what did you stumble over?"

"What?" Kelly sits very straight, eyes wide. "What?"

"You were running scared, and you didn't watch where you were going, and you stumbled over the body of a man down on the road."

"Hell," Kelly says. "How did you know?"

"Your hands are scraped and scabby from falling on pavement," Bohannon says.

"And I'm afraid," T. Hodges says, "the thought that jumped into your mind was that your father had killed that man, and that he'd changed more than you'd thought in those twenty years, and you were suddenly very much afraid of him."

"And didn't want to stay anywhere near him anymore," Bohannon says. "You were on your way. Which is why you didn't take time even to write me a note."

"I stopped to see Stubbs," Kelly says defensively.

"Sixty-five miles down the road," Bohannon agrees. "And George didn't describe it as a long visit."

"What will they do to my dad?" Kelly asks anxiously.

"You love him in spite of everything," T. Hodges marvels.

"Don't worry about him," Bohannon says. "I don't think he killed the man. But it would help if I knew who did."

T. Hodges puts out her cigarette. "You didn't see anyone around there? An expensive car, maybe?"

Kelly laughs, but there's no humor in it. "I was so scared I didn't see nothin'. Man, I was outta there. I mean, we're talkin' roadrunner here." They watch him without comment, and he pauses and blinks to himself seriously. "Wait. No. You're right. There was a car. Other side of the road. Mercedes. Parked wrong way."

"No driver?" Bohannon says.

"Not that I saw." Kelly turns pale. "The killer, you mean?"

"The killer, I mean," Bohannon says.

For a long time, he didn't want and didn't keep a phone by the bed, but when Stubbs got to the wheel-chair stage, it helped to have it there in case of emergencies. After Stubbs went to the nursing home, Bohannon just kept the phone. And now it rings. Early morning. He's overslept. He groans, gropes out, gets the receiver, and mumbles "Bohannon" into it.

"The gun was the proud possession of the deceased," Gerard says. "Cedric Lubowitz. But the only fingerprints on it were Steve Belcher's."

"The good news," Bohannon croaks, "and the bad news all in one package?"

"No, the bad news is I know all about Teresa's activities last night, and she is on leave till this case is over with. I'm holding Kelly for at least seventy-two hours. The provenance of the gun suggests he could have been the killer. Motive, robbery. The vic's wallet hasn't turned up."

"Kelly got money on him?"

"Not very much," Gerard says. "You should pay your help better."

"I'd have thought a man like Lubowitz would keep a couple hundred bucks cash on him." Bohannon throws off the blankets and sits on the edge of the bed. "Well, since you haven't got the wallet, that means it wasn't in the camper. And that clears Steve, anyway." He reaches to get a cigarette from his shirt which hangs on a painted straw-bottom Mexican chair. "Of course, you checked to see whether the killer threw the wallet away along the roadside."

"That's what the citizens pay me for," Gerard says. "Me, not you, Hack. Will you stay out of this now?"

"I keep trying," Bohannon says. "Don't worry. I haven't got time. Not with my stable hand in jail." And he hangs up.

"He didn't tell you about Lubowitz's car?" T. Hodges says. She is at the stove cooking breakfast for him again. Earlier, she cleaned out the box stalls, fed, watered, and groomed the horses while he slept. Now she puts plates of ham and eggs and fried mush on the table. "They found it at the Tides Motel on the beach where he was staying."

Bohannon raises his eyebrows. "Not in the guest room at the beautiful home of his sister-in-law and her eternal friend Dr. Combs?" Bohannon pitches into his breakfast. Mouth full, he says, "So much for the love story motive."

T. Hodges quietly pours syrup on her slabs of fried mush. "Don't jump to conclusions," she says. "His first night, they all had dinner together at the Brambles. Very pleasant. Fresh salmon, champagne. Lots of laughter and jokes about him sweeping Mary Beth off to Paris on the Concorde. The check went on his credit card."

Bohannon chews a chunk of ham. "And afterward?"

"The waiter at the Brambles said they took Mr. Lubowitz home with them afterward, for dessert, and to listen to some new Mozart CDs on the stereo. The motel says he didn't get back there until midnight."

"Mozart. You remember when Steve Belcher camped up in the Mozart Bowl?" It's a little natural amphitheater among the pines in Sills Canyon. "Dr. Combs got on his case hot and heavy for that."

T. Hodges laughs. "She'd taken some possible large contributors to the Canyon Mozart Festival up to see the place in all its unspoiled loveliness. Sasquatch was not what she'd expected to find. She could have killed him."

"You don't mean that," Bohannon says.

She wags her fork in denial. "Figure of speech. When our team examined the Lubowitz Mercedes," she says, "it had no fingerprints on it. Inside or out. Not the victim's, not anyone's."

"A careful murderer," Bohannon says, and tries his coffee. "A schemer, a planner-ahead. Wore gloves. Nothing spontaneous about this killing, Teresa." He sets his cup down and lights a cigarette. "Nobody at the motel saw who returned the Mercedes?"

She shakes her head. "Not the day man, not the night man. None of the guests Vern could find to question."

"Yup," Bohannon says, looking across at the sunlit kitchen windows. They are open. Smells of sage and eucalyptus drift in on a cool breeze. The sky is clear blue above the ridges. "Craftily plotted. An organizing mind, used to managing people and events."

"But insane," she says. "Cedric Lubowitz was a gentle old man."

"Yup." Bohannon scrapes back his chair and goes to stand looking out the door. "Nobody's given me the medical examiner's findings. No, don't say it. Let me guess. He was shot at close range, right? Only a few feet. And through the chest. He was facing his killer. His killer was a friend."

"He must have thought so." T. Hodges gathers up the plates and carries them to the sink. "What a horrible way to die."

"Sure as hell too late to learn anything from it."

Water splashes in the sink. "You go along and find out what you want to find out," she calls. "I'll look after things here."

"On a day like this," he says, "there'll be lots of people wanting to go horseback riding. You'll be run off your feet."

"Be careful," is all she says.

And he takes down his hat and goes.

Steve Belcher sits on the bunk in his cell and glowers. Outside the windows, towering old eucalyptus trees creak in the breeze. Fat Freddie May stands leaning against the sand-colored cinderblock wall. Bohannon leans back against the bars. Down the way, someone is softly playing a harmonica. A hard song. "I'm comin' back, if I go ten thousand miles . . ." A dimestore mouth organ can't handle it, but the player keeps trying.

Bohannon repeats his question: "You said there was a prowler, and you shot the gun to scare the prowler off. What did the prowler look like, Steve?"

"How do I know? It was midnight. It was pitch dark."

"Tall, short?" Bohannon says. "Thin, fat? Wearing what?"

"I only heard him tramping around," Belcher says.

May says in his gentle voice, "It was Kelly, wasn't it? Your son, Kelly?"

"Oh, hell," Belcher says, and runs a hand down over his face. "Is he messed up in this, too, now?"

"Since last night," Bohannon says. "He went up there, and you shot the gun off. So it was after Mr. Lubowitz was killed, after the killer threw the gun at your camper."

But Belcher is shaking his shaggy head. "It wasn't him. This one was bigger. Taller. Heavier. Kelly's head is shaved. This one had hair."

"That's all?" Bohannon asks. "Clothes? Voice? Anything?"

"Went crashing down through the trees." Belcher grins. His teeth are in poor shape. "Maybe it was a bear."

"You don't want to help us get you off the hook? Okay." Bohannon sighs, straightens, peers through the bars. "Vern?"

Fred May says, "And Kelly. You don't want to help him?"

A guard with a big gun in a holster on his hip comes and unlocks the cell door. Bohannon goes out, May after him. The door closes. They follow the guard along the hallway.

And Belcher calls, "It could have been a woman."

Bohannon doesn't break stride, but he smiles and says, "Ah!"

He noses the green pickup truck into a diagonal slot in front of the drugstore. A pair of sleepy old huskies with pale eyes look at him as he passes. One of them sniffs his boots. He pushes into the gleaming shop and stands looking for Mrs. Vanderhoop. There she is, at the back, by the prescription counter. When he nears, he sees she is talking with a bald little man who plays cello in local music ensembles. Mrs. Vanderhoop, wife of the pharmacist who owns the only drugstore in Madrone, is a busy part-time musician herself. Piano. Though Bohannon seems to remember she once sang. She sees him and gives him a smile, excuses herself to

Mr. Cello, and comes to him, gray-haired, thin, running to homespun skirts, Navajo blouses, Indian jewelry.

"Mr. Bohannon?" Her expression is concerned. "Isn't it terrible about that poor man, Liebowitz?"

"Lubowitz," Bohannon says. "Listen. You can correct something I heard. That he came up here to see his sister-in-law, Mary Beth? Wouldn't he have seen her at her sister's funeral, his wife's funeral?"

"Oh, no." Mrs. Vanderhoop shakes her head firmly. "Not that Mary Beth did not love her sister. But Dolores wouldn't allow it. They had a terrible argument about it. I came back for something I'd forgotten after a rehearsal. Mary Beth was in tears."

"I don't understand." Bohannon pushes back his hat. "I heard they were all close friends together when they were young."

Mrs. Vanderhoops's smile is bleak. "Yes, well, for some of us, young was rather a long time ago. No, there was no love lost."

"But they had dinner with Mr. Lubowitz only the night before he was killed," Bohannon says. "Very friendly and good-humored, I'm told. Laughing over old times."

"Did they? Really." Mrs. Vanderhoop blinks thoughtfully to herself. "Do you know, if it wasn't you telling me, Mr. Bohannon, I wouldn't believe that. Dolores Combs despised Mr. Liebowitz. And once her sister Rose took sick, she wouldn't let Mary Beth near him."

Bohannon circles the house, a sprawling redwood place with windows that stare at the ocean. It's isolated on its hill, land once owned by Henry Madison III. Big pines shelter it. Nobody is around. Cars? The garage doors are closed. He parks his green pickup truck, gets out, and looks down the road. Only a short walk to the beach, only another short walk to Cedric Lubowitz's motel room. You could do it in ten minutes. He hikes up through the trees around the back of the house, where he spots the structure he wants and goes toward it, waiting for some reaction if he's been seen. He doesn't hear or see any. The enclosure of redwood plank fencing he has had his eye on has a gate, but it isn't locked. He works the latch quietly, opens the gate, and sees inside what he expected. Trash barrels. Two are filled with yard trimmings, and their lids are propped against the enclosure, but the third has its lid in place. Heart beginning to beat fast, he pries the lid off. Inside is a large green plastic bag. He undoes the wire twist that closes it, pulls the bag open, reaches inside, and a voice behind him says: "What the hell do you think you're doing?"

He turns. It's Gerard. He looks stern.

Bohannon says, "Collecting trash? Is that against the law?"

"You haven't got a license to collect trash," Gerard says. "What you are doing is breaking and entering, conducting a search of private property without a warrant."

Bohannon pulls a white cableknit sweater out of the bag and holds it up. It has bloodstains on it. And next, a brand new pair of women's jeans, also splashed with blood. "Hundred to one," he says to Gerard, "those will match Cedric Lubowitz's blood type. And his DNA." He brings out a pair of expensive low-heeled women's walking shoes. Turns the soles up. "More of same off the road." With a fingernail, he pries out scraps of oak and eucalyptus leaves, pine needles. "Stuff like this lay all around the body." He looks at Gerard, whose face is expressionless. "What you're saying is that I've made this inadmissible evidence."

"It would be," Gerard answers, "except when I learned you were out and around, talking to prisoners behind my back, checking out the tires on Lubowitz's car at the impound, generally acting your usual hot-dog self, I got a warrant." He pulls the folded paper from inside his uniform jacket. He edges Bohannon aside and rummages in the trash bag for himself. "The wallet," he says, and holds it up.

"Isn't it disgusting," Bohannon says, "how right I always am?"

Gerard starts off. "Bring that stuff. Let's go arrest her."

He presses a bell button on the wide, redwood-beamed porch. Handsome stained glass frames the doorway. The motif is California wildflowers. Yellow poppies, blue lupine, white yucca. Suddenly, the door flies open, and Dolores Combs stands there angry, a big-boned woman, white hair cropped handsomely. Arty women in Settlers Cove run to sweatshirts, but not she. A shirtwaist of brown shantung. Tailored slacks. A jade necklace. From Gump's, probably.

"I warned you," she begins. "It's you, Lieutenant Gerard. Forgive me. I thought it was more news people. They've been pestering the life out of us."

"Morning," Gerard says. "We're here about the death of your friend Cedric Lubowitz. This is Hack Bohannon, investigator for the public defender's office."

She glares at Bohannon. "You're defending that animal Belcher?"

Bohannon tugs his hat brim. "Ma'am."

"These things belong to you?" Gerard takes sweater, jeans, and shoes from Bohannon and holds them out to her. She blinks at them and turns pale. "N-no. Certainly not. Where did you get them?"

"Out of your trash barrels back of the house," Bohannon says.

She acts indignant. "You had no right to—"

"We have a search warrant." Gerard hands her the sweater, jeans, and shoes and produces the paper again, unfolding it, holding it up for her to read. "It covers the grounds, the house, and all outbuildings."

She eyes it and seems to shrink a little. But she braves up in a second. "I have no idea how these got there. No idea." She drops the clothes and snatches the paper, reading it closely. Her head jerks up. "Harold Willard? Why—why—Judge Willard is a close personal friend. He's one of the principal contributors to—" She thrusts the paper back at Gerard. "Why would he sign such a warrant? What lies did you tell him about me?"

"It's not going to be hard to prove those are your clothes, Dr. Combs, your shoes. And they have bloodstains on them. We can trace the clothes to where you bought them. We can trace the bloodstains to Mr. Lubowitz. And"—he flashes it—"Mr. Lubowitz's wallet."

"Dolly? What's wrong?" A dainty pink and white woman appears behind the doctor of music. *Fluffy* would describe her. Curvacious once, now pudgy. Her voice is little-girlish. "Who are these men?" Her blue eyes widen, looking at them. "What do they want? Is it about poor, dear Cedric?"

"Go away, Mary Beth. Let me handle this."

Mary Beth Madison sees the clothes. She stoops and picks up the sweater.

"Why, where did you find this? I've been looking all over for it. I was going to take it to the cleaners days ago." She draws in her breath. "Why, just look at those stains. Now, those were not on it when I—"

Dr. Combs tries to kill her with a look. "Will you be quiet?" she says. "Do you have to rattle on and on constantly?"

The plump little woman is amazed. "But, Dolly, I only—"

"Shut up, can't you?" The Combs woman is trembling. "Mary Beth, please go away, now. You're only making things worse." But Mary Beth simply stands, holding the sweater, totally bewildered.

Gerard asks her, "Is that Dr. Combs's sweater?"

"Oh, yes." Mary Beth nods. "Hand-knitted. From Ireland. We were there two years ago." She looks adoringly at her big friend. "Dolly played an organ recital in Dublin. Beautiful old church." Her small hands are stroking the sweater. She looks at it again. "Dolly, what are these awful splotches? Will they ever come out?"

Her lifelong friend lets out a snarl and strikes Mary Beth Madison hard across the face. The little woman staggers backward, appalled, holding her bruised cheek.

"Dolly." She gasps. "You hit me. What's happened to you?"

Gerard steps forward, taking handcuffs off his belt. "Dolores Combs, you are under arrest for the murder of Cedric Martin Lubowitz." He reaches to turn her around, but she swings at him, too. He dodges the blow, but she is running away, down a long living room where a Bosendorfer grand stands glossy in stained-glass gloom. Bohannon takes after her. Oriental carpets slide under his boots. She has reached French doors at the end of the room and is tugging at the latches before he can grab her. She is strong and flails and kicks, but he gets her arms behind her, finally, and swings her—she's a good weight, is Dr. Combs—back toward Gerard, who now manages to cuff her wrists. Behind her, as if she were some L.A. street tough.

He half nudges, half lifts her down the room, toward the front door, droning the Miranda warning, grunting with the effort she is costing him. Bohannon goes ahead to gather up the jeans and shoes from the floor. He reaches out to Mary Beth for the sweater. She hands it to him, but she is listening to the outraged Dr. Combs.

"This is grotesque," the big woman says. "Why would I kill Cedric Lubowitz? Why would I kill anyone? No jury in the world will believe Dr. Dolores Combs is a murderer. When Judge Willard hears—aah! Let me go. You're hurting me."

Mary Beth begins beating on Gerard with her little fists. "Stop it," she says. "Stop hurting Dolly." Bohannon pulls her off the lieutenant. She clutches his arms. "Where are you taking her?"

"Just down to the sheriff station." Gerard grunts, wrestling the large woman through the doorway, out onto the porch. "For a nice talk."

"I'll come, too," Mary Beth says. "Dolly, what shall I wear?"

"No, dearest," the handcuffed woman says. "You stay here and feed the cats." And she goes with Gerard down the plank steps to the path, no longer resisting, lumpish, defeated.

The little pink and white girl of sixty gazes wanly after her. "When will you come home, Dolly?" Her question drifts off into the noon silence of the woods, as sad a sound as Bohannon has ever heard.

It is sundown. T. Hodges is washing down Twilight, while Mousie stands by, reins loosely knotted to a post of the long stable walkway. Before Bohannon has fully stopped the truck, Kelly is out of it, running to help the deputy. She smiles at him, hands him the sponge, walks toward Bohannon, wearily brushing a strand of hair off her face.

"Boy, am I glad to see you." She gives him a hug.

"You okay?" he says.

"I think," she says thoughtfully, taking his hand and walking toward the ranch house, "you work much too hard for a living."

"I'm sorry I stranded you here." They go along the house porch and in at the kitchen screen door. "I didn't know so much would happen so soon. And Gerard wanted me there for the interrogation."

"It was Dolores Combs, then?" She drops onto a chair. "Oh, am I going to be sore tomorrow."

"It was Dolores Combs." Bohannon fetches Old Crow and glasses and sits down opposite her at the table. "She thought we'd never guess, so she didn't bother to hide her bloodstained clothes." He pours whiskey into the glasses and hands her one. "She just threw them in the trash."

"How did she get him to drive her up the canyon?"

"Some romance about Mary Beth being stranded up there. I don't know why he believed her. But he did. And took along his gun."

"Odd." She frowns. "A man like that carrying a gun."

"One of his fellow stockbrokers got mugged and badly beaten recently. It upset the firm, and Cedric Lubowitz not least. Another lesson for society. Leave the guns to law enforcement. But they won't learn."

She tastes the whiskey and again reaches for Bohannon's cigarettes on the table. "And the prowler Steve Belcher shot at?"

"Combs. After she'd driven halfway down the canyon, she worried whether he'd find the gun and pick it up. She turned the car around and drove back. Well, he'd found it all right, hadn't he?" He gives his head a wondering shake. "She and Kelly must have missed each other by inches, running away in the dark."

She laughs briefly, grows somber again. "We know why she hated Steve. Why did she hate Cedric Lubowitz?"

"*Fear* is the word you want." Bohannon stretches an arm and switches on the lamp. "She was convinced, as Mrs. Madison, the girls' mother, had been, that that Jew scoundrel only married Rose for her money."

"Please, Hack. Belle Hesseltine says the Lubowitzes were rich."

"If you want to hate Jews, sweet reason is meaningless, Deputy."

She sighs. "I guess so. So . . . Dolores was convinced once Rose was dead, and Cedric came up here, and immediately started wining and dining Mary Beth, he meant to marry her and take over her fortune, too?"

Bohannon nods. "And put Dolores Combs out to starve and freeze in the cruel world. And she didn't want to give up the beautiful house, the antiques, the jewelry, the Cadillac, the parties and banquets. And most of all the power. Money is power, Deputy. Ever hear that before?"

"Mary Beth's love didn't count for anything?"

Bohannon shrugs, sighs. "Who knows? Maybe once long ago. But Dolores learned how nice being rich was, and, face it, she didn't do much with all that talent she kept raving about this afternoon." He adopts a plummy elocutionary voice. " 'I could have been an international star. But I gave that up for Mary Beth. Stayed here in this backwater . . . ' et cetera, et cetera." He resumes his normal voice. "Hell, a backwater was what she needed. Organizing her little ensembles, festivals, concerts. She swayed around here like a duchess. You've seen her."

"And she thought Cedric Lubowitz would end all that?"

"Thought so enough to kill him," Bohannon says.

T. Hodges sits studying her hands around the glass for a long minute. "It's pitiful," she says. She raises her head, looks into his face. "And Mary Beth? Mary Beth worshipped her. What will she do now?"

"Wait for her to come home," Bohannon says.

# Christine Matthews

## Character Flaw

ROBERTA STANTON, a crazy lady P.I., was born out of a real-life situation and made her first appearance in the anthology *Deadly Allies II*. Her creator, Christine Matthews, is a veteran short story writer with more than fifty to her credit. Her mysteries have appeared in dozens of anthologies, and the best of them were recently anthologized in the short story collection, *Gentle Insanities and Other States of Mind*. An erotic thriller, *Scarred for Life* will be released later in 2001. "Character Flaw," first published in *The Shamus Game*, has Roberta at her wild and woolly best.

# Character Flaw

*Christine Matthews*

If it hadn't been for the blood matted in her hair, I would have noticed Skye Cahill's turquoise eyes first.

"Miss Stanton?" she asked in such a calm voice. "Are you *the* Roberta Stanton? The one from TV?"

"Yes."

"I just killed someone—well, not just someone . . . I'm pretty sure he was my father."

I stood back from the door. "Get out of the hall." I let her into my apartment so easily. I wasn't the least bit frightened. Not even after noticing the gun in her right hand.

I guess I was at that raw patch in my life. There didn't seem to be a clean spot left on my body or psyche that hadn't been hurt. It felt like I'd been frightened for years. Then one day I just got pissed off. But the terror returned. In tidal waves. Then suddenly . . . it passed. All of it—the good and the bad. Nothing mattered. And it was at that point in my life I let a frightened stranger enter my apartment.

She stood in the middle of the kitchen, unsure where to turn. Like a dog circling until he finally plops down for a nap.

I pointed to a dining room chair. "Why don't you sit there?"

"Yeah. Okay . . . I'll do that . . . I'll . . ."

"How about if I take this?" I reached for the gun hanging from her limp hand.

"Okay." No struggle. She let me take it and then eased herself onto the stiff chair. "Could I have some coffee? A Coke? I need caffeine. All the way over here I felt so tired, like I was going to fall asleep. Isn't that crazy?" She looked at me, realizing how her last word stung and quickly added, "Sorry."

I laid the gun on the counter, in plain sight, but closer to me just in case I needed to go for it. Then I poured last night's coffee into a clean mug and set it in the microwave. "Well, I did spend time in a mental hospital."

She took the coffee from me and shrugged. "So you hired a hit man, big deal. If I had the money, I wouldn't have had to kill my father myself."

"But I was messed up back then . . ."

"That's why I came to you. I remembered reading all about your trouble growing up, how they took your license away, and how you finally got out last year. I knew you—of all people—would understand how I feel."

I sat down across from her, folding my hands on top of the table. "Understand what?"

"That it was *his* fault, not mine."

Before we got any deeper into our new relationship, I thought it best to tell her, "I have to call the police, you know. If what you're saying is true and you killed a man?"

She looked at me like I was an idiot. "Of course. But I came to hire you first."

I picked up my cordless, curious to see her reaction. "I make the call first and *then* we talk while we wait."

"Fine." She gulped the hot coffee down; I wondered how she managed without burning her throat. "Call."

"I figure we've got at least ten minutes—tops," I told her after hanging up.

"It won't even take that long," she said, reaching for her purse.

I jumped for the gun then, and she grinned like I'd fallen for the punch line of a tired old joke. While I held it on her, she groped around in her tote bag.

"I made this on the way over here." She handed me a cassette tape.

I took it with my free hand. Turning it over, I asked, "What is it?"

"Details. I thought it was important you have my side of the story before you go investigate."

"So you're hiring me to establish the fact that you killed your father? I don't get it." I put the gun back on the table, feeling foolish pointing the thing at her that way.

"No, I want you to check out the man. You'll find his body at the address I wrote on the tape. I can stall the police for a while. You go there, look around . . . to make sure."

"He's dead, right?"

She nodded.

"Then I still don't get it."

Suddenly she was a little girl. "I need you to tell me that there is no doubt—whatsoever—he was my father."

Before I could ask any more questions, the police were knocking at my front door.

Reaching in her pocket, Skye pulled out two hundred-dollar bills. "Here"—she thrust them at me—"for gas, your time, whatever. Please."

I lied . . . so sue me. I managed to convince the police that Skye Cahill and I had been friends for years, explaining we were practically sisters. I handed over the gun, and they took her in for questioning. Then I promised to come down after I could arrange bail. Another lie? It all depended on what I found at the address she'd written on the tape.

Elkhorn is a small town about twenty minutes outside of Omaha. The only thing I had ever heard about the place concerned its strip clubs. Since time was definitely not on my side, I decided the quickest and straightest shot would be Maple

Road, which I steered toward while listening to Skye's voice coming out of my cheap car speakers.

> My name is Skye Louise Cahill, I'm twenty-five years old. I'm a filmmaker and I live in Los Angeles—in the Valley. The only way I know how to do this effectively is to pretend this recorder is a camera. Maybe if I distance myself, you can understand better.

Her voice took on a tone that was both detached and informative. I felt as though I was listening to a documentary.

> The trailer sits by itself in a vacant lot. There are no trees for shade, not one blade of grass for color. It's gray now, but she assumed it used to be silver.

I was taken by surprise when she referred to herself in the third person but soon got used to it. . . .

> A small window on the side that faced her had a box pushed against it, blocking anyone from looking inside. The only thing adhering to the structure was dirt. No antennas, no paint, not even an address.
>
> She stood a few feet from the door, kicking a large dirt clump, watching it crumble into the air. Trying unsuccessfully to walk a few feet without stepping into a hole, she made her way to the side, to an entrance. It took her a few more minutes before she knocked.
>
> "Yeah? What do you want?" a man yelled.
>
> "I'm looking for Edward Blevins. Is this number three-twenty-nine?"
>
> She could feel him on the other side of the door, could hear him shift his weight. If he thought making her wait would discourage her, he was very wrong. She sat down on the wooden box which served as a stair.
>
> He couldn't leave without her seeing him. She'd circled the lot several times and knew for a fact there was only one door. He couldn't even move around inside without jostling the trailer. The late afternoon sun was at her back, and she could feel her blouse sticking to her damp neck.
>
> "Is this three-twenty-nine Oak or isn't it?"
>
> "Who wants to know?"
>
> The immediate response startled her enough to make her stand. Facing the door, she shouted, "I do!"
>
> Only silence filtered from inside the trailer. She hoped he was spying on her, searching to make sure she was alone, or harmless—worth the effort to answer. She had turned to sit down again when the door suddenly opened.
>
> "Get your ass off my property. I don't know who the hell you are,

what you're selling, or what church you're collectin' for, and I don't give a damn—"

"I'm not collecting or selling anything! I just came to talk to Edward Blevins. Is that you or not? Just tell me so we can both stop yelling!"

The heavy-set man stepped out onto his wooden step and slammed the door behind him. Easing onto the ground, he forced her back a few steps. "So what if I am?"

"I'd look you straight in the eye and tell you I'm your daughter."

"Helena's kid?"

"Yes."

"How the hell is she?" he asked without smiling or softening his face in any way.

"I wouldn't know. We've never met."

"What the hell you talkin' about, girl?"

"She put me up for adoption."

"Then how do I know you're Helena's . . . and mine? What the shit you trying to pull here?"

She shoved the birth certificate in his face. "Here. It says you're my father."

"Look, it's too goddamn hot to stand around. I guess it would be all right if you came inside. Just till I get a good look at that."

It was roomier than she expected. Dark, except for one lamp in the corner, by the kitchen area. A bit of sunlight managed to filter through the skylight between dirty streaks and bird shit.

He pointed her toward a folding chair teetering against a wall while he threw himself onto a stained sofa. "Says here you was born in May of seventy-four."

"In Ardmore, Oklahoma."

"I can read," he snapped. "Suppose I am this Edward Blevins. What do you want? It sure don't look like you suffered none. I bet you had real nice folks an' a pretty little room all to yourself. Your mama done the right thing, givin' you away."

"How long did you know her?"

"A few months was all. But that don't mean shit. Lots of guys knew Helena." He laughed.

"And you got her pregnant?"

"Hell, sweetheart, I got six kids in town that I know of, if you get my meanin'?" He laughed again, and she thought she'd be sick. "Helena got herself knocked up if you so much as shook her hand. She already had four kids when I knew her. Workin' the hell outta welfare; she was really somethin'."

They stared at each other for a while before she asked, "Haven't you ever wondered about me? Even for one minute?"

"It might surprise you, girlie, sittin' there with your pink frills an' shiny shoes, but I got a lot more important things on my mind. Things ain't been all that easy for me."

She pulled her chair closer to him.

"What now?" he complained. "Lookin' for your roots ain't gonna make things easier for any of us. You came to see me—you seen me. Guess we're finished."

"Do you ever think about my mother?"

"Jesus H. Christ, give me a fuckin' break here." His voice rose as his face grew red. He lifted himself off the couch and took a few steps toward the small refrigerator. Pulling it open with the toe of his shoe, he groaned as he reached down for a beer. Returning to his seat, he twisted off the cap, tossed it onto the floor and took a swig.

She watched him.

"Is that all you think I got to do with my time? Sit and wonder about some whore I slept with once or twice? Shit, I got better things to do. Not like you."

"You can't begin to understand me."

He grunted. "Look, I'm just tryin' to survive out here. Takin' any job I can to keep the electricity on. Sure, I had some good times with your old lady. So what? I earned 'em. An' I had me a good job down at the lumber yard. Even a car. Then that load of two-by-fours fell on top of me. Now it's beggin' each month for comp checks those lousy bastards owe me. In case you ain't heard, baby, life ain't stinkin' fair."

She watched him drink half his beer down in one long gulp and was glad he hadn't offered her one. Any act of kindness would have thrown her concentration off.

While I marveled at the dramatic flair Skye had for telling a story, the tape stopped. I waited for the cassette player to click to the other side. A semi came speeding past the passenger's side, splashing my car. That's when I realized what didn't feel right about the recording. Right before it started up again.

"I've had my problems, too."

He threw the bottle, and the remaining beer spattered across the wall behind her as well as on her clothes. But she never took her eyes off him. She could tell her defiance startled him.

"Now, just what kind of troubles do you have, Skye Blue? Just what the hell is it you have to worry about?"

Her eyes fogged over with rage, and she could hear it pulsing in her ears. "Why, just last year I was worrying about where I could go to get an abortion. I think it was just after my husband skipped town. And before that I was a little concerned about a vacation I was planning. Just a few weeks to myself to get away from the beatings, some time to let the bruises heal. I worry about a lot of things, Mr. Blevins. I try to imagine what kind of a tramp my mother was and could my father possibly be the asshole I imagine? I can feel you inside me, and I wonder if I just sit here quietly and listen to you, will this anger go away? Ever?"

He sneered. "Well, lookin's free. But I ain't never said if I is or I ain't your daddy. Even though I do see my likeness a little around your mouth. Whooo boy, what your mama could do with her mouth."

"I've wondered about you on Father's Day, birthdays and at Christmas. Especially while I was cleaning up the broken glass from all those happy family gatherings. And while I was pushing slop down the disposal, I wondered what kind of scum could spawn a piece of garbage like me. Because, dear father, I enjoyed it. I actually enjoyed pushing everyone around me. It didn't matter how much they said they loved me or how kind they were. I pushed until they had no choice but to fight."

"Good God, I do believe you are my daughter." He smiled. "Now get outta here." He worked his way up to a standing position.

She slid the small revolver out of the pocket of her jacket and into his gut. "For years and years, more years than I can remember, I've thought about this. I've thought that if you were dead, maybe . . ."

He grabbed her hand, squeezed it inside his large meaty paw and pushed the gun deeper into his belly. "Do it, then."

There wasn't a struggle, it was more of a standoff. He glaring down at her, she glaring back.

"Are you deaf *and* stupid? I said do it!"

There was a slight hesitation. Then her voice changed.

I pulled the trigger. His stomach exploded. The small room echoed, God, it was loud. Then I pulled the trigger over and over. It felt wonderful.

"I guess that's all of it, Miss Stanton. There's no question I killed someone. I just need to know if he was really my father. I'd hate to have gone through all this for the wrong person. I'm sure you know how I feel, after what you did to your own father—framing him for a murder you arranged, setting him up like that. But somehow I don't think it was a fair trade-off considering you got put away and he just had to suffer a little bad press. They never get what they deserve, do they?"

I waited for more, but the rest of the tape was blank.

I knew Elkhorn wasn't large enough for me to get lost too badly. But just to save time, I pulled into a gas station. I was directed toward West Papillion Creek where it intersected with the Old Lincoln Highway. After that it was just a few turns before I found myself on Oak.

I checked the address again. Three-twenty-nine was a blue split-level colonial house on a freshly mowed lot. It sat on the edge of a cul-de-sac, and as I stood there rechecking my directions and the address on the tape, I can't really say I was surprised. Puzzled would have been a more accurate way to describe my feelings.

"Beep! Comin' through!" a little boy warned as he peddled close to my toes on his Big Wheel.

"Do you know who lives in this house?" I asked before realizing he shouldn't be talking to a stranger.

"My girlfriend, Tiffany Thompson." And he was off, beeping a man mowing his lawn.

I started back to my car but hesitated. How many times had I stopped for directions only to find out the thing I was seeking had been right in front of me? I turned back toward the blue house and walked up the flagstone path to the front door.

A teenage boy answered the bell. "Yeah?"

I flashed my suspended license. "My name is Roberta Stanton, I'm a private investigator."

"Look, the cops already been here. My dad told them all he knows. Which ain't much."

"Can I speak to your father, then?"

"He's watching a game now, and if I interrupt him, he'll get pissed. Why don't you just go ask the cops about that crazy lady?"

The word "crazy" flew out of his mouth and slapped me in my ego. For two years I had been trying to get on with my life, all the while being labeled crazy by the press. And at that moment I knew why I was standing in front of that door in a small town asking a snotty kid for help. Skye Cahill and I had this very tiny character flaw in common. Maybe I had felt sympathy for her from the start. But I knew one thing for sure. I wasn't crazy. Now I had to find out about her.

"Is Tiffany your little sister?" I tried a different angle.

He rolled his eyes. "No. She's my mother."

"Can I talk to her?" I tried returning his sarcastic tone. "Or is she watching a game, too?"

"Wait here," he said, and slammed the door.

Not even a full minute passed before Tiffany Thompson came to the door. She was petite and very pretty with auburn hair pinned up on her head. She waved her hands, trying to dry her long purple nails. "Yes? My son said you wanted to ask me some questions."

I opened my mouth to start, but she talked right over me.

"My husband told the police everything he knows. I don't appreciate you coming here and bothering us. We've lived in this house for almost five years now. I remember the day we first saw it. We were out driving around, and I told my husband—well, he wasn't my husband then—I said Jack, this is my dream house. This is the place—"

"Mrs. Thompson, I'm not with the police. I'm a private investigator." She stopped waving her nails, and I knew now that I had her attention, I had to keep talking and not come up for air until I was finished.

After my brief chat with Mrs. Thompson, I realized there was nothing for me to uncover at 329 Oak. And when Mr. Thompson came to the door looking for his wife, I was more convinced than ever.

Jack Thompson must have stood all of five feet five inches tall and weighed in at considerably less than I did. No way could he have been the Edward Blevins Skye had described.

Driving back toward Omaha, I caught sight of the gas station I had stopped at on my way through. Suddenly craving a candy bar, I thought it wouldn't be a bad idea to call the police.

While I waited for the phone to be answered, I peeled back the silver paper covering the Hershey bar. Its dark brown texture brightened my spirits. The detective who had given me his card after he'd cuffed Skye picked up on the fifth ring. After inquiring about the case, I was told she had been released.

"What about the blood in her hair?" I asked.

"There was a deep gash right at the hairline, over her left eye."

"And the gun?"

"It was registered in her name—she had all the papers with her. There was no sign of it having been fired," he added.

"You checked out the address she gave you?" I asked, already knowing the answer.

"Yes." A heavy sigh. "Yes, Miss Stanton, we checked it all out."

"So where is Ms. Cahill now?"

"She was escorted to Douglas County to have her wound stitched up, and then she'll be evaluated."

I knew he couldn't tell me how long any of it would take. "Thanks."

He hung up.

A breeze came up; I felt a chill on the back of my neck and along my arms. Wishing I'd thrown on a jacket, I was again struck with another inconsistency in Skye's tape. She'd said how dry and hot it had been outside the trailer. Even inside. I remembered thinking how it sounded like she was somewhere in the desert. Maybe she had become disoriented and was talking about an Oak Street in California; that's where she'd said she was from. And the sun shining so brightly had rung a false note. The closer I'd gotten to Elkhorn, the wetter the ground had appeared. It had obviously rained earlier that day.

I tossed the candy bar wrapper into a trash can, licked my fingers clean and brushed a few stray slivers from the front of my khakis. Before getting back into my car, I scanned the directory chained to the phone for the name Blevins. There was no listing.

As I shifted into third gear, I slid the tape into the player to listen to Skye Cahill's story another time.

When I was first released from the state psychiatric facility, I lived in a hotel. Being surrounded by generic paintings, lamps and furniture, I could logically assess my situation while not being influenced by anything familiar. My sister had put my things in storage, and I didn't even know if I wanted to remain in Omaha after the tabloids got through with me.

But the public does indeed have a short memory, and I managed to lay low, finally settling into a small apartment on Q Street. I found comfort in once again having my own things in my own place.

I made a cup of tea and was wondering what to do next, or even if I should do something, when the phone rang.

"Miss Stanton? This is Dr. Paige at Douglas County. Miss Cahill asked me to call to let you know we'll be keeping her overnight for observation."

"How's she's doing, Doctor?"

"Well, calmer than her previous visits. I think she's finally starting to resolve some issues."

Now I was surprised. "You've seen her before?"

"Oh yes, I was working with her in group until we found Ann."

"Who's she?" I held my breath.

"Her second personality. Why, I assumed you knew. Aren't you Roberta Stanton? The one from TV?"

"Yes. But I don't understand what that has to do with this."

"Miss Stanton, I was under the impression you were somehow related to Miss Cahill." I could hear him shuffling papers. "Yes, here it is. She has you listed as her next of kin, a cousin . . . on your father's side."

It took me a minute to mentally climb up and down my family tree. "I think there's been a mistake here, Dr. Paige. And even if it were true, why haven't you notified me before this if you thought I was a relative?"

"Miss Cahill has sessions twice a week with me. She is well over the age of twenty-one, and there have never been any problems. Besides, if I remember correctly, you were 'out of town' for about a year?"

He was diplomatic, I gave Dr. Paige credit for that. "Sorry, Doctor, but Ms. Cahill and I just met this morning. We are not related in any way. And the only reason we met at all is because she came to hire me. . . ." Suddenly I decided I was saying too much about a woman I hardly knew to a man I wasn't sure actually was who he claimed to be.

"Hired you to do what?" he calmly asked.

"That's confidential. Sorry."

"Well, Skye asked me to give you a message and I've delivered it. I guess that's it, then. Have a good evening."

"You, too." I hung up before he could. That always made me feel just a little superior, and after getting the runaround all day, I needed the boost.

Walking back into the living room, I propped myself on the couch. Holding the hot cup of tea between my hands, I studied the mug painted with tiny brown teddy bears, then stared at the blank screen of the television, and I started planning what I would do tomorrow.

Maybe it's true what they say. That if you think about a problem before going to bed, you'll wake up with the solution. Because while I brushed my teeth, I suddenly knew. I had to go to Ardmore, Oklahoma.

Skye Cahill had mentioned being born in Ardmore. No mention of where she was raised. I could have gone on-line, I guess. But no matter how proficient I became on my new computer, it was still a piece of plastic. Like the phone, I considered it just an impersonal tool. Something told me that if I looked up Skye's past, actually smelled the Oklahoma air, I'd learn something.

After checking my trusty Rand McNally, I figured it was about 570 miles from my front door to Ardmore. With the two hundred-dollar bills my client had paid me still folded in my wallet, I stuffed clean underwear and a few T-shirts into a small suitcase and felt excited at the idea of a road trip.

My Toyota was starting to show its age. A tire on the passenger's side was missing its hubcap. The faux leather interior was split in spots where the sun had baked it during last summer's excruciating heat. But for now I couldn't even think about replacing the blue Tercel. Besides, it ran like it had just glided off the showroom floor. And the best part—it was paid for.

Before heading out of town, I stopped by the hospital. It took awhile, but I managed to snag a nurse.

"It's very important Ms. Cahill gets this," I said for the second time and then handed her the letter I'd written that morning.

"She'll get it, don't worry." She looked at me with such pity. "We're all professionals here; we operate very efficiently."

It took every bit of self-control I could muster not to respond sarcastically. From clerks who couldn't make change to doctors who prescribed the wrong medication even after I told them repeatedly about my allergy to penicillin. The older I got, the more it became clear to me that very few "professionals" did their job the way I thought it should be done.

"Okay then, I guess I'll be going." I started to walk away, knowing in my gut that something would happen to my letter. "Remember . . ." I started.

"I know, I know. I'll give this to Miss Cahill." The nurse shoved it deep into her pocket and waved me good-bye.

My first impulse had been to distance myself from Skye, at least until I knew a little more about her situation. That went for Dr. Paige, too. In the letter I assured her I was working on her behalf and would return in a few days. Attached was my card with all sorts of numbers where I could be reached. I then pulled out of the hospital parking lot and got on the highway with a clear conscience.

The trip was an easy, uneventful one. Turning on the radio, I caught up on world events, switching stations as soon as one faded out and another came in clearer. Country music and sermons seemed easiest to find the farther south I got. It was technically winter, mid January. But other than the trees looking scratchy and bare, that day was a clone for one in early spring or fall. I had gotten by for months with a light fleece jacket, and now had to pull my sunglasses out of the glove compartment as the glare from other cars reflected into my eyes.

After hearing the tinny twang of one too many soulful guitars, I slipped Skye's cassette into the tape deck and listened to it for the fifth time in two days.

It took about eight hours to get to Ardmore, and I was pooped when I crashed onto my bed in the Okay Motel off Highway 35.

I slept for ten hours straight. Waking up early the next morning, I walked next door for breakfast and got into an easy conversation with the waitress. Between snapping her gum and scratching her head, Fern finally remembered the Blevins family.

"Lived here my whole life. But can't say as how I remember an Edward. There was Doreen, her twin boys Joe and Beau. Over to the other side of town was Fat Gator and his mama, Beatrice.

"Fat Gator?" I asked, trying not to be rude.

"Called him that on account of his summer jobs down at Disney . . . on the Jungle Ride. An' him also bein' a bit . . . oversized."

I stirred the grits around on my plate, wondering who ever thought to serve the white mush like it was real food. "What was Gator's legal name?" I asked.

"How 'bout that. I don't know. Hey, Dot!" she shouted to the hostess with the sixties hairdo. "You know what Fat Gator's Christian name might be?"

"Edward," she shouted back.

I couldn't believe my luck. What were the odds of coming up with a hit first time out? I quickly thanked the cosmos and pushed for a little more. "I don't suppose you'd know where he lives." When she cocked a suspicious eyebrow at me, I added, "I'm a friend of his daughter's."

"That man did have a passel of kids. But you're not gonna find ole Gator home, I'm afraid."

"Oh?" I looked up from my breakfast.

"He got hisself killed 'bout ten years back. Yeah, it was right about the time I started workin' here."

I had dreaded a day schlepping myself around from newspaper office to library to county records, and here all had been eliminated while I talked to Fern. She knew everybody's business and wasn't afraid to tell what she knew. Praise the Lord and pass the information!

By the time the lunch crowd started showing up, I had a map sketched on a paper napkin giving me detailed directions to the murder scene. Fern couldn't remember ever meeting Skye. But as she told me many times, Fat Gator was a "genuine lady's man." When I smirked, she assured me, "Gator could get real ornery, 'specially when he was drinkin'. But when that man was sober, he was a real sweetheart. He made a lady feel special, know what I mean?"

Blevins and Fern had gone all through grammar school together until Gator dropped out in the seventh grade. She wasn't sure what had become of his trailer or even if it was still hooked up on the lot outside town close to Enville, near Lake Murray.

Fern had also been kind enough to give me the name of the chief of police, his age, marital status and year of graduation. She warned me he was a snot at eleven years of age and was still one. That I shouldn't expect much more out of him than a grunt. I checked in with him before driving the ten miles south toward the lake.

When I had heard the word "lake," my brain did a free association: speedboats, skiers, cottages, wooded areas, concession stands, motels. But those were summer images and this was winter, a weekday. The skiers were in school or at offices. The only thing lit up in front of motels were their vacancy signs.

After finding the dirt road, I drove for a few minutes hoping my tires wouldn't blow out. My body jiggled up and down on the seat while I held tightly to the steering wheel, forcing my car to stay in the deep ruts. Just when I was getting ready to find a clearing to turn around in, I saw a large silver mailbox leaning to one side from too many side swipes. The name, painted sloppily in red paint, read: BLEVINS. I made a hard left.

There was the trailer exactly the way Skye had described it. The only discrepancy was the rusted lawn chair sitting in front of the single step. I didn't see any vehicles parked in the area, and as I got out of my car I reexamined the copy of the newspaper story Chief Jackson had given me. Contrary to what Fern had said, the chief had been gracious and very helpful. I could tell the unsolved murder had haunted him for years.

As I put my hand on the dirty knob, the door was yanked out of my hand.

"What the hell do you think you're doin'?" a frightened woman wearing a floral printed house dress asked. "This here's private property. You cain't go prancin' up to someone's private home and walk in pretty as you please."

"I'm sorry." I fumbled in my purse. Flashing the suspended license, I said, "I'm a private investigator working for Miss Skye Cahill."

"Let me see that." The woman grabbed my ID and brought it closer to her face. "This here's no good, missy." After looking me up and down, she finally said, "But if you say Skye sent you, I guess I can hear ya out. Come on in here." She stood back and motioned impatiently for me to enter.

The inside of the trailer wasn't anything like Skye had described. But then, if Blevins had been murdered ten years ago, there had to be some changes made. Chief Jackson had gone on and on about what a bloody scene the trailer had been after the murder. My eyes scanned the floor for traces of scarlet. But, in sharp contrast to the disheveled woman wearing grimy tennis shoes, the interior was immaculate.

"Can I offer you a cup of coffee?" she asked.

"That would be nice."

While she filled two cups she asked my name.

"Roberta Stanton, I'm from Omaha."

"So how would you hook up with Skye, her livin' out in Los Angeles?"

I took the cup she handed me and seated myself on the leather sofa.

"Well, that's kind of a long story, Mrs. . . . ?"

"Sorry, I'm Beatrice."

I sat a little straighter. "Edward's mother?"

She slowly lowered herself onto a folding chair. "My only child."

"I'm so sorry; you have my sympathy."

"Honey"—she blew on the hot coffee—"it was the best thing for all of us. I only wish I'd never brought him into the world is all." She waited for my reaction. When it was obvious I didn't know what to say, she asked, "Ain't that a terrible thing for a mother to say?"

"A few years ago I would have said it was. But not now. Being related to someone doesn't mean you automatically love them."

"Amen!" She smiled at me, and I could see she didn't have any teeth. "Now, Miss Stanton, tell me what it is you came all this way to find out."

"Well, I understand your son fathered several children with various partners."

She cackled at my civility. "You're bein' very polite, but there ain't no need. Eddie was a pig. He poked anything and anybody. I know what they says about him havin' all these children, but the only one I ever seen was Skye. She was a beautiful baby . . . a real Kewpie doll."

"You saw her? I was under the impression your son never met his daughter."

"Far as I know, he never did."

"Mrs. Blevins, the reason Skye hired me was to find out if Edward Blevins was in fact her real father."

"Oh, he surely was."

"You're absolutely positive?" I asked.

"It took some convincin'. Even after I got a letter from Helena—that bitch. Thought she was just stirrin' up the shit like she always done. She said she wanted money for the baby and didn't care if it come from the family or some stranger in the gutter. She was gonna sell the poor little thing. There was a picture stuck inside the envelope. 'Course, I had to be sure if it was true or not. Called me a lawyer, the one in them TV commercials. He said he'd check it out."

"And you never told your son?"

The old woman seemed weary at the memory. "I tried. Brought the letter for him to see. I was livin' up at the house back then, it's 'bout a mile from here. That way he never got wind of my mail, liked to keep my private affairs away from him. But when I told Eddie, he didn't wanna hear nothin' 'bout no kid. He just laughed, went on how I should be proud that the ladies loved him so much. That kinda talk always made me sick."

"So what did the lawyer find out?"

"Took 'bout ten days, but they said it was all true. My grandbaby was livin' in back of some bar in El Paso. Said that the place was a real hole and I should try to get her outta there. But I was too old to care for a baby myself. An' I certainly did fear for her if Eddie got wind of the situation.

"So I cleaned out my savin's. All twenty thousand of it. Mr. Blevins left me a little and there was government checks. It took everything I had."

"What happened to Skye?"

"The lawyer gave Helena the money and arranged for the poor child to be adopted."

"Did you have any idea where she was living?"

Beatrice Blevins looked at me for a long moment, studied my brown boots, then the hems of my jeans. "I knew all along. I fixed it so the pastor and his wife down at the Methodist church who had just moved to California got her. What better people for parents than those God-fearin' Cahills? They was such a sweet couple."

"Did they turn out to be the perfect parents you thought they'd be?" I wondered out loud, not expecting an answer.

"I figured they was till some woman called me one day—oh, it must have been 'bout five years ago. She told me Skye was in danger and asked me to help."

"What kind of danger?" I asked.

"That's what I wanted to know. But she just kept goin' on, like she was a doctor or somethin'—real quiet and listin' off how she had been beat up an' hurt."

I did the math. "Five years ago Skye would have been twenty."

Beatrice scrunched up her face while she did her own calculations. "She was married by then. To some important guy in the movies. Not anyone famous, some big cheese that did all the dealin'. I thought for sure she struck it rich."

"Apparently not." I could hear Skye's own words replaying as she told her father about her unhappy marriage. That poor kid never had a chance, and I wondered how much worse off she would have been if Beatrice hadn't tried so hard to save her. "Did you help?"

"There wasn't nothin' I could do. She was an adult, with her own life to live, and I was stone broke. Had to sell the house an' move down here. Eddie was long gone, but even if he was still around, he wouldn't of done nothin'.'"

"You did your best." I leaned across and patted her hand.

"Don't stop me from feelin' bad. But now ya say Skye come to see you? How did she look?"

I remembered those turquoise eyes. "Beautiful," I told her.

I stood to leave. Beatrice walked me out to my car and asked that I give her granddaughter her regards.

I was buckling myself into the front seat when something made me ask, "Do you happen to remember the name of the woman who called you about Skye?"

"Sure. Have a hard time with faces, but names stick in there pretty good." She tapped her right temple. "It was Ann. Never did give me a last name."

Dr. Paige wouldn't give me Skye's home address, and since there was no message from her when I returned home, I was forced to plant myself in his waiting room.

"The doctor only sees patients with appointments," his pretentious receptionist told me. "And he *never* sees investigators. If you have a legal matter, we advise you to take it up with the police. In turn, we will be more than happy to cooperate with them."

After that speech I went out to get a hamburger, bringing it back to eat, loudly and slowly, while I waited. I was slurping at the bottom of the ice in my plastic cup when the doctor came out.

"Five minutes," Dr. Paige said as I slid into the chair across from his desk. "Please remember I'm seeing you only out of respect for Miss Cahill."

I checked my watch before asking, "When you called me the other evening, you said you've been seeing Skye for two years."

The jerk just stared at me and nodded.

"I assume that means she lives here, in Omaha?"

"Elkhorn."

Now it made sense why she'd sent me out there. Maybe seeing the street name had triggered off a repressed memory. "According to her grandmother, Skye was raised in Los Angeles?"

"Yes."

"Would it be breaking any great ethical code to tell me the last address you have for her in California?"

He rolled his eyes in such a way that made me want to harm him. "Miss Stanton . . ."

"Look, you can either cooperate with me now or later. Now will only take up"—I checked my watch again—"four minutes and thirty seconds. Later could take days. I'm a bullheaded German with free hours to spend haunting your office."

He pounded his fist down on the date book in front of him. "Yes! Of course I know her address!" He swiveled his chair angrily around and started punching numbers into his computer. When the screen was lit up with Skye Cahill's history, he read the address: "Three-twenty-nine Oak Street. She lived there with her husband for three and a half years." Then he closed the file and defiantly turned toward me. "What else?"

"Three minutes left for you to listen to a theory of mine."

He sat back nodding, at first bored and then stunned to hear that I suspected Skye Cahill of murdering her father, Edward Blevins, when she was sixteen years old.

410    |    CHRISTINE MATTHEWS

"Miss Cahill is incapable of such a violent act."

"What about Ann?"

The doctor's ears perked up then. "Now, that's an interesting thought." I must have struck a nerve; all of a sudden he wanted to talk. I leaned back and listened.

"The personality of Ann is the idealized mother figure. She protects and loves Skye, unconditionally. I would suspect she is capable of doing whatever it takes to keep Skye safe. But if that was the case, why hadn't she struck out sooner, try to harm the unstable parent or abusive husband?"

"When was Ann . . . born?"

"As far back as Skye can remember," he said.

"Then wouldn't it make sense that the mother would blame the father for putting the child in danger?"

"Very good, Miss Stanton."

"How long did Skye know she was adopted?"

"As far back as she could remember. Yes, it all makes sense."

I picked up my purse and pulled out a copy of the original cassette Skye had given me. I started to stand, and the doctor looked disappointed. "You're not going so soon? Look, I apologize for my bad manners."

I tossed the tape at him. "Listen to this and see if you agree with me that Skye was confessing to protect Ann, the personality who actually pulled the trigger."

He was excited now. "Sit, we can listen together."

I started for the door. "Dr. Paige, I'm really not interested in helping you make a name for yourself by exploiting this young woman. The chief of police from Ardmore, Oklahoma, has also received a copy of that tape and will be contacting you, as will the detective who booked Skye here, in Omaha. I have no interest in the outcome of this case. That will be left to the three of you."

I hurried out of the door before he could say anything else. When the elevator doors opened, I thought I was home free until I saw those frightened eyes.

"Miss Stanton." Skye grabbed my arm and nudged me to a corner in the hall. "I've been waiting outside your apartment for hours. Where have you been?"

"Working on your case," I told her gently.

"So? What did you find out? Was that man my father?"

"Yes, Skye, he was." I watched her expression and it never changed. I wasn't sure if I was talking to Skye or Ann. I felt so sorry for her.

"I need to see Dr. Paige," she said, and walked away as if I had suddenly gone invisible.

"And I need to make a call," I said to myself, dialing the police.

Someone once told me that the second most important thing about doing a job is knowing when you are finished. As I forced myself back into my car, I kept telling myself I'd done only what Skye Cahill had hired me to do. My job was done. What happened to her as a result of my investigation was of no concern to me.

But still I felt guilty.

# Jürgen Ehlers

## Golden Gate Bridge——A View from Below

JÜRGEN EHLERS is one of the rising stars of the German literary scene. With the trials and tribulations the German mystery publishing field is going through right now (see the World Mystery Report for Germany), one can only hope that this will not diminish this terrifically talented author's output. Only time will tell, but for now, enjoy this suspenseful tale of people loving, living, and dying in San Francisco. "Golden Gate Bridge—A View from Below," was first published in the anthology *Crime Scenes*.

# Golden Gate Bridge—
# A View from Below

*Jürgen Ehlers*

How nice to see you again!" Thus the reunion with my brother began with a lie. I had not been looking forward to seeing him for the first time in fifteen years. His telephone call the day before, and instantly it was all there again, everything I had tried to push out of my mind ever since. He had been giving a lecture at Hamburg University and wanted to call briefly before flying back. "You look fine," I said. And that was not a lie. He did not look his age, forty-seven. I wondered if he had dyed his hair.

He looked about my room. Of course, he spotted the photo at once. The only souvenir of my trip to California fifteen years ago. The photo that still kept its place in my study was a picture of the Golden Gate Bridge. No ordinary picture, though. None of those you can buy at any souvenir shop in San Francisco. It just showed part of the steel construction of one of the piers. My brother had taken it. "Just give me your camera!" he had demanded and then held it obliquely downward into the gap between footwalk and driveway, and pushed the button. "Farewell to California, I would call the shot," he had suggested. This being the ultimate view of the sun-kissed state for the several hundred suicides who had jumped off the bridge so far. That was typical of my brother. Always good for some bizarre action, clever, fast, unpredictable. The years spent together had never been sufficient for me to grasp more than half of his mind. In the meantime I had stopped trying to understand him.

"You should have thrown it away," he said. He took the picture off the wall and tore it to pieces. As if that could make any difference.

Many people assume it would be a great advantage to have a big, strong brother. That is only half true. Certainly, I used to admire and envy him not only for being ten years my senior but also for his intelligence. He had his diploma in economics when I had just passed my O-levels. But at times I had also hated him, especially when he had said things like "You would not understand that!" in such an arrogant manner that only big brothers are capable of. Naturally he had got that job in California, picked out of a crowd of over two hundred applicants, whereas I had to be glad to find any job at all.

My invitation to California had arrived when I had almost given up hoping for it. He had announced that he had quit his job and was about to do something different, somewhere else in the U.S., but before leaving San Francisco he intended to show me around. He couldn't spare much time, but an extended weekend would be fine. The plane tickets? It would be his pleasure. He had always been a show-off.

I might have forgotten some of the details if I had not kept a diary in those days. We had never been able to afford major trips. The flight to the U.S. was the most exciting event of my life. I simply had to write it down. There I was, standing on the Golden Gate Bridge, together with my brother and Nick Mintford, his land-lord, and with Parker, the guide dog. Mintford was about my brother's age. "I am Nick," he had introduced himself. We all called each other by our first names, which was completely new for me. I felt part of a big family.

"Over there, I think that is Fisherman's Wharf, and the tiny island in the middle of the Bay, that is Alcatraz." Nick pointed exactly in the right direction. I was impressed. Of course, my brother had told me in advance that Nick was blind. Nick, the freelance journalist and landlord of a little appartment in the attic of his house in Oakland. I was impressed at how independently he could find his way around. Only after a closer look did I grasp that his seeming independence was carefully orchestrated. Part of his freedom of movement, of course, he owed to Parker, his mongrel guide dog. His ability to point out the tourist spots to us, however, he probably owed to the fact that he had not been blind all his life. Right now he was holding on to the railings for orientation, and I was sure that he had not made this tour for the first time, and he might well have rehearsed his act with Marie, his wife.

Nick was clearly proud to show me his town. To be honest, I was pretty tired after the twelve hours' flight and would have preferred to get some sleep first. However, Nick's enthusiasm just carried me along.

Our sightseeing tour ended abruptly, when all of a sudden a heavy shower of rain poured down upon us. I had seen the clouds well in advance, but my brother had swept away my concern saying "Not at this time of year!" Obviously, there were exceptions, and even my big brother did not know everything. We were completely drenched by the time we reached our car. Parker shook his coat and jumped onto the backseat. Nick took the seat next to his companion. My brother pushed back his wet hair and sat down behind the wheel. Probably only I could hear that he was humming at a very low key: "It Never Rains in California."

Marie I did not meet before the evening. She was a nurse. We collected her at the hospital and drove to a small Afghan restaurant near the university to have a meal. After dinner we went to Nick and Marie's place.

The house was over in Oakland, halfway up the hill, and from the back you had an astounding view of San Francisco and the Bay. Nick moved about in his house like a seeing man. Without hesitating he found the right drawers, and I would not have been able to open a bottle of wine more expertly than him. We drank Californian red wine. Nick knew all about it. I liked the wine; we emptied several bottles.

We talked about all sorts of things. Of course I had to appreciate Nick's col-umn that had appeared in *The New Yorker* a year ago. The central part was the description of a sunrise in San Francisco. Those guys over in New York apparently had been unaware that their author was blind.

Later I helped Marie with the washing up. "That is one of the things Nick hates to do," she said. "He is afraid of breaking something. To be honest, he probably doesn't drop any more plates than I do. But it doesn't bother me much. Just carelessness, nothing more. But he always blames it on his blindness."

"I think he takes it marvelously," I said.

Marie smiled. "A lot of it is just facade. He tries to make it all look light and easy, but really it bothers him a lot. You can see that from the fact that he drinks too much."

I fell silent, because I had also drunk too much. Did that show? Did I talk too much? Was Marie's remark aimed at me rather? I watched her putting the glasses up onto the highest shelf. She was a beautiful woman, although she must have been well beyond thirty which was old for me at the time. How lucky Nick had been to have found such a companion!

"Was Nick already blind when you first met?" I asked.

She nodded.

"Some kind of illness?" I asked. At that moment I sensed already that she did not want to talk about it.

She answered in a single word: "Vietnam."

I fell silent. What could I possibly say? All of a sudden I became fully aware of the wonderfully innocent country I was living in. Eternal peace all my life. Other people had been less lucky. But at least Nick was still alive, and he had found Marie. I envied him for Marie.

America is the land of firearms. Nick had one, too. He showed it to us the same evening, when we touched on the question of security. Him being in the house on his own most of the day, what if a burglar came?

Nick grinned. "I would shoot him! Just like this!" He had jumped to his feet. His chair fell over. Just two steps to the sideboard and he had pulled open the drawer and produced a gun, which he now trained at us. Not just vaguely in our direction, but at every single one of us, one after the other.

We had all jumped up. I held my breath. After all, Nick had drunk a lot, and we had to assume that the gun was loaded. It seemed rather large and menacing, but I had never seen a gun before. Except on TV, of course.

For a few seconds we all stood as if frozen. I do not know why, but all of a sudden I felt the urge to test Nick. Very cautiously I slid sideways. Inaudible, as it seemed to me. But not so for Nick. The muzzle followed my move.

"It's not easy to trick you," I said. My voice sounded strange.

"No." Nick put the gun down. "And it is not advisable to try." He felt for the chair that he had pushed over. Uneasy silence.

"How about a cup of coffee?" asked Marie. The spell was broken. We spent a long evening in easy chat together.

It was well after midnight when we clambered up the stairs to my brother's flat. I was dog-tired. Right next to me the springs creaked when my brother flung himself on his bed. "Nick is quite a character, isn't he? By the way, do you know how he became blind?

"Vietnam," I said. I had nearly been asleep.

My brother looked at me. "Good joke!"

I hated it when he talked down to me like that. After all, I was almost twenty, and apart from that in this case I was pretty sure. "Marie told me so."

"All right, it had to do with Vietnam," he conceded. And then he let me in: Nick had not been wounded in the war, as I had assumed. He had not been to Vietnam at all. He had fired a bullet through his head when they had come to draft him.

"My God," I said.

Again I thought of myself. How easy had it been to dodge the draft in Germany, even for me, who had only half believed in being a conscientious objector. And the risk of ever having to go to war had appeared so remote that I had never considered it seriously.

Again my brother looked down at me. "You think now that it's ever so cool to protest against war like that. Kill yourself in order to avoid killing others."

Indeed I had thought along those lines. "But—couldn't he have simply gone to Canada? I mean, others have done that, as far as I know."

He had gone to Canada. Staying with friends near Ottawa. But then his mother had died and he had thought it essential to be present at her funeral. That was not in San Francisco but someplace in the North, the name of which I have forgotten. Nick's father was the mayor. They say he had not agreed with his son's decision to flee to Canada. They say he hadn't known that he would come down for the funeral, just for the day. The family reunion took longer than he had expected, and eventually Nick was talked into staying overnight. And then, next morning, there was the police.

"Nick assumes that his father had turned him in. That in the course of the night, all of a sudden, he had realized that as mayor he had no choice but to enforce the law. And after all, everybody had seen that his son was back. Nick locked himself into his father's study. When the cops threatened to force the door open, he had taken the pistol out of his father's desk, put the muzzle at his temple and pulled the trigger."

He had been lucky. The bullet had penetrated his skull too far to the front and caused no lasting brain damage. Only that he was blind. And at that, of course, unsuitable for military service. He was lucky twice. At the hospital where he was nursed he met Marie. She was a young probationer then, and of course she was also fervently against the war. They got married three months later.

After breakfast my brother and I went out to explore. The university and botanic gardens. Nick did not want to join us. The sun was shining. Only too soon would I be on my way back home to Hamburg. To drizzling rain and 17 degrees centigrade. I congratulated my brother on his wonderful life here in California. If I were him, I would never leave the place.

My brother looked at me. "You wouldn't believe how lonely I felt over here for the first few months. Sure, all the people I had met were nice and friendly, but most relationships are rather superficial. If it hadn't been for Nick and Marie, I would have despaired." That was something he had never mentioned in his phone calls. But there had been frequent calls during the first months. Suspiciously frequent calls, I would say with hindsight. When the calls got less frequent, our mother concluded that he had found new friends. Or a friend rather.

"You have really been lucky with Nick and Marie," I said. "Such nice people. I think it's marvelous how compatible they are."

My brother nodded. "So it seems, doesn't it? But all the same they will split up later this year!"

I thought I couldn't trust my ears. "What do you mean by that?"

"Marie will leave him," he said.

I stared at him.

"You can't see it yet, can you? She's pregnant, into the fourth month. And not by Nick."

No, I had not realized that. "And she chose you to confess that to?" I could not get over it.

My brother nodded. "Of course. It is my child, after all."

"Your child!" I exploded. Oh, yes, I could easily imagine how it had happened. My brother, the charming boy, the heartbreaker. Whenever he wanted a woman, he just had to look at her with his big dark eyes. Irresistible. At least that's how it seemed to me. He had once demonstrated this glance to me, just for fun, and I had spent hours in front of the mirror afterward, practising. I had no chance. My eyes were lighter, smaller, and on top of that I lacked his maturity, as I know now, which gave him this air of superiority. Sure, he was a good-looking guy and an able scientist. Why else would they have called him to Berkeley?

I might have hit him. In fact, I should have done it, although it would have been futile because it would not have changed anything. And on top of that he was the stronger, so in the end I would have got a beating.

"You consider me a pig?"

I spared him my reply.

My brother lit a cigarette. He had never smoked back home. He was nervous. "Dear little brother, you must know that it always takes two," he said. "To make love, I mean. And I can assure you, I didn't rape Marie."

I said nothing. Not raped but seduced, I thought. With your eyes. That was something poor Nick was unable to compete with.

"You're outraged, I can see that." That didn't require much. I blush easily when I'm excited, and apart from that my lips get quite thin. My brother tried hard to explain that Marie would have left Nick anyway; it was just a matter of time. That their marriage had been a romantic mistake from the very beginning. Only later had it occurred to Marie that his attempted suicide had not been a heroic act at all—otherwise he would not have run away to Canada in the first place. Grabbing the gun had been nothing but a panic reaction.

And the relationship between my brother and Marie, that was no romantic mistake? Wasn't it perhaps just an easy escape from her unattractive everyday life with a cripple? Because a cripple he was, regardless of all his skills and his charm. But I didn't mention it, as it was too late anyway. The baby was on its way; the decision had been made. "When are you going to tell him?" I queried.

My brother could not conceal a hint of uncertainty. "In a few weeks, I think. At least we didn't want to bring the issue up before your visit. We wanted to show you a little bit of California without any problems."

The next few days passed like a dream. We rode the cable car, took a short and very cold bath in the Pacific and payed a visit to the sea lions at Fisherman's

Wharf. In the evening, drinking wine in Nick's living room, we talked and laughed a lot, and during all this I nearly forgot the dark clouds that were gathering over the three of them. When on the last evening late at night a hailstorm swept over the house, Nick and my brother sang loudly and rather out of key "It Never Rains in California". My brother shouted so loudly that Parker, the dog, looked at him reproachfully. I have no idea what became of Parker afterward.

The last entry in my diary describes the flight back home. However, that was by no means the end of the story. Three weeks later. The short note was on the last page of my newspaper, which I used to look at first, for the weather. Under the heading "The World in Brief" there was an entry saying that in San Francisco a blind man had shot his wife by mistake. The man's name was given as de Boer. No first names were mentioned. I was alarmed. Of course, Nick's and Marie's second name was Mintford, but de Boer sounded familiar, too. Marie's maiden name, perhaps? And the house was owned by her parents, as far as I knew. You couldn't trust a newspaper in such matters, and surely there could not be all that many blind men in San Francisco.

I rang up Nick. Or I tried. I let the telephone ring over twenty times, but nobody answered. I checked the time. Early morning in San Francisco. Nick and Marie would still be at home normally. I tried again, dialing with greater care, but to no avail. Nobody lifted the receiver.

The next day, when the original events were already two days old, the *Abendblatt* gave a more detailed report, and this time there could be no doubt. The names had been corrected. They said, Nicolas Mintford had mistaken his homecoming wife for a burglar and shot at once. Marie had not realized the danger because the flat had been in total darkness. She had been dead by the time the ambulance arrived. There was no mention of any unborn baby. A tragic accident.

Accident? I had my doubts. Had Nick not moved about in his flat in light and dark with absolute confidence and recognized every sound? Was it possible that he might have mistaken Marie for a burglar at any time of day? Was it not much more likely that Marie's intention of leaving him had triggered the same kind of panic as the cops had done with his suicide attempt? That he had knowingly shot at Marie? And, if so, wasn't then my brother in extreme danger, too? If Nick had killed his wife in anger, wouldn't he possibly or even most likely try to kill my brother as well? After all, he had caused Marie's decision.

I tried to call my brother at his job. In vain. Finally I got hold of the operator. The girl tried to put me through, but again with no result. The phone kept ringing in my brother's office. Then the girl's voice again: "Mr. Berger is not in his room; do you want me to leave him a message?"

I asked her to put a note on his desk, saying would he please ring me back at once. I did not leave the house for the next few hours. In vain. My brother did not call. Perhaps he spent the weekend with friends somewhere in the country. Perhaps he had hidden in some hole in mournful misery over the death of Marie and refused to hear or see anybody. Or he was dead already. I was helpless. I could only wait for him to call.

When he eventually called, very much later, everything was clear anyway, even without him admitting anything. We did not even touch on the issue, and police investigations had been closed some time since. Again I had not understood anything. One thing I know by now, however: Nick's revolver, of which I had been so afraid for my brother's sake, had been confiscated by the police, of course.

Hamburg, today. My big brother, nervously pacing the room. And me, just as nervous, watching him. "I just had to come," he said. "You are the only person to whom I can talk about this."

But, of course, I would not be able to help him, and he knew it. "The air mail letter then," I said, "that came from you, right?" He nodded. The envelope had contained nothing but a newspaper clipping. The article said a blind man had jumped off the Golden Gate Bridge at dawn the previous morning. Suicide no. 828. By chance the fall had been witnessed from a passing coast guard vessel; they had eventually pulled the man out of the water, but he was dead by then. A probable cause for the suicide had been the death of his wife, whom the blind man— as reported yesterday—had accidently shot dead.

"What did you think?" he asked.

I shrugged. To be honest, initially I had been relieved. Suicide. And my brother would not be in danger anymore. But then I had my doubts. Suicide? Sure, Nick knew his way around the house perfectly well. He went everywhere and did anything he wanted. But the Golden Gate Bridge was at the other end of the town. It was much beyond Parker to take his master there. Even if Nick had taken a taxi it would have been difficult to get on the bridge without help.

"There is only one possible reason why you had sent me that letter," I said.

He avoided my eyes. "Police investigations found no traces of foreign inter-ference."

"You didn't come all the way to tell me that," I said.

My brother did not say anything for a while. Then, finally: "He did not even put up a fight." I looked up. He wept. My big, strong brother. My poor brother.

# Richard Laymon

## Boo

RICHARD LAYMON'S first novel was the now-notorious *The Cellar*, as heart-stopping a mix of noir, woman-in-peril, and horror as has ever been concocted. In the ensuing quarter century, his worldwide reputation as a true master of dark suspense—albeit one with a truly sly sense of humor—made him a brand name in England. His books were just beginning to find wide favor in the States before his untimely death last year. "Boo," which first appeared in the anthology *October Dreams*, shows his sense of humor running dead even with his sense of the macabre.

# Boo

*Richard Laymon*

The last time I ever went out trick-or-treating, it was with my best friend Jimmy and his sisters, Peggy and Donna. Peggy, Jimmy's kid sister, had a couple of her little friends along, Alice and Olive. There was also Olive's older brother, Nick.

Donna, Jimmy's older sister, was in charge.

We all wore costumes except Donna. Being sixteen, Donna thought of herself as too old for dressing up, so she went as herself in a plaid chamois-cloth shirt, blue jeans, and sneakers.

Peggy wore a Peter Pan outfit. When I saw her in the green elf outfit and feathered cap, I said, "Peter Pan!" She corrected me. "Not Peter Pan, Peggy Pan."

One of her little friends, I don't remember whether it was Olive or Alice, sported a tutu and a tiara and carried a wand with a star at one end. The other girl wore a store-bought E.T. costume. Or maybe she was Yoda. I'm not sure which.

Nick I remember. All of fourteen, he was a year older than Jimmy and me. He was supposed to be a Jedi warrior. He wore black coveralls, a black cape, and black galoshes. No mask, no helmet. We only knew he was a Jedi warrior because he told us so. And because he carried a "light saber," pretty much a hollow plastic tube attached to a flashlight.

Jimmy was "the Mummy." Earlier that night, Donna and I had spent ages wrapping him up in a white bedsheet that we'd cut into narrow strips. We kept pinning the strips to Jimmy's white longjohns. It took forever. It would've driven me nuts except for Donna. Every so often, she gave Jimmy a poke with a pin just to keep things interesting. We finally got it done, though, and Jimmy made a good-looking mummy.

My costume was easy. I was Huck Finn. I wore a straw hat, an old flannel shirt, and blue jeans. I had a length of clothesline over one shoulder, tied at the ends to a couple of my belt loops to look like an old rope suspender. As a final touch I had a corncob pipe that my dad let me borrow for the night.

So that was our group: who we were and how we were dressed that night.

Jimmy and me, Donna and Peggy, Alice and Olive and Nick.

Seven of us.

Except for Donna, we carried paper bags for our treats. Donna carried a flashlight. For the most part, she took up the rear. She usually didn't even go to the doors with us but waited on the sidewalk while we rang doorbells, yelled "Trick or treat!" and held out our bags to receive the goodies.

For the first couple of hours that night, everything went along fine. If you don't count Nick going on occasional rampages, bopping us on the heads or prodding us in the butts with his light saber, proclaiming, "The Dark Side rules!" After a while, Jimmy's bandages started to come off and droop. At one point, ET (or Yoda) fell down and skinned her knee and spent a while bawling. But nothing major went wrong and we kept on collecting loot and roaming farther and farther into unknown territory.

It was getting very late when we came to a certain house that was not at all like the others on its block. Whereas they were brightly lighted and most had jack-o'-lanterns on their porches, this house was utterly dark. Whereas their shrubbery and lawns were neatly trimmed, this house seemed nearly lost in a jungle of deep grass, wild foliage, and brooding trees. It also seemed much older than the other houses on the block. Three stories high (not two like its neighbors) and made of wood (not brick), it looked as if it belonged to a different century.

The houses on both sides of the old one seemed unusually far away from it, as if whoever'd built them had been afraid to get too close.

Though Nick usually ran from house to house without returning to the sidewalk, cutting across lawns and brandishing his light saber with Peggy and Olive and Alice chasing after him, this time he thought better of it. All four of them came back to the sidewalk, where Jimmy and I were walking along with Donna.

"What's with that house?" Nick asked.

"It's creepy-eepy-eepy," said either Olive or Alice, whichever one was the fairy godmother princess ballerina.

"It doesn't look like anyone lives there," Donna said.

"Maybe like the Munsters," I said.

"I think maybe we should skip this one," Donna said.

"Hey, no," Jimmy protested. "We can't skip this one. It's the best one yet!"

I felt exactly the same way, but I never could've forced myself to disagree with Donna.

She shook her head, her bangs swaying across her brow. "I really don't like the looks of it. Besides, it'd be a waste of time. Nobody's there. You won't get any treats. We might as well just—"

"You never know," Jimmy interrupted. "Maybe they just forgot to turn their lights on."

"I think Donna's right," I said. "I don't think anyone's there."

Jimmy shook his head. By this time, all the "bandages" had slipped off his head. They dangled around his neck like rag necklaces. "If somebody does live in a place like that," he said, "wouldn't you wanta meet him? Or her. Maybe it's a creepy old woman. Just imagine. Like some crazy old witch or hermit or something, you know?"

For a while, we all just stood there and stared at the dark old house—what we could see of it through the bushes and trees, anyway, which wasn't much.

Looking at it, I felt a little shivery inside.

"I think we should just go on," Donna said.

"You're in charge," Jimmy muttered. He'd been ordered by his parents to obey Donna, but he sounded disappointed.

She took a deep breath and sighed. It felt good to watch her do that.

"It's probably deserted," she said. Then she said, "Okay, let's give it a try."

"All *right!*" Jimmy blurted.

"This time, I'll lead the way. Who else wants to come?"

The three girls jumped up and down, yelling, "Me! I do! Me! Me-me-me!"

Nick raised his light saber, and said, "I'll come and protect you, Princess Donna."

"Any trouble," I told him, "cut 'em to ribbons with your flashlight."

"Take that!" He jabbed me in the crotch.

He didn't even do it very hard, but the tube got me in the nuts. I grunted and gritted my teeth and barely managed not to double over.

"Gotcha!" Nick announced.

Donna bounced her flashlight off his head. Not very hard, but the bulb went dark and Nick yelped, "*Ow!*" and dropped his light saber and candy bag and grabbed the top of his head with both hands and hunched over and walked in circles.

"Oh, take it easy," she told him. "I barely tapped you."

"I'm gonna tell!" he blurted.

"Tell your little ass off, see if I care."

The ballerina fairy-godmother princess gasped.

ET or Yoda blurted, "Language!"

Little sister Peggy Pan almost split a gut, but seemed to know she shouldn't laugh at Nick's misfortune so she clamped a hand across her mouth.

Jimmy, more concerned about my fate than Nick's, patted me on the back and asked, "You okay, man?"

"Fine," I squeezed out.

Donna came closer. Looking me in the eyes, she said, "Did he get you bad?"

I grimaced and shrugged.

"Right in the nads," offered Jimmy.

I gave him a look.

Instead of killing him, as intended, my look seemed to inspire him. "Donna's a certified lifeguard, you know. All that first-aid training. Want her to take a look?"

"Shut up!" I snapped at him.

"Stop it, Jimmy," she said.

"How'd you like to have her kiss—"

I punched his arm. He yelled, "Hey!" and grabbed it.

"Okay, okay," Donna said. "Everybody calm down. No more hitting. How are you doing, Matt?" she asked me.

"Okay, I guess."

"Nick?" she asked.

He was standing nearby, gently touching the top of his head. "I've got a bump."

"Well, that's too bad, but you asked for it."

"Did not."

Donna said, "You busted my damn flashlight."

Jimmy and I laughed. So did Peggy Pan.

ET or Yoda blurted, "Language!"

"You shouldn't go around whumping people on the head," Nick explained. "You can cause 'em brain damage."

"Not you!" Jimmy said. "You haven't got one."

"That's enough," Donna said. "Come on, are we gonna check out this house or aren't we?" Without even waiting for a response, she stepped off the sidewalk and started trudging toward the creepy old place.

I went after her, hurting. Each step I took, it felt like a little hand was squeezing one of my balls. But I didn't let it stop me and it seemed to pretty much go away by the time we reached the porch stairs.

Donna stopped and turned around. She still held the flashlight in one hand, though it wasn't working anymore. With her other hand, she put a finger to her lips.

In a few moments, everyone was standing in front of her, motionless and silent.

Donna took the forefinger away from her lips. She pointed it at each of us, counting heads the way a school bus driver does before bringing a bunch of kids back from a field trip. Done, she whispered, "Okay, six."

"Seven," I said.

She turned her head toward me. The moon was full, so I could see her face pretty well. She raised her eyebrows.

"You," I whispered.

"Ah. Okay. Right." In a somewhat louder voice, she said, "Okay, there're seven of us right now. Let's hope and pray there're still seven when we get back to the street."

Her words gave me the creeps.

One of the girls made a whiny sound.

"I wanna go back," said one of them. Maybe the same one who'd whined. I don't know whether it was Alice or Olive. It wasn't Peggy Pan, though.

Peggy Pan whispered, "Wussy."

Jimmy chuckled.

And I saw the look on Donna's face and realized she was trying to psych us out.

Not us, really. Them.

Nick had made her mad, and she wasn't exactly tickled by Alice or Olive, either, so she figured to make life a little more interesting for them.

"If anybody wants to go back and wait for us on the sidewalk," she said, "that's fine. It'd probably be a good idea. No telling what might happen when we go up and ring the doorbell."

One of the girls whined again.

"You're just trying to scare us," Nick said. In the full moon, I could see the sneer on his face. "Can't scare a Jedi," he said.

Donna continued, "I just think . . . everyone needs to know the score. I wasn't planning to mention it, but . . . I've heard about this house. I know what happened here. And I happen to know it isn't deserted."

"Yeah, sure," Nick said.

Lowering her voice, Donna said, "A crazy man lives here. A crazy man named . . . Boo. Boo Ripley."

I almost let out a laugh, but held it in.

"Boo who?" Jimmy asked.

I snorted and gave him my elbow.

"Ow!"

"Shhh!" Donna went. "Want Boo to hear us?" She looked at the others, frowning slightly. "When he was only eight years old, Boo chopped up his mom and dad with a hatchet . . . and ate 'em. Gobbled 'em up! Yum yum!"

"Did not," Nick said.

"I wanna go home!"

"Shut up," Nick snapped.

"But Boo was a little boy, back then. And his mom and dad were very large. Even though he gobbled them day and night, night and day, there was always more that needed to be eaten.

"Well, Boo's mom was a real cat lover. She had about a dozen cats living in the house all the time and stinking it up, so finally Boo started feeding his folks to the cats. Day and night, night and day, Boo and the cats ate and ate and ate. At last, they managed to polish off the last of Boo's mom and dad. And you know what?"

"What?" asked Peggy Pan. She sounded rather gleeful.

"I don't wanna hear!" blurted tutu girl.

"Knock it off, pipsqueak," Nick snapped at her.

"Boo and the cats," Donna said, "enjoyed eating the mom and dad so much that they lost all interest in any other kind of food. From that time forth, they would only eat people. Raw people. And you know what?"

"What?" asked Peggy Pan and I in unison.

"They still live right here in this house. Every night, they hide in the dark and watch out the windows, waiting for visitors."

"You're just making this up," Nick said.

"Sure I am."

"She isn't, man," said Jimmy.

"They're probably up in the house right this very minute watching us, licking their lips, just praying we'll climb the stairs and go across the porch and ring the doorbell. Because they're very hungry, and you know what?"

"*What?*" asked Peggy Pan, Jimmy, and I in unison.

In a low, trembling voice, Donna said, "The food they love most of all is . . ." Shouting, *"Little girls like you!"* She lunged toward Alice and Olive.

They shrieked and whirled around and ran for their lives. Yoda or ET waved her little arms overhead as she fled. The fairy dancer whipped her magic wand as if swatting at bats. One of them fell and crashed in the weeds and started to cry.

Nick yelled, "Fuck!" and ran after them, his light saber jumping.

"Language!" Jimmy called after him.

Donna brushed her hands together. "Golly," she said. "What got into them?"

"Can't imagine," I said.

"What a bunch of wussies," said Peggy Pan.

"I can't stand that Nick," said Jimmy. "He is such a shit."

"Language," Donna told him.

We laughed, all four of us.

Then Donna said, "Come on, gang," and trotted up the porch stairs. We hurried after her.

And I'll always remember trotting up those stairs and stepping onto the dark porch and walking up to the door. Even while it was happening, I knew I would never forget it. It was just one of those moments when you think, *It doesn't get any better than this.*

I was out there in the windy, wonderful October night with cute and spunky little Peggy Pan, with my best buddy Jimmy, and with Donna. I was in love with Donna. I'd fallen in love with her the first time I ever met her and I'm in love with her to this day and I'll love her the rest of my life.

That night, she was sixteen and beautiful and brash and innocent and full of fun and vengeance. She'd trounced Nick and done quite a number on Alice and Olive, too. Now she was about to ring the doorbell of the creepiest house I'd ever seen.

I wanted to run away screaming myself. I wanted to yell with joy. I wanted to hug Donna and never let her go. And also I sort of felt like crying.

Crying because it was all so terrifying and glorious and beautiful—and because I knew it wouldn't last.

All the very best times are like that. They hurt because you know they'll be left behind.

But I guess that's partly what makes them special, too.

"Here goes," Donna whispered.

She raised her hand to knock on the door, but Jimmy grabbed her wrist. "That stuff about Boo and the cats," he whispered. "You made it up, didn't you?"

"What do you think?"

"Okay." He let go of her hand.

She knocked on the door.

Nothing.

I turned halfway around. Beyond the bushes and trees of the front yard, Nick and the two girls were watching us from the sidewalk.

Donna knocked again. Then she whispered, "I really don't think anyone lives here anymore."

"I hope not," I whispered.

Donna reached out and gave the screen door a pull. It swung toward us, hinges squawking.

"What're you doing?" Jimmy blurted.

"Nothing," said Donna. She tried the main door. "Damn," she muttered.

"What?" I asked.

"Locked."

*Oh,* I thought. *That's too bad.*

The wooden door had a small window at about face level. Donna leaned forward against the door, cupped her hands by the sides of her eyes, and peered in.

Peered and peered and didn't say a word.

"Can you see something?" Jimmy asked.

Donna nodded ever so slightly.

"What? What's in there?"

She stepped back, lowered her arms and turned her back to the door and said very softly, "I think we'd better get out of here."

Peggy Pan groaned.

Jimmy muttered, "Oh, shit."

I suddenly felt cold and shrively all over my body.

We let Donna take the lead. Staying close behind her, we quietly descended the porch stairs. At the bottom, I thought she might break into a run. She didn't, though. She just walked slowly through the high weeds.

I glanced back at the porch a couple of times. It was still dark. Nobody seemed to be coming after us.

Entering the shadows of some trees near the middle of the lawn, Donna almost disappeared. We all hurried toward her. In a hushed voice, Jimmy said, "What did you see?"

"Nothing, really," she said.

"Yes, you did," Peggy Pan insisted.

"No, I mean . . ." She stopped.

The four of us stood there in the darkness. Though we weren't far from the sidewalk where Nick and the girls were waiting, a high clump of bushes blocked our view of them.

"Okay," Donna said. "Look, this is just between us. They ran off, so they've got no right to hear about it, okay?"

"Sure," I said.

Peggy Pan nodded.

Jimmy whispered, "They'll never hear it from me."

"Okay," Donna said. "Here's the thing. It was really dark in the house. I didn't see anything at first. But then I could just barely make out a stairway. And something was on the stairway. Sitting on the stairs partway up, and it seemed to be staring straight at me."

"What was it?" Peggy Pan whispered.

"I'm not really sure, but I think it was a cat. A white cat."

"So?" Jimmy asked.

I felt a little letdown, myself.

"I think it was sitting on someone's lap," she said.

"Oh, jeez."

Peggy Pan made a high-pitched whiny noise. Or maybe that was me.

"He was wearing dark clothes, I think. So I really couldn't see him. Or her. All I could see was this darkness on the stairs."

"How do you know it was even there?" Jimmy asked.

"The cat was white."

"So?"

"Someone was petting it."

"Let's get outta here," Jimmy said.

Donna nodded. "Remember, not a word to Nick or Alice or Olive. We'll just say nothing happened."

We all agreed, and Donna led us through the trees. Out in the moon-light, we walked around the clump of bushes and found Nick and the girls waiting.

"So what happened?" Nick asked.

We shrugged and shook our heads. Donna said, "Nothing much. We knocked, but nobody was home."

Smirking, he said, "You mean Boo and his cats weren't there?"

Donna grinned. "You didn't believe that story, did you? It's Halloween. I made it up."

Nick scowled. The ballerina fairy godmother princess looked very relieved, and Yoda or ET sighed through her mask.

"Good story," I said.

"Thanks, Matt," said Donna.

"Can we still trick-or-treat some more?" Peggy Pan asked.

Donna shrugged. "It's getting pretty late. And we're a long way from home."

"Please?" asked Peggy Pan.

Her little friends started jumping and yelling, "Please? Please-please-please? Oh, please? Pretty please?"

"How about you, Nick?"

"Sure, why not?"

"Guys?" she asked Jimmy and me.

"Yeah!"

"Sure!"

"Okay," Donna said. "We'll go a little longer. Maybe just for a couple more blocks."

"Yayyy!"

The girls led the way, running up the sidewalk to the next house—a normal house—cutting across its front lawn and rushing up half a dozen stairs to its well-lighted porch. Nick chased them up the stairs. Jimmy and I hurried. By the time the door was opened by an elderly man with a tray of candy, Jimmy and I were also on the porch, Donna waiting at the foot of the stairs.

We were back to normal.

Almost.

We hurried from house to house, reached the end of the block, crossed the street, and went to the corner house on the next block. It was just after that house, when we met on the sidewalk and headed for the next house, that Donna, lagging behind, called out, "Hang on a minute, okay? Come on back."

So we all turned around. As we hurried toward the place where Donna was waiting on the sidewalk, she raised her hand, index finger extended, and poked the finger at each of us. Like a school bus driver counting heads before starting home from a field trip.

She finished.

"Seven," she said.

"That's right," I said as I halted in front of her.

"Seven not including me," she said.

I whirled around and there was Jimmy the woebegone mummy dangling loose strips of sheet, some of which by now were trailing on the sidewalk. There was Nick the Jedi warrior with his light saber. And Peggy Pan and the ballerina fairy princess godmother and Yoda or ET and—bringing up the rear but only a few paces behind the girls—someone else.

He carried a grocery bag like any other trick-or-treater, but he was bigger than the girls, bigger than Nick, bigger than any of us. He wore a dark cowboy hat and a black raincoat and jeans. Underneath his hat was some sort of strange mask. I couldn't tell what it was at first. When he got closer, though, I saw that it seemed to be made of red bandannas. It covered his entire head and neck. It had ragged round holes over his eyes, a slot over his mouth.

I had no idea where he'd come from.

I had no idea how long he'd been walking along with us, though certainly he'd shown up sometime after we'd left the dark old house.

Is that where he joined us? I wondered.

Speaking in his direction, Donna said, "I don't think we know you." Though she sounded friendly and calm, I heard tension in her voice.

The stranger nodded but didn't speak.

The girls, apparently noticing him for the first time, stepped away from him. "Where'd you come from?"

He raised an arm. When he pointed, I saw that his hand was covered by a black leather glove.

He pointed behind us. In the direction of the dark old house . . . and lots of other places.

"Who are you?" Donna asked.

And he said, "Killer Joe."

Alice and Olive took another step away from him, but Peggy Pan stepped closer. "You aren't gonna kill us are you?" she asked.

He shook his head.

"Cool costume," Jimmy said.

"Thanks," said Killer Joe.

"So who are you really?" Donna asked.

Killer Joe shrugged.

"How about taking off the mask?" she said.

He shook his head.

"Do we know you?" Jimmy asked.

Another shrug.

"You wanta come along trick-or-treating with us?" Peggy Pan asked.

He nodded. Yes.

Donna shook her head. No. "Not unless we know who you are." Her voice no longer sounded quite so calm or friendly. She was speaking more loudly than before. And breathing hard.

She's scared.

And she wasn't the only one.

"I'm sorry," she said, "but you'll either have to let us see who you are or leave. Okay? We've got little kids here, and . . . and we don't know who you are."

"He's Killer Joe," Nick explained.

"We know," Jimmy said.

"But he's all by himself," Peggy Pan said. "He shouldn't have to go trick-or-treating all by himself." She stepped right up to him and took hold of a sleeve of his raincoat and tilted her head back.

"Peggy," Donna said. "Get away from him. Right now."

"No!"

Killer Joe shrugged, then gently pulled his arm out of Peggy's grip and turned around and began to walk away very slowly, his head down.

And I suddenly figured this was some poor kid—a big and possibly somewhat weird kid, granted—but a kid nevertheless without any friends, trying his best to have fun on Halloween night, and now he was being shunned by us.

I actually got a tight feeling in my throat.

Peggy Pan, sounding desolate, called out, " 'Bye, Killer Joe!"

Still walking away, head still down, he raised a hand to acknowledge the girl's farewell.

"Come on back!" Donna called.

He stopped walking. His head lifted. Slowly, he turned around and pointed to himself with a gloved hand.

"Yeah, you," Donna said. "It's all right. You can come with us. But we are almost done for the night."

Killer Joe came back, a certain spring in his walk.

Though he never removed his strange and rather disturbing bandanna mask and never told us who he was, he stayed with us that night as we went on from house to house, trick-or-treating.

Before his arrival, we'd been on the verge of quitting and going home. But even though he rarely spoke—mostly just a gruff "Trick or treat" when people answered their doors—he was so strange and friendly and perky, we just couldn't seem to quit.

This had been going on for a while and I was about to follow the bunch toward another house when Donna called softly, "Matt?"

I turned around and went back to her.

She took hold of my forearm. In a quiet voice, she said, "What do you think of this guy?"

"He's having a great time."

"Do you trust him?"

I shrugged.

"I don't," Donna said. "I mean, he could be anyone. I think it's very weird he wouldn't take off his mask. I'm afraid he might be up to something."

"Why'd you let him come with us?"

She shrugged. "Guess I felt sorry for him. Anyway, he's probably fine. But how about helping me keep an eye on him, okay? I mean, he might be after the girls or something. You just never really know."

"I'll watch him," I promised.

"Thanks." She gave my arm a squeeze. "Not that we'd be able to do anything much about it if he does try something."

"I don't know," I said. "I know one thing, I won't let him do anything to Peggy. Or you."

She smiled and squeezed my arm again. "Sure. We'll let him have Alice and Olive."

"But we'll encourage him to take Nick."

Donna laughed. "You're terrible."

"So are you," I said.

After that, I joined up with the rest of them and kept a close eye on Killer Joe as we hurried from door to door.

Sometimes he touched us. He gave us friendly pats. But nothing more than what a buddy might do. I started to think of him as a buddy, but warned myself to stay cautious.

Finally, Donna called us all over to her. She said, "It's really getting late, now. I think we'd better call it quits for the night."

Sighs, moans.

"Just one more house!" the girls pleaded. "Please, please, just one more house? Pretty please?"

"Well," said Donna. "Just one more."

Olive and Alice went, "Yayyyyy!"

Killer Joe bobbed his masked head and clapped his hands, his gloves making heavy whopping sounds.

We all took off for our final house of the night. It was a two-story brick house. Its porch light was off, but one of the upstairs windows glowed brightly.

All of us gathered on the porch except Donna, who waited at the foot of the stairs as she often did.

Peggy Pan rang the doorbell. Olive and Alice stood beside her, and the rest of us stood behind them. I was between Mummy Jimmy and Killer Joe.

Nobody came to the door.

Peggy jabbed the button a few more times.

"Guess nobody's home," I said.

"Somebody has to be!" said Peggy. "This is the last house. Somebody has to be home."

Olive and Alice started shouting, "Trick or treat! Trick or treat! Open the door! Trick or treat!"

Killer Joe stood there in silence. He seemed to be swaying slightly as if enjoying some music inside his head.

"Maybe we'd better give it up," Jimmy said.

"No!" Peggy jabbed the doorbell some more.

Suddenly, the wooden door flew open.

We all shouted *"Trick or treat!"*

An old woman in a bathrobe blinked out at us. "Don't any of you kids know what time it is?" she asked. "It's almost eleven o'clock. Are you out of your minds, ringing people's doorbells at this hour?"

We all stood there, silent.

I felt a little sick inside.

The old woman had watery eyes and scraggly white hair. She must've been eighty. At least.

"Sorry," I muttered.

"Well, y'oughta be, damn kids."

"Trick or treat?" asked Peggy Pan in a small, hopeful voice.

*"No! No fucking trick or treats for any of you, you buncha fuckin' assholes! Now get the fuck off my porch!"*

That's when Killer Joe reached inside his raincoat with one hand and jerked open the screen door with his other.

If the door had been locked, the lock didn't hold.

The woman in the house yelled, *"Hey, you can't! . . ."*

Killer Joe lurched over the threshold and the woman staggered backward but not fast enough and I glimpsed the hatchet for just a moment, clutched in Joe's black leather glove, and then he swung it forward and down, chopping it deep into the old woman's forehead.

That's all I saw.

I think I saw more than most. Then all of us were running.

We were about a block away and still running, some of the girls still screaming, when I did a quick head count.

Seven.

Including Donna.

Not including Killer Joe.

Joe had still been in the house when we ran off.

We never saw him again. He was never identified, never apprehended.

That was a long time ago.

I never again went trick-or-treating after that. Neither did Donna or Jimmy or Peggy. I don't know about Nick and Alice and Olive, and don't care.

Now I have a kid of my own. I hate for her to miss out on the strange and wonderful and frightening joys of dressing up and going house to house on Halloween night.

Trick-or-treating . . .

Sometimes, what happens on Halloween is as good as it gets.

Sometimes not. Judy agrees.

"What the hell," she said, "let's go with her, show her how it's done."

Judy's not Donna, but . . . she's terrific in her own ways and I have my memories.

# John Lutz

## Veterans

*SWF SEEKS Same* was a popular novel that resonated with the troubles of its era. Filmed as *Single White Female*, the popular movie brought its author, John Lutz, to greater prominence than at any time in his long career. His novel is as rewarding to readers as it has been to John himself. One of the smoothest stylists and tart (but forgiving) observers of contemporary American culture, Lutz has won both the Edgar and the Shamus awards and built up a substantial following. From modern day to the Civil War era, few can match his gift for mystery and characterization. "Veterans," first published in the anthology *Murder Most Confederate*, proves this in spades.

# Veterans

*John Lutz*

It began because Confederate Major General Henry Heth's troops needed boots.

In search of a new supply in a town called Gettysburg, Heth's men marched unknowingly toward death and history. They were noticed by Union soldiers serving under Brigadier General John Buford, who were bivouacked on a nearby hill. Buford sent for Union reinforcements. The ensuing Union troop movements were observed by Heth, who attacked. The newly arrived First Corps, led by Major General John Reynolds, took the brunt of the assault on McPherson's Ridge. Casualties were high, the Union's crack Iron Brigade lost more than half its men, and Reynolds was killed.

Corporal Will Faver, born in Oak River, Missouri, and a Union volunteer, survived. Grape shot had grazed his head, leaving a nasty gash, and a minie ball had taken a bite out of his left arm, but he was alive and still full of fight. Bandaged and determined, he rejoined Union forces on Cemetery Ridge, where they'd been driven backward to hold after fierce fighting.

The Rebs decided not to press the attack in the evening's waning light, so during that night the Yanks regrouped and waited. Reb troops were moving in from the north and west. Pickets were needed to take up position in those directions, well away from the main body of troops, to act as isolated lookouts and give warning of approaching Confederate forces. Dangerous assignments. Which was why Will Faver, wounded but not seriously, and mostly unknown by the men around him, was given picket duty. With a youth named Elliott Nance, a lean and sad-faced Pennsylvanian, Will was sent about half a mile north to take up position in a peach orchard.

There was a moon that night, and the two men were spotted near the orchard and had to break into a run when Confederate light artillery opened fire on them.

Will, who'd won many a picnic foot race in Oak River, simply put his head down and sprinted for the trees. Nance decided to weave to avoid the Rebel fire. Entering the cover of the orchard, Will heard the young trooper's shrill scream.

Will found himself alone in the orchard.

He moved farther into the shelter of the trees. It was June and they'd borne early fruit. The sweet scent of peaches rotting on the ground spooked him, reminding him of decay and death. His lost comrades in the First Corps . . . young Nance. Morose and afraid, he stumbled through the darkness beneath the tree cover, waiting for the artillery to be trained on the orchard. Will had seen wooded areas assaulted by artillery, leafless, blackened skeletal ruins where no life could survive. He hadn't much hope.

The ground dropped out from beneath him, and with a gasp of surprise he slid on his back into a dry creek bed. It would provide him some cover if the artillery decided to open up on the entire orchard. He scooted around to sit with his back braced against the slope of the hard dirt bank. And there he sat listening to his harsh, ragged breathing, living his fear, knowing his duty.

As he had so many times in danger, he slid his hand beneath his shirt and caressed the silver locket with Sharleen's curl of blonde hair tucked beneath its oval lid. The metal warmed to his touch and calmed him. His faith returned. He would survive this night, this war, and get back to Oak River and live out his life with his wife and the children they planned on having. He knew at that moment that Will and Sharleen Faver would grow old together.

Then his brother said, "Move a muscle, Yank, and I shoot you dead as a stump."

Terror froze Will so he couldn't have moved if he tried. Then through his cold panic seeped warm realization. *The Reb's voice! He couldn't mistake that voice!*

"Luther?"

Luther Faver, Will's older brother, had taken sides in the war first, and joined the Tennessee Volunteers. He'd been in the tobacco business with partners in Memphis, and that was where his loyalties lay. Will was the brother who took over the family farm rather than let it lie fallow, married Sharleen, and sank his own roots deep and forever in Oak River.

"Luther? That you, Luther?"

The dark form of the Reb aiming his musket down at Will didn't move. Then slowly the long barrel of the gun dropped low and to the side.

"My God, it *is* you," Luther said, and scampered down into the gouge of the creek bed with Will. "How in the hell you been, boy?"

"Stayin' alive, I guess."

"Good thing we had orders to bring back prisoners if we could find 'em, or I'da surely opened fire on you when I saw you here." Luther, a tall man with a lean face and darker hair than his brother's, wiped the back of a hand across his forehead and took a swig from a canteen. He recapped the canteen and tossed it over to Will. "Seen Ma lately?"

And Will remembered that Luther wouldn't know their mother had died six months ago. Will had managed to return briefly to Oak River for her funeral. "Gone . . . ," he said, and took a long pull of water from the canteen.

Luther didn't say anything, just stared up at the night sky beyond the peach tree branches. "How 'bout Sharleen?" he asked at last.

"Good. Seen her last six months ago. Me an' her been workin' the farm. She's keepin' it goin' till I come back for good."

"Why'd you ever leave her, Will. You didn't have to fight in this war."

"Neither did you," Will said.

Luther looked surprised. "Me? Why, I had financial considerations."

Will nodded, understanding. "I plumb forgot you were a businessman." He capped the canteen and tossed it back to his brother. "Thing is, Luther, what are we gonna do now."

"Now?"

"I mean, about this here situation."

"I still don't understand why you ever left Sharleen," Luther said.

Will was trying to think of a good answer when Luther shot him between the eyes.

Luther survived the rest of the war, sustaining only a slight gunshot wound in the Battle of Kennesaw Mountain the following year.

He returned to Oak River a hero. The Mason-Dixon Line ran close to the town, and veterans of both armies were welcomed home. People were eager for healing.

The second day home, Luther rode the aging horse he'd been allowed to keep the three miles out of town to the farm. It was where he'd grown up none too happily. He'd always been jealous of Will, who was the favorite and had gotten everything, from their parents' attention to . . . Sharleen.

Sharleen must have seen him from a window. She came out onto the porch as he approached the log house. The house itself didn't look bad, though it could use a little upkeep, some chinking between the logs and some paint on the shutters. And the porch roof sagged some.

Sharleen had aged better than the house. Though she looked older, she was still trim and beautiful, with her calm blue eyes, and her wonderful blonde hair pulled back now and tied in a swirl atop her head. She was wearing a faded flower-print skirt and a white blouse molded to her by the prairie breeze.

Luther reined in the horse a few feet in front of the porch and gave her back her smile. Then he stopped smiling. "I sure am sorry about Will."

Her smile left her face as if caught by the breeze. "So'm I, Luther. More'n you can know."

He dismounted and walked to stand at the base of the three wooden steps to the plank porch. "Place looks good, except for the fields for this time of summer."

"Frank Ames helps out some. Did some mending and painting last month."

Luther looked at her, fingering the brim of his hat held in front of him. "Ames survived the war?"

"He come back to Oak River six months ago. Lost him a leg at Gettysburg."

"Then he's lucky to be alive."

"He 'peers to think so," Sharleen said. She seemed to shake off her sadness and managed a bright smile that brought back memories to Luther. The smile had been there the night Sharleen had taken the walk with him among the cottonwoods in the moonlight, the times at the local dances when she whirled gaily to the music. The smile that was so uniquely hers was there when she'd won the turkey shoot one cold Thanksgiving, and when she filled in teaching at the schoolhouse, and when she and Will surprised everyone by saying they were getting married. The smile had been there on her wedding day. And no doubt on her wedding night . . .

". . . my manners."

Luther realized she was speaking.

"Do come on into the house," she was saying. "Luther?"

"Sorry," he told her. "My mind was wandering."

"It's no wonder," she said solemnly, "after what all you been through." Over her shoulder, as she led him into the house, she said, "Least it was over and final for Will after Gettysburg. Some small comfort in that."

The inside of the house was neat and clean if sparsely furnished. Will sat in a wooden chair at a square oak table in the kitchen. Sharleen had been cooking. The scent of baked bread was in the air, along with that of brewed coffee.

He watched the sway of her hips beneath her skirt as she moved to the wood stove and poured coffee into a tin cup. She set the cup in front of him, then sat down across from him at the table.

"Gotta be a rough life here for a woman alone," Luther remarked.

"Oh, I'm not alone." Her glance slid to an open doorway.

Luther didn't understand at first. Then he stood up, walked over, and peered into the room. A small child was sleeping in a wooden crib.

"That's Samuel," Sharleen said, when Luther had sat down again at the table.

"Will's son," he said with a forced smile.

"The precious thing he left me," Sharleen said. "I got Samuel. And I got Frank Ames."

Luther took a deep breath. "Sharleen, is Ames . . . ? I mean, are you and him . . . ?"

She appeared surprised, touching the side of her neck lightly in a way he remembered she'd done long ago when she was embarrassed. "Oh, no! It's nothing like that, Luther."

"Maybe not to you, but what about to him?"

She seemed to think on the question. "I don't believe so, and a woman oughta know. I think it's just he's a kind man and he runs the bank and's in a position to help out now and again. I know I'm not the only one he's helped."

Luther raised his eyebrows. "Runs the bank, does he?"

"Surely does. You remember he worked there before leaving to fight. Well, old man Scopes retired and sold his interest to Frank. There's partners and a board, but Frank's president and makes the decisions."

"I'll talk to him," Luther said, and took a sip of coffee.

" 'bout what?"

"Getting a loan to run some irrigation to the fields, turn the soil, and put in some good seed for spring planting. That horse I got out there ain't worth much, but he surely can pull a plow."

He couldn't read the expression on Sharleen's face.

"Luther . . ."

"Remember," he said, "I was raised here on this land. It ain't that I see it as mine, but you and Samuel are family, and nothing can change that." He gave her a reassuring smile. "With what happened to Will and all . . . I mean, I feel duty bound to help."

She studied his face, then nodded, stood up, and poured him some more hot coffee. "It ain't as if we don't need it," she said.

"You done all right," Luther said.

"The Lord knows I tried." She lowered her head, almost as if she were going to pray, but she began to cry quietly.

Luther got up, strode around the table, and hugged her to him until her back stopped heaving and she wiped her nose and was calm.

He caressed her cheek with the backs of his knuckles and she turned her face away. He walked back to his chair and sat down.

"Coffee was something we could never get enough of during the war," he told her. "Towards the end, we'd make it outta most anything we could grind between two stones." He shook his head glumly. "There was lots of things we couldn't get enough of."

"I just bet there was," Sharleen said.

Luther went to see Frank Ames the next morning at the Oak River Bank. Ames was a small man with a jutting chin and bushy dark mustache. He looked startled to see Luther, then stood up behind his desk and shook hands with him. That he'd stood up surprised Luther, as Sharleen had said Ames lost a leg to the Yanks.

"I'm real glad to see you made it back here safe and sound," Luther said.

Ames smiled. Though his angular face hadn't changed much, his gray eyes were a lot older than when he and Luther had competed in the county games five years ago. "Safe, maybe. But I'm not exactly sound, Luther. Lost a leg."

"Wouldn't guess it."

"Got a wood one, foot and all," Ames said, and limped out from behind the desk. "Don't have to work my boot off and on it, anyway. Silver lining." He motioned for Luther to sit in a nearby chair, then went back to sit behind the desk. He ducked his head and looked strangely at Luther. "I heard you were dead, killed at Chickamauga."

Luther raised his eyebrows in surprise, then smiled. "Don't look that way, does it?"

"Nope. Don't have to touch you to know you're real and still among the living."

"War was hell," Luther said.

Ames nodded. "Damned Sherman." He made a pink steeple with the fingers of both hands. "This visit about business, Luther?"

"It is. I understand you been helping my sister-in-law Sharleen. We appreciate that, but now that I'm back, I want to do my duty to her. After all, she's my brother's widow. Family's all that's left after this war, and for lots of folks not even that."

"It was a shame about Will. He was a good boy."

"He was that."

"His widow deserves better than what she's got," Ames said. "What do you have in mind, Luther?"

"A loan for a decent plow my horse can pull, for some irrigation work, a new barn and chicken coop, a well that ain't run dry, and good seed come the spring."

"That's a lot," Ames said.

"Sharleen needs a lot."

"Gettysburg was hell worse than Sherman," Ames said. "Made a lot of Southern widows."

"Northern ones, too."

Ames nodded. "Carpetbaggers are gonna come in here from the North, change this country. Oak River is gonna grow. Guess Sharleen's farm can grow with it."

"You'll help, then?"

"I'll loan you the money, Luther. The work's up to you."

"And I'm up to it," Luther said.

"Just figure out what you need."

Luther drew a sheet of paper from his pocket and unfolded it. "I got it right here."

Oak River grew just as Frank Ames had predicted. And Sharleen's farm prospered. Luther worked hard and became a substitute father for young Samuel, and stayed in the old barn while he built a new one. By late fall the farm had new or repaired outbuildings, but the harvest was meager.

Winter was cold and with more than the usual snow, but Luther kept at his work. Before spring planting, he located water with a divining rod fashioned from a forked branch from a peach tree, a talent that had always been his, and with help from town dug a new well. The spring planting produced a rich harvest that late summer and fall, and Luther and Sharleen began to repay Frank Ames's bank.

At the beginning of their second winter together Luther and Sharleen were married. By that time, nobody was much surprised, and the wedding was a joyful event. The farm became known to the townspeople as the Faver Place.

Both Luther and Sharleen continued to work hard, and when Samuel got old enough he took to farm work. Besides farming, Luther gained a reputation with his dowsing, and the carpetbaggers moving into Oak River paid him handsomely to locate water with his divining rod so they'd not waste time and money digging dry wells.

Frank Ames was soon paid off, and with profits no longer going toward the loan, Luther and Sharleen began to grow rich by Oak River's standards. They replaced the log farmhouse with a fine two-story frame home with a green marble fireplace and a wide front porch.

At the turn of the century Luther had lived longer than he imagined was possible, almost to sixty. But he was healthy and saw more good years ahead for him and for Sharleen.

Samuel had become a tall, handsome man who looked more like Luther than Will, and moved with his young bride to Joplin where they managed a dry goods emporium. One day he appeared at the farm with a fancy carriage pulled by two fine horses, and in his wife's arms was Luther's grandson.

Will's grandson.

"We named him Will!" Samuel said proudly. Then he asked how they liked the carriage and said, "I seen 'em with motors in Kansas City. Nothin' else pullin' 'em!"

"Horseless carriages?" Sharleen asked in amazement. Though graying and thicker through the middle, she was still a beautiful woman, and her eyes widened with the enthusiasm of a youthfulness that would always be hers. The past lived with her and in her.

"So they're called," Samuel told his mother. "I'm gonna talk to a man about a dealership. The carriages might be horseless, but they ain't without profit." He grinned at Luther. "And Dad taught me the value of plannin' ahead."

That evening, sitting before the warm blaze in his marble fireplace, Luther Faver considered that he was one of the luckiest men alive.

The next morning his illness introduced itself, and it never left him. His stomach was never right, and he lost weight until his elbows and knees made sharp angles. Then his hair began to fall out.

Doc Newsner in town didn't know what to make of it. He tried different medications on Luther and bled him with leeches. Nothing seemed to help.

Only Sharleen could comfort him. She stayed awake through the night with him at times, holding his hand while the pain wracked him and caused him to moan and draw up his knees. The nights were the worst time. She would place a folded damp cloth on his forehead and croon softly to him. But the pain persisted.

When Sharleen suddenly came down ill, Doc Newsner figured maybe it was something in the well water.

It wasn't, though. Two days later she died from a burst appendix.

Luther was too ill to attend the funeral. He lay bedridden and alone in the big farmhouse on the Faver Place. Samuel was coming in from Joplin to take him back there to die. Nobody had any illusions about that. They would travel by train to Joplin so Luther could pass while among family.

The night before Samuel was to arrive, Frank Ames paid Luther a visit.

Ames hadn't aged well. He was bent at the waist, walking with the aid of a walnut cane, and his face was deeply lined. His mustache had become gray and scraggly above bloodless lips. As he limped into the bedroom, Luther thought Ames probably wouldn't live much longer than he would.

"Some whiskey in the kitchen," Luther offered.

"Can't drink the stuff anymore," Ames said. His voice had become older than he was, hoarse and so soft you had to listen hard to whatever he was saying.

Luther weakly waved an arm toward the easy chair alongside the bed, and Ames settled into it with a long sigh, his wooden leg extended straight out in front of him.

"Sharleen was buried well," he told Luther. "She was a good woman."

"Always," Luther said. "I hope I did right by her."

Ames drew a briar pipe from his pocket and gave his wooden leg a sharp rap with it. "We came a long ways from Gettysburg," he said, and began packing the pipe's bowl with tobacco from a leather pouch.

"War's a long time ago now," Luther agreed.

"To some it is." Ames struck a wooden match to flame with his thumbnail and held fire to tobacco. He puffed until he got the pipe burning well, then he shook out the match and put the blackened remains of it in the vest pocket of his banker's suit. The room filled with the acrid-sweet scent of the smoldering tobacco leaf.

"Long time ago for everyone," Luther told him. "Time buries everything."

"Sometimes it takes a while, though," Frank Ames said. He reached into the pocket where he'd slipped the burnt match, withdrew an object and laid it on the nightstand alongside the bed where Luther could see it.

Luther raised his head and peered to the side at the glittering object.

"I shined it up for you," Ames said.

"What is it?"

"A locket. Silver. Pretty old now. There's a lock of Sharleen's hair in it."

Something dark and immortal stirred in Luther.

"Your brother Will wore it for good luck in the war: Had it on him when he died."

"Did they send his personal effects to Sharleen?"

"Nope." Ames settled back in his chair and spoke around the pipe stem clamped in his teeth. "I was with Longstreet's troops at Gettysburg, camped near Cemetery Ridge and waiting for morning and the hell it'd bring, when we spotted a couple of Yanks headed for picket duty. The moonlight made them good targets, and some artillery pieces opened fire on them. Killed one of them. The other made it to cover in a peach orchard. I was one of three men sent to capture that lone picket so he wouldn't give information to the Yanks. We didn't know another patrol was sent from Heth's First Corps to capture him. You were in that patrol." The burning pipe tobacco made a soft whispering sound in the quiet room. "I was in the peach orchard and saw what happened that night, Luther. I saw you shoot your brother."

Luther's heart seemed to shrivel. He was having even more difficulty than usual breathing. Possession of the locket was proof of Ames's story. Proof that he was in the peach orchard that night and proof enough of murder. Luther knew that he'd come close to being hanged long ago.

"Why didn't you tell someone?" he heard his own rasping voice ask. "Why didn't you tell Sharleen what happened?"

"I never told her nor anyone else because I knew she needed you," Ames said. "And Samuel needed a father. Me with my missing leg, there was no way in hell I could help her enough, no way I could farm crops and build and be a father to a son not my own. But I loved Sharleen and wanted to do something for her. I couldn't bear to sit and watch her live such a hard life and fall ill and die, or bend beneath her load and become an old woman before her time. You were the answer, Luther. The solution to the problem you created."

"I killed Will so I could have Sharleen," Luther said feebly. There were tears in his eyes. He hadn't cried in decades, not even when Sharleen died.

"That was easy to figure," Ames said. "You always loved her, and you were always jealous of your brother."

"I was a good husband to Sharleen," Luther said. "A good provider, and a good father to her son. Maybe I made it up to her, in a way. Maybe I made amends for what I did."

Ames drew on his pipe and exhaled a cloud of smoke. "I don't think so. I don't think that was enough."

"At least she never found out."

"I didn't say that, Luther."

Luther couldn't lift his head, but he craned his neck painfully so he could see Ames. He didn't like what he saw in Ames's face.

"I told her 'bout a year ago," Ames said. "Showed her the locket."

Luther felt himself go cold from the inside. "She never said anything to me."

"She decided to poison you instead."

Now Luther did manage to raise his head. "Wha . . . ?" The back of his head sank back into his sweat-soaked pillow.

"She's been feeding you arsenic, Luther. Exacting her revenge little by little for what you did to her young husband. Exacting justice. Nothing you can do about it now. It's too late to fix the damage that's been done to you or reverse the process. The poison'll soon have its way."

Luther struggled to speak but could only croak weakly and gasp.

"I thought you oughta know," Ames said, bracing himself with his cane and standing up from his chair with difficulty. "Maybe because I'm a banker and I believe there needs to be an accounting. It's only right. You haven't got much longer and things oughta be settled."

Ames made to leave, then paused and turned. "We were on the losing side, Luther, but you thought you won your own personal war. It took a long time, but you lost just like the rest of us."

Ames limped toward the door. His cane clattered like dry bones as he clumped down the stairs.

Then there was complete silence.

Luther lay with ghosts in the darkening room.

# Jan Burke

## The Abbey Ghosts

JAN BURKE'S second story in this year's collection is every bit as good as her first, "The Man in the Civil Suit," but in a very different vein. "The Abbey Ghosts" is more in line with her historical novels, and equally gripping. It was first published in the January 2001 issue of *Alfred Hitchcock's Mystery Magazine*, which bore a 2000 copyright. We're glad to have it, regardless of which year they call it.

# The Abbey Ghosts

## *Jan Burke*

I did not meet the Eighth Earl of Rolingbroke until he was twelve years old. I was in some measure compensated for the lack of our acquaintance during those first dozen years of his life, not only by the deep friendship my stepbrother and I formed over the years we did have together, but also by occasionally being allowed to spend time with him after his death.

His death had come unexpectedly and before he attained his thirtieth year. That first evening after his funeral I sat before the fire in The Abbey library, weary and yet certain that my grief for him would not allow me to sleep. Not many hours earlier my late stepbrother had been laid to rest in the family crypt. Lucien's body was placed next to that of his wife—who had died five years before, shortly after giving birth to Charles, their only child.

Lucien's orphaned son was much on my mind. Candle in hand, I had looked in on Charles just before ten o'clock that night. The day's events had been exhausting for him as well, and he slept, though his young face seemed sad even in repose. He stirred, perhaps because of the light, so I extinguished it. I waited, but he did not waken, and I crept silently away in the darkness, softly shutting his door before relighting the candle. I returned to the library.

I poured another glass of port as the mantel clock struck eleven. I had dismissed the servants for the evening, not able to bear their solicitude or their misery. They had loved Lucien as much as I, and the strain of this terrible day was telling on us all. I chose to spend the last few hours of it alone, thinking of Lucien and the years we had shared as brothers. How I would miss him!

When Lucien's father married my widowed mother, my mother and I went to live at The Abbey. I'd met the Seventh Earl of Rolingbroke, my new stepfather, on only two previous occasions—brief interviews that had put me quite in awe of that forceful man. I entered his home knowing I was without a champion—my mother, for all her beauty and good-heartedness, was a timid soul, more likely to suffer a fit of the vapors than to defend me.

The Abbey itself was daunting—a rambling structure larger by far than the small estate where I had been reared, and very much older. I sincerely believed that a boy of my size might be lost within it, and even if his newly remarried mother should take the trouble to look for him, she might never discover which winding staircase or long gallery held his remains.

Not the least of my anxieties concerned my new stepbrother. I expected resentment from Lucien, then twelve and two years my senior. My first impression of him led me to believe that he was a cool and distant fellow. As we entered The Abbey, he stood back from the others, regarding me lazily from his greater height. I was afraid and trying not to show it—but I must have failed, for his father muttered something about "Master Quake-boots."

Lucien's expression changed then, and he welcomed me by bowing and murmuring for my ears only, "Lord Shivershanks, at your service." I choked back a laugh, received his rare but charming smile in return, and, like any recipient of that smile, knew all would be right with the world.

Lucien soon became both friend and brother, offering wise-beyond-his-years guidance and his seldom bestowed affection. He taught me how to get on well with my stepfather, protected me against a bully or two, and allowed me to accompany him in every lark imaginable. He taught me the ways and traditions of The Abbey. He also taught me how to find several secret passages within it and told me stories of its past, thrilling me with tales of ghostly, headless monks haunting the north (and only remaining) tower, of hidden treasures and ancient curses.

"And we must not forget the Christmas Curse," he whispered to me one chilly evening in late November—when as usual he had made use of a priest's hole to come into my room and visit long after the servants believed him abed.

"Can there be such a thing?" I asked.

"Oh yes," he said with one of his mischievous smiles. "You, my dear Edward, have not had the felicity of meeting my Aunt and Uncle Bane and their pack of hellborn brats—Henry, William, and Fanny. Utter thatchgallows."

"Thatchgallows!" I laughed.

"Shhh! Yes. Born to be hanged, every man Jack of them—and Fanny, too. We shall have to prepare for their arrival. They'll try to harass you, of course, but don't worry. Every time one of them behaves odiously, you are to remind yourself that soon we will be handing them a reckoning."

He was not mistaken. Lord and Lady Bane brought their three interesting offspring to The Abbey not two weeks later. The servants had prepared for their visit by carefully removing the most treasured and fragile objects of the household from sight. From the moment the Banes passed through the imposing entrance of The Abbey, our home was turned upside down. Henry and William, true to Lucien's prediction, made it their business to make me suffer. Henry was my own age, William a year younger, but they were both taller and stronger than I. All three children favored their father, Lord Alfred Bane, who was both brother-in-law and cousin to the earl—though I could perceive no family resemblance. Lord Bane was a redhaired man whose countenance could easily be brought to match it in color. His softest whisper was nothing less than a shout—and he seldom whispered.

His sons were equally loud and seemed never to stand still for a moment. They contrived to poke, pinch, trip, and jostle me at every opportunity. By the end of their second day among us, I was quite bruised but did not doubt for a moment that Lucien would come to my aid. In his quiet way he often did so, surprisingly able to control them as no one else could—giving a quelling look to Henry or William that always made them desist until they chanced to find me apart from him.

When those opportunities arose, any feeble attempt on my part to defend myself caused them to set up a caterwauling that served as a siren call to Lady Sophia Bane. This fond mother relished coming to their aid and invariably boxed my ears as she rang a peal over my head. On these occasions my own mother, who knew better than any general how to retreat in good order, always announced that she felt a spasm coming on, and—clutching her vinaigrette to her bosom—excused herself from the battlefield.

Lady Bane complained constantly, perceiving faults everywhere. The food was not to her liking. The servants were never to be found when needed. The room in which she sat was too chilly. When the fires were made larger, she was too warm and protested that the chimneys smoked. The rooms where they had been installed were uncomfortable for this reason or that. "Not what we are accustomed to at Bane House!" was a refrain we soon wearied of hearing.

When she declared that their rooms were inconveniently located, my stepfather raised his brows.

"But my dear Sophia!" he said. "They are the very rooms you insisted upon after refusing the ones you had last year, claiming I was trying to banish you to a far wing of The Abbey."

It made no difference.

Lucien later told me that his father and aunt had been reared separately—the earl had spent most of his childhood at The Abbey with Lucien's grandfather. Lucien's grandmother, who disliked life in the country nearly as much as she disliked her husband, lived in Town with her daughter, Sophia.

I was grateful for these insights. We had little opportunity for private speech such as this, however, for Fanny constantly spied on Lucien and me. Since I had been almost constantly in his company during the previous months, suddenly being unable to share confidences with Lucien gave me a sense of loneliness the depth of which surprised me, as I had often been alone before we came to live at The Abbey.

Then one evening, just as I was feeling quite sure this would be my most miserable Christmas ever, Lucien winked and smiled at me. I immediately understood this to mean that he had devised a remedy for our troubles. I was not mistaken.

We had been engaged in playing jackstraws, but Fanny's governess, who had been overseeing our activities that evening, called the proceedings to a halt—perceiving, I suppose, that this was not the sort of game the Banes could play without violence. As she moved across the room to put the game away, Lucien turned to me and said, "Edward, do you suppose the ghost will walk tonight?"

"What ghost?" the Banes said loudly and in unison.

"The Headless Abbot, of course," he replied.

Fanny's eyes grew round.

"What nonsense is this?" asked the governess, but with an air of interest.

"Long, long ago," Lucien said, casting his spell over us, "a castle was built here—its ruins form part of the north tower. But the castle itself was built over ruins—ruins of an even older abbey, which is how our home came to be named.

"In the days when The Abbey was truly an abbey, a war broke out between two powerful lords. One winter's night, not long before Christmas, the abbey came under attack, which was a shocking thing because this was then considered a holy place, with relics and the like. Knights in armor rode their horses into the chapel, where the abbot was leading the evening prayer. The captain of these rogues took out his broadsword and—*swoosh!*" He made a slicing motion with his hand.

All three Banes and the governess gasped—and I believe I did, too, for though I had heard this tale before, never had Lucien related it in such a dramatic manner.

"Yes," Lucien said darkly, "he beheaded the holy man where he stood, and his knights murdered all the other monks—defenseless men at their prayers."

This earned another gasp.

"But why did they do such a thing?" the horrified governess asked.

Lucien seemed to hesitate, his manner that of one who was deciding whether he should impart a great secret. "The attackers," he finally said, "had heard a legend, a tale of a treasure kept in the abbey. It probably wasn't true, for although they examined every cupboard and cabinet and pulled at loose stones and tiles and looked in every room and hall for its hiding place, they could not find the treasure." He paused. "The powerful lord to whom the knight had sworn his loyalty sent a messenger to the captain, saying that he needed his warriors and so they must make all haste to the battlefield. The greedy captain did not want to abandon his treasure hunt, so he pretended to have an illness. He sent all but a small number of the knights to join their lord in battle while he remained with a small band—the most black-hearted of the lot—to continue his search."

He lowered his voice. "But during the night on the very first evening this small company stayed in the abbey, the men who stood guard were startled to see a strange sight—a man wearing a monk's robes, his face hidden by its cowl, seemed to appear out of nowhere. Unlike the brown-robed monks they had slaughtered so mercilessly, this one was dressed all in white save for a splash of red on his chest. 'Who goes there?' cried one of the knights. The figure in white halted and lowered his cowl. With horror the knights saw that the apparition *had no head*."

"The abbot!" William said breathlessly.

"Yes," Lucien said. "The guards screamed in terror, awakening the others. The knights were frightened, but their captain tried to brazen it out. 'Show us your treasure!' he shouted. And the abbot began to lead the way. The captain called to his five bravest men, and they followed the monk into a secret passage. The others were too frightened to go near him and waited."

Again Lucien paused.

"Yes, yes! Then what happened?" Henry insisted.

Lucien smiled. "They were never seen again!"

There was a suitably awed silence.

"But the treasure!" William said. "What happened to the treasure?"

"It was never found. Accidents befell any who tried to discover it—especially those who ventured near the old sanctuary. Eventually this land was given to one of our ancestors. He had the portion of the abbey that had been the sanctuary sealed off and built his castle over it. But the local people will tell you that the Headless Abbot still walks on winter nights. Some say they've heard the sound of hoofbeats coming from the part of the abbey that lies nearest the sanctuary—the ghostly horses of the accursed knights."

"Which part of this old pile is that?" Henry asked, trying for nonchalance.

Lucien appeared to reflect. "Why, I believe it is very near your rooms."

All Henry's bravado disappeared. "Mother!" he screamed, running from the room. Fanny burst into tears and soon followed him. William hurriedly escaped on her heels.

"My word!" the governess said, rather pale, although perhaps she feared her employer's displeasure more than headless monks, for she hastened after her charges.

"My compliments," said Lucien calmly. "You appeared suitably frightened. If you continue to play your part so well, my dear Edward, I believe we can have them on their way by first light."

I decided not to admit that I was genuinely frightened, but I think he knew in any case, for the delightful prospect of the Banes' departure made me smile, and when he saw it, he said, "That's the barber! They've been beastly nuisances to me, but worse to you, poor boy." He looked closely at my face, which had served as a target for Henry's fists a little earlier in the day. "Daresay you'll have a mouse under your right eye. Was it Henry who tried to darken your daylights?"

I nodded, fairly certain that Henry had indeed given me a black eye.

"Nasty fellow, Henry. I'll have to think of some special treat for him. But never mind that—you've got more bottom than the lot of them. Game as a pebble, you are!"

Such praise, delivered for the most part in cant expressions he had learned from one of the stable lads, delighted me so much he had to remind me to appear to be frightened.

"We must be prepared, for my father will be demanding an explanation of us soon, I'm sure."

The thought of being called before the earl was enough to restore my pallor.

"Excellent," Lucien said, his smile broadening when Fibbens appeared at the door.

"If your lordship and Master Edward would be so good as to come with me?" the young footman said, his face revealing nothing. "Your lordship's father asks that you join the other members of the family in the drawing room."

"To receive a rare trimming from my Aunt Sophia?" Lucien asked.

There was the slightest twitch at the corner of Fibbens' mouth before he answered, "I'm sure I could not say, your lordship."

As we approached the drawing room, Lucien whispered to me, "It is absolutely essential, dear Edward, that you stand as close to my father as possible."

A daunting instruction indeed. Summoning all my courage, I did as he asked, making my way to the earl's side as Lady Bane began to deliver herself of what promised to be a lengthy speech on the lack of manners of certain members of the younger generation. Henry, William, and Fanny eyed us with smug satisfaction.

"Never mind that, Sophia!" Lord Bane interrupted, loud enough to cause my mother to shrink back against the cushions of the sofa she occupied but silencing—however briefly—his own wife.

No sooner had I taken up my position near the earl's chair than he stood, picking up a decanter and walking toward Lord Bane as though none of the havoc in the room were actually taking place. I looked to Lucien, who subtly signaled me to stay where I was.

"Lucien," the earl said quietly as he finished refilling Lord Bane's glass, "I don't suppose you would mind troubling yourself to give me a brief summary of the events of this evening? I am particularly interested in those that caused your cousins to fly to their mama and hold to her skirts."

Lord Bane laughed at this, even as his wife protested. As my stepfather walked back toward me, he seemed to study me for a moment before refilling his own glass and returning the decanter to the drinks tray. "Edward," he said, in the gentlest voice I had yet heard him use, "come stand here with me by the fire. My sister tells me all our chimneys smoke, but I fear I'll need to feel some warmth while Lucien recites his chilling tale."

So we moved nearer the fireplace with its holly-draped mantel. The warmth of the fire felt good, and so did some nearly imperceptible change in my stepfather's manner toward me. Lucien began his tale, but the earl kept his eyes on me.

"As you have so often told us, Aunt Sophia," Lucien said, "you are a woman who is accustomed to finer treatment than we can afford you here at The Abbey, in part because you consider London your home and were not often here as a child. That being so, I do not imagine the tale of the Headless Abbot has come to your ears."

"I should say not!"

Lucien turned to his father. "I thought it only fair to warn my dear cousins about him, sir."

"Your dear cousins," the earl repeated. "Just so."

Lucien again recounted the legend, this telling no less unnerving than the previous one. My mother had recourse to her vinaigrette no fewer than five times but was an avid listener.

"Poppycock!" Lord Bane declared. "Fairy tales."

"I used to think so," Lucien said. "But if it's just a fairy tale, there ought to be a good earl in it. But there isn't, you see."

"A good earl?" his father asked, looking sharply at him.

"Yes, Father. The abbey should have been protected by a good man, someone who cared about the defenseless men who lived there. He would not have let the ruffians who descended on them have their way."

"Perhaps he was otherwise occupied," the earl said.

Lucien shrugged. "Perhaps he did not see his duty."

The earl raised a brow. "Perhaps he was taking a switch to the backside of his impertinent son."

Lucien gave a little bow. "I trust in your wisdom, sir. You must have the right of it."

"Doing it much too brown, Lucien!" the earl said, but there was a twinkle in his eye that did not abate even as his sister upbraided him for using such terms.

"And why you talk of earls, which has nothing to do with the case, I'm sure

I don't know!" Lady Bane protested. "You seem to forget, dear brother, that Lucien has frightened poor Fanny and her brothers half to death!"

"I beg your pardon, Aunt Sophia," Lucien said when she paused to draw breath, "if I've caused you or my cousins any fright. But I do think the experience of seeing the ghost or hearing the hoofbeats is much less frightening if one is *prepared*. Imagine the shock one might feel if he were to see a bloodstained, headless apparition floating outside his window at midnight if he *didn't* know the legend."

"Nonsense!" Lady Bane declared. "We've spent Christmas here these past three years and more. Why have we never heard this legend before now?"

"If I may offer an explanation, Aunt Sophia?" Lucien said. "Only one section of The Abbey is haunted—beneath the chambers you occupy. No one is ever disturbed in any other part of the house, so we did not wish to frighten you with the tale. But since you wished to have the rooms nearest the north tower—"

"Oh! So this is my fault is it? Well, I'll tell you why we are just now hearing of your ghost, my good fellow! Because some who've never been here before this year have invented tales. Outsiders!" She rounded on me, pointing. "It's you!"

She received a chorus of approval from her offspring. I quailed before them, but then I felt the earl's large hand on my shoulder. I winced a bit as he touched a bruise, and his hand shifted slightly. At that moment I became aware that the room had fallen silent. Everyone was looking at the earl, whose face was a mask of cold fury.

"Are you assuming that my wife's son has no place in our family?" he asked icily. "I assure you, Sophia, he is not an outsider here. Lucien thinks of Edward as his brother, and I as my son. Indeed, there are blood relations I would much liefer disown—and may."

I could hardly believe my own ears, which were soon assaulted.

"No offense meant!" Lord Bane shouted. I was sure he'd spoken loudly enough to startle the villagers from their beds several miles away.

The earl, however, appeared not to have heard him. "Perhaps, Sophia, you would find Christmas in Town more to your liking."

"La!" she said nervously, "how you do take one up! Prefer Christmas in London to being with family—indeed, no! Bane is right—I meant no offense. Lucien's lurid tale has quite overset me!"

With that, she snapped at her children, telling them it was long past time for them to be abed, remonstrated with the governess for not having seen to it, and said, "Bane!" in a commanding tone that had her husband soon bidding all a good night.

"You too should be in bed, Edward," my mother said.

"Time we all were," my stepfather said. "Go on up if you like, my dear. I shall have a brief word with the boys before I retire."

As soon as she had left, the earl turned to Lucien and said in a lazy voice, "I trust Act III of your little drama will be staged later this evening?" Despite his tone I could see the amusement in his eyes, and for the first time, I perceived a likeness between the earl and his son that went beyond Lucien's physical resemblance to his father.

"Tomorrow evening, sir. Tonight would be too soon. They are Banes, and being such, need time to think."

"You frighten me far more than your telling of the legend did—though I credit you with an admirable performance."

Lucien bowed again. "I had an excellent teacher."

The earl gave a sudden shout of laughter. "Impossible boy!"

"Again, sir—"

"No, don't say I taught you to be such an impudent hellion, for I'll swear I did not!"

"Then I shall say nothing, sir—except—except—thank you, sir!"

" 'Tis the other way 'round, I believe." The earl turned back to me and gently lifted my chin. "I see I have been remiss in your education, Edward. Or perhaps—yes—Lucien, you must teach your brother to be handy with his fives." He paused. "Lady Rolingbroke need not be apprised of it."

"Thank you, sir!" I said.

"Oh, I demand a high price! If you fail to rid me of the Banes, you and that makebait Lucien will be served gruel for Christmas dinner—by whatever headless monk I can find to take it to the dungeon!"

We were destined to eat a sumptuous feast. Before Lucien and I sought our beds, he enlisted my aid in creating a few hoofbeats along the secret passages near each of the Banes' bedchambers. Henry had awakened to feel a ghostly presence in the form of a room that was suddenly terribly cold, not knowing that Lucien had merely left the entrance to one of the draftiest passages open for a time.

We left it at that. The next morning, of course, we denied hearing anything like hoofbeats. When Henry swore he had felt the ghost but no other member of his family told a similar tale, Lucien grew thoughtful. "I wonder why he would single you out?"

This made Henry go very pale and ask again if no one else had felt a bit chilly last night.

No one had, of course. The earl went so far as to say he had rarely slept so well.

Lady Bane was perhaps made suspicious by this remark, for she gave her husband a speaking look and asked him to accompany her into the village. Henry was rather quiet that day, if a little jumpy. William, owing to the increased watchfulness of several footmen and others, did not have any chances to harm me that morning. He later confided to us that Lord and Lady Bane had found the villagers ready to repeat all the salient points of the legend and in many cases to enlarge upon it. After hearing something of this at luncheon, the earl strode up to Lucien and me as we were on our way to the stables. "Lucien, dear boy, I take it I am going to be generous to my tenants this Boxing Day?"

"Extremely, sir. But it should interest you to know that Aunt Sophia's dresser has told Bogsley that she doesn't expect the Banes to remain in this, er 'accursed place' another day."

"Don't tell me you've enlisted my staid butler in your schemes? I'd think it beneath Bogsley's dignity."

Lucien seemed to ponder before answering. "Perhaps, Father, it would be best not to inquire too closely on some matters."

"Good God!" the earl declared and walked away seeming shaken.

The following night I helped again with hoofbeats, and later to make howling sounds as Lucien—and Fibbens—contrived to swing a headless "apparition" past their windows. Bogsley had recommended the village seamstress who made the monk. Each Bane caught no more than a fleeting glimpse of this phantom, but judging from the pandemonium, this glimpse was more effective than a full night's haunting. The Banes, looking haggard, were on the road to London before noon, swearing never to return to The Abbey.

The earl declared it the most delightful Christmas gift his son had ever bestowed upon him, causing my mother a great deal of puzzlement.

As we grew older I learned how rare a gift I had received in Lucien's affection for me and saw how infrequently he troubled himself to form friendships. He nevertheless grew into a man who was invited everywhere. While his fortune, breeding, and rank might have guaranteed that in any case, there was a vast difference between the welcome Lucien was given by leading members of the *haut ton* and that afforded others. That I benefited from my connection to him is without doubt and was decried by Lord Henry Bane, Mr. William Bane, Miss Fanny Bane, and the Dowager Lady Sophia Bane, who made no less imposing a widow than a wife. Lucien's aunt might complain all she liked about "persons who were no blood relation" enjoying "privileges above their station," but she found few who paid heed to her.

Our parents died together in a carriage accident when Lucien was but twenty-two. He succeeded to his father's dignities and two years later married well. His wife was a young beauty with a handsome dowry, although his own wealth prevented anyone from imagining him a fortune hunter. Lucien, unlike so many of our order, married for love.

I was myself by no means penniless, provided for both by my late stepfather and, having come into an inheritance, through my mother's family. Not long after Lucien's wedding, feeling restless, I used some of my own fortune to buy colors and left for the Peninsular War to see what I could do to hamper Boney's efforts in Portugal and Spain. Lucien and I exchanged letters, and although the mail was not always reliable, his correspondence made my soldier's life easier to bear. The letters made me long to be home, of course. Of all of these, the most heartrending was the one in which he told me of both the death of his wife and the birth of his son.

It was not his way to be effusive—either in grief or in joy—but in this letter he wrote a litany of all the small pleasures he would miss—hearing the soft rustle of her skirts as she entered the library while he read, watching her blush at an endearment, listening to her sing softly to herself as she walked through The Abbey gardens, unaware that he was near—and I came to a new understanding of how deeply he had cared for her. Beyond that one letter he never wrote to me again of her, though across the great distance between us I could sense his sadness.

Gradually, over the next two years, I began to see that he had found a new source of joy as well. Letter after letter gave the latest news of Charles Edward Rolingbroke, my nephew and godson. Lucien clearly doted on his heir. I saved these letters as I had every letter before, reading them again and again.

I next saw Lucien when he approached my bed in a dismal London hospital. He looked for me there after Ciudad Rodrigo. He had seen my name among the lists of wounded and used his influence to discover what had become of me. I heard someone say, "Captain, you've a visitor." I opened my eyes, and there stood Lucien, looking ridiculously worried. Delirious with fever, nevertheless I recognized him—at least for a few moments, when he seemed to me some last vision granted to me before dying. I was too weak even to speak to him and remember nothing more than smiling foolishly at him. Nor do I remember being moved from that place and taken to Rolingbroke House, his fashionable London residence. The quality of my care improved immeasurably, and eventually the fever subsided.

Though at last I no longer burned alive with it, I was still weak and somewhat confused about my change of circumstance. I knew I was in Lucien's home and fell asleep not long after a recollection came to me of Lucien arguing with a doctor, refusing to allow me to be bled. This was confirmed by the doctor when I awoke the next morning. He chuckled. "No, wouldn't let me bleed you, and offered to—how did he put it now? Oh yes, he promised to draw my own claret if I caused you to lose one more drop of yours. Well, my fine captain, I'd as soon fight Boney himself than cross swords with the earl." My wounds, he told me, would leave me with a few scars and a permanent limp. "But only two days ago I tried to convince his lordship that your funeral service should be arranged, so you are in far better case than expected."

Not much later Lucien himself came into my room, under strict orders not to make his visit a long one. I told him I did not want to burden him with the care of a lame stepbrother who was weak as a cat and not of as much use.

"I shall fetch that doctor back," Lucien said, "and demand a return of his fee. He distinctly told me you were no longer delirious, but here you are, speaking utter nonsense!"

"Lucien—"

"No, wait! Tell me you aren't feverish, for I'm only allowed a short visit and I shall be driven mad by your nephew if he isn't allowed to at last lay eyes on his Uncle Edward."

"He's here?" I asked.

But my question was answered by the entrance of a small boy who, over his nursemaid's protests, opened the door and ran toward his father. He was the spit and image of Lucien. "Papa!"

"Your lordship," the flustered nurse said, "I beg your pardon! I'll take him right out again."

"Oh no, madam!" Lucien exclaimed in mock horror. "Leave him with me. My brother has seen enough warfare as it is."

She left us, and no sooner had the door closed than Charles's questions began.

Did I feel better? Yes.

Had I hurt my head? Yes, that was why I wore a bandage.

Had I hurt my leg, then, too? Yes.

Did a Frenchy hurt me? Yes.

He offered to send his father to hurt the Frenchy in return. I thanked him but said I would prefer we all just stayed home together for a time, for I had missed my brother, and would like to become acquainted with his son.

Why was my skin so brown? A soldier spends a great deal of time in the sun.

454 | J A N  B U R K E

"That will do, Master Pokenose," Lucien said, causing his son to giggle. Obediently, though, Charles ceased asking questions. He sat quietly while Lucien discussed plans for removing to the countryside. Quite against my will I began to fall asleep. Charles brought this to his father's attention, which brought a rich laugh from Lucien. "Indeed, youngster, you are right. We'll let him rest for now."

I murmured an apology, stirring awake as I felt a small hand take my own.

"Papa says you're a great gun and we must help you to get better."

"My recovery is assured, then," I said, "but it is your papa who is the great gun."

Over the next three years, I would come to believe more and more in the truth of that statement. Fibbens was made my valet, a job that for some months involved the added duties of attending an invalid. I came to value him greatly. As my physical strength returned, though, it was Lucien and his son who would not allow me to retreat from the world. Charles's energetic encouragement and Lucien's refusal to permit me to mope over my injuries kept me from falling into a fit of the dismals. Before long I seldom thought so much of what I could not do as of what I could. Charles continued to delight me—I could not have been more attached to him if he had been my own boy.

On the night following Lucien's funeral, recalling my brother's life, I wondered how I would be able to comfort Charles over the days to come when the numbness I felt now would undoubtedly wear off.

When Lucien's horse, Fine Lad, had returned riderless to the stable three days earlier, a large group of men began a frantic search—servants, tenants, and neighbors. It was I who found him. I'd followed a route he often took through the woods when he rode for pleasure and discovered his motionless form along this path. He lay pale and bleeding beneath a shady tree—a thick, broken, bloodstained branch beside him. I did my best to staunch the wound on his head and to keep him warm even as I shouted for help.

All along the way back to The Abbey, the men who helped me carry him on a litter, and then to place him in a wagon, recounted several strange riding accidents of which they had heard. It was their way, I realized later, of trying to make sense of what seemed impossible—that Lucien, an excellent horseman, would be so careless while riding among low-hanging branches.

I had the broken branch with me, though, to prove it, as much to myself as anyone. And I would show it to Lucien, I vowed, and ask him what the devil he was about.

A fractured skull, the doctor said. Lucien never regained consciousness.

I knew the sort of blind rage that is the consort of our worst grief. I thought of burning the branch that had struck him. I thought of taking an axe to the tree, felling that which had felled him. I thought of shooting the horse.

I did none of these. Perhaps it was the horse's name that cleared my mind: Fine Lad.

Charles needed me.

That single thought cooled my rage.

Lucien's will made me Charles's guardian and trustee. I knew he did not merely want me to keep Charles's fortune safe and take care that he was sent to the best schools. I was to teach him what The Abbey meant to his family, what it meant to be the Earl of Rolingbroke, what he owed to his name, and owed to the memory of two good men who had held the same long list of titles before him. I had no fear that Charles would fail to be a credit to them—he was already so much his father's son.

That evening sitting before the fire remembering Lucien, I knew I would protect my young godson with my life. As the clock struck midnight, I vowed I would do my damnedest to keep Lucien alive in his memory.

I had no sooner made this vow than the library door flew open, startling me. Charles, pale and tearful, ran toward me, frantically calling my name. I opened my arms to him, taking him up on my lap and waving away the small army of concerned servants whose grasp he had eluded.

As the door to the library closed again, I tried to soothe him. "What's wrong, nipperkin?" I asked, certain that I already knew the answer.

"Papa's alive again," Charles sobbed.

"What?" I said, thinking I must have misheard him.

"Papa's alive. But he was dead, and now he scares me."

Was this some strange manifestation of a child's grief, I wondered? "What do you mean, Charles?"

The boy shivered. "I mean I saw him. His ghost."

I sought an explanation. "You were sleeping—"

"It was not a dream!" he insisted, with a familiar obstinacy.

I hesitated, then asked, "Charles, have you been speaking to the Banes?" The odious family was there—the dowager, Henry, William, and Fanny. The Banes had insisted on sleeping in a different wing from the one they had last occupied, although Henry now pooh-poohed the ghost story, saying it was undoubtedly one of Lucien's larks.

They had arrived, clearly, not so much for the funeral as for the reading of the will, and to say they were angry with its terms is to vastly understate the matter. Had William not intervened, the dowager, it seemed, would have been carried off on the spot by an apoplexy. "It is of no use, Mama," he said. "You should have known how it would be."

The dowager continued to bemoan her faithless nephew's lack of consideration for his own family, but not quite so intensely. Nevertheless, there was enough ill-concealed venom among the Banes to recall to me my first encounter with them, and I made sure Charles was never left alone with them.

"No," Charles said now. "I don't like them."

"You are a wise young man."

"Then why don't you believe me?"

"Did I say I did not believe you? Kindly refrain from making assumptions."

"What are those?"

"Er—don't believe you know something until you're sure you do know it."

He frowned as he puzzled this out, but he had stopped crying.

"Do you know, Charles, the more I think about this, the more I'm sure there is nothing to be frightened of here. Your father loved you very much and would never harm you."

"Yes," he said slowly. "And I have a great many things I should like to say to him that I have been thinking of these past few days. But one can't help but be frightened of ghosts, even good ghosts."

"No one can blame you for feeling frightened. I'm glad you came to me. I promise I'll protect you, Charles. Your father asked that of me, and I gave him my word that I would."

He sat quietly with me for a time, lost in his own thoughts. He was past the age when he wanted to be carried or held, which gave me some idea of how terrified he was now. I was sure he had merely dreamed of Lucien, but I knew he did not believe this to be the case.

"Do you think he was trying to tell me something?" Charles asked.

"Perhaps he was," I said.

"What?"

I reached for a packet of fragile papers lying on the small table next to us. "Let's see if we can guess. When I was fighting in the Peninsula, and your father and I were far away from one another, he wrote these letters to me. Would you like me to read them to you?"

He nodded, and I chose one of the letters Lucien had written about him. He was pleased and laughed at Lucien's comical descriptions of him as an infant, then asked me to read another. So we continued, until he suddenly said, "I smell smoke."

"You *have* been listening to your Aunt Sophia."

But before he could protest, I heard the shouts of the servants, and cries of "Fire!"

"We must help them put it out!" Charles said, jumping up from the chair.

I knew the same impulse, but what came quickly to mind were a series of drills that Lucien had insisted upon. I had always had the role of finding Charles in whatever room he might be in and taking him to safety. I used to argue with Lucien, saying that a man with a pronounced limp was hardly the most suitable person to be saving his heir, but he remained stubborn on this point. Remembering my vow of hardly more than an hour before, I grabbed Charles's hand before he was out of reach. "Your lordship," I said sternly, using the form of address which he knew to be a command to be on his best behavior. "You must not run toward the fire. You must allow me to keep you safe—just as we practiced. Come now."

I saw the briefest mulish cast to his face before he relented and allowed me to lead him out of the library. Fibbens, his face blackened with soot, was rushing down the stairs. "Oh, thank goodness!" he cried in relief. "Forgive me, captain—we feared the young master had returned to bed! His chambers are on fire!"

"My room!" the young master wailed.

"He will tell you more when we are all safely outside," I said, more shaken by Fibbens' announcement than I cared to admit. "What of the staff and the other guests?" I asked as we made our way.

"Everyone accounted for, sir. The fire has not spread beyond the young master's chambers. If you do not mind, I'd like to assure the others that his lordship is safe—"

"Yes, of course."

"Thank you, sir. Those who are not attempting to put out the fire should be downstairs shortly."

At the front steps it occurred to me that we were without cloaks, and Charles was without shoes. A fault in our drills, which had taken place in summertime. There had been little snowfall of late, but it was cold. I placed my coat around Charles's small shoulders—much to his delight—and lifted him into my arms.

Soon the Banes began to join us on the front drive. Aunt Sophia was wrapped in what I recognized to be William's many-caped driving coat. She'd not had time to put on her wig and looked a positive fright. Fanny seemed to have borrowed boots from one of her brothers but wore no coat—she shivered in a rather unbecoming nightgown. Henry appeared before us still fully dressed but rather well-to-live as the saying goes—from his unsteady walk, I suspected he had made substantial inroads on The Abbey's wine cellars. William too was dressed, although from his mother's criticisms, it was clear that he had remained in the building longer than she believed safe.

"And look! Your new coat from Weston—ruined!"

The expensive coat of blue superfine was indeed smudged. "Unlike others I could name," he sneered, looking reproachfully at Henry, "I attempted to make sure the old pile didn't burn down around my family's ears!"

Henry waved a vague hand of uninterest and stared at the building. Smoke had stopped billowing from the window of Charles's room. I prayed that meant the fire was under control.

"Here, Fanny," William said, taking off the coat. "You wear it. You look as if you're likely to freeze to death."

But Fanny, after bestowing a grateful smile on him, proved to be her mother's daughter. "Ugh!" she said, wrinkling her nose. "It smells of smoke."

William rolled his eyes.

"I do not know why I allowed you to talk me into staying at this accursed place!" his mother said to him.

"*I* talked you into it! That's a loud one!"

"Do not use that horrid cant with me, my young man! I won't have it!"

I realized that Charles was providing an interested audience to this byplay. Still holding him, I walked a bit apart from them.

Bogsley and Fibbens appeared, bearing cloaks and blankets. Fibbens attended the Banes while the elderly butler approached us.

"Bogsley, please tell me what has happened!" Charles said.

"I am pleased to say, your lordship, that the fire is out and little damage done. Your dear father had made preparations, you know, and the staff responded in a way that would make him proud if I do say so myself."

"The next time I see him, I shall tell him how well you did," Charles said.

Bogsley, that most self-controlled of all God's creatures, did not blink an eye, but I heard the slightest catch in his voice as he answered, "Thank you, your lordship. I pray that will not be for some time yet."

"One never knows," Charles said.

Worried over the effect these words seemed to have on the butler, I quickly said, "You've given us good tidings indeed, Bogsley. I trust none of the staff took any hurt?"

"None whatsoever, sir."

"Please thank everyone for saving our home," Charles said, then turned to me. "Perhaps Cook could give a jam tart to each of them."

"Yes, or whatever other treat might be managed," I said, pleased with his show of manners but hard pressed to maintain my gravity.

"Your lordship is very kind," Bogsley said.

"Thank you so much for the cloak, Bogsley," I said. "I do not think his lordship intends to return my coat."

At this Charles laughed, and we made our way indoors.

Only the promise of a jam tart persuaded Charles to spend a few moments with Fibbens while I inspected the damage. The hallway reeked of smoke, but the flames had been confined to one portion of Charles's room.

"I'm afraid his lordship won't be able to sleep in here this evening, sir," Bogsley said.

"You remain the champion of understatement, Bogsley." Charles's bed had been reduced to ashes.

"Thank you, sir. It would seem that a candle or lamp was left burning on his nightstand and ignited the bed curtains."

"Except that being something of a little lion, his lordship does not suffer a fear of the dark as some children do. He *prefers* a dark room and has never required any sort of candle or lamp to be lit in his room. And in fact he closes his bed curtains about him to keep out the light."

"Yes, sir."

"I looked in on his lordship earlier this evening. He was sound asleep. There was no candle burning in here at that time. I brought one in with me and extinguished it while I was here, fearing the light would wake him. Has anyone else been here this evening?"

"Until we were engaged in extinguishing the fire, no, sir. I should say no member of the *staff* entered this room after his lordship called for you, Captain Edward. But by that time his lordship was rather determined to find you on his own."

"And the Banes?"

"I'm afraid I couldn't say, sir— not just at this moment."

I knew he would discreetly question the Banes' servants. After a moment's silence I said, "I will speak plainly to you, Bogsley. I am concerned for his lordship's safety."

"Understandably so, sir."

"I will do my best to resolve this matter as soon as possible. In the meantime—"

"You may rely on me, sir—indeed, on all of us."

"For which I'm grateful. Please have a truckle bed placed in my room until we can make other arrangements. I need not add that I would prefer we do not alarm his lordship with our concern."

I thanked him again and fetched my nephew from the kitchen, where he was, as usual, being cosseted past redemption.

Charles, pleased that we would be sharing a room, nevertheless protested my plan to place him in my bed, while I slept on the truckle bed.

"But Charles," I said, "there are no bedcurtains on the truckle bed, and as you can see, there is a great deal of moonlight tonight."

He had no argument against this and thanked me politely before allowing me to tuck him in. "But keep the curtains open just a bit if you please. Then I shall know you are here, keeping me safe." So much, I thought, for hiding our concern.

I lay awake on the truckle-bed listening to his breathing settle into the rhythms of sleep. My feet suddenly felt a little cold, and then I heard a voice whisper, "Well done, Master Quakeboots."

I sat bolt upright. By the light of the moon I could make him out, a faint but definite image of my dead brother sitting at the foot of my bed.

My heart pounding, I opened my mouth to let out a cry, but I was frozen with fright.

"Please don't," he said. "I frightened Charles so badly early this evening I don't think I can forgive myself if I do so again. I cannot tell you how awful it is, Edward, to become a spectre of horror to those you love. It nearly puts me in sympathy with aunt Sophia, parading about without her wig."

I felt a giddy sensation but stopped myself short of laughing aloud. "By God, it *is* you!" I whispered.

"Lord Shivershanks, at your service." He gave his familiar little bow.

"Oh, Lucien, how I've missed you already! How shall we contrive to get along without you? Whatever possessed you to ride so carelessly?"

He gave me a look as cold as the winter night. "My dear Edward, do not be a sapskull! Would I have endangered my life—to say nothing of the future of that precious boy sleeping next to you? Carelessly tossed away my days with him? When since his arrival have you ever known me to take foolish chances?"

"Exactly my thoughts, Lucien, truly—"

"Yes, I heard you say so not long before I—well, I haven't completely departed, now have I?"

"How good it is to be able to speak to you again! But—is it terrible for you?"

"Not in the least—well, no, that isn't true. There are things that one longs for and can never have in this state, so one certainly feels a desire to—to get on with it, shall we say? As much as I am loath to leave you—and I promise you, I did my best to stay—now I feel something like a traveler who has harnessed his horses, placed his trunks on the coach, and climbed within—but sits in his own drive, not going forward."

"Not—not unsure of his destination!"

He laughed, and said, "Hardly gratifying that you have doubts! But you may be at ease on that score. I'm quite curious about the place, but my departure has been delayed. I gather I have some unfinished business here, and it isn't difficult to see what it is. First, we must find my murderer, for that person is threatening my son's life now that I am—supposedly—out of the way."

"Your murderer!" I said blankly.

"My dear Edward, have you not been attending?"

"The branch—"

"Was off the tree before it struck my head."

"But I saw the place on the tree where the branch had broken off. It was not cut clean, as it would have been if cut off the tree with an axe."

"I'm not saying my murderer was stupid. I'm only saying that the branch was already broken off the tree before it was applied—with some force—to my head."

"Then how—"

"I'm not sure of all the particulars, but I'll tell you what I do know. Examine Fine Lad, if you would, please—why are you looking so pale? You aren't going to faint on me, are you?"

"The horse—I almost had him shot."

He studied me for a moment, then said, "If I could have found a way to leave you without grief, Edward, I would have."

I could not speak.

"I take it the poor creature has not been sent to his equine reward?"

"No, I decided that I needed to think of Charles and not of killing horses or felling trees."

"Dependable Edward. I could not have left Charles in better hands. Still, what impressive vengeance you planned on my behalf! I'm touched, truly. Now—let us channel that determination toward saving my son."

"Yes. Tell me more about what happened to you—and your horse."

"I was about to slow him, knowing we were coming up to that tree, when something slowed him for me—rather abruptly. Without the least warning, Fine Lad—who is quite surefooted—stumbled hard near that tree. I flew from his back, landing flat on my face, the wind knocked out of me—disgraceful, but please note that I was still holding fast to the reins. I had slowly raised myself to my hands and knees—a bit unsteadily—when suddenly a cloaked figure stepped out of the trees and knocked me senseless with that blasted branch. Hurt like the very devil—briefly."

"A cloaked figure?"

"I'm afraid he was off to one side—the better to swing that branch, I suppose. All I saw were a pair of men's boots—rather expensive Hessians if I'm any judge—and the front of a large, black cloak. I was struck down before I saw a face, but I'd lay odds my attacker was wearing a mask."

I considered this. "Can you travel from The Abbey grounds?"

"I'm not sure. I can move within The Abbey and at least as far as where you were standing tonight. I'm rather new at this," he added apologetically.

"Were you in Charles's room when the fire started?"

"No, although—it's the strangest thing, Edward. I was merely looking in on him, watching him sleep, when I felt this urgent need to appear to him even though I knew it would scare him—as if it were so vital to awaken him I could not remain hidden."

"It was vital," I said. "Had he not come to me in the library, he might have perished in that bed."

"And Henry Bane would have become the Earl of Rolingbroke."

"Yes. But it was William whose coat smelled of smoke and showed signs of being singed."

"Hmm. How disappointing. William has actually spoken kindly to me once or twice in the past few years. But then, he needed to borrow money." He sighed. "He's not immediately in line for the title, but I suppose if two Rolingbrokes could be disposed of, Henry might have a short tenure as well."

"Who are you talking to?" a child's voice asked.

I looked in some dismay at Charles peering at me sleepily from the bed. I glanced toward Lucien, but he had disappeared.

"Myself, Charles."

"That's a loud one," he said, yawning.

"I beg your pardon?" I said, and thought I heard a ghostly chuckle near my ear.

But Charles had fallen asleep again, and though I whispered Lucien's name, he did not reappear that night.

Charles was still sleeping peacefully when I bestirred myself just before dawn the next morning. I awakened Fibbens, who gladly kept watch over him while I went to the stables. I went down the row of stalls until I came to that of Lucien's favorite, Fine Lad. An old groom was with the big dark bay, applying fomentations to his legs.

"I'm afraid he'll be scarred, sir," the old man said, showing me the horizontal cuts that neatly crossed the front of Fine Lad's forelegs. "But he should be right as rain otherwise."

"Those wounds—could they have led to the late earl's injuries?"

"I wondered about it, sir, and thought p'haps he'd been tripped up like. But then there was that branch, so I figgered our Fine Lad here hurt himself on the way home."

"Tell me—what do you mean, tripped up?"

"It's an old bad 'un's trick, sir—they puts a rope across the road."

"But the earl would have seen such a rope."

"Beggin' your pardon but no, sir. The way it works is, Mr. Thief finds a place near a tree like and ties th' rope around its trunk. Then he lays the rope across th' road, and covers it with leaves so it's hidden. Along comes a fine gentleman like our lordship. Mr. Thief waits until he's near abreast of 'im and yanks hard as hell— beggin' your pardon—he pulls it tight, see, and the horse can't stop nor mebbe even knows what's hit 'im, and while all's confusion, he coshes th' fine gentleman—if he ain't already knocked in the cradle by the fall. Then he robs him, and that's that."

"How do you know of this 'tripping up'? Has this ever happened near here before?"

"Oh, not near here, sir. But I remember it did happen to the earl's—beggin' your pardon—the late earl's uncle."

"Lord Alfred Bane?"

"Yes, sir. 'Is lordship's groom told me of it. Said that when 'is lordship were a young man, he was served just such a nasty trick and took an awful blow to the side of 'is brainbox—and that's how he went deaf in one ear, which is why 'is lordship was forever shouting. I used to hate it when that man came near our horses—his late lordship, I mean, no disrespect intended—but y'see, ours t'weren't used to all that shoutin' and carryin' on. So his groom tells me what happen'd t'him, and tells me that the robbers got to look nohow anyways 'cause Lord Bane hadn't more'n a few shillings on 'im, whilst they were caught and hanged, which is what they deserv'd."

I rode my own horse back to the place in the woods where I had found Lucien. I searched for a likely place for an ambush and found it just a few feet away. I did not find a rope, but one tree bore a mark on its trunk, a line that might have been made by a thin rope being pulled taut—and within the bark near that line I found strands of bristly fiber as from a cord or rope.

I searched the side of the path directly opposite as I might have searched for signs of an enemy's camp during the war. My search was rewarded—I discovered another tree, with similar marks and fibers, as well as a spot with a good view of the path, where sticks and leaves had been crushed. It was a place near a fallen log where fragments of brown shell told me that someone had eaten walnuts while he waited for the sound of an approaching rider, a place where someone's boots had made marks in the soft, damp earth.

I spent a little time also in studying a third tree—the tree that had supposedly caused Lucien's injury—and the place where its deadly branch had broken off. I rode my horse slowly down the path, halting in front of the tree, which allowed me an even better view of the point of breakage.

Back at The Abbey I again examined the branch. I spoke to Bogsley and two other servants before I went to my room and changed out of my riding clothes—which had become somewhat soiled during my explorations. I cleaned up in time to join Charles for breakfast. By then most of the family was in the breakfast room. Lady Bane—wearing a purple turban—declared that the previous evening's disturbance had quite ruined her appetite.

I thought Charles might make some remark about this, as her plate was quite full, but he seemed lost in his own thoughts, not even responding to her lecture about young children never being allowed to dine with their elders at Bane House. At one point he looked up and smiled and winked at me just as his father might have done. But before I could respond with more than an answering smile, my attention was drawn back to Lady Bane, who asked why I was smiling and if I thought fires in the middle of the night were amusing.

"Mother!" William said desperately, "Your breakfast grows cold. Do try to eat something."

She ignored him. She had other complaints to make and ended her lengthy list of criticisms by saying, "We are leaving immediately after breakfast, Edward, and I cannot tell you what a relief it will be!"

"I'm sure it defies description," I said.

She eyed me in an unfriendly manner but was distracted when William said, "I am staying—if it will not be an imposition, Edward?"

"Staying!" Lady Bane thundered. "Why?"

"To better acquaint myself with my cousin," he said.

"Edward is not your cousin!"

"I meant Cousin Charles," William said, then added, "And Edward, too, of course."

Henry, who entered the room at just that moment, said, "An excellent notion, William! I believe I will join you."

William seemed displeased but said nothing. There was no opportunity for him to speak. Lady Bane found their plans extremely objectionable. However, when Fanny said, "I'll leave with you, Mother," the matter was decided.

It was decided because Lady Bane, ever contrary, said, "No, I'll not have it said that I was backward in any attention due to my family. We'll all stay."

Into the awkward silence that met this decision came Charles's voice. "I wish to discuss a private matter with Uncle Edward," he said, then, frowning, added, "If you will excuse us, please?"

He took my hand and led me to the library. He closed the doors, then said, "All right, Papa!"

"Excellent, youngster!" Lucien said. "My son, as you can see, Edward, is a stout-hearted fellow."

"I've known that for some time now," I said.

"He whispered to me during breakfast!" Charles said gleefully. "He was with me while you were out riding this morning."

"And Fibbens?"

"I believe he has recovered from his initial shock," my brother said. "I've asked him to break it gently to Bogsley."

" 'Zooks, Lucien! Is this wise?"

"I'd prefer they knew rather than come across me, er—accidentally. Fibbens will be here shortly to take Charles through one of the passages to the servants' quarters. Charles will be my ambassador."

"That means I'm going to tell them *I'm* not scared of Papa, so then they won't be either. I'm helping."

"Yes," I said, "you are."

As soon as Fibbens—amazingly at home with members of the spirit world, it seemed to me—had led Charles from the room, I told Lucien what I had learned. He listened thoughtfully.

"I took another look at the branch this morning," I said. "I realized that the bloodstains were on a section of the branch that you could not have struck with your head while riding, a part of the branch that was too close to the trunk of the tree—close to where it broke off from the trunk."

"A part of the branch much thicker, I suppose, than the section I would have struck if I *had* ridden into it."

"Yes. The Banes undoubtedly heard the story of their father's encounter with ruffians many times. And of the persons currently staying or working at The Abbey, only the Banes and their personal servants would not know that Charles prefers his chambers to be darkened."

"It could be one of the Banes' servants, I suppose," Lucien said, and I did not miss the note of hopefulness in his voice.

"No servant would gain from your death, Lucien. I don't like the idea of scandal in the family any more than you do, but Charles is very young, and by the time he is in society, this will be long forgotten."

Lucien gave a bitter laugh. "Murder is unlikely to pass so quickly from even the *haut ton's* collection of shallow minds. But for no, our first thoughts must be for Charles's safety."

"Yes."

"So it's a Bane," he said. "I don't believe it was Lady Bane—she would have made sure her wig was on."

I laughed. "Nor can I picture her waiting patiently in the woods or wearing Hessians."

"But now what?"

"I'm not certain which of the three 'thatchgallows,' as you once called them, it is."

"Surely not Fanny?"

"I would have ruled her out until you told me of the boots. She was wearing a pair of them last night—and William and Henry were each already wearing their own. She's strong. And remember how she used to spy on us?"

"But what would she have to gain?"

"I don't know. Does she bear you any grudge?"

"Nothing to signify." He couldn't exactly blush, but he was obviously embarrassed.

I raised a brow. "She had a *tendre* for you?"

"She believed we ought to marry. It was certainly not out of affection—it was a stupid idea placed in her head by her pushing mama. Aunt Sophia also tried to persuade my father that I should marry Fanny, but he was opposed—said he had seen at least three bad results of a marriage of first cousins. Alfred Bane was their first cousin, you will remember. Aunt Sophia was quite insulted, and nothing was said for years, but shortly after he died—let us say I told them I would respect my father's wishes on the matter. When I became a widower, I almost thought Fanny would raise the subject again, but I think the notion of being stepmama to Charles put an end to her pursuit. Now—let's look at Henry and William, then. William's coat reeked of smoke."

"According to Fibbens, William did attempt to help put out the fire. But since he was not trained in one of your drills, he was more a nuisance than a help, and Bogsley, in his inimitable Bogsley way, persuaded him to leave before he caused harm. Still, how did he find out about the fire so much sooner than the others?"

"And Henry?"

"Supposedly drunk."

"Supposedly?"

"Oh, several bottles of your finest port are missing."

"Charles's port! But you sound as if you doubt Henry drank them."

"I'm not sure. I find myself wondering where the empty bottles are and why, at breakfast this morning, he did not appear to be suffering any ill effects after such a binge."

"A veteran drinker might be able to manage both the bottles and the morning."

"True. And since I have long avoided the Banes, I have no idea if our cousin is a souse or abstemious."

"Which leaves us where we started."

"Do you know, this morning I found myself thinking like a soldier for the first time in a long time."

"Meaning?"

"We must use strategy, Lucien. And I believe we would do well to take the offensive rather than wait for the murderous Bane to make another attempt on Charles's life."

"Ah!" he said, smiling. "You want to set a trap."

"Yes. We will each have a role—including Charles. Do you suppose, dear Lucien, that you could play the part of a headless monk?"

Act I, Scene I, took place just outside the morning room door. Lucien told us that Henry had settled into a chair before the fire to read a newspaper there, thus determining where we must stage our play. Charles proved to be his father's equal as an actor. He acted out a perfect tantrum, with Fibbens providing able support.

"There's no such thing as ghosts!" Charles shouted angrily.

"Perhaps not, your lordship," Fibbens said anxiously, "but the north tower is dangerous. Your father meant to undertake repairs but—"

"*I'm* not afraid. It's *my* treasure!"

"Not so loud, please, your lordship!" Fibbens said, knowing perfectly well that Henry Bane was undoubtedly pressing his ear to the door.

"Uncle Edward knows how to find it." Charles declared. "We're going treasure hunting!"

"Not with a houseful of guests, your lordship. It would be—er, impolite."

That was my cue. "Charles, Charles! Are you talking that treasure nonsense again?" I asked. After a brief pause I said, "Fibbens, I believe I will need my heavier cloak—and his lordship will need his own as well."

"Yes, sir," Fibbens said and, treading heavily, left the hallway.

"Charles, what have I told you about the treasure?"

"That we will find it tonight because you promised Papa you would show me where it is."

"Yes. And what else?"

"Not to tell the Banes. But Fibbens isn't the Banes."

"Fibbens is entirely trustworthy, but you never know who might be listening. So please don't discuss it with anyone else. Now, here's Fibbens with our cloaks. Have you your gloves? Excellent. Let's go for our walk."

Two slight variations on this performance were given—one for the benefit of Fanny and one for William.

Only Lady Bane seemed to enjoy a normal appetite at dinner that evening. Charles kept looking conspiratorially at me, which required no real acting.

Lucien's role was proving the most difficult. To our dismay he could not move objects, and any attempt to dress him in something other than the riding clothes he had been wearing on the day of his accident met with utter failure. Bogsley had unearthed the old headless abbot—the one the village seamstress had manufactured for that long ago Christmas haunting. It was losing its stuffing and looked a little aged, but we only needed the robe itself. When Lucien tried to put it on, however, it simply fell to the ground.

Making the best of what he could do, he practiced materializing and soon had the knack of partial materialization. "I do so hate the prospect of being dead from the neck up," he said when he'd managed to appear before us without a head. Charles, who had been rather thrilled with our story of swinging the "headless monk" past the Banes' windows, asked the housekeeper if it might be possible to repair it. She stuffed a few pillows into the old costume, and our headless abbot had yet another round of life. Before falling asleep Charles enjoyed playing with this large, if rather gruesome, doll.

"Boys is all alike" was the housekeeper's assessment, with a nod toward Lucien and me.

At ten o'clock that evening I awakened Charles from his brief slumbers. Bundled up in warm clothing, we carried shielded lanterns as we went through one of the secret passages to the North Tower. The tower was built into the rise on which The Abbey stood. Perhaps at one time, it had indeed towered over the castle that had been here, but very little of the castle remained. Now the only apparent entrance to the tower was near the top of what remained of it—the tower was more akin to a well than a tower: more of it was reached by descending a staircase than by climbing. It was dank, musty smelling, and of no practical use.

I knew of no Rolingbroke who would dream of tearing it down.

After the treasure story had been spread about, Fibbens, several footmen, and other servants had taken turns keeping an eye on the Banes. None of them had yet been seen at the only tower entrance—the only entrance they would know of.

In addition to that entrance, there were two means of reaching the tower by secret passage. The one we were in ended on a sturdy, wide, stone platform, about halfway up (or down, as it seemed) the tower. Above us a relatively new wooden staircase led to the usual tower entrance, off one of The Abbey hallways. Below us, at the foot of a crumbling stone staircase, was the other secret passage. As boys, Lucien and I had explored it, half-hoping, half-dreading we'd encounter the Headless Abbot. We found damp stones and little else.

Charles and I waited in relative comfort, hidden from view, our lantern shielded. We soon knew who the first of our arrivals would most likely be— Lucien came to report that within a few minutes of one another Henry and Fanny had each softly knocked at the door to my room and peered inside. They had then hurried back to their own rooms.

But it was William who opened the door at the top of the stairs, carrying a candle. He was halfway down the stairs when the door opened a second time. He turned to see Fanny. "What on earth are you doing here?" he asked her.

"I might ask the same of you."

"I'm looking for Henry. Do you know where he is?"

"I haven't the vaguest. Where are Edward and the brat?"

In the darkness of our hiding place I laid a finger to Charles's lips. He nodded his understanding.

"How should I know?"

"I should have known it was all a Banbury tale," she said.

"What are you talking about?"

"Don't try to gammon me, dear brother. You're here looking for the treasure, too!"

"I'm not worried about any treasure—"

"Not worried about any treasure! That's a loud one! You who've been punting on River Tick for I don't know how long!"

"If Mama could hear you using such terms—"

"Mama is sound asleep. Go on, deny that you're one step ahead of the bailiff."

"All right, I deny it. I'm not in debt. I've come about—thanks to Cousin Lucien."

"What!"

"I never told you or Henry, but it's true. He helped me, Fanny."

"Why you?"

"Because he cared about the family, bacon-brain! Wasn't just the money—he talked to me. Made me think, I tell you. So anyone planning further mischief around here will have to come through me. I was too late for Lucien, and last night I was sure I was too late to help Charles. But now I've caught you, and I tell you I won't allow it!"

"Help Charles? Mischief? What on earth are you talking about?"

"My horse is in the stall next to Fine Lad. I think you know what that means."

"That he's eating his head off at his lordship's expense."

"Fanny!"

She eyed him malevolently.

"Enough of your nonsense, William. Let me by. Edward and the brat will be here any minute—probably working their way through the secret passage now."

"Secret passage!" William said. "What secret passage?"

"The place is full of them. Don't you remember my telling you so when we were down here that last Christmas?"

William frowned. "No."

"Well, maybe I told Henry, then. Which is of no importance in any case! Move off this staircase before I have to shove you off!"

"Touch me, and I'll tell Mama that nothing pleases her spinster daughter so much as to dress up like a man and ride astride!"

"Oh! You won't be alive to tell her! They'll burying you next to Lucien!"

*"Now!"* I heard Lucien say, and I pulled the shield off the lantern.

The sudden light caught the attention of the two Banes. But it was Lucien who caused William to give out a bloodcurdling scream.

Charles clung to me, apparently more frightened by the scream than anything that had gone before.

"Lord Almighty!" Fanny said. "You frightened the life right out of me. What's gotten into you! You'll bring the whole house down on us!"

William, the color gone from his face, pointed a shaking hand toward Lucien.

"What?" Fanny said. "Speak up, now!"

"The Headless Abbot."

"Headless Abbot! I don't see any Headless Abbot! It's just a light coming from one of those passages I told you about."

"Don't you see him?" William cried. "In riding clothes!"

"Are you back to giving me trouble over that? What's it to you if I find men's clothes more sensible for riding?"

Lucien tried moving closer to her. But while William swayed on his feet, Fanny was oblivious to him.

"William?" she said. "Are you feeling quite the thing?"

In frustration Lucien materialized completely.

"Lucien!" William said and fainted. Unfortunately, he was still on the stairs when this happened. Lucien tried to make a grab for him, but William fell right through him, tumbling down to the ledge.

Now Fanny screamed, but obviously she still could not see my brother.

"Fibbens, please take his lordship to safety," I said over Charles's protests. "Ask Bogsley to bring some men with a litter to me." And picking up a lantern, I limped out as quickly as I could to the landing, where William lay in a heap.

"Edward!" Fanny called, hurrying down the stairs and straight through Lucien without so much as a blink, "Oh, help him, Edward!"

She stood nervously watching me. William made a groaning sound and opened his eyes. "Edward?" he said dazedly. "Was it you all along?"

He then caught sight of Lucien standing behind me, though, and fainted once again.

I did my best to make him more comfortable. "Help will be here soon, Fanny," I said.

"He's broken his arm," Lucien said, "but I don't think he has any more serious injuries. Why do you suppose he could see me but she can't?"

"I don't understand it," I said.

Fanny, thinking I spoke to her, said, "Well! I understand it! It's all because of Lucien's stupid story about the monk. He thought he saw the ghost. Just your lantern light, I daresay."

We heard a sound then, a faint cracking noise from below.

Fanny's face grew pale. "The abbot!" she said weakly.

"Henry," I called, "are you down there in the dark eating walnuts?"

A long laugh echoed up the tower.

"Henry!" Fanny exclaimed.

"Get help," I said to Lucien.

"I'll stay here, thank you," Fanny replied. "Besides, you said help is already on the way."

"Oh, it is, dear Fanny, it is!" Henry said, lighting a lantern. He started up the stone stairs. "Where's Charles?"

Lucien made a wild banshee sound and swooped toward Henry. Nothing.

"Never mind the brat," Fanny said impatiently. "Here's your brother broken to bits!"

"I wouldn't trouble yourself too much over William, Fanny," Henry said. "He discovered my little plan, so I think it's best if the next accident concerning an earl has something to do with trying to save my brother. Edward and Charles make a valiant, combined effort. Alas, it will be unsuccessful."

"Will no one talk sense to me?" Fanny asked.

"Your brother Henry wants to be an earl," I said. "So he murdered Lucien—right, Lucien?"

"Right."

But Henry laughed and said, "Don't tell me you think you can try that ghost business on me at this age, Edward! Now where's that treasure? I warn you, I'm armed."

"You'll never own The Abbey's treasure," I said. "The Abbey's treasure then, as it is now, was in the good men who have lived here—Lucien and his father and Charles."

"Henry," Fanny said, "tell me you didn't harm Lucien!"

"Lucien? Oh, not just Lucien. Don't forget his father and his ninnyhammer of a stepmother—you didn't think that carriage overturned by chance?" I heard the sound of rock falling, and Henry said, "When I am earl, I shall have these steps repaired."

"You'll never be earl!" Lucien vowed.

I heard a commotion in the passageway. Fibbens' voice was calling desperately, "Your lordship, no!"

Suddenly a white, headless figure with a bloodstained cassock came barreling onto the landing. Fanny, who did not see me grab hold of the small boy who carried it, let out the fourth scream to assault my ears in nearly as many minutes.

Lucien grabbed the pillow ghost, and went flying off the landing. Literally. Previously unable to support it, this time—perhaps somehow strengthened by his need to protect Charles—he was able to make the Headless Abbot billow impressively and to aim it directly at Henry Bane. Henry fired his pistol at it, but the stuffed costume came at him inexorably and knocked him from the stone stairs. His fall was harder than William's, and fatal.

I called to Lucien, but he had disappeared.

Two weeks later, William, recovered enough to be moved, left with his sister and the much quieter dowager for Bane House. They wanted to be home in time for Christmas, which was drawing near. William and his sister were getting along fairly well by then—as we all were—and none of us told the dowager about her daughter's clothing preferences. Although a scandal of a far more serious nature had been avoided, both Henry's duplicity and his death had left Lady Bane shaken.

But even with the Banes gone and the immediate crisis over, I was feeling dismal, as was Charles. One night he came to the library at midnight, upset—not because he saw a ghost, but because it had been so long since he *had* seen one. I tried to explain his father's traveling coach analogy, but Charles wanted that coach to return. "At least for visits," he said tearfully.

I took out the packet of letters again, and read to him—this time, the letter Lucien had written to me on the death of his wife.

"I used to be able to picture her so clearly after she was gone," a familiar voice said. "To feel her watching over Charles and me, sharing our joys. Do you know, I believe I now know why Fanny and Henry couldn't see me but you who've loved me can?"

"Papa!" Charles cried out.

"Yes, my boy, I'm back—for a visit."

Gradually, over the years, we saw less and less of him. By the time Charles had grown into a man, it was no longer necessary to trouble Lucien to be our ghost. By then we knew how to recall his spirit in other ways—through fond remembrance, and the knowledge that we can never be truly parted from those we love.

And that, I've come to believe, is the true spirit of Christmas.

# Doug Allyn

## The Country of the Blind

DOUG ALLYN is not only one of our most prolific short story writers but one of our best, as his Edgar Award for best short story of 1994 with "The Dancing Bear" and several Edgar nominations demonstrate. He is also a first-rate novelist, with books such as *Motown Underground* and *Icewater Mansions* proving that the dazzle of his short stories can also be found in his longer works. His series character, the bard Tallifer, makes another welcome appearance in our year-end collection in "The Country of the Blind," solving a tale of children lost and hope regained in the Scottish Highlands in the Middle Ages. This story first appeared in *Murder Most Medieval*.

# The Country
# of the Blind

*Doug Allyn*

I've never much cared for my own singing. Oh, I carry a tune well enough, and my tenor won't scare hogs from a trough, but as a minstrel, I would rate my talent as slightly above adequate. Which is a pity, since I sing for my living nowadays.

As a young soldier I sang for fun, bellowing ballads with my mates on battlements or around war fires, amusing each other and showing our bravery, though I usually sang loudest when I was most afraid.

The minstrel who taught me the finer points of the singer's art had a truly fine voice, dark and rich as brown ale. Arnim O'Beck was no barracks room balladeer; he was a Meistersinger, honored with a medallion by the Minstrel Guild at York.

An amiable charmer, Arnim could easily have won a permanent position in a noble house, but he preferred the itinerant life of the road, trading doggerel tunes in taverns for wine and the favors of women.

My friend ended dead in a cage of iron, dangling above the village gate of Grahmsby-on-Tweed with ravens picking his poor bones. I hadn't bawled since my old ma died, but I shed tears for Arnim, though I knew damned well he would have laughed to see it. In truth, he ended as we'd both known he would.

But it wasn't only for my friend that I cried. I was a soldier long years before I became a singer. Death has brushed past me many times to hack down my friends or brothers-in-arms.

I mourned them, but I never felt their passing had dimmed the light of the world. A soldier's life counts for little, even in battle. His place in the line will be filled.

But when a minstrel like Arnim dies, we lose his voice and all the songs in his memory. And in these dark times, with the Lionheart abroad, Prince John on his throne, and the Five Kings contending in Scotland, this sorry world needs songs to remind us of ancient honor all the more.

My friend the Meistersinger knew more ballads of love and sagas of heroes than any minstrel I've ever known.

But even he was not the best singer I ever heard. . . .

•   •   •

I'd been waiting out a gray week of Scottish drizzle, singing for sausages in a God-cursed log hovel of an alehouse at the rim of the Bewcastle wastes. If the muddy little village had a name, I never heard it nor did I inquire. I was more concerned with getting out of it alive.

The tumbledown tavern had too many customers. Clearly there was no work to be found in the few seedy wattle and daub huts of the town, yet a half dozen hard-bitten road wolves were drinking ale in the corner away from the fire. They claimed to be a crew of thatchers, but their battle scars and poorly hidden dirks revealed them for what they were: soldiers who'd lost their positions. Or deserted them. Men whose only skill was killing.

Bandits.

Ordinarily, outlaws pose no problem for me. Everyone knows singers seldom have a penny, and brigands enjoy a good song as readily as honest folk. If I culled the gallows-bait from my audiences, I'd sing to damned skimpy crowds indeed. But along the Scottish borderlands, thieves are more desperate. And as ill luck would have it, I had some money. And they knew it.

I'd earned a small purse of silver performing at a fest in the previous town. One of the border rats jostled me, purposely I think. Hearing the clink of coins, he hastily turned away. But not before I glimpsed my death in his eyes.

And so we played a game of patience, whiling away the hours, waiting for the rain to end. And with it, my life and possibly the innkeeper's. Cutthroats like this lot would leave no witness to sing them to a gallows tree.

My best hope was sleep. Theirs. And so I strummed my lute softly, murmuring every soothing lullaby I could remember. And praying they would nod off long enough to give me a running start.

And then I heard it. I was humming a wordless tune when an angel's voice joined my own in perfect harmony, singing high and clear as any Gregorian gelding.

Startled, I stopped playing, but the melody continued. For a moment I thought it was a voice from heaven calling me to my final journey. Then the innkeeper, a burly oaf with a black bush of a beard, cursed sharply and ended the song.

"Who was that singing?" I asked.

"My evil luck," he groused. "A nun."

"A nun? In this place?"

"Well, an apprentice nun anyway, a novice or whatever they're called. There were a fire at the abbey at Lachlan Cul, twenty mile north. Most died, but one aud bitch nun stumbled here with her charge before death took her, saddling me with yon useless girl."

"She has a wonderful voice."

"It's nought to me. I've no ear for song, and my customers don't care much for hymns. She's heaven's curse on me, I swear. She's blind, no good for work, nor much inclined to it neither."

"Bring her out, I would like to hear her sing more."

"Nay," he muttered, glancing sidelong at the louts in the corner. "That's a bad lot there. I'll not risk harm coming to a nun under my roof. My luck's foul enough as 'tis."

"I'm sure you're wrong about those fellows," I said a bit louder. "I have plenty of money, and they've not troubled me. Buy them an ale, and bring the girl out to sing for us. I'll pay." I tossed a coin on the counter, snapping the thieves to full alert.

The innkeeper eyed me as though I'd grown a second head, but he snatched up the coin readily enough. Brushing aside the ratty blanket that separated his quarters from the tavern, he thrust a scrawny sparrow of a girl into the room. Sixteen or so, she was clad in a grimy peasant's shift, slender as a riding crop with a narrow face, her eyes wrapped in a gauze bandage.

"What's your name, girl?"

"Noelle," she said, turning her face to the sound of my voice. The landlord was right to worry. She was no beauty, but she'd pass for fair with the grime wiped away.

"Noelle? You're French?"

"No, the sisters told me I was born at Yuletide."

"Ah, and so you were named Noelle for Christmas, and your holiday gift was your lovely voice."

"You're the singer, aren't you?" she asked with surprising directness. She hadn't the mousy manner of a nun. "What are you called?"

"Tallifer, miss. Of Shrewsbury and York; minstrel, poet, and storyteller."

"I've been listening to you. You seem to know a great many songs."

"I've picked up a tune or two in my travels. Most aren't fit for the ears of a nun, I'm afraid. Nor is it proper for you to stay at an alehouse. There is an abbey a few days to the west. I'll escort you there if you like."

"Hold on," the innkeeper began, "I shan't let—"

"Come now, friend, the girl can't remain here, and I need a good deed to redeem my misspent life. I'll pay for the privilege." Pulling the purse from beneath my jerkin, I spilled the coins in a heap on the table. "Consider this as heaven's reward for your kindness to this poor waif. Have we a bargain?"

Stunned, the innkeeper stared at me, than hastily glanced at the crew in the corner. Their eyes were locked on the silver like hounds pointing a hare.

"There's no point in haggling," I continued. "Search me if you like, but I haven't one penny more. Come girl, we'd best be going."

"But it's still raining," the innkeeper protested, eyeing the outlaws, afraid of being left alone with them. "Surely you'll wait for better weather?"

"Nay, I've no money to pay for your hospitality now, and I wouldn't dream of imposing further. Has she any belongings?"

"Belongings? Nay, she—"

"This will do for a cloak then," I said, ripping the blanket from the doorway, draping it about her. Snatching up my lute, I paused at the door long enough for a 'God bless all here,' then I dragged the girl out into the drizzle. But after a few paces she pulled free of my grasp, whirling to face me, her narrow jaw thrust forward.

"Kill me here. Please."

"What?"

"If you mean to dishonor me, then kill me now where I can be buried decently. Sister Adela warned me about men like you."

"And rightly so, but I'm no one to fear. I'm old enough to be your father, girl. I was a soldier once, and I swear my oath to God I mean you no harm. Unfortunately, I can't swear the same for that lot back there. We've got to get away from here and quickly, or we'll both be dead."

"Then stop pulling me along like a puppy. I can walk. Fetch me a slender stick."

Cursing, I hastily cut an alder limb, and she used it as a cane to feel for obstructions in her path. Though she stumbled occasionally, she had no trouble maintaining my pace. Coltish legs, young and supple.

We marched steadily through the afternoon, moving north on a rutted cart track through the forest. Tiring as dusk approached, I began casting about for shelter.

"Why are we slowing?" Noelle asked.

"It'll be dark soon."

"Darkness is nothing to me. Continue on if you like."

"No need. The rain will wash out our tracks, and they may not follow us at all. If I can find a copse of cedar—"

"That way." She pointed off to our left. "There's a cedar grove over there."

She was right. Peering through the misty drizzle, I spied a stand of cedars some twenty yards off the path.

"How could you know that?"

"Scent. We've passed cedars several times in the last hour, though the wood around us is mostly alder, yew, and ash. Each has their own savor. Gathering osier wands for baskets was my task at the abbey. I often did it alone."

Taking her hand, I threaded my way through the brush to a cedar copse with a soft bed of leaves beneath and heavy boughs above that kept it relatively dry. I cut a few fronds to make our beds, then used flint and steel to kindle a small fire.

Leaving Noelle to warm herself, I scouted about and found a dead ash tree with a straight limb as thick as my wrist. Twenty minutes whittling with my dirk produced a usable quarterstaff, a peasant's pike.

Returning to the fire, I was greeted by the heavenly scent of roasting meat. Noelle was holding two thick blood sausages over the fire on the end of a stick, sizzling fat dripping into the flames.

"You came well prepared," I observed, sliding a sausage off the spit, blowing on it til it cooled enough to chew.

"In the country of the blind, one learns to cope."

"But surely you were well treated at the convent?"

"They were kind, but their lives were so . . . stifling. I was always pestering new novitiates for songs they knew and news of the outside world. Have you traveled far?"

"Too far. From London to Skye and back again many times, first as a soldier, now a singer."

"Would you sing something for me? A song of some faraway place?"

"Is France distant enough?" Sliding my lute from its sheepskin bag, I tuned it and began the "Song of Roland," a war ballad from the days of mighty Charlemagne. In the streets or a stronghold, I sing it lustily, but huddled near the fire as dusk settled on the wood, I sang softly. For Noelle only.

A dozen verses into the ballad, she raised her hand.

"Stop a moment, please." And then she sang it back to me, echoing my every word, every inflection in her crystalline angel's voice, ending the refrain at the same place I had.

"Sing on, girl. Your voice does wonders for that song."

"I can't. I've ne'er heard that tune before, and I can only memorize a dozen or so verses at a time. But at the end I'll remember it all."

"Truly? You can learn an entire ballad with one hearing?"

"There are no books or signposts in my country. Memory is everything. Sister Adela said Homer was blind, yet he sang ballads of ten thousand verses."

"Homer?"

"A poet, a Greek I think."

"I know who Homer was. I was bodyguard to the young Duke of York during his schooldays at London. I'm just surprised that nuns study Homer."

"I'm not a nun. I was a ward of the convent, a lodger. I had my own quarters and Sister Adela to teach me and help me get about."

"How long were you there?"

"Always," she said simply. "My whole life."

"But no bairns are born in convents. Where are your parents? Your home?"

"The convent was my home," she said, with a flash of anger. "They had other guests, an idiot girl and a boy so deformed he had to be wheeled about in a barrow. If I had parents, I know nothing of them, nor care to. In the country of the blind all men are handsome, all ladies lovely."

"But all is in darkness?"

"Not all, I can see the changes 'tween day and night readily enough and some colors and shapes, though not clearly. I wear this ribbon to spare confusion and let my other senses compensate. That's how I knew the cedar was near. And that someone is coming now."

"What? Where?"

"Behind us, on the track we left."

"I hear nothing."

"Sight is no help in the dark. He's on horseback, moving slowly."

"I hadn't counted on horses," I said, rising, seizing my cudgel. "The louts from the inn—"

"No," Noelle said positively. "There were no horses at that place. And I hear only one animal now."

And then I heard it as well, the soft *tlot, tlot* of hooves on the muddy trail. Then they stopped.

Silence. Only the drip of the rain.

"Hellooo, the fire," a voice called. "I'm a traveler, wet and in need of direction. I have food to share. May I approach?"

"Come ahead, and welcome," I replied, moving into the shadows.

He walked in warily, leading his animal, a plowhorse from the look of it. Our visitor had much the same look. Heavily built, stooped from farm work, his face was obscured by the cowl of his rough woolen cloak. He appeared to be unarmed, though with his cloak pulled tight I couldn't be sure. I stepped out to face him, quarterstaff in hand.

"God bless all here," he said, glancing about. "I'm John of Menteith, a reeve for Lord Duart. No need for that stick, friend. I mean no man harm."

"You're far from Menteith," I said.

"Aye," he nodded, warming his hands at the fire, "I'm bound for the fair at

Grahmsby. Hope to trade this sorry nag for a bullock and a few cups of ale. Who might you folk be?"

"Tallifer of York," I said. "Traveling to Strathclyde with my daughter."

"A blind girl, by chance?"

Sweeping off his cloak, he revealed a sword, a crude blade, standard issue at any barracks.

His bush of a beard split in a gap-toothed grin. "Drop the stick, fellow, or I'll cleave you in two."

If he expected me to wet myself or scamper off, he was disappointed. I've seen blades before; I've even faced one or two with nought in my hand but sweat. I had a stout cudgel and Menteith had the look of a farmer, big but clumsy. I waited.

So did he. His eyes flicked from me to Noelle and back again. He licked his lips, unnerved by our stillness, gathering himself. Then with a roar, he lunged at me, swinging his blade like a field sickle.

He'd have done better with a sickle. Jabbing the cudgel butt between his shins, I sent him sprawling into the fire. He moved quickly for a big man, though. Rolling with the fall, he scrambled clear of the flames, crouching on the far side, panting.

Unable to tell what was amiss, Noelle stood frozen as Menteith began sidling around the fire toward her. I thought he meant to seize her as a shield. I was wrong. Eyes wild, he charged again, this time at Noelle!

He was almost on her, blade raised high to hack her down, when I rammed the pole hard into his gut, doubling him over. Gasping, he staggered back, slashing at me. A mistake. Blocking a blow with one end of my staff, I swept the other around full force, catching him squarely on his bull neck just below the ear.

He stared at me a moment, surprised. Then his eyes rolled up like a hog on a hook, and he toppled backward into the fire. I stood over him, taut as a drawn bow, ready to finish him if he moved. But even the flames couldn't rouse him.

Kicking the blade out of his fist, I prodded him out of the fire with my staff.

"Tallifer? What's happened?"

"Our guest had no manners, and it worked out poorly for him. Do you have any idea who he might be?"

"I've ne'er heard his voice before. Why?"

"He seems an unlikely thief. He was armed with a yeoman's blade, but he was no soldier."

"He said he was a reeve, perhaps he spoke true. He smells of cattle."

"He fought like one, all bull, no skill. He was definitely seeking us, though. He knew you were blind though he could see neither of us clearly."

"I don't understand."

"Nor do I, yet. I'll persuade him to explain when he wakes."

But he didn't wake. As I stripped off his belt to tie his hands, his head flopped unnaturally. I checked his pupils. Dead as a goose on Saint Margaret's Day.

"God's bodkin," I said softly.

"What is it?"

"The bastard's dead. Damn me, I didn't think I hit him that hard. And damn him for an inconsiderate lout. Not only does he keep his secrets, I'll have to haul his useless carcass into the wood. We don't want him found near our camp."

After dragging his dead weight for what seemed like a mile, I used his sword to dig a shallow grave, rolled the reeve in it, and threw his blade in after him. Weapons are outlawed for common folk in Scotland and the sword surely hadn't done the reeve much good. His purse held a few shillings, fair payment for a burial.

I slept poorly, restless from the fight and the death of the reeve. As a soldier I was no hero. I fought for my life and my friends, killed when I had to but took no satisfaction in it. In battle I was always afraid. And afterward, though I survived, I knew how easily it could have been me bleeding out while my enemies divided my gear and had a drink on my luck.

The reeve's death was doubly troubling, though. He was no vagrant bandit. Only a fool travels this country at night, yet he'd arrived at our camp well after dark. He must have been hunting us though I couldn't imagine why.

Had the cutthroats from the inn set him on us? Unlikely. Why hire out work they could easily do themselves?

Odder still, in the midst of the fight, he'd lunged at Noelle when she was clearly no threat. It made no sense. Unless she was the one he came for, and I was just in his way. But who would kill a blind nun?

"Tallifer? Are you awake?"

"Yes."

The fire had burned to embers, and her face was only a vague shape in the shadows. As all faces were in her world.

"I've been thinking. You can't leave me at an abbey."

"Why not?"

"Without money to pay for my lodging, they won't accept me."

"How were your expenses paid before?"

"I don't know, by a kinsman, I suppose. It was a private arrangement with the abbess and she was lost in the fire. I have an idea, though."

"Such as?"

"Take me with you," she said in a rush. "I can earn my way. I sing fairly well and you can teach me to—"

"It's out of the question. Life on the road is too hard; it's nothing for a girl."

"All roads are hard in the country of the blind. I heard you breathing heavily this afternoon, when I could have walked another day without tiring. I can carry burdens, wash clothes. I'll be your woman if you want."

"My what? Good lord, Noelle, what do you know of being a woman?"

"The novitiates seldom talked of anything else, and I know a few songs of love."

"I know songs about dragons, girl, but I can't breathe fire. And I'm much too old for you anyway."

"I wouldn't know."

"Yes, you would. Trust me on that."

"You don't want me? Am I too plain, then? Or does my blindness offend you?"

"Neither, but—"

"Then what is it? You've saved my life twice. Why did you bother if you mean to cast me off?"

"Noelle—"

"A minstrel came to the abbey once. He had a little dog who danced when he played the fife. I can't dance, but I can sing a bit. And I promise to be no more trouble than a little dog. Please, Tallifer."

"Enough!" I said, throwing up my hands. "The sun is rising and we'd best be away from here. We'll talk more of this later."

But we didn't talk. We sang instead. We took turns riding the reeve's mount, entertaining each other, with Noelle memorizing each ballad I sang, then vastly improving it with her marvelous voice.

I skirted the next few hamlets, afraid the reeve's horse might be recognized. But in the first town of any size, I found a tailor and squandered our inheritance to buy Noelle a decent traveling garment.

After the measurements, Noelle and the tailor's wife disappeared into the family quarters for a final fitting. I waited with the tailor, exchanging news of the road and the town. And then Noelle stepped out.

The dress wasn't fancy. It had no need to be. In pale blue woolsey, and with her face scrubbed and shining, my grimy foundling was transformed. And I was lost.

The tailor's wife had replaced her blindfold with a blue ribbon that matched the dress. She was a vision as lovely as the damsels of a thousand ballads. But no mirror could ever tell her so.

My throat swelled and I could not speak. Mistaking my silence for displeasure, the tailor's wife frowned.

"If the color is too dark—"

"No," I managed. "It's perfect. Wonderful. No man ever had a more lovely—daughter."

And so it seemed. Born restless, I've never had a family of my own nor much felt the lack. Yet after a few weeks with Noelle I could scarce remember life without her.

As summer faded into autumn, we worked our way southwest toward the border, singing for our supper. And prospering.

My performances have always been well received, but Noelle brought freshness and sparkle to songs I'd sung half my life, her youth and zest a sprightly contrast to my darker presence.

Audiences responded to her and she to them, basking in the applause like a blossom in the sun. The waif from the convent was fast becoming an assured young beauty. And though she never raised the subject of being more than a daughter to me again, neither was she interested in the young bloods who lingered after our performances to chat her up.

She was always courteous but never a whit more than polite as she dismissed them. When I asked why she showed no curiosity about boys, she replied that they were exactly that. Boys. For now, the music and freedom of her new life were more than enough. She'd never been happier.

Nor had I. The last large town we worked was Strathclyde, a performance in the laird's manor house for his family and kinsmen that was well received. Afterward, his steward offered us a year's position in his household as resident artists.

A month earlier I'd have leapt at the chance, but no more.

I've always felt comfortable amongst Scots. Their rough humor and love of battle songs suits both my art and my temperament, but Noelle was changing that.

As her talent and skills improved, I noted the magical effect her singing had on village folk and was certain she could charm larger, more worldly audiences south of the Roman walls just as easily. Newcastle, York, perhaps even in London itself.

For the first time in years I allowed myself to consider the future. We could become master minstrels, winning acclaim and moving in finer circles than either of us had known before.

But to reach that future, we'd have to survive the present. There are always rumors of war in the Scottish hills, but I was seeing more combatants than usual, not only Scots and their Irish cousins, but also hard-bitten mercenaries from France and Flanders.

In earlier years I would have been pleased at the chance to entertain soldiers far from home with fat purses and dim futures. Lonely troops are an amiable audience, easily pleased and generous with applause and coins.

But I had a daughter to worry about now. So after politely declining the steward's offer, we began working our way south toward the border and England. Perhaps we could even journey to my family home at Shrewsbury after long years.

Traveling was a pure pleasure now, singing through the lowlands, describing the folk and the scenery to a girl who savored every phrase like fine wine. My sole regret was that Noelle remained in her country of the blind and I could do nothing to light her way out.

But there is little difference between a lass born sightless and a fool befuddled by dreams. Though I recall those days as the happiest I've ever known, in some ways I was more blind than my newfound daughter.

The first frosts of autumn found us moving steadily south and into trouble. We were entering the country of the true border lords now, nobles with holdings and kinsmen on both sides of the river Tweed and loyalties as changeable as the lowland winds. Arnim once described the Scottish border as a smudged line drawn in blood that never dries.

Perhaps someone was preparing to alter the mark once again.

As we neared the Liddesdale, traveling from one small hamlet to another, we often took to the wood to avoid troops, well mounted and heavily armed. Skirmishes between Norman knights on the Tyne or the Rede and restive Scots along the Liddel Water are common in a land where cattle raids are lauded in song. Still, with war in the air, crossing the border would be dangerous. We might be hanged as spies by one side or another.

But our luck held. As we approached Redheugh, I spotted a familiar wagon in a camp outside the town wall, a bright crimson cart with a Welsh dragon painted boldly on its sides.

After changing from our traveling garments into performing clothes, I led Noelle on our mount into a world unfamiliar to most folk, a traveling circus.

Most minstrels, especially in the north, ply their trade alone or in small family groups. But a few singers earn enough renown to gather a larger assemblage, a troupe of musicians, jugglers, and acrobats whose appearance at a town is reason enough to declare a feast day.

One such is Owyn Phyffe, Bard of Wales and the Western World as he calls himself. A small, compactly built dandy, blond-bearded and handsome as the devil's cousin, Owyn is a famed performer on both sides of the border and on the continent as well. A son and grandson of Welsh minstrels, he's a master of the craft. And well aware of it.

His camp was a hive of activity, cookfires being doused and horses hitched for travel. I found Owyn strolling about, noting every detail of the preparation without actually soiling his hands. He dressed more like a young lord than a singer, in a claret velvet doublet and breeches of fine doeskin. His muslin shirt had loose Italian sleeves. And not just for fashion.

Owyn carries a dirk up one sleeve or the other, perhaps both, and I once saw him slit a man's throat so deftly that the rogue's soul was in hell before his heart knew it was dead. Owyn dresses like a popinjay, but he's not a man to take lightly.

Our paths had crossed a number of times over the years, usually on friendly terms. Or so I hoped, because I needed him now.

He scowled theatrically as I approached leading the mount.

"God's eyes, I believe I spy Tallifer, the croaking frog of York. I can't tell which is uglier, you or that broken-down horse. Here to beg a crust of bread, I suppose."

"Not at all. In the last town, folk told me of a perky little Welsh girl who dresses like a fop and calls herself Owyn Phyffe the poet. Is she about?"

"Aye, she's about, about to thrash you for your loud mouth," Owyn said, grinning, seizing my arm in a grip of surprising strength for a small man. "How are you, Tallifer?"

"Not as well as you. The years have been kind to you."

"You were always a poor liar. How goes the road?"

"We've been doing quite handsomely. We've played Ormiston, Stobs, and a half dozen rat-bitten hamlets between, to very good response."

"We?"

"May I introduce my daughter, Noelle, the finest singer in this land or any other."

"I'm sure she is," Owyn snorted, then read the danger in my eyes and hastily amended his tone. "Because, as I said, your father is an inept liar, my dear. Honest to a fault."

Taking her hand, he kissed it with a casual grace I could only envy, favoring her with the smile that melted hearts on two continents. If he noted her blindness, he gave no sign. Owyn is nought if not nimble-witted.

"I would gladly offer you the hospitality of my camp, Tallifer, but we're making ready to leave."

"I see that. Well, there's no point in our playing yon town now. A performance by Owyn the Bard is impossible for lesser minstrels to follow."

"Even shameless flattery is sometimes a Gospel truth," Owyn grinned wryly. "Do we meet by chance, Tallifer, or can I be of some service to you and your . . . daughter?"

"We meet by God's own grace, Welshman. Over the past weeks the roads have grown crowded with soldiers. I'm hoping we can travel with your troupe across the border. I can pay."

"Don't be an ass, come with us and be welcome. We're not bound directly for the border, though. I've an agreement to perform in Garriston for Lord DuBoyne on All Saints Day. Do you still want to come?"

"Why shouldn't we?"

"Because the soldiers you've been seeing likely belong to DuBoyne or his enemies. Whatever the trouble is, we're wandering merrily into the heart of it, singing all the way."

"We're still safer traveling with you than on our own."

"That may be," Owyn conceded grimly. "But I wouldn't take much comfort in it. The sooner we're south of the Tweed, the happier I'll be, and devil take the hindmost."

Owyn's company traveled steadily for the next few days, stopping only at night to rest the animals. If anything, we encountered more soldiers than before, but with wagons, we couldn't cede the road. Troops simply marched around us.

Owyn's fame is such that even warriors who hadn't seen him perform greeted us cheerfully. After chatting with one grizzled guards' captain at length, though, the Welshman's gloom was palpable.

"What's wrong?" I asked, goading my mount to match pace with Owyn's. Noelle was riding on one of the wagons with Owyn's wife, or perhaps his mistress. His two companions looked much alike to me, small, dark women, with raven hair. Sisters perhaps? Some things you don't ask.

"Everything's wrong," Owyn said glumly. "You were a soldier once, Tallifer, have you noted anything odd about the troops we've encountered?"

"Mostly Scots, supplemented by a few mercenaries. Why?"

"I was talking about their direction."

I considered that a moment. "We haven't met any for the past few days," I said. "They've all been overtaking us."

"Exactly," Owyn sighed. "They're traveling the same way we are, and the only holding on this road is Lord DuBoyne's. But when I offered to buy the captain of that last lot an ale at the festivities, he declined. He said he wouldn't be there."

"So?"

"So there's nowhere else for him to be, you dolt, only Garriston. And if he's not bound for Garriston to celebrate . . ." He left the thought dangling.

"Sweet Jesus," I said softly.

"Exactly so," Owyn agreed.

"Perhaps they'll delay the bloodletting until after the holiday."

"That would be Christian of them," Owyn grunted, "though I'm told good Christian crusaders in the Holy Land disembowel children then rummage in their guts for swallowed gems."

"You're growing gloomy with age, Owyn."

"Even trees grow wiser with time. And I wouldn't worry much about old age, Tallifer. We're neither of us likely to see it."

Arriving at Garriston on the fourth day did little to lift Phyffe's spirits. It was a raw border town on a branch of the Tweed, surrounded by a high earthen wall braced with logs. Its gate was open but well guarded. Noelle was riding at the front of the train with Owyn as I trudged along beside.

"What do you think, Tallifer?" he asked, leaning on his pommel, looking over the town.

"It seems a small place to hire such a large troupe."

"So it does. The DuBoyne family steward paid us a handsome advance without a quibble, though."

"Is it a pretty town?" Noelle asked. "It feels lucky to me."

Owyn shot a quizzical glance at me, then shook his head.

"Oh, to live in the country of the blind, where every swamp's an Eden. Aye, girl, it's a fine town with gilded towers and flags on every parapet. But perhaps you'd better stay in the camp, while your father and I taste the stew we've got ourselves into."

Leaving instructions with his wives to camp upstream from Garriston near a wood, Owyn, myself, and Piers LeDoux, the leader of the Flemish jugglers, rode in together. In such a backwater, well-dressed mounted men are seen so rarely we were treated like gentry. The gate guards passed us through with a salute, saying the manor's steward could be found in the marketplace.

An old town, Garriston was probably a hamlet centuries before the Norman conquest. Houses were wattle and daub, set at haphazard angles to the mud streets. It was a market day and the air was abustle with the shouts of tinkers and peddlers, the squeal of hogs at butchering, hammers ringing at a smithy, and, beneath it all, the thunderous grumbling of a mill wheel.

A month earlier I wouldn't have noted the noise, but after traveling with Noelle I found myself listening more, trying to savor the world as she did.

A stronghold loomed over the north end of the town. Crude, but stoutly built in the Norman style, the square blockhouse sat atop a hill with corners outset so archers could sweep its walls. And even in peaceful daylight, sentries manned its towers.

The street wound into an open-air market in the town square, with kiosks for pottery, hides, and leatherwork, an ale-house, and a crude stone chapel. Owyn spied the DuBoyne family steward, Gillespie Kenedi, looking over beeves for the feast day.

Heavyset, with a pig's narrow eyes and a face ruddy from too much food, too little labor, Kenedi wore the fur-trimmed finery of his station and its airs as well. He was trailed by a rat-faced bailiff who bobbed his head in agreement whenever his master spoke. Or farted, probably.

Kenedi talked only with Owyn, considering the Fleming and myself beneath notice. But as the haggling progressed, he kept glancing my way, as though he might know me from somewhere.

When their bargain was struck, Owyn and the steward shook hands on it, then Kenedi beckoned to me.

"You there! Where did you get that horse you're holding?"

"From a crofter north of Orniston."

"And how did the crofter come by it?"

"As I recall, he said he traded a bullock for it. Why?"

"It resembles one of our plowhorses that went missing some time ago."

"I'm sure Tallifer acquired the horse fairly," Owyn put in. "If you have a problem, it's with the man who took it from you."

"Unless you believe I'm that man," I said, facing Kenedi squarely, waiting. But he was more beef than spirit.

"Perhaps I'm mistaken," he said, glancing away. "One spavined nag looks much like another. I'll let it pass, for now." He turned and bustled off with his bailiff scurrying after.

"Nicely done," Owyn sighed. "It's always good business to antagonize one's host before getting paid. So? Did you really get the horse at Orniston?"

I didn't answer. Which was answer enough.

As dusk settled on our camp like a warm cloak, townsfolk and crofters from nearby farms began gathering to us. Dressed in what passed for their best, carrying candles in hollowed gourds or rutabaga hulls to light their way, they brought whatever small gifts they could afford, a flask of ale, bread or a few pickled eggs, walnuts, even a fowl or two.

Drawn by the noise, Noelle came out of the women's tent. I led her to a place near the fire as Owyn entertained the gathering throng, singing in Italian love songs to folk who barely understood English. And winning their hearts.

"What's afoot, Tallifer?" Noelle whispered. "What is all this?"

"We were hired to perform tomorrow at the DuBoyne castle for All Saints Day. But among Celtic peoples, tonight is a much older celebration called All Hallomas Eve, or Samhain, the festival of the dead."

"The dead? But I hear laughter and the music is gay."

"Life is so hard for borderland peasants that death isn't much feared. For the rest of us, Samhain is for remembering those who are gone. And to celebrate that we're not among them yet."

"Owyn is a fine singer, isn't he?"

"Aye, he's very good. He's an attractive man, too, don't you think?"

"Owyn?" she snorted. "You must be joking. He's a snake. His glib tongue and smooth hands put me in mind of the serpent of Eden. And you should hear what his wives say about his love-making."

"You shouldn't listen to such things."

"What do you think women talk about when we're alone? They asked me about you as well. About what we really are to each other. They noted we bear little resemblance."

"What did you tell them?"

"The absolute truth, of course. That you are the only father I've ever known and that you never speak of my poor mother."

"Very poetic. And ever so slightly misleading."

"Thank you. I have a good teacher. What's happening now?"

"Piers and the Flemish acrobats are putting on a tumbling show. It's not so fine as they will do for the nobility, but it suits this lot. Some of the women are cracking walnuts to read the future."

"Can they foresee it? Truly?"

"Certainly. A peasant's future is his past, and any fool who trusts a walnut has no future at all."

The crowd continued to swell with folk from the town, tradesmen, manor servants, even a fat priest who mingled with his flock quaffing ale as heartily as the rest. The steward too made an appearance with his rat-shadow of a bailiff, standing apart from the rest, aloof.

"Horses," Noelle said quietly.

"What?"

"I hear horsemen coming. Many. Moving slowly."

For a moment I thought she was mistaken, but then I saw them, moving out of the woods in a body toward our fires. A mounted troop, battle-weary from fighting by the look of them. Their horses were lathered and played out, and the men weren't much better, slumped in their saddles, exhausted, some wounded.

Their leader was young, less than twenty, but he was no boy. Dressed in mail with a black breastplate, he sat on his horse like a centaur. His armor was spattered with blood, not his own, and a broken arrow was stuck in his saddle.

A shaggy mane of dark hair obscured his eyes, but as he scanned the camp, I doubt he missed a thing. Including Noelle. His glance lingered only a moment, but I've seen the look before. In battle. We'd been marked.

"God's eyes," Owyn said, sidling over to us. "Here's trouble if I ever saw it."

"Who are they?"

"Milord DuBoyne's men. That's his eldest son, Logan. Black Logan he's called, both for his look and his sins."

"What sins?"

"Cattle raiding's a national sport in Scotland, but instead of beating or ransoming the thieves Logan hangs them, then guts them to make easy feeding for the ravens."

"I can see why he'd be unpopular with cattle thieves, but that's hardly cause for sackcloth and ashes."

"He's a hotspur, gives battle or extracts a tax from anyone found on DuBoyne lands, even neighbors. He's killed three men in single combat and God knows how many more in frays. There's already a ballad about him."

"He seems a bit young for a song."

"The legend is that after two babes were stillborn, his mother made a Christmas wish for a healthy son. Instead, the devil sent a demon child who sprang full-grown from the womb, called for his armor, and rode off to fight the Ramsays. Villagers hide their children when he passes."

"They hide from thunder as well." I spoke lightly, but in truth I was growing concerned. Black Logan was conferring with Kenedi, and both of them were glancing our way.

"Perhaps you'd better take Noelle . . ." I began. Too late. The steward was bustling toward us, looking altogether too pleased.

"I'm told this girl is with you, minstrel," he said without preamble. "How much for her?"

"What?"

"The girl. Young DuBoyne wishes to buy her for the night. He's willing to pay, but don't think you can—"

And then he was on the ground, stunned, his lip split open. It happened so quickly I didn't even realize I'd hit him.

"Damn," Owyn said softly. "Now we're in for it."

Logan strode angrily to us, his hand on his sword. "What madness is this? You struck my father's steward!"

"He asked my daughter's price and paid a small part of it. Are you here for the rest?"

He blinked, eyeing me more in surprise than anger. "Are you offering me a challenge, commoner?"

"He asked the price, I'm simply telling you what it is. Your life. Or mine. Is that plain enough?"

It was a near thing. Young or not, he was a warrior chief with a small army at his back. I was but a cat's whisker from death. He cocked his head, reading my eyes.

"Do you know who I am?" he asked quietly.

"I only know I'm not your man, nor do I owe that hog on the ground any fealty."

"I'm Sir Logan DuBoyne—"

"He's lying!" Noelle snapped, pulling free of Owyn's grasp.

"What?" DuBoyne and I said together.

"Any DuBoyne would be noble," she continued coldly. "At the convent they said I could tell the nobility by their scent and fine manners. You smell like a horse and show your breeding by insulting my father who was a soldier before you were born. Yet you claim to be a knight? I think not."

For a moment, I thought he might butcher us both. His eyes darkened, and I could see why the villagers hid their children. But the rage passed. He shook his head slowly, as if waking from a dream.

"You were convent raised, miss? Then clearly I've . . . misunderstood this situation. I apologize. I've fought two skirmishes today, and I'm not as young as I used to be. I meant no offense to you. But as for you," he said, turning to me, "if you ever lay hands on a man of mine again, I'll see your head on a pike."

Reaching down, he hauled Kenedi to his feet. "Come on, Gillespie, let's find some ale."

"The bastard struck me!" Kenedi said, outraged.

"He saved your life," DuBoyne said, leading him off. "The girl would have cut our hearts out."

"You idiot," Owyn said angrily, spinning me around. "You could have gotten us all killed!"

"And if she were yours? Would you have sold her?"

For a moment I thought I'd pushed him too far. But Owyn is nothing if not agile. "Sweet Jesus, Tallifer. You may not be the world's greatest singer, but by God you're never dull. And you, girl, you've enjoyed my hospitality long enough. It's time to earn your keep. Come, sing for us. If I'm to be slaughtered defending your honor, you'd better be worth it."

I wanted to fetch my lute to accompany her but I was afraid to risk letting her out of my sight, even for a moment. Black Logan was prowling the camp, talking with pedlars and travelers. And glancing my way from time to time.

It didn't bode well. Most men with black reputations have earned them. His own people shied from him as if he wore a leper's bell and I knew that if he snatched up Noelle, none but me would oppose him.

And so I watched tensely as Owyn led Noelle into the ring of firelight, introduced her, then stepped back. It was an impossible situation. Drunken revelers were bellowing jests, laughing, groping their women. A clown troupe juggling lions with their manes ablaze wouldn't satisfy this lot.

Yet, as that slip of a girl began to sing, the crowd gradually fell silent, listening. She sang a simple French lullaby in a voice so pure and true that my heart swelled with longing, not for Noelle but for all I'd lost in my life. And would lose.

When she finished there was a long moment of stone silence, then the crowd erupted with a roar of applause and cheers. They called for more and she gave it, singing a rousing Irish war ballad I'd taught her and then a love song that would have misted the eyes of a bronze idol.

I was as transfixed as the rest, until I realized that Black Logan was standing a few paces to my left. He was eyeing Noelle like a lion at mealtime, but if her song moved him he gave no sign, not even applauding when she finished. He turned to me instead.

"I didn't know the girl was blind."

"What difference does it make?"

"I don't know. But it does. I've asked around the camp. Folk say you truly were a soldier once. Whom did you serve?"

"I was a yeoman for the Duke of York, bodyguard to his son for a time. Later I fought for Sir Ranaulf de Picard."

"At Aln Ford?"

"I was there, and at a hundred other scuffles you've never heard of."

"Then you must know troops. Whose men did you pass on the road here? How were they armed?"

"I was a soldier once and now I'm a singer. But a spy? That I've never been."

"Minstrel, you're trying my patience at a bad time. My father's health is failing, and his neighbors and enemies have begun raiding our stock and gouging taxes from our people. When I answer their aggression with my own they whine to Edinburgh, branding me an outlaw. My father has invited some of those same neighbors to the feast in hopes of a truce, but I know they've brought troops with them. Perhaps they fear treachery. Perhaps they plan it. Either way, you'd best tell me what you've seen."

"Suppose we compromise, and I tell you what I didn't see instead? We saw no heavy cavalry on the road, nor any siege engines, nor did we encounter any supply trains. The soldiers were carrying a few days' provisions, no more."

"Then they aren't planning a siege; they're escort troops only. Good. How many men did you see, and whose were they?"

"I took no count, and I don't know the liveries of this land well enough to identify them."

"And wouldn't if you could?"

"They did us no harm, DuBoyne. We've no quarrel with them."

"Nor with me. Yet." The camp erupted in a roar as Noelle finished her song, with Owyn standing beside her leading the cheers.

"Your daughter sings well."

"Yes, she does."

He started to say something else but his voice was drowned by the throng as Owyn led Noelle back to me. DuBoyne turned and stalked off to rejoin his men.

"Tallifer, did you hear?" Noelle's face was shining and Owyn's grin was as broad as the Rede.

"You were in wonderful voice, Noelle, and they knew it. What was that French lullaby? I've never heard it before."

"A woman sang it to me when I was small. I don't know why it came back to me tonight. Was I foolish to sing it?"

"*Au contraire, cherie*, it was brilliant," Owyn countered. "By singing softly, you made them quiet down to hear. You won many hearts tonight, little Noelle, including mine."

"All of it?" she asked sweetly. "Or just the parts your wives aren't using at the moment?"

"Get back to your tent, imp," Owyn snorted. "I swear, if you weren't so pretty I might believe you really are Tallifer's child. Your tongue's as sharp as his." Laughing, Noelle set off, but Owyn grasped my arm before I could follow.

"What did Black Logan want? More trouble?"

"He has trouble of his own." I quickly sketched the situation DuBoyne had described.

"I've heard the old laird's mind is failing," Owyn nodded. "And vultures gather early along the borders. Do you think there will be quarreling at the feast?"

"I hope not. That boy may be young, but he's already a seasoned fighter. I half believe that nonsense about him leaping from his mother's womb to his saddle and riding off to fight the Ramsays."

"He won't have far to ride tomorrow," Owyn sighed. "The Ramsays are among the honored guests. A baker's dozen of them. And that captain I spoke to yesterday, the one who's probably watching us from the hills at this moment? He was a Ramsay man."

"Damn it, you should have warned me away from this, Owyn."

"I tried to, remember? Besides, Noelle likes it here. Thinks the blasted place is lucky."

"She may be right. But good luck or bad, I wonder?"

The evening feast of All Saints Day was a rich one, probably to atone for the carousing and deviltry of the night before. It was also a display of wealth and power by the laird of Garriston, Alisdair DuBoyne. Food and drink were laid on with a will, steaming platters of venison and hare and partridge, wooden bowls of savory bean porridge spiced with leeks and garlic; mulled wine, ale, or mead, depending on the station of the guest.

The great hall, though, was great in name only, a rude barn of a room, smoky from the sconces and cooking fires, its walls draped with faded tapestries probably hung when the DuBoynes first came to this fief a generation ago.

Seated at the center of the linen-draped high table, flanked by his wife and two sons, Laird DuBoyne was even older than I'd expected, seventy or beyond, I guessed. Tall and skeletal with a scanty gray beard, it was said he'd once been a formidable warrior, but his dueling days were long past. He seemed apathetic, as though the juice of life had already bled from him and only the husk remained.

His wife was at least a generation younger. Dressed in green velvet, she was willowy as a doe, a striking woman with aquiline features and chestnut hair beneath a white silken cap. Her youngest son, Godfrey, nine or so, had her fairness and fine features, while his brother, Black Logan, with his dark beard and burning eyes, sat like a chained wolf at the table, seeing everything, equally ready for a toast or a fight.

Kenedi, the stocky steward, and his wife sat at the far end of the high table beside the chubby priest I'd seen at the Samhain fest. Father Fennan, someone had said, was a local man who'd risen from the peasantry to become both parish priest and chaplain to the DuBoynes.

Two lower tables, also decked in fine linen, extended from the corners of the high table to form a rough horseshoe shape, which was appropriate since the guests were probably more familiar with war saddles than silver forks.

Three family groups of DuBoyne's neighbors, the Ramsays, Duarts, and Harden clans, nearly thirty of them, were seated in declining order of status. A hard-eyed crew, wary as bandits, they'd brought no women or children with them. Nor had they worn finery to honor their hosts, dressing in coarse woolens instead, clothes more suited to battle than a banquet.

Randal Ramsay was senior among them. A red-bearded descendent of Norse raiders, Ramsay conversed courteously with his host and the other guests but kept a watchful eye on Logan, an attention the younger man returned.

In England, strict protocols of station would have been observed, but along the borders the Scots and their English cousins act more like soldiers in allied armies, jests and jibes flying back and forth between high and low tables. But I noted the exchanges were surprisingly mild and politely offered, lest harmless banter explode into bloodshed.

Owyn delayed beginning the entertainment as long as he dared. Scots at table can be a damned surly audience, and the tension in DuBoyne's hall was as thick as the scent of roasting meat. Later, with full bellies and well oiled with ale, DuBoyne's guests might be more receptive.

Not so. When Piers LeDoux and his troupe of Flemish acrobats opened the performance, their energetic efforts received the barest modicum of applause.

After a juggler and a Gypsy woman who ate fire fared equally poorly, Owyn took the bull by the horns and strode to the center of the room. He stood silently for a bit, commanding attention by his presence alone. Then, instead of singing, he began to recite a faerie story of Wales and then ghostly doings in the Highlands and Ireland, delivering the tales with such verve and drama that even the blood-thirsty warriors at the low table leaned forward to hear.

It was a masterful performance. Owyn entranced the DuBoynes and their restive neighbors alike, holding them spellbound for the better part of an hour. He finished to rousing cheers and applause, the first enthusiastic response of the night.

"Match that if you can," Owyn whispered with a grin as he passed us in the doorway.

The minstrelsy is a free-spirited life, but it has protocols of its own. As Noelle and I had joined Owyn's troupe last, we were scheduled to perform last, the toughest position of all.

Ordinarily, I warmed up a crowd with a few rowdy ballads before bringing on Noelle, but after the way she won over the revelers at the Samhain, I simply introduced her and began strumming my lute, softly, softly, hoping the crowd would quiet.

Facing her unseen audience, Noelle sang the French lullaby, even more beautifully than the previous night. And with the same wondrous effect. The room fell utterly silent, every eye fixed on Noelle as she poured all the pain and longing of her blighted life and our own into that song. Angels on high couldn't have sung it one whit better. My eyes grew misty as I played the accompaniment, and I wasn't alone.

As I glanced about, reading the room, I noted Randal Ramsay's fierceness had softened, Lady DuBoyne was crying silently, while her husband . . . was up and moving. Laird DuBoyne was shuffling past the low table, coming toward us.

Unaware of his approach, Noelle sang on. I couldn't guess his intentions, but he seemed anguished and angry. Brushing past me, the old man seized Noelle's arm, startling her to silence.

"My dear, this is not fitting. You sing as beautifully as ever, but it's not proper for my lady wife to—"

"Let go of me!" Noelle shouted, pulling away. "Tallifer!"

"Come back to the table, milady, we'll—"

"Milord Alisdair!" Lady DuBoyne's voice snapped like a whip, cutting off her husband's ramblings. He stared up at her, shocked, then turned back to Noelle, eyeing her in wonder.

"I . . . but you're not my lady," he said slowly. "I thought . . . Your voice sounds much like hers did. Long ago. I'm sorry. I've ruined your song . . ."

And then Black Logan was at his father's side. Firmly disengaging his hand from Noelle's arm, he led Laird DuBoyne from the room. But at the door, the old man stopped, turning back to stare at Noelle in confusion.

"Who are you?" he asked, his voice barely a whisper. "Who are you?"

With surprising gentleness, Logan ushered him out, leaving us in stunned silence.

"What was all that?" Lord Ramsay said, rising. "Is our host going mad, then?"

"He had a bit too much wine, that's all," Lady DuBoyne said coldly. "It's a celebration, Ramsay, and you're falling behind. Continue the music, minstrel. Play on!"

And I did. Striking up a merry Scottish reel on my lute, I played as though the strings were on fire. To no avail. The spell of Noelle's song was shattered, and the guests were only interested in discussing their host's behavior with one another.

Owyn led Noelle quietly out of the hall, then after letting me twist in the wind alone for a time, he called the rest of the company back for a final song and bow before we all beat a hasty retreat to a smattering of applause.

Noelle was waiting for us in the outer hall. "Tallifer, what happened? Who was that man?"

"Our host, my lark," Owyn said. "The man who is supposed to pay me tomorrow. Assuming he doesn't mistake me for a tree and have me cut down."

"Is that what happened?" I asked. "He mistook her for someone else?"

"For his lady, I believe. There's a vague resemblance, and a man addled by age could mistake them. Still, if DuBoyne's neighbors came to take his measure, they just saw the ghost of a man who's still alive, but only barely. I don't like the feel of this a damned bit. We're breaking camp at first light, I—"

"Good sirs, hold a moment, please." It was the pudgy priest, red-faced and puffing as he hurried after us. "I'm Father Fennan, Mr. Phyffe, chaplain to the DuBoyne family. Milady DuBoyne would like a word. And with these other two as well, the blind girl and her father."

"It's late," I said. "Noelle should—"

"It's not that late and I want to be ten miles south of here tomorrow," Owyn interrupted. "Lead on, Father."

"You must be a busy man," Noelle said, as we followed the friar. "From what I hear of Black Logan, he badly needs a priest. Or is it already too late for him?"

"It's never too late for salvation, miss," Father Fennan said, eyeing her curiously. "You sang in French very well. Where did you learn?"

"I know only the one song. I grew up in the convent at Lachlan Cul and must have heard it there."

"I see," Fennan said curtly. Too curtly, I thought. Either the song or the mention of the convent seemed to trouble him. I knew the feeling. Everything about this place was worrying me.

We followed the priest down a shadowed corridor lit by guttering sconces, arriving at a windowless room at the west corner of the fortress. Vellum scrolls and ledgers filled pigeonhole racks against the walls.

"A library?" Noelle asked. "Linseed and charcoal. I love the ink scent. It smells like knowledge."

"Nay, it's a counting room," I whispered. Though such a place was normally a steward's lair, Lady DuBoyne was seated alone at his desk with a ledger open before her.

"According to Kenedi's accounts, this was the sum agreed on," she said brusquely, pushing a purse of coins toward Owyn. "Count it if you like."

"That won't be necessary, milady," Owyn said, touching his forelock. "I'm only sorry that—"

"Our business is concluded, Mr. Phyffe. Wait outside with Father Fennan, please. I want a private word with these two."

"As you say, milady." Giving a perfunctory bow, Owyn followed the priest out. Fennan swung the oaken door closed as he left.

Lady DuBoyne eyed me a moment, lips pursed, then pushed a small purse toward me. "This is for you, minstrel. And your daughter."

"I don't understand."

"It's money for travel, the farther the better. And for your silence. My husband is no longer young and has no head for wine, but he's still my husband. I will not have him ridiculed."

"I saw nothing to laugh at, milady, and Noelle saw nothing at all. You need not pay us."

"The girl is truly blind then? I thought the ribbon might be an artifice. Come closer, child. You have a beautiful voice."

"Thank you. Do you know me, lady?"

"I beg your pardon?"

"Have we met? You seem . . . familiar to me, though I can't say why. Have you ever visited the convent at Lachlan Cul?"

"No, and I'm sure we've never met. You're very lovely. I'd remember."

"I must be mistaken, then. Forgive me, the country where I live is a land of shadows. It's confusing sometimes. But Tallifer is right, there's no need to buy our silence."

"Then consider it a payment for your song."

"The song was for any who listened, not for you alone. You needn't pay for it and you have nothing to fear from us. We'll not trouble you again."

She turned and started for the door so hastily I had to grab her arm to save her from injury. I glanced back to make our goodbyes, but Lady DuBoyne didn't notice. She was leaning forward on the desk, her face buried in her hands.

"Well?" Owyn said when we joined him in the hall. "What did she want?"

"Not much," I said. "She asked us to be discreet."

"Discretion is always wise," Father Fennan agreed. "We live in fearsome times."

"That lady has nought to fear," Noelle said sharply. "Her son has a ballad of his own already. Tell me, Father, did Logan fight those battles or just bribe minstrels to praise his name?"

"Hardly," the priest said, surprised. "As his confessor, I assure you the song doesn't tell half the carnage he's wrought, and he despises it. He once struck a guardsman unconscious for singing it."

"I'm surprised he didn't hang the poor devil," Noelle snapped. "This is an unlucky town for singing, gentlemen. We'd best be away from here."

Owyn glanced at me, arching an eyebrow. I shrugged. I had no idea why Noelle was so angry. Or why Lady DuBoyne had broken down. Women have always been an alien race to me, as fascinating as cats and no more predictable.

Noelle was right about one thing, though: Garriston was unlucky for us. The sooner we saw the back of it, the better.

Pleading the lateness of the hour, the priest led us to the chapel, which had its own exit through the town wall. He seemed uneasy, eager to have us gone.

"Good luck and Godspeed," he called, as he strained at the heavy door. "And remember, discretion!" The armored door clanged shut like the gates of hell.

"Paid to the last penny," Owyn said somberly, hefting his purse. "A successful engagement, I suppose. At least we finished with a profit."

But we weren't finished with Garriston, nor it with us. We'd scarcely retired to our tents when a commotion arose from behind the city walls. Shouting, men running. A raid? Trouble between the DuBoynes and their guests?

I was pulling on my boots when horsemen thundered into our camp followed by foot soldiers on the run, shouting for us to come out, tearing open the tents and wagons. My first thought was to reach Noelle, but I was seized as soon as I showed myself.

"Hold him! He's one of them!" The rat-eyed bailiff who'd been with Kenedi the first day was on horseback, armed with a poniard, directing the search. Owyn stalked boldly out to demand an explanation, but the bailiff ordered him seized as well. Then they dragged Noelle out and marched the three of us back to the stronghold under guard, directly to the great hall.

The linens were gone now and the high table was occupied by the steward, Kenedi, Black Logan, his younger brother Godfrey, and the heads of the guest families, Randal Ramsay, Nicol Duart, and Ian Harden. Red-eyed, disheveled, and still half-drunk from the feast, they were in an evil mood, eyeing us like wolves 'round a wounded calf.

Armed guards ringed the room and blood was in the air, real blood. A body was laid out on a trestle table in the center of the room covered by a sodden sheet, bleeding gore onto the flagstones.

"What is the meaning of this?" Owyn said coldly. "Why have we been unlawfully seized?"

"You've been brought to answer, Mr. Phyffe," Randal Ramsay said coldly. "For murder."

"Whose murder?"

"See for yourself." The squat soldier holding Noelle thrust her forward, banging her into the corpse. She recoiled, and as he reached for her again, I pulled free and tackled the lout from behind, slamming his face into the floor! Once, twice, and then the others were on me, dragging me off him, kicking me down.

"Enough!" Black Logan's bark stopped the beating instantly. "This is a court, not a damned alehouse brawl!"

"What kind of court?" Owyn said coolly. "I see no townsmen here to act as a jury."

"This isn't a hallmote hearing for selling bad ale, Phyffe," Ramsay said. "As the crime is against a peer of the realm, only his equals can sit as judges."

Jerking his arm free of his guard, Owyn strode boldly to the table with the corpse. Noelle helped me to stand as Owyn drew the sheet back. His mouth narrowed, but he gave no other sign.

"Who's been killed?" Noelle whispered to me. "Is it the steward?"

"God rest him," Owyn said quietly, gazing at the corpse. "Father Fennan seemed a good man, but he was only a parish priest, unlettered and coarse of speech. I doubt he was of noble birth."

"Fennan was not the only one attacked," Ramsay said. "The laird of Garriston also lies wounded and is unlikely to—"

"He's not dead yet," Logan snapped. "He's survived worse."

"When he was younger, perhaps," Ramsay countered, "but he's been failing for some time. No one of sound mind would have loosed you to ravage the countryside!"

"Gentlemen, please," Owyn interrupted. "Could you save your private quarrel for a more convenient time? My friends and I have been hauled from our beds to no good purpose I can discern. There are any number of folk here with cause to harm Laird Alisdair while we have none. If you wish us to testify, let's get on with it."

His sheer audacity stunned the room to silence.

"Testify?" Gillespie Kenedi sputtered. "You are charged with the crime!"

"On what basis?"

"You are the only strangers here, and you were last seen with the priest. Money was found in your tent."

"Money paid to me by the lady of the manor for the night's performance," Owyn replied. "As to the priest, when last we saw him he was alive and well. He saw us out through a portal at the rear of the chapel and bolted it behind us. Once outside the walls, we could not return, and since you found me abed with my wife who will swear I never left once I'd arrived—"

"Your *wife* will swear," Kenedi sneered.

For a moment Owyn stood silent, his eyes locked on the steward's until Kenedi looked away. "Gentlemen, I have been falsely charged with murder. I have answered that charge with truth. I can have six free men in this room in half an hour to vouch for my word. But there is a simpler way. You have impugned my wife's honor, Mr. Kenedi. Suppose we put the question to the test in the courtyard? With any weapons you choose."

It was a bold move, and pure bluff. Owyn was a lover, not a fighter. Though lightning quick with a dirk, he had no real skill with weapons. But he was a master at reading audiences. The Scottish lords, tired and surly, brightened at the idea of a trial by combat. And he read Kenedi correctly as well. The steward had the arrogance of his high office, but no belly for a fight.

"No offense was intended to your wife," Kenedi muttered.

"Then you accept my word and my explanation?" Owyn pressed.

"Yours, yes. But what about the other minstrel? Who was he abed with? His daughter?"

Owyn glanced at me, warning me with his eyes to control my anger. But he wasn't the only one who could read people. Owyn was about to lie for me and I couldn't let him. Nothing but the truth could save us now.

"My daughter was with Owyn's family," I said. "I was quite alone."

"Then you could have returned," Kenedi said intently. "The gate guard has admitted he drowsed off. You could easily have passed by him to commit the crime."

"To what end? I have no quarrel with anyone here."

"You were sent by Lord Alisdair's enemies," Kenedi countered. "You arrived on a stolen horse. My bailiff can testify that the horse came from Garriston."

"No need. I accept your word that the horse came from Garriston. Was the reeve who rode it a Garriston man also?"

The question surprised him. It surprised me as well, but there was no turning back now. Murder had been done, and someone would pay for it before first light. Denials were useless. I had neither witnesses nor friends to vouchsafe my word. I had only my road-weary wits and the glimmer of an idea.

"Aye," Kenedi conceded, "the reeve was from Garriston. Why?"

"Because he attacked me in a wood on the way to Orniston. I buried him there." That woke them up.

"You admit you killed the reeve?" Kenedi said.

"In self-defense, yes."

"Why would a reeve attack you?" Black Logan asked. "Did you quarrel?"

"No, we hardly spoke. And he seemed more interested in killing Noelle than me."

"Same question: Why would he attack your daughter?"

"Much as it pains me to admit it, Noelle is not my daughter. She was a resident at the convent at Lachlan Cul until recently, when it burned."

"All was lost," Noelle put in. "A sister was taking me to her family when she died of injuries. Tallifer saved me."

"A touching tale but irrelevant," Kenedi sneered. "After killing the reeve, you likely came to Garriston for revenge."

"If I'd known the lout came from Garriston, I would hardly have ridden his horse here. Chance brought us to this place, or perhaps fate."

"An ill fate," Kenedi snorted. "You rode here on the horse of a murdered man yet claim you know nothing of the attacks on our laird and his chaplain?"

"I didn't say that. I had no part in what happened tonight, but I believe we may have caused it."

"Don't bandy words, minstrel," Randal Ramsay demanded. "What are you saying?"

"I think what happened tonight was the echo of another crime, one that occurred many years ago."

"What crime?" Logan asked.

"Before I answer, I have a question of my own." Turning to Noelle, I quietly asked her something that had troubled me. Then I turned back to the court. "Gentlemen, I believe the explanation lies in a ballad I heard when I came to this town—"

"What nonsense is this?" Kenedi sputtered. "You stand accused of murder—"

"Let him talk," Randal Ramsay interrupted. "His life is in the balance. But bear in mind, minstrel, if we don't care for your tale, you'll never tell another. Go on."

"The song is one you all know, the "Ballad of Black Logan," the boy warrior. Like most songs, it's part fancy, part truth.

"For example, it speaks of his birth at Christmas. Is this true? Was he born at Yuletide?"

"What difference—?" Kenedi began.

"Aye, it's true enough," Nicol Duart offered. The lanky clan chief had a buzzard's hook nose, and the same implacable eyes. "It was a damned black Christmas for this country. But the rest is a lie. Young Logan never leapt from his crib to raid Lord Randal's lands. He were at least a year old before he turned outlaw." The third lord, Ian Harden, guffawed. Neither Logan nor Ramsay smiled.

"Then the ballad is partly true. And the rest of it, the myth of a bairn riding off to war, is to explain a thing seen but not understood."

"What was seen?" Logan demanded.

"Here is what I believe happened. Seventeen years ago, a young wife who'd lost two stillborn children feared she might be put aside if she didn't deliver her lord an heir. So when she was expecting again, she arranged to obtain a male child. When her own child came, a frail girl born blind, she replaced it with the other and sent her true daughter off to a convent. At Lachlan Cul.

"The boy became a fearsome warrior. But his size at birth did not go unremarked, and a local legend sprang up to explain it. A ballad that grew with his exploits."

"You lying dog," Logan said coldly. "You dare insult my family by—"

"Hold, hold, young Logan," Ramsay said, his face split by a broad grin. "Perhaps you haven't fully grasped the implications. If the minstrel's tale is a lie, his life is forfeit. But at least part of his story *is* true. And if the rest is, then you have no right to threaten anyone, nor even to a seat at this table. And fool can see you don't favor your father, and the girl looks so like Lady DuBoyne that her own husband mistook her earlier tonight."

"My father is not well—"

"*If* he is your father."

"By God, Ramsay, step into the courtyard, and we'll see which of us doesn't know his father!"

"I don't brawl in the street with common louts, boy. We'll hear the rest of this before I consider your offer. What of it, minstrel? Have you any proof of your tale?"

"Lady DuBoyne knows the truth of it," I said.

"My mother is keeping vigil with her dying husband," Logan snarled. "Anyone who dares disturb her grief for this nonsense will deal with me first."

"I admit it's inconsiderate to trouble the lady now, but neither is it fair to condemn me without asking the one person who knows the truth."

"We needn't hear any more," Kenedi snapped. "The minstrel has admitted to killing a reeve from this town. As steward of Garriston and head of this court, I say we condemn him for that murder and dismiss the rest of this nonsense as a pack of lies told to save himself. We can hang him straightaway unless . . . any of you gentlemen truly wish to dispute the birthright of Lord DuBoyne's son and heir?"

The Scottish lords exchanged glances, and I read my fate in their eyes. Death. They couldn't risk challenging Logan in his own hall with his men about. They might raise the matter another time but that would be far too late for me.

"Well, gentlemen?" Kenedi said. "Shall we put it to a vote?"

"No," Logan said, his face carved from oak, unreadable. "We've gathered to resolve the murder of a priest and assault on my . . . on the laird of Garriston, not the death of a reeve many miles away. If we condemn the minstrel for killing the reeve, the rest remains unresolved and I will not have any stain on my name nor any question of my rights of inheritance. But I see a way to settle this. We'll send my younger brother Godfrey to ask Lady DuBoyne the truth of the minstrel's tale. If she denies it, he stands condemned out of his own mouth. Unless any man here doubts the lady's honor?"

"The minstrel's the one who'll be dancing the hangman's hornpipe if she misleads us," Ramsay noted dryly. "He may have a misgiving or two."

I considered that a moment. "No, as it stands, only a few know the truth of what happened, and the lady is the one most likely to tell it. I agree to the test. Send the boy."

"So be it," Ramsay said, eyeing me curiously. "Duart will accompany the lad to vouch that all is done properly."

"Agreed," Logan nodded, "with one stipulation. If my mother denies Tallifer's lies, he will not hang. One of you will loan him a blade, and we'll settle our differences in the courtyard. If he kills me, you can hang him afterward."

"Or gift him with silver and a fast horse," Ramsay growled. "Duart, take the boy to speak with his mother. And listen well to her answer."

The whey-faced youth and the burly border lord exited, and I resigned myself to wait. Perhaps for the rest of my life.

The reply came sooner than I expected. A stir arose at the back of the room, which grew to an uproar. Logan bolted to his feet, his face ashen. "Help him to a chair, forgodsake!"

I turned. Lord Alisdair had tottered into the hall, supported by Godfrey and Duart. He looked even more ancient than before, as though he might fade to smoke any moment. His muslin nightshirt was bloodstained, hanging loosely over a poultice.

A servant fetched him a chair and Alisdair eased painfully down, but as he looked about him, his eyes were bright and alert.

"Milord," Logan said, "you should not be here."

"Miss a trial for my own murder?" Alisdair asked, his voice barely a whisper. "Not likely. Is this the man accused of the attack?" He gestured weakly at me. "Well, sir, speak up. What have you to say for yourself?"

"Me? Nothing!" I said, dumbfounded. "You know damned well I didn't attack you!"

"I fear not. I sleep like the dead nowadays, especially after wine. Someone jammed a pillow over my face, and when I struggled against it I was stabbed. And woke in the arms of my wife. A most agreeable surprise. I expected to wake in hell."

"Sir," Ramsay said, "perhaps your lady can better answer our questions. You should be resting."

"I'll be at rest soon enough, Ramsay," DuBoyne said. "And my lady is at chapel, praying for my soul. Prematurely, I hope. I've survived cuts before; God willing, I'll survive this. Nothing like a good bleeding to clear a man's senses. And his wife's as well. As I lay a-dying, my lady confessed to a deception long ago, a wondrous tale of a child put aside and another put in its place."

"My God, it is true then?" Ramsay breathed. "Black Logan is not your son?"

"My family tree is no concern of yours, Ramsay, only the murder of my priest."

"But surely they are related!"

"Perhaps, but . . ." DuBoyne winced, swallowing. "It is the minstrel's life and his tale. Let him finish it. If he can."

"As you say, lord," I said. "The exchange of the children took place years ago. But when word came of the fire at Lachlan Cul, a reeve was sent to end the threat the girl represented. He failed. Later, when we arrived, someone realized who she was."

"Who?" Ramsay asked.

"The priest knew, for one. As milady's confessor, he would have heard the tale long since. But only one person stood to lose everything if the truth came out. Not the lady. Her deception was done for love of her husband, and she has borne him a second son since."

"Only Logan stood to lose all," Ramsay said, turning to the youth. Black Logan met his stare but made no reply.

"True, Logan had everything to lose," I agreed, "and he's surely capable of any slaughter necessary to protect himself or his family. But only if he knew the truth of his birth. And he didn't."

"How can you know that?" Ramsay countered.

"Because I'm still alive. A moment ago, the steward could have hanged me for the death of the reeve. Logan prevented it, something a guilty man would never have done."

"Who then?" Ramsay demanded.

"Only one other person had everything to lose if the truth came out. The one who arranged the original substitution. A foundling child couldn't come from this village, too many would know. Who can travel his lord's lands at will to deal with peasants who might sell a babe? And later, when word of the fire came, who could send a reeve to do murder?"

Ramsay swiveled slowly in his seat, to face Kenedi.

"It's a lie," Kenedi breathed.

"Is it? If Lord Alisdair learned the truth he might forgive his wife, and even the foundling boy who came here through no fault of his own. But he would never forgive the man who betrayed him for money by arranging the deception. His steward."

"But killing his lord wouldn't save his position," Logan said coolly. "Surely the lady would guess what happened and confess the truth."

"Only if she knew there'd been a murder. Lord Alisdair said he woke beneath a pillow. If he'd smothered, everyone would believe he died in his sleep. But when the priest surprised him, Kenedi lashed out in desperation."

"All lies," Kenedi said, "a tale told at bedtime. There's not one shred of proof."

"Actually, there is," I said. "When Noelle and I were first brought into this room, she asked if you'd been killed, Kenedi. Tell him why, girl."

"When the soldier pushed me against the body, I smelled linseed and charcoal. Ink," Noelle said, stepping forward. "The scent was unmistakable."

"And the priest was unlettered," I finished. "As are most of us here. Only you have the gift of literacy, Kenedi. And the smell of ink on your hands. Only you."

"It's not true."

"Do you dare say my daughter lies?" Lord Alisdair asked weakly. "If I were hale I'd kill for that alone. But as things are. . . . Logan, see to him."

"Wait," Ramsay interjected. "If Logan is not your blood, he has no standing in this court, no right to be here at all."

"Sir," Alisdair said, rising unsteadily, "the offense was against me and mine in my own hall, so the justice will be mine as well. Gentlemen, I invited you here to celebrate All Saints Day in a spirit of fellowship. The banquet and the . . . entertainment are finished now. And I am very tired."

Ramsay started to object, but a glance at Logan changed his mind. We were still in DuBoyne's hall, surrounded by DuBoyne's men.

"As you wish, milord," Ramsay said, rising. "My friends and I thank you for the fest and pray for your speedy recovery. For all our sakes."

Ramsay stalked from the hall with Harden and Duart close behind, joined by their clansmen at the rear. At Logan's nod, a guardsman led the steward away.

Their departure sapped the fire from DuBoyne. Wincing, he sagged back in the chair. Logan eyed him but didn't approach.

"Where is the girl?" DuBoyne asked quietly. "The one who claims to be my daughter?"

Warily, Noelle stepped forward. DuBoyne raised his head to observe her, then nodded slowly.

"So it is true. You look very like my lady wife did once. A great, great relief."

"Relief?" Logan echoed.

"Aye, that I wasn't completely bereft of my senses last night when I mistook them. And a relief that so late in my life, my daughter has been returned to me."

"And relief that I am no son of yours?"

"That too, in a way. In truth, a part of me has always known you weren't mine, Logan. My young wife lost two sickly babes before the miraculous birth of a strapping lad the size of a yearling colt, a boy who looked not at all like me. I feared she'd taken a lover to get the son I couldn't give her. I'm relieved to be wrong.

"But if you're not my blood, you're still my creation, the son I wanted. And needed. My daughter's birthright will be worthless if our land is lost. Fiefs are bestowed in Edinburgh or London, but they can only be held by arms. Your arms, Logan. You remain lord here in all but name, and for now that is enough. I'm tired, boy. Help me to my bed. Perhaps my daughter can join us later. We have much to talk of, lost years to make up for."

As Logan led the old man out, I touched Noelle's hand.

"I must be going as well, Owyn will be breaking camp. But you needn't stay here unless you choose to. We'll find a way to—"

"No," she said, stopping my lips with her fingertips. "I have always known I belonged somewhere and for good or ill, I've found that place. In the country of the blind, places are much alike, only people are different. Besides, if I go with you, I may end up as Owyn's third wife."

"There are worse fates. It won't take long for that young border wolf to realize he can reclaim his inheritance by marrying the lord's newfound daughter."

"And is he truly such a monster?"

"No, but . . . why are you smiling? My God, Noelle. You've thought through this already, haven't you?"

"At the convent, the young girls talked of little but love, love, love. I can never have love at first sight, but I know Logan wanted me before he knew who I was."

"He wanted to *buy* you! And you said he smelled of horses."

"I suspect he will always smell of horses. I like horses."

"The poor devil," I said, shaking my head in wonder. "He has no chance."

"Perhaps I'm his fate. He may only own his armor now, but he has a song. And you've said I'm a fair singer."

"You have the loveliest voice I've ever heard, Noelle, on my honor. I shall miss you greatly."

"We'll sing together again, whenever the wind or the road bring you to me. Perhaps one day we can sing to my children."

"We will. I promise."

We said our good-byes in the great hall, and I took to the road, leaving my foundling child with strangers. And yet I did not fear for her. She grew up in a harsher land than any can imagine and flourished there. She would have no trouble coping with her new situation, of that I was certain.

And she would have Black Logan. But not because of her family or position. Love at first sight is more than a legend or a girlish fancy. It happens rarely, but it does happen.

I'd seen Logan's face at the Samhain as he listened to Noelle's wondrous voice. He had the look of a starving wolf at a feast, a turmoil of hunger, love, and lust.

I remember that terrible yearning all too well. I felt it for a woman once myself, long years ago.

But that is another tale . . .

# Joyce Carol Oates

## Happiness

JOYCE CAROL OATES is one of the dominant literary voices of
the latter half of the twentieth century. She has written in so many
styles, forms, and voices that it is impossible to define an "Oates"
novel or short story. From gritty urban realism to dark flights of
the fantastic, Oates had always been bold, restless, and brilliant in
her attempt to make peace with our troubled times. "Happiness,"
dealing with a family in turmoil, is a shining example of her work
in the crime field. It first appeared in the August issue of *Ellery
Queen's Mystery Magazine*.

# Happiness

*Joyce Carol Oates*

*In the harsh sunlight on the pebbly southern shore of Lake Ontario. All objects are sharp and clear as if drawn with a child's crayon. Colors are bright, bold, unambiguous. Always there's wind. No shadows. Maybe the wind blows shadows away?*

*This story is written with a child's crayon. Matte black, or purple, with a faint oily sheen. Crayolas like the kind we played with when we were small children.*

*What did you see that day?*

*Kathlee.* What did I see that day, I saw nothing. I saw the sharp edges of things. I heard a dog snarling and whining but I saw no dog. I was headed into the house because I was looking for Irish. He wasn't my fiancé then. He was not. Somehow I was in the house. And passing through the kitchen, and saying *Irish? Where are you, Irish?* because maybe it was a game, Irish was a boy for games, you couldn't look at him for more than a minute before he'd get you to smile, and there came Irish stepping out of nowhere, behind me I guess, in the hall, and catching my arm, my bare forearm, between two of his big callused fingers, and I stopped right there on my toes on the threshold of that room (did I smell it, yes I guess: the blood: a rich dark-sickish smell, and the buzzing! yes I guess it must've been flies, on the McEwan farm there were horse flies big as your thumb) like a dancer, and his arm around my waist quick to turn me toward him, and he said *Kathlee, no you don't want to see* and right there I shut my eyes like a scared little girl, pressed against his chest, and he held me, oh I felt his heart beating hard and steady but what did I see that day at the McEwan farm, I saw nothing.

Irish McEwan was my first love, and my only. I would believe his innocence all my life. I was sixteen, that day at the farm.

*Nedra.* What did I see that day, *I don't know!* It was the start of my nervousness. My bad eyes. Even now I hate a surprise. If I'm back from school and it's winter and dark and nobody's home I'm half scared to go inside. After that day at the Mc-Ewan farm, I couldn't sleep a night through for years. And if Red, our border collie, began barking it's like *I might jump out of my skin!* People joke about things like that but what's funny? I'd go upstairs in our house and if it was dark, somebody'd have to come with me. For a long time. Almost, I couldn't use the bathroom during the night. Couldn't sleep, thinking of what I'd seen. No, not thinking: these flashes coming at me, like a roller-coaster ride. And Kathlee across the room sleeping. Or pretending to sleep. *Kathlee didn't see, she has sworn that on the Holy Bible. Her testimony at the courthouse. Her affidavit.*

These are words not a one of us knew before. Now we say them easy as TV people.

*Kathlee.* What did I see that day, I saw nothing. Swore to the police and then to the court ALL I KNEW EXACTLY AS I RECALLED IT. Placed my hand on the Holy Bible so help me God. I had prayed for help and guidance in remembering but when I tried there was a buzzing in my head, a fiery light like camera flashes.

*Kathlee, no you don't want to see. C'mon!*

Even now, it's years later. I will get sick if I try.

No, Holly will *not be told.* If I learn of anyone telling her, I will be madder than hell! That's a warning.

*Nedra.* What did I see, Oh God: I looked right into the room. I ran to the doorway, couldn't have been stopped if even Irish had grabbed me, which he did not, hadn't seen me I guess where I'd been sort of hiding behind the refrigerator. Half-scared but giggling, like this was a game? Hide-and-seek.

I'm like that. I mean, I was. A tomboy. Pushy.

At school I always had to be first in line. Or raising my hand to answer the teacher. I was quick, and smart. It wasn't meant to be selfish—well, maybe it was, but not only that—but like I was restless, jumpy. Mexican jumping bean, Grandma called me. Like a watch wound so tight it's got to tick faster than any other watch or it will burst.

How long we were driving the back-country roads, I don't know. Started out in Sanborn, around 2 P.M., I mean Irish and Kathlee picked me up then. We drove to Olcott Beach, then the Lake Isle Inn where Irish was drinking beer and Kathlee and me Cokes, and we played the pinball machines and Irish played euchre with some older men and it happened he won fifty-seven dollars. The look on his face! Kathlee and I counted it out in mostly ones and fives. Irish kept saying he wasn't any card player, must've been luck like being struck by lightning.

Kathlee said then we'd better go home, Nedra and her. And Irish right away agreed. We'd been with him all that afternoon. And I was worried that Grandma might've called home to tell Momma—or what if Daddy answered the phone!— how we'd gone off with somebody in a pickup truck she hadn't caught a clear glimpse of (from the front window where she was looking out) but believed it was an older boy, not Kathlee's age. And that swath of dark-red hair, maybe one of the McEwans? (The McEwans were well known in the area. Mostly, the men had bad reputations. Not Irish McEwan, everybody liked Irish who'd played football at Strykersville High, but the others, especially the old man Malachi.)

So Irish treats everybody at the Lake Isle Inn to drinks, roast beef sandwiches, and French fries. Spent more than half of his winnings like he needed to be rid of it.

When we left it was a little after 5 P.M. Though I could be wrong. It's summer, and bright and glaring-hot as noon. A kind of shimmery light over the lake, and a warm briny-smelling wind, and that smell of dead fish, clams. Irish is driving us home and there's a good happy feeling from him winning at euchre, he's saying maybe his luck has changed, and it's strange to me, to hear a boy like Irish McEwan say such a thing, like his life is not perfect though he is himself perfect (in the eyes of a thirteen-year-old, I mean). In the front seat Kathlee is next to Irish, squeezed between him and me, and her hair that's the color of ripe wheat is blowing wild. And her skirt lifting over her knees so she's trying to hold it down. And she's sneaking looks at Irish. And him at her. They'd danced a little at the tavern, dropping coins in the jukebox. And on the beach, I'd seen him kissing her. And I'm NOT JEALOUS, I'm only just thirteen and would be scared to death I KNOW if any boy let alone Irish McEwan asked to dance with me, or even talked to me in any special way. I'm this jumpy homely girl, immature my mother would say, for my age. Maybe I like Irish McEwan too, more than I should, but I know he'd never glance twice at me, and it's a surprise even he seems interested in Kathlee who's never had a boyfriend, she's so sweet and nervous and shy and flushes when boys talk to her, or tease her, though she can talk okay with girls, and adults, and gets B's in school. *Simple!* some of the kids say of my sister and that is absolutely untrue. Now Irish McEwan is asking politely where do we live, exactly?—he thinks he knows, but better be sure. And Kathlee tells him. And we're on the Strykersville Road, a two-lane blacktop highway leading away from Lake Ontario where the tavern is. It would be said of Irish McEwan that he'd had a dozen beers that afternoon, the alcohol count in his blood was high, but Irish never drove recklessly all the hours we were with him and has been polite not just to Kathlee and me, but to everybody we met. He's a muscle-shouldered boy you might compare to a steer on its hind legs. He's strong, and can be a little clumsy. He's got pale skin, for a boy who works outdoors, with smatterings of freckles, and thick dark-red hair straggling over his ears and down his neck. He would've been good-looking except for his habit of frowning, grimacing with his mouth, as bad as my father who's hard of hearing and screws up his face trying to figure out what people are saying. Irish McEwan is twenty-three years old and already his forehead's lined like a man's twice that age.

Then on the Strykersville Road, Irish says suddenly he has a feeling he'd better drop by his own house first. Because his father has been sort of expecting him and he hasn't gone. Because of meeting up with Kathlee, and then with me. And his father was expecting him around noon but he'd been with Kathlee then, and lost track of time. And Kathlee says okay, sure. So that's what we do. Where the McEwans live, or used to live, it's on the Strykersville Road about two miles closer to the lake than our house, and we live on a side road, so it makes sense to drop by Irish's house before he takes us home. The McEwan house (that would be shown in newspapers and on TV always looking better, more dignified than it is) is back from the highway about a quarter-mile. One of these bumpy rutted dirt lanes. Except the house is on a little rise, and evergreens in the front yard are mostly dead, you couldn't have seen it from the road. One of those old faded red-brick houses along Lake Ontario that look larger from the outside than they actually are, and sort of distinguished, like a house in town, except the shutters and trim are rotting, and the roof leaks, and the chimney, and there's no insulation, and the plumbing (as my father who's a carpenter would say) is probably shot to hell. And the outbuildings in worse shape, needing repair. The McEwans are farmers, or were, but hadn't much interest in farm work, at least not Malachi and Johnny who worked odd jobs in town, but never kept them long. These McEwans were men with quick tempers who didn't like to be bossed around, especially when they'd been drinking. So we're driving up the rutted lane and on one side is a scrubby cornfield and on the other is a rock-strewn pasture, and some grazing guernseys that raise their heads to look at us as Irish bounces past raising clouds of dust. *My pa is gonna be madder than hell* Irish says with this nervous laugh, *he wanted me here by noon.* Parking then in the cinder driveway. And there's an old Chevy sedan, and another pickup in the drive. And nobody around. Except scruffy chickens pecking in the dirt unperturbed, and a dog barking. This dog is a black mongrel-labrador cringing by the rear door of the house, and when Irish climbs out of the pickup the dog shies away, barking and whining, as if it doesn't recognize him. Irish calls to the dog *Mick, what's wrong? Don't you know me?* But the dog cringes and whimpers and runs away around the corner of the house.

And that's the first strange thing.

This gaunt ugly old faded red-brick house. Plastic strips still flapping over the windows, from last winter. Missing shingles, crooked shutters. The back porch practically rotted through. Streaks down the side of the house below the second-floor windows from, it would be said in disgust, men and boys urinating out the windows. *A house with no woman living in it you can tell.* (Because Irish's mother had died a few years ago, and the family split up. In the papers and on TV it would seem so confusing, who lived in this house, and who did not. Suspicious-sounding like the way they'd identify Irish as *Ciaran McEwan* which was a name nobody knew, and always giving his age as *twenty-three.* Strange and twisted such facts can seem.)

That day, August 11, 1969, only just the old man Malachi and the oldest brother Johnny were actually living in the house. But other McEwans, including Malachi's thirty-six-year-old biker son from his first marriage, might drop by at any time or even stay the night. And there might be a woman Malachi'd bring back from a tavern to stay a few days. At one time there'd been six children in the family, four brothers and two sisters, but all except Johnny had moved away. Irish moved away immediately after his mother died to live alone, aged seventeen, in Strykersville, in a room above the barbershop, and to work at the lumberyard where my dad knew him, and liked him. Most Saturdays in August, Irish had off. And so he happened to turn up in Sanborn, a small town six miles away, near the lake, where it just happened that Kathlee was working in our aunt Gloria's hair salon like she does some Saturdays, but not every Saturday, and I was at the library for a while, and then at our grandma's. *These things just happened, like dice being shaken and thrown, or like a pinball game, no more intention than that. I can swear!*

Irish enters his father's house by the rear door saying he'll be right back. The black Lab (that Irish would say he'd known since it was a pup) is hiding beneath the porch. Kathlee says, *Oh Nedra, d'you think Irish likes me?* She's excited, can't hardly sit still, licking her lips, peeping at herself in the dusty rearview mirror, and out of meanness I say guys like any girl who'll make out with them. Though I know it isn't true, an older guy like Irish would be used to kissing girls, and girls kissing him back, and plenty more beside that Kathlee, who's shocked by just words some of the boys at school yell, would never consent to. Kathlee says,

*Nedra, you're not nice*. And I say, nudging her, in the waist where there's a pinch of baby fat Kathlee hates being teased over, *I guess you think you are? Kiss-kiss*. I'm puckering my lips making the ugliest face I can.

Kathlee says, *Sometimes I hate you.*

So Kathlee's fired up and huffy, and climbs out of the pickup, and goes to the screen door that's rusted and has a broken spring, swinging open from where Irish has gone inside. She's wearing that blue-striped halter-top sundress with the elastic waist and short skirt that makes her look like a doll, and her fluffy-wavy hair to her shoulders, and her cheeks sort of flushed and slapped-looking from the excitement. *Because Kathlee Hogan isn't the kind of nice girl you'd expect to be seen with a boy like Irish McEwan.* She's calling, *Irish? Irish?* in a breathy little voice nothing like you'd hear from her if it was just me, her sister, close by. And after a minute or so, she goes to look inside the screen door, saying, *Irish? Can I come in?* and I'm surprised, Kathlee opens the door and turns back to me and sticks out her tongue, and disappears inside like this is a house she's been inside before, and I know for sure *it is not.* And I jump down out of the pickup, too. And (not knowing how stupid this behavior is, as I'd realize later) I'm squatting by the porch trying to see the black dog that's hiding beneath it, that I can hear panting and growling, and I'm cooing *Mick! Good dog! Don't be afraid, it's just Nedra.*

Like I'm God's gift to animals. If Irish McEwan is going to be Kathlee's boyfriend, I'm not jealous for I can talk to animals, some animals at least. As I don't wish to talk to humans.

But the dog won't come to me, and I'm fed up and restless, and I follow Kathlee into the McEwan house, like this is a kind of thing I'm accustomed to doing. And stepping inside I feel shivery right away, and my heart starts kicking in my chest. That kitchen! A real old refrigerator, and a filthy gas stove, and a plastic-topped table covered with dirtied plates, and more dirtied plates in the sink, and grease-stained walls and a high ceiling that's all cobwebs and cracks. A sickish smell of old burnt food. And a darker smell like fermenting apples. And worse. And I'm wiping at my eyes, and almost can't see. You'd think I would be calling *Kathlee? Kathlee? Irish?* but it's like my tongue has gone numb. I'm wearing just a tank top and denim cutoffs and rubber-thong sandals from the discount bin at Woolworth's. Wet from Olcott Beach where we'd been running in the surf. And my straggly hair that's dishwater blond, not a soft pretty color like Kathlee's, sticking in my face. And there's Kathlee in the doorway, her back to me. She's looking into the front room (that would be called in the news stories the "parlor," not the living room) and it seems to me I can see her spine shivering, though she isn't moving just standing there, and what I'm seeing also that's unexpected is a grandfather clock in the hall, not ticking, pendulum still, a tall handsome wood-carved clock with Roman numerals and afterward I will learn that the clock belonged to Irish's mother, she'd brought it with her when she married Malachi McEwan. *Of course it's broken. Like everything in this house.* And there comes Irish up behind Kathlee. From a room off the hall. The bathroom, I'm thinking, because Irish is wiping his hands on his thighs like he's just washed them. Or maybe his hands are sweaty, he's sweated through his T-shirt. And there's this look on his face, hungry and scared, but when he touches my sister he's gentle, takes hold of her wrist between two of his big fingers, and Kathlee turns right away to look up at him, blank and trusting as a baby, or maybe she's stunned, in a state of shock, and Irish slips his arm around her waist, and says words I can't hear, and Kathlee presses against him and hides her face and when Irish turns to walk her away, back through the kitchen and out of the house, I hide from them in a corner of the kitchen, and they don't see me. And I'm excited, I know there's something in the front room *I have to see.* I can smell it, I'm so scared I'm shaking, or maybe it's just excitement, like our cats excited and yellow-eyed and their tails switching when they smell their prey invisible and indiscernible to us, and irresistible. I'm Nedra, the pushy one. I'm Nedra, all elbows. Lucky your sister came first, folks teased, 'cause your mother might not've wanted a second one of you. I'm Nedra, I would've pushed past Kathlee in the hall if Irish hadn't stepped out of that room. So I run to the doorway in a house strange to me, pushy and nosy. And I see. I'm panting like that dog under the porch, and I see. I don't know what I am seeing, what the name or names for it might be, this sight is no more real to me than flicking through TV like I do when I'm restless and nobody's there to scold me. Maybe I'm smiling. I'm a girl who smiles when she's nervous or scared, for instance if boys look at me in a certain way and I'm alone, and nobody close by to define me, to know not *who I am* (because I would not expect that) but *whose daughter.* My nostrils are pinching with the strong smell, and I'm beginning to gag. There's something sickish-rotten like guts, and human shit, a shameful smell you recognize without putting a name to it. And I hear the flies. And see them. Where they're a buzzing cloud like metal filings on the broken heads of two men. Men I don't know. Adult men, one of them with thick white bloodstained hair. Blood and brains on the filthy carpet of this room that would be called the parlor. Like a child had smeared crimson Crayola marks across a picture. Splashed onto a worn-out old sofa and chairs. The bodies looked like they'd crawled to where they were. Blood-soaked workclothes, and blood in the ridges and crevices of what had been faces. Yet they were lying easy as sleep. The weirdness was to me, seeing adult men lying on the floor, and me standing over them almost! Thinking, *Except for those horseflies they'd be at peace now.*

*Kathlee.* No, Irish McEwan was not my fiancé that day. Nor my boyfriend. All that, I explained.

I explained we'd been together every minute. Since late that morning around eleven, or eleven-thirty. To whenever time it was when the sheriff's men came, with their siren blasting, to the house. Irish was the one to telephone for help. He'd gone back inside the house, to use the phone. Yes: All those hours I was in his company. At first it was just Irish and me, then we went to pick up Nedra at Grandma's. Oh, all the places we drove, I don't know . . . We were talking and laughing. Listening to Tommy Lee Ryan, "Just Kiss Goodbye," and the Meadowlarks, "Sweet Lovin' Time." And the Top Ten.

A dozen times I would be questioned, and always I would swear. I began to get sick, fainting-sick, in just entering one of their buildings. My parents would take me of course. But you never get used to it. People looking at you like you're not telling the truth. Like you're a criminal or murderer yourself! *Don't be afraid of them, honey,* Irish would console me. *They can't do anything to you. They can't do anything to me either, I promise.* And I knew this was so, but I was filled with worry.

The last customer's hair I rinsed for my aunt Gloria was about ten o'clock, a walk-in. Then I did sweeping and cleanup and taking out trash et cetera into the alley. An hour of this, maybe. That's when I saw Irish McEwan driving past. On Niagara Street. Around eleven o'clock. A little later, I saw him parked by the bridge. Gloria said it was all right if I quit a little earlier, that time of summer is slow in the beauty salon. So I left around quarter to twelve, I'm sure. If Aunt Gloria remembers later, around one, oh she is mistaken but I never wanted to argue face-to-face. Always I was polite to older relatives, always to adults. You weren't rude, not in my family. I ran down the street to say hello to Irish McEwan who my father knew. Yes, that was the first time. Like that. Yes, but I knew him. From Strykersville. No, I never knew his father or brother. His father they called old man McEwan. (Not that Malachi McEwan was truly old: In the paper, his age was given as fifty-seven.)

Yes, Irish knew my name. He said it—*Kathlee*. It was my baby sister's name for me from when she couldn't pronounce *Kathleen*. So everybody called me *Kathlee*, that was my special name and I liked it.

We were talking and kidding around and Irish asked if I'd like to ride a little and I said yes, so we did, then he asked how'd I like to drive to Olcott Beach, which is nine miles away, and I said yes I would except we have to take my little sister Nedra, she's at our grandma's. So we went to pick up Nedra, where she was slouched on the glider on Grandma's porch reading. What time was this, maybe twelve-thirty. That Nedra! She was a fanatic about books. Every Saturday she'd return books to the library and take out more books and she had cards for two public libraries, and still that was hardly enough for her. She would go to college and be a librarian or a teacher everybody predicted. The first in the Hogan family to go away to school. I would have been the first to graduate from high school, except marrying Irish McEwan like I did in my junior year, I had to drop out. You couldn't be married at that time and remain in school. It just wasn't done. You'd be expelled. Nobody questioned this just as nobody questioned the Vietnam War. (Remember that war?) These days a girl can be pregnant and unmarried and she'll be welcome to stay in school, nobody protests. At least, not officially. It's an enlightened time today in this new century, or a fallen time. It's a more merciful time, as a Christian might see it, or it's a time of no shame. But then, in the early 1970s where we lived in Eden County in upstate New York, we were the people we were, and when Irish McEwan and I married I dropped out of school, and was happy to be a wife to him, and soon a mother. Good riddance was how I felt, leaving Strykersville, people talking about us like they were. Even so-called nice people. Even my friends. Because they were jealous. Because I was so happy, and had my baby thirteen months after we were married (I know, everybody was counting months), and nobody was going to cheat me of what I deserved. I swore on the Holy Bible that Irish McEwan had been in Sanborn by eleven o'clock that morning and he'd been in my company for hours and when we drove to his father's farm he was never out of my sight for more than a few seconds, and never until then saw what was inside the house. It was a pure shock to him. But his first thought was for me. *Kathlee*, he said, *no, you don't want to see*. He was white-faced and trembling but his first thought was of me. He pulled me from the doorway, and I didn't see. He said they'd been struck down by shotgun blasts, that was what it seemed to him. He was not excited or hysterical but calm-speaking, yet he was mistaken about this. Also, Irish said he knew who'd done it, but afterward he wouldn't repeat these words, he'd never repeat them again even to me, even after we were married. And moved away from Strykersville. And the farm (which was mostly mortgaged) was sold.

No. Nedra never went into that house. She was in Irish's pickup in the driveway. She was afraid to get out because of the dog barking. She says she followed me inside, and she saw the dead men, but that's just Nedra making things up. She was always nervous, and saw things in the dark.

Anything physical, that wasn't in a book, Nedra could not handle. For all her pushy behavior and sarcasm. Yes, she was smart, she got high grades, but there were things she didn't comprehend. She'd never have an actual boyfriend. The boys who might've liked her, she scared off with her smart-aleck remarks, and the other boys, they'd never give a plain skinny girl like Nedra a second glance. She was scornful of them too, or pretended to be. Saying to me, after Irish and I were married and living in Yewville, and Holly was about a year old, in this earnest quivering voice *Kathlee, how can you let it be done to you? What a man does? Doesn't it hurt? Or do you get used to it? And having a baby, doesn't it hurt awful?* I was so surprised at my sister saying such things, I laughed, but I was angry, too. I said *Nedra! Watch your mouth. This baby could pick up such talk, and remember years later.*

*Nedra.* And somebody comes up behind me to touch my shoulder. Where I'm just standing there. And it's Irish, and he's gentle with me like he'd been with Kathlee, saying my name, Nedra, which was strange on his lips, saying I'd better come outside with him, and not look anymore.

Like there's danger he must rescue me from. There *is* danger, and he will rescue me from it.

Not holding me as he'd held Kathlee. But he took my hand, that was numb as ice, like I'm a little girl to be led away. He brings me dazed and blinking and stumbling back outside where Kathlee is crying and whimpering, saying *Oh! oh! oh!* but I'm not crying, and I won't cry, it wasn't real to me yet. Or, I was thinking, *Who are they, nobody I know. Why should I cry.* But a hot acid mash comes boiling up out of me, my stomach, and I'm vomiting, spattering the ground at my feet and onto my yellow rubber-thong sandals from Woolworth's I would throw away forever, after that day.

I would not be a witness. I would not give a statement. I was thirteen years old and the county argued I was not a child, I was old enough to provide a statement they argued, but my parents told them yes I was too young, I was an immature girl for my age, and what I believed I might have seen wasn't necessarily to be believed. For Kathlee swore she'd seen nothing inside the house, and Kathlee insisted I had not even gone inside. *Because she was jealous. Irish McEwan leading me out of the house, holding my hand. That red-haired boy with the dark eyes, treating her sister tenderly.*

My eyes were never the same since. In the fall, I would be diagnosed as myopic in both eyes, and would have to wear glasses, and nobody can believe my eyes were perfect before what I was made to see, and my life changed. In a few years, I would "see" without glasses just vague blurry things, and partly this was my habit of reading, reading, reading all the time including late at night, with just a single lamp burning, but mostly it was because of what I saw at the McEwan farm that day, that my sister Kathlee would deny I ever saw! *Nedra you know you're imagining it. You never went anywhere near that house. Irish says he doesn't remember you inside. There was so much happening, and none of it had to do with you.*

I would wish to God I'd never gone to Sanborn that day. Or I would wish I'd stayed at Grandma's. I had my library books, and I was helping Grandma cut out a dress pattern in tissue paper, sticking in the straight pins, and holding it up against me. (A wool plaid jumper for me. That ever afterward, when I wore it, I would have a sickish feeling.) When Irish and Kathlee came by to get me, I would not know what time it was. It was after lunch, but how long, I don't know. They would inquire of Grandma, too, and she was confused and obstinate, and finally they gave up in disgust because if Grandma said one thing, next morning she would wish to change it, and finally they gave up on me. Because I could not contradict my sister who was so certain what she knew. I could not contradict my sister who swore what she believed to be true while in my state of nerves I could not swear what was true, nor even what I believed might be true. Was it past two o'clock they came for me, in the steel-colored Ford pickup with rusted grillwork, pulling up at the curb outside Grandma's house, or was it before noon, *I could not swear.* I would not say either time. For what a surprise to see my sister Kathlee with any boy, happy and waving at me, let alone that red-haired Irish McEwan everybody knew. When you're thirteen, being driven around in a twenty-three-year-old's pickup, and at Olcott Beach on the boardwalk and running along the beach laughing and squealing like girls you've seen all your life, with guys, but never dreamt it could be you, you are not able to retain a clear picture of what did, or did not, happen. Especially if it is hurtful of those close to you.

*Nedra, you know. Just tell the truth.*

*It was before noon Irish came for me. It was only just a few minutes later, we came for you at Grandma's. You know!*

*He couldn't have been at the farm. When it happened. He was with me at the time they said it happened. Every minute, Irish was with me. Nedra, you know!*

But I wish I didn't. Even now a long time later. Mr. McEwan and his son Johnny had been seen alive by a neighbor around noon of that day. The coroner ruled they'd been killed between that time and approximately 2 P.M. But Kathlee had seen Irish in Sanborn as early as 11:30 A.M. She would swear. So Irish could not have been the murderer, that was a fact. *Nedra, you saw him, too. Say you did. Say you did! Just say what's TRUE.*

But I could not. I became dizzy, and stammered; and shook so bad, it was speculated I might be "epileptic." That was when my eyes began to worsen. For I could not swear what I had seen, because Kathlee insisted I had not seen it, how then could I swear what I had not seen?

The look in my sister's eyes! Like mica glinting in the sun.

The change that came over my sister, and would never go away.

*She is in love. She isn't Kathlee now.* So fierce, I believed she might have clawed out my eyes like a cat. But even earlier, at Olcott. A wildness in her. For no boy had ever kissed her before that day as Irish McEwan kissed her (I'm sure of it!) where they drifted off away from me. Where I stood barefoot in the smelly surf tossing broken clamshells out into the lake. Calling after them jeering *Kiss-kiss! You're disgusting! I hate you both!*

But the wind blew my words away.

Wished I hadn't gone to Olcott with them that day. And on that ride to the McEwan farm! Irish had been drinking but was not drunk I'm sure. He was excitable, and jumpy, but you could say that was only natural because he feared the old man who was known for his bad temper and his cruelty to his wife and children. For sure, Irish's father had beaten them all. It would come out in the papers. And you could say that the dog Mick, who'd known Irish all its life and was frightened of him that day and ran under the porch to hide, had been terrified by the murders, the screaming and shouting, and by the awful smell of death that all animals can identify.

The flies! I feel them brushing my lips sometimes. My eyelashes. Wake up screaming.

The ax, no I did not see any ax. (Never would the *murder weapon* be found. People said he'd buried it or dropped it in the Yew River.) I saw no ax in the front room, but I would later learn the murder weapon was a double-edged ax, investigators concluded; and the McEwans' ax was missing from the farm, never to be found. In the first shock of seeing the bodies Irish would think his father and brother had been killed by shotgun blasts. And Irish would say to us, he knew who the murderer was. He knew! Saying in a dull slow voice *There's somebody wanted Pa dead for a long time, now it's happened.* But when police came, Irish would not tell them this. He would tell no one these words, ever again.

I never lied, because I never gave testimony. And if I had sworn, I would not have lied because I could not remember except what was confused and rushing as a bad dream. I was a plain girl with a silly streak and I would grow into a plain woman with a melancholy heart. Except when I look at my niece Holly, then my heart swells with something like happiness. For I love this child like my own. For I have never had any daughter, and never will. It's true that I have a certain weakness for my students (I teach seventh-grade English at Strykersville Junior High) and in their eyes I am Miss Hogan, one of the no-nonsense, funny, enjoyable teachers, for I hide my melancholy from them, but my affection isn't very real or lasting and as soon as school ends in June, I cease to think of the children and will scarcely remember them in the future. Maybe I am not a happy woman but I believe that happiness is a region in which we can dwell, if only for brief periods of time. And when I am with Kathlee and Holly my niece, I dwell in such happiness. For they are my family, mostly; and when I am with them I behave like a happy woman, and so it might be so.

*Kathlee.* The fact is, Irish McEwan *had not been* at his father's house that morning, he *first saw the bodies past 5 P.M.* of that day, stopping at the farm with Nedra and me. But many were doubtful of him, at first. For a long time it was hard. How people want to believe the worst, oh I came to know how people are, even Christians: in your hearts mean and malicious and hurtful. And yet—meeting Irish as people did, looking into his eyes that were a warm rich brown, a burning brown, almost black, those beautiful eyes, you would see the goodness in him, and come to believe him, too.

The police questioned so many men, why'd anybody wish to focus upon Irish? Yet there are people who wish to believe the worst: that a son would murder his father (and his older brother!) in such a terrible way. But what about Melvin Hooker who lived next door, it was known there was an old feud between him and the McEwans, Malachi had shot one of Hooker's dogs claiming it had killed some of his chickens. And there were men Malachi owed money to, scattered about. And his son Petey he was always fighting with. And the Medinas, the family of Malachi's deceased wife Anne, who bitterly hated Malachi for his treatment of her. It was said that Malachi had ceased to love and respect his wife during her first pregnancy, and she would have six children! By the time she was wasting away with breast cancer, and bald from chemotherapy, Malachi made no secret of his revulsion for her, even to their children. And made no secret of his affairs with women.

Like the wind in the dried cornfields the whisper came to me. *If ever a man deserved death. And a hard death. If ever a man deserved God's vengeance.*

But Irish was not one to speak ill of the dead. In all things, Irish was respectful. We were married in the Methodist Church and our baby baptized in that faith. In time, my mother came to accept my husband and even, I believe, to love him. My father, being ill with diabetes, and set in his mind against us, never came to truly know Irish nor even, to that old man's shame, his beautiful granddaughter.

Irish said, *He's a good man, Kathlee. But troubled in his heart.*

Irish said, *He's an old man. It isn't for us to judge him.*

It was a fact, Irish McEwan and I were deeply in love when we got married. But it was not to be an easy marriage, with such a shadow over us, like great bruised-looking clouds over Lake Ontario you look up and see, surprised, where a few minutes before the sky had been clear. For people persisted in saying mean things behind our backs. For it was not easy for Irish to keep a job, which was why we moved so often. And there was Irish's weakness for drinking, like all the McEwan men, his only true reliable happiness he spoke of it, shamefacedly, wishing he might change, yet finding it so very hard to change, as I could sympathize, for I had such a bad habit of smoking, like a leech was sucking at me with its ugly lips, for years. Yet it was a fact: Irish was a good husband, and a good father, as far as he could be. I understood he was troubled in his mind, that the true murderer of his father and brother was never arrested. He seemed to know and to accept who it was. That first hour, at the farm, when he'd discovered the bodies, and shielded me from seeing, where I had come up behind him like a silly little fool, he'd known who it was, most likely, the murderer, but never would he say. Never, questioned by police, would he accuse another, even to defend himself.

*Tell them what you know, honey.* I begged him.

*What do I know?* Irish asked, lifting his hands and smiling. *You tell me, baby.*

Of course, all the McEwan sons were questioned by police. The thirty-six-year-old biker who lived in Niagara Falls, and had a criminal record, Irish's half-brother, was a strong suspect. But nothing was ever proven against him. Like Irish, Petey McEwan could account for where he was at the time of the murders. And it was miles away. There was a woman who claimed he was with her, and maybe this was so.

The family farm was only twelve acres. Mostly mortgaged from a Yewville bank. In time, the property would go to Malachi McEwan's surviving sons and daughters, but it would be near-worthless after taxes and other assessments, and not a one of the heirs would wish to live there, nor even to visit it, as I said to Irish we might do, one day, a crazy idea I guess it was, but an idea that came into my head, and I spoke without thinking, *Honey, why don't we drive out to the farm before it's sold, and show Holly?*

Holly was just two years old then. We were living in Yewville.

Irish said, *Show Holly what?*

*The farm. Where you grew up. The land, the barn . . .*

*The house? You'd want to show her the house?*

*It's been cleaned, hasn't it?*

*Has it?*

*Well, I mean,* and here I began to stammer, feeling such a fool, and Irish staring at me with this tight little smile of his meaning he's pissed, but trying not to let on,—*hasn't it? Been cleaned?*

I had not looked into the front room. As Nedra claimed she had. I saw only just a blur, a dizziness before my eyes. There were vivid crimson blotches and a frenzied glinting (I would learn later these were horseflies! ugly nasty horseflies) but I saw nothing, and I did not know. And now Irish was waiting for me to answer—what? I could not even think what we'd been speaking of! My thoughts were so confused.

Then I remembered: Yes, the house had been cleaned. Of course! How could such a property be sold, otherwise? After the police took away what they wished. Nobody in the McEwan family wished to do such a task, so the janitor at the high school was hired, and scrubbed the floorboards and the walls and whatever. And the filthy old blood-soaked carpet had been hauled away by police, for their investigation. So the "parlor" might now be clean. But we would never step into that place of death of course, I never meant that Holly would see that room! This I would have explained to Irish except—where had Irish gone?

Out in the driveway I heard the pickup start. He'd be gone through the night probably, and one day, some years into the future, when Holly was in junior high, he wouldn't come back at all.

That night I watched Holly sleeping in her little bed as often I did. Not in concern that she would cease breathing, as nervous mothers do, but in a trance of love for her. *Your grandfather had to die,* the sudden thought came to me, *that you might be born.* A great happiness filled my heart. A great calmness came over me. What I knew seemed too great for what I could comprehend in an actual thought, as a mother knows by instinct her child's need. As when I was nursing Holly, in a distant room I could feel her waking and hungry for the breast, and my breasts would seem to waken too, leaking sweet warm milk, and in my trance of love I would hurry to her.

For my life is about her, my baby. It is not about Irish McEwan after all.

*Nedra.* Those nights! When I couldn't sleep. When Kathlee didn't want to share a room with me any longer, saying I made her nervous, so I had to sleep in a tiny room hardly more than a closet, in the upstairs hall. When my eyes began to go bad, from so much reading. Bright-lighted pages (from a crooknecked lamp by my bed) and beyond the pages darkness. My eyes stared, stared at the print until it melted into a blur. And a faint buzzing began I would refuse to hear knowing it was not real. Sometimes then I would jump from bed to use the bathroom, or I would tiptoe to a window on the landing where some nights, by moonlight, you could see the lake a few miles away, a thin strip of mist at the horizon. Most nights there was only a thickness like smoke and no moon, and no stars.

For my niece Holly's second birthday I would give her a big box of Crayolas. Like the crayons I'd loved when I was a little girl. And we would draw together, my niece and I, and tell each other silly stories.

Holly used to laugh, and touch my cheek. "Auntie Neda, I love you!"

The story of what I saw but had not seen. And what I had not seen, I would see and tell myself all my life.

# Ian Rankin

## The Confession

PROBABLY NO suspense writer has attracted as much attention as Ian Rankin in these past few years. He has brought his own voice, style, and viewpoint to the police procedural in particular, and to crime fiction is general. He is one of those rare writers who is as good with the short story as he is with the novel. One senses even greater days ahead for him. "The Confession," which first appeared in the June issue of *Ellery Queen's Mystery Magazine*, showcases a master at work, with the plot and characterization compacted down to the bare essentials, all the while revealing an incredible depth in every line.

# The Confession

*Ian Rankin*

It was Tony's idea," he says, shifting in his seat. "Tony's my brother, a couple of years younger than me, but he was always the brainy one. It was all his idea. I just went along with it."

He's still trying to get comfortable. It's not easy to get comfortable in the Interview Room. The CID man could tell him that. He could tell him that the chair he's wriggling in has been modified ever so slightly, a quarter-inch taken off its front legs. The chair isn't designed with rest and relaxation in mind.

"So Tony says to me one day, he says: 'Ian, this is one plan that cannot fail.' And he tells me about it. We spend a bit of time bouncing it around, you know, me trying to pick holes in it. I have to admit, it looked pretty good. Well, that's the problem really. That's why I'm here. It was just too bloody good all round. . . ."

He looks around again, studying the walls as if expecting two-way mirrors, secret listening devices. The one thing he's not been expecting is the quietness. It's eleven-thirty on a weekday night. The police station is like a ghost town. He wants to see lots of activity, lots of uniforms. Yet again in his life, he's being let down.

Tony had noticed the slip-road. He drove from Fife to Edinburgh most Saturday nights, taking a carful of friends. They went to pubs and clubs, danced, chatted up women. A late-night pizza and maybe a couple of espressos before home. Tony didn't drink. He didn't mind staying sober while everyone around him had a skinful. He always liked to be in control. On the A90 south of the Forth Road Bridge, he'd seen the signpost for the slip-road. He'd seen it before—must've passed it a hundred times—but this one night something about it bothered him. The next morning, he headed back. The sign said: DEPART-MENT OF TRANSPORT VEHICLE CHECK AREA ONLY. He took the slip-road, found himself at a sort of roundabout in the middle of nowhere. He stopped his car and got out. There was grass growing in the middle of the road. He didn't think the place got used much. A hut nearby, and a metal ramp that might have been a weighbridge. Another slip-road led back down onto the A90. He stood there for a while listening to the rush of traffic below him, an idea slowly forming in his head.

"See," Ian went on, "Tony had worked for a time as a security guard, and he still had a couple of uniforms hanging in his wardrobe. He's always had the idea of robbing someplace, always knew those uniforms would come in handy. One of his pals, guy called Malc, he works—I should say worked—in a printing shop. So Tony brought Malc in, said we could trust him. Have you got a cigarette?"

The detective points to the No Smoking sign, but then relents, hands over a packet of ten and some matches.

"Thanks. So you see," lighting up, exhaling noisily, "it was all Tony's idea, and Malc had a certain expertise, too. I didn't have anything. It was just that I was family, so Tony knew he could trust me. I haven't worked in eight years. Used to be in heavy engineering up in Leven, got laid off in the slump. If somebody could do something about the manufacturing industry in this country, there'd be a lot less crime. Bit of advice there, free of charge." He flicks ash into the ashtray, brushes some stray flecks from his trousers. "I'm not saying I didn't play a part. Obviously, I wouldn't be here otherwise. I just want it on record that I wasn't the brains of the operation."

"I think I can go along with that," the detective says. Ian asks him if he shouldn't be taking notes or something. "We're trained, lad. Elephant's memory."

So Ian nods, goes on with his story. The interview room is small and airless. It carries the aromas of every person who's ever been through it, all of them telling their stories. A few of them even turning out to be true . . .

"So we make a few recces, and never once do we see the place being used. We stopped the car on the slip-road a few nights. Plenty of lorries steaming past, but nobody so much as notices us or asks what we're up to. This is what Tony wanted to know. We set the thing up for last Wednesday."

"Why a Wednesday?" the detective asks.

Ian just shrugs. "Tony's idea," he says. "All I did was go along with him. He was the mastermind: That's the word I've been wanting. Mastermind." He shifts again in his chair, stares at the walls again, remembering Wednesday night.

Tony and Ian were dressed in the uniforms. Tony had a friend with a haulage truck. It had been easy to borrow it for the night. The story was, they were helping someone move house. Malc had come up with IDs for them: They'd had their photos taken at a passport booth, and the laminated cards, each in its own wallet, looked authentic. They took the truck up to the roundabout, left the car near the bottom of the slip-road. Malc was dressed in a leather jacket and baseball cap. He was supposed to be a truck driver. Tony would head back down the ramp and use a torch to signal a lorry onto the slip-road. Then he'd ask the driver to go to the test area, where Ian would be apparently interviewing another lorry driver. This was so the real driver wouldn't suspect anything.

"It worked," Ian says. "That's what's so unbelievable. First lorry he stopped, the driver brought it up to the roundabout, stopped it, and got out. Tony comes driving up, gets out of his car. Asks to see the delivery note, then says he wants to check the cargo."

The detective has a question. "What if it turned out to be cabbages or fish or something?"

"First thing Tony asked was what he was carrying. If it had been something we couldn't sell, he'd have let him go. But we came up gold at the first attempt. Washing machines, two dozen of them at three-hundred quid apiece. Only problem was, by the time we'd squeezed them into our own lorry, we'd no room for anything else, and we were cream-crackered anyway. Otherwise, I think we could have kept going all night." Ian pauses. "You're wondering about the driver, aren't you? There were three of us, remember. All we did was tie him up, leave him in his cab. We knew he'd get himself free eventually. Quiet up there; we didn't want him starving to death. And off we went with the haul. We had about fifteen of the machines and were already thinking of who we could sell them to. Storage was no problem. Tony has a couple of lockups. We left them there. There's a local villain, name of Andy Horrigan. He runs a couple of pubs and cafes, so I thought maybe he'd be in the market. We were being careful, see. Once the news was out that someone had boosted a consignment of washer-dryers . . . well, we had to be careful who we sold to." He pauses. "Only, we'd already made that one fatal mistake. . . ."

One mistake. He asks for another cigarette. His hand is shaking as he lights it. He can't get it out of his head, the insane bad luck of it. Even before he'd had a chance to say anything to Andy Horrigan, Horrigan had something to ask him.

"Here, Ian, heard anything about a heist? Washer-dryers, nicked from the back of a lorry?"

"I didn't see anything in the papers," Ian had replied. Quite honestly, too: It had surprised them, the way there had been nothing in the press or on radio and TV. Ian could see Horrigan was bursting to tell him. He knew right away it couldn't be good news, not coming from Horrigan.

"It wasn't in the papers, never will be neither."

And as he'd gone on to explain it, Ian had felt his life ebb away. He'd run to the lockup, finding Tony there. Tony already knew: It was written on his face. He knew they had to get rid of the machines, dump them somewhere. But that meant getting another lorry from somewhere.

"Hang on, though," Tony had said, his brain slipping into gear. "Eddie Hart isn't after the machines, is he? He only wants what's his."

Eddie Hart: At mention of the name, Ian could feel his knees buckling. "Steady Eddie" was the Dundee Godfather, a man with an almost mythical status as mover and shaker, entrepreneur, and hammer-wielding maniac. If you crossed Steady Eddie, he got out his carpentry nails. And according to the local word, Eddie was absolutely furious.

He'd probably put a lot of thought into the scheme. He needed to move drugs around, and had hit on the idea of hiding them inside white goods. After all, a lorryload of washer-dryers or fridge-freezers—they could saunter up and down every motorway in the country. All you needed were some fake dockets listing origin and destination. It just so happened that Tony had hit on one of Eddie's drivers. And now Eddie was out for blood.

But Tony was right: If they handed back the dope, got it back to Eddie somehow, maybe they'd be allowed to live. Maybe it would be all right. So they started tearing the packing from the machines, unscrewing the back of each to search behind the drum for hidden packages. And when that failed, they emptied out each machine's complimentary packet of washing powder. They went through both lockups, they checked and double-checked every machine. And found nothing.

Ian thought maybe the stuff had been hidden in one of the machines they'd left behind.

"Use your loaf," his brother told him. "If that were true, why would he be after us? Wait a minute, though . . ."

And he went back, counting the machines. There was one missing. The brothers looked at one another, headed for Tony's car. At Malc's mother's house, Malc had just plumbed the machine in. The old twin-tub was out on the front path, waiting to be junked. Malc's mother was rubbing her hands over the front of her new washer-dryer, telling the neighbours who'd gathered in the kitchen what a good laddie her son was.

"Saved up and bought it as a surprise."

Even Ian knew that they were in real trouble now. Everyone in town would get to hear about the new washing-machine . . . and word would most definitely travel.

They took Malc outside, explained the situation to him. He went back indoors and maneuvered the machine out of its cubbyhole, explaining that he'd forgotten to remove the transit bolts. His hands were trembling so much, he kept dropping the screwdriver. But at last he had the back of the machine off and started handing brown-paper packages to Tony and Ian. Tony explained to the neighbours that they were weights, to stop the machine slipping and sliding when it was in the back of the lorry.

"Like bricks?" one neighbour asked, and when he agreed with her, sweat pouring down his face, she added a further question. "Why cover bricks in brown paper?"

Tony, beyond explanations, put his head in his hands and wept.

The detective brings back two beakers of coffee, one for himself, one for Ian. He's been checking up, using the computer, making a couple of phone calls. Ian sits ready to tell him the last of it.

"We couldn't just hand the stuff back, had to think of a way to do it. So we drove up to Dundee, night before last. Steady Eddie has a nightclub. We put the stuff in one of the skips at the back of the club, then phoned the club and told them where they could find it. Thing is, the club gets its rubbish collected privately, and the company works at night. So that night, the skip got emptied. Well, that wouldn't have mattered, only . . . only it was me made the call . . . and there were two numbers in the phone book. Instead of the office, I'd got through to the public phone on the wall beside the bar. It must have been some punter who answered. I just said my piece then hung up. I don't know . . . maybe they nipped outside and got the stuff for themselves. Maybe they didn't hear me, or thought I was drunk or something. . . ." His voice is choking; he's close to tears.

"Mr. Hart didn't get the stuff?" the detective guesses. Ian nods agreement. "And now your brother and Malc have gone missing?"

"Eddie got them. He must have done."

"And you want us to protect you?"

"Witness relocation: You can do that, can't you? I mean, there's a price on my head now. You've *got* to!"

The detective nods. "We can do it," he says. "But what exactly is it you're a witness to? There's no record of a lorry being hijacked. Nobody's reported such a loss. You don't seem to have any evidence linking Mr. Hart to anything illegal—

much as I'd love it if you did." The detective draws his chair closer. "It wasn't a slump that led to you losing your job, Ian. It was threatening your foreman. He didn't like your attitude, and you started spinning him some story about having a brother who's a terrorist, and who'd stick a bomb under his car. You scared the poor man half to death, until he found out the truth. See, I've got all of that in the files, Ian. What I don't have is anything about washing-machines, drugs wrapped in brown paper, or missing persons."

Ian leaps from his seat, begins pacing the room. "You could send a team out to the dump. If the drugs are there, they'll find them. Or . . . or go to the lockups, the washing machines will still be there . . . unless Steady Eddie's taken them. I wouldn't put it past him. Don't you see? I'm the only one left who can testify against him!"

The detective is on his feet now, too. "I think it's time you were off, son. I'll see you as far as the door."

"I need protection!"

The detective comes up to him again. Their faces are inches apart.

"Get your brother the terrorist to protect you. His name's . . . Billy, isn't it? Only you can't do that, can you? Because you haven't got a brother called Billy. Or a brother called Tony, if it comes to that." The detective pauses. "You haven't got *anybody*, Ian. You're a nobody. These stories of yours . . . that's all they are, stories. Come on now, it's time you were home. Your mum will be worrying."

"She got a new washing machine last week," Ian says softly. "The man who delivered it, he said sorry for being so late. He'd been stopped at a checkpoint."

It is quiet in the interview room. Quiet for a long time, until Ian begins weeping, weeping for the brother he's just lost again.

# Peter Lovesey

## The Perfectionist

PETER LOVESEY won a mystery novel writing contest in 1969 and has never looked back. The numerous awards and distinctions heaped upon his work continue to accrue, his latest being the Diamond Dagger for Lifetime Achievement from the Crime Writers Association. He has balanced his love of historical England (both his Prince of Wales and his Sgt. Cribb–Constable Thackery series) with a more dispassionate, harsher eye for his own times as seen in several novels, including his latest, and many, many outstanding short stories. As in "The Perfectionist," which first appeared in issue 4 of *The Strand Magazine*.

# The Perfectionist

*Peter Lovesey*

The invitation dropped on the doormat of The Laurels along with a bank statement and a *Guide Dogs for the Blind* appeal. It was in a cream-coloured envelope made from thick, expensive-looking paper. Duncan left it to open after the others. His custom was to leave the most promising letters while he worked steadily through the others, using a paper knife that cut the envelopes tidily. Eventually he took out a gold-edged card with his name inscribed in the centre in fine italic script. It read:

> The most perfect club in the world
> has the good sense to invite
> *Mr. Duncan Driffield*
> a proven perfectionist
> to be an honoured guest at its biannual dinner
> Friday, January 31st, 7:30 for 8 pm
> *Contact will be made later*

He was wary. This could be an elaborate marketing ploy. In the past he'd been invited—by motor dealers and furniture retailers—to parties that had turned out to be sales pitches, nothing more. Just because no product or company was mentioned, he wasn't going to be taken in. He read the invitation through several times. It has to be said, he liked the designation "a proven perfectionist." Couldn't fault their research. He was a Virgo—orderly, a striver for perfection. To see this written down as if he'd already achieved the ideal was especially pleasing. And to see his name in such elegant script was another fine touch.

Yet it troubled him that the club was not named. Nor was there an address, nor any mention of where the function was to be held. Being a thorough and cautious man, he would normally have looked these things up before deciding what to do about the invitation.

The phone call came about 8:30 the next evening. A voice that didn't need to announce it had been to a very good school spoke his name.

"Yes?"

"You received an invitation to the dinner on January 31st, I trust?"

"Which invitation was that?" Duncan said as if he received invitations by every post.

"A gold-edged card naming you a proven perfectionist. May we take it that you will accept?"

"Who are you, exactly?"

"A group of like-minded people. We know you'll fit in."

"Is there some mystery about it? I don't wish to join the Freemasons."

"We're not Freemasons, Mr. Driffield."

"How did you get my name?"

"It was put to the committee. You were the outstanding candidate."

"Really?" He glowed inwardly before his level-headedness returned.

"Is there any obligation?"

"You mean are we trying to sell something? Absolutely not."

"I don't have to make a speech?"

"We don't go in for speeches. It isn't like that at all. We'll do everything possible to welcome you and make you feel relaxed. Transport is provided."

"Are you willing to tell me your name?"

"Of course. It's David Hopkins. I do hope you're going to say yes."

Why not, he thought. "All right, Mr. Hopkins."

"Excellent. I'm sure if I ask you to be ready at 6:30 that as a proven perfectionist, you will be—to the minute. In case you were wondering, it's a dinner jacket and black tie affair. I'll come for you myself. The drive takes nearly an hour at that time of day, I'm afraid. And it's Dr. Hopkins actually, but please call me David."

After the call, Duncan, in his systematic way, tried to track down David Hopkins in the phone directory and the Medical Register. He found three people by that name and called them on the phone, but their voices had nothing like the honeyed tone of the David Hopkins he had spoken to.

He wondered who had put his name forward. Someone must have. It would be interesting to see if he recognised David Hopkins.

He did not. Precisely on time, on the last Friday in January, Dr. David Hopkins arrived—a slim, dark man in his forties, of average height. They shook hands.

"Is there anything I can bring? A bottle of whisky?"

"No. You're our guest, Duncan."

He liked the look of David. He felt that an uncommonly special evening was in prospect.

They walked out to the car—a large black Daimler, chauffeur-driven.

"We can enjoy the wine with a clear conscience," David explained, "but I would be dishonest if I led you to think that was the only reason we are being driven."

When they were both inside, David leaned across and pulled down a blind. There was one on each window and across the partition between the driver and themselves. Duncan couldn't see out at all. "This is in your interest."

"Why is that?"

"We ask our guests to be good enough to respect the privacy of the club. If you don't know where we meet, you can't upset anyone."

"I see. Now that we're alone, and I'm committed to coming, can you tell me some more?"

"A little. We're all of your cast of mind, actually."

"Perfectionists?"

He smiled. "That's one of our attributes."

"I wondered why I was asked. Do I know any of the members?"

"I doubt it."

"Then how . . ."

"Your crowning achievement."

Duncan tried to think which achievement could have come to their notice. He'd had an unremarkable career in the civil service. Sang a bit with a local choir. Once won first prize for his sweet peas in the town flower show, but he'd given up growing them now. He could think of nothing of enough merit to interest this high-powered club.

"How many members are there?"

"Fewer than we would like. Not many meet the criteria."

"So how many is that?"

"Currently, five."

"Oh—as few as that?"

"We're small and exclusive."

"I can't think why you invited me."

"It will become clear."

More questions from Duncan elicited little else, except that club had been in existence for over a hundred years. He assumed—but had the tact not to ask—that he would be invited to join if the members approved of him that evening. How he wished he was one of those people with a fund of funny stories. He feared he was dull company.

In just under the hour, the car came to a halt and the chauffeur opened the door. Duncan glanced about him as he stepped out, wanting to get some sense of where he was. It was dark, of course, but they were clearly in a London square— with street lights, a park in the centre, and plane trees at intervals in front of the houses. He couldn't put a name to it. The houses were terraced, and Georgian, just as they are in almost every other London square.

"Straight up the steps," said David. "The door is open."

They went in, through a hallway with mirrors, brightly lit by a crystal chandelier. The dazzling effect, after the dim lighting in the car, made him blink. David took Duncan's coat and handed it to a manservant and then opened a door.

"Gentlemen," he said. "May I present our guest, Mr. Duncan Driffield."

It was a smallish anteroom, and four men stood waiting with glasses of wine. Two looked quite elderly, the others about forty or so. One of the younger men was wearing a kilt.

The one who was probably the senior member extended a bony hand. "Joe Franks. I'm president, through a process of elimination."

There were some smiles at this that David didn't fully understand. Joe Franks went on to say, "I qualified for membership in 1934, when I was only nineteen, but I didn't officially join until after the war."

David, at Duncan's side, murmured something that made no sense about a body left in a trunk at Brighton railway station.

"And this well set-up fellow on my right," said Joe Franks, "is Wally Winthrop, the first private individual to put ricin to profitable use. Wally now owns one of the largest supermarket chains in Europe."

"Did you say *rice?*" asked Duncan.

"No, *ricin*. A vegetable poison."

It was difficult to see the connection between a vegetable poison and a supermarket chain. Wally Winthrop grinned and shook Duncan's hand.

"Tell you about it one of these days," he said.

Joe Franks indicated the man in the kilt. "Alex McPhee is our youngest member and our most prolific. Is it seven, Alex?"

"So far," said McPhee, and this caused more amusement.

"His *skene-dhu* has more than once come to the aid of the club," added Joe Franks.

Duncan wasn't too familiar with Gaelic, but he had a faint idea that the *skene-dhu* was the ornamental dagger worn by a Highlander in his stocking. He supposed the club used this one as part of some ritual.

"And now meet Michael Pitt-Struthers, who advises the SAS on the martial arts. His knowledge of pressure points is unrivalled. Shake hands very carefully with Michael."

More smiles, the biggest from Pitt-Struthers, who squeezed Duncan's hand in a way that left no doubt as to his expertise.

"And of course you've already met our doctor member, David Hopkins, who knows more about allergic reactions than any man alive."

With a huge effort to be sociable, Duncan remarked, "Such a variety of talents. I can't think what you all have in common."

Joe Franks answered, "Each of us has committed a perfect murder."

Duncan played the statement over in his head. He thought he'd heard it right. It had been spoken with some pride. This time no one smiled. More disturbingly, no one disputed it.

"Shall we go in to dinner, gentlemen?" Joe Franks suggested.

At a round table in the next room, Duncan tried to come to terms with the sensational claim he had just heard. If it was true, what on earth was he doing sharing a meal with a bunch of killers? And why had they chosen to take him into their confidence? If he shopped them to the police, they wouldn't be perfect murderers any longer. Maybe it was wise not to mention this while he was seated between the martial arts expert and the Scot with the *skene-dhu* tucked into his sock.

The wineglasses were filled with claret by an elderly waiter.

"Hungarian," Joe Franks confided. "He understands no English." He raised his glass. "At this point, gentlemen, I propose a toast to Thomas de Quincey, author of that brilliant essay, "On Murder, Considered as one of the Fine Arts", who esteemed the killing of Sir Edmund Godfrey as the finest work of the eighteenth century for the excellent reason that no one was able to determine who had done it."

"Thomas de Quincey," said everyone, with Duncan just a half-beat slower than the rest.

"You're probably wondering what brings us together," said Wally Winthrop across the table. "You might think we'd be uncomfortable sharing our secrets. In fact, it works the other way. It's a tremendous relief. I don't have to tell you, Duncan, what it's like after you commit your first—living in fear of being found out, waiting for the police siren and the knock on the door. As the months pass, this panicky stage fades and is replaced by a feeling of isolation. You've set yourself apart from others by your action. You can only look forward to keeping your secret bottled up for the rest of your life. It's horrible. We've all been through it. Five years have to pass—five years without being charged with murder—before you're contacted by the club and invited to join us for a meal."

David Hopkins briskly took up the conversation. "It's such a break in the clouds, to discover that you're not alone in the world. To find that what you've done is valued, in some circles, as an achievement which can be openly discussed. Wonderful. After all, there is worth in having committed a perfect murder."

"How do you know you can trust each other?" Duncan asked, without giving anything away.

"Mutual self-interest. If any one of us betrayed the others, he'd take himself down as well. We're all in the same boat."

Joe Franks explained, "It's a safeguard that's worked for over a hundred years. One of our first members was the man better known as Jack the Ripper, who was, in fact, a pillar of the establishment. If his identity could be protected all these years, then the rest of us can breathe easy."

"That's amazing. You know who the Ripper was?"

"Aye," said McPhee calmly. "And no one has ever named the laddie."

"Can I ask?"

"Not till you join," said Joe Franks.

Duncan hesitated. He was about to say he had no chance of joining, not having committed a murder, when some inner voice prompted him to shut up. These people were acting as if he was one of them. Maybe, through some ghastly mistake, they'd been told he'd once done away with a fellow human being. And maybe it was in his interest not to disillusion them.

"We have to keep to the rules," Wally Winthrop was explaining.

"Certain information is only passed on to full members."

Joe Franks added, "And we are confident you will want to join. All we ask is that you respect the rules. Not a word must be spoken to anyone else about this evening, or the existence of the club. The ultimate sanction is at our disposal for anyone foolish enough to betray us."

"The ultimate sanction—what's that?" Duncan huskily enquired.

No one answered, but the Scot beside him grinned in a way Duncan didn't care for.

"The *skene-dhu.* . . . ?" said Duncan.

". . . or the pressure point," said Joe Franks, "or the allergic reaction, or whatever we decide is tidiest. But it won't happen in your case."

"No chance," Duncan affirmed. "My lips are sealed."

The starters were served, and he was pleased when the conversation shifted to murders in fiction, and some recent crime novels. Faintly he listened as they discussed *The Silence of the Lambs*, but he was trying to think what to say if someone asked about the murder he was supposed to have committed. They were sure to return to him before the evening ended, and then it was essential to sound convincing. If they got the idea he was a mild man who wouldn't hurt a fly he was in real trouble.

Towards the end of the meal, he spoke up. It seemed a good idea to take the initiative. "This has been a brilliant evening. Is there any chance I could join?"

"You've enjoyed yourself?" said Joe Franks. "That's excellent. A kindred spirit."

"It will take more than that for you to become a member," Winthrop put in. "You've got to provide some evidence that you're one of us."

Duncan swallowed hard. "Don't you have that? I wouldn't be here if you hadn't found something out."

"There's a difference between finding something out and seeing the proof."

"That won't be easy."

"It's the rule."

He tried another tack. "Can I ask something? How did you get on to me?"

There were smiles all round. Winthrop said. "You're surprised that we succeeded where the police failed?"

"Experience," Joe Franks explained. "We're much better placed than the police to know how these things are done."

Pitt-Struthers—the strong, silent man who advised the SAS—said. "We know you were at the scene on the evening it happened, and we know no one else had a stronger motive or a better opportunity."

"But we must have the proof," insisted Winthrop.

"The weapon," suggested McPhee.

"I disposed of it," Duncan improvised. He was not an imaginative man, but this was an extreme situation. "You would have, wouldn't you?"

"No," said McPhee. "I just give mine a wee wipe."

"Well, it's up to you, old boy," Winthrop told Duncan. "Only you can furnish the evidence."

"How long do I have?"

"The next meeting is in July. We'd like to confirm you as a full member then."

The conversation moved on to other subjects and then a lengthy discussion ensued about the problems faced by the Crown Prosecution Service.

The evening ended with coffee, cognac and cigars. Soon after, David Hopkins said that the car would be outside.

On the drive back, Duncan, deeply perturbed and trying not to show it, pumped David for information.

"It was an interesting evening, but it's left me with a problem."

"What's that?"

"I—eh—wasn't completely sure which murder of mine they were talking about."

"Do you mean you're a serial killer?"

Duncan gulped. He hadn't meant that at all. "I've never thought of myself as one." Recovering his poise a little, he added, "A thing like that is all in the mind, I suppose. Which one do they have me down for?"

"The killing of Sir Jacob Drinkwater at the Brighton Civil Service Conference in 1995."

*Drinkwater.* He had been at that conference. He remembered hearing that the senior civil servant at the Irish Office had been found dead in his hotel room on that Sunday morning. "That was supposed to have been a heart attack."

"Officially, yes," said David.

"But you heard something else?"

"I happen to know the pathologist who did the autopsy. A privileged source. They didn't want the public knowing that Sir Jacob had actually been murdered, and what means the killer had used, for fear of creating a terrorism panic. How did you introduce the cyanide? Was it in his aftershave?"

"Trade secret," Duncan answered cleverly.

"Of course the security people in their blinkered way couldn't imagine it was anything but a political assassination. They didn't know you'd had a grudge against him dating from years back, when he was your boss in the Land Registry."

Someone had their wires crossed. It was a man called *Charlie* Drinkwater who'd made Duncan's life a misery and blighted his career. No connection with Sir Jacob. Giving nothing away, he said smoothly, "And you worked out that I was at the conference?"

"Same floor. Missed the banquet on Saturday evening, giving you a fine opportunity to break into his room and plant the cyanide. So we have motive, opportunity. . ."

"And means?" said Duncan.

David laughed. "Your house is called The Laurels, for the bushes all round the garden. It's well known that if you soak laurel leaves and evaporate the liquid, you get a lethal concentration of cyanide. Isn't that how you made the stuff?"

"I'd rather leave you in suspense," said Duncan. He was thinking hard. "If I apply to join the club, I may give a demonstration."

"There's no *if* about it. They liked you. You're expected to join."

"I could decide against it."

"Why?"

"Private reasons."

David turned to face him, his face creased in concern. "They'd take a very grave view of that, Duncan. We invited you along in good faith."

"But no obligation, I thought."

"Look at it from the club's point of view. We're vulnerable now. You're dealing with dangerous men, Duncan. I can't urge you strongly enough to co-operate."

"But if I can't prove that I killed a man?"

"You must think of something. We're willing to be convinced. If you cold shoulder us, or betray us, I can't answer for the consequences."

A sobering end to the evening.

For the next three weeks he got little sleep, and when he did drift off he would wake with nightmares of fingers pressing on his arteries or *skene-dhus* being thrust between his ribs. He faced a classic dilemma. Either admit he hadn't murdered Sir Jacob Drinkwater—which meant he was a security risk to the club—or concoct some false evidence, bluff his way in, and spend the rest of his life hoping they wouldn't find him out. Faking evidence wouldn't be easy. They were intelligent men.

*"You must think of something,"* David Hopkins had urged.

Being methodical, he went to the British Newspaper Library and spent many hours rotating the microfilm, studying accounts of Sir Jacob's death. It only depressed him more, reading about the involvement of Special Branch, the Anti-Terrorist Squad and MI5 in the official investigation. Nothing he had read, up to and including the final pronouncement in the papers that the death had been ruled a heart attack and the investigation closed, proved helpful to him. How in the world would he be able to acquire the evidence the club insisted on seeing?

More months went by.

Duncan weighed the possibility of pointing out to the members that they'd made a mistake. Surely, he thought (in rare optimistic moments), they would see that it wasn't his fault. He was just an ordinary bloke caught up in something out of his league. He could promise not to say anything to anyone, in return for a guarantee of personal safety. Then he remembered the eyes of some of those people around the table, and he knew how unrealistic that idea was.

One morning in May, out of desperation, he had a brilliant idea. It arose from something David Hopkins had said in the car on the way home from the club: *"Do you mean you're a serial killer?"* At the time it had sounded preposterous. Now, it could be his salvation. Instead of striving to link himself to the murder of Sir Jacob, he would claim another killing—and show them some evidence they couldn't challenge. He'd satisfy the rules of the club and put everyone at their ease.

The brilliant part was this. He didn't need to kill anyone. He would claim to have murdered some poor wretch who had actually committed suicide. All he needed was a piece of evidence from the scene. Then he'd tell the Perfectionists he was a serial killer who dressed up his murders as suicides. They would be forced to agree how clever he was and admit him to the club. After a time, he'd give up going to the meetings and no one would bother him because they'd think their secrets were safe with him.

It was just a matter of waiting. Somebody, surely, would do away with himself before the July meeting of the club.

Each day Duncan studied *The Telegraph*, and no suicide—well, no suicide he could claim was a murder—was reported. At the end of June, he found an expensive-looking envelope on his doormat and knew with a sickening certainty who it was from.

> The most perfect club in the world
> takes pleasure in inviting
> *Mr. Duncan Driffield*
> a prime candidate for membership
> to present his credentials
> after dinner on July 19th, 7:30 for 8 pm
> *Contact will be made later*

This time the wording didn't pamper his ego at all. It filled him with dread. In effect it was a sentence of death. His only chance of a reprieve rested on some fellow creature committing suicide in the next two weeks.

He took to buying three newspapers instead of one, still with no success. It seemed as if there was no way out. Mercifully, and in the nick of time, however, his luck changed. News of a suicide reached him, but not through the press. He was phoned on the afternoon of the 19th by an old civil service colleague, Harry Hitchman. They'd met occasionally since retiring, but they weren't the closest of buddies, so the call came out of the blue.

"Some rather bad news," said Harry. "Remember Billy Fisher?"

"Of course I remember him," said Duncan. "We were in the same office for twelve years. What's happened?"

"He jumped off a hotel balcony last night. Killed himself."

"Billy? I can't believe it!"

"Nor me when I heard. Seems he was being treated for depression. I had no idea. He was always cracking jokes in the office. A bit of a comedian, I always thought."

"They're the people who crack, aren't they? All that funny stuff is just a front. His wife must be devastated."

"That's why I'm phoning round. She's with her sister. She understands that everyone will be wanting to offer sympathy and help if they can, but for the present she'd like to be left to come to terms with this herself."

"Okay." Duncan hesitated. "This happened only last night, you said?"

Already, an idea was forming in his troubled brain.

"Yes. He was staying overnight at some hotel in Mayfair. A reunion of some sort."

"Do you happen to know which one?"

"Which reunion?"

"No. Which hotel."

"The Excelsior . . . 1313. People talk about thirteen being unlucky. It was in Billy's case."

Sad as it was, this had to be Duncan's salvation. Billy Fisher was as suitable a murder victim as he could have wished for. Someone he'd actually worked with. He could think of a motive later—make up some story of an old feud. For once in his life, he needed to throw caution to the winds and act immediately. The police would have sealed Billy's hotel room pending some kind of investigation. Surely a proven perfectionist could think of a way to get inside and pick up some personal item that would pass as evidence that he had murdered his old colleague.

He took the 5:25 to London. Most of the other travellers were going up to town for an evening's entertainment. Duncan sat alone, avoiding eye contact and working out his plan. Through the two-hour journey he was deep in concentration, applying his brain to the challenge. By the time they reached Waterloo, he knew exactly what to do.

A taxi ride brought him to the hotel, a high-rise building near Shepherd Market. He glanced up, counted the wrought-iron balconies until he reached number thirteen, and thought of Billy's leap. Personally, he wouldn't have gone up so high. A fall from the sixth floor would have done the job just as well, and more quickly, too.

Doing his best to look like one of the guests, he walked briskly through the revolving doors into the spacious, carpeted foyer and over to the lift, which was waiting unoccupied. No one gave him a second glance. It was a huge relief when the door slid across and he was alone and rising.

So far, the plan was working beautifully. He got out at the 12th level and used the stairs to reach the 13th. It was now around 7:30, and he was wary of meeting people on their way out to dinner. He paused on the landing to let a couple pass by him on their way downstairs. They didn't seem to notice him. He moved along, looking for room 1313.

There it was. He had found Billy Fisher's hotel room. No policeman was on duty outside. What a stroke of luck, thought Duncan, it wasn't even as if a man had killed himself in there.

He went back down to the foyer, marched coolly up to the desk and looked at the pigeonhole system where the keys were kept. He'd noticed before how automatically reception staff hand over keys when asked. The key to 1313 was in place. Duncan didn't ask for it. 1311—the room next door—was also available and he was given its key without fuss.

Up on the 13th floor again, he let himself into 1311, taking care not to leave fingerprints. His idea was to get out on the balcony and climb across the short gap to the balcony of 1313. No one would suspect an entry by that route.

The plan had worked brilliantly up to now. The curtains were drawn in 1311. He didn't switch on the light, thinking he could cross to the window and get straight out to the balcony. Unfortunately his foot caught against a suitcase some careless guest had left on the floor. He stumbled, and was horrified to hear a female voice from the bed call out, "Is that you, Elmer?"

Duncan froze. This wasn't part of the plan. The room should have been unoccupied. He'd collected the key from downstairs.

The voice spoke again. "Did you get the necessary, honey? Did you have to go out for it?"

Duncan was in turmoil, his heart thumping. The plan hadn't allowed for this.

"Why don't you put on the light, Elmer?" the voice said. "Now I'm in bed I don't mind. I was only a little shy of being seen undressing."

What could he do? If he spoke, she would scream. Any minute now, she would reach for the bedside switch. The plan had failed. His one precious opportunity of getting off the hook was gone.

"Elmer?" The voice was suspicious now.

In the civil service, there had been a procedure for everything. Duncan's home life was similar—well ordered and structured. Now he was floundering, and next he panicked. Take control, something inside him urged. Take control, man. He groped his way to the source of the sound, snatched up a pillow and smothered the woman's voice. There were muffled sounds, and there was struggling, and he pressed harder. And harder. And finally it all stopped.

Silence.

He could think again, thank God, but the realization of what he had done appalled him.

He'd killed someone. He really had killed someone now.

His brain reeled and pulses pounded in his head and he wanted to break down and sob. Some instinct for survival told him to think, think, think.

By now, Elmer must have returned to the hotel to be told the room key had been collected. They'd be opening the door with a master key any minute.

Must get out, he thought.

The balcony exit was still the safest way to go. He crossed the room to the glass doors, slid them across and looked out.

The gap between this balcony and that of 1313 was about a metre—not impossible to bridge, but daunting when you looked down and thought of Billy Fisher hurtling towards the street below. In his agitated state, however Duncan didn't hesitate. He put a foot on the rail and was up and over and across. Just as he'd hoped, the doors to the balcony of 1313 were unfastened. He slid them open and stepped inside. And the light came on.

Room 1313 was full of people. Not policemen or hotel staff, but people who looked familiar, all smiling.

One of them said, "Caught you, Duncan. Caught you good and proper, my old mate." It was Billy Fisher, alive and grinning all over his fat face.

Duncan said, "You're . . ."

"Dead meat? No. You've been taken for a ride, old chum. Have a glass of bubbly, and I'll tell you all about it."

A champagne glass was put in his shaking hand. Everyone closed in, watching his reaction—as if it mattered. Their faces looked strangely familiar.

"Wondering where you've seen them before?" said Billy. "They're actors, mostly, earning a little extra between engagements. You know them better as the Perfectionists. They look different out of evening dress, don't they?"

He knew them now: David Hopkins, the doctor; McPhee, the *skene-dhu* specialist; Joe Franks, the trunk murderer; Wally Winthrop, the poisoner; and Pitt-Struthers, the martial arts man. In jeans and T-shirts and a little shame-faced at their roles in the deception, they looked totally unthreatening.

"You've got to admit it's a brilliant con," said Billy. "Retirement is so boring. I needed to turn my organising skills to something creative, so I thought this up. Mind, it had to be good to take you in."

"Why me?"

"Well, I knew you were up for it from the old days, and Harry Hitchman—where are you, Harry?"

A voice from the background said, "Over here."

"I knew Harry wouldn't mind playing along. So I rigged it up. Did the job properly, Civil service training. Got the cards printed nicely. Rented the private car and the room and hired the actors and stood you all a decent dinner. I was the Hungarian waiter, by the way, but you were too preoccupied with the others to spot me in my false moustache. And when you took it all in as I knew you would—being such a serious-minded guy—it was worth every penny. I wanted to top it with a wonderful finish, so I dreamed up the suicide," he quivered with laughter.

"You knew I'd come up here?"

"It was all laid out for your benefit, old sport. You were totally taken in by the perfect murder gag, and you were bound to look for a get out, so I fabricated one for you. Harry told you I'd jumped off the balcony, and when you asked in which hotel, I knew you took the bait."

"Bastard," said Duncan.

"Yes, I am," said Billy without apology. "It's my second career."

"And the woman in the room next door—is she an actress, too?"

"Which woman?"

"Oh, come on," said Duncan. "You've had your fun."

Billy was shaking his head. "We didn't expect you to come through the room next door. Is that how you got on the balcony? Typical Duncan Driffield, going the long way round. Which woman are you talking about?"

From the corridor outside came the sound of hammering on a door.

Duncan covered his ears.

"What's up with him?" said Billy.

# Edward D. Hoch

## A Wall Too High

ED HOCH doesn't seem to be resting on his laurels. In addition to producing the steady stream of fiction that has helped garner him his recent awards, he has been kept busy by his work in compiling a bibliography and the obituaries for the volume you hold in your hand. But the story is always the thing for Ed, as "A Wall Too High," first published in the June issue of *Ellery Queen's Mystery Magazine*, amply demonstrates.

# A Wall Too High

*Edward D. Hoch*

I understand you are a Gypsy king," the uniformed man addressed Michael Vlado, not without an edge of contempt in his voice. He was seated across the desk in an unadorned office fifty kilometers north of Prague. It was a sunny afternoon in early autumn, and Michael would rather have been back in the village with his wife and their horses.

He smiled, trying to cooperate with his inquisitor. "I am only a king to my people back in Romania. Here in the Czech Republic I am merely a tourist."

The man, taller than Michael, had slicked-back hair and a tiny black moustache. He said his name was Lieutenant Lyrik and he spoke German after learning that Michael's knowledge of the Czech language was limited. "More than a tourist. Our police computer lists you as a trouble-maker, an agent provocateur."

"Hardly that, Lieutenant! I have not traveled this distance to incite anyone to anything. As you must have guessed, I've come about the wall. The European Roma Rights Center in Budapest has commissioned me to act on its behalf, to request that the wall separating the Roma section of town from the rest be torn down at once."

"What you refer to as a wall on Masarak Street is no more than a fence."

Michael had dealt with this type of official before. It was never pleasant. "A seven-foot-high fence made of concrete?"

Lyrik shrugged. "There is a similar structure in Ústí nad Labem and that is called a fence too. You must realize that these Gypsies are criminals, beggars, thieves, and fortunetellers squatting in decrepit apartment buildings, usually without paying rent. Can we do nothing to protect the decent neighbors who live just across the street?"

Michael Vlado was growing impatient with this man. He had traveled from his village to do some good, not to hear a diatribe against the Roma. "You must know that seventy percent of Gypsy children in this country are shunted off to special schools for the mentally retarded. In many cases, their parents have been fired from their jobs, beaten, and killed. The police do nothing."

"What do you want?" the lieutenant asked. "Why have you been sent here?"

"The Roma Rights Center wants the walls here and in Ústí nad Labem torn down. They want the Gypsies free from segregation and persecution."

"This is strictly a local matter. You have no authority here." After a moment's thought he stood up. "But we do not wish to seem uncooperative. Let me speak to my superior."

Left alone, Michael let his eyes wander over the slate-gray walls and the framed photograph of the country's president, Václav Havel. The single window offered a view of the parking lot, and he noticed a uniformed officer checking his license plate and peering into the car. He wondered if they'd ask his permission to search it.

Presently Lieutenant Lyrik returned. He resumed his seat behind the desk and smiled. "I have been given permission to take you to the Gypsy quarter and show you the fence."

"Very good. That's what I wanted."

Michael followed along to the officer's car, where the man who'd been inspecting his vehicle joined them. "This is Sergeant Cista. He will accompany us," the lieutenant said. Cista was a grim sort who shook hands and then rested his palm on the holster flap of his pistol. Michael was given the front passenger seat and he was well aware that Cista was seated directly behind him with the weapon.

The small city's commercial and shopping district covered only a half-dozen blocks and within minutes they'd reached an area of decrepit apartment buildings, two stories in height. He saw at once that a solid concrete wall had been erected down the center of the wide street, effectively separating the apartment block from the two-family homes on the other side. As Lyrik started down the better side of the avenue, Michael said, "I'd like to visit the Roma side first."

"Very well." The lieutenant backed out, made a sharp turn, and then proceeded past the Gypsy apartments. Behind him, Michael heard the snap as Sergeant Cista opened the flap on his holster.

Some of the Gypsy women were on the sidewalk clustered in small groups. One older woman in a colorful skirt spit at the police car as it went by. Further along there were a few men and boys, too, shouting their defiance at the wall. "Can you stop?" Michael asked. "I wish to speak with them."

"That's not allowed," was the answer.

"What about that woman?" He indicated a fair-skinned redhead in her thirties. "Surely she's not a Roma."

"Mrs. Autumn," Cista muttered from behind him.

"Is that her name?"

Lyrik snorted. "She is sent by an Irish relief agency to work with the Gypsies. We call her that because she comes every autumn."

"I'd like to meet her."

Lyrik dismissed the suggestion. "She's an agitator." They pulled around the end of the wall and started down the other side. "As you can see, this is no Berlin wall. Your Gypsies need merely to walk around it. But it does offer the neighbors some respite from their noise and rubbish."

He stopped the car and they got out. The wall rose higher than Michael's head, probably seven feet. As they approached it, Lyrik explained that it was constructed of cinder blocks with cement facing. Michael wondered how long it would be before graffiti began to appear on it.

Sergeant Cista had remained behind them near the car while Lyrik and

Michael walked up to the wall. "Perhaps the noise and garbage you fear so much would be less if the children were not denied a proper education," Michael told the lieutenant, reaching out to touch the rough concrete of the wall.

Lyrik opened his mouth as if to reply when a sudden sound like the crack of a rifle reached them from the distance. Lieutenant Lyrik gasped and his right hand flew to his face. He sank to his knees and toppled forward into the wall. Michael could see blood on the pavement even before Sergeant Cista ran up and turned him over.

There was a bloody wound over Lyrik's right eye. Michael had no doubt that the shot had killed him instantly.

Cista's hand came up from his holster, holding the pistol he'd been so anxious to draw. "Back up," he ordered Michael.

"I didn't kill him. I have no weapon." Not knowing how well the sergeant understood him, he raised his hands above his head.

Cista unhooked the cell phone from Lyrik's belt and called for help. Already a few neighbors had ventured forth from the two-family homes that lined the street on this side of the wall. "I heard the shot," one man said. "The Gypsies killed him!"

Michael was kept well away from the body as an ambulance and police car arrived on the scene. The body was quickly removed as the gathering crowd increased in size, and Cista escorted a police officer over to where Michael waited. "I am Captain Mulheim," the officer said briskly. "Do you wish to make a statement?" He was older and stouter than Lyrik had been, perhaps reflecting his higher rank.

"I have no statement to make. I'm sure you are aware that I came at the request of the European Roma Rights Center. Lieutenant Lyrik was showing me your wall when he was shot."

"By a bullet from the Gypsy side of the wall."

"We don't know that," Michael insisted. "I heard the shot but couldn't tell its direction."

The police captain glowered. "You will accompany me to headquarters while we check your story," he said, making it clear there was no room for negotiation.

Michael Vlado sat on a hard wooden bench for two hours outside Captain Mulheim's office. Finally, at five o'clock, he was summoned inside. "Your story checks out," the captain told him. "I also have the medical examiner's report. The fatal bullet passed through Lieutenant Lyrik's head and was not recovered, but it came from a high-powered rifle some distance away, probably equipped with a telescopic sight. An hour from now, at six o'clock, I am going on television to issue an ultimatum. If the killer of Lieutenant Lyrik does not surrender within twenty-four hours, the police and militia will clear all Gypsies from the apartments on Masarak Street. The message will also be broadcast by loud-speakers on the street."

"You can't do that," Michael said, trying to keep his voice under control.

"Can't?" The captain smiled. "You seem to forget that I am the law in this city. I have full authority in all criminal matters."

"Let me speak to the Rom. Let me get to the bottom of this."

"Certainly," Captain Mulheim said, getting to his feet. "You have twenty-four hours to deliver the murderer."

Michael left police headquarters and walked back several blocks through the decrepit city. To his eye, the area being protected from a Rom incursion was little better than the Gypsy section itself. The wall was not a matter of economics but rather of fear. As he passed the wall itself he could still see the stain of Lyrik's blood on the pavement where he'd fallen. Michael rounded the end of the wall and walked up to the first house. It was a two-story apartment like the others, although a broken front window on the second floor told him that apartment was probably unoccupied. From downstairs came the sound of off-key music, perhaps played on an accordion.

A young woman wearing a full red skirt came to the door, frowning at him. She had the dark features of a Gypsy, though her manner almost suggested a Western upbringing. "Are you police?" she asked immediately. "They have already questioned us about the shooting."

"My name is Michael Vlado," he told her. "I have been sent by the European Roma Rights Center in Budapest. It's about the wall."

"You are Rom?"

"Yes."

"Come in," she said reluctantly, stepping aside. The outlines of her long legs were visible against the thin fabric of the skirt.

The music grew louder as he entered a small, neat living room. He saw at once that it was coming from two boys about nine or ten years old. The younger was playing a small violin while the other had an accordion. It was little more than a toy but he was coaxing passable music from it.

"These are your sons?"

"Yes."

"Your husband?"

"He is at work." She brushed the dark hair back from her face, then added, "I am Rosetta. My sons are Erik and Josef." She signaled to the boys. "Go practice in your room."

They disappeared through the kitchen. Michael sat down on the nearest chair. "They play well for children."

"Gypsies love music, but you must know that. They say a violin in the hands of a Gypsy produces purer and more passionate sounds than for anyone else."

"That is true," Michael agreed. Then, "I have disturbing news. The police captain, Mulheim, is threatening to clear this entire block if the killer of Lieutenant Lyrik does not surrender within twenty-four hours."

"Of course!" She showed a flash of anger. "We are easy people to blame for any crime. He sent you to tell us this?"

"No. You will learn it soon enough." Already, far in the distance, he could hear the blare of an approaching sound truck, its message not yet clear. He glanced toward the ceiling, where the sound of the children's music had resumed. "Does someone live upstairs?"

Rosetta shook her head. "It's empty. The children play there and practice their music."

"Josef shows great promise for his age. Is he around ten?"

"He is twelve. I know he looks younger. Sometimes we cannot afford the food a growing boy needs. His father beats him if he catches him begging in the streets with the other Rom children. He wants to support us through his own work, but that is not always possible."

"Do the police bother you?"

"All the time," she acknowledged. "But we are used to it. My husband says it is the price we must pay for living in the city."

"How many of you are living here?"

"About seventy. There were more, but the police harassment has driven many away. That is their goal, of course."

The sound truck was on the street now, blaring its message for all to hear.

Captain Mulheim had seen to it that the announcement was read in Czech, followed by a translation into Rom. Michael lifted the curtain on the front window and looked down the street. A few men and some women had come out of the apartments and were gathering in small groups. "I'd better go out there," he told her. "I may see you again later."

The Irish woman that Lyrik had pointed out to him had emerged from one of the houses and was pleading with the Rom to remain calm. One man, taller and bulkier than the rest, already held a slender dagger in his hand. "I am calm until they drive me from my home," he told anyone who would listen. "Then I am angry."

Others clustered around and when there was an opportunity Michael spoke to the Irish woman and introduced himself. "I'm glad they've sent someone," she told him. "I can't handle this alone." Up close he judged her age to be around forty, but the long red hair had given her a younger appearance when he saw her from the patrol car.

"The police call you Mrs. Autumn," he said.

"They usually call me worse than that. My name is Mary Baxter. Come inside where we can talk."

"Do you live here?"

"I stay in one of the empty apartments when I come each year."

"Is this a fairly stable Rom community?" Michael asked, following her up the steps to one of the apartments. The inside walls were greasy from years of cooking. Peeling paint hung from the ceiling.

She shrugged. "Some Gypsies are meant to wander. I do believe it is in their blood."

"My wife and I have lived in the same Romanian town for more than fifteen years. We have a farm where we raise horses."

"Ah, but you're here now, aren't you?" Mary Baxter said. "I imagine this position with the Roma Rights Center keeps you away from home much of the time. It is your own form of wandering."

"It is a new thing for me. But I admit to being away frequently. Perhaps you are right. But I'm interested in this particular community. Is there anyone you know who resents the wall enough to shoot a police officer over it?"

"Many."

He gestured out the window toward the man with the dagger. "That one?"

"His name is Mathias. He is their protector and he takes the job seriously."

"Might he have killed the lieutenant?"

Mary Baxter shook her head. "That dagger is his weapon. I have never seen anyone on the block with a firearm."

He motioned toward the peeling paint. "This place needs work. The house at the end of the block is in much better shape."

"Rosetta Lacko. She has a husband and two fine children. They're not all that lucky. But I hope to find time to paint these walls while I'm here."

"Who lives upstairs?"

"Mathias."

"The one with the knife?"

"He doesn't worry me. Next year it'll be someone else."

"Why do you keep coming back?" Michael asked.

"Because the job is never finished, is it?"

"No," he agreed.

Mary Baxter prepared something for them to eat, and they talked into the evening hours. "Michael is an unusual name for a Rom," she observed.

"Not in Romania. I was named for their last king, deposed by the Communists after the war and still living in exile. We were ruled with an iron fist until recently."

"Sometimes I wish for a strong president here to keep the local police under control."

"I thought Václav Havel was a strong leader. He's highly regarded in other countries. Can't he control them?"

She shook her head. "Havel has lost much of his popularity with the Czech people. He seems to do nothing toward helping the Gypsies."

The conversation shifted to the murder of Lieutenant Lyrik, and who might have fired the fatal shot. "There aren't a great many men on the street," Michael observed. "Is there a tribal king?"

"The last one moved away. Rosetta's husband Bruno will probably replace him."

"Where does he work?"

"He has a booth at the fun fair on the outskirts of the city, one of those where you hit the target and win trinkets or stuffed animals. He should be home soon."

Michael glanced at his watch. "I must be going. I hadn't realized it was so late."

"Where will you stay?"

He smiled. "The Roma Rights Center arranged for a hotel room. I have two beds if you'd care to sleep in comfort for one night."

She smiled and shook her head. "It is a kind offer, but my place is here."

"When does Mathias return with his dagger?"

"When he's so drunk I have to help him upstairs to his bed."

"Before I leave, could you show me the upstairs apartment? The side facing the wall?"

"Follow me."

She snapped on the stairway light and led him up to Mathias's place. The door was unlocked, and as they entered Michael could smell the odor of beer and stale tobacco smoke. He stood at the window for a moment, trying to gauge the angle down to the wall in the center of Masarak Street. "I need more light," he decided. "Could I return in the morning?"

"Certainly. It may be our last day here if the police drive us out."

"You don't think Lyrik's killer will confess?"

"Whoever did it, he is not a Gypsy. He is not here."

Michael looked again at his watch. "I really must leave. I'll be back in the morning."

She saw him to the door and he headed down the street the way he had come, nodding to some of the Gypsy families lounging in front of their apartments. Though it was after nine o'clock, Rosetta's children were still practicing on their instruments and she was seated on the front steps. As he stopped to say hello, a well-built man with glasses and a moustache loomed up beside her. "Bruno," she said, "this is the man from the Roma Rights Center that I told you about."

"Bruno Lacko," he said, extending his hand to Michael. "Rosetta tells me you've come to help."

"If I can. Mary—Mrs. Autumn—tells me you're in charge here."

"When I can be. I work long hours for my family."

"What is the feeling among your people? Might one of them have killed Lieutenant Lyrik?"

"In a fair fight, certainly. No one on this block would have fired a rifle at him. No one owns a rifle that I'm aware of."

Michael nodded. "I'd like to return tomorrow and take some measurements from your upstairs window to the wall. Would that be all right?"

"Certainly, so long as you make it before the police deadline. We don't know what will happen then."

Michael slept well in the strange bed and ate breakfast at the hotel. As he retraced his route to Masarak Street he was aware of the police cars slowly circling the blocks. One of them came to a stop at a corner, blocking his route across a street. The window rolled down and Captain Mulheim peered out.

"I did not expect you to be here still, Gypsy. At six this evening Masarak Street will not be a safe place."

"I'm hoping I can help settle this matter before your deadline. Would it be possible for me to examine the lieutenant's body?"

Mulheim shook his head. "It was cremated this morning. He had no wife or close relatives."

"Captain, I ask that you consult with me before moving against those Gypsies."

"I can make no promises," he said, and the car window slid silently shut.

Michael continued on his way, aware that he was never out of sight of at least one patrol car. He entered Masarak Street from the other end, but the street showed little difference when approached from that direction. The first adult he saw was Mary Baxter, directing children into a small van that he guessed must function as a school bus.

"You've come back," she said.

"Of course. Are these children schooled by the state?"

"Not so they learn anything. I've managed to enroll them in a private school for half days. We have to provide our own transportation, but it's better than nothing."

Once the van pulled away from the curb, crowded to overflowing, she relaxed with a sigh. "I don't want them here this evening, in case there is violence. No one knows how serious the police are about evicting us."

"They're serious," he said, following her into the apartment. "If they are driven out, will you return to Ireland?"

"Not until Christmas, whatever happens. My husband—"

"Then there is a Mr. Autumn?"

She laughed. "Yes, there is. He teaches the autumn semester each year at Trinity College."

Michael stood by the front window, staring at the wall again. "Would you happen to have a ball of string or twine?"

"I think there's one in the kitchen. I'll get it."

She returned with it and they went upstairs together. "Is Mathias still here?" he asked quietly.

She nodded. "He came in late, and drunk as usual. He'll still be sleeping."

He followed her inside and opened the parlor window. They were just about opposite the spot where Lyrik had been shot. Hefting the ball of twine about the size of his fist, he said, "I'll see how my pitching arm is." Holding one end, he threw the ball out the window, aiming for the other side of the wall. Leaving a trail of twine as it unwound, the ball just cleared the seven-foot wall.

"What's all this?" a voice growled behind them.

It was Mathias, wearing a dirty nightshirt, his tall hulk filling the bedroom doorway. He had the dagger in his hand, as if facing some threatening intruder, but Mary quickly disarmed him. "You met Michael yesterday, Mathias," she reminded him. "He is trying to find out who killed the police officer."

He grumbled something but returned to his bedroom. "Here," Michael said, handing the end of the twine to Mary. "Hold this while I go around to the other side of the wall."

He then hurried downstairs and circled the end of the wall to the other side. About halfway along he found the ball of twine, much reduced in size. He pulled it taut so that it just cleared the top of the seven-foot wall. If the fatal shot had been fired from Mathias's apartment, or any of the other second-floor rooms in mid block, this was the path it would have taken. Michael had been standing right next to the victim, and he remembered holding out his hand to touch the wall. They'd been thirty inches away from that wall, probably a bit less.

But that close to the wall, the fatal shot would have passed nearly a foot over their heads. Any lower and it wouldn't have cleared the wall at all. It was a simple matter of geometry. The wall was too high.

Michael backed up until he could see Mary Baxter in the apartment window, holding the end of the twine. He knew a high-powered rifle can be accurate at a distance of a mile or more, but there were no taller buildings even at that distance. There was nothing but sky, gray with the threat of approaching rain.

He tried reexamining the facts. There'd been the sound of a distant rifle shot and Lieutenant Lyrik had fallen dead. The fatal bullet could not have come from in front of him because of the height of the wall, but Sergeant Cista was behind them. Could he have killed his superior with a pistol shot?

No, because Lyrik was facing the wall at the time. There'd been no blood on the back of his head, only on the front, where he'd been hit over the right eye. Michael turned to the right, looking over the wall at the last house. It had been the first house when he entered the street the previous day, Rosetta and Bruno Lacko's apartment, with its empty second floor.

He tossed the ball of twine over the wall and walked around to retrieve it. "Drop the end," he called up to Mary. "I want to try it again down the block at Rosetta's place."

The children were at school but Michael found Rosetta hanging out the wash. Bruno was in the small kitchen, preparing to go off to his job at the fun fair. "What will you do with that ball of twine?" the man asked.

"I'm trying to determine where the fatal shot might have come from. I ran a line from Mary Baxter's second floor over the top of the wall where Lyrik was standing. Now I want to try it from here."

Bruno Lacko nodded. "I must go," he called to his wife. "I will return before five."

Rosetta came in with her wash basket. "He doesn't want me alone if Captain Mulheim makes good on his threat."

"He cares about you," Michael said.

"He cares about all of us. Too much, I fear. If the police come as they threaten, Bruno will be standing in front of them, blocking their path. I worry about what will happen then."

Upstairs, in the empty apartment, he opened the window next to the broken one and hurled his ball of twine again, aiming down the street toward the center of the wall. This time his aim was a bit short. It hit the wall and came down on their side. "I'll go get it and throw it over," Rosetta said. "Stay here and hold the end. You can tell me where to put it."

He agreed and stood by the window with the end held firmly in hand. Out in the street, Rosetta hurried to pick up the end and then flipped it over the wall. He saw at once that she had not thrown it far enough along for a proper measurement and he sought out a way to help her. The end of the twine could be tied to something in the empty apartment and he could join her at the wall. But what?

He opened a closet door, thinking that even a clothes hook might serve as an anchor, and that was when he found it. A rifle, standing in the corner.

Rosetta watched him approach her with a grim expression written on his face. "I tied the twine to a hook in the closet," he told her. "I found something there."

"What do you mean."

"A rifle. Is it your husband's?"

She shook her head, confused. "Bruno never goes up there. Only the boys use it, for their practice."

"Could one of them, Josef perhaps, have fired the rifle? Is that how the window was broken?"

"That window was broken by a rock hurled by one of the boys across the street, before they put up the wall to protect them from us." She handed him the end of the twine. "Do your measurements. Tell me if a bullet from our rifle could have killed Lieutenant Lyrik."

He strode further down the wall but he saw at once that in order to clear the top a bullet would still have passed well above Lyrik's head. "No," he told her. "The fatal shot couldn't have come from over the wall. But it also couldn't have come from any other direction. Are you sure one of your boys couldn't have—"

"Come with me, Michael Vlado!" She walked quickly around the wall with long strides that he had difficulty matching. They climbed the stairs to the empty apartment. "Now show me this rifle."

He went to the closet and lifted it gently from the corner. She took it from him, her concern vanishing, pointed it at the ceiling and pulled the trigger. Nothing happened. "My boys would have difficulty shooting anyone with this. It's an air rifle from Bruno's fun-fair booth. He brought it home for them months ago because it was broken and not worth fixing."

"I'm sorry," Michael told her. "I don't usually jump to conclusions like that."

Her mood turned somber again. "We are only a few hours from the police deadline. What will happen then?"

"Perhaps someone will come forward and confess."

She shook her head. "How is that possible? No one is guilty."

"That's true," he agreed, and left her standing alone in the empty apartment with a promise to return.

The rain had started by the time he reached the street, not the hard, driving sort that autumn sometimes brought to his home in the foothills of the Carpathians but a misty, sweeping shower that warned of worse to come. He bundled his jacket around him and saw at the opposite end of the block the sudden appearance of a police armored vehicle. Go away, he wanted to yell as if confronting the angel of death. It's not yet time! But instead he hurried along in the opposite direction.

It was the sight of Sergeant Cista parked in a police car across from his hotel that told Michael what he must do. The officer had obviously been assigned to keep track of him, and Michael made certain he was seen entering the place. Then he retrieved the raincoat from his luggage and left the hotel by a rear door. He came up to the police car from the rear and was into the front passenger seat before Cista knew what was happening.

"What are you doing?"

"You should keep your doors locked, Sergeant. I want to talk to you."

Cista squirmed about, trying to reach his holstered weapon, but Michael laid a hand on it first, yanking it free. "You don't need this. I only want to talk."

"I'm just following orders. I have nothing against the Gypsies."

"I know what happened at the wall yesterday."

"I don't know what you mean."

"Lyrik was standing too close to the wall to have been hit by a bullet from one of the Gypsy apartments. I know because I took measurements of the angles today. The bullet couldn't have come from behind, where you stood, because there was no blood on the back of his head. The wound was over his right eye, yet I was standing on his right side, shielding him from that direction."

The sergeant ran his tongue over dry lips. "What are you trying to say, that his murder was impossible?"

"Exactly. It was impossible, and therefore it didn't happen. Lieutenant Lyrik is still alive and you're going to take me to him."

The rain had let up by the time they reached the little farmhouse some distance from the city. With his raincoat bundled around his face, Michael was unrecognizable until Lyrik had already opened the door to admit Cista. Then he shoved his way inside, knocking the lieutenant to the floor. "Don't go for a gun," he warned. "We wouldn't want the report of your death to be proved correct after all."

Lyrik rolled over on the floor, cursing his sergeant. "You told him! Mulheim will have our heads for this!"

"No, no! He already knew!"

"How could he know, unless someone told him?"

"Someone told me today. Someone told me that no one could have killed you and they were right. Captain Mulheim said the fatal bullet passed through your head, yet there was no blood on the back of your head, only on the forehead. The bullet couldn't have passed through. I remembered too that I heard the shot a split-second before you grabbed your forehead and the blood appeared. A bullet from a high-powered rifle would travel faster than the sound. You had a capsule of blood hidden in your hand, and when one of Mulheim's men fired a shot in the air you squashed the capsule against your forehead and fell over. Sergeant Cista came running and the captain was summoned with an ambulance. I was kept away from the body, so I wouldn't discover that you were still alive. The whole thing was a plot on Mulheim's part. He wanted an excuse to rid that block of Gypsies."

"And he'll do it," Lyrik said with a smile. "In less than two hours."

Michael showed him the sergeant's 9 mm automatic pistol. "I have this now. And you're coming with us to Masarack Street."

It was a wild ride back to the city, but they reached the street with ten minutes to spare. Every Rom was outside, facing the police, and Mary Baxter stood at their front with Bruno Lacko, not twenty feet away from Captain Mulheim. Cista had to blow his horn to cut a path through the waiting police and militiamen.

Michael was the first out of the car, and Mulheim raised his pistol to face him.

"You arrived just in time for the evacuation," he said, "unless you've come to confess to Lyrik's murder yourself."

"Hardly that! I have Lieutenant Lyrik alive and well in this car, and you have a great deal of explaining to do."

When they saw Lyrik, the residents of Masarak Street shouted and cheered, knowing the threat was ended. Captain Mulheim hesitated just an instant, perhaps contemplating the killing of them all. Then he turned and waved his men back. "There'll be other days, Mr. Vlado," he promised.

It was not a promise he was fated to keep. In the morning, as Michael prepared to return home, Mary Baxter brought him the good news. President Havel and the government had negotiated the removal of the walls in the Gypsy sections of their city and Ústí nad Labem to the north. The wall was already being torn down and the Czech government had promised to give both cities money to improve social conditions. Meantime, a formal investigation had been opened into the faking of Lieutenant Lyrik's murder and the plot against the Gypsies of Masarak Street.

"If I'm ever in Ireland I'll visit you," Michael told her as he prepared to leave for home.

Mary Baxter smiled. "So long as it's not in autumn."

# Kristine Kathryn Rusch

## The Silence

QUITE UNLIKE her other story, with which Kristine Kathryn Rusch led off this volume, "The Silence" is a quiet yet chillingly effective story. It first appeared in the June 2000 issue of *Ellery Queen's Mystery Magazine*.

# The Silence

*Kristine Kathryn Rusch*

It was the city's fifteenth day without a homicide. The tabloids blared the news, almost daring the crazies to break the streak. I worried too, worried that there were deaths we weren't seeing, worried that something had turned, making the world into a strange and unrecognizable place.

I missed the mayhem. I didn't want to admit it, to myself or anyone else, but I missed the uncertainty of walking into a murder scene and feeling that edge of violence still lingering in the air. Not that there wasn't violence. In New York, violence is as common as air, but during the last fifteen days, it hadn't led to anything. People got mugged, just like always, beaten, just like always, but no one seemed to have the urge to haul out a gun and fire it at someone else.

And they should have. That's what got me. It was August—hot, stinking, humid August—and we'd just come off a full moon. The lunatics should have been out in force, and they weren't.

For the first time in years, I wished I was a flatfoot and not a member of the mayor's special Homicide task force. I wanted to ride a car, have a partner, walk a beat. I wanted to bust up a few fights, threaten a few crackheads, rescue a kid from a tree.

I wanted something, anything, except the old cases in front of me, the ones whose trails were so cold that the ice on the files was thick and blue. On day three of The Silence, as the *Daily News* was calling the strangeness, the chief called the entire Homicide task force into his office and gave us options: We could assist some of the other task forces—Narcotics or Robbery or, God forbid, Missing Persons—or we could close some cases we didn't normally have time to close. Me, I thought closing would be good. It would keep the task force together, and the task force was one of the few things from the mayor's anti-crime initiatives that was working. Closing would also prove what I had always said, that a good cop could solve any case given enough time.

A man should carry a tape recorder around to know how fatuous he sounds when he makes pronouncements like that. Then he wouldn't have to eat his words twelve days later when not one cold case had turned hot, when not one file, iced open, warmed shut.

I didn't even have anything promising: not the Puerto Rican wife stabbed fifteen times in her apartment; not the street thug shot once through the heart and left inside a dumpster on 42nd; not even the bloated, naked, fish-belly-white corpse that had floated up the East River one July afternoon. On him, I couldn't even get an ID.

So it didn't seem strange when Evelyn sauntered over to my desk wearing a light brown suit that made her look as if her mother had dressed her in her older sister's clothes. She slapped her hand on the gray Formica surface, and the sound echoed in the nearly empty House.

Three other Homicide detectives looked up. They were surrounded by stacks of files, just like I was. Only the five of us remained. The others in our task force had scattered like the winds, knowing early that the need for action was much more important than the need for closure.

"I say what we need is a wager." She leaned against my desk because I was best known as the task force's betting man. I'd wager on anything legal, and even some things that weren't, given Vice didn't hear about it.

Because I was intrigued and because I didn't want to show it, I gave her a good old-fashioned up and down. "What do you need a wager for?" I asked. "You got court today. That's enough excitement for any person."

She snorted through her nose, an unladylike habit that somehow made her more appealing. "Shows what you know," she said. "I got an interview on WPIX about The Silence."

"What's the wager?" Bob asked. He was a skinny man with too much hair and a deceptively relaxed air about him. Beneath it was one of the best detectives I ever knew.

"First one to close a case buys a round?" she said, although she sounded uncertain.

"Hell," Weisburg said, tugging on his coffee-stained yellow jersey, "the way things've been going, the first one to close should get a medal."

"Yeah." Hawkins slammed a hand on top of his files. "These things are colder than a witch's tit."

I would have expected a cliché from him, just like I would expect him to lose the wager. Hawkins was a political appointment who rose in the ranks because he knew how to play the game—and how to take more credit than he was due. He'd done that to me once; he wasn't ever going to do it again.

"Glad to hear I'm not the only one having trouble closing," Evelyn said.

"Maybe this is part of The Silence," Bob said. We all stared at each other. Cops were just superstitious enough to worry about such things. This dry spell, this Silence, or whatever you wanted to call it, was making us nervous; to think our own inability to close was tied to it only made us even more nervous.

Finally it was Hawkins who broke the mood. "Yeah," he said. "Tell that to the chief."

And we all laughed, not because he was being funny—he wasn't—but because we needed to.

"Whatcha working on, Spence?" Evelyn asked, leaning over my desk.

"Nothing great. How 'bout you?"

"Same," she said. "You guys?"

The other three shrugged in unison. It almost looked as if they'd planned the gesture.

"Narc arrests are up," Bob said.

"Vice arrests are down," Hawkins said.

"None of our people went to Vice," I said.

"There you go," Evelyn said with a smile. "What we gotta worry about is when all them missing persons get found."

This time we matched her smile, and meant it. "So what's going wrong here?" I asked. "Did only the incompetent ones vote to remain in Homicide?"

"That's what the chief's gonna think," Hawkins said.

Bob shook his head. "Chief knows these cases are cold."

"You'd think at least one would break, though," Weisburg said.

"You'd think," Evelyn agreed.

I pushed my chair away from the desk. "Maybe we're going about this wrong."

"You up for the wager?" Evelyn asked.

"Maybe," I said. "How're you approaching cases?"

"Traditionally. Newest to oldest."

"Bob?"

"Same."

"Weisburg?"

"Same."

"Hawkins?"

"Yeah, man, me too."

I sighed. "And me too. Maybe that's what's wrong."

"Go again?" Evelyn said.

I leaned forward. "What's your favorite case?"

"Favorite how?"

"Weirdest, strangest, most intriguing. Most unsolvable. I don't give a damn. Whatever rings your bells."

She didn't even have to think for a minute. "I got a shoe on Fifty-third, middle of the damn street. Some bike messenger picked it up, was gonna give it to his girlfriend, I don't know. But it's full of blood. He don't drop it. He carries it to the curb and uses his cell to call the cops. They show up, order a DNA on the blood, find it matches the interior of a bloody car found on Lex three days before. Car belongs to a young married over Central Park West. The wife's been missing two weeks. She takes fifty grand in cash and disappears, and the husband don't think nothing of it."

"You think the husband did it?" Hawkins asked.

"I think we got strange breaks in the case. The DNA on the blood, for one. Who'da thought there'd be a match?"

"Who thought to look?" Weisburg asked.

"I did," she said. "I figure you got a blood-filled shoe, you gotta have other blood-filled items."

"The problem is," I said, "how'd the shoe get to Fifty-third, full of blood, three days later?"

"Give the man a cigar," she said. "That's the most interesting case to me."

This last she said almost as a topper, as if she dared someone to do better. Of course, Hawkins tried.

"I got that torso found in the Hundred-and-tenth Street station."

"Some jumper," Weisburg said.

"Yeah, they probably couldn't find the rest of him 'coz it was mashed against some subway car."

"I think it's more than that," Hawkins said.

"Why?" I asked, more to find out how Hawkins's brain worked than out of any real curiosity about the torso.

"Because the cuts was real neat. Jumpers, they get ragged sheer. This looked like it was done with one of them surgeon's knives. And the skin was clean, too. No dirt, except where it was on the floor. And no blood."

"When was this?" Weisburg asked.

"May. About the fifth. You know, that freaky rainstorm?"

"No wonder I didn't hear," he said. "I was upstate with the kids." Weisburg usually got the body parts.

"Well, I think it's damn strange," Hawkins said.

Weisburg leaned forward a little. "A torso with arms or a torso without?"

"Without. What do you think, I'm some kind of idiot? I'd'a known to run the prints."

Weisburg shrugged. "I'll look at it if you want."

Hawkins looked at me. "If he helps me close, does that make it his case or mine?"

"What are you looking at me for?" I asked. "The wager's Evelyn's idea."

"But you're the one who mentioned favorite cases," she said. "Right, Weisburg?"

He scrunched up his narrow little face. "I think having favorite homicide cases is sick."

"Yeah, like you didn't just get jealous that Hawkins has a torso and you don't," Evelyn said.

I leaned back in my chair. "Come on, Weisburg. You must have a case that intrigues you."

"It's not a favorite," he said a bit defensively.

I shrugged. "I phrased it wrong."

He ducked his head, and I could have sworn that he was blushing. "It's the puppies."

I'd never heard of this one. "The puppies?"

He nodded, raised his head, and sure enough, there was color in his pasty white cheeks. "Outside the Port Authority Terminal, in April, you know that really sunny stretch around tax time?"

We all nodded. Who could forget that weather?

"Some woman calls Animal Control because there's eight German shepherd puppies, about six months old, just sitting curbside. They're well behaved, ain't doing nothing, but they was there all day, and this lady got worried. So Animal Control shows up and finds they're sitting in a ring around this corpse. Now you'd think the guy was homeless except for the dogs. They're purebred, or so the pound tells me, and they have on expensive collars but no tags. It took Animal Control a long time to round 'em up, too. They was guarding this guy, so they were attached."

"What happened to the dogs?" Bob asked.

Weisburg grinned. "I gave 'em to my daughter." His daughter had married money and had a country house near the Catskills. "They're great dogs."

"Nothing on the guy?" I asked.

"No missing breeders, no nothing. We didn't even know it was a homicide for two days."

"What was it killed him, then?" Evelyn asked.

"Choked."

"Choked?" Bob asked.

Weisburg nodded. "On some woman's left index finger."

We let that sit for a few minutes, then Evelyn said, "Bob?"

"I ain't got nothing to compare to that."

"But you have a favorite case?"

He shrugged. "I got one that bugs me. But it's just simple."

"Simple how?" I asked.

He shrugged again. "Or maybe it's not so simple. I don't know."

*"Bob,"* Evelyn said.

"Okay," he said. "Husband and wife in the Village are having this argument. They live in a walk-up and their fights are always interesting enough to draw the neighbors. This time, the wife has had it, and she grabs a gun, tries to shoot the husband, but before she can pull the trigger, he grabs her arm and they flail around. Of course, the gun goes off, and one of the neighbors gets it smack in the face. Dies."

"Seems straightforward," Hawkins said.

"Don't it?" Bob said. "Until you come to find that the neighbor owns the apartment building and in his will he leaves it to the couple. Now everyone swears they didn't know he owned it, and everyone swears that no one knew the contents of that will."

"You think it was deliberate?"

"I *know* it was," Bob said. "Just can't prove it. At least, not enough to get the D.A. to look at the case."

Evelyn shook her head. "See? Impossible cases, all of them."

"Yeah, but I'd'a said it was impossible for there to be no murders in the Big Apple for one day, let alone fifteen," Weisburg said.

"So what are you saying?" I asked.

"I'm saying maybe this is our chance. Maybe we can solve these things."

"So what's the wager?" Evelyn asked.

"One week," Bob said. "We get one week to solve our baby or we gotta trade it to someone else."

"If they solve it, we'll look like a putz," Hawkins said.

Bob grinned and pointed at him. "You got it in one."

"Don't get all excited," Evelyn said. "We ain't heard from Spence yet."

I held out my hands. "You guys get all the interesting cases."

"And you're holding out," Evelyn said.

Indeed I was. But she caught me. I felt the color rise in my cheeks.

"Ah, he's got an embarrassing one too," Hawkins said.

I shook my head. "It's the image that got me, not the case."

"Image?" Evelyn asked.

I took a deep breath. Sometimes revealing yourself to your colleagues wasn't all it was cracked up to be. "There's a doll hospital just north of Bloomies—"

"A doll hospital?" Hawkins asked.

"Yeah," Weisburg said. "A place you can take favorite toys to be repaired."

"Or antique toys," Evelyn said.

"Anyway," I said, feeling the heat deepen, "they had this guy. They called him the wiz because he could fix damn near anything. You'd bring in a turn-of-the-century Steif, no stuffing, no arms for God's sake—"

"Stiff?" Hawkins whispered to Weisburg.

"Steif," Weisburg said.

"It's a collectible stuffed bear," Evelyn snapped. "Now shut up and let him talk."

"Anyway, he could turn it around in a day or two and have the thing looking like it just come off the assembly line. He was a master, the best, they all said that."

"And he was murdered," Bob said.

"You got it," I said. "I'd'a thought it was simple burglary too—they had a load of collectibles from Sotheby's that disappeared that night—except for the dolls."

"The dolls?" Hawkins asked, obviously willing to work for every detail.

"The dolls. When the staff came in the next morning, they found dolls all over him—no blood on them, even though he'd been stabbed in an artery and there was blood everywhere. The dolls were hooded and masked in surgical clothes and they were poised over the body like they was trying to fix him."

Hawkins snorted and looked away. "Nice try, but you could've made up something better than that."

I stared at him. He slowly looked back at me. Then he frowned. "You mean you weren't making that up?"

"Nope. They left the body as it was, and the call came in here. I got photos."

"But no suspects."

"No suspects, no motive, no nothing."

"The stolen collectibles?"

"Never were shipped. It was clerical error. Sotheby's dropped them off the day *after* the murder."

"So not even a robbery."

"Nothing," I agreed.

"When was this?" Evelyn asked.

"Valentine's Day," I said. "I remember because we were having that deep freeze."

"Oh, yeah," Bob said.

"So," Hawkins said. "The wager?"

Weisburg shrugged. "I'm willing to give it a shot. I have a fondness for those dogs."

"You gonna mind if someone else cleans up your mess?" Bob asked with a grin.

"I figure The Silence is gonna end by tomorrow morning and this is all gonna become moot," Weisburg said.

Evelyn grinned. "That's his way of agreeing to the proposition. We all in?"

I glanced around the room. Everyone was nodding. "We're all in," I said.

I had never worked on a case that was six months old before. I'd never had the luxury. But as I reviewed my notes, I realized that the case had only intrigued me in hindsight. I would find myself thinking of those dolls, poised over the body like a Lilliputian surgical team, and smile.

Smile.

Sometimes this job got to me.

I had actually only spent an afternoon on the case, even though when the dead guy's family called long distance every few weeks, I would tell them the file was still open. In truth, the next day I got slammed with three drive-bys, a potential serial, and a famous floater, and the doll-hospital murder got shoved aside by more pressing—and more easily solvable—cases.

I think that's often the way. We usually close about seventy-five percent, but that's because most murderers are stupid. Think about it: The best way to solve a problem is not to take out a gun and blow someone away. The twenty-five percent unsolved are either lost in the shuffle, committed by a professional who knows how to hide his tracks, or done by someone smart who has been thinking of the crime for a long, long time. That's one thing we rarely tell people: If the killer's smart, chances are he'll get away.

The doll-hospital murderer had been smart, or in the very least, lucky. There were no fingerprints in the place, except for the ones that needed to be there, and despite all the blood, there wasn't a decent shoe or hand print either. No murder weapon, and no motive, at least not one I could find.

I stared at the photos. The victim, one Joel Dudich, was slender to the point of gauntness, balding, and had a tattoo of a teddy bear on his right forearm. I took out a magnifying glass and examined the tattoo. The work was fine, even artistic, and bore a vague resemblance to the posable doctor bear who was sitting on the edge of the table, his furry arms crossed as if he were denying the patient treatment.

In fact, the doctor was the only bear, even though I had made a note in my case file that Dudich specialized in bears. The other creatures around him, the ones who were trying to save him, were dressed as orderlies or nurses—no doctors at all. I recognized a ripped Raggedy Ann, an early 1960s Barbie that was missing one arm, and a headless G.I. Joe.

The others had their little backs to me, but I could probably identify them if I tried hard enough. My father had owned a toy store in the small Pennsylvania town where I grew up, and he treated each doll and stuffed animal as if it had a presence all its own. He was a good and gentle man, and he had always seemed astonished that his only son had taken to the violence of police work, ending in the most violent side of all—chasing difficult homicides in the mean streets of New York.

I turned the large glossy photograph of the corpse facedown, skipped the autopsy photos for the moment, and reread my case notes.

Dudich had lived alone in a fifth-floor walk-up that he couldn't afford. His most recent roommate, a woman, had left him abruptly, at least according to the super, two weeks before the murder. The super figured they were lovers, and there was nothing in the record to confirm or contradict that. Dudich's name was the only one on the lease, and none of his friends knew who the girl was.

His coworkers found him strange and fey, his habits those of a prima donna in a small pond. They claimed they never spoke to him about his personal life. He came in late, snapped at anyone who interrupted him, and didn't care who he insulted. But everyone put up with it because his work was so beautiful. Clients came back, asking for him by name: parents wanting their children's toys repaired; collectors wanting their valuables restored to mint condition; and, in the end, galleries and auction houses taking advantage of his relatively cheap services.

"Could've gotten more money," I had written in the margin. It was a reference to an interview with one of Dudich's colleagues, who couldn't understand why Dudich stayed at the hospital when he had been offered a much higher salary with several of the antique shops on the Upper West Side.

I circled the comment and underlined it, thinking it a place to start. But before I went further, I finished with the file, making sure my memory was jogged. The family was out of state—Iowa—and they confessed that they hadn't seen him since he graduated from a cow college at which he had shown no sign of his particular gifts. I had covered a lot of ground that first day. It was too bad that I hadn't followed up on it.

Just before I left the House, I noted that the others were looking more excited than they had since The Silence began. Evelyn had put all her files under her desk. She had gone to her interview, but she had left on her desktop a computer-generated list of all the blood-spattered unidentified objects found around the time her shoe had been located.

Hawkins was on the phone with the forensic pathologist, talking about the possibility of matching a severed arm to the mysterious torso. Weisburg was typing on the task force's computer, doing an Internet search of New York area dog breeders. And Bob was poring over a copy of the dead landlord's will, making notes and circles and lines, and muttering to himself.

Finally, it looked like a normal day in the task force. We hadn't had one for more than two weeks.

I walked down the faded wood steps and through the double doors out to the city. It didn't look different. Horns honked, brakes squealed as taxis nearly rear-ended real cars. Pedestrians didn't even look. They walked, heads high, to their next destination. It was hot, of course, being August, and the men wore short sleeves and slung their suitcoats over their shoulders with one hand and clutched their briefcases with the other. Women wore dresses and no nylons and clutched their briefcases too. A car backfired as I reached the end of the block and everyone ducked, just like they always did, thinking it was a gunshot.

I walked to the doll hospital. It wasn't too far from the House, and I liked to keep a finger on the city's pulse. The heat was unbearable, and within minutes, I had my suitcoat off too. The stink was worse, though. New York always smells bad in the height of summer: garbage sitting on the curbs waiting for collection; the way the exhaust from cars hangs in the air; and the general odor of sweaty humans who have no business being so close to each other, but because of the nature of the city, are.

I didn't have a formal line of questioning ready when I reached the hospital. All I knew was that I wanted to see what had happened since the loss of their star, since Dudich had died on them and taken away so much lucrative business.

When I reached the building, saw the small sign covered with dirt and flies,

I had a bad feeling, but it wasn't until I walked up the narrow stairs into a growing darkness that I knew.

The hospital was gone. Not vanished-gone, but out-of-business gone. I stopped at the glass door with the For Rent sign taped in a corner of the window, and peered through the soaping someone had done to prevent just this sort of snooping.

The tables were gone inside, and all that remained was a gray vinyl floor covered with thin midafternoon sunlight. A doll's arm lay in a corner, and a high-heeled shoe, probably from an early Barbie doll, had a spot all its own beneath a wall. Otherwise, there was no evidence that the doll hospital had been there. The tidy place with the bewildered employees, the ones who had described their job as a happy one until Dudich died, had vanished as if it had never been.

I moved away from the door and went back down the stairs. The tenant below was a women's boutique with about 500 square feet of floor space. It probably cost a fortune just to maintain that, even though this wasn't one of Manhattan's priciest neighborhoods. I let myself in.

The dresses were all variations on the same theme, a drapey disco sort of dress that I thought had gone out of style twenty years before. Some were decorated with shell necklaces. Others had scarves for accents. The woman behind the small table that served as a counter wore her long hair in a thousand beaded braids. She wore orange lipstick that set off her dark skin, and her inch-long nails, which looked real, were painted orange to match.

"Help you?" she asked in a disinterested New York tone that belied the Jamaican melody in the vowels.

"I was wondering what happened to the doll hospital."

"Closed." She hadn't even looked up yet.

"When?"

"Ah, March. The last day was the freak snowstorm on the third. I remember because they were setting toys out in the snow."

"Is there anyone I can talk to connected with the hospital?"

She pulled open a drawer in the table, and using those long fingernails like pincers, removed a cream-colored business card. "Don't blame me if she doesn't get back to you," the woman said. "She's the only one now, and she's working out of her home."

I took the card. Apparently this boutique got a lot of inquiries about the doll hospital. She hadn't even asked for my ID.

"Do you have any idea why it closed?"

She raised her eyes to mine. They were magnificent, the stunning centerpiece to what I just realized was a remarkable face. "Why, the murder, of course."

"The murder?"

"Of the wiz boy. The one who could repair anything. They say the dolls surprised him in the middle of the night, but I don't believe it."

"You don't?" I asked in a tone that I hoped didn't sound patronizing.

"No. If they killed him, why were they found trying to save him, now? They were found all around him, like little doctors. But they couldn't do anything."

"So, they didn't find out who did it?"

She shrugged. "I don't think they ever will. The police have too much to do to look into the death of one pimply-faced guy with a fascination for teddy bears."

Ouch. That one hit too close to home. I took a step away from the table, as if I were getting ready to leave. "Aren't you afraid to work here, after someone got murdered upstairs?"

She laughed. "Mister, I live in New York. If I was afraid of everything that happened, I'd move to somewhere where nothing happened."

I smiled in response. "Good point," I said, and thanked her for her time. Then I left the store and stepped back into the oven that was the street.

Halfway down the block, I paused and looked at the card. It had a name—Lena O'Dell; an occupation—toy repair; and a contact phone number with a Manhattan exchange but no address. I walked back to the House and used the number to trace the address. She lived in the Village. I thought of calling before I went to see if she was home, but then I changed my mind.

She was the only lead I had, and I didn't want to scare her away.

Evelyn was just arriving as I was leaving. She had changed out of her power suit and into her usual jeans and blouse. She was whistling as she came up the stairs.

"What're you smiling about?" I asked as we passed.

"Found the other shoe," she said.

"Really?" I stopped on the way down.

"Yep. Recovered from a dumpster on Fiftieth, same area. Forms a triangle with the first shoe and the car. And, get this, there's a bloody handprint on the back. That's why the station kept it."

"Lucky break."

She grinned over her shoulder at me. "You don't know the half of it."

She was close. She had to be or she wouldn't be in such a good mood. "Give."

She shook her head. Then she turned and jogged up the stairs before I could ask the next question.

She did that on purpose, of course. I sighed, and walked down the rest of the way, wishing my luck were running the same as hers.

I took my company car to the Village because I didn't want to hassle with getting a cab. Parking was hell, even on days like this, but I squeezed into a spot on a side street without denting any bumpers. Then I walked around the corner to the address I had.

It was a dilapidated building with a recessed steel door with a 1970s security system. Someone had propped the inner door open with a brick and I suspected it was often left that way. I glanced at the names penned beside the row of doorbells and saw O'Dell in Number 3. I slipped through the door into the hallway and started up the stairs.

The place felt like a sauna. A window on the landing was painted shut and caked with dirt. Not that it mattered. It provided a view of the building across the back alley and nothing more. I doubted that opening it would provide a breeze.

The second floor smelled of garlic and feta cheese. There was a narrow hallway that ran the length of the floor, and the stairs continued up one side. Apartment 3 was just beyond the railing, the door firmly closed.

I knocked.

I heard a small scraping against the wood as someone peered through the peephole. Then a woman's voice said, "What?"

I held up my badge. "Miss O'Dell. I'm Detective Spencer Gray. I'm handling the murder of Joel Dudich."

"God," she said. "And here I thought you were gonna wait until the Second Coming before you continued your investigation."

I heard several locks click and then the door opened, sending frigid air into the hallway. A window air-conditioning unit hummed in the background.

O'Dell leaned against the door frame. She was slender and barefoot, wearing jeans and a ratty T-shirt that was covered with bits of thread. Her hair was red and curly, her skin nearly as dark as the boutique owner's.

I didn't remember seeing her before, but that had been months ago, in a case I normally would have forgotten.

"Gray," she said. "You were there asking questions when they took Joel's body away."

I nodded. I guess I had seen her.

"You wanna come in, or you gonna interrogate me in the hall?"

"It's not an interrogation, Miss O'Dell. I just need information."

She stepped away from the door. I went inside, glad for the icy air. Her apartment was a clutter of books and spider plants, with plush toys on every available surface. A coffinlike box stood against one wall. It was filled with broken toys like the ones I had initially seen in the hospital. A thick wooden door was braced on cinder blocks and on top of it were several stuffed dogs, all missing the right leg. A series of half-finished legs sat in a row beside them.

She took a doll off a caftan-covered armchair and asked me to sit. I did and nearly sank to the floor. The chair had no springs. I tried not to show my surprise.

"What happened to the hospital?" I asked.

She glared at me, then sat on the blanket-covered couch, next to a group of limbless dolls. "It didn't go without Joel."

"One employee couldn't be that important."

"He had a talent, he did, and everyone came for him. When he died—" She held out her hands and didn't finish the sentence.

"What kept him at the hospital? I heard he could have worked for Sotheby's or any of the antique stores at a much higher rate."

Her face softened. She had been a beautiful woman once, several years of stress ago. "The kids," she said.

"You had children in the doll hospital?"

She nodded. "They came with their parents, mothers usually. It took some work to get men to come into a place devoted to dolls." And then she looked at me like that was the reason I hadn't finished the investigation. "Joel liked watching their faces when he gave them the fixed toy. Said it made his entire week."

"Know anyone who would want to kill him?"

"Just about everyone," she said, and her answer surprised me. Then she looked down at her hands. "Except the customers, of course."

"Of course," I said.

"Look," she said. "He wasn't the nicest guy. I think he hung out with dolls because he didn't much like people. There was something in his past, in his childhood, he never talked about, and he said he could get the sweetness he was denied then when he looked at kids' faces. That's the part of Joel I like to remember."

"And what's the part you want to forget?"

She flinched, then smoothed the faded denim on her jeans. "He had a temper," she whispered, as if, even now, he could hear her.

"He ever inflict it on you?"

"On anyone who wasn't as good as he was. Or as quick." She glanced up, her dark eyes haunted. "I didn't like him much, and at first, I was glad he was dead."

I waited again. She would say more if I just gave her enough time.

"Then I learned how much I had come to depend on him. Closing the hospital was the toughest thing I've ever done."

I nodded. "Where were you the night he died?"

"You asked me that the first time," she said.

"Tell me again."

"Here." She closed her eyes and leaned her head back against her couch. "Unfortunately, I was here. Alone."

"And your other employees?"

"You'll have to ask them."

"Do you have a list of names?"

She nodded, seemingly grateful to get off that couch and be busy. I took the moment to scan the apartment more carefully. There were no photographs behind the spider plants, no signs that anyone except O'Dell had ever been in this apartment. After a moment, she handed me a carefully lettered piece of paper with six names on it.

"All but one are still in the city," she said.

"And where's the one?" I asked.

She shrugged. "She disappeared the day after Joel was killed."

News of the disappearance should have excited me, but it didn't. Not really. It was too easy, for one, and for another, it was too convenient. Not that murders ever go the way you want them to. But when I heard about the employee that got away, I didn't feel those stomach butterflies that usually told me things were going well. I felt a shiver travel down my spine, so strong that I wondered if O'Dell had seen me shake.

The disappeared was named Melanie Glisando, and she had been Dudich's on-again off-again lover, something none of the employees had bothered to tell me in the first investigation. I didn't yell at O'Dell for that. I also didn't yell at her for failing to tell me that Glisando hadn't shown up for work on the day of my investigation. I would save the rougher emotions for later, in case I needed them.

Instead, I had her tell me more about Glisando, and from what I heard, she was Dudich's perfect match—a woman who was interested in toys, a woman who could repair even the most stubborn of tears, a woman who didn't mind spending her days on a pursuit most considered frivolous. She had kept an apartment two buildings down from O'Dell, although she rarely used it. I stopped at the apartment after I left O'Dell's, and the super mentioned that he had thrown Glisando's things away just the week before.

"Hard to tell whether she was really gone or not. She had this lover, see, and she spent time there, and you know how it is. This place gets to be where she stores her stuff. Not that she had a lot of stuff."

"Did she take anything with her when she left?"

The super shrugged. "How'm I supposed to know? I don't case my people's places, you know? I don't compare before and after."

"Anything unusual in her apartment?"

The super wrinkled his nose. I braced myself. "Naw," he said. "Not unless you count all them toys."

"Toys?"

"Yeah." His grimace grew. "They was posed all over the place. Little scenes, like you'd find in store windows."

Scenes. I should have felt the butterflies then, but I didn't. Something was off with this case, something intangible.

"What did you do with the toys?" I asked.

"I was gonna toss 'em, but the missus, she said no, kids would want them. I gotta listen to her, you know how it is, so I take 'em to one of them specialty shops and they was glad to have 'em. Made a few bucks off 'em and put that against the rent."

He told me this last as if it would shock me. It didn't.

"What shop?" I asked.

He told me, and I made a note, although I wasn't sure I would go.

"How'd you know Glisando was gone?" I asked.

"No rent in the mail," he said. "That's the one thing she was good at, paying her rent."

"When did the payments stop?"

"Last month," he said.

I blamed my growing depression on the heat. The pieces of information I got were the kind a detective wanted to have, the bits of another person's life, the fragmented details that constituted part of a puzzle and led me to believe I could solve this. The House was even hotter than the street, and as I came in our sarge informed me that the air conditioning was out, and they already had someone upstairs working on the problem.

I wiped the sweat off the back of my neck with a handkerchief that had seen better days, and then I went up the stairs, expecting to be the only detective in that steamy place. Instead the entire crew had gathered, bottles of water in a bucket on the floor, like someone was holding a party without the booze.

Everyone looked as down as I felt.

I picked up one of the water bottles and held it to my forehead. It felt like a blast of frigid air. "Who do I have to thank for this?"

"Hawkins," Evelyn said.

I opened my eyes. Hawkins didn't even bring in donuts on his assigned day. The man was cheaper than any skate I'd ever seen.

He met my gaze, then looked away, as if he knew what I was thinking.

"What's the occasion?" I asked, thinking this was almost as strange as the damn Silence.

"No occasion," he said.

"He found one of the arms that matched that torso," Weisburg said.

"Got an ID?" I asked.

Hawkins took a swig of his water, making me think of booze yet again. Only in a heat wave could a man approach water like it was wine.

"That's the problem," he said. "I been wanting to talk to you guys. Any of you think that maybe we shouldn't solve these cases?"

I rolled my eyes. Evelyn sat down behind her desk so hard that the wheels on her chair moved and she spun. Bob shook his head ever so slightly. Only Weisburg didn't move.

"All right," I said. "I give. Why shouldn't we solve these cases?"

"Because," Hawkins said. "Maybe they're what's causing The Silence."

"So, lemme get this straight," Evelyn said. "If we solve these cases, The Silence ends and we got a new crime wave on our hands."

"Hell," I said. "That means we're directly responsible for all future homicides."

"You know," Bob said, "I knew you liked slacking off, Hawkins, but I didn't think you'd go to these lengths."

"I'm serious," he said. "These're all strange cases, and what if they're the key?"

"Yeah," I said. "Sure. It'd be our cases, not the ones at the hundred-and-sixth or the ones in Brooklyn or somewhere else. And out of all the unsolved we got, we just happened to pick the five that were the cause of The Silence, and if we solve them, then well, sorry New York, it's business as usual?"

Hawkins flushed. "Put that way, it sounds kinda funny."

"Yeah, it does," Bob said.

"So you think I should solve the jumper?"

"Isn't that what we're here for?" I asked. "Or are we really the waste of funds the tabloids been saying we are?"

"I was just thinking maybe—"

"That's the problem," Evelyn said. "You were thinking." She grabbed a water bottle. "Thanks for the refreshment," she said, and left the floor.

Bob closed his file and left too. After a moment, Hawkins shuffled off in the direction of the men's room. That left just me and Weisburg. Strangely, he had said nothing.

"You don't buy that argument, do you?" I asked.

He shrugged. "It's as good as any. I mean, we ain't never seen nothing like this. Anything could be causing it. I think maybe if Hawkins believes it's our unsolveds, then maybe he's right. If the tabloids think it's the heat, maybe they're right. If I believe maybe the city's hit its personal limit, maybe I'm right. You know, in unusual situations, you can't close your mind."

"It's not logical—"

"It's not logical for a man to choke to death on a woman's finger outside Port Authority in the presence of his very expensive dogs and not have identification on him or the animals."

"Unless it was a smuggling operation," I said.

"Shit," he said and sat up straight. I couldn't believe he hadn't thought of that.

"You see?" I said. "There's got to be a logical explanation for anything."

"The finger?" he asked. "He'd'a had to bite it off in the presence of witnesses."

"Maybe he didn't. He had dogs."

"And what, he picked it up like it was a sausage?"

"Was there bread around him, a bun maybe?" I was wondering how far I could yank him.

Apparently not that far. Weisburg winced. "You're disgusting, Spence."

"I'm just looking for logic."

"In all the wrong places," he said and stood. After grabbing his own water, he too left me alone.

For all my talk of logic, the conversation with Hawkins left me unnerved. Maybe there was something that we were missing, some tie, some reason that things had gotten so strange. Or maybe the ancients were right, and life revolves around the phases of the moon. I know my ex-wife's did. Why shouldn't a city be the same?

That morning's *Times* had some scholar saying things like this happen before every millennium. Some twerp in the *Daily News* was saying that New York had entered its own alternate timeline, a timeline parallel to the one in which Berlin had found itself more than ten years before when the Wall suddenly came down. And the guy on the street corner outside my building was yelling that we were all victims of some secret government experiment in behavior control.

Those ideas were as plausible as Weisburg's, certainly more plausible than Hawkins's, and I didn't buy any of them. We had just hit a statistical anomaly, that was all. The odds that no murders would take place couldn't be calculated accurately by looking at the entire city. Each murder was its own event, with its own probability. Or, if you wanted to look at it another way, each country had its own murder rate, and just because no one was dying by a human being's hands in New York, didn't mean it wasn't happening in L.A. or New Orleans or D.C. In fact, at that moment, I would have laid money on the idea that the national murder rate was the same as it had ever been. The murders just weren't happening here.

I didn't want to think about it. The Silence made me nervous enough as it was. Thinking about its causes made it worse.

I took a sip of that delicious cool water that Hawkins had tried to bribe us with, and then I realized what I had missed earlier. I picked up the phone and called the super for Glisando's building.

"You said that Glisando paid her rent up to last month," I reminded the super, "but that she was never in the building. Where'd the money come from?"

"I dunno where my tenants work," the super said.

"No," I said, clarifying. "Where did she send the checks from?"

"Upstate," the super said. "Her parents' farm."

Normally, I don't like to leave the city, but in that August's record heat wave, I was glad to leave the island of smog and tall buildings for the fresher and somewhat cooler air upstate.

Glisando's parents had what might once have been a working farm, but what was now called a farm only out of tradition. The house had been restored by some *Architectural Digest* wannabe, and the barn had been remade into a guesthouse more beautifully apportioned than most of Manhattan's hotels. I pulled up in the clearly regraveled driveway, probably kept that way for "authenticity," and headed straight for the barn, which was where some folks in the nearby town had told me I'd find Glisando.

They weren't lying. She came to the door barefoot, her hair gone and her face so skeletal and covered with melanoma that it was clear she was dying. Mom and Dad, apparently, had decided to take her in and give her what little comfort they could in her last year of life.

"I'm sorry," I said, after I'd introduced myself. "If I'd known I wouldn't have bothered you with this."

Glisando shrugged a bony shoulder as if to say that questions like mine no longer mattered. She motioned me into the coolness of the barn and its lovely central air, and led me into the living room. The chairs were leather, obviously part of the decor, but someone had put in a ratty fabric sofa, on which was an Amish quilt. Dolls decorated all the surfaces. The television was still playing directly in front of the sofa, and as we went into the room, Glisando grabbed the remote and shut the set off.

"No one's ever talked to me about Joel," she said as she sat on the couch and wrapped the quilt around herself. "At least, not officially."

"According to your super and your employer, you disappeared right after the killing."

Glisando laughed. It had the empty quality of a once-hearty chuckle; she didn't seem to have the energy to go full strength. "I hadn't disappeared at all. My doctor's in the city, and I kept using the apartment off and on until last month. I just stopped going to work. I couldn't. Not after Joel died."

"You were evicted, did you know that?" I asked. "Your landlord sold all your things."

"Joel's things," Glisando said, and she didn't sound sad. "I hadn't the strength to move them."

"Why didn't your parents help you move?"

Her smile was small. "They didn't even know where I was until I showed up here in March. I didn't want them to see how I'd been living."

"So Joel had AIDS."

Glisando shook her head. "He was one of the lucky ones. He never got infected, no matter how many times he was exposed. He was a carrier only. A researcher was going to use him as a test subject and then—" Her lower lip trembled and she stopped, swallowing hard.

"It must have been hard to lose his things."

Glisando looked at the dolls, then back at me. "Do you ever feel watched, Detective?"

"No," I said.

"I do. These are Joel's. It's like they see right through me." She coughed, then pulled the blanket tighter.

"What do they see?" I asked.

"I was so angry at him."

I felt the hair on the back of my neck rise.

"He didn't get sick and I did, and when we found out, I thought it wasn't fair. Why did he get to live and I didn't?"

I waited. I threaded my fingers together, wondering in this time of strangeness if something even stranger would happen: a confession.

"And then we had that cold spell, remember? So cold that the air felt brittle."

I did remember. It had been a memorable weather year.

"He didn't come home. They said on the news there had been a rash of killings that night. Like a full moon. Everyone had gone berserk."

I nodded. Most were easily solved. Husbands killing wives, wives killing husbands. A video-store clerk shooting a client who looked like he was pulling a gun from his jacket when actually he had been trying to return a tape.

"My father—" Glisando shivered slightly when she mentioned her father— "he's into weather. He said that those kinds of killings usually happen only in hot weather. But now the papers say there's been no killing at all."

A response felt appropriate here. I tried to keep it short. "We have had a reprieve."

"So you can investigate old cases."

"Yes."

She closed her eyes, leaned back. "I don't remember that night. God's truth. I woke up unable to remember going to bed."

I waited.

She swallowed. "But positioning the dolls." She opened her eyes. "It was something he used to do for me after I got sick. Only they didn't make me better."

There was fear in her eyes, fear I didn't dare assuage. She said nothing more. Finally, I said, as carefully as I could, "You know that makes you a suspect."

"To everyone," she said. "Including myself."

In the end, I didn't take her in. I thought about it, but I needed to back up my suspicions with physical evidence, and I wasn't sure I was up to the task. Not in this case. Because once I'd seen Glisando, I realized that whatever I did wouldn't really matter. She would die a horrible death. I'd find another case to pursue, something easier, something that would convince the captain that the task force still had it, that we could still solve the old cases. It wasn't time to disband us yet.

I thought about all that on the drive back to the city. The light over Manhattan was hazy and thick, and as I drove into it, I felt as if I were driving into soup. I went to the precinct, thinking that I would type up my notes and then double-check forensics in the morning.

When I got in, I discovered Weisburg at his desk, hands in his hair. Bob was packing up, heading home for the evening. Hawkins, apparently, hadn't returned. Evelyn was following a lead.

I didn't say much to Bob or Weisburg. I started typing my notes, unable to shake the uncomfortable feeling in my stomach.

Here's what I know: I know that anyone can kill, given the right circumstances. I know that we all have it in us; it's bred into the genetic code. We do it when we're threatened, when we need to survive, when we need food. There are sick people whose genes are malfunctioning, guys like Speck and Dahmer, who like to kill for the hell of it. And some folks, well, the civility gets trained out of them, and they become soldiers for hire, assassins, or worse. And then there's the folks who will kill accidentally at least the first time: They're beating their wife or their boyfriend, and the whole thing gets out of hand. The death wasn't planned. It was, literally, a crime of passion.

Killers. They all have a look, and you learn to recognize it when you've been in the business as long as I have. Folks who've killed to survive never think of it again. Or, if they have a finely tuned conscience, they spend lots of money on therapy or booze, but at first glance, you can't tell them from you or me.

Then there's the sick ones so clearly abnormal that you can feel it when you come into a room. I was never sure how they lured their victims. Maybe those folks had poor survival skills or were good at denial or simply didn't have the time to defend themselves. I always bet on the latter, that twisting feeling in the stomach when you realize you've made a mistake and there's no way out.

And then, finally, there's the crime-of-passion folks. Most of them don't meet your eyes. Most of them, they carry this little thread of guilt in them, and if you look hard enough, you see it: in their posture, in their gestures, in the way they look away at the very last moment, the deep moment, when you can really see inside someone's soul.

Glisando wasn't a Speck or a Dahmer, and she didn't look like a person who had killed to survive. In fact, it was hard to believe that, even a few months before, she'd had the strength to kill anyone. Oh, she said the right things; that comment about the dolls was close, but it was what she said later, about suspecting herself. No guilty person would ever give that much, dying or not. She had the guilt, but it was the guilt of a person who'd thought of killing another and then that other died. It wasn't the guilt of someone who'd actually committed the act. Glisando really and truly didn't remember, and it tore her up.

It was bothering me, too. It just didn't fit, somehow.

Nothing did. Nothing seemed to work the way I understood it at all anymore.

The next morning I arrived at the House late, deciding to treat myself to coffee at an expensive restaurant just so that I could cool down. As I walked upstairs, I heard raucous laughter accompanied by someone pounding on a desk.

I came in to see Evelyn playing the desk like a tom-tom and laughing as she did so. The others were crowded around her.

When she saw me, she stood up and grinned. "Pay up," she said.

"You solved it?"

She nodded. "Kid named Jack Davis was the shooter, and he came clean the moment I found him. He was hired by the husband to kill the wife. Which he did. The problem was, the family dog attacked in the middle of the shooting, so he had to shoot the dog too. Tore the kid up. Seems he likes dogs. But being the little psycho that he is, he blamed the husband for making him shoot the dog. And he knew better than to shoot the husband too, so he started leaving clues all over the city. First thing he said when I brought him in was, 'Shit, bitch, I was beginning to think I needed a friggin' neon sign.'"

I laughed like I was supposed to, but it made me uncomfortable. "Contract killers usually don't advertise," I said.

"The kid's a flake," she said. "But even he admitted his behavior was a bit strange, although he attributed it to something else. He said he never missed. He shoulda been able to shoot the wife and leave the damn dog alone."

I turned to Hawkins. "I thought you were going to be first."

"Arm matched," he snapped. "Hand was missing."

"Does this mean the rest of us give our cases to Evelyn?" Bob asked.

Weisburg shook his head. "We said a week."

"You guys at least owe me a round," she said.

"Seems like a round is small payoff for solving that one," Bob said.

"We didn't agree to a round," Hawkins said. He stood. "I'm near closing too. I got one more lead to follow."

He hurried out the door. Evelyn's grin widened. "Touchy, touchy."

"He hates to lose," Weisburg said.

"He should be used to it by now," I said.

"Hell, I think that's the problem. He's always losing," Bob said. "At least on the things that count."

"Excuse me." The voice came from the stairs. A middle-aged couple stood there. The wife had artificially blond hair that didn't match her sun-wrinkled face, and the husband had his arm around her protectively. "We're here to see Detective Gray."

"That's me," I said. The group silenced behind me and went to their desks. "How can I help you?"

The man looked at the woman. He cleared his throat. "I'm Nic Glisando, and this is my wife Anne."

I didn't let the surprise I felt show on my face. "Let's go somewhere private," I said.

I took them to one of the interview rooms and closed the door. They remained standing, as if the place were disgusting to them, and it probably was. Glisando's polo shirt had a designer label and his wife's hands were covered in jewelry worth more than I'd earn in the next fifteen years.

"We're Melanie's parents," Mrs. Glisando said, as if I hadn't already put that together. "She told us you'd been to see her."

"Yes," I said, not sure how this related to me. I hadn't taken Glisando into custody, and I wasn't planning to. But the parents were clearly frightened.

"When I heard that, I told my husband Nic that he had to talk to you." She turned to him. "Nicky. Please."

Glisando wiped his hands on his trousers, then glanced at the tape recorder in the center of the table. "That's not on, is it?"

"No," I said. My heart was pounding. I didn't know what I had stumbled into.

"What I have to tell you is in the strictest confidence. I could get fired for revealing this to anyone."

This was good. I pointed to the chairs. The wife sat, and then her husband. I sat too. "I'm not really in the business of keeping confidences."

"If I tell you something, and I give you documentation, will you promise me you won't say where it came from?"

"Why would you do this?" I asked.

"So that you don't charge my girl. She's dying as it is." Glisando said that as if he'd had practice, but his wife looked down. They traded strengths in this family.

I sat still for a moment, thinking. Then what Glisando said registered with me. The parents thought that my charging Melanie with Dudich's murder was a foregone conclusion.

I sighed. I had already made up my mind about Glisando. She wouldn't be killing anyone else, not in her condition, and what she had already done would soon be taken up between her and her maker. I didn't have to tell these folks that, of course, but I didn't have to leave them hang either.

"Tell you what," I said. "If I think the information you have is compelling, I won't charge your daughter."

"And you won't tell anyone where you got this?"

"No."

Glisando nodded and then handed me a computer disk.

I took it and slapped it against my palm. "You want to tell me what's on it?"

His eyes met mine. They were a pale blue, almost clear, and the whites around them were lined with red. "I used to work at Columbia. Meteorology. Then I got hired by—"

"Nic," his wife said warningly. He nodded to her.

"—I got hired by a private company that has a defense contract. We've been working on this project for years, but we've been doing field work since January."

I waited. I didn't see how this fit in.

"Experimenting. In Manhattan." He stopped then, as if I should understand. I didn't.

"How does this relate to Melanie?" I asked.

"No one's been murdered in the city in three weeks."

"Yes," I said.

"It's the heat."

"Beg pardon," I said, "usually heat causes people to go crazy, not to stop going crazy."

"I know," Glisando said. "But we've been studying the effect of weather on the human killing impulse."

"It's a defense contract," his wife said softly, as if I hadn't heard it the first time. It was all I could do not to snap at her. She apparently thought public servants didn't have the intelligence of a gnat.

"As a rule, human beings don't kill each other when the temperature goes below zero," Glisando was saying, "even if they can't leave the house for days. It just doesn't happen. But if the mercury is above ninety degrees for a long time, murder rates climb. We thought if we could isolate the impulse, we could negate it."

"We?"

"We," he said. "I can't go into all of this. I don't understand much of it myself. I was there to be the forecaster, and the predictor, and to help develop computer models on weather patterns. But to make a long story short, we thought we'd isolated the impulse—we had in lesser mammals—so we field-tested on Manhattan."

That woke me up. "Manhattan?"

He nodded. "It's an island, which means it's controllable, and it's got fairly predictable weather patterns. We knew, for example, there'd be a long heat spell this summer. We just didn't know when."

"So you're not causing the heat?"

He laughed, a mirthless sound that was more a reaction to my ignorance than any amusement on his part. "No. Of course not."

"You're causing the murder rate to go down?"

"Actually, my colleagues are. They're biologists and psychologists. I simply worked on the weather aspects of it." He'd said that already. I just hadn't understood it before. Maybe I did need Mrs. Glisando as an interpreter.

"And they do this through—?"

"A combination of chemicals and hormones that have to do with the brain. I don't understand much of this myself, but it's on the disk."

"So they're spraying the city with some kind of chemical?"

"It's not that simple, Detective," he said. "Like I said, it's on the disk."

"The disk is in my hand, not the computer. You can explain it to me."

Glisando shook his head. "I'm not here to talk science. I want to get my daughter cleared."

The man was loony, and his wife wasn't much better. I wanted them out of the precinct. I wanted the case closed.

"In order to clear her, you have to tell me how all this science is relevant," I said.

Glisando glanced at his wife. "We had to test our theory," he said, "in all kinds of weather. Take the fourteenth of February, for example."

The night Dudich had died. The night of the cold spell. The night of all the homicides. I remembered that even before Melanie Glisando had mentioned it to me.

"We had to see if we could make people behave contrary to our assumptions," Glisando said.

"People don't usually kill on cold nights," his wife said, as if I hadn't understood.

I had. I was just in shock. I couldn't believe they'd haul this out to protect their daughter. I couldn't believe anyone would believe I'd believe this.

"If what you're saying is true," I said slowly, "then all the deaths in the city that night could be laid on your doorstep."

"The company's," he said, as if he'd already thought of that.

"And the government's."

He shrugged. "They said it all balances. No one's been dying all summer."

I stared at them. They stared at me. I had nothing to say to them. If his theory was true, then this was something as big as the atomic-bomb tests with human guinea pigs at ground zero, the ones that happened in the fifties. If it wasn't true, it was the strangest story I'd ever heard anyone make up to get someone else off the hook.

And The Silence lent just enough credence to it. More than enough.

There were butterflies in my stomach.

It was my turn to clear my throat. I did, and swallowed hard. "So your program works," I said, trying to keep my voice calm. "And since it does, is it going to spread from city to city? Are you going to cover the countryside with this—chemical?"

He shook his head. "It didn't work."

I frowned. "You just said it did work. No one died."

"But the violence continues. That's what we missed. We didn't change peo-ple's basic nature. We just muted it."

"Or made it quirkier," I said, thinking not of this heat wave and The Silence, but of all the bizarre deaths all winter long.

His wife bowed her head. He closed his eyes and turned away from me. I waited, but that last shut them up. They seemed to have nothing more to say.

"I'm keeping the disk," I said finally.

Glisando turned back to me. "Illness makes people think irrational thoughts."

"And drugs make them act on it," I said. "That's never really been an excuse before."

*I don't remember that night*, Melanie Glisando had said to me. *God's truth. I woke up unable to remember going to bed.*

God, I was in the wrong place to hear this conversation. Too many strange things had happened. Too many strange things were still happening.

"I'm not going to charge Melanie," I said. I stood and opened the door. "But that's only because I can't do anything worse to her than is already being done."

"She's not a bad person," Mrs. Glisando said.

I turned to her. "Let's say for a moment that I believe your husband. Let's say that he did something to this city to make the murder rate climb in cold weather. Whatever he did wasn't one hundred percent effective, or we'd all be dead. It only allowed those with a predisposition to murder to commit the act."

Glisando shook his head. "You don't understand," he said.

I looked at him. "Yes," I said. "I'm afraid I do."

That night, I watched the weather on television. The first hurricane of the season was blowing up from the Carolinas, and the heat wave, so stifling and oppressive, was at an end. I kept my windows open and, sure enough, about 3 A.M., the wind howled through the building canyons and the rain pelted the streets and the air got cool.

Blissfully cool.

That morning, a man jogging despite the rain (or maybe because of it) through Central Park was mugged and beaten to death. A drug runner for one of the local gangs was shot on 42nd Street, and a broker was found strangled near the Exchange. By the time I got up, the news was already blaring on the radio.

The Silence was over.

Within days our caseload filled back up. But that didn't stop Bob from find-ing the evidence he needed to pin the murder of the neighbor on the husband and wife. Nor did it stop Weisburg from identifying the man who'd swallowed the finger as the head of a smuggling ring that had double-crossed the mob. The finger still had prints, and it belonged to the man's wife, who was alive and will-ing to talk if she was sent to witness protection.

Only Hawkins didn't solve his crime, which was no surprise. It's hard to make a case with just a torso and part of an arm for evidence. All the other body parts floating around the city didn't match.

The team thought I'd failed too, and I let them. I didn't say anything about Glisando or her nutty parents, at least not to the other wagerers. I did some double-checking, found out where Nic Glisando worked, found out, too, that he'd been there all night the night Dudich had been murdered. So Nic Glisando hadn't killed his daughter's lover, and neither had the wife. She'd been out of the country, visiting relatives in Europe.

Maybe it was that news that made me make three copies of the disk on the department's computer. Or maybe it was my innate caution. I gave one copy to my captain and the second to the *Daily News*. The *Daily News* apparently read the disk and printed the speculation that Glisando had laid on me, but by then, The Silence was long forgotten. The story ended up on page ten, bottom, a two-inch column that no one seemed to notice.

My captain thought the information on the disk as strange as I did and wrote it off to the flakiness some people could exhibit when under stress.

That's what I told myself too. But I keep the third copy of that disk in my desk and the original in a safety-deposit box because I'm as superstitious as the next guy. Maybe more so. And I'm keeping a graph now too. On one line is the ambient temperature in Manhattan, on the other, the number of homicides. I tell you, if things start looking strange, or we get some more Silence, I'm marching up to that farm upstate and getting more information, like what the government is really going to do with the knowledge if the experiments succeed.

What I'll do with that information, I haven't a clue. And at this moment, it's not really an issue. Things are back to normal. I'm overworked, overloaded, and suffering from stress. When a car backfires, I duck like I always have, knowing that random gunshots are happening again, and that people are dying at the hands of other people, just like they have from the time Cain had it in for his hapless brother Abel.

Hard to believe, even for myself, that I'm praying there won't be another Silence. Statistics experts say there won't, that this was just one of those anomalies that happen from time to time, something strange for the record books. The religious nuts blame the millennium, as they always do, and the change back to man's inherent evil nature. The alternate-timeline folks say that we'd been in a bubble, and now we're back on track.

I like those ideas a lot better than Glisando's. Glisando's means that human mind-control is possible, and that would put people like me, people who know but aren't affected, under an obligation to stop whatever's going on. And I don't like moral conundrums like that. I don't want my mind controlled any more than the next guy, but I also don't want the guy next to me to haul out his daddy's hunting knife and carve me into Sunday dinner because he's sick of sweating too much for the eighth day in a row.

So far my chart has shown nothing, and I doubt it ever will. People will say anything when their kid's dying, and could be up for murder at the same time. People'll say anything.

But what crosses my mind, usually at night, usually before I fall asleep, is that little thread of guilt that showed itself in Nic Glisando's face every time he frowned, the way he wouldn't quite look at me, the way he protected his soul. I believe his daughter killed Joel Dudich. Glisando believes it, too. Only he thinks that she did it because he was working on some strange government experiment.

I think she did it because, at home, she'd never learned how to take responsibility for herself.

The Silence was one of the strangest things I've ever seen on the job. But, you know, it wasn't the strangest. Because in our ice-blue files, there are a million

things that one human being has done to another for reasons only those two people fathom, and maybe not even they do. And we're just supposed to solve cases;
we're not supposed to understand them.

That's the hardest thing of all, realizing, when you come down to it, that
every human being is a mystery to others. Maybe people like Glisando believe
someday they'll find a way to make people do whatever they want. But I just
don't believe it.

# Bill Pronzini

## The Big Bite

BILL PRONZINI has lately concentrated his career on such award-winning mainstream suspense novels as *Blue Lonesome* without forgetting his role as one of America's preeminent private detective authors. The Nameless series grows richer, wilier, and crustier with each new outing. A Balzacian take on one working-class man's life in contemporary San Francisco—spanning thirty-some years now—the series grows in importance as the years tick by. Many flavors-of-the-month will fade. Nameless will stand for decades and perhaps longer as a vital, original part of crime novel heritage. "The Big Bite," published in *The Shamus Game*, sees Nameless's welcome return to the short form after a five-year vacation.

# The Big Bite

*Bill Pronzini*

I laid a red queen on a black king, glanced up at Jay Cohalan through the open door of his office. He was pacing again, back and forth in front of his desk, his hands in constant restless motion at his sides. The office was carpeted; his footfalls made no sound. There was no discernible sound anywhere except for the faint snap and slap when I turned over a card and put it down. An office building at night is one of the quietest places there is. Eerily so, if you spend enough time listening to the silence.

Trey. Nine of diamonds. Deuce. Jack of spades. I was marrying the jack to the red queen when Cohalan quit pacing and came over to stand in the doorway. He watched me for a time, his hands still doing scoop-shovel maneuvers—a big man in his late thirties, handsome except for a weak chin, a little sweaty and disheveled now.

"How can you just sit there playing cards?" he said.

There were several answers to that. Years of stakeouts and dull routine. We'd been waiting only about two hours. The money, fifty thousand in fifties and hundreds, didn't belong to me. I wasn't worried, upset, or afraid that something might go wrong. I passed on all of those and settled instead for a neutral response: "Solitaire's good for waiting. Keeps your mind off the clock."

"It's after seven. Why the hell doesn't he call?"

"You know the answer to that. He wants you to sweat."

"Sadistic bastard."

"Blackmail's that kind of game," I said. "Torture the victim, bend his will to yours."

"Game. My God." Cohalan came out into the anteroom and began to pace in front of his secretary's desk, where I was sitting. "It's driving me crazy, trying to figure out who he is, how he found out about my past. Not a hint, any of the times I talked to him. But he knows everything, every damn detail."

"You'll have the answers before long."

"Yeah." he stopped abruptly, leaned toward me.

"Listen, this has to be the end of it. You've *got* to stay with him, see to it he's arrested. I can't take any more."

"I'll do my job, Mr. Cohalan, don't worry."

"Fifty thousand dollars. I almost had a heart attack when he told me that was how much he wanted this time. The last payment, he said. What a crock. He'll come back for more someday. I know it, Carolyn knows it, you know it." Pacing again. "Poor Carolyn. High-strung, emotional . . . it's been even harder on her. She wanted me to go to the police this time, did I tell you that?"

"You told me."

"I should have, I guess. Now I've got to pay a middleman for what I could've had for nothing . . . no offense."

"None taken."

"I just couldn't bring myself to do it, walk into the Hall of Justice and confess everything to a cop. It was hard enough letting Carolyn talk me into hiring a private detective. That trouble when I was a kid . . . it's a criminal offense, I could still be prosecuted for it. And it's liable to cost me my job if it comes out. I went through hell telling Carolyn in the beginning, and I didn't go into all the sordid details. With you, either. The police . . . no. I know that bastard will probably spill the whole story when he's arrested, try to drag me down with him, but still . . . I keep hoping he won't. You understand?"

"I understand," I said.

"I shouldn't've paid him when he crawled out of the woodwork eight months ago. I know that now. But back then it seemed like the only way to keep from ruining my life. Carolyn thought so, too. If I hadn't started paying him, half of her inheritance wouldn't already be gone. . . ." He let the rest of it trail off, paced in bitter silence for a time, and started up again. "I hated taking money from her—*hated* it, no matter how much she insisted it belongs to both of us. And I hate myself for doing it, almost as much as I hate him. Blackmail's the worst goddamn crime there is short of murder."

"Not the worst," I said, "but bad enough."

"This *has* to be the end of it. The fifty thousand in there . . . it's the last of her inheritance, our savings. If that son of a bitch gets away with it, we'll be wiped out. You can't let that happen."

I didn't say anything. We'd been through all this before, more than once.

Cohalan let the silence resettle. Then, as I shuffled the cards for a new hand, "This job of mine, you'd think it pays pretty well, wouldn't you? My own office, secretary, executive title, expense account . . . looks good and sounds good, but it's a frigging dead end. Junior account executive stuck in corporate middle management—that's all I am or ever will be. Sixty thousand a year gross. And Carolyn makes twenty-five teaching. Eighty-five thousand for two people, no kids, that seems like plenty but it's not, not these days. Taxes, high cost of living, you have to scrimp to put anything away. And then some stupid mistake you made when you were a kid comes back to haunt you, drains your future along with your bank account, preys on your mind so you can't sleep, can barely do your work . . . you see what I mean? But I didn't think I had a choice at first, I was afraid of losing this crappy job, going to prison. Caught between a rock and a hard place. I still feel that way, but now I don't care, I just want that scum to get what's coming to him. . . ."

Repetitious babbling caused by his anxiety. His mouth had a wet look and his eyes kept jumping from me to other points in the room.

I said, "Why don't you sit down?"

"I can't sit. My nerves are shot."

"Take a few deep breaths before you start to hyperventilate."

"Listen, don't tell me what—"

The telephone on his desk went off.

The sudden clamor jerked him half around, as if with an electric shock. In the quiet that followed the first ring I could hear the harsh rasp of his breathing. He looked back at me as the bell sounded again. I was on my feet, too, by then.

I said, "Go ahead, answer it. Keep your head."

He went into his office, picked up just after the third ring. I timed the lifting of the extension to coincide so there wouldn't be a second click on the open line.

"Yes," he said, "Cohalan."

"You know who this is." The voice was harsh, muffled, indistinctively male. "You got the fifty thousand?"

"I told you I would. The last payment, you promised me . . ."

"Yeah, the last one."

"Where this time?"

"Golden Gate Park. Kennedy Drive, in front of the buffalo pen. Put it in the trash barrel beside the bench there."

Cohalan was watching me through the open doorway. I shook my head at him. He said into the phone, "Can't we make it someplace else? There might be people around. . . ."

"Not at nine p.m."

"Nine? But it's only a little after seven now—"

"Nine sharp. Be there with the cash."

The line went dead.

I cradled the extension. Cohalan was still standing alongside his desk, hanging onto the receiver the way a drowning man might hang onto a lifeline, when I went into his office. I said, "Put it down, Mr. Cohalan."

"What? Oh, yes . . ." He lowered the receiver. "Christ," he said then.

"You all right?"

His head bobbed up and down a couple of times. He ran a hand over his face and then swung away to where his briefcase lay. The fifty thousand was in there; he'd shown it to me when I first arrived. He picked the case up, set it down again. Rubbed his face another time.

"Maybe I *shouldn't* risk the money," he said.

He wasn't talking to me so I didn't answer.

"I could leave it right here where it'll be safe. Put a phone book or something in for weight." He sank into his desk chair, popped up again like a jack-in-the-box. He was wired so tight I could almost hear him humming. "No, what's the matter with me? That won't work. I'm not thinking straight. He might open the case in the park. There's no telling what he'd do if the money's not there. And he's got to have it in his possession when the police come."

"That's why I insisted we mark some of the bills."

"Yes, right, I remember. Proof of extortion. All right, but for God's sake don't let him get away with it."

"He won't get away with it."

Another jerky nod. "When're you leaving?"

"Right now. You stay put until at least eight-thirty. It won't take you more than twenty minutes to get out to the park."

"I'm not sure I can get through another hour of waiting around here."

"Keep telling yourself it'll be over soon. Calm down. The state you're in now, you shouldn't even be behind the wheel."

"I'll be okay."

"Come straight back here after you make the drop. You'll hear from me as soon as I have anything to report."

"Just don't make me wait too long," Cohalan said. And then, again and to himself, "I'll be okay."

Cohalan's office building was on Kearney, not far from where Kerry works at the Bates and Carpenter ad agency on lower Geary. She was on my mind as I drove down to Geary and turned west toward the park; my thoughts prompted me to lift the car phone and call the condo. No answer. Like me, she puts in a lot of overtime night work. A wonder we manage to spend as much time together as we do.

I tried her private number at B & C and got her voice mail. In transit probably, the same as I was. Headlights crossing the dark city. Urban night riders. Except that she was going home and I was on my way to nail a shakedown artist for a paying client.

That started me thinking about the kind of work I do. One of the downsides of urban night riding is that it gives vent to sometimes broody self-analysis. Skip traces, insurance claims investigations, employee background checks—they're the meat of my business. There used to be some challenge to jobs like that, some creative maneuvering required, but nowadays it's little more than routine legwork (mine) and a lot of computer time (Tamara Corbin, my techno-whiz assistant). I don't get to use my head as much as I once did. My problem, in Tamara's Generation X opinion, was that I was a "retro dick" pining away for the old days and old ways. True enough; I never have adapted well to change. The detective racket just isn't as satisfying or stimulating after thirty-plus years and with a new set of rules.

Every now and then, though, a case comes along that stirs the juices—one with some spark and sizzle and a much higher satisfaction level than the run-of-the-mill stuff. I live for cases like that; they're what keep me from packing it in, taking an early retirement. They usually involve a felony of some sort, and sometimes a whisper if not a shout of danger, and allow me to use my full complement of functional brain cells. This Cohalan case, for instance. This one I liked, because shakedown artists are high on my list of worthless lowlives and I enjoy hell out of taking one down.

Yeah, this one I liked a whole lot.

Golden Gate Park has plenty of daytime attractions—museums, tiny lakes, rolling lawns, windmills, an arboretum—but on a foggy November night it's a mostly empty green place to pass through on your way to somewhere else. Mostly empty because it does have its night denizens: homeless squatters, not all of whom are harmless or drug-free, and predators on the prowl in its sprawling acres of shadows and nightshapes. On a night like this it also has an atmosphere of lonely isolation, the fog hiding the city lights and turning street lamps and passing headlights into surreal blurs.

The buffalo enclosure is at the westward end, less than a mile from the ocean—the least-traveled section of the park at night. There were no cars in the vicinity, moving or parked, when I came down Kennedy Drive. My lights picked out the fence on the north side, the rolling pastureland beyond; the trash barrel and bench were about halfway along, at the edge of the bicycle path that parallels the road. I drove past there, looking for a place to park and wait. I didn't want to sit on Kennedy; a lone car close to the drop point would be too conspicuous. I had to do this right. If anything did not seem kosher, the whole thing might fail to go off the way it was supposed to.

The perfect spot came up fifty yards or so from the trash barrel, opposite the buffaloes' feeding corral—a narrow road that leads to Anglers Lodge, where the city maintains casting pools for fly fishermen to practice on. Nobody was likely to go up there at night, and trees and shrubbery bordered one side, the shadows in close to them thick and clotted. Kennedy Drive was still empty in both directions; I cut in past the Anglers Lodge sign and drove up the road until I found a place where I could turn around. Then I shut off my lights, made the U-turn, and coasted back down into the heavy shadows. From there I could see the drop point clearly enough, even with the low-riding fog. I shut off the engine, slumped down on the seat with my back against the door.

No detective, public or private, likes stakeouts. Dull, boring, dead time that can be a literal pain in the ass if it goes on long enough. This one wasn't too bad because it was short, only about an hour, but time lagged and crawled just the same. Now and then a car drifted by, its lights reflecting off rather than boring through the wall of mist. The ones heading west might have been able to see my car briefly in dark silhouette as they passed, but none of them happened to be a police patrol and nobody else was curious enough or venal enough to stop and investigate.

The luminous dial on my watch showed five minutes to nine when Cohalan arrived. Predictably early because he was so anxious to get it over with. He came down Kennedy too fast for the conditions; I heard the squeal of brakes as he swung over and rocked to a stop near the trash barrel. I watched the shape of him get out and run across the path to make the drop and then run back. Ten seconds later his car hissed past where I was hidden, again going too fast, and was gone.

Nine o'clock.

Nine oh five.

Nine oh eight.

Headlights probed past, this set heading east, the car lowslung and smallish. It rolled along slowly until it was opposite the barrel, then veered sharply across the road and slid to a crooked stop with its brake lights flashing blood red. I sat up straighter, put my hand on the ignition key. The door opened without a light coming on inside, and the driver jumped out in a hurry, bulky and indistinct in a heavy coat and some kind of head covering; ran to the barrel, scooped out the briefcase, raced back and hurled it inside; hopped in after it and took off. Fast, even faster than Cohalan had been driving, the car's rear end fishtailing a little as the tires fought for traction on the slick pavement.

I was out on Kennedy and in pursuit within seconds. No way I could drive in the fog-laden darkness without putting on my lights, and in the far reach of the beams I could see the other car a hundred yards or so ahead. But even when I accelerated I couldn't get close enough to read the license plate.

Where the drive forks on the east end of the buffalo enclosure, the sports job made a tight-angle left turn, brake lights flashing again, headlights yawing as the driver fought for control. Looping around Spreckels Lake to quit the park on 36th Avenue. I took the turn at about half the speed, but I still had it in sight when it made a sliding right through a red light on Fulton, narrowly missing an oncoming car, and disappeared to the east. I wasn't even trying to keep up any longer. If I continued pursuit, somebody—an innocent party—was liable to get hurt or killed. That was the last thing I wanted to happen. High-speed car chases are for damn fools and the makers of trite Hollywood films.

I pulled over near the Fulton intersection, still inside the park, and used the car phone to call my client.

Cohalan threw a fit when I told him what had happened. He called me all kinds of names, the least offensive of which was "incompetent idiot." I just let him rant. There were no excuses to be made and no point in wasting my own breath.

He ran out of abuse finally and segued into lament. "What am I going to do now? What am I going to tell Carolyn? All our savings gone and I still don't have any idea who that blackmailing bastard is. What if he comes back for more? We couldn't even sell the house, there's hardly any equity. . . ."

Pretty soon he ran down there, too. I waited through about five seconds of dead air. Then, "All right," followed by a heavy sigh. "But don't expect me to pay your bill. You can damn well sue me and you can't get blood out of a turnip." And he banged the receiver in my ear.

Some Cohalan. Some piece of work.

The apartment building was on Locust Street a half block off California, close to the Presidio. Built in the twenties, judging by its ornate facade, once somebody's modestly affluent private home, long ago cut up into three floors of studios and one-bedroom apartments. It had no garage, forcing its tenants—like most of those in the neighborhood buildings—into street parking. There wasn't a legal space to be had on that block, or in the next, or anywhere in the vicinity. Back on California, I slotted my car into a bus zone. If I got a ticket I got a ticket.

Not much chance I'd need a weapon for the rest of it, but sometimes trouble comes when you least expect it. So I unclipped the .38 Colt Bodyguard from under the dash, slipped it into my coat pocket before I got out for the walk down Locust.

The building had a tiny foyer with the usual bank of mailboxes. I found the button for 2-C, leaned on it. This was the ticklish part; I was banking on the fact that one voice sounds pretty much like another over an intercom. Turned out not to be an issue at all: the squawk box stayed silent and the door release buzzed instead, almost immediately. Confident. Arrogant. Or just plain stupid.

I pushed inside, smiling a little, cynically, and climbed the stairs to the second floor. The first apartment on the right was 2-C. The door opened just as I got to it, and Annette Byers put her head out and said with excitement in her voice, "You made really good—"

The rest of it snapped off when she got a look at me; the excitement gave way to confusion, froze her in the half-open doorway. I had time to move up on her, wedge my shoulder against the door before she could decide to jump back and slam it in my face. She let out a little bleat and tried to kick me as I crowded her inside. I caught her arms, gave her a shove to get clear of her. Then I nudged the door closed with my heel.

"I'll start screaming," she said. Shaky bravado, the kind without anything to back it up. Her eyes were frightened now. "These walls are paper thin, and I've got a neighbor who's a cop."

That last part was a lie. I said, "Go ahead. Be my guest."

"Who the hell do you think you are—"

"We both know who I am, Ms. Byers. And why I'm here. The reason's on the table over there."

In spite of herself she glanced to her left. The apartment was a studio, and the kitchenette and dining area were over that way. The briefcase sat on the dinette table, its lid raised. I couldn't see inside from where I was, but then I didn't need to.

"I don't know what you're talking about," she said.

She hadn't been back long; she still wore the heavy coat and the head covering, a wool stocking cap that completely hid her blond hair. Her cheeks were flushed—the cold night, money lust, now fear. She was attractive enough in a too-ripe way, intelligent enough to hold down a job with a downtown travel service, and immoral enough to have been in trouble with the San Francisco police before this. She was twenty-three, divorced, and evidently a crankhead: she'd been arrested once for possession and once for trying to sell a small quantity of methamphetamine to an undercover cop.

"Counting the cash, right?" I said.

". . . What?"

"What you were doing when I rang the bell. Fifty thousand in fifties and hundreds. It's all there, according to plan."

"I don't know what you're talking about."

"You said that already."

I moved a little to get a better scan of the studio. Her phone was on a breakfast bar that separated the kitchenette from the living room, one of those cordless types with a built-in answering machine. The gadget beside it was clearly a portable cassette player. She hadn't bothered to put it away before she went out; there'd been no reason to, or so she'd have thought then. The tape would still be inside.

I looked at her again. "I've got to admit, you're a pretty good driver. Reckless as hell, though, the way you went flying out of the park on a red light. You came close to a collision with another car."

"I don't know what—" She broke off and backed away a couple of paces, her hand rubbing the side of her face, her tongue making little flicks between her lips. It was sinking in now, how it had all gone wrong, how much trouble she was in. "You couldn't have followed me. I *know* you didn't."

"That's right, I couldn't and I didn't."

"Then how—?"

"Think about it. You'll figure it out."

A little silence. And, "Oh God, you knew about me all along."

"About you, the plan, everything."

"How? How could you? I don't—"

The downstairs bell made a sudden racket.

Her gaze jerked past me toward the intercom unit next to the door. She sucked in her lower lip, began to gnaw on it.

"You know who it is," I said. "Don't use the intercom, just the door release."

She did what I told her, moving slowly. I went the other way, first to the breakfast bar, where I popped the tape out of the cassette player and slipped it into my pocket, then to the dinette table. I lowered the lid on the briefcase, snapped the catches. I had the case in my hand when she turned to face me again.

She said, "What are you going to do with the money?"

"Give it back to its rightful owner."

"Jay. It belongs to him."

I didn't say anything to that.

"You better not try to keep it for yourself," she said. "You don't have any right to that money. . . ."

"You dumb kid," I said disgustedly, "neither do you."

She quit looking at me. When she started to open the door I told her no, wait for his knock. She stood with her back to me, shoulders hunched. She was no longer afraid; dull resignation had taken over. For her, I thought, the money was the only thing that had ever mattered.

Knuckles rapped on the door. She opened it without any hesitation, and he blew in, talking fast the way he did when he was keyed up. "Oh, baby, baby, we did it, we pulled it off," and he grabbed her and started to pull her against him. That was when he saw me.

"Hello, Cohalan," I said.

He went rigid for three or four seconds, his eyes popped wide, then disentangled himself from the woman and stood gawping at me. His mouth worked but nothing came out. Manic as hell in his office, all nerves and talking a blue streak, but now he was speechless. Lies were easy for him; the truth would have to be dragged out.

I told him to close the door. He did it, automatically, and turned snarling on Annette Byers. "You let him follow you home!"

"I didn't," she said. "He already knew about me. He knows everything."

"No, you're lying . . ."

"You were so goddamn smart, you had it all figured out. You didn't fool him for a minute."

"Shut up." His eyes shifted to me. "Don't listen to her. She's the one who's been blackmailing me—"

"Knock it off, Cohalan," I said. "Nobody's been blackmailing you. You're the shakedown artist here, you and Annette—a fancy little scheme to get your wife's money. You couldn't just grab the whole bundle from her, and you couldn't get any of it by divorcing her because a spouse's inheritance isn't community property in this state. So you cooked up the phony blackmail scam. What were the two of you planning to do with the full hundred thousand? Run off somewhere together? Buy a load of crank for resale, try for an even bigger score?"

"You see?" Annette Byers said bitterly. "You see, smart guy? He knows everything."

Cohalan shook his head. He'd gotten over his initial shock; now he looked stricken, and his nerves were acting up again. His hands had begun repeating that scoop-shovel trick at his sides. "You believed me, I know you did."

"Wrong," I said. "I didn't believe you. I'm a better actor than you, is all. Your story didn't sound right from the first. Too elaborate, full of improbabilities. Fifty thousand is too big a blackmail bite for any crime short of homicide, and you swore to me—your wife, too—you weren't guilty of a major felony. Blackmailers seldom work in big bites anyway. They bleed their victims slow and steady, in small bites, to keep them from throwing the hook. We just didn't believe it, either of us."

"We? Jesus, you mean . . . you and Carolyn . . . ?"

"That's right. Your wife's my client, Cohalan, not you—that's why I never asked you for a retainer. She showed up at my office right after you did the first time; if she hadn't, I'd probably have gone to her. She'd been suspicious all along, but she gave you the benefit of the doubt until you hit her with the fifty-thousand-dollar sum. She figured you might be having an affair, too, and it didn't take me long to find out about Annette. You never had any idea you were being followed, did you? Once I knew about her, it was easy enough to put the rest of it together, including the funny business with the money drop tonight. And here we are."

"Damn you," he said, but there was no heat in the words. "You and that frigid bitch both."

He wasn't talking about Annette Byers, but she took the opportunity to dig into him again. "Smart guy. Big genius. I told you to just take the money and we'd run with it, didn't I?"

"Shut up."

"Don't tell me to shut up, you son of—"

"Don't say it. I'll slap you silly if you say it."

"You won't slap anybody," I said. "Not as long as I'm around."

He wiped his mouth on the sleeve of his jacket. "What're you going to do?"

"What do you think I'm going to do?"

"You can't go to the police. You don't have any proof, it's your word against ours."

"Wrong again." I showed him the voice-activated recorder I'd had hidden in my pocket all evening. High-tech, state-of-the-art equipment, courtesy of George Agonistes, fellow P.I. and electronics expert. "Everything that was said in your office and in this room tonight is on here. I've also got the cassette tape Annette played when she called earlier. Voice prints will prove the muffled voice on it is yours, that you were talking to yourself on the phone, giving yourself orders and directions. If your wife wants to press charges, she'll have more than enough evidence to put the two of you away."

"She won't press charges," he said. "Not Carolyn."

"Maybe not, if you return the rest of her money. What you and baby here haven't already blown."

He sleeved his mouth again. "I suppose you intend to take the briefcase straight to her."

"You suppose right.

"I could stop you," he said, as if he were trying to convince himself. "I'm as big as you, younger—I could take it away from you."

I repocketed the recorder. I could have showed him the .38, but I grinned at him instead. "Go ahead and try. Or else move away from the door. You've got five seconds to make up your mind."

He moved in three, as I started toward him. Sideways, clear of both me and the door. Annette Byers let out a sharp, scornful laugh, and he whirled on her—somebody his own size to face off against. "Shut your stupid mouth!" he yelled at her.

"Shut yours, big man. You and your brilliant ideas."

"Goddamn you . . ."

I went out and closed the door against their vicious, whining voices.

Outside, the fog had thickened to a near drizzle, slicking the pavement and turning the lines of parked cars along both curbs into two-dimensional black shapes. Parking was at such a premium in this neighborhood, there was now a car, dark and silent, double-parked across the street. I walked quickly to California. Nobody, police included, had bothered my wheels in the bus zone. I locked the briefcase in the trunk, let myself inside. A quick call to Carolyn Cohalan to let her know I was coming, a short ride out to her house by the zoo to deliver the fifty thousand, and I'd finished for the night.

Only she didn't answer her phone.

Funny. When I'd called her earlier from the park, she'd said she would wait for my next call. No reason for her to leave the house in the interim. Unless—

Christ!

I heaved out of the car and ran back down Locust Street. The darkened vehicle was still double-parked across from Annette Byers' building. I swung into the foyer, jammed my finger against the bell button for 2-C and left it there. No response. I rattled the door—latched tight—and then began jabbing buttons on all the other mailboxes. The intercom crackled; somebody's voice said, "Who the hell is that?" I said, "Police emergency, buzz me in." Nothing, nothing, and then finally the door release sounded; I hit the door hard and lunged into the lobby.

I was at the foot of the stairs when the first shot echoed from above. Two more in swift succession, a fourth as I was pounding up to the second-floor landing.

Querulous voices, the sound of a door banging open somewhere, and I was at 2-C. The door there was shut but not latched; I kicked it open, hanging back with the .38 in my hand for self-protection. But there was no need. It was over by then. Too late and all over.

All three of them were on the floor. Cohalan on his back next to the couch, blood obscuring his face, not moving. Annette Byers sprawled bloody and moaning by the dinette table. And Carolyn Cohalan sitting with her back against a wall, a long-barreled .22 on the carpet nearby, weeping in deep, broken sobs.

I leaned hard on the doorjamb, the stink of cordite in my nostrils, my throat full of bile. Telling myself it was not my fault, there was no way I could have known it wasn't the money but paying them back that mattered to her—the big payoff, the biggest bite there is. Telling myself I could've done nothing to prevent this, and remembering what I'd been thinking in the car earlier about how I lived for cases like this, how I liked this one a whole lot . . .

# Les Roberts

## The Gathering of the Klan

LES ROBERTS has had several careers, both as Hollywood producer (the original producer of *Hollywood Squares*), screenwriter (*The Man From U.N.C.L.E.*), restaurant critic, and now full-time crime novelist. From the critical and public acclaim he's received, it's doubtful he'll be changing careers anytime soon. His latest Milan Jacovich novel was cited by *People* magazine as "the page-turner of the week" and offers further evidence that the Milan novels are among the most unique and important in contemporary crime fiction. Roberts is equally good in the shorter form, as "The Gathering of the Klan," first published in *The Shamus Game*, illustrates.

# The Gathering of the Klan

*Les Roberts*

Just about the biggest controversy to hit Cleveland since the old Browns released Bernie Kozar in mid-season back in the early nineties was the announcement that our African American mayor had granted a permit for a rally outside the Cleveland Convention Center on a Sunday afternoon in August to an out-of-town contingent of the Ku Klux Klan.

Probably no one was as surprised as the klunks, klowns and kleagles themselves; their usual M.O. was to apply for a permit in some northern city and then sue for the right to free speech when the permit was denied. They had accumulated quite a comfortable little nest egg from collecting such judgments in towns in Michigan, Pennsylvania and Minnesota over the last several years, and they were probably planning on collecting big from liberal and heavily black-populated Cleveland.

Everyone was mad at the mayor. The police department's union, the black community, the city council and the county commissioners, all of his many political enemies and rivals, and most of the media had taken the opportunity to try to shoot him down. Everyone was terrified that Cleveland would once again become a national laughingstock, to say nothing of the genuine fear that one hastily hurled racial slur or one thrown beer can could set off a riot that would see the city go up in flames.

The mayor pleaded that his hands were tied and talked a lot about the First Amendment, and begged the citizenry to behave itself and not give the national media any sound bites with which to tarnish the image that Cleveland had taken such pains to rebuild and polish over the past twenty years.

I try to stay out of politics; as the sole owner of a small business—Milan Security, which I christened after my own first name, Milan, since my surname is almost impossible for many people to pronounce—supplying industrial security and private investigations, I have enough to do just trying to keep solvent. My natural dislike and loathing for anyone promoting racial hatred made me follow the story closely in the newspapers, but I had no intention of getting involved in it one way or the other.

Until Earl Roy Ruttenberg, the regional president and exalted Grand Dragon of a southern Ohio branch of the Klan, walked into my office five days before the rally, wanting to hire me as his personal bodyguard for the weekend of the rally.

He was close to fifty, some forty pounds overweight, slightly balding, and had a complexion like four-day-old cottage cheese. He came in flanked by two over-muscled young men who were twenty years younger; both had bad hair and Elvis sideburns and UP WITH WHITE PEOPLE T-shirts, and looked as though they were totally ignorant of even the whereabouts of the nearest dentist. One of them had a girlish, soulful look like Paul McCartney. Ruttenberg sat in one of my client's chairs, but his two trained orangutans positioned themselves on either side of the door.

I listened to his offer of a two-day job as his bodyguard and turned him down flat.

"I'm truly sorry to hear that, Mr. Jacovich," he said, his accent that blend of Southern and Midwestern that you hear down near the Kentucky-Ohio border and which is referred to as "briar," after the somewhat disdainful sobriquet "briarhopper."

"Sorry," I said.

"I've asked around, believe me, gotten lots of recommendations, and you're definitely my first choice."

"I can't imagine why," I said. "First of all, I'm Catholic, and secondly, I despise everything you stand for and I have nothing but contempt for the line of shit you're trying to sell."

Ruttenberg smiled easily. "A lot of people feel that way."

"Maybe you should go find a bodyguard that doesn't."

"You're not saying that you'd like to see me dead, are you?"

"I don't want to see anybody dead, Mr. Ruttenberg. But if the whole world was on the *Titanic* and I was in charge of the lifeboats, I don't think you'd get one of the first seats."

He laughed; he had a *yuk-yuk-yuk* kind of laugh that grated on my nerves almost as much as his racial attitudes. The T-shirt muscle boys guffawed, too, but I don't believe they got the humor; they were programmed to laugh when the Grand Dragon did.

"You seem as if you're pretty well protected already," I said.

"Oh, Ozzie and Jay are great for the everyday stuff. But I know that our being here on Sunday has caused a lot of controversy, and I was hoping to find someone who really was plugged in to Cleveland, who knew the crazies to look out for."

"From where I stand, it seems to me that the crazy we have to look out for is *you*."

"Ah-ha-ha," he said, but it wasn't a laugh this time. "I'm a crazy who's prepared to pay you very well, though."

"If I tried to spend your kind of money, Mr. Ruttenberg, I'm afraid I'd disappear in a puff of sulfurous smoke."

"You'd druther see some wild-eyed funky nigger with a razor cut my throat?"

I glanced out my office window at the Cuyahoga River, which ran past the building. As a big guy who used to play defensive tackle on the Kent State football team, I figured that with a good enough throw I could probably toss Ruttenberg into it with ease. "Say that word again in here, Mr. Ruttenberg, and you're going to have to swim home." The muscle guys stirred uneasily at the threat. "And the same goes for Ozzie and Harriet over there, too. Try me if you think I'm kidding." I fantasized the scenario for a few seconds and added, "Please try me." Hope springs eternal.

"I am truly sorry I offended you, Mr. Jacovich," Ruttenberg said. "It's just a word, after all."

"It's an ugly, hate-filled word that I never allow in my presence. I can't fault you for being stupid, because you probably can't help it. I can, however, blame you for being rude. Remember that. Or don't bother, you're leaving anyway."

"I think you owe me the courtesy of a hearing, at least."

"I don't owe bigots the sweat off my ass."

"Looky here," he said. "We're entitled to our b'liefs just like anyone else. And I can assure you that my people are completely under control and will cause no trouble at all unless they are physically provoked. *Physically* provoked, you understand. We've been called names by the best of them; that doesn't bother us."

"Then you won't have any trouble and you won't need me. Besides, this city is going to great expense to make sure nobody offs your sorry ass when you put on your clown costumes and wave the flag."

"They are at that, and I appreciate it." He said the next-to-last word like Andy Griffith used to, without the first syllable. "It's the time leading up to the rally that has me worried.

"We don't want any riots. That'd run counter to our purposes. But d'you have any idea what might transpire here if anything happens to me? Or to *anyone?* Chaos," he intoned, pronouncing both the *C* and the *H* like he would if he were saying "chicken." He leaned back in the chair and crossed his legs. "People will get hurt, maybe innocent people, maybe some of your tippytoe-dancing liberal and black friends. You see the truth in that?"

I did, but I didn't tell him so.

"You want that happening here in your city? I don't b'lieve you do, do ya?"

Once again, I wouldn't give him the satisfaction of answering a question that was, after all, rhetorical.

"So here's the deal. The city of Cleveland is providing security at the rally, but before that we're on our own. Now, we're gonna check into our hotel on Sat-tidy afternoon. We want you there just to make sure there isn't any trouble. We eat dinner, you join us—dinner is on me, of course—and at nine o'clock we turn in. We're country people, we go to bed early. Sunday morning you meet us at the hotel, you escort us to the rally, and then the Cleveland po-lice take over and per-tect us from those people who don't like what we have to say and wanna deny us our right to free speech under the First Amendment of the Constitution of the United States. You're free to leave then. You don't even have to stay and listen to the speeches." He gave me what he thought was a winning smile. "Although you really oughta, you might learn somethin'."

"I could learn the same things from the wall of a truck stop men's room."

His mean little eyes got even smaller; he didn't like that. He didn't like *me.* I could live with it.

He was a gamer, though, I had to grant him that. He didn't give up. "So you gonna he'p us out here? Or are you willin' to jus' sit back and maybe watch your hometown burn?"

Now, I am not possessed of sufficient hubris to think that the safety of Cleveland's citizenry depended on me. But the son of a bitch did have a point. American cities today are as volatile as gasoline fumes, and it wouldn't take much of a spark at a public breast-beating where one group disses another in the ugliest of racial terms to set off a conflagration for which Cleveland would have to apologize for the next thirty years.

Maybe I could make a very small contribution toward keeping a spark from striking.

"All right, Mr. Ruttenberg, I'll do it. As long as we completely understand each other."

"What's there to understand?" Ruttenberg asked, taking a checkbook out of the breast pocket of his discount-store suit.

"That I despise everything about you," I said.

My pal at *The Plain Dealer*, Ed Stahl, whose column used to grace page two every morning but, due to the paper's new format, was now buried deep inside where nobody could find it, was frankly appalled. Over the past three weeks since the rally was announced, he had filed several scathing columns excoriating the Klan and the mayor for granting them access to public space, along with the mayor's political enemies who protested that he was coddling bigots and racists who were using the opportunity to savage him for their own aggrandizement, and just about everyone else in town, too. Ed had received several ugly and even threatening voice mails for his pains, most of them from gravel-voiced men who sounded, he said, like refugees from *Deliverance*.

"I think you're making a mistake, Milan," he told me over pasta at a table by the window in the front room of Piccolo Mondo on West Sixth Street. "Those people are pigs. You know what happens when you lie down with pigs."

"I do," I said. "But it seems preferable to a riot."

"That Earl Ruttenberg is bad paper."

"He's a fat clown, Ed. And the only people who will listen to his crap are the morons who think like he does in the first place. He's preaching to the choir."

"If that's true, Milan, you win. So why are you worried about rioting?"

"Because there's a hell of a lot of people in this town, of all colors, who think Ruttenberg and his people should be used as garden fertilizer. If rocks and bottles and bullets start flying, there won't *be* any winners."

He gulped down a slug of his favorite poison, Jim Beam on the rocks, and grimaced. Ed has an ulcer, and has no business drinking anything stronger than buttermilk.

"Is the money enough that you can live with yourself afterward?"

"I'll let you know Monday morning," I said.

He glanced up at the door and his shoulders grew rigid. "Oh my," he said. "Oh my fucking stars . . ."

I followed his gaze. Entering the restaurant was one of the most familiar faces—and loudest voices—on the local scene. After a long tenure as de facto leader of Cleveland's African American community, Clifford Andrews had been elected to a lively and volatile mayorship for four years that were characterized by violent temper tantrums and black-power rhetoric, before losing City Hall in a close election seven years ago to the current two-term incumbent, a setback for which he had never forgiven his former friend, and had been not-so-subtly trying to undermine his successor ever since. Now forced into the private practice of law on Cleveland's largely black east side, Andrews had made enough political hay out of the issuance of the KKK permit to last the farmers of Kansas several lifetimes.

He bore down on us, eyes lasering into Ed Stahl, his cocoa-brown face glistening with perspiration, flanked by two very large black men one might be forgiven for mistaking as Cleveland Browns offensive linemen, and stopped at our table.

"Hello, Clifford," Ed said.

"Stahl, don't you 'hello-Clifford' me, you race-baiting son of a bitch." Andrews was enough of a presence that most people look up when he enters a room, but the volume of his voice made sure that anyone who had missed his grand entrance at first corrected their oversight.

Ed just smiled up at him with the innocence of a Christmas-card cherub. "I'm glad to know you're still reading my column, Clifford. Although only you would call it race baiting."

"You say I'm trying to start a riot in this city just to make myself look good? I ought to crack you across the face."

I shifted uneasily in my chair. Clifford Andrews was sixty-three-years-old and suffered from arthritis, but was not beyond the bar-fight stage, not by a long shot. During his administration he had been known to throw ashtrays, crockery, and on one occasion, a folding chair at people who angered or disagreed with him. He also outweighed Ed Stahl by about eighty pounds.

"Clifford," Ed said, remarkably calm under the circumstances, "if I only wrote my column so that no one ever got their feelings hurt, I'd wind up selling ties at Dillard's. I think you acted irresponsibly, and whether you like it or not, it's my job to say so. Nothing personal."

"We'll see about that," Andrews said. Then he looked at me and his eyes blazed even more. "You're Jacovich, right?"

"Close enough, Mr. Andrews," I said. He had incorrectly pronounced the J; the correct way is YOCK-o-vitch. But I sensed Clifford Andrews didn't care one way or the other.

"I hear that you're the son of a bitch who's actually gonna protect those scum."

"Word gets around."

"How can you even look in the mirror?" He sneered. It was almost funny coming from him, the man who'd fanned media fever and street anger over the triple-K hate hoedown from a warm coal to a white-hot ember.

Almost.

"I guess from time to time we all have trouble looking in mirrors, Mr. Andrews," I said.

His dark skin grew even darker as the blood rushed to his face. Then his lips tightened into a smile that could best be described as satanic. "You'll get what's coming to you, too. You and your honky racist employer, too. I'll see to it," he promised, and stalked off into the inner dining room. His two companions gave me a lingering look before they followed him.

Everybody else in Piccolo Mondo was giving *us* the looks. I just ignored them, but Ed boldly stared them down until they went back to their pizza and pasta.

"Move over, Ed. I guess I've just joined you on Clifford Andrews's shit list."

Ed laughed. "Welcome to the club. His shit list is longer than the one that tells who's naughty and nice." He took a carbon-crusted briar pipe out of his pocket and stuck the well-chewed stem between his teeth. No smoking was allowed in the dining room, but there was no law against pretending to. "I have to say that as mad as Clifford has ever been at me, he's never threatened me before, Milan."

"That bothered me, too," I said. "Well, look on the bright side—he didn't throw any furniture."

But Andrews did hurl a good bit of invective my way when he spoke to the Channel 12 news anchor, Vivian Truscott, on the six o'clock news that evening, calling me an even worse racist than Earl Ruttenberg, who, in Andrews' words, "at least has the guts to be up-front about it." I've been called dirtier names, I suppose, although rarely with less justification, but I still had to hope that my two sons didn't hear it.

Those particular three of my allotted fifteen minutes of fame on the news show did prompt two unexpected office visits the next morning, one from a longtime business associate and the other from someone I had heard about but never met.

The business associate was Willard Dante, who ran the largest manufacturing company of residential and security devices in Ohio, in the not-too-close exurb of Twinsburg. He garnered national recognition a few years ago with his development of a stun belt that had civil libertarians picketing outside his factory, but my relationship with him was based more on the alarm systems, surveillance cameras and security paraphernalia which I purchased from him on occasion for my more paranoid industrial clients. He was the kind of church-tithing, flag-waving super patriot I didn't have anything to do with socially, but our business dealings had always been cordial.

"I was on one of my rare trips downtown anyway today, Milan," he said heartily after I'd poured him a cup of coffee, "so I thought I'd pop in and tell you in person that I thought what Cliff Andrews said about you on TV last night really stinks the big stink. You deserve better."

I shook his outstretched hand. "Thanks, Will, I appreciate it. But I can't say it really bothered me. Andrews rants and raves all the time. Not that many people listen to him anyway."

"Well, I think you're doing the right thing. Somebody somewhere is going to blow Ruttenberg away for his sins one of these days, but I'd just as soon it didn't happen here. I'm glad you're on board to see it doesn't happen."

"The police are going to baby-sit him in public on Sunday," I said. "There's more security planned than if the pope was going to show up."

"I know," he said. "The mayor is breaking out the tear gas, and I heard a rumor there would be snipers up on the rooftops. Snipers, for God's sake, In *Ohio*! So what does Ruttenberg want *you* to do for him?"

"Make sure he and his Keystone Klunks check into their hotel with no problem, for one thing. And then I have to eat dinner with them. The next morning I drive him downtown to his slimefest, and then I'm through."

"I'd think that they would be staying at a downtown hotel, for the sake of convenience," Dante said.

"They're too cheap for that, Will. They've booked twenty-five rooms at a dinky little motel out by the airport."

"My stars," he said. He was the only person I'd ever met who said "my stars" as an exclamation and didn't sound like somebody's grandmother. "That's tacky. Where are you going to eat with them? McDonald's?"

"No, they picked this little low-end steak house close to their motel, a place called Red's, for God's sake. I think I'm going to eat before I go."

He laughed. "Anything I can do to help out? Want to rent some security cams?"

"I don't think we'll need them, Will."

He nodded, looking a little disappointed. "Well, listen, pal, I just wanted to let you know that I'm with you a hundred and ten percent on this one, and that what old windbag Andrews said about you last night is not going to affect our business relationship in the slightest."

"I appreciate the support, Will."

"What are friends for?" he said.

Well, it was nice to get an attaboy when the rest of the world seemed ready to hang me on the wall. A few of my friends had called me at home the previous evening to complain about Andrews' vilification of me on television, but no one had dropped in except Willard Dante. I had visited his Twinsburg plant several times, but I don't think he'd ever been in my office before.

About five minutes after he left, my second visitor arrived, and I wondered if they had crossed paths in the parking lot. I'd seen him on television, seen his photo in the newspaper countless times, and had even heard him speak once when he made an unsuccessful run for the office of county commissioner a few years earlier. The Reverend Alvin Quest of the Mount Gilead Baptist Church on Cleveland's east side was a moral and spiritual leader in the black community who had also made a brief and spectacularly unsuccessful run for a U.S. Senate nomination a few years earlier. He was a consistent voice of reason and, when the occasion called for it, of fire.

In my office, however, he spoke with warmth and courtesy in a soft and well-modulated voice, his dark eyes sparkling behind his small, thick-lensed spectacles.

"It's a pleasure meeting you, Reverend Quest," I said. "I've been an admirer of yours."

He smiled. "Thank you," he said. "That's good to hear."

"So I hope you haven't come up here to give me a spanking about this Klan thing."

"Just the opposite," he assured me. "To be sure, Clifford Andrews and I share the same goals, but we usually differ sharply in how we want to accomplish them. I apologize for his rashness on the news last night."

"No harm, no foul."

"Actually I came here to offer you any help I can."

That one brought me up short. "Help?"

He nodded. "It would be very destructive to what our people have tried to accomplish in Cleveland if anything untoward were to happen to Mr. Ruttenberg or any of his minions. To say nothing of tarnishing the name of a city that has come so far in the last twenty years. So it is vitally important to me that Earl Ruttenberg stay safe as long as he is in our city. I'm more than happy to dispatch some of our people to help you with your security."

"You think that's such a good idea, Reverend? Letting the world see black men actually protecting the head of the KKK?"

"Oh, we'll be there having our say as well. The city of Cleveland has set aside a special area for protesters, just like they have for the Klan supporters. I'm sure you read that in the papers."

I nodded.

"But it will be a peaceful, quiet, dignified protest. I want to let everyone know that there are other avenues besides violence, that we defy those sad, silly, misguided fools in their sheets and hoods. That there is sanctity in human life, and that under the skin, people are all the same. Isn't that what Martin Luther King preached?"

"Martin Luther King," I said, "never met Earl Roy Ruttenberg."

Not knowing, of course, that soon Dr. King was to have his chance.


It was Saturday afternoon and I was sitting in the so-called lobby of the Pine Rest Motel on Brookpark Road near the Cleveland Airport. I don't know why they had named it that; there wasn't a pine tree within ten miles, and if the lobby furniture was of the same quality as the beds in the rooms, it wasn't very restful, either. It wasn't the kind of hot-pillow joint where hookers plied their trade in cubicle rooms and pushers passed dime bags down by the ice machine, but it wasn't exactly the Ritz Carlton, either.

I was wearing a .357 Magnum in a shoulder harness under my sports jacket, but nobody seemed to notice that. Maybe sitting in the lobby heeled was the Pine Rest's dress code.

For the past hour there had been a trickle of rough-looking white males with one piece of luggage apiece checking in at the desk; a few of them gave me suspicious glances bordering on hostile, but I suppose when your main source of recreation is running around wearing sheets and hoods and foaming at the mouth about blacks and Jews and Catholics, suspicion and hostility are your daily portion.

Finally, at a few minutes after four, a vintage Cadillac pulled up in front of the motel office. Earl Roy Ruttenberg got out of the backseat, and Ozzie and Jay exited from the front. I walked out of the lobby into the heat of August.

"I see you got here all right," I said to Ruttenberg. I made no effort to shake hands, nor was he expecting me to do so.

"So far, so good. Kind of a boring trip up from Medina, with all that highway construction. All quiet around here? Any suspicious-looking characters?"

"A bunch of them," I said, "but they're all with your group."

"Heh-heh," he said. "No, I was thinking of those folks of the Negro persuasion."

I assured him that no "folks of the Negro persuasion" were in evidence except the room maids, walked him in to the front desk, followed by Ozzie and

Jay, who today were sporting mirrored sunglasses in a pathetic attempt at looking cool, macho and bad-ass. I watched while they checked in. It had been pre-arranged that the boys of bummer would share a room next to Ruttenberg's, which turned out to be a suite, a sitting room with a bedroom attached.

I sat on the sofa and watched him unpack. He had brought a brown suit, white shirt and an ugly tie, which he put in the closet, extra socks and underwear and a pair of brown shoes that went in the dresser drawer, and a sports jacket, gray slacks and a bilious green polo shirt, which he laid out on the bed. Then I watched in amazement as he lovingly unpacked and hung up his white robe and hood. It was almost funny.

Almost.

"Tell me," I said, "do you have those sheets laundered commercially, or does your wife wash and iron them for you?"

"Go ahead and have your fun, Mr. Jacovich," he said good-naturedly. This time he pronounced it correctly.

"Where did you learn the correct pronunciation of my name?"

"Oh, I heard some loud-mouthed boogie talking about you on television the other night."

I started to get up from the sofa, but he raised a hand like a traffic cop stopping a line of cars. "Take it easy, now. You just told me I couldn't use the N-word; you didn't say nothing about boogie."

I just sighed. When he's right, he's right.

From his briefcase he took several stacks of flyers and brochures of racial filth and put them on the table near the window. I avoided them the way I would a pile of rancid garbage.

He pulled a silver hip flask from his pocket and unscrewed the top. "Join me?"

"No thanks."

He laughed. "Fussy who you drink with, huh?"

"Something like that."

"Don't be that way. No reason we can't be friends, is there?"

"There are a thousand reasons. I'm here to see no one takes a shot at you or sticks a knife in your eye, and I'll do that to the best of my ability. If you were looking to hire a friend, you dialed the wrong number."

"Your loss," he said. He unscrewed the top of the flask and took a long pull at it. "Aaaaahhh," he breathed in satisfaction. The smell that wafted across the room told me it was not very good bourbon.

"What do you get out of this, Mr. Ruttenberg?" I said, partly to make conversation and partly because I really wanted to know. "You have to be aware that here at the beginning of the twenty-first century, the vast majority of the people are either hating your guts or just laughing at you."

"Some folks do," he admitted. "Like you. But I think you'd be s'prised at how many folks are starting to think my way. *Our* way."

"That's why you travel with two bone breakers and hired me as extra security, huh? Because everyone loves you."

"Of course not. Not the kikes or the spics or the pope lickers. And certainly not the mud people."

"Damn," I said.

"What?"

"We're going to have to amend our little agreement, Mr. Ruttenberg, and put a moratorium on all the racial and ethnic slurs, or I'm not going to be able to keep from pounding the piss out of you."

"Just trying to get your goat, Jacovich. And I seem to have done a good job of it. Well, okay, I'll be good. But I can't guarantee what kind of words my friends might say at dinner tonight. You gonna pound the piss out of all of them?"

I didn't respond.

"But let me answer your question. What do I get out of it? The, um, *minorities* in this country are going to take over if we're not careful. The Jews have all the money and they control all the newspapers and television, the blacks have all the jobs, and the Catholics keep on grinding out new little Catholics like sausages to suck up our tax money in welfare. This country was founded by white men. What I get out of it is reminding the white people of this country of that fact so they don't let the U.S. of A. slip out from between their fingers. And to remind the *others* that there's a whole bunch of folks who just aren't about to let them take our birthright from us."

"I see," I said, feeling as if an elephant had just stepped on my chest. I'd heard this kind of foamy-mouthed crap before; all of us have. But I never looked at it across the same room before, and it was causing me difficulty in breathing.

"So what I get out of it," he went on, "is a U.S. of A. that I'll be proud to leave to my children and grandchildren."

I suppressed a shudder. The thought of Earl Roy Ruttenberg actually breeding and reproducing was an unsettling one.

I had brought a paperback along with me, figuring I'd rather read than have to talk to him, so I sat by the window, occasionally glancing up from the page and out into the parking lot to make sure no one was out there with a bazooka, while Ruttenberg went into the bedroom to make some phone calls. He emerged at a quarter to seven in the sports jacket and snot-green shirt, his jowly face glistening from a very recent shave.

"Let's eat!" he said, and actually rubbed his hands together.

Red's Steak House is for people who have arteries like firehoses. Gnarly steaks, french fries, meat loaf, roast duck, pork loin, and anything else one might cook with grease were featured prominently on the menu. For those who don't eat red meat, there was fried perch. Other than the desserts, there was not much else. There is a lounge attached to the dining room, the kind of bar where ordering a frozen daiquiri is indicative of either seriously impaired judgement or a death wish.

The Klan had been relegated to what Red's laughingly called their banquet room, a private dining room with two long tables—each table was actually five tables pushed together—that seated sixteen people each. Ruttenberg ensconced himself at the head of one of them and indicated that I should sit next to him. But frankly, I didn't think I could eat a thing, despite Ruttenberg's generous offer to pay for my dinner. It was less the prospect of a heart attack on a plate that engendered a loss of appetite, frankly, than the company. I opted instead to stand at the door, just in case I had to earn my money, and unbuttoned my jacket in the event I had to draw my weapon quickly. Ruttenberg actually seemed a little hurt, but Ozzie and Jay flanked him and made him feel safe, so he didn't need me.

Most of the flint-eyed, slack-jawed men I'd seen checking into the Pine Rest had showed up, some of them tackily and gaudily dressed for the occasion. I guess they operated on the theory that you can't spew misanthropic hatred at the dinner table if you aren't gussied up for the part.

After everyone had enjoyed a pre-dinner cocktail or four, the first course was brought out. As befitting his exalted station in life, Ruttenberg was served first. It was soup, chicken noodle from the look of it, and for a while the only sound in the room was sucking and slurping, like standing next to a sewer grating after a heavy rain. Then, when the soup plates had been cleared away, Earl Roy Ruttenberg tapped on his water glass with a fork, waited until his followers had quieted down, and rose.

"My fellow patriots," he said when he had everyone's attention. "First off, I wanna thank y'all for being here. The camaraderie of white men is something special—warm and loving and strong in its devotion to a righteous cause. And I am reveling in that camaraderie right now."

Applause, heartfelt and enthusiastic. Nothing like a warm-and-fuzzy to fire up a lynch mob.

"Naturally, we're hoping for a big turnout tomorrow," Ruttenberg went on. "But that really isn't important anymore. Because just by *being* here, we've won the game. The Negro politicians who run this town are at one another's throats already, and we couldn't have asked for more help from the liberal news media than if we'd paid for it!"

"Hear! Hear!" somebody said.

"But I wanted to give each and every one of you my personal and sincere thanks. We are the last line of defense in the United States, and I am just damn proud of all of you for—"

He stopped, got a strange look on his face, and burped.

" 'Scuse me," he said. "I am proud of each and every . . ."

And then his face got very flushed, his eyes grew wide, and he bent over almost double from the waist and vomited down the front of his green shirt.

If you've ever given serious thought to putting rat poison in your basement, you would probably rethink it if you'd watched Earl Roy Ruttenberg die. It took him about seven minutes, and from his roars of agony, his writhing on the floor, his vomiting black bile, and the horrible contractions that sent his body into spasms every few seconds, it was not an easy seven minutes. Someone called the paramedics, but they arrived far too late.

The Klansmen were bumping into each other in panicked disarray, but they were muttering darkly about revenge and payback as well. It's apparently true that when you cut off the head of a snake, the rest of the body lives on.

Lieutenant Florence McHargue of the Cleveland P.D.'s Homicide Division arrived a few minutes after the paramedics. She was cranky because such a high-profile victim had dragged her away from her Saturday night, and even crankier because she was a black woman whose duty had thrown her among a rattled mob of Ku Kluxers. She temporarily ordered them all out into the main dining room of Red's Steak House, where they milled around bumping shoulders like nervous steers in a slaughterhouse pen.

She wasn't exactly overjoyed to find me there, either. Lieutenant McHargue doesn't like me very much, but as far as I've been able to tell she isn't really fond of anyone.

"I heard on TV that you were going to hold Ruttenberg's hand," she said. "This serves you right." She looked down at the body, which had been hastily covered with a couple of tablecloths until the coroner's technicians could arrive. "Serves him right, too."

"And there are only about three hundred thousand people in greater Cleveland with a motive, too. This should be a slam-dunk for you, Lieutenant."

"Let's start with slam-dunking *you*," she said. "Talk to me."

"I can start with Clifford Andrews. I suppose you know about him hanging me out to dry on television the other night. Did you also hear that he threatened both me and Ruttenberg publicly in Piccolo Mondo the other day?"

"Oh, yes," she said. "That got back to me in a hurry."

"I'd think, then, that you'd start with slam-dunking *him*."

"I will, believe me. But the fact is that while in public Andrews is a fire-breathing race baiter, privately he is a very logical, reasonable, and even charming man. Most of the time, anyway."

"When he's not throwing furniture."

"At his age, he's lucky he can still lift it, much less throw it."

"Nobody had a better motive," I reminded her. "It kills two birds with one stone. He rids the world of Earl Roy Ruttenberg, and he makes the mayor look like a doofus."

"The mayor does that himself without anyone's help," she observed dryly; the mayor and the police rank and file regarded each other the way the Albanians do the Serbians. "What else?"

"Not much," I said. "Ruttenberg was a little obsessed about his safety, but obviously just because he was paranoid, it didn't mean someone wasn't after him. Hate has a way of blowing up in your hand."

"We're questioning all the kitchen help and the wait staff. Who knew the Ruttenberg crowd would be eating here?"

"I have no way of knowing who they told. I know I didn't tell anybody." Then the skin prickled on the back of my neck. "Except Willard Dante."

"The stun-gun guy?"

"That's the one. I happened to mention to him that the Kluxers were going to be having dinner here. But he's a Pat Buchanan conservative; why would he want to kill Ruttenberg?"

"Why indeed" she said, and jotted his name down in her notebook. "This town catches fire this afternoon and his phone will be ringing off the hook with people wanting security cameras and alarm systems and even stun guns to protect themselves from rioters. What made you tell him and no one else?"

I had to think about that for a while. "Because he asked."

"Uh-huh," McHargue said.

Willard Dante's house was in the elegant little village of Gates Mills. Apparently the stun-gun business was a lucrative one. He seemed surprised to see me on his doorstep, because I hadn't called first. From what I could see over his shoulder into the formal dining room, he and his wife were apparently hosting a dinner party for two other couples, a casual one because he was wearing white sailcloth slacks and a fuschia polo shirt.

He looked shocked when I told him about Ruttenberg.

"But why come all the way out here to tell me?" he wanted to know. "I had nothing to do with him."

"Is there someplace we can talk?"

He looked nervously back at his guests. "Sure, in the garden room."

Which turned out to be a quaint little utility room that had been done up with white wicker furniture and trellises against the walls. It was a peaceful room, the kind of room one sits in when the pressures of business are great and the batteries need a little peaceful recharging.

"Will," I said after we were both sitting down, "why did you come to my office the other day?"

"I told you. I was in the neighborhood, and I thought what a lousy deal you'd gotten from Clifford Andrews's talking about you on TV like that, and I wanted to drop by and show you some support."

"Support because I needed it, or support because you thought Earl Ruttenberg was a patriot?"

His face flushed. "That's a shitty thing to say, Milan. Sure, I'm a right-wing conservative, and sure, I've lived in Cleveland all my life and my favorite color isn't black, but I'm no Kluxer. I thought Ruttenberg was pig shit, to tell you the truth."

"Enough to slip rat poison into his chicken soup?"

"You aren't serious!"

"You made a point of asking me where Ruttenberg was staying and where they were going to eat. Why would you want to know that?"

Out in the dining room, everyone laughed. They were having a lot better time than their host. "I told you I dropped by for support and friendship," Dante said, "and that's true. But I also came to see if I could do a little business. Remember I asked you if you wanted hidden cams put up?"

"I remember," I said.

"So trying to turn a buck or two makes me a bad guy?"

"Not necessarily."

"It sure doesn't make me a murderer."

"Who else did you tell about Red's Steak House and the Pine Rest motel?"

"Nobody," he said. "Who the hell would I tell?" Then his eyes got big and round. "Oh, wait," he said. "In the parking lot outside your office. I just happened to mention it in passing. Reverend Quest. Was he coming to see you, Milan?"

Lieutenant McHargue wasn't glad to see me the next morning; she never is. And she was overwhelmed with work, trying to coordinate the police presence at the Klan rally for that afternoon. But I had, after all, cracked her case for her, and she couldn't be downright rude and toss me out of her office.

"Go figure," she grumped. "A man like Alvin Quest. God!"

"He made a full confession?"

She nodded. "He sent one of his people in to Red's Steak House and got him a job as a busboy—using a phony name, of course; that's how the rat poison got in the chicken soup. The kid is long gone from the city and Reverend Quest will go to the execution chamber before he'll tell us his name. Quest's lawyer will probably plead temporary insanity. He may have something at that. Find me twelve jurors in this town who are going to send Alvin Quest to death row." She took a deep breath. "Frankly, I'm more pissed off at him for trying to incite a riot in my city than for ridding the world of garbage like Ruttenberg."

"It's the same scenario as Clifford Andrews," I said, "only Quest's was more dignified and with a little come-to-Jesus thrown in. Certainly Quest had every reason in the world to hate Earl Roy Ruttenberg and want him dead. And if things blow up this afternoon, the mayor is going to have a whole Western omelet on his face. And that would give Quest the wedge he needed to run for mayor himself."

"Well, the joke's on him, Jacovich, and you, too. Because there isn't going to be any blowup. We've got every cop who can drag his or her ass out of bed with riot gear and tear gas, ready to uphold the Constitution and protect the rights of a bunch of mouth breathers with pillow cases over their heads. Or we will have," she said pointedly, "if you get the hell out of my office and let me do my job."

"Good luck this afternoon."

"Are we going to see you at the rally?"

"And listen to that kind of filth? No, thanks. I have better things to do with a summer Sunday afternoon."

"Like what?" she said.

"I was thinking about straightening out my sock drawer."

I didn't go near my sock drawer, after all, but I did stay home and watch the Indians play the Oakland A's on television. Jim Thome didn't hit a dinger, but the Tribe won anyway.

I stayed around for the six o'clock news, though, and was delighted to hear that the Klan rally passed without incident that afternoon. Less than a hundred Klan supporters showed up, probably because the keynote speaker was in cold storage with a tag on his toe. About twice that many anti-Klan protesters linked arms and sang "We Shall Overcome." The biggest contingent of all was the press, and they had precious little to write about when it was all over. No incidents whatsoever, no sound bites for the networks to use to castigate poor old Cleveland, and when it was all done, the mayor came out smelling like the Rose of Tralee.

I was damned proud of my city that day. Cleveland can be a tough town, but it's always, always fair.

# Clark Howard

## When the Black Shadows Die

THIS SECOND of the brilliant Clark Howard's stories to grace our collection this year, "When the Black Shadows Die," shows off his strengths in full force as he chronicles the lives of several outsiders in southern California. This piece first appeared in *Mystery Scene Magazine*, issue 67.

# When the Black Shadows Die

*Clark Howard*

As Tony parked his rented car on the East Los Angeles funeral home parking lot, he saw that he was being observed by two men posted at the entrance driveway. One of them spoke at once into a palm-size two-way radio. It did not surprise Tony. He was a stranger, an outsider. Strangers did not attend the wake of a man like Frank Barillas. Not if they were smart.

Tony locked the car and walked toward the funeral home, a tall, lean man with the easy movements of someone with self-confidence and skills, someone who did not fear to walk an unknown path, such as the one to the wake of Frank Barillas. He wore a dark suit and dark tie, which made his light nutmeg complexion seem even lighter; much lighter, for instance, than the darker brown men at the parking lot driveway.

There was a small group of people congregated outside the funeral home entrance, a few of them smoking, all talking in subdued voices. They stopped when Tony approached, their eyes appraising him, the women because of his clean, handsome features, the men because of his obvious *macho* bearing. Tony made his way through the group without making eye contact with any of them.

Inside, in the silent foyer, there was a directory that read:

FRANCISCO BARILLAS
SLUMBER ROOM 3

At the open double doors to Slumber Room 3 were two more sentry types, one with another palm-size two-way radio in his hand. Just inside the doors, at a podium holding a large open book, were two scrubbed, dark young women in plain black dresses with white orchids pinned to them.

"Good morning," one of them greeted him in English, as if he might not understand Spanish. "Will you sign the visitors memory book, please."

"*Si gracias,*" he replied. She offered him a pen but he removed a Mont Blanc from his inside coat pocket and signed with that: Antonio Marcala.

The slumber room was softly lit, cool and quiet, with only barely audible organ music coming from unseen speakers. The fragrance of flowers permeated the room. As Tony walked toward the bier where the open casket rested, he saw that the mourners already in the room also wore orchids of various colors, larger ones pinned to the dresses of the women, smaller ones on the lapels of the men's coats. The bier and the casket were likewise trimmed with trains of multi-colored orchids, and when Tony stepped up to the casket he saw that the dead man in it had a white orchid on his lapel and held a larger purple one in his clasped, embalmed hands.

Frank Barillas, Tony thought, looking down, a legendary killer of men, was leaving the world surrounded by many of the two hundred different species of orchids indigenous to his homeland of El Salvador. Back there, he likely would have been tortured to death and thrown in a ditch. In the U.S. he had the luxury of dying in a clean hospital bed of kidney failure and having the privacy of his wake protected by somber men with two-way radios. Lucky. Very lucky.

Tony knelt at the bier, made the sign of the cross, and lowered his head. But he did not pray. What good would it have done? After all, the soul of Frank Barillas, if he ever had one, had already gone to wherever it was supposed to go, so prayers after the fact of death seemed pointless. But since Tony knew he was being observed curiously by every pair of eyes in the slumber room, he simulated prayer for what he deemed to be an appropriate period of time, then made the sign of the cross again and rose.

Walking back up the aisle toward the scrubbed, dark young women, ignoring the inquisitive eyes that followed him. Tony wondered how far he would get before being stopped and queried. Not far, he guessed. And he was right. Before he reached the funeral home's foyer, he was stopped by three men, one in front and one on each side, all wearing orchids in their lapels.

"Excuse me, would you mind coming with us?" said the one facing him.

"Where to?" Tony asked.

"Just in here." The man indicated the open door of an anteroom.

Tony let the men walk him inside and close the door. It was a small room, comfortably furnished for use during moments of unmanageable grief. Two more men and a woman were already in the room, standing, waiting for him. They all wore orchids and were not friendly looking.

"Who are you?" one of the men asked. He was about Tony's age, twenty six or so, and had the same look of confidence that Tony had.

"My name is Antonio Marcala," Tony said.

A hint of irritation flashed in the other man's eyes. "I know your name, *hombre*," he said quietly. "I read it in the visitors book. What I want to know is who *are* you? Why are you here?"

"I am here to pay my respects to my *patron, Senor* Barillas."

"Your *patron*?"

"Yes. The man who got my mother and me out of El Salvador. The man who gave us a place to live in the U.S. The man who sent me to college."

Looks of incredulity seized the expressions of everyone in the room. They exchanged glances of complete disbelief. *Brief* disbelief, that quickly became doubt, then even more quickly suspicion.

"He's lying," said the lone woman. "He's an agent."

"Shut up, Tela," said the other man who had been waiting in the room.

"Don't tell me to shut up, Perico," the woman snapped. "Shut up yourself!"

"Both of you shut up," the first man said firmly.

"Okay, Monte," the other man said quickly.

"Sure, Monte," the woman called Tela said.

"Show me some ID, man," Monte ordered.

"Why should I?" said Tony.

Monte nodded to the man called Perico. He immediately drew a Glock 17 automatic from under his coat and placed its muzzle against Tony's temple.

"Why? Because," said Monte, "if you don't, I will tell my friend Perico to kill you."

"Will he do it?" Tony asked calmly.

"Yes, I think so," Monte replied, just as calmly.

Pursing his lips just slightly, Tony said, "I am convinced." He unbuttoned his coat and indicated his inside pocket. "May I?" Monte nodded. Tony brought out his wallet and handed it over. "Would you tell him to take the gun away, please?" Another nod from Monte and Perico lowered the automatic.

Monte examined Tony's drivers license, voters registration, draft card, medical insurance card, American Express and Visa cards, ATM card, Blockbuster Video rental card, and an employee ID card from a firm named EBC, Inc., in San Francisco. "What is this EBC?" he asked Tony.

"Executive Business Consultants," Tony said. "It's a firm that helps businesses improve their operations."

After looking at each card, Monte passed it to the woman called Tela. She was young and thin, with not much figure, and one cheek carried a small patch of pock marks. Her eyes were cold and critical, the line of her jaw rigid, the curve of her lips severe. But there was something about those lips, something about her mouth, a slight overbite, that made her also look pensive, vulnerable. As she finished examining everything in Tony's wallet, she shook her head resolutely.

"He's an agent."

"An agent of what?" Tony asked.

"How the hell do I know, man?" she challenged. "Why don't you tell us? Immigration? FBI? ATF? State Department?"

"Why would I be an agent?" Tony challenged back. "Are you criminals?"

Monte got right in his face. "No, man, we're not criminals. We're revolutionists. And if Francisco Barillas was really your *patron*, you would know that."

"I know nothing like that," Tony said adamantly.

"What do you know, then?" Tela demanded. "Tell us what you know about Francisco Barillas!"

Tony shrugged. "As a boy growing up in San Francisco, I knew that he was my mother's friend—"

"Friend?" Tela's eyes flashed. "What kind of friend?"

"Good friend." Tony glanced down. "Lover. She slept with him. He visited us a couple of times a month. My mother told me that he had been a friend of my father and had helped us get out of El Salvador during the civil war. She said I should think of him as an uncle—"

"Ha!" Perico cackled. "An uncle who slept with your mother!"

Tony turned icy eyes on him. "That gun in your hand does not mean that I will allow you to disrespect my mother. If you think it does, then shoot me now."

Monte reached over and touched Perico's arm. "Put the gun away, Perico." Then, to Tony, "What else did you know?"

"I thought that he was a successful importer of Central American handicrafts. When I was older. I presumed that he was probably married and had a family down here somewhere—"

"He never married," Tela declared. "We were his family. The movement. The Mara Salva—"

"Tela, shut up!" Monte ordered.

"What is the Mara Salva?" Tony asked.

"Nothing to concern you," Monte said, "unless, as Tela believes, you are an agent of some kind."

"Look," Tony tried to reason, "I would be lying if I said I had no knowledge of Frank Barillas being involved at one time in the trouble in El Salvador. I know he was a member of Farabundo Marti, the National Liberation Front. I know he was a guerilla fighter. At my mother's funeral last year, he said—"

"Your mother is dead?" Tela asked suddenly, frowning.

"Yes. She died of pancreatic cancer. At her funeral, Uncle Frank told me that in El Salvador he had killed many men, and that he was a fugitive down there. He said that was the reason he had never married my mother, and he asked my forgiveness for that. Of course, I forgave him. But I thought all that was in the past, twenty years ago. I had no idea he was still involved."

"He was never *not* involved," Monte said quietly. "Freeing El Salvador from the rich landowners and the military was his whole life." Monte held out his hand. "I am Monte Copan. Francisco Barillas was my *patron* also. I understand your loss."

"And I yours," Tony said, shaking hands.

"You *believe* him?" Tela bellowed.

"I do, yes." Monte gathered all of Tony's cards together and handed them and his wallet back to him.

"Monte, this is insanity!" Tela pleaded. "He is an *agent!*"

"I am now the leader of this organization," Monte stated unequivocally, locking eyes with the woman. "That was the wish of Francisco Barillas. Would you question his judgment if he were alive?"

Tela lowered her eyes. "No."

"Then do not question mine, please." He turned again to Tony. "You have my apology."

"Not necessary," Tony said. "It was an honest mistake, nothing more." He shook hands with Perico and the other men in the room, but when he offered his hand to Tela, she refused to take it and looked away.

"I'm sorry you don't trust me," Tony said.

Then he left.

Monte returned to the slumber room where Frank Barillas lay. Tela, with two of the others, Benito and Armando, remained in the anteroom and watched from a window as Tony left the funeral home and walked across the parking lot.

"He is an agent," Tela said, quietly but grimly. "I can *feel* it." Turning to the two men, she said, "Benny, you and Mando must follow him. We've got to find out more about him."

"I don't know, Tela," Benito said reluctantly. "Maybe we ought to clear it with Monte—"

"Monte is grieving," she said. "Much more than we are. Francisco was like a father to him. His mind is not as alert right now as it should be. We must help him through this trying time by thinking for him."

"I don't know, Tela," said Armando, as hesitantly as Benito.

"Jus' do it," Tela directed. "I am a senior captain in Mara Salva. I will take responsibility for it." Out the window, she saw Tony reach his car. "Move, before he is gone!" she insisted, and sent the two men hurrying from the room.

Tela watched as Tony backed out and drove off the lot, then waited to be sure Benito and Armando left quickly enough in one of their own cars to follow him. Satisfied, she went back into the slumber room with Monte and the other official attendants at the wake.

Benito and Armando were gone for nearly four hours. Tela saw them when they returned and motioned for them to join her in the anteroom again.

"Well?" she asked impatiently. Both men shrugged.

"Nothing, Tela," reported Benito. "He drove to LAX, turned in the car at Avis, and got on the next commuter flight up to San Francisco."

"He didn't stop anywhere? Speak to anyone. Make any phone calls?"

"Nothing, Tela," Armando confirmed.

"Damn!" She slammed a fist into the palm of her other hand. "Now, he's gotten away from us."

"We're sorry, Tela," Benito said, as if he and Armando were ashamed of their failure.

"No, no, it's not your fault." Tela assured them. "It's mine. I should have shot him right here in this room when I had the chance, regardless of what Monte said."

"How can you be so sure that he's an agent?" Armando asked.

"I'm just sure, that's all. Two things I can always tell: a federal agent and a *Sombra Negra*. Both make my heart skip beats. It never fails."

Benito and Armando nodded gravely. *Sombra Negra* was the name of the government death squads in El Salvador.

"Maybe we'll get another chance at him," Benito tried to placate Tela.

"Maybe," Tela said quietly.

If they did, she would not let him get away again. She would kill him herself whether Monte ordered it or not.

Four nights later, the doorbell rang in Tela's apartment.

"Yes, who is it?" she asked through the door.

"Tony Marcala."

"Who?" The name did not immediately register.

"The agent." Tony said wryly.

Shocked, Tela opened the door on its safety chain. "What are you doing here?" she asked indignantly. "What do you want? How did you know where I live?"

"Frank Barillas told me where you lived," said Tony. He held up an envelope. "This was delivered to me yesterday. Frank left it with someone in the hospital to mail after he died. Your address is in it, and instructions to come see you."

"Let me see that," she said, frowning coldly. He handed the envelope through the narrow opening. Tela removed the letter and quickly scanned it. The handwriting was that of Francisco Barillas, there was no doubt. She would have recognized it anywhere. Slightly shaky from his weakened condition, it was his penmanship nevertheless. She had known the man's precise script since she was a high school girl and took letters to the mailbox for him every day.

Closing the door, Tela removed the chain and opened it again. "Come in." she said resignedly. Her eyes swept over Tony as he entered. He wore a sport coat now, with a casual black shirt under it, gray slacks and loafers. Somehow he looked less like an agent, but her suspicions did not diminish. Her heart *did* skip a beat, but perhaps, she grudgingly thought, it was because he was close to her for a moment, and he smelled of bay rum, and it had been a long time between men. "May I read the letter?" she asked.

"Of course."

"Thank you. Please sit down."

Tony sat on her couch in the modest but tidy little living room he had entered. There was nothing of *her* in the room that he could see, only things of her *cause*. On the walls were El Salvadoran Liberation posters in striking graphics of red, white, and black. In a nearby bookcase, he could see books with names on their spines like Zapata, Castro, Mao, and Biko. A few framed photographs showed men and women in camouflage fatigues holding automatic weapons; one of the men he recognized as a young Frank Barillas. Two Spanish-language newspapers lay on the coffee table. The only thing feminine was a silky white blouse with a sewing kit next to it, lying on one of the end tables where she apparently meant to mend it.

Finished with the room, Tony studied the woman herself. She was wearing a flimsy spaghetti-strap house dress of some Aztec pattern, and was barefoot. He decided that she probably had nothing on under the dress because she sat defensively, knees pressed together, elbows at her sides, leaning forward slightly as she read the two-page letter. When she finished, she put it back in the envelope and handed it over to him. In the same movement, she reached for a tissue and dabbed at her eyes.

"It is like a voice from the grave," she said.

"Yes," Tony agreed quietly.

Her sadness faded as quickly as it had appeared. "He said he was sending you to me because I was the one least likely to trust you. He was right."

"Yes, you've made that obvious."

"He wants me to arrange a meeting for you with Monte and the other captains of Mara Salva. He says he thinks you might be of significant help to us in what we do. Do you agree with him?"

"I can't answer that," Tony said, "until I know exactly what it is that you do."

"And you expect us to tell you?" Tela asked incredulously.

"I don't expect anything, and I'm not asking for anything," Tony told her evenly. "I am simply responding to a deathbed request from a man to whom I owe a great debt. He saw to it that I was fed, clothed, and sheltered as a child, and in my later life he provided me with an outstanding education. He sent me to Stanford University for six years to earn a master's degree in business administration. Do you have any idea what that is worth?"

"No." Tela admitted. "I do not. I am not a formally educated person." She saw Tony's eyes shift to the bookcase containing volumes on history, government, and revolution. "I teach myself," she answered his unasked question. Tony nodded.

"You seem to be well along. I had some political science courses; those books are used in advanced studies."

"I try," she said, raising her chin an inch.

"Perhaps," he suggested, "that is why Frank wanted us to meet. Perhaps he felt that you could overcome your distrust if we could meld intellectually."

"What is 'meld?'" she asked.

"To come together," he said quietly, his eyes holding to hers. She tried to stare him down, but could not. After a moment, she rose and walked around to stand behind her chair.

"Perhaps you would like something cold to drink?"

"No, I wouldn't." Tony stood and removed his coat. "And neither would you."

He stepped over and took her in his arms and kissed her for a long time until she finally kissed him back. He felt her overbite with his upper lip and it increased his arousal. His hands went all over the flimsy dress she wore and felt nothing underneath it except her thin, angular body. In one fluid movement, he peeled the dress over her head and swung her up into his arms. He carried her back around to the couch and turned off all but one small lamp as he undressed.

Watching him from where she lay, Tela thought: *This is not for the cause. This is for me. It makes no difference if he is an agent.*

Two hours later, in an exhausted afterglow, Tony lay stretched out on the couch, Tela on the floor next to him, legs curled under her, the side of her face resting on his hip, one finger idly tracing an appendectomy scar on his side. She had already asked him when his appendix had been removed, and he had told her it had been in his sophomore year at Stanford. Then he had asked her if she was Monte's girlfriend, and she had laughed and said no, her best friend Amelia was Monte's wife, and that she and Monte were more like brother and sister. Then she had asked him how many girlfriends he had in San Francisco, and he had told her twelve or fourteen, he wasn't sure, after ten it was hard to keep track. For that answer she had slapped him on the shoulder, not too softly either. Then he had asked her if she still thought he was an agent. She thought about it for a time, then admitted she wasn't *as* sure, but still was not prepared to say he definitely *wasn't* one. And what about the letter from Frank Barillas? "It could be a forgery," she reasoned. "You people have the resources to do anything."

"You people? What people?" he wanted to know.

"The U.S. government."

Tony could not argue with logic. They fell silent for a while then, with only one small lamp on and the window open a few inches behind closed blinds, hearing an occasional muted voice from the street, listening to barely audible *salsa* music being played somewhere, feeling the fleeting brush of a breeze now and then.

After a few minutes, Tony asked, "What is Mara Salva?"

Tela did not answer for so long that he almost decided she was not going to. But presently she turned with her back to the couch, put her head against his side, drew one of his arms down around her, and told him.

"During the civil war in El Salvador, there were two major groups that opposed the military dictatorship of the government. The first was La Mara. It was a well-organized and very violent urban gang that terrorized the streets of San Salvador, the capital. Second, there was the FMLN, the Farabundo Marti National

Liberation Front, that Francisco belonged to. It was made up primarily of rural peasants trained as guerilla fighters, men and women who eventually became very adept in the use of small arms, explosives, and booby traps. The FMLN opposed the military in the outlying areas.

"The war went on a dozen years. The military could not suppress the two groups, no matter how hard it tried. Even when it formed the death squads, the *Sombra Negra,* to take people from their homes in the middle of the night to be tortured and killed, the people of the resistance never gave up. More than one hundred thousand people were killed during that war, a thousand a week, and a million Salvadorans fled the country to escape torture and death, as you and your mother did. As I did, and Monte, and many others that you saw at the wake, and Francisco himself.

"Here in southern California, the refugees from Salvador were not welcomed by the Latinos and Asians already here; we were harassed and abused in many ways. But since there were many who had been members of La Mara, and many others who had been with the FMLN, Francisco saw the opportunity to band them together into one organization for the protection of *all* Salvadorans. So he formed the Mara Salva, and we soon became strong enough to protect ourselves against any other ethnic group trying to take advantage of us. At first, that was the sole purpose: protection only. Later, when the organization grew and became stronger, Francisco saw ways for us to become diverse, ways for us to help our people back home, ways to prepare to overthrow the government."

"But I thought the war had ended," Tony said. "I thought the government was all straightened out."

"You are naive," Tela told him quietly, patting fondly the arm she had drawn across her thin body. "In 1983 a new constitution was drawn up for a representative government like you have here in the U.S. Three branches: executive, legislative, and judicial. An elected president serves a single five-year term. It sounds very good, no? And on the surface, it *looks* very good. But the fact remains that even with an elected president, the government is still dominated by a small, elite group of incredibly wealthy landowners *and* high-ranking military officers. Poverty is more widespread today among the rural peasants and urban poor than it was *before* the civil war began. The government itself is flourishing because it is nationalizing land for export crops, and the world says. 'See how well Salvador has recovered.' But every hectare of land taken by the government, is one less hectare for people to grow their own crops on. Malnutrition among the peasants increases constantly; infant mortality rates increase constantly. Tens of thousands live without electricity, running water, or adequate sanitation. And," Tela's voice became even quieter, "the *Sombra Negra* still terrorizes the people."

"*Sombra Negra,*" said Tony. "That means 'black shadows.' What is it?"

"The death squads," she said. "The men who come in the night and take people away. Men who abduct student demonstrators, union activists, priests, women who organize and demand more for their children. Sometimes the people they take are never heard from again; other times they are found dead somewhere after being horribly tortured—" She shuddered involuntarily and became quiet, shivering slightly as if cold. Tony took her arms and drew her up onto the couch to lie with him, holding her close to warm her.

"I'm sorry," he whispered. "I had no idea that any of that still went on."

"It is odd," she said, suspicion surfacing, "that Francisco never told you."

"Perhaps he wanted me to get my education first, without any preconceived ideas about the plans he had for me later."

"What do you think those plans were?"

"Apparently to have me come into Mara Salva with him."

"To do what?"

"I don't know. Streamline the operation, maybe, like I would a business that hired me as a consultant. Make Mara Salva more efficient, more profitable."

"For you to do that, we would have to tell you everything we do, no?"

"Yes."

"If we did that, and you were an agent, it would mean the end of us, wouldn't it?"

"I suppose. But if I were *not* an agent, and could help, it might be just the beginning for the organization." He brushed his fingertips over the small patch of pock marks on her cheek. "Are you going to take me to Monte and the others?"

"Don't touch me there," she said, pushing his hand away. "I don't know yet. I must think on it."

He kissed her where his hand had been and she turned her face away. "I said I don't like to be touched there. It is embarrassing to have a scarred face."

Rolling on top of her, Tony looked down. "There are no scars on your body. No flaws, no imperfections. Every inch of you is beautiful. And I will touch you wherever I wish."

Reaching over, he turned off the lamp again.

The next afternoon, Tela had Tony take her to a long abandoned drive-in movie theater on the edge of Anaheim. The entrance and exit gates were chained shut, but she had the key to a lock on one of the rear exits and let them in, leaving the gate unlocked behind them. She had Tony park his rental car directly in the center of the big open space in front of the high structure where the screen had once been.

Earlier that morning, while Tony showered and dressed in fresh clothes from the suitcase he had in the car, Tela had called Monte and told him about the letter Tony had brought her. Monte sent someone to pick it up, then called back a couple of hours later to arrange a meeting at once. It irritated Tela that Monte wanted a meeting so soon. She and Tony had made love a second time the previous night, and again in the morning when they woke up. The sessions had been strenuous, fiery, full of passion—and exhausting. Tela was tired, and when she was tired, she was irritable and cross. It did not help at all that Tony, with his perfect, toned body, was full of vim and vigor and sang in the shower. That was all she needed in her life right then, she groused silently to herself: a *macho hombre* who knew all fifty-two positions. Still—it *had* been exquisite lovemaking.

"When are they supposed to get here?" Tony asked when he parked.

"They'll get here when they get here," she replied sullenly.

"What's the matter?" he asked.

"What's the matter with what?" she challenged. "With me? With you? With the world? What do you want to know from me?"

"Hey, forget I asked," he said, shaking his head in annoyance.

Fortunately, they did not have long to wait. Two cars came through the gate and drove over to where they were. Monte, two other men, and a woman got out of one, three men got out of the other. One of the men with Monte was Perico, who had held the gun on Tony at the funeral home, and two of the others were Benito and Armando, who had followed Tony to the airport when he left.

"We meet again," said Monte, offering his hand.

"Yes." Tony shook hands.

"I apologize, but I must have you thoroughly searched for a wire. Go with these two men, please."

Benito and Armando escorted Tony to what had once been a men's room when the theater was open, but was now empty of fixtures and in total disrepair. Tony was instructed to strip, which he did, to allow the two men to closely examine every garment he wore, then to scrutinize his body the same way. Tela could have told them that they would find nothing, but she dared not. It would have been mortifying to let the men know that she had slept with a man she suspected of being an agent. So she only confided in Amelia, the woman in the group, who was her best friend and Monte's wife.

The two women were standing off to themselves, talking, when Benito and Armando returned with Tony. Tela would not meet Tony's eyes when he came back, but Amelia looked him up and down at once and raised her eyebrows approvingly at Tela, making her blush and turn away from the men.

"These people here," Monte said to Tony when he returned and was declared clean of a wire, "are the officers and leaders of Mara Salva, the organization that Tela has already explained to you. Perico, Armando, Benito, and myself you already met at the wake. This," he introduced, "is my wife, Amelia. Tela you also already know. These other two are Ruben and Reynaldo. The eight of us were Mara Salva captains under Francisco Barillas, who was our leader. I was chosen by him to be leader when he died. While he lived, he allowed all of us to vote on any important step the organization considered taking. His vote, of course, was the tie-breaker, if it was needed, which was rarely."

Monte removed from his coat pocket the letter Tony had brought to Tela the previous night, and which she had sent to Monte that morning to evaluate. Now he handed it back to Tony.

"We have all read the letter and believe it was written by the hand of our late leader, Francisco Barillas. The purpose of this meeting is to vote whether to take you into the confidence of Mara Salva, as Francisco apparently wished us to do, or to reject you. But I must ask you first whether you yourself desire to become one of us. Do you?"

"I wish to honor the dying request of my *patron*," Tony said simply. "If I can be of benefit to you in a cause to which he was dedicated, then I will do so."

"Very well," said Monte. "Then we will vote. Each of the captains here will vote to accept or reject you. Amelia, I begin with you. Accept or reject?"

"Accept."

"Tela, accept or reject?"

"Reject."

Both Tony and Amelia looked at Tela in astonishment. She ignored them.

"Armando?"

"Accept."

"Benito?"

"Accept."

"Perico?"

"Reject." He sneered at Tony to punctuate his vote.

"Ruben?"

"Accept."

"Reynaldo?"

"Accept."

"Five to two to accept." Monte said. "I also vote to accept, so it is six to two." Again he held out his hand to Tony. "Welcome to Mara Salva."

From the drive-in, they all went in the three cars back to East Los Angeles to a storefront location with a sign above the door which read: EL SALVADOR RELIEF ASSOCIATION.

"We have this as a legal, registered humanitarian organization," Monte explained as he led them all inside. The front room was an office set up with desks, computers, printers, and other equipment to function as a legitimate operation. "Here we print and distribute material to raise money for needy people back home. We raise very little money, of course, but what we do raise is distributed by the churches in poor areas. Our main work, as you have probably guessed, is altogether different."

The group followed Monte to a separate room in the rear, which was furnished with a large meeting table, and its walls covered with area maps of California from the northern limits of Los Angeles county south to the southern city limits of San Diego, and east to the Arizona state line. Other maps, on the opposite side of the room, showed the southwestern United States border areas of California and Arizona, next to maps of Mexico, Guatemala, and El Salvador.

"Our business," Monte said simply, "is the exportation of stolen automobiles, which we sell to the twenty percent of the population of El Salvador that can afford to buy them. We then use the proceeds to buy weapons and munitions to stockpile for the next revolution. This is the way it works—"

Using the various maps, Monte explained how subordinate members of Mara Salva were trained to steal medium-size sedans from shopping malls and theater parking lots all over southern California. Luxury automobiles were never taken, no Lincolns or Cadillacs, no fancy sports cars, just moderately valued midline Buicks, Oldsmobiles, Pontiacs, Chryslers, and other dependable makes. Four Mara Salva members would go out in two teams in separate cars. When a suitable vehicle was seen being parked, its make, model, and color would be noted by one of the teams, which would immediately leave and begin to search other lots for a similar make and model. When they found one, they would steal its license plates. Then they would search until they found a third similar car, steal its plates, and replace them with the first set of stolen plates.

"It is tedious, but very confusing to the police," Monte said. The first set of plates is reported stolen, but many times the owner of the second set of stolen plates does not even notice that he now has *different* plates on his car. So for a period of time, we have a safe set of plates for a matching stolen car—because by then the other team has stolen the original car that was decided on earlier. The theft of the car is easy: one member of the team follows the driver into the mall or wherever, with a cell phone with a line already open to his partner. The partner jacks open the car door, rams the ignition, starts the car, notifies his partner inside, and picks him up at a different entrance while the real owner of the car is still inside.

"And we have rules," Monte emphasized. "We take no cars from older people or women with children. Mostly we look for guys alone, or two younger women shopping together."

The safe plates were put on the stolen car, and it was immediately driven out of California into Mexico the same day.

"There are many places to cross," said Reynaldo. "Tijuana and Mexicali, of course, are the busiest ports of entry from California. Then there are Nogales and Agua Prieta in Arizona. But in addition to those main crossings, there are many smaller ones: little towns like San Luis Rio, Sonoyta, Escabe, Naco. And they all connect to Mexico Route 2, which connects to the Mexican national north-south toll road, Route 15."

"There is never a problem crossing the border," Armando took up the narrative. "U.S. Border patrol guards have no interest in what *leaves* the U.S., only what comes in. And Mexican border guards let all vehicles in without question."

"Less than two hundred miles south into Mexico," said Monte, "is the city of Hermosillo. It's a nice little city, surrounded by many cotton farms. In this city is a man who has mastered the art of producing counterfeit vehicle identification number plates that are fastened to the top of the dashboard to allow law enforcement officers to immediately identify the automobile's origin and registration. When our people steal the second set of license plates, they also write down the VIN from that car. In Hermosillo, we stop and get a VIN plate with a number that corresponds with the license plate. Then, a hundred and fifty miles farther south, in the town of Los Mochis, is a very talented printer who has duplicate blanks of California certificates of title identical to those issued by the department of motor vehicle. In less than an hour, the driver of our car has a certificate of ownership, with no lien, on a car that now has license plates that match the VIN number."

"In short," said Tony, "it is now a car that can be sold."

"Exactly," said Monte. "It is two thousand miles down the length of Mexico to Guatemala, and two hundred more across Guatemala to El Salvador. There we sell the car to a used car dealer. There is no problem finding a buyer; about eighty percent of the late-model cars being driven in El Salvador were stolen in the U.S."

"And the money from the sale?" asked Tony.

"A percentage is brought back here to run the organization. The rest is used to buy automatic weapons and munitions in Honduras, smuggle them back into El Salvador, and stockpile them in various places throughout the country."

Tony paced the length of the room, then turned to face the group. "Do you honestly think that by stealing cars and buying weapons that you can overthrow a *government?* That you can take over a *country?*"

They all exchanged looks and Monte shrugged. "Why not? It is a very small country: only one hundred sixty miles long and ninety miles wide. Right now the military has about twenty-three thousand soldiers. By the year 2000, there will be six *million* people in the country—and nearly *five* million of them will be living at the very edge of poverty." He smiled a cold smile. "If we can arm fifty thousand peasants, *senor*, believe me, we can take the country."

"But how will you reach that many people? You are so few."

"When Fidel Castro started, there were only three: himself, his brother Raul, and the woman, Celia Sanchez. We, like they, are only the nucleus, Antonio. Besides the people in this room, we have more than fifty other members in southern California. And we have members in all fourteen districts of El Salvador, and their number is increasing all the time. We know that the church will stand behind us, the students will join us, and the unions will support us once we are in power. This is not a daydream, *amigo*; this is an obtainable goal—and we are dedicating our lives to it." Monte walked over and stood before Tony. "Now that you know everything about us, I must ask you two questions. Can you help us? And *will* you help us?"

Tony's eyes swept the room. Everyone was looking at him, the six men, the two women: their collective gaze was fixed on him like an unseen laser, their presence as a group seeming to charge the little meeting room with energy and intensity. He looked at Tela, at her stark eyes, behind which he knew lay a fierceness and a strength unlike he had ever seen in a woman. If anyone in that room could kill him without a second thought, it was Tela. She who still did not trust him—no matter that she had surrendered her lissome body to him.

Tony knew that he had to speak, that he had to commit, or he would not leave the room alive.

"Yes," he said simply to Monte, to them all, "I can help you." His eyes shifted to Tela. "And I will."

Tela's eyes told him that his words only strengthened her distrust.

Immediately following the group meeting, Monte and Tony had a private conversation in a small office Monte had in the rear of the big room, an office that until recently had belonged to Frank Barillas. The new leader of Mara Salva and its newest member talked for nearly an hour, and then Tony came out and asked Tela to come with him back to her apartment so that he could pick up his suitcase.

In the car, Tela asked, "You are leaving?"

"Yes."

"Where are you going?"

"Monte will tell you," Tony said. "He is meeting with all of you this afternoon and then he and I will be leaving together tonight. We will be gone for about two weeks."

"And you won't tell me where?"

He shook his head. "It is up to Monte to tell you and the others what he wants you to know."

In the passenger seat, Tela stared straight ahead, wary and suspicious. "I don't like this."

"There don't appear to be too many things that you *do* like," Tony replied quietly, without malice.

"Just what does that mean?" she demanded.

"It means that you seem to be mistrustful and skeptical of everything most of the time. You never seem to be happy."

"You say that to me after last night? And this morning?"

"That was not happiness, Tela. That was passion. Even after this morning, you voted against me. And you have been unhappy all day."

"I am the way I am," she declared doggedly.

They said nothing more to each other for the rest of the drive.

At her apartment, Tela watched silently as Tony gathered his previous day's clothes and put things back in his shave kit. He opened his suitcase on the bed in her tiny bedroom. For the first time, he noticed a small, framed photograph of a girl about twelve, with a slight, pleasant smile.

"You were a pretty child," he said. "Not so unhappy then, I guess."

"That is not me," she told him. "That was my little sister, Felia."

Tony felt a tightening in his stomach. He stopped packing. "Was?"

Tela looked away. "She is dead. At least, I assume as much. One night the *Sombra Negra* came to our home looking for my father. He was up in the mountains with the Farabundo guerillas. So one of them said take his wife instead, and tell him he can come claim her at our headquarters. But another one said no, take one of the daughters, it will make him surrender faster. Then the leader said—I remember his words exactly—'Take the younger one. That will make him respond very quickly, because he knows how much we like these very young ones'. So they took her."

Tela's eyes had moistened and a single tear streaked her cheek and spread out over the pockmark. Tony put an arm around her and sat with her on the bed as she finished her story.

"My mother and I went at once to the guerilla contact in our village to get word to my father. Two days later, he came down and surrendered. My mother left me with a neighbor and went to the headquarters to see him. The *Sombra* accused my mother of trying to smuggle a gun in to him. They shot them both."

"And your sister?"

"She was never seen or heard from again. The *Sombra* were notorious for taking very young girls. Some of the stories that came out later about what they did to them were—were—"

Tela broke into sobs and Tony held her tightly with both arms as her thin body wracked and shuddered against him for long minutes until she had cried as much grief and anguish out of herself as she could at that moment. Then she slowly came out of the convulsion, catching her breath, swallowing hard, and mopping her eyes with Kleenex. Pulling slightly away from him, she said, "I'm sorry. I got your shirt all wrinkled."

"It's nothing." He pushed her hair back off her forehead, and touched her cheeks and patted her arms. "How did you get out of Salvador?"

"The neighbors took me to the guerillas and they took me across the Guatemala border to a refugee camp. Some nuns that had been working there were going back to the states. They took me with them. Immigration held me in Los Angeles for a few days while the church applied for me to be given asylum. Then the church sent me to live with a Salvadoran couple who took in refugee children. Francisco lived next door. After school, I would go to the mailbox for him. I stayed there until I was old enough to work. I was a counter girl at Taco Bell for a while, then Francisco recruited me for Mara Salva."

Tony gave her a final hug and rose. "I understand now why you aren't more trusting. I'm sorry for what I said earlier." He finished packing his suitcase and closed it. She followed him as he walked to the living room door with it.

"Tony, please, I want you to tell me where you are taking Monte."

"I am taking him on a business trip. It has to do with improving the efficiency and profitability of the Mara Salva operation. There is nothing for you to worry about."

"I can't *help* worrying," she asserted. "With Francisco dead, Monte is the only one qualified to lead Mara Salva. If you are an agent and—"

"Please, Tela, don't start with that again," he said impatiently.

"But you *could* be an agent," she said, wringing her hands, "and if Monte never came back, it would ruin us—"

Tony kissed her lightly on the lips. "Don't worry about Monte; he'll be all right. I promise you. I have to go now. I'll see you soon."

It was only after Tony was gone that Tela realized that the only assurance he had given her was that Monte would be all right. He had not once said that he wasn't an agent. As a matter of fact, it suddenly dawned on her, he had *never* said he wasn't an agent.

Tony stayed gone for ten days. Then one morning just after three o'clock he showed up back at Tela's apartment, suitcase in hand, clothes wrinkled, needing a shave, looking very, very tired.

"Where is Monte?" Tela demanded first thing as she let him in.

"I missed you too, Tela *mia*," he said wryly.

"Tony, where *is* he? Tell me!"

"Lower your voice. He's in San Salvador."

Tela turned as pale as a Latina can turn. San Salvador was the capital of El Salvador, stronghold of the wealthy landowners, the military, and the *presidente*.

"Why?" she asked urgently. "Why is he there?"

"Because that is where he is needed most at the moment."

"You promised he would come back!"

"I promised he would be all right," Tony pointed out. He went into the bedroom, set his suitcase in a corner, and began undressing. "I'm worn out, Tela," he said. "I need a hot shower and a few hours sleep. I want you to contact all the captains and arrange a meeting for ten o'clock this morning. I will explain everything then."

"You have no authority to call a meeting," she bristled. "Only Monte can call a meeting."

"I speak for Monte," he said, handing her a folded sheet of paper. It read: 'To all captains—Obey Antonio Marcala's instructions as you would my own.' It was signed, 'Monte Copan.'

The note only made Tela seethe. "Why should I believe this? It could be a forgery, just like the letter from Francisco!"

"Tela, Tela, Tela," he said tolerantly, "what am I to do with you? It is said that we all have a cross to bear; you must be mine." He looked at her as she paced agitatedly around in bikini panties and a tank top in which she had been sleeping. "I could become very upset with you if you weren't so cute in your underwear."

As she glared irately at him, Tony finished undressing, stepped into the shower, and turned on the water. Tela watched him stand with his head bent under the spray, arms braced against the wall, his usually groomed face haggard, the muscular, toned body she remembered from their lovemaking now lax with fatigue. He's thrashed, she thought, really whipped. Quickly she stripped her bed and from a dresser drawer took fresh sheets and spread them in place, turning them back neatly, invitingly. She put fresh cases on the pillows and fluffed one up for him. She lighted a fat, scented candle on the nightstand and turned out all the lights in the apartment. And she turned on her little bedside radio and tuned it to the softest music she could find. Then she sat cross legged on the bed and waited for him.

When Tony came out of the bathroom, still drying himself with one of her multicolored towels, he saw what she had prepared for him and smiled a tired but pleased smile.

"Maybe," he said, "you are not my cross to bear, after all. Maybe you are an angel sent to care for me. What do you think?"

"I don't know what I am with you," she said unguardedly. "The only thing I am sure of with you is that I am very confused."

Tony dried his hair a little, tossed the towel back into the bathroom, and stretched out on his stomach on the bed. "I am so tired, Tela—so very tired—"

Immediately he was asleep, soundly, deeply. Tela looked over at the suitcase he had set in the corner. She should probably search it, she thought, for some clue to what was going on, to who he really was, *what* he really was. But she decided not to. For tonight she did not want to know anything except that he was there and that he needed her.

Tela pulled a sheet up to his shoulders, slipped under it, and blew out the candle. She lay up against him very closely so that if he awoke he would know she was there.

Tela arranged the meeting with the captains as Tony had asked her to do, and at ten o'clock they were all gathered in the back room of the El Salvador Relief Association offices. Tony's letter of authority from Monte was passed around for all of them to read.

"There's something very odd about this," Perico said bluntly. "I don't like this one little bit, Amelia." He asked Monte's wife, "Is this truly Monte's handwriting?"

Amelia glanced at Tela, then Tony, and shrugged nervously. "It *looks* like Monte's writing."

"I think we have to accept it as such," said Benito, "unless we can prove that it is not."

"I agree," Reynaldo said. "How do you feel about it, Tela?"

Tela shook her head. "I don't know. I'm not sure. I'm not sure of anything."

Tony stood up at the head of the table. "Let me tell you what Monte and I have been doing for the past ten days. Perhaps that will do away with some of your worry. There is a term in business called 'reengineering.' It means to reorganize and restructure a business operation so that it functions more efficiently and more effectively, and ultimately more profitably. That is what Monte and I have started doing for Mara Salva."

Tony walked along one wall where there were various maps. "From now on," he said, "we will discontinue concentrating our automobile procurement exclusively in southern California. That is far too risky and at some point will create an obvious pattern that both local and federal law enforcement will begin to track. Instead, we will expand our operation into the metro areas of Phoenix, Albuquerque, and El Paso. Armando, you will be in charge of California and Arizona; Benito, you will have New Mexico and Texas.

"We have purchased small auto body repair and painting shops in each of the three cities I mentioned, as well as in San Diego. There will be no more license plate switching from cars of the same make, model, and color; the risk of getting caught at that is too high—and, again, it begins to create a pattern. Instead, we will simply bring the cars that we select to the nearest shop that we own, and they will be painted the same day. We will have a list of colors of cars that are not to be taken; these are the colors we will then paint them.

"As soon as the cars are dry, they will be driven immediately to Tucson, Arizona. In transit, they will still carry the original plates they had on them. Highway patrols do not check plate numbers unless the color of the car matches the color reported stolen. Ours will no longer match.

"Once in Tucson, the cars will be taken to a newly formed company called Ari-Mex Auto Exporting Company. This is a legitimate firm owned by a parent company called Salvadoran-American. Incorporated, a Delaware corporation formed through the mail last week. Ruben, you will run Ari-Mex. The firm will legitimately purchase automobiles for export to Mexico; the cars that we acquire other than by purchase will be merged with the legitimate purchases. Two auto transport trucks, each with a capacity of eight cars, have been purchased for this exporting. Monte will select eight Mara Salva members to be sent to long-haul highway truck drivers school to learn to operate these trucks.

"From Tucson, the cars will be transported into Mexico at the Nogales port of entry. We will have legitimate certificates of title for the purchased vehicles: counterfeit COTs for the others will have come up by courier from the printer in Hermosillo, whose business is now called Salvo Printing, and is a subsidiary of Salvadoran-American, Inc., and he is a member of our board of directors—as, incidentally, all of you will also in time become.

"After entering Mexico at Nogales, the auto transport trucks, which will leave on Tuesdays, Thursdays, and Saturdays of each week, will drive one thousand miles south along the Mexican limited-access toll highway, Route 15, to the Pacific seaport of Mazatlan. There they will be loaded onto freighters belonging to the Lago Shipping Company, in which SA. Inc., now owns a sixty percent share. Reynaldo, you will become general manager of Lago Shipping's office and berths in Mazatlan.

"From Mazatlan, the vehicles will go by sea approximately fourteen hundred nautical miles south to the Salvadoran port of Puerto Cutuco. There, they will be off-loaded and driven individually to either Santa Ana in the north, San Miguel in the south, or the suburbs of the capital, Nueva San Salvador. Reynaldo, you will have an assistant who will be in charge of Lago Shipping's new offices and berths in Puerto Cutuco.

"In each of the cities just mentioned, SA, Inc., through another subsidiary called U.S. Cars, owns a used-car dealership which we just put into operation last week. We are, as required by Salvadoran law, in partnership with a Salvadoran company, that being the Liberdad Holding Company, a firm formed by a retired army general for the express purpose of expediting foreign investment. We have made him a director of U.S. Cars and he will receive generous compensation for his assistance. He is, of course, our enemy, and not to be trusted, but we will use him as we must.

"Since we will now be retailing the cars ourselves, profits will no longer have to be shared with any middlemen, and more can be diverted into other profitable ventures which will ultimately generate more funds with which to buy arms. To that end, our Delaware corporation will open a branch office in one of the modern, new high-rise office buildings in San Salvador. Monte will have an office there, and both Amelia and Tela will work there. I will have offices in the same building, for another subsidiary to be known as Delaware Investments, Limited, a secondary corporation under SA, Inc., which will invest profits from U.S. Cars in other ventures. For instance, I am already looking into a balsam forest in the Chula region, because balsam resin is now being used extensively in the manufacture of cosmetics. I am also looking at stock in a new hydroelectric plant being planned."

Tony walked back to his chair and sat down. The others were stone silent, obviously overwhelmed by what they had heard, more so because it applied to them, and because this business wizard sent to them from the grave of Francisco Barillas could recite it all without notes or papers or figures of any kind. They felt like kindergartners on the first day of school.

"I know it all sounds very complicated." Tony said to allay some of their unease, "but I assure you that no one will be required to do anything that he or she has not been trained to do. Temporary consultants will be in place to teach each of you everything you need to know about the responsibilities you will have and how to cope with them." He looked around the table. "Does anyone have any questions?"

"I do," Tela said. "What about Perico?"

"Perico?"

"Yes. Perico and I are the two who have been against you all along. You mentioned a place for me and for everyone else in the room, except Perico. What about him?"

Tony shrugged. "I have no information about Perico. Monte made all the assignments among you; I merely described the various jobs and what they would entail. Monte did not mention Perico to me."

"And you did not inquire?"

"It is not my place to inquire about matters involving Mara Salva *people*. I am a business consultant, not a revolutionist."

"Perhaps, then," Perico said, speaking for himself for the first time, "you do not belong among us."

"That," Tony countered, meeting Perico's cold stare with one of his own, "is a matter for you to take up with Monte. Unless, of course, you wish to overthrow him in his absence. Perhaps you would like to take a vote among the people here to challenge the leadership passed on to him by Francisco Barillas?"

Perico's stare turned into a look of open malevolence. He would kill me here and now, Tony thought, if he could get away with it. But the others, including the always mercurial Tela, were staring at their comrade with expressions that said he dare not try to seize control from Monte Copan.

Finally, after a deep breath of resignation, Perico yielded. "I will await my orders from Monte," he said quietly.

"Good," Tony nodded curtly, and rose. "Monte will return from San Salvador in two or three days and begin putting everything in order here. I will attend to some financial matters today and will go back down there on this evening's flight. Tela, Monte has given permission for you to accompany me, to assist in setting up the new offices in San Salvador. You have a valid passport, do you not?"

"Ah—yes, I do," Tela replied hesitantly, perhaps even suspiciously.

"Good. Amelia, will you please arrange for two first-class tickets to be held at the AeroMexico check-in counter?"

"Yes, Tony," Amelia said. It was the same tone she used when speaking to Monte.

"I guess the meeting is over, then," Tony said. "Tela, I'll pick you up at your place at six for the flight. You'll be ready?"

"I'll be ready, Tony," she said.

Tony frowned. There was something about the way she said it, something in her voice, an intonation or pitch, that he had never heard before, or at least never noticed. But her expression was inscrutable; nothing in her eyes told him anything.

"Okay, see you then," he said, and left.

At four o'clock that afternoon, Tony came out of the Los Angeles federal building with another man. They stood at the top of the steps for several moments, talking, then shook hands. The other man went back inside and Tony came down the steps and walked to the parking lot. Before he reached his car, Tela stepped from the doorway where she had been watching and fell in beside him. He felt the muzzle of a gun against his side, concealed by a sweater she carried over her arm.

"Don't make me kill you in public, on a parking lot," she said.

Halting, Tony replied, "I'm not going to make you kill me anywhere, Tela. You followed me?"

"I had you followed."

"Not Armando and Benito again? I would have spotted them."

"No. A loyal young couple with a baby, whom you had never seen. They watched you go into the FBI office, then called me. So, you were an agent all along?"

"Yes."

She prodded him with the gun. "Walk to your car."

In the car, Tela had him leave the Civic Center and drive back toward East L.A.

"It's been a trap from the very beginning, hasn't it?" she asked, putting the sweater aside to reveal a four-inch barreled revolver with a two-inch Stifler silencer attached.

"That's how it started out," Tony admitted.

"You never knew Francisco Barillas."

"No."

"The letter you showed me was a forgery."

"Yes."

"And your name is not Antonio Marcala."

"No. Antonio Marazan."

"When you trained to become an FBI agent, did they give you special love-making lessons to use on foolish women like me?"

Tony's expression tightened. "Tela, I'm going to pull over and park. There are things that I must tell you. If you do not want to hear them, you will have to shoot me."

"Keep driving," she ordered.

"No." He slowed and pulled out of traffic. Tela cocked the hammer of the pistol.

"I warn you, keep driving!"

"Shoot if you must," Tony said grimly, and eased the car to a parking place at the curb. Turning off the ignition, he sat with both hands on the steering wheel, looking straight ahead, waiting to see if the bullet came. It did not.

"You son of a bitch," she said tearfully. "You made me fall in love with you even when I knew—I *knew*—that you were an agent."

"Tela, listen to me," he turned to her. "I *was* an agent; I'm not any longer. I've resigned from the bureau. From now on, I am the president and chief executive officer of Salvadoran-American, Incorporated, the new Delaware firm we formed for Mara Salva last week. I will also be president of the other businesses we now have: Ari-Mex, Salvo Printing, Lago Shipping, U.S. Cars, and Delaware Investments. I'm going to do exactly what Frank Barillas would have wanted me to do if we had known each other. Within a year or two, Tela, I can turn Mara Salva's operation into a completely legitimate multi-diversified business that someday will be able to finance a revolution *without* its leaders being outlaws or criminals. In the meantime, we can use profits to make life better for our people now."

"*Our* people?"

"Yes, of course." He was slightly taken aback. "I am a Salvadoran, just like you. Why do you think the bureau selected me for the assignment?"

"I don't know. I guess I didn't realize—"

"Tela, uncock the gun. Please."

"No."

"All right. But please be careful. As I was saying, the revolution may be far in the future, but we can begin laying a foundation for it *now*, with something besides hidden stock-piles of weapons. We can build small, private schools in the rural areas to educate the peasant children. We can establish private utility firms to provide electricity and running water. We can open co-operative food warehouses through the church to import non-profit food products to stop the malnutrition among the poor. There are dozens of other ways that Monte and I have been discussing—"

"Monte will kill you when he learns that you are FBI."

"*Was* FBI. And Monte already knows it."

"You tol' him?" she asked, aghast.

"Yes. When we arrived in San Salvador, I told him the entire truth. I even told him who among his ranks was an informant."

"Informant? In Mara Salva?"

"Yes. How do you think I was so well briefed about Frank Barillas? Where do you think the bureau got all its information?"

"Who is it?" Tela asked, almost in a whisper.

"Who do you think?"

"Perico?"

"Yes."

"Then Monte will kill *him* when he gets back."

"Monte already *is* back," Tony told her. "He is with the others right now. And I imagine Perico is already dead."

Tela lowered the pistol and uncocked it. For several minutes, she stared straight ahead, as if in a trance. All of the strength Tony normally saw in her seemed to have drained away, leaving her traumatized and unable to function. After a while, she said simply, "Take me home, please, Tony."

That night, thirty thousand feet in the sky, as the AeroMexico jetliner cruised toward Mexico City where they would change planes for San Salvador, Tony and Tela relaxed over drinks in the Aztec-decorated first-class cabin. Tela had been quiet and subdued back at her apartment when she packed a small bag and got her passport out. As Tony drove them toward LAX, she made only light, inconsequential conversation about things like weather, traffic, the increasing smog problem in the Los Angeles basin. It was as if all the sudden and significant changes about to occur within Mara Salva, therefore within her life, were weighing on her so heavily that she had been forced, in the interest of her own emotional well-being, to put everything of any importance on hold, and allow herself to mentally consider only the most trivial and common of subjects. She remained in that repressed mode as they checked in at the Bradley International Terminal, went through security, and finally boarded the plane. It was only after they were airborne and had each finished one margarita and began sipping their second, that the alcohol helped Tela return to her old self, albeit a much less inflexible self. From her window seat, she reached over and brought Tony's left hand across to her lips, kissed it, then held it comfortingly to her cheek.

"You know, you are really the very best," she said softly, her voice shaded, almost nostalgic. Tony leaned his head toward her.

"The best? You mean the best lover?"

"No, I mean the best liar. You're an excellent lover, don't misunderstand me. But telling lies is your talent."

"There will be no more lies between us," he promised.

"That," she said, rolling her eyes, "might be the biggest lie of all."

"You still don't trust me completely." It was a statement, not a question. Tela shrugged.

"If you were only an agent, how could you have done all the things you did with Monte? All the business things? Where did you get such knowledge?"

"What I told you about my education was the truth; I do have a master's degree in business administration from Stanford. In the bureau, I was assigned to the CRBA Division; that stands for Covert Racketeering Business Affiliations. Our work was to uncover legitimate businesses that were fronts for organized crime or terrorist organizations. I've investigated enough front businesses to be very familiar with them. The one I set up for Mara Salva is complex and very elaborate; I don't think anyone will catch onto it before we become completely legitimate. Does that satisfy you, my angel?"

"I don't know," Tela said. "I mean, suppose you were part of an even larger sting operation than simply infiltrating Mara Salva in southern California? Suppose this is a joint undertaking involving the CIA, the state department, and the

Salvadoran government, with the goal being to expose all undercover members in Salvador, all hidden arms, all supporters in the church, the unions, the universities? Suppose you are but one of many agents involved?"

Tony shook his head helplessly. "Tela, my sweet, is there nothing I can do to prove myself to you once and for all?"

"Perhaps." She took a sip of her drink. "If you would do it."

"Tell me what it is."

"You said that I never seemed happy. Do you know what would make me happy?"

"What?"

"What would make me happy would be to see the end of the *Sombra Negra*. The end of the death squads. The way you and Monte are going, the Mara Salva will become like some giant corporation. You seem to be thinking only of profits and expansion, becoming legitimate. But, Antonio, there is still much killing to do."

She took Tony's hand from her cheek, put it to her lips, and kissed it again. And she bit one of his knuckles, just enough to hurt. Tony frowned.

"I want to begin killing the *Sombra Negra*," she said. "I want to see all the black shadows die. That would make me happy."

In the muted light above the seats, Tony saw in Tela's eyes a consuming desperation, not just a desire but a *need* to kill. Perhaps, he thought, it was in revenge for her parents and little sister, or for the thousands she had spoken of who died in the long Salvadoran civil war. Perhaps it was because she did not understand all the complicated things that were going on within Mara Salva, and she did understand the simplicity of killing. Whatever the reason, Tony sensed that it was a deep, deep paranoia, one that had not yet reached the plateau of madness, but seemed so near as to be irreversible. He suddenly knew that through whatever was to come in El Salvador, that he had to protect her. He had to remain at her side, doing as she wished, even if she slipped farther into the dementia that was decaying her mind.

"All right, that is what we will do," Tony said.

"Yes, you and I together, Antonio. We will find members of the *Sombra Negra* and execute them, one by one. Promise me."

"I promise, my love." Now he drew her hand to his lips, and kissed it as if taking an oath. "And when the black shadows die, you will trust me completely?"

"Yes, Antonio. Completely."

"And you will be happy?"

"Oh, yes! I will be very happy when they are all dead."

Her eyes became fierce again as she spoke. Her bloodlust stirred in him a more intense loyalty than he had ever known.

For her, he silently swore, he would do whatever he had to.

# Miguel Agustí

## Rebirth (Cain and Abel)

MIGUEL AGUSTÍ published his first story at nineteen and, since then, he has written more than a hundred articles and short stories for magazines such as *Nueva Dimensión, Bazaar, Spirit, Rufus, Playboy* and others. Agustí has also contributed to newspapers and has cultivated many different genres, including thrillers, fantasy, science fiction, and comic strips. He has been editor in chief for several Spanish magazines and also worked as a script writer for the TV series *L'Ofici d'Aprendre,* broadcast by the Catalan regional channel. All of which has given him a unique way of looking at the world. In his story "Rebirth (Cain and Abel)," first published on the Web site Mysterypages.com, he takes a look at a very different kind of sibling rivalry.

# Rebirth (Cain and Abel)

*Miguel Agustí*

It could not be hell, but he had dreamed that silence and darkness has enveloped him. It was a silence that was almost a vacuum but not quite nothingness.

He was not alone. In this dream he sensed a very slight presence of someone or something watching him, attempting to probe inside him but in vain. For a moment he thought that the silence had taken on a tangible form. Maybe that was it. He rejected the idea. All forms are tangible yet this one was not. Silence lacks form and can only be measured by its intensity. It must be someone who, like himself, was dreaming. The thought appealed to him: two beings who found themselves in the same dream. Was it possible?

"Who are you?" he asked without speaking. Would silence answer him? No, it would have been too human a reaction, befitting only a living being, and he guessed that he had ceased to live as had the other thing who remained hidden and spied upon him.

Perhaps the other presence was so distant that it could not eavesdrop. That would mean he had tried to draw closer to nowhere because the vacuum that surrounded him had no direction or beginning and was vague and unfathomable.

For a brief instant there was a flash of light. It was not the presence but something else. A brief instant. At least time existed, he told himself. The light had seemed like a flower. Do flowers flash?

"Who are you?" he asked.

Another thought welled up. Perhaps he was awakening, although he was not aware of sleeping or even drowsing. But this was no dream. What was it? What is most like to a dream?

The light flashed again—this time more intensely—and began to move. Nothing around him indicated this was the case, rather he was convinced it was so. Concern gripped him as the vacuum began to fade. He felt it was not the first time and that he had suffered in that silence on other occasions. How many times? The belief began to grip him, like waves running ahead of a storm, harbingers of panic and shipwreck.

He realized that he still had memories, leftovers from some previous existence, that threatened to bear down on him in some crushing avalanche. He felt he was getting tangled in an awful web from which there could be no escape.

The light winked again. It was not exactly a wink, more a pulsing, a palpitation, like a heartbeat, evoking something.

He remembered. Understanding dawned as he relived the experience. A tongue of flame had frozen his heart. The lover had killed him out of love—for her. Love, the reason for everything: life, madness, death. Love, the everlasting excuse and justification.

So that was death . . . light, silence, light, vacuum, light, nothingness. The presence became more oppressive and drew closer. The other being also moved toward the flower of light, toward him.

He could not remember the lover's face. He had hardly glimpsed him before the man brandished the knife, before he could even imagine his existence. She had always shown herself to be so sweet, so in love, even after the abortion when she finally broke down and wept. How could he have guessed that she planned his murder and wanted him dead. Maybe he was not yet dead and the silence that enveloped him just the last thread by which his life hung while she and the lover dragged his body to some hiding place.

He should have guessed. The curtains in the living room were almost always drawn open until well into the evening. The light streamed in through the open windows. She disliked the shade and a game of shadows on the wall terrified her—some remnant of childhood nightmares. That evening she had kissed him and led him into the darkened living room—circumstances that he had read wrongly. Even the kiss, which was unusually passionate, should have led him to suspect something. She had been distant of late, wrapped up in herself. He had thought this to be just one of her frequent changes of mood. Being used to her mercurial nature, he had thought nothing of it. It was just the way she was. However his killer was there, lurking behind the curtains. It was like something out of a B-movie thriller but no less effective for all that. When she hugged him and opened his mouth with her tongue, the hand that held the knife parted the curtains and stabbed him in the back. He was speechless, his last breath of air escaping between his teeth, a bite on emptiness. The air spilled out and he sagged into her arms. The shadows in the living room turned into the blackness of nothingness. Where had he awoken?

What had they planned to do with his corpse—put it in the car and fake an accident? His carbonized body would be rendered unrecognizable as would the wide, deep stab wound. Tongues of flame would blister his flesh, consume him, turn him to ashes. The deed done, there would be nothing to spoil the happiness of the two killer-lovers. They would never be found out—she was too clever, slippery, and single-minded. She was a superb liar, it simply came naturally. It was now all so clear.

He had met her two years ago and fallen hopelessly in love. She had broken up a long relationship that had shackled her to the point where she exhibited signs of schizophrenia. Her partner was a drunk and she had sexual problems that went way back, making her timid to advances and off-putting to the opposite sex. Despite that, she remained beautiful, her white skin and slightly darkened eyelids emphasising the black voracity of her eyes and her pale rose-colored lips. He had fallen for her immediately and quickly went from protector and confidant to doting husband with dizzying speed, scarcely without realizing it. It had to be admitted that it was a happy marriage, while it lasted. He had never suspected her of the least unfaithfulness. She had proved herself a skilled lover in bed, had grown more passionate and overcome her old inhibitions. Daily life had gone by with no upsets worthy of mention, except when it came to the abortion.

He had forced her to abort, persuading her that it was for the best, that children destroy their parents and only serve to deprive others of their freedom through their relentless cruelty and selfishness. He had never been a child. It was the right choice. She had resisted the abortion out of religious conviction and also because she desperately wanted to be a mother. Motherhood was what she most yearned for, a kind of saving grace in her life. However she finally gave in to his threats. He made her give up the baby. She cried for some time after that and then the tears finally dried up.

Why had she sought a lover? Why had they both planned his murder? He had saved her, redeemed her soul, dragged her from a hellish life. He had provided for her and satisfied her least whim. She had no grounds for complaint.

A wave of hatred overcame him, thrusting him deeper into his dark agony. The pain almost made him shout in that deathly silence. His soul, what of his soul? He looked inward in a desperate attempt to resist the evil that was trying to tear him apart and emanated from the other presence. The hatred was accompanied by deception, frustration, falling out of love, a savage lethal instinct as the tongue of flame pursued him beyond death, without letting up.

Finally he saw the tongue of flame, the lover. Another intangible form. He was filled with wonder, joy, euphoria. The lover had just been a plaything in her hands, they were both little more than dismembered rag dolls in the hands of a lascivious, ruthless child who killed those whom she snared. He had fallen into her sticky web of deceit and a cloying fear had overtaken him since he began his voyage into darkness.

She had killed him for his money, what other reason could there be? The lover moved toward him, he wanted to kill again.

At the end of nothingness the light had grown as he drew closer to it. He realized as he got nearer that the light did not flash but simply grew and shrank.

What was happening in the silence? There was no longer a vacuum, he was surrounded by a something tangible that acted as a balm. Was it the last rites? Oil smeared on the forehead of a newborn child? Life and death at the heart of nothingness, the successful sperm fertilized the egg, the death rattle transformed into birth pangs.

The darkness began to oppress him. He no longer floated in a vacuum but swam in a warm, thick, all-enveloping liquid. Silence had given way to an irregular, deep heartbeat that changed in intensity, sometimes solemn, sometimes flighty, but always disturbing. A heartbeat that recalled other heartbeats, just as the earlier silence recalled other silences.

He looked behind him at his killer. Direction and distance, endings and beginnings, epilogues and prologues existed once more. Everything was left behind: his regrets; chronic loneliness (until she appeared on the scene); a life enslaved by work; the family's emigration in the lean postwar years in search of a crust to feed too many mouths; his hatred for the unbearable and shameful mediocrity of his parents and brothers; the desperate search for brighter social circles; the little steps made toward some greater end that were merely a product of his overweening ambition; and finally his contempt for women who, despite their shammed deference and manners, had always treated him as some kind of low-life.

How he had come to hate them! Until he met her, that was. Everything had gone swimmingly until she became pregnant. She had wanted a child. What nonsense! He had not given in to her foolishness. The son had grown inside her womb but the child was never born.

Tearful, she had accused him of murder as they left the clinic.

He had swiftly forgotten the episode. Women, after such an occurrence, become hypersensitive, hysterical, the eternal female. Forget about children, they come packaged with shit, just like when he was born.

She cried for a while after and then her tears dried up.

The warm thick liquid in which he floated had gone, drained away toward the pulsing flower. The parched atmosphere was unbearable.

Ba-boom, ba-boom. The beating sound was deafening, as if that pulsing infinity in which he found himself trapped with his murderer could no longer contain so much hate and was collapsing inward, painfully crushing him and crunching the cartilage in his tiny skull.

Something moved in front of him, so close he could almost touch it. He could feel it. He once more had a body and the movements that had surprised him were his own limbs, those of a foetus. An umbilical cord floated from his belly. The amniotic liquid and sack surrounded him, making him seem like an outsized goldfish in a plastic bag—but one made for two.

His murderer was upon him now and was trying to strangle him with his umbilical cord. Hate overtook him. He desperately tried to place his hand between his neck and the other's umbilical cord. He managed—God knows how!—to kick out with his legs and the pressure abated for a moment and both foetuses faced each other in their ever-shrinking human cell. However the cord still threatened to tighten round his neck while an irresistible force pulled him toward the winking light. The cord tightened again like a hangman's noose and he felt himself being strangled once again. The killer was stronger than he and had greater freedom of movement. He kicked forlornly. Almost half his head was now wedged between living walls, which relentlessly sucked him in. What unbearable pain! Perhaps death was not the end but merely the endless prolongation of the throes of agony? How many times must a man die and how man times shall he rise again? He was overcome with panic and thrashed desperately, doubling up his tiny body in his frantic struggles. The pressure round his neck ceased and he was immediately sucked into that pulsing maelstrom. Panic, it seemed, had saved him. The killer foetus's umbilical cord had slipped off and released him during his last sudden contortion. Then the ghastly truth dawned—panic had not saved him but rather condemned him to live again. He lost consciousness and forgot everything of his former existence. At that precise moment God's voice boomed out, "Twins!" His murderer was born just after him.

# Denise Mina

## Helena and the Babies

DENISE MINA hails from Glasgow, Scotland. She has won the John Creasey Golden Dagger Award, and has just started to dazzle American critics, who get all breathless and misty-eyed when her name comes up. Not that she doesn't deserve it, however, because yes, she's that good. Her story here won the The British Crime Writers' Association Award for Best Short Story. As always—the Brits being the excellent short story writers they are—the competition was intense. In "Helena and the Babies," first published in *Fresh Blood III*, three generations of women collide at a crossroads of mystery.

# Helena and the Babies

*Denise Mina*

Auxiliary Nurse Bentham unpacked Helena Lawrence's suitcase. They were fine clothes, silk slips in peaches and pinks, cotton blouses and linen suits. Bentham stacked them on the bed, stroking the soft material, letting her fingertips linger.

"I'm sure Mum'll like it here," said Alison Lawrence to Matron. She hadn't looked at Bentham once. "She chose this very bed for Grandma."

"You have my sympathy." Said Matron gently, "This must have been a very hard time for you."

"It has," said Alison tearfully. "First Grandma dying and now Mum getting so bad so suddenly. At least she's somewhere familiar."

The nurses called it the Babies' Room because it had been a nursery and the occupants were all confused and doubly incontinent. Set at the very top of the big house with a low arched ceiling, it had a cozy, enclosed feel. During the winter the room filled with warm yellow light, and the tops of the trees filled the windows, keeping the room cool in summer. There were six beds in the room. At the end of each sat an old woman in a comfy, urine-proof armchair. Creeping blindness and wild confusion meant that, despite months of intimate proximity, the Babies were hardly aware of one another's existence.

Helena's own mother had spent three months sitting at the end of this bed by the window. Helena adored her mother and had chosen the home and the bed carefully. The summer light had warmed dear Elizabeth's feet at teatime, just as it did Helena's now. The tapping of the tree branches against the window caught Elizabeth's attention, as it did Helena's now. Elizabeth had died within three months of moving in. It was often difficult, said Matron, for older residents to make the transition from home. And now, only one month after her death, Elizabeth's only daughter was here to take her place.

Alison bent down to the wheelchair and took her mother's hand. The bones and veins and sinews were visible through the paper skin. Helena looked vacantly upward, her mouth hanging open, knowing that her hand was being touched, unaware of why or by whom.

"Mum," said Alison, "It's me, Mum."

Matron noticed the likeness between them, from their slight physiques to their long, angular faces and coifed white hair. She was secretly surprised that

Elizabeth had declined so quickly, she seemed a robust little woman with a strong heart but over a single cold winter weekend she declined and her heart failed.

A young nurse bustled into the room. She was short and had a punky black hairdo. She blushed when she saw Matron with a visitor,

"Sorry, Matron. I'm . . . I'm here to do the afternoon teas."

"Very good, Nurse. Nurse Thomas, this is Helena Lawrence and this is her daughter, Mrs. Tombery." Matron turned to Alison, "This is one of our newest nurses. Nurse Thomas looks young but she has a lot of experience, don't you, Nurse?"

Nurse Thomas smiled shyly as she moved quickly around the room, clearing the tables for the tea trays.

"Where did you work before this?" asked Alison.

"Oadby Hospital," said Nurse Thomas quietly.

"Well, I hope you're happy here," said Alison. "And I especially hope you'll take good care of my mum."

Alison took her mother's hand again, patting it and smiling sadly. Sour, hot urine flooded Helena's wheelchair, cascading onto the linoleum floor, splashing on Alison Tombery's linen dress. She dropped her mother's hand and leaped back from the splattering spill, frantically brushing at the piss on her dress. She looked at her wet hand and laughed weakly. "I'm so sorry," she said to Matron. "It smells . . . terrible."

Matron cupped her elbow. "It smells like that because Helena's slightly dehydrated, Mrs. Tombery."

"I don't understand, she used to be so fastidious."

"Incontinence is never deliberate," Matron said. "You mustn't feel ashamed. Let's go downstairs and finish the paperwork. Nurse Bentham will help your mother get cleaned up."

Matron led her from the room, nodding at Bentham to attend to Helena.

"Thomas," said Bentham when they were out of the room, "take your break before the afternoon tea."

Thomas cleared the final table and went upstairs, leaving Bentham alone in the room. She leaned over Helena, stroking her cheek slowly with the back of her hand. "I knew your mother," she said.

Thomas was hiding in the staff toilet, smoking a cigarette. She couldn't smoke in the staff room. The other nurses stopped talking when she went in there, and sat looking at her, waiting for her to leave. They all knew about the Annex because it had been in the papers, they knew about the alleged beatings, they knew nothing was ever proved against anyone and they knew that Thomas had left suddenly. They resented her even more when they found out she was working for nothing.

Thomas had left because she couldn't take it anymore. She found herself unemployable, everywhere she applied to knew about the Annex. But she was desperate to remain in nursing, so desperate that she offered to work at Roseybank on a voluntary basis for three months. If it went well she would be offered a job. Otherwise she could leave with new references. She was spending her meager savings on bus fares.

She had spent the first month working as a floater between the floors, fetching and carrying from the kitchen, making the beds and toileting when the other shifts were running slow. After a month Bentham actually requested her as a shift partner for the Babies' Room. Thomas was amazed, no one else wanted to be associated with her.

Bentham didn't trust Thomas at first. She wouldn't let her do any patient care, not even the bed baths. She gave Thomas all the heavy work to do, the toileting, the bed changes and the laundry. It only took a week for Bentham to come around and trust her: every afternoon, without fail, she left Thomas alone with the patients for an hour to manage the afternoon teas. Thomas was deeply grateful for the gesture. It sent a message to the others.

So Thomas hung on. In less than a month and a half she'd be out of there, she'd have references and she wouldn't need to mention the Annex on her CV or get references from Staff Nurse Evans. She heard the other nurses talking about Bentham. They said she was a misery because she'd worked the Babies' Room for so long and so many of them died.

The cold urine was seeping into Helena's legs, burning her. Without a word, Bentham slipped both her arms under Helena's and lifted her up, perching her on her stiff, unsteady legs. Locked together like marathon dancers, they staggered slightly while Bentham reached behind and tugged down Helena's sodden underpants. "Dirty, dirty," murmured Bentham. "Dirty, dirty bitch."

She lifted Helena's dress, baring her backside to the world. A hot flannel hit Helena's back and the nurse scrubbed hard, washing, drying and dusting her with talc. She pulled fresh incontinence pads onto the chair and sat Helena down, pulling her wet dress up at the back, sitting a crocheted blanket on her lap to hide her naked legs.

"Don't be a dirty bitch like your mother." Bentham's face was inches from Helena's. "D'you understand? I looked after your mother. She was a dirty bitch as well."

She reached down below the arm of the chair and pinched the skin on Helena's boney hip, twisting it between her fingers. Helena jumped, not understanding what she was feeling but knowing it was pain.

"Yes," said Bentham softly, "you understand that, don't you?"

Bentham walked over to a fat woman sitting directly across from Helena. "This is Mrs. Hove. And this is what happens to dirty old bitches," she slid her fingers deep into Mrs. Hove's thick white hair. It was as soft as duckling fluff. Bentham tightened her fingers into a fist and tugged, jerking Mrs. Hove's head back. Mrs. Hove squealed with surprise and swung her fat arm back, trying to hit her assailant but it was the wrong arm on the wrong side. Nurse Bentham watched her and sniggered.

The door opened. Matron came in followed by Alison Tombery. They saw Bentham standing by Mrs. Hove, holding her hair, and stopped dead. "What are you doing there, Nurse?"

"I was going to set Mrs. Hove's hair this afternoon, Matron." Nurse Bentham stroked Mrs. Hove's hair, "But it doesn't seem to need a wash."

"Good, well, perhaps we could leave it until tomorrow."

Helena was staring at the crocheted blanket, picking thoughtlessly with arthritic fingers.

Alison Tombery came to visit on the second day, fussing around her mother and trying to feed her lunch. Helena wouldn't take anything. Alison smiled at Bentham.

"Is she eating, Nurse?"

Bentham looked at Helena.

"She isn't eating much but she's drinking a lot, aren't you, ducks?"

"Are you all right, Mum?"

Helena smiled to the air, showing off her ragged yellow teeth. The summer light played softly through the trees outside the window and Helena lifted her hands, reaching out to the thing she was smiling at. The backs of her hands were peppered in little purple bruises, like splashes of ink on tissue paper.

"What happened here?" Alison asked Bentham.

Bentham held Helena's fingers and looked sad.

"She banged them on the cot sides last night. We tried putting padding on the bars but she pulled it off."

"Oh, dear. What have you done to yourself?"

Helena looked Alison full in the face and smiled, drawling a strangled "Yaaaaanng."

Alison sat back and looked despondent.

"She wasn't always like this. She was a journalist, you know. The first woman ever to edit the *Leicester Mercury*."

"We have many professional ladies in this room," said Bentham. "Mrs. Hove over here was a furrier. Mrs. Clutterbuck over there"—she pointed to a skeletal woman slumped in an armchair in the corner—"was a GP."

"Illness is a great leveler, isn't it?"

"Yes," said Bentham, "it certainly is."

Alison Tombery didn't come on the third day. Or the fourth. Or the fifth. She phoned on the sixth to say she was going on holiday and wouldn't be in for a week, could Matron phone this number in Portugal if her mother's condition changed.

Helena Lawrence had been in the Babies' Room for a week. Thomas was in a good mood. She had counted the days and had exactly one month and one week left before she could leave. She wanted to leave Roseybank, the staff hated her. Just over a month and the Annex would be behind her, Staff Nurse Evans couldn't touch her.

It was early morning. Thomas was making the beds up while Bentham washed and changed the babies. They were waiting for the breakfasts to come up from the kitchen. It was quiet in the room and the Babies gurned contentedly as warm water sloshed in the basins and fresh sheets flapped over beds. Quite suddenly a shriek erupted in the far corner. Thomas dropped the clean sheet and spun around.

Bentham was standing over little Mrs. Clutterbuck, holding her arm. Mrs. Clutterbuck's mouth gubbed silently but her blank-eyed stare was eloquent. She was in so much pain she couldn't breathe. Bentham turned slowly. "Go back to your work, Thomas."

Horrified, Thomas walked over to them, "What on earth are you doing to her?"

"Go back to your work."

Mrs. Clutterbuck's arm was wrong, it was hanging wrong, at an absurd angle. "You've dislocated her shoulder, Bentham, how the hell did you do that?"

Bentham let go of the arm carelessly, it fell crazily, twisting forward. Mrs. Clutterbuck closed her eyes, tilted her head back and let out a high, shrill whinny. Bentham seemed very calm.

"Go back to your work. Mrs. Clutterbuck fell over."

"How could she fall over?" Thomas snorted indignantly. "She's sitting down."

Bentham watched Thomas's face and reached around, yanking Mrs. Clutterbuck out of the chair by her dislocated arm and dropping her on the floor. Mrs. Clutterbuck landed on her good shoulder and panted with pain. Quiet suddenly, she stopped panting and gurgled. Her good arm crept up to her chest, her little hand contracting like a dying flower. Expressionless, Bentham watched her.

"Okay, now she has fallen over," said Bentham slowly. "You'd better go and get Matron."

Thomas staggered backward out of the room, running when she got to the stairs. She came back with Matron.

"What has happened?" demanded Matron.

Thomas didn't know what to say. "She's on the floor," she said stupidly.

Matron saw Bentham at the far end of the room, crouching next to the slight little body by the bed. She bent down and took Mrs. Clutterbuck's pulse. Thomas stared at Bentham. Bentham had murdered Mrs. Clutterbuck and she was standing casually, watching Matron, her arms folded, one foot resting on the other. Matron stood up slowly.

"How did she manage to fall?" Her voice was hoarse. "She couldn't stand up."

Thomas waited for Bentham to own up but she didn't. She looked at Thomas, licking her lips, raising an eyebrow, waiting for her to speak.

"I was making the beds," said Thomas finally, "and Nurse Bentham was washing her—"

"No," interrupted Bentham, turning to Matron, "I was making the beds. She was washing her and then I heard a terrible noise. I came over and she was lying on the floor."

"That's a lie," shouted Thomas, "Matron, I was making—"

Matron raised her hand,

"First, let's get her into bed and pull the screens."

Matron pulled the screens around the bed as Thomas and Bentham lifted Mrs. Clutterbuck's body into the bed, her dislocated shoulder hanging wildly at the side.

"You bloody idiots," muttered Matron. "Do you two have any idea how serious this is? She's had a heart attack and her shoulder's dislocated. Her children and her grandchildren are doctors, they gave her a medical a month ago and there was nothing wrong with her." She rubbed her eyes hard and sighed. "Thomas, undress Mrs. Clutterbuck and lay her out. Bentham, you come with me."

Matron stormed out with Bentham at her heels, leaving Thomas alone with Mrs. Clutterbuck. She only had a month and a week left. If they pressed charges Thomas would lose more than her references. Mrs. Clutterbuck lay on the bed, tiny and helpless, her gumsy mouth hanging open like a baby bird waiting to be fed.

Gently, Thomas rolled the nightie over Mrs. Clutterbuck's bony legs and up to her waist. Sliding her left hand under the small of her back, she lifted her slightly, pulling the nightie up with the other hand. She stopped. Mrs. Clutterbuck's skinny legs were covered in bruises, bruises shaped like four-fingered slaps, bruises like knuckle dents and small cuts like compass scratches. Losing her breath, Thomas pulled the rest of the nightie off Mrs. Clutterbuck and stood back. Her sagging tummy was worse. A large, deliberate cross was cut into the blackened skin. Mrs. Clutterbuck's chest heaved and she burped a stinking black liquid, it splattered out over her lips. It smelt like liver. Thomas blinked and it came to her: Bentham had asked for her, knowing about the Annex, knowing that Thomas would be blamed. She let Thomas do the teas on her own so that she could have had time to do it. Bentham had been planning the whole thing.

Thomas darted across the room to Mrs. Hove. Mrs. Hove looked up at her, smiling beatifically. "Mrs. Hove," she whispered. "Mrs. Hove, let me see you."

Thomas took the travel blanket from Mrs. Hove's lap and lifted the dress. Above the knees, around her groin, rolls of flesh were covered in red and black welts.

"Oh, Mrs. Hove." Thomas took her plump face in her hands, "Poor, dear, Mrs. Hove."

Thomas went over to Helena, who was picking at an invisible thing on the table. "Can I see? . . ."

She lifted the dress. Helena's hips and thighs were red and yellow. Matron came through the door, looking stern, with Bentham in tow. They stopped and stared at Thomas.

"What are you doing?" demanded Matron.

"I was looking—"

"You're in a lot of trouble. Get back behind that screen. Small wonder you're crying."

Thomas hadn't realized that she was crying. Bentham trotted across the room and pulled back the screen, gasping melodramatically,

"Oh. My. God," she said, and slapped her hand over her mouth.

Matron looked at Mrs. Clutterbuck. She stepped forward, reached out and gently closed the dead woman's eyes. She turned to Thomas,

"You evil little shit."

"It wasn't me, it was her," gabbled Thomas. "She wouldn't even let me wash them, Matron, I swear to you, Matron, I swear on my life."

"How dare you?" Matron was beside herself. "With your history—"

"No, Matron, no," said Thomas, sobbing now, struggling to speak through the tears, "I didn't touch anyone in the Annex. I told on the others and they couldn't prove anything and I had to leave because they made my life hell. Matron, I told on them, that's why I had to leave."

Matron wasn't listening. She was staring at Mrs. Clutterbuck,

"How could anyone . . . Unbelievable."

She pulled the sheet up and over Mrs. Clutterbuck's face. Bentham patted Matron's shoulder and Matron acknowledged the kindness with a long, slow nod.

"I'm going to phone the police." She said, "Nurse Bentham, bring Thomas to the office."

Bentham wrapped her big hand around Thomas's upper arm, digging her nails into the skin, as venomous as a playground bully, sneering at her when Matron wasn't looking. She dragged Thomas down the short flight of stairs to the small office. Matron picked up the phone and dialed.

Matron couldn't bear to stay in the same room as Thomas. She was downstairs, waiting by the door for the police. Thomas was looking out of the window trying to think. She heard Bentham hissing at her,

"You're the next Beverley Allit."

Thomas looked at her.

"You *are* fucking Beverley Allit."

"They'll hate you, the police, when they find out what you've done."

"I haven't done anything, Bentham. They'll find out it was you when they measure the bruises. My hands are too small to make bruises that big." She could see Bentham glancing at her hands and thinking about it. "You're a mental case, Bentham."

Bentham slid toward the door and took hold of the handle. She turned and grinned. "Be a shame if you got away now, wouldn't it?"

She opened the door, looked outside, and crept out of the room.

Thomas could run. If she got downstairs she could get out of the kitchen door. Over the back wall. She stood up suddenly but stopped at the office door. If she left they'd think she was guilty. Bentham would never get caught. She sat back down. That's what Bentham wanted, that's why she left her alone. She'd be standing in the kitchen, waiting to catch her and make herself the hero. Thomas looked out of the window. The fire escape. There were fire exits all over the house, Bentham couldn't cover them all. She was standing behind the door, sweating and tremorous, wondering which exit to take, when the door opened. Matron was there with two policemen. Her face was very red. She raised her hand and slapped Thomas across the face as hard as she could. *"What,"* screamed Matron, *"have you done with Helena Lawrence?"*

Beyond the door Matron was ticking Bentham off for leaving Thomas alone and the other nurses were gathering, quizzing each other and expressing dismay. The sun shone in through the office window, yellowing one of the policemen's trousers. He fumbled in his pocket and leaned across the desk,

"Cigarette, miss?"

Thomas took one and the policeman lit it for her.

"We know you can't have taken her far," said the policeman, "you were only left alone for three or four minutes."

"I stayed in here," said Thomas, knowing they wouldn't believe her, knowing they would have checked with Staff Nurse Evans at the Annex and knowing Evans would relish the chance to drop her in it. "You want to talk to Bentham, not me."

The policeman sighed. "You know, in ten minutes we'll have a full team of officers here and we'll find her anyway. You might as well tell us."

"I don't know where she is. Ask Bentham."

"It'll look better for you if you do tell us."

"I don't know where she is, I swear."

He sat back in his chair and looked out of the window.

"What happened at the Annex, Sarah?"

"You mean you haven't already phoned them? Don't listen to Staff Nurse Evans, speak to someone in admin."

"I'd rather you told me."

Thomas slumped back in her chair. It sounded ridiculous.

"I reported senior members of staff for hitting the patients. The inquiry couldn't prove anything and I was hounded out of my job."

"You didn't hit them yourself?"

"No."

"Why didn't you tell Matron that when you came for the job here?"

She shook her head, "It's harder to get a job as a whistleblower than as an abuser."

The policemen didn't believe her.

"If you were a boss," she said, "would you give a job to someone who snitched on their last boss?"

"Yes," said the policeman, without pausing to think. "Yes, I would. Where is Helena? Is she in a cupboard somewhere?"

They didn't believe her. The inquiry didn't believe her and Matron didn't believe her and the police didn't believe her. Thomas couldn't think of anything to say,

"Can I have another fag, please?"

"Did you kill her, Sarah?"

"I know—"

The policeman cut her off with a raised hand. He cocked his head and listened to a small army of feet jogging noisily up the stairs.

"You've almost missed your chance, miss, d'you want to tell me now?"

The crowd on the stairs arrived outside the door and Thomas heard Matron let out a wordless exclamation. A silence fell over the nurses. The policemen in the office looked at each other. The one with the fags stood up and opened the door a crack, peering out into the hall. Thomas could see Matron's back. She was standing with her arms out at the side, stiff with surprise, staring at something in front of her. The door swung open revealing four tall uniformed policemen standing around Bentham. Two of them were holding her by the arms while another said she didn't have to say anything. Bentham wasn't listening. She was staring ahead, just like Matron, frozen.

"You're on holiday," said Bentham.

Alison Tombery slid into view and smiled as Helena Lawrence stepped into the doorway. She was still wearing her nightie but was standing tall now, wearing incongruous court shoes with a low heel.

"And what," said Helena, quite clearly and distinctly, to Bentham, "Did you do to my mother?"

# Brendan DuBois

## Old Soldiers

THIS VERSATILE writer enjoys writing about the men and women of the government and what happens when the world passes them by, like in the following story, "Old Soldiers," which first appeared in the May issue of *Playboy*.

# Old Soldiers

*Brendan DuBois*

When performing a boring chore like splitting wood, you tend to dwell on trivia to pass the time, such as the two distinct sounds you encounter during the job. The first is a thump, when the maul you're using makes a slight indentation into the wood. The other is a sharp crack, when you've started a major split that means you're almost finished with that chunk of soon-to-be firewood. Thoughts like these were going through my mind as I was about an hour into my morning woodcutting routine one spring Saturday.

Then a dark blue Ford LTD with government plates bumped its way up my dirt driveway, and I wasn't bored anymore.

And when Special Agent Cameron of the FBI and a companion got out of the car, I momentarily wondered what kind of sound a maul would make while being buried in the base of someone's skull.

Cameron carried a slim leather briefcase and his white hair was combed carefully over the back of his head, as if he had just had his picture taken for his official government ID. He had on a charcoal gray suit, unlike his companion, about 20 years younger, who wore blue jeans, white polo shirt and a dark brown leather jacket.

"Owen," Cameron said, as I rested near the woodpile. "I'd like to present Mr. . . . Smith. Mr. Smith works for another government agency."

I stuck out my hand and as Smith came forward to shake it, I wiped it off with my handkerchief, and Smith paused, the slight grin on his face steady under my insult. His dark brown hair was cut short and his blue eyes were bright, brittle and sharp. Underneath his polo shirt there seemed to be hard muscles. He looked like a guy who would spend his vacation in Europe, retracing Wehrmacht invasion routes through Poland with a smile on his face.

"Really?" I said. "And would that government agency be the GAO? Is your work being audited, Agent Cameron?"

Cameron didn't look pleased. "No. And this meeting has nothing to do with my previous visits. Mr. Smith has a matter to discuss with you, in private. When the two of you are finished, I'll take him back to Portland. That's it."

When the government pays your bills and keeps you alive, year after year, after any competent actuary would have written you off as dead long since, then I guess listening is the polite thing to do. So I shrugged and said, "All right, why don't the both of you come in."

Smith spoke for the first time. "That sounds grand." He came forward, but Cameron shook his head. "No," he said. "I want no part of this."

So Smith followed me into the farmhouse as Cameron trudged back to the LTD.

In the kitchen, I poured myself a tall glass of lemonade, offering nothing to my uninvited guest, and we sat at the round oak table. Perhaps I was being childish, but Smith didn't seem to notice. He leaned back in his chair and rested his hands on his flat stomach.

"Agent Cameron gave me a thorough briefing on the way over here," he said. "You certainly have a fascinating past, Mr. Taylor."

"Ain't I lucky," I said.

"And it's that past that has brought me here," he said. "Your talents. We want to use them, just for a short time."

"Sorry, I'm retired."

His smile was wide and merry. "Sorry, in return. You've been unretired and turned over to us. And if you don't care to cooperate, we can make your life quite miserable very quickly. I know what you've got here. In return for certain past services, you live here in total freedom, save for a few minor restrictions. Like staying within the town limits. Which brings me to my next point. Ever hear of Marion?"

Something seemed to wiggle around in my throat. "Maximum security prison."

He waved a hand in the air. "No, not maximum. Maximum is a dime a dozen. I'm sure even this rural wonderland has a maximum prison. No, Marion is the ultimate federal penitentiary. An inmate lives alone in a concrete cube eight feet in each direction. Once a week, you get out for an hour for some sunshine and fresh air. That's it. No radio, no television, newspapers and books strictly controlled, and the food is government-supplied. So. We reach an understanding here, everything's fine. If not, tomorrow at this time, you'll be staring at concrete."

I tried to stay calm. "Special Agent Cameron—"

"Look," he interrupted. "Some time ago Cameron made a mistake. A big one. In a little Texas town called Waco. Ever wonder why he's way out here in this area? Waco is why. And Waco is why Cameron cooperates. Which includes lending one of his charges for a while. So, Owen. What's it going to be?"

I put my hands under the table because they were clenching into fists so hard that I could feel fingernails starting to break skin. "What do you want?"

He waggled a finger in my direction. "No, no, no. I want to hear the words from your mouth that you're on board. Then I will tell you what we have planned."

I nodded, and then said, "All right, I'm on board."

Smith's grin got wider. "Thanks. And I also won 20 bucks. Cameron bet me you'd say no. OK, here's the drill." He reached into his jacket and pulled out a small slip of paper and tossed it over. "There's a man named Len Molowski, lives up in Cardiff, about an hour north of here. He's in his mid-60s, owns a small farm. That's his address."

I glanced at the paper. "And what's so special about Len Molowski?"

"What's special is that his real name is Leorud Malenkov. He's a Soviet military intelligence operative, placed here in deep cover almost four decades ago. You know those Jap soldiers who lived on in Guam and the Philippines, years after the war was over, who didn't give up? Same story, except they're here and they're Russian."

"So?"

I guess that wasn't the response Smith was looking for, as his smile faded. "Some old records we've kept over the years, we've managed to finally decode them. You'd be surprised what's for sale now over in Moscow. We found Len's name and a bunch of other names, all Soviet military intelligence, all placed into this country at about the same time, during the late Fifties."

"And what was he going to do while in Maine? Burn down a forest?"

"Who knows and who cares," Smith said. "That he's still here is what counts. And that's why I'm here with you."

"At the risk of repeating myself, I'll do just that," I said. "So what? Hasn't the news gotten to you folks yet? The Cold War's over. They lost. We won. We have a hell of a budget deficit to pay, but they have McDonald's in Red Square, their nuclear subs are rusting and sinking at dockside and their soldiers spend their time harvesting potatoes and trying to stay alive. What's the point of going after this guy?"

His eyes flashed at me. "The point is, *we* know we won the Cold War, but some people in Moscow haven't gotten the message. They don't like having NATO move in next door. They don't like having American fast food next to Lenin's tomb. They don't like American game shows on their TV. And we want to send them a message."

I picked up the paper again. "And how does Len become part of this message?"

Smith's gaze was steady, unblinking. "We want you to go up to his farm. Pay him a visit. Confirm his background. And then handle it."

I was suddenly aware of how tired I was, from chopping all that wood and from talking to this awful young man. "Handle it how?"

"Don't play wedding night virgin with me, Owen. I've read your record, know your background. You know exactly what I meant by handle it."

I slowly nodded. "So I do. *Mokrie dela,* right? Russian for wet work. After all, blood is wet and tends to get on your shoes and clothing. A nice piece of euphemism from Department V of the old KGB. And by handling an old man who's probably clipping newspaper coupons, and wondering how to pay for fertilizer this spring, this is going to do just what for you and your friends?"

"A message," Smith said slowly. "A demonstration. By retiring this old network of theirs, we make an effective demonstration to the right people with a minimum of fuss. More efficient and cheaper than flying over the Secretary of State to talk about trade issues or some other goddamn nonsense."

I crumpled up the paper. "And part of the minimal fuss is me, right? Deniability in case anything goes wrong. If I'm caught, I'm a career criminal with mysterious ties who one day killed a Maine farmer for no good reason. Right?"

"Who says retirees are losing their marbles," Smith said.

I looked out the window at the parked LTD and the man inside. "Part of my agreement with the Department of Justice is that I—"

"I know, I know," he said. "You're not allowed to leave the confines of this lovely little town without express prior permission, blah blah blah. All taken care of. You have a week, Owen. Seven days from now we'll be back for results, or your bag better be packed. And that bag should contain a toothbrush and nothing else. The clock is running. Understood?"

"Understood."

Smith slapped his hands together and stood up. "Great. Glad we could reach agreement."

He walked out of the kitchen, and as he strolled to the LTD, I had a fantasy of running downstairs to retrieve one of my slightly illegal weapons and blowing away Mr. Smith before his hand reached the car door. I replayed it in my head as the car left my property.

There are negatives associated with life in a small town. The local cable provider thinks one channel from Boston is stretching its cultural limits. No bookstores. And the nearest supermarket has boiled ham and American cheese as the extent of its deli offerings.

But there are some advantages, too, and one of them owns and works at the Pinette General Store. Miriam Woods is my oldest and dearest friend in town, and she winked at me as I finished a late lunch of tomato soup and a BLT. She's a widow, several years younger than I am, with dark brown hair and even darker eyes that are lightly framed by wrinkles. She owns the store, she runs the town post office out of a storefront window off to the side, and she's also one of the town's three elected selectmen.

As she picked up plates, her son Eric was restocking shelves in one of the far aisles. She looked over at him and then at me and lowered her voice.

"This Tuesday," she said. "Eric has basketball practice and I was thinking of coming over to your place for dinner."

"Really?"

"Really. You supply the dinner and I'll supply the desserts. One of them will be in an ice cream container." She lowered her voice even more and winked again as she started wiping the counter.

I said slowly, "But I won't be home."

"Well, there's always Thursday night, because—"

"Miriam, I won't be home all next week."

She stopped wiping the counter. "Oh?" And my dear Miriam was able to stuff about a ton of frost, disappointment and inquiry into that little two-letter word.

"That's right. I have . . . I have business to attend to."

Her wiping cloth was clenched in a fist. "I see. What kind of business?"

"I'm sorry, I really can't say. It'll take less than a week and then I'll be back."

She managed a smile and shook her head and went over to the cash register, counting and recounting bills, all the while talking, as if talking to herself. "You've never once agreed to go away with me for a trip to somewhere, even if it's just Portland or Bar Harbor. You've always said you couldn't leave the town, that you wouldn't feel comfortable."

Then she looked at me and slammed the cash drawer shut. "Now you tell me you're leaving town for a week, and you can't tell me why. To hell with that and to hell with you."

She marched to the rear of the store and I followed, but she locked herself into her little post office cubicle. I suppose it would have taken me all of 30 seconds to get through the lock, but I knew I would pay for those 30 seconds for a very long time.

Instead, I went outside to my truck and was climbing in when I heard a familiar voice.

"Owen? Got a sec?"

I rolled down the truck's window as Eric approached in his white store apron. He's about as tall as I am but gangly, with the loose limbs of a 15-year-old. He shares his mother's hair and eyes, and those eyes were troubled now.

"Sure," I said. "More than a sec, whatever you need."

"Just wanted to see how you're doing with the Internet. Got any more questions for me?"

I did at that, and we talked techno-speak for a while, him using phrases like HTML and links and hypertext with practiced ease, while I struggled along like a backwoodsman who's entered sixth grade at the age of 40. Eric had helped introduce me to the joys of cyberspace and was my own personal tech help line. I asked him a few questions and he gave me more than a few answers.

Then he nodded back toward the store. "I heard most of what went on back there, though I wish I hadn't."

"I wish I hadn't taken part in it, so don't worry."

Quick nod as he smoothed down the front of his store apron. "Mom gets like this, around this time every year. This is when dad died, and it bothers her still, though she never says a word."

"Does it bother you?" I asked.

He shrugged. "Not like it bothers her. I don't remember him that well. He spent most of his time either out in the woods or in a bar. Best memory I have is him lying on the couch, trying to balance a Coors can on his forehead and yelling at mom when she didn't move fast enough to get him another one. That's about it."

I started up the truck and he said, "Don't worry, she'll be fine in a bit."

"Honest?"

A wide smile. "Gosh, I don't know, Owen. I just thought that would make you feel better."

"Thanks," I said. "It did, just for a moment."

I then drove home, where I packed up and left the next morning to murder an old Soviet spy.

The day was warm, and I drove with the windows open, enjoying the wet smell of spring, of hidden whispers of trees and grass and crops ready to grow, ready to get back to life. As I drove out of town I felt a tingle along my hands, as an old and deep part of me appreciated that I was leaving the reservation. Mysterious Mr. Smith had been correct. There were certain things I could not do as part of my agreement with the Department of Justice, and one of them was to cross the boundaries of the township of Pinette. Even thinking of the bad business ahead of me, I couldn't help grinning as I watched the miles roll up on the odometer. For at least this day, I was free to go where I wanted. It was a heady feeling, and if I had found the right tune, I would have been singing. But the only thing on the radio was a syndicated pop psychologist who seemed to gauge her success by seeing how many of her callers burst into tears.

About halfway to Cardiff, I pulled over at a minimall and bought a strawberry ice cream cone. I strolled inside, checking out the stores and the people moving about, young and old, families and single men and women of all ages and sizes. I sat on a bench and finished my cone, thinking about the pundits who carped about the "malling" of America. A serious problem, I'm sure, but on this spring day I was happy to be here, free to go into any one of half a dozen stores.

Which I did. I bought a dozen new hardcover books and put them in the truck, went into a computer store and picked up some software, and then went over to an electronics store where I acquired a digital camera and a nice cassette tape recorder. Elsewhere, I spent an obscene amount of money on clothes, and when I left the minimall, my credit card was almost smoldering at the unfamiliarity of so much use.

I continued north and came to a tiny county airport. A sign outside said FEARLESS FERN'S FLYING SERVICE and I had a neat little thought of renting Fern and his Flying Service and heading out to British Columbia. Instead, I kept on the job.

While the day had been warm, the night was cold indeed, and lying on the dirt and leaves in a copse of birch trees outside a Cardiff farmhouse was making my bones ache to the point where I wondered if they'd ache forever, or if a long hot bath would set things straight. I was wearing a "gillie suit," a camouflage outfit with such varied colors and strips of netting and cloth that even in daytime I would melt against the backdrop of the forest. With a good gillie suit and the patience to keep still, a hunter can be damn near invisible, even with the target standing next to him.

My target wasn't standing next to me, though. He was walking around in his old farmhouse about 100 feet from my hiding spot, alone except for an old collie dog that cowered whenever Len Molowski—or Leonid Malenkov—approached. The man appeared to be in his mid-60s, with thick white hair combed to one side and black-rimmed glasses. His face was red and fleshy, and he wore a checked flannel shirt and brand-new blue jeans. I had been watching him since dusk, watching him cook and eat dinner by himself, toss a bag of trash on the porch, kick the dog when it got in his way and then sit on a couch to pass a few hours in the ghastly blue light of the television.

There were some things I did not see. I didn't see him cleaning a Kalashnikov AK-47 by lamplight. I didn't see a flag of the old Soviet Union flapping in the breeze from a flagpole. And I didn't see an Order of Lenin pinned to his thick chest.

I lifted my binoculars so I could scan the property. The farmhouse was larger than mine, with two stories and a wraparound porch that went around three sides of the house. There was a barn off to the right—also larger than mine, but I didn't have barn envy—and then what looked like a few dozen acres of fields beyond to the east. The nearest neighbor's house was about a half mile away. Everything on the property was neat but shabby, like he was doing all right but didn't want to show up the local populace.

I put the binoculars down, exchanging them for a handheld nightscope. The scenery flashed into pale green as I scanned. Two pickup trucks—one on cement blocks—and a tractor and other equipment in the barn. Nothing out of the ordinary—nothing, of course, except for me in the backyard, lying on the cold ground, 9mm Smith & Wesson Model 915 holstered to my side, water bottle, binoculars, nightscope and some hard candies all within easy reach. If I had been younger and more eager, I suppose I could have handled this job immediately and been back home by morning.

But, among other things, I wasn't that person anymore. So I waited. The night air was still and it was so quiet that I could hear the drone of engines far off in the distance, and the murmuring of Len's television set. Eventually, Len got up from the couch and went upstairs. An upstairs light went on and I heard the flush of a toilet, and then all the lights went off and I stayed in the cold woods for another hour. Something rustled behind me, but I ignored it. I listened to the frantic hoo-hoo-hoo of an owl and heard a crash of wings and a squeaking noise as something was killed just a few yards from me.

And then I crept away, moving slowly. Getting out is as important as getting in.

For the next couple of nights and days I kept watch on Len's house and discovered he had a pattern. He worked in the barn in the mornings or went out into the fields with a tractor, turning up the earth. At noon, he finished and went into town for lunch at the Cardiff Café. In the late afternoon, he spent his time around the house, and by the time evening rolled around it was the same routine: make dinner, kick the dog, watch television and go upstairs.

I envied his bed and his home. I was living out of the back of my truck, for I wanted no record of my stay at any hotel or motel in the area. After my nights of surveillance outside his house, I slowly and carefully trekked my way back through the woods to my truck and drove to a place I'd picked out earlier. In these woods were many dirt paths and logging roads, and from one of these, a different one each night, I backed into the woods until I was sure I couldn't be spotted. Then I slept poorly in the rear of the truck on a foam mattress wrapped in a sleeping bag, and while Len had a cozy hot breakfast, I made do with coffee from a little camp stove and cold cereal. Fires mean smoke and smoke in the woods gets noticed, which is not what I planned for this little adventure.

His midday journeys into town, which I timed, each lasted more than an hour. On day three I waited till after he drove off and then I rose from my hiding spot. I shed the gillie suit for what would pass for a disguise in these woods: a pullover jacket (the better to hide my holstered 9mm), a long-billed cap, binoculars around my neck and a Roger Tory Peterson bird book in my hand. I sauntered into Len's backyard as if I belonged there, went up to the rear door and in a few seconds I was inside. Len hadn't even bothered to lock the door.

Inside and off to the left was a large kitchen. The collie looked up from the kitchen floor, eyes curious, and thumped his tail as I murmured softly and rubbed his head. The tail thumped a few more times and he licked my hand and rolled over as I scratched his belly. Poor guy. Based on his treatment, I'm sure the collie would have helped me shift the furnishings into a moving van, but I had other plans.

I moved quickly, starting in the basement. It took just a few minutes to peg Len as a neat freak, his basement tidier than my kitchen. Boxes of clothing and canned food were stacked on the shelves, and there was an oil furnace that looked as if it had powered the 1939 World's Fair. Upstairs, the collie wagged his tail again as I went through the kitchen, the living room and the downstairs bathroom. Len had a few books, recent best-sellers, in the living room and the usual news and sports magazines and newspapers. No *Khrushchev Remembers*. No *Gulag Archipelago*. No *History of the Communist Party of the Soviet Union*.

On the second floor, I found his bedroom and a spare room, and, besides neatly made beds, bureaus and closets filled with clothes, and a few more magazines, nothing else. I checked the time. I had been in the house about half an hour. Time to leave.

Downstairs, I gave the collie another belly scratch and went back to the woods to put on the gillie suit. Forty-five minutes later, Len came home. As I waited for him, I thought about what I had not seen in the house. Quite a lot.

There were no family pictures on the walls or the bureaus.

No collections of letters or scrapbooks of photos.

No framed certificates of achievement from 4-H or the Grange or the Future Farmers of America.

In short, the things that should have been there, if Len were a usual Maine farmer.

From inside the house came the yelp of the collie, and I refocused my binoculars.

The next day I picked up a few groceries and made a quick phone call from a pay phone at a combination gas station and convenience store, a new one. I had not shopped at the same store twice, because I didn't want to be remembered, not even for a moment. When Miriam picked up the phone, she said, "Owen, I apologize."

"Oh," I said. "Very well. Apology accepted."

A sigh from the other end. "Don't you even want to know what I'm apologizing for?"

I turned and looked at a large Agri-Mark dairy truck rumbling by. "You're right. I should have asked."

Another sigh, but lighter than the first one. "Look, I was having a bad time the other day. Some old memories."

"I hear you."

"Of course you hear me, but I don't think you understand. When you said you were leaving and you couldn't tell me much—well, I don't like being left high and dry twice in the same decade."

"I understand."

I could hear voices in the background. "Maybe you do, Owen. All right?"

"Absolutely, Miriam," and I was going to say something else when I heard a few more voices and then hers, saying, "Gotta-go-bye" all in one breath as she hung up.

When Len next went back into town, I wandered around the reaches of his property in my bird-watcher's disguise. He had enough acreage for one man to farm, if he hired help in the spring and fall. Beyond the edge of one of the fields, I found a dump, where he had trashed a few appliances, a box spring and some worn truck tires. When I walked up to investigate, a chipmunk jumped on a rusting washing machine and chattered at me.

"Oh, hush up," I said. "Don't you see I'm trying to uncover a dangerous Soviet spy?"

And I laughed.

Heading back, I saw something behind the barn that I hadn't noticed before, a worn path leading into the woods. I followed it, looking for a stream or a fishing hole, but instead it went deeper into the pine forest and then up a slight incline. The trail was old and well maintained, with branches and brush cleared away from the tree trunks. Last year's leaves crackled under my feet as I made my way. I stopped for a moment to note a red driveway reflector light nailed into a tree trunk. The nails were rust-red from being outside a long time. Farther up the trail were more reflectors. The trail was marked for someone traveling through here at night.

The climb got steeper and I rested for a few minutes, taking a swig of water from my bottle, before following the path through a series of switchbacks. After a few minutes of climbing that made my thighs twitch, I was on the top of the hill, breathing hard. "Excelsior," I muttered, as I sat down on a fallen tree log.

The view was not what I expected. An airport was down there, with a long concrete runway that ran at an angle to the hill. A control tower and a number of hangars were in the distance, together with enough buildings for a small town. It was a much bigger airport than the one I had passed on the drive out, and also much bigger than such a remote and rural area would seem to need.

From the knapsack, I pulled out my binoculars and a map of the county. I scanned the few small private planes parked near the hangars. Those hangars were scaled for aircraft much bigger and faster than these Cessnas and Piper Cubs.

On the map, the marker for the town of Cardiff had a stylized aircraft symbol nearby. Below the cartoon plane were the words:

Raymond Air Force Base

Strategic Air Command

(Closed and now available for civilian use)

Looking down at the old Air Force base as I sat there, the damn spring sun didn't warm me a bit.

That night in my gillie suit, I watched Len go through his routine. Tonight was a bit different. At the kitchen table, he tossed down shot glass after shot glass of something from a clear bottle. Vodka was my guess. Then he started singing, a morose tune that I couldn't make out. It could have been in a foreign language, or it could have been that the breeze was blowing away from me, softening the sounds from the house. I waited for long hours as he gently placed his head on the kitchen table and fell asleep, and my hands and feet were trembling from cold before he woke to stagger upstairs.

The night after the drinking bout, after Len left for town, I stepped right up in my bird-watcher's outfit. I whistled as I walked through his yard and through the open sliding barn door. Ain't rural life grand, where people keep their outbuildings wide open for the benefit of would-be assassins?

A John Deere tractor was parked in the center of the barn, along with a collection of tills, spreaders and harvesters. Everything looked to be in good working condition. There were a few bags of fertilizer and seed, and a ladder going up to the loft. I climbed it—wincing as a splinter dug into my hand—and on the second level found a collection of tools, leather harnesses, rolled blankets and more bags of fertilizer. I went back down and outside past the tractor. Something was wrong, something was quite wrong.

I looked around, picking at the splinter on my hand. My internal alarm bells were jangling and everything felt odd, as though my inner ear balance had gone haywire. I squinted at the barn. It was bigger outside than it was inside.

I went back inside and paced the interior, counting off my steps, and then I came outside and repeated the process.

The dimensions were wrong.

Something was hidden inside.

And it didn't take long to find. To the left as I went back in was an empty stable. I ran my fingers around the wood of its far wall and quickly located an eye-bolt and heavy iron ring. I twisted and tugged and something went click, and I was able to swing the door open. Inside was a room with some boxes and a low table.

A faint light flickered from overhead, and I looked up to see a wire running from the fixture down to a car battery. A light that automatically came on whenever the door was opened. How convenient. The wooden table was built right up against the wall, and an old kitchen chair was slid underneath. On the wall were thumbtacked photos, old black-and-white pictures that were curling at the edges, of Air Force aircraft: KC-135 and KC-10 tankers, and B-47 and B-52 bombers.

Squatting in the middle of the table was a dusty shortwave radio and receiver, about 20 or 30 years old, it looked like. Beside it was a desk calendar from 1979. Next to that was a small collection of books, cheap drugstore paperbacks. I opened one and saw rows of numbers, line after line. There were a few books in Russian, the Cyrillic writing looking odd in this place. There was also a small leatherbound notebook, which I scanned. The first brief entry was dated to 1959 and the last to 1981. The handwriting was in Cyrillic, tight and nearly illegible.

Maybe it was the dust or the flickering light, but a headache, a powerful one, started throbbing at the base of my skull. To the left, leaning against the wall, was a large pack frame with webbed straps that looked as if it were designed to carry a heavy load, and next to the frame were four wooden boxes, about two feet deep, three feet wide and five feet long. The covers weren't nailed shut; they had fasteners that allowed the boxes to be opened quickly. I had a pretty good sense of what I would find when I opened the first box.

There, nestled in a dry and cracked Styrofoam casing, was a long dark green metal tube, with a handle about a third of the way from one end. There was also a sighting mechanism and a few other odds and ends, and a projectile with fins, about 30 inches long. More Cyrillic writing decorated the tubing.

I closed the cover.

And it was the creaking floor that saved me.

I spun on my feet, ducking my head and raising my left shoulder, as Len Molowski charged in, swinging an ax. The blade bounced off my raised shoulder, sliced into my left ear and struck the wall. Len was shouting something incomprehensible and I backed away, tripping over the kitchen chair and falling flat on my ass on the barn floor. With a triumphant bellow, he took three steps toward me, ax raised high in the air, eyes glaring, face red, mouth twisted in anger, and by then I had frantically dug under my coat and pulled out my 9mm.

I pointed it up at him, both hands tight in the approved shooting grip, and snapped back the hammer. The clicking sound seemed to echo in the tiny room and he paused, ax in midair, the portrait of a frustrated lumberjack.

My voice was calmer than I thought possible. "Right now I'm bleeding, Len, and when I'm bleeding, I tend to get upset, and when I'm upset, my trigger finger gets shaky. So toss the ax out into the barn and I won't be upset anymore. Understand?"

He stood there for just a moment, puffing and breathing hard, face still red. Then he tossed the ax, where it clanged off the John Deere tractor, and said, "You're trespassing. You're on my property. You get the hell off before I call the cops."

"Sure," I said. "Sounds like a good idea. And when you tell them about the trespasser in your barn, I'll tell them about the Soviet military officer named Leonid Malenkov, who owns said barn with surface-to-air missiles and other delights, and who's been in this country illegally for about 40 years. Care to guess who'd they be more interested in?"

His eyes flickered to me and then to the ax, and I knew he was regretting having tossed it. Then he collapsed. His face whitened, his shoulders slumped and he nodded, a sharp little motion.

"So, you've come," he said. "CIA? FBI? What is your name? What do you want?"

I motioned to the kitchen chair. "The name is Owen. I want you to sit down on that chair. And then we'll talk. And please don't insult me by thinking I work for either of those agencies. Right now I'm an independent contractor who's feeling particularly ornery."

A couple of minutes later, I had sloppily tied my handkerchief to my left ear, which was throbbing and hurt like hell but offered the advantage of allowing me to focus my mind. Len sat in the chair, thick hands folded on his lap. I sat on the table next to the radio, gently swinging my legs beneath me as I kept my 9mm pointed in his direction.

"Bomber gap, right?" I asked.

He looked at me, brow furrowed, eyes unblinking. "I don't know what you mean."

"Look, this will go a hell of a lot easier if we don't play games, Len. I know your background, your real name." I waved my pistol in the general direction of the hill I had climbed earlier. "You've got half a dozen handheld surface-to-air missiles—they look like an experimental version of the SA-7 Grail, right? And you're living next door to a Strategic Air Command base, supposedly chock-full of nuclear-armed B-52 bombers, just waiting for the word to take off and head up over the Arctic Circle and incinerate your motherland."

I waggled the pistol back and forth. Deep cover mission, right? You and probably a couple of dozen comrades, you took up residence near Air Force bases in the U.S., maybe even Britain and Turkey and other places. You wait for the word, and when the word comes, and when those B-52s are rolling down those runways during an alert, you're ready for them. A couple of surface-to-air missiles later, you've got flaming B-52 wreckage everywhere. You and your comrades have taken care of the situation, right here in the enemy's backyard."

Len was quiet, but his head moved just a bit, as if he were nodding. "Bomber gap," I said. "Back in the Fifties and early Sixties, the U.S. thought there was a bomber gap, that you folks had more and better bombers than we did. And you know what? There *was* a bomber gap, but on the other side. We had bigger and better bombers, and your leaders, they must have been scared. They must have looked for something to tip the balance in their favor. Something quick and dirty and cheap. And they came up with you, am I right?"

A quick, almost embarrassed nod, and then he talked rapidly, like he was finally glad to tell someone of what he had done. "Yes. We were young, committed, all volunteers. We were told it would be a long, hazardous mission. But we did what we had to do. You had us ringed with bases, your NATO, your missiles. Your generals boasted of destroying us in a fortnight."

He folded his arms and stared at the far wall. "We were sworn to secrecy and taken to a remote area in Soviet Asia, near Alma-Ata. We were trained and retrained on how to fire our missiles. We fired them in the air at first, and then at drones, and then. . . ." He looked up at me. "Hard to say now, even years later. Last, we fired them at aircraft piloted by real pilots. American pilots, captured during the Korean War a few years earlier. They were told that if they could fly these jets and survive, that they could go home." A shrug. "None did, of course."

I touched the bloody handkerchief on my ear. "Of course. And so you were sent here, to wait. And wait some more. What was that like?"

"I lived as a Maine farmer, every day hating this place and its people. Bah. No culture, no sense of family, no real life. Just scratch a living out of this poor dirt and screw your neighbors."

"Why didn't you go home?"

"Home," he said, twisting his face as if the word itself was sour. "First, I have no money for such a trip." He looked up at me, fists clenched. "And what kind of home awaits me? The stupid bastards! They gave it all up. All of it! And without a fight."

"Miss the old Soviet Union, do you?" I asked.

Len glared at me. "What do you think, you fool? At one time we were the mightiest empire in the world. We started with nothing, nothing at all. A backward peasant country dismembered by war, and in less than a decade, we were making you and your allies tremble. We meant something. We were powerful, we strode across the world stage, and now. . . ." He nearly spat out the words. "Then we gave it all up, and for what? We have a drunken clown as a president. We have whores in Red Square and the Mafia ruling our cities, and that is what we have as we leave this century."

I looked around at the old gear and the radio and said, "How long since you've had contact from home? Five years? Ten?"

A shrug. "That sounds about right."

"In case you haven't noticed, your target air base has been closed for some years now," I said. "And the country you worked for doesn't even exist. There are ways of getting money. Why in hell didn't you pack it up and leave?"

He folded his arms, jutted out his jaw. "Because I am a Soviet soldier. I follow my orders. And my orders are to stay here and keep watch on this base. I cannot predict the future. The old Communists may come back into power. This air base may be used again by your Air Force. I am not a coward, and I do not shirk my duty. I stay here and follow my orders."

I shook my head. "You know, there's a guy I just met that you should talk with. You two would probably get along. Old soldiers from old empires, still fighting in the middle of the wreckage and debris."

"And you, you are not an old soldier?"

"At one time I was, but things have changed."

"Then why are you here? To arrest me? Bring me back to your superiors?"

I lowered my pistol, aimed in his direction. "You see, that's the problem. I was sent here to kill you."

And with that, I pulled the trigger of the 9mm twice.

Back at home and exhausted after my nights and days in the Maine woods, I slept late. After I unloaded the new clothing and toys I had bought up on my way to Cardiff, I went to my little upstairs office and my computer, and, remembering certain things that Eric had taught me, did a little research in the wild reaches of the world wide web.

Mr. Smith was as good as his word and arrived the next day. I watched from my upstairs office, flanked by my new toys, as the dark blue LTD bumped up the dirt driveway, and the two men started walking to the house. Old master and new master. They weren't very different.

I waited for the knock on the door before I wrapped some things up and went down to the kitchen. Special Agent Cameron and Mr. Smith stood at the door, the FBI man looking like he was on his way to the dentist, the government man with a large grin on his face.

"Am I being graced with both of you today?" I asked.

Cameron said, "I'll wait on the steps." He sat down gingerly on the stone steps to my house as Smith came into the kitchen. We sat at the table and I said, "Later this morning someone's coming to pump out my septic tank, and I'd rather spend the time looking into my septic tank than at you, Mr. Smith, so let's make this quick."

He smiled, self-satisfied. "You did well. Very good."

I made a show of looking surprised. "Surveillance. You guys were watching me."

A happy nod. "That we were."

"Your folks were good. Didn't notice a thing."

"They're the best."

"And what did they notice?" I asked.

Smith leaned back in the kitchen chair, the old wood groaning under the pressure. "They saw you conduct yourself well, performing a surveillance of the property for three days. They saw the target return early, and they heard two gunshots. They then saw you back up the target's pickup truck to the barn, stuff him in an old feed bag in the rear of the truck and then drive out at about midnight. On a bridge spanning the Queebunk River, you dumped your load, returned to the property. Then you left. Our team moved in, checked the bullet holes in the wall and the blood on the floor. We also found the evidence of the target's connection to Soviet military intelligence. Like I said, nicely done. There was even a typewritten note for the mailman, asking him to take care of the dog. You're an oldie and a softie, Owen."

I kept my hands steady on top of the table. "So I did a good job for you and your government friends, killing an old man who's no longer a threat to this country?"

The chair came down with a thunk. "Owen, in our little agency, we decide who's a threat or not. And then we decide what to do. And in this case, you did exactly as we asked by killing that old man. Very good."

"Really?" I asked.

"Not bad at all. In fact, we may extend our little agreement with you, have you perform a few other . . . unusual tasks."

My voice was flat. "In other words, you want to hire a killer."

"If you want to be blunt."

I looked down at the table, slowly shook my head. "Sorry. I'm not feeling well, and I have to go to the bathroom." I looked up and said, "Being retired and all, sometimes your body betrays you."

He waved a hand in the air. "Sure. You run along. We'll talk in a few minutes."

I got up from the kitchen table and went upstairs. Ten minutes later, I flushed the toilet and went to the head of the stairs. "Smith!" I called down. "Come up here for a moment, will you?"

I went into my office and was rummaging around in the closet as he came in and looked at my bookshelves and my humble computer, humming along on my desk. I came out of the closet with my 9mm and in one snap-quick motion, I inserted the barrel into his left ear.

"Hey!" he said, hands raised. With my free hand, I put a finger to my lips.

"Shush," I said. "Come over here and sit down. That's right, in front of the computer."

We moved slowly and I tried to keep everything focused, for I could feel something from him, a coiled sense of energy like a rattlesnake ready to strike. I said, "In less than five minutes, Smith, you'll be free to go, but if you try anything sneaky, anything at all, I'll blow your damn head off. Understand?"

"You'd be in a world of hurt," he said, no longer smiling.

"Not really," I said. "I don't think Special Agent Cameron would miss you that much, and in this county, I would only have to explain to the police and my neighbors and a couple of lawyers how I came to shoot a trespasser in my house. Perhaps I'd get a stretch, but in less than a month everything would be back to normal again, except that salesmen wouldn't dare come down that driveway. Have a seat."

He did, settling himself heavily into the chair. I pushed the pistol into his ear just a little more for emphasis, and I said, "Take hold of the mouse, and double-click on that little icon in the upper left-hand column."

Smith did, and through the connection of the pistol against his head, I felt his body tense up. "What the hell is this?" he demanded, his voice a step above a strained whisper.

"Oh, I'm quite proud of it," I said. "This is my very first webpage. See the nice headline, about a government conspiracy to murder old Soviets? Pretty catchy, don't you think? And right below that are half a dozen little thumbnail pictures of you, Smith, as you came up to my house a while ago. Digital cameras are amazing, aren't they? You can process and download pictures instantly. And you'd be surprised at what you can do with a microphone, some long wire and a cassette recorder. See those little speaker icons on the bottom? Double-click on the left one, why don't you."

His hand moved grudgingly and after the little snap-snap of the mouse came Smith's voice, coming from my computer's twin speakers. "Owen, in our little agency, we decide who's a threat or not. And then we decide what to do. And in this case, you did exactly as we asked by killing that old man. Very good."

I took a deep breath, feeling that intoxicating rush of putting everything on the line against a dangerous foe. "To repeat something you said, first time we met, the clock is running. You don't have any time for arguing. This page is up and active. I've posted messages to a dozen Internet discussion groups, inviting them to check out my webpage. And every second you argue, every second you try to wiggle out of what's going on, that means dozens and hundreds and thousands of visitors are going to see your lovely face and hear your thoughtful words. Think your bosses will be impressed next time they do your employee evaluation?"

"What do you want?" he asked, and as his shoulders sagged, I knew I had won.

"I close down the webpage, and you leave here and never come back, and none of your friends ever bother me again. Agreed?"

"Agreed," he said with about as much enthusiasm as a man agreeing to have a toenail removed with a chisel.

"Oh," I said. "One more thing. Stop bothering Special Agent Cameron. He's no friend of mine, but I'm used to him."

I pulled the pistol out of his ear and stepped back. He stood up, his face mottled red, his fists clenched. "Agreed."

I went over to the computer, double-clicked that, downloaded this, and in a moment the screen was blank.

Smith said, "You bastard."

I smiled. "That's the nicest thing that you've ever said to me."

Outside, as Smith stomped his way over to the parked LTD, I said to Cameron, "A moment of your time, Agent Cameron."

He looked over at me with tired eyes, and for the first time since he had first come to check up on me, I felt sorry for him.

"Yes? What do you want?"

What I wanted was to sit him down in my kitchen and talk to him, to find out what he saw in his mind's eye, his memory of that awful time in Waco and what happened that caused the torching of scores of people, setting off fuses that killed hundreds of people more, and to find out how he made it through, day after day.

But I said, "You owe me."

A slow nod. "You may be right. What do you have in mind?"

I told him. He thought about it for a moment, cocked his head.

"You got a deal," he said.

The LTD's horn blew twice as Smith leaned over and hammered the steering wheel, and Cameron managed a wan smile as he walked away.

"I don't envy you the ride back," I called out.

"Actually, I'm looking forward to it," he said.

Two days later I was driving north, Miriam at my side, holding my hand. She said, "I know Eric's big enough to hold down the store and close it up by himself tonight, but damn it, I don't like being kept in the dark like this."

"In a few minutes, all will be revealed," I said, driving easily with one hand. "I have a secret plan, m'dear."

"You do?" she asked, eyes a touch playful. "And what's that?"

I squeezed her hand. "If I told you, it wouldn't be a secret, now, would it."

She shook her head, muttered "you" and looked out the window.

But she didn't take her hand away.

After a while of driving, I turned right into the parking area of a small airport. The familiar sign said FEARLESS FERN'S FLYING SERVICE. She looked over at me, surprised. "What are we doing here?"

"You'll see soon enough," I said.

We got out of my truck and I grabbed her hand again as we walked around a small hangar. A Cessna was waiting, engine grumbling, propeller turning, and a bearded man standing under the wing nodded at me and I nodded back. Miriam tried to say something, but I pretended the noise of the engine was too loud. A few minutes later, seated in the rear and with earphones on and seat belts fastened, we were in the air, the bearded man piloting.

"Owen," she said to me, her voice static-filled over the intercom system. "What's this all about?"

I gently reached over and grasped her hand. "It means a number of things. It means you and I are going to Portland tonight, for dinner and to see a musical. We'll also be spending the night at a beautiful bed-and-breakfast near the harbor."

And savoring the new agreement I had with Cameron, I added, "Why don't we plan on getting away at least once every month? And you can name the place."

She nodded, blinked hard a few times and then looked out the side window. She held my hand all the way until we landed.

Some nights later I was in my pickup, engine idling. Next to me, a small ruck-sack in his lap, sat Len Molowski—or Leonid Malenkov, if you prefer.

"My ears are still ringing from when you shot at me," he said, looking out across at the barn where he had lived in the upstairs loft for the better part of a week.

"You're a farmer. Ever hear the proverb of how a farmer gets a mule to pay attention?"

Even in the darkened truck cab, I could tell that he was grinning. "Yes, I have. You strike him over the head with a wooden plank."

"So consider those shots two whacks over the head, Len. I had to make you understand that you'd been noticed, and that the next guy to come to your farm wouldn't be as thoughtful or as charming as I was. Frankly, all that talk about being a good Soviet soldier was a bit boring."

The man sighed. "Perhaps you are right. But after decades of keeping such a secret, I had to talk and talk, and I had to convince you and myself that what I did was right. I had to know that these years had a purpose. That they were not a waste."

"Did it work?"

Another sigh. "No, I do not think so. When you spread your blood on the floor, told me to play dead so you could put me in the truck in a feed bag, and when you dumped your camping gear in another feed bag and threw it into the river, I was humiliated. A man who was supposed to be my enemy was trying to help me. Why did you do that?"

I rubbed at the steering wheel. "It was a long war, the Cold War. There had to be an end to it, the last two old soldiers coming to an understanding. It just made sense. That's all I can say."

I reached into my coat pocket, pulled out a thick envelope and passed it over. "Here. Inside's a goodly amount of cash. Pay me back whenever you can. About a half mile down this road is the center of town. There's a Greyhound bus station, bus leaves in an hour to Portland. From there . . . well, you can go anywhere you want. But if I were you, I might head to New York City. Go to a place called Brighton Beach. There's a lot of Russian émigrés who live there. You might find a way to get home if you ask the right people."

"This money, this is charity, and I cannot—"

"Oh, shut up. You're still a marked man, and it's in both our interests that you get the hell out of here. All right? Now, get. Before you miss the bus."

Len waited for a moment, and then the envelope rustled as he packed it into his rucksack. He held out his hand to me. "I never forget. *Da svidaniya.*"

"*Da svidaniya* to you, too."

He got out of the truck, a stranger in an odd land, and I watched him as he walked down the road, rucksack on his back. I thought about what lay ahead of him. A bumpy bus ride to Portland. Then another long ride to New York, to a city full of strangers. Then . . . who knows. Perhaps he would try to make a living with the rest of the émigrés in that crowded city. Perhaps he would go home, try to adjust to a motherland that had changed so much. It seemed inevitable that he would face poverty and loneliness, with no one to care where he went or where he stayed.

I started up my truck and headed back home.

God, how I envied him.

# Ed McBain

## The Victim

ED MCBAIN is Evan Hunter. Hunter wrote *The Blackboard Jungle* and the screenplay for Alfred Hitchcock's classic suspense movie "The Birds." McBain is the author of the 87th Precinct series. Taken together, McBain/Hunter have had lasting effects on their society and their times. Perhaps the most inspiring aspect of his/their whole career is that the books continue to get better, richer, deeper in every way. His recent novel *Candyman*, written as a collaboration between Hunter/McBain, is a tour de force and one of the most stunning literary gambits of the year. In "The Victim," published in the collection *Running from Legs and Other Stories*, Ed/Evan are both in top form.

# The Victim

*Ed McBain*

An afternoon in October, ten years ago. She was nineteen years old, and a storm broke just as she was leaving the Columbia campus. She tried to cover her head with her notebook, but she was soaked to the marrow within minutes. Standing helplessly in the middle of the sidewalk, not knowing whether to run back for the shelter of one of the buildings or ahead to the subway kiosk, she noticed a red Volkswagen at the curb, its door open. A young man was leaning across the front seat.

"Hey!" he shouted. "Get in before you drown!" Then, seeing the look of hesitation on her face, he immediately added, "I'm not a weirdo, I promise."

She got into the car.

"My name's Bobby Hollis," he said.

"How do you do, Bobby?"

"What's *your* name?"

"Laura Pauling."

"Laura and Bobby."

"Yes. Laura and Bobby."

Wide grin, mischievous blue eyes, straight brown hair a bit too carelessly combed, falling onto his forehead, long and lanky Bobby—oh, how the girls on campus went for Bobby! Laura had hooked herself a big one out there in the rain. A young man who'd been on the dean's list for three successive semesters, wrote a column for the school newspaper, played the lead in the drama group's presentation of *Arsenic and Old Lace*, and also played the clarinet. "Would you like to hear the glissando passage at the beginning of 'Rhapsody in Blue'?" A young man who, most important of all, was absolutely crazy about—

Her.

Wow.

Little Laura Pauling. Five foot four, mousy brown hair that sort of matched her brown eyes. Fairly decent figure but not anything anyone in his right mind would rave about. Except Bobby Hollis, who maybe *wasn't* in his right mind.

Wow.

Laura had hooked herself the seventh wonder of the *world* out there in the rain. When at last he asked her to marry him, she accepted at once. Of *course*, she accepted! And before she knew it, she had two children who were surely the eighth and *ninth* wonders, and eventually she forgot what she'd been doing up there on that uptown campus. Forgot she'd been studying to . . . well, become something. Well, that wasn't important. Well, yes, it was important, but the hell with it.

Laura had been willing to go along with changing dirty diapers and wiping runny noses so long as she believed Bobby loved her. After all, somebody had to do those things while Bobby was busy making a career for himself. Somebody had to keep those old home fires burning while Bobby was out chasing—

Out chasing.

Period.

She learned about it from a well-meaning associate of his who'd had too many martinis.

"Laura," he'd said, "forgive me if I'm brutally frank, okay?"

"What is it, Dave?"

"I know a man's supposed to look the other the way and keep his mouth shut when a friend of his is . . . well . . . playing around. Supposed to nudge the guy in the ribs, wink at him, gee, you son of a gun. But I like you too much to . . ."

"I don't want to hear it," she'd said.

But he'd told her, anyway.

Five years ago.

Tonight, she watched her husband in action at her own dinner table.

A fierce September rain lashed the window panes of their sixth floor apartment, and far below she could hear the sound of automobile tires hissing on wet asphalt. The clock on the dining room wall read exactly ten o'clock. Over coffee and dessert, Bobby was telling a New York atrocity story to their guests. Laura watched him from the opposite end of the long table, listening only distractedly. She knew it was happening again, and that she was helpless to stop it.

Bobby's eyes twinkled as he told the story. He liked New York atrocity stories, especially those about cab drivers. A smile was forming on his mouth now in anticipation of his own punch line. She knew he would burst into immodest laughter the moment he finished the story. She knew him so well. She'd been married to him for nine years. He was her beloved Bobby. Her spouse. Her mate. The father of her two adorable children. Under the table, his left hand was resting on Nessie Winkler's thigh.

"By now, this is the *fifth* time we've circled the Plaza," he said. "Now even if I were fresh off the banana boat, I'd begin to recognize the same hotel going by five *times*, wouldn't you think? I'd begin to maybe *suspect* a little something?"

Had he just squeezed Nessie's thigh under the table?

If not, why had she turned to him in that quick conspiratorial way and looked dopily into his face? Nessie. For Agnes. But you could not call a lissome blonde Agnes. Agnes was for the comic characters of the world. There was nothing funny about Nessie Winkler or the fact that Bobby had his fingers spread on her thigh under the table.

"So finally I tapped on the glass—they're all so terrified of getting held up these days—and he slid open the partition, and I told him he'd better take me to Forty-seventh and Fifth *immediately*, and do you know what he said?"

Lucille came in from the kitchen just then, and stood immediately inside the swinging door, visibly nervous. She was a plain, brown-haired, pudding-faced woman of perhaps twenty-six and Laura suspected this was the first dinner party she'd ever served. Everyone at the table was watching Bobby, waiting to hear the end of his cab-driver story.

Lucille said, "Ma'am?" and Bobby turned to her immediately and snapped, "Would you *mind*, please?"

He leaned toward his guests then, and grinned, and in the heavy Brooklyn accent the cabby must have used, delivered the long-awaited zinger to his story.

"He looked me straight in the eye and said, 'Look, mister, you shoulda *tole* me you was a New Yorker!' "

He burst out laughing, just as Laura knew he would. Nessie burst out laughing, an instant later. Laura laughed, too. Politely. Everyone was laughing but Lucille, who was standing just behind Nessie's chair now, looking somewhat bewildered.

"Yes, Lucille?" Laura said.

"Ma'am, shall I start clearing?"

"Please."

Bobby's hand was still under the table. Laura watched him incredulously. A fork slid off the plate Lucille was lifting from the table, clattering to the floor. She flushed a deep red and immediately knelt beside Nessie's chair to retrieve it. When she rose again, her eyes met Laura's.

There was knowledge in those eyes.

She had seen.

"Delicious," Nessie said, and folded her napkin.

At five minutes to twelve, Laura went into the kitchen to pay Mrs. Armstrong and Lucille and to thank them for helping to make the dinner party such a success. Mrs. Armstrong accepted her check and told Laura what a pleasure it always was to work for such a fine lady. Lucille took her check and said nothing. Her eyes avoided Laura's.

Mrs. Armstrong and Lucille were wearing almost identical black topcoats and carrying black handbags. Mrs. Armstrong was carrying a red umbrella. Lucille had no umbrella, and when Laura asked her if she'd like to borrow one, she replied, "No, thank you, ma'am, I'm only catching a bus on Fifth," which was the longest sentence she'd uttered all night long.

Her eyes still avoided Laura's.

It was as if she were somehow blaming Laura for what she'd seen earlier.

When the two women left the apartment, Laura double-locked the service door behind them. Bobby was sprawled on the living room sofa, sipping a cognac and watching an old cowboy movie on television.

"Nice party," he said.

"I thought it went smoothly," Laura said.

"Want a nightcap?"

"Thanks, no. Are the kids okay?"

"What?"

"I asked you to look in on them while I . . ."

"Slipped my mind," Bobby said. "Got involved in the movie here."

"I'll do it," Laura said, and went out of the room and down the corridor to the children's bedrooms.

Both of them were asleep. Seven-year-old Jessica had the blanket twisted around her like a strait jacket, and Laura had difficulty unwinding it without awakening her. She extricated her daughter at last, and then kissed her on the forehead and went next door to where five-year-old Michael was sleeping with his face to the wall. Laura touched his brow, smoothed his hair, kissed him on the cheek, and tucked the blanket tighter around his shoulder.

When she came back into the living room, Bobby was still watching television. He did not look at Laura as she came into the room.

She sat beside him on the sofa and, without preamble, said, "About Nessie."

"What about her?" Bobby asked.

He still did not turn away from the screen, where a band of hapless cowboys were being ambushed at a waterhole by a larger band of Indians.

"Do you find her attractive?" Laura asked. She was not at all asking about Nessie Winkler's attractiveness; only a blind man would not have noticed her startling beauty. She was simply asking whether Bobby was sleeping with her. Nor was she even asking that. She didn't know *what* she was asking. Maybe she only wanted to know if he still loved her.

"I think she's a good-looking woman, yes," Bobby said.

"That doesn't answer my question," Laura said, and became immediately frightened of what might follow. She did not want this confrontation. She had been foolish to bring it to this dangerous point in the short space of several sentences.

Bobby turned from the television screen. His eyes met hers. Blue, steady, level—challenging. Evenly spacing his words, stretching them out interminably, he said, "What, exactly, *is*, your, question?"

Tell him, she thought.

Tell him the question is one of trust; you either trust someone completely, or you don't trust him at all.

Tell him you stopped trusting him five years ago.

Tell him you would appreciate it if he kept his whores out of your home where they only embarrass and humiliate you before the hired help.

*Tell* him, damn it!

"Well?" he said.

She was trembling.

She smiled and said, "I forgot the question."

His eyes held hers a moment longer, as if to make certain the matter had been finally and irrevocably put to rest. He turned back to the television screen.

"I think . . ." Laura started.

"Yes?" he said.

"I think I'll go down for a walk."

"At this hour?"

"I need some air."

"It's still raining, isn't it?"

"I think it's let up."

"Suit yourself," Bobby said, and shrugged.

Laura walked out into the entrance foyer. She took her yellow slicker and rain hat from the closet, put them on, and let herself out of the apartment.

The streets glistened with reflected light, green and yellow and red from the traffic signals, white from the overhead street lamps, a warmer white from the headlights of infrequently passing automobiles. The rain had indeed stopped. The city smelled fresh and clean.

Laura walked.

There was something evocative about the scent of the streets and the sound of rainwater rushing along the curbs. She could remember coming downstairs after summer thunderstorms when she was a child, taking off her shoes and socks against her mother's wishes, splashing in the curbside puddles. She could remember being fifteen and wildly infatuated with a boy named Charlie, with whom she'd walked dizzily through a springtime city washed by rain. And she could remember meeting Bobby—in the rain.

What do I do now? she wondered.

Do I confront him the way I started to do five minutes ago?

What do I say?

Look, Bobby, enough is enough, I want out. I'm thirty-one years old, there's still a life ahead of me if I can find the courage to reach out for it. I don't have to stay married to a man who's got his hands all over every new girl in town, the hell with that.

But is that what I really want to do?

Throw away nine years of marriage because my husband has a few minor flirtations . . . or adventures . . . or affairs . . . or *whatever* the hell you choose to call—damn it, I choose to call them infidelities! He has been *unfaithful* to me!

But . . .

Even so . . .

Do I . . . do I break up a marriage because of infidelity? Even the word sounded old-fashioned. Wouldn't it be better, really, to look the other way, pretend it never happened, pretend it wouldn't happen again?

Like the rainstorm, she thought.

It had been raining at ten o'clock when Bobby explored Nessie's smooth white flesh under a similarly white tablecloth. But the rain had stopped shortly after midnight, and now the streets smelled fresh and clean. There was hardly even a memory of the storm now.

Wasn't that the best way, after all?

Banish each sudden storm to a safe distance in the past, and then quickly forget it?

Bobby was a good provider. The children had a good father. He was handsome, witty, hard-working, and fun to be with most of the time.

Count your blessings, she thought. You've got everything you want or need. He probably loves you to death. It's just that he has a roving eye. It's the same in every marriage. Live with it. Forget it.

The hollow reassurances echoed noisily in her mind, raising a mental clatter so overwhelming that at first she wasn't certain she'd heard the other sound at all. She stopped mid-stride, stood stock still on the sidewalk, heard the click of the traffic signal as the light changed to red at the end of the block.

Silence.

And then the sound again.

A whimper.

She turned toward the brownstone on the right.

The woman lay crouched in the far corner of the small courtyard, in the right angle formed by the facade of the building and the side of the stoop leading to the front door. She was wearing a black coat, and Laura could barely see her until she moved closer to the low iron railing that surrounded the courtyard.

She peered deeper into the gloom.

The woman whimpered again, and Laura went immediately to her. The woman's coat was open, her clothes disarrayed, her dress pulled up over rain-spattered pantyhose.

The pantyhose were jaggedly torn.

At first, they didn't recognize each other.

The courtyard was quite dark, and the woman was crouched into the deepest corner of it, as if seeking anonymity there. She looked up as Laura knelt beside her, and flinched as though expecting to be struck. Her eyes were unfocused, she continued whimpering piteously, and then the whimper changed to a name, and she repeated the name over and over again—"Oh, Mrs. Hollis, oh, Mrs. Hollis, oh, Mrs. Hollis"—as if the litany would invoke the past and somehow change it to a brighter present. Laura was startled at first to hear her name, and then she looked into the woman's face—and saw that it was Lucille.

She leaned in close to her.

Lucille was trying to tell her what had happened. She was not articulate to begin with, and shock now rendered her almost unintelligible. Laura gathered that she and Mrs. Armstrong had parted outside the building, the cook to walk toward Lexington Avenue to board a subway train, Lucille toward Fifth to catch a downtown bus. The man had confronted her suddenly . . . stepping out of a doorway . . . ramming his forearm across her throat . . . knife point coming up, gleaming in the dull glow of the street lamp further up the street. He'd forced her into the courtyard, into the darkness . . . forced her legs apart . . . slashed her pantyhose . . .

"I didn't know anybody was on the street with me, I didn't hear a thing, didn't see a thing until he . . . until he . . ."

Suddenly Lucille was sobbing.

And Laura began to tremble.

She trembled with rage and with fear.

Seeing Lucille this way, vulnerable and exposed, whimpering like a small animal that had been mercilessly beaten, Laura wanted only to kill whoever had done this, find the man who had so abused this woman and simply and swiftly kill him.

At the same time, she was terrified that the man might suddenly appear again, spring out of the darkness to claim her as his next victim, overpower her as he had Lucille, leave her quaking and whimpering on the stone floor of the same courtyard.

"I'm going to call the police," she said. "If I leave you for a minute, will you be all right?"

"No, please," Lucille said.

"I'm only going as far as the nearest telephone."

"No. I'm bleeding, I think. Oh God, Mrs. Hollis, I'm bleeding."

"The police will send an ambulance."

"No, I don't want the police."

"What?"

"No police. Please."

"Why not?"

"They'll think it was me."

The two women looked at each other, their eyes searching in the darkness.

Somewhere a rainspout poured water into a catch basin. There was the sound of the steady splashing, and then the sharp click of the traffic signal changing again. Their faces were suddenly tinted green.

"I didn't do nothing to cause it," Lucille said.

"I know that."

"The police'll think . . ."

"No, Lucille. They'll think you were victimized."

"No. My husband'll . . ."

"Lucille, we've *got* to call the police."

"No, ma'am, please."

"Did you get a good look at him?"

"Yes."

"Then you've got to describe him to the police."

"No. No, ma'am, please, I can't do that. I can't let my husband find out about this."

"Lucille . . ."

"Ma'am, if you'll help me find an open drugstore . . ."

"Lucille, listen to me . . ."

"If I can maybe stop the bleeding and get some new pantyhose, then my husband won't know what . . ."

"Your husband's *got* to know, damn it! You were *raped!*"

The force of her own voice surprised her.

"He raped you," Laura said.

"I know, ma'am, but . . ."

"You've got to report it to the police."

"Then my husband'll know."

"Yes, Lucille. He'll know you were raped."

"But then he'll think . . ."

"It doesn't matter *what* he thinks. You were a victim, Lucille."

"They won't find him, anyway," Lucille said, shaking her head. "I'll tell them, and they'll know what he looks like, but they won't find him, it won't do any good, they'll think I wanted what happened, they'll . . ."

*"Stop it!"* Laura said.

The courtyard went silent.

Lucille's eyes met Laura's. They were the same eyes that had seen Bobby's hand in Nessie Winkler's lap. They searched Laura's face skeptically now, almost accusingly.

"If it was you," she said, "would *you* go to the police?"

"Yes," Laura said.

Yes, she thought. I would march into a police station and up to the polished brass railing and I would say to the desk sergeant, "I want to report a rape. I've been raped." Yes, she thought. I would.

They continued staring at each other.

Lucille nodded almost imperceptibly.

"Yes," Laura said. "Believe me, I would."

Lucille nodded again, more firmly this time.

Laura helped her to her feet and together they walked toward Fifth Avenue in search of a taxi. She had no idea where the local police station was but she expected the cab driver would help them find it. She would stay with Lucille while she talked to the detectives. She would remain by her side and see her through this.

And then she would go back to the apartment where she would hang her yellow slicker and rain hat in the hall closet. And she would go into the bedroom where Bobby would be lying asleep snoring lightly—he always snored so lightly, she knew so much about this man she was now ready to leave.

I want to report a rape, she would say. I've been raped.

A taxi was approaching.

Laura nodded, and then raised her hand to hail it.

# Pete Hamill

## The Poet of Pulp

WHILE WE don't often run nonfiction in this collection, "The Poet of Pulp" is such a fine piece of writing by Pete Hamill we felt duty bound to include it. Rarely has a crime writer been profiled in such depth or with such elegance. To complement an especially compelling Evan Hunter story, here is Hamill's article from *The New Yorker*.

# The Poet of Pulp

## How Ed McBain Made the Precinct House a Respectable Place

*Pete Hamill*

For decades, I've had a secret literary pleasure: the novels of Ed McBain. As far as I know, they're not taught; they're not part of the canon. But, in some strange way, McBain and I have been pilgrims together on a long journey through what he calls the big, bad city; the novels are as woven into my life as the Lexington Avenue express. No matter where I live, part of me is always in the 87th Precinct.

I began reading the McBain novels in the late '50s, when I was starting out as a writer. The first one I read was *The Mugger*, which started this way, from inside the head of a criminal:

> The city could be nothing but a woman, and that's good because your business is women.
> You know her tossed head in the auburn crowns of molting autumn foliage, Riverhead and the park. . . . She is a woman, and she is your woman, and in the fall she wears a perfume of mingled wood smoke and carbon dioxide.

The paragraphs that followed were a rhapsodic and gritty evocation of the city and its female nature, written in a shade of purple; today they seem more than a little ripe. But when I first read them, in 1958, they pulled me swiftly into the story and kept me there. Unlike so many of the books I was reading—by Hemingway, Fitzgerald—these novels were not set in Pamplona or Antibes; they were about the city where I lived. I stayed up most of the night reading the short novel, moving through the city with the detectives of the 87th Precinct.

As an apprentice, I admired McBain's solid paragraphs and the absence of

waste or decoration. I admired his dialogue, too. McBain understood that a specially tuned ear was essential to defining the people of the city that he called Isola.
He showed that speech on a printed page depended upon rhythmic approximation, and not the exactitude of a transcript. Yet McBain wasn't asking the reader to
pause and take note; he was asking the reader to keep reading. Everything in
McBain's work served the story.

In time, I learned that Ed McBain was a pseudonym for the mainstream
novelist Evan Hunter, who had established himself in 1954, with *The Blackboard
Jungle*. (Hunter's many other credits include the novel of '50s suburban adultery
*Strangers When We Meet* and the screenplay for Alfred Hitchcock's *The Birds*).
But for me the McBain novels came first. They usually started with a corpse—on
the floor, on the street, in a snowbank—and then moved swiftly into answering
the classic questions about how the body got there. The process of unraveling the
mystery was never mechanical, and the novels were at once surprising and familiar. They were about a world I knew as a New Yorker and a newspaperman—
they took me to places that I'd seen a dozen times as a young reporter—and, like
any great journalist, McBain gave life to that world through details. *In Long Time
No See*, published in the late '70s, a building superintendent named Reynolds lets
two detectives into a third-floor apartment. A blind woman is lying on the floor
beside a refrigerator.

> Her throat had been slit, her head was twisted at an awkward angle in
> a pool of her own blood. The refrigerator door was open. Crisping trays
> and meat trays had been pulled from it, their contents dumped onto the
> floor. There were open canisters and boxes strewn everywhere. Under-
> foot, the floor was a gummy mess of blood and flour, sugar and corn-
> flakes, ground coffee, and crumpled biscuits, lettuce leaves and broken
> eggs. Drawers had been overturned, forks, knives and spoons piled hap-
> hazardly in a junk-heap jumble, paper napkins, spaghetti tongs, a
> corkscrew, a cheese grater, place mats, candles all thrown on the floor
> together with the drawers that had contained them.

The victims, of course, are not always dead, as in *Blood Relatives*:

> The front of her dress had been ripped, and she tried to hold the
> torn sides of the *V* closed over her brassiere as she ran through the
> rain. It had been raining since 10 o'clock. The rain was neither cruel
> nor driving now; it had changed to a gentle drizzle that sent mist
> drifting up from the pavement. In the distance, the green globes of the
> 87th precinct shone through the rain and through the mist.

In McBain's city, the precinct house is an outpost of civilization. To be sure,
the cops of the 87th Precinct are not saints. Their private lives are often untidy.
There are racists among them, and fools and schemers, too. They would not be
surprised by the cases of Abner Louima or Amadou Diallo. But such aberrations
would outrage most of them; even the most racist of McBain's cops, Fat Ollie
Weeks, recognizes that there are lines he cannot cross. McBain's cops work in a
city where it would be entirely plausible for a crackhead to hit a stranger in the

head with a brick. And without cops, McBain implies, there would be no city at all. In that sense, his novels speak for conservative values. In the end, we have cops because we have bad guys. The cop, like the novelist, can bring sympathy, even compassion, to his pursuit of even the most atrocious killer.

The lead detective of the 87th Precinct novels is Steve Carella, but the job of detection and pursuit is done by a team that includes detectives, forensic specialists, lab technicians, psychologists, and a cast of informants. This reflects actual police work, and it also follows the novelist's plan. From the first of the McBain novels, Hunter's design was to feature what he calls a "splintered" hero.

In clumsier hands, splintering the tasks and talents of the squad could lead to novelistic anarchy. That never happens in McBain's narratives, which are carefully focused on the quest for understanding and resolution; they are as simple as myths. Carella, who is usually at the center of each novel, is the best detective on the squad—intelligent, skeptical, proud of what he knows, modest about what he doesn't, at peace with the bad hours and the lousy pay. He knows that he must work with all the other cops. They include Bert Kling, whose doomed romantic life provides a continuing narrative; Detective Meyer Meyer, a patient, serious, and gutsy cop who is Jewish and prematurely bald, and whose sense of humor helps him through the inevitable bad patches; Cotton Hawes, a big, handsome, sometimes reckless bachelor with many women in his life; and Artie Brown, the only black man on the squad, who often struggles with bigotry, black and white. In minor roles there are women cops, police brass, and technicians.

The characters, in short, are part of an ensemble; as in life, the stories may be overlapping, unconnected, and parallel. In McBain's 1971 *Hail, Hail, the Gang's All Here!* there are (if I've counted accurately) fourteen plot lines. If this sounds familiar, it's because the concept has been appropriated in various ways by television cop shows like *Homicide* and *N.Y.P.D. Blue*. In *Hill Street Blues*, the main policeman was named Furillo, in what I took to be an homage to Carella.

Hunter did not invent what came to be known as the "police procedural" (a label believed to have been coined by Anthony Boucher, who reviewed crime novels for the *Times Book Review* from 1951 to 1968). He doesn't like the term; it makes the novels sound as if they were about the mere clerking of crime. There were police detectives in American letters well before the first McBain novels began appearing, and readers and writers of crime fiction were also aware of Georges Simenon's Inspector Jules Maigret, the pipe-smoking French detective who was featured in more than seventy books written between 1931 and 1972. But McBain's novels were more realistic than their predecessors, in that he used a full range of the modern tools of detection. Above all, they were much better written. And, beginning with the first McBain, *Cop Hater*, published in 1956, the novels moved beyond the archetype of the Master Detective, a literary tradition that included Maigret (although Simenon and McBain resemble each other in several ways: productivity, craft, professionalism). McBain's people were cops—real cops. And when a crime is committed in the real world cops, not amateurs, are called in to deal with the mess.

This had not usually been the case in American crime fiction. During Prohibition and the Depression, the private eye—Sam Spade, Philip Marlowe—had come to dominate the popular imagination. Most urban police departments—along with big-city political machines—had been corrupted by the easy money that flowed from the bootleggers during the '20s; in many towns during the Depression, police power was marshaled against unions, leftists, protesting war veterans. The private eye was not an agent of the state, and thus had a special appeal for the children of Irish, Jewish, and Italian immigrants—that is, of people who came from countries where the police were an oppressive force. Many Americans grew up, as I did, wary of ever going to the police for help.

But readers and writers of crime novels were changed by the experiences of the Second World War and Korea. In the armed forces, they learned that winning a war required the skills of many specialists. For such men (and many women), the platoon was the central unit of survival—and of eventual triumph—in the same way that the family was the basic unit of civilian society. The men of the 87th Precinct are described in the early books as veterans, and they form their own platoon. They are also a kind of family.

The precinct's job is to ward off threats to the family of the squad and the wider family of the city. The city around the detectives changes; they do not. In more than forty years, Carella has aged only a decade. In the fiftieth 87th Precinct novel, *The Last Dance*, being published this month by Simon & Schuster, Carella's fortieth birthday is behind him, barely.

But, if the elasticity of the calendar reminds us that we are reading fiction, McBain's picture of the dense, layered, sometimes scary city suggests that his achievement is much bigger than its fifty parts. In fact, I read this latest McBain as if it were a piece of a larger project: a multipart novel about New York in the second half of the century. That grand novel is now about 3 million words, and it does not seem too much of a stretch to compare it to, say, Eugene Sue's *The Mysteries of Paris*, in which crime and misdeeds and the pursuit of the guilty are used to illuminate a great city during a particular era. Sue—and Balzac—took readers to places where nobody else could go. In his own way, in our time, so does Ed McBain.

Over the past four decades, McBain has taken us into boardrooms and crack houses; into glossy law offices, the Broadway-like theater (which he revisits in *The Last Dance*), import-export firms, the music business, publishing, network television, art galleries. He has made vivid the lives of strangers, various and bizarre. He has challenged us to think about the precarious value of human life in a huge American city—a place populated by blind beggars, youth gangs, predatory rapists, Jamaican drug posses, con men, blackmailers, race hustlers, kidnappers, burglars, and stool pigeons.

Along the way, the reader can see how the city's language changes: the topical references change; the immigrants change; the names change. There are seven daily newspapers in the early novels; by the time of *The Last Dance*, there are three. One can trace the arrival of television, drugs, and racism. Almost from the beginning, the books are imbued with a nostalgia that is the permanent curse of so many native New Yorkers. In a city where all is in flux, New Yorkers of every generation carry around the memory of a lost city. In 1977, Carella (in *Long Time No See*) was feeling nostalgia even about murder:

> There used to be a time when most murders started as family quarrels resolved with a hatchet or a gun. Find a lady dead on the bathroom floor, go look for her husband. Find a man with both legs

broken and a knife in his heart besides, go look for his girlfriend's husband, and try to get there fast before the husband threw her off the roof in the bargain. Those were the good old days.

Still, McBain is too much of a New Yorker to become maudlin. Near the end of *The Big Bad City*, the forty-ninth 87th Precinct novel, published last year, Carella sits with the black detective, Artie Brown. Carella is remembering old cases, riffing about cops who died and bad guys who were punished:

> Jesus, remember the times? I remember them all, Artie. I remember all of it, all of it. Every single minute. It goes by too fast, Artie. I'll be forty in October. Where did it all go, Artie?"
> He looked up.
> "Artie?" he said.
> Brown was snoring lightly.

Several times in the past year, I met with Evan Hunter in his apartment, on the twenty-second floor of a building in the East Seventies. He is seventy-three but talks with the restless energy of a much younger man. He is lean and trim, with thinning hair and a neat beard that is scratched with gray. He usually wore a sweater, slacks, and loafers, and was at once relaxed and focused. He used to smoke, but three heart attacks have cured him of the habit.

Hunter has published more than ninety works of fiction, including four children's books, and his publisher says that he has sold more than a 100 million books around the world. He has won the Grand Master Award from the Mystery Writers of America and the Diamond Dagger from the British Crime Writers Association. He's had good luck with film. Both *Strangers When We Meet* and *The Blackboard Jungle* became films, and the director Frank Perry made a lovely small movie from Hunter's 1968 novel *Last Summer*. In 1963, Akira Kurosawa transformed an 87th Precinct novel called *King's Ransom* into a thriller called *High and Low*, starring Toshiro Mifune; it has been remade three more times in Japan, and Martin Scorsese is planning to produce another version.

"It's always been an odd kind of success," Hunter told me. "*The Blackboard Jungle* was a blockbuster success, but I was hardly attached to it—it wasn't my movie. *Strangers When We Meet* made a lot of money; and I got to write the screenplay, but still . . . *Last Summer* was a good film, but it came in second to *Easy Rider* that season. I always felt like an outsider in Hollywood. I always felt like I was going out to do a job, putting on the leather gloves, and, you know, get the money and go home." In 1997, Hunter published a short memoir, *Me and Hitch*, about working with Hitchcock. The laconic ninety-page book is devoid of illusions, either about the British director or about Hunter's own career in Hollywood.

Hunter talked in a rueful way about other unsatisfactory parts of his writing life. "The experiences I had in the theater never resulted in a hit play," he said. "So I never felt part of that inside theatrical community where you call Orso's and reserve three tables and rush right over. I never felt that." He shook his head and shrugged. "And I never felt the sort of acceptance one gets from the literary community. It's as if Evan Hunter got dismissed along the way. And, with Ed

McBain, I've never felt quite accepted in the mystery writers community because they go, 'He's Evan Hunter slumming.' It's a strange thing. I never felt that niche that would make me feel enormously comfortable."

Hunter was married for the third time in 1997. His wife is an elegant, dark-haired Yugoslavian woman named Dragica Dimitrijevic, and he has dedicated both *The Last Dance* and its predecessor to her. (His second marriage, to Mary Vann, ended several years ago.) On this morning, Dragica was out shopping. Their dog, a five-year-old Maltese, Sasha, began barking at a cable that was whipping around outside the window. Hunter shushed the dog, then stood up and explained the harmlessness of the cable to Sasha. He paused at the window. The East River was below us, and a barge was moving sluggishly on its opaque surface. Queens was on the right, the Bronx in the distance. "It's a beautiful view, isn't it?" he said.

The beautiful view was due north along the edge of Manhattan to East Harlem, where Hunter was born, in 1926, and where he lived until he was twelve. His name at birth was Salvatore Lombino; he was the only child of Charles F. and Marie Coppola Lombino.

"My father was a substitute letter carrier," he told me. "In those days, when you joined the Post Office Department, you had to be a substitute for a certain amount of time before you became a quote regular unquote. But when the Depression started they froze the list, and he was stuck, earning eight bucks a week. We moved in with my grandparents. My grandfather was a tailor, and he made all my clothes. I had tailor-made suits when I was eight years old. I was the best-dressed kid in the slums."

The family lived on 120th Street between First and Second Avenues, two blocks from Sal's grandfather's shop. "There were people from all the immigrant groups," Hunter said. "There was a German lady who lived on the third floor, Jewish people elsewhere in the building. It was a very quiet neighborhood at that time, in terms of crime. Although it wasn't just an Italian neighborhood, there was an Italian feeling to it. When I went to Italy for the first time, in 1949, and I got to Naples, I heard the same sounds I heard in the streets when I was growing up. The same street sounds, the peddlers . . . There was no violence then. There were no street gangs. Sure, it was divided. There was East Harlem, where we lived, and then you crossed Lexington Avenue and you were in black Harlem. And I used to go with my father all the time to the Apollo, way over on the West Side, with a largely black audience. We used to get out of there at midnight and walk back home and there was never a problem. Never."

He has a great affection for his father. Clearly, Charles Lombino was responsible for encouraging his son's creative side. "My father had a band," Hunter went on. "He played drums. He supplemented his income by playing weddings, engagement parties—he met my mother at an engagement party where he was playing. He had bands called the Louisiana Five and the Louisiana Rhythm Kings. He had a band called the Phantom Five, where they all came out in white hoods. They must've looked like Ku Klux Klan members. That's how he met my mother. He took off the hood and said 'Hi!' "

Hunter smiled broadly remembering Charles Lombino in the years of the Depression. "He was a very smart man," he said. "Totally uneducated, but very inventive and creative. He started businesses all the time. He started something called the Ace Bureau of Clippings—the A.B.C. He'd look in newspapers and find an article, say, about somebody whose wife had just given birth to a baby boy. He'd clip it out. Then he'd send a letter saying, 'I have some articles about you in the newspaper, would you be interested in having them?' And they paid him for the clippings. It was like a clipping service, and he was doing it out of his own kitchen. He started a pool hall. Failed. He started a crochet-beading business. At that time, in the twenties, all the women were wearing crocheted beaded dresses. They were high fashion. But then they went out of fashion—and that failed. The only thing that paid any money was his band."

In 1938, the family moved to the Bronx. Hunter's father encouraged him in many ways; together they mounted puppet shows and printed their own newspaper. When Sal was a teenager, he announced that he wanted to be an artist. He'd been drawing for as long as he could remember, sometimes copying characters from the comics, and subliminally learning the fundamentals of narrative from such strips as *Terry and the Pirates.* The hobby became a skill and the skill evolved into a wider ambition: to be a painter. He finished high school at sixteen, in 1942, and won a scholarship to the Art Students League; a year later, he was accepted at Cooper Union.

"My mother was always more pragmatic than my father," Hunter said. For a while, she worked as a clerk in the mail room of the publishing house Harcourt, Brace. "She'd say, 'Why don't you go to engineering school like all your friends? Why do you want to go to art school?' 'Cause I want to be an artist, Mom.' "

Then, as now, the Cooper Union art school was a rigorous place, its scholarship students drawn by competitive examination from the elite of the city's talented young. Sal Lombino soon discovered that it was one thing to be the best artist on East 120th Street, or even in the entire East Bronx, and quite another to go up against the students at Cooper Union. He worked hard. Influenced by such Disney films as *Snow White and the Seven Dwarfs, Pinocchio,* and *Fantasia,* he began designing a layout for an animated film. But he was also getting discouraged. In 1944, with the war on, he joined the navy.

For the first time, at the age of eighteen, he was away from home, meeting people from the world beyond Manhattan and the Bronx. For the next two years, as a member of the crew of a destroyer, he saw Norfolk, Boston, and San Diego, Pearl Harbor and the Pacific. After the war ended, he spent time among the bombed-out ruins of Yokohama and Nagasaki. He painted most of the ship's signs. He drew pictures of shipboard life and of his shipmates. More important, he began to read, greedily, eclectically, as eighteen-year-olds do, and recorded his favorites in a diary: Dashiell Hammett's *Red Harvest.* Richard Wright's *Black Boy.* Hemingway's *The Sun Also Rises.* James M. Cain's *The Postman Always Rings Twice,* novels by Lloyd C. Douglas, Willa Cather, Ngaio Marsh, G. K. Chesterton, Pearl Buck, and James Hilton. Inspired by his reading, and bored with his artwork, he started writing short stories and sent them off to *The Saturday Evening Post, Colliers, Ladies' Home Journal,* and, finally, the pulp magazines; they all came back, rejected. He kept working, helped by a former professor who was on the ship, determined to be a writer.

"There was a thing that happened when I started writing, and when I began to read so much," he said on this morning, more than half a century later. "I began to realize that there was no longer a *frame* around things. You weren't limited to that frame they were teaching in art school. I could go *anywhere*. I could go from a dust speck in the eye to a battlefield"—he snapped his fingers—"in a flash, in an *instant*!"

In June of 1946, Sal Lombino was offered a bonus to reenlist in the navy; he turned it down. "I said, Sorry, I really want to get on with my life. Because I really felt, okay, now I start." Back home, he used the GI Bill to matriculate at the Bronx campus of Hunter College, and began making friends with "guys who had high aspirations." He took every writing course he could find in the curriculum, playwriting, poetry, short stories. His mother, now persuaded of his seriousness, bought him his first typewriter. He wrote a weekly column for the school newspaper. With some friends, he started a drama group called the Powdered Wig Society and did everything from acting to writing press releases. The Wigs were soon known all over the Hunter campus. "If ever I had celebrity in my life," he said, smiling, "it was then, in college."

In 1949, he married a woman named Anita Melnick. He had found an apartment on North Brother Island, and to get there you had to take a bus and a ferry. "It was the same ferry that went to Riker's Island. We'd be going to our apartment and all the women would be going to see their boyfriends and husbands on Riker's Island. But it was a *great* apartment. It was like this, right on the river."

He now had a plan for the future. "My dream was that I was going to do what Hemingway did," he told me. "As soon as I graduated, I was going to go to Paris and live on the Left Bank and write a novel." But, almost immediately, his wife got pregnant. Sal Lombino graduated with honors from Hunter in January of 1950; a son, Ted, was born in August. "There was no way we could go to Paris. I had a family now."

He scrambled for work. He had taken an education minor at Hunter, which allowed him to obtain an "emergency license" that September and a teaching job at Bronx Vocational High School. "I couldn't stand it," he said. "I'd go in and give them everything I had. I would use all my acting talents, all my creative talents, trying to make interesting assignments for them. They weren't buying. They didn't give a rat's ass. All they wanted to do was fix automobiles and airplane engines."

He remembers one student who sat in the back of the classroom. "He used to come in and read the newspaper every day," he said. "He was waiting to get drafted. Then one day I said, 'You, in the back row; put down that newspaper. I'm trying to teach a class here.' He pointed the newspaper at me, and said, 'You don't bother me, I won't bother you.' " Hunter acted out the sense of menace in the young man's challenge. "I didn't bother him. I didn't care what he did for the rest of the term."

By Christmas of 1950, he had quit Bronx Vocational. He took a job answering telephones for the Automobile Association of America, and, when that didn't last, a job selling lobsters. Then he read an ad in the *Times* and his life changed abruptly.

"It was an ad for an editor," Hunter recalled. "No experience necessary. So I went to the address in the ad—580 Fifth Avenue. I went up and looked for the number on the door. It was a frosted door and it said 'Scott Meredith Literary Agency.' I almost made the biggest mistake of my life. I had my hand on the doorknob and I thought, *Aw, gee, this isn't what I want.* I started to turn away from the door. But then I said, What the hell, I'm here. I was on my lunch hour from the lobster place. I went in and they said sit down."

Meredith wasn't present, but his employees told Lombino they were looking for an executive editor. They handed him a story without telling him that it had been written by one of their own editors. "It was a model of ineptness," Hunter recalled. "He did it deliberately, but I didn't know that. They said, 'Read the story and tell the writer why you think it's salable or unsalable.' I said, 'Okay.' It was a dreadful story and I wrote exactly what I thought of it. Told whoever wrote it, 'Burn it,' and told him exactly why."

Then Hunter went back to the lobster place. A few days later, he got a call from the agency, which wanted to interview him. He met the man who was leaving the editor's job. There were, the departing editor explained, two kinds of clients at the Meredith agency: amateurs, who paid fees to get their manuscripts critiqued, and professionals. The latter included P. G. Wodehouse, Mickey Spillane, Arthur C. Clarke, and Poul Anderson. Spillane's almost comically hard-boiled Mike Hammer novels, which had started with *I, the Jury,* in 1947, were a huge success; Anderson and Clarke were bringing new vitality and sophistication to science fiction; Wodehouse was trying to recover from the scandal of his naive broadcasts from Nazi Germany. Sal would handle the professionals, writing critiques as if they had come from Scott Meredith himself. The pay was forty dollars a week.

"I said to him, 'Why are you leaving the job?' He said, 'I'm selling so much of my own work it doesn't pay to stay here anymore.' Puh-kooo. My ears went up, and I said, 'I'll take it.' "

The Scott Meredith Agency was Evan Hunter's graduate school. "I learned everything there was to know about writing there," he told me. "Not only by reading stories by professional writers but by hearing the comments of editors." Often, he was the middle-man, taking notes from editors and passing them on to the writers. He saw that professionals always took advice from editors; only insecure amateurs protested about trimming or rewriting. After a few months, Sal Lombino brought in some stories of his own for Meredith's scrutiny. The agent took them home for the weekend.

"On Monday morning he said, 'Can you come in for a minute?' Sure. I went into his office. He said, '*This* you should burn. This is no good. *This* I think I can place. This—if you want to rewrite the thing—we can try it. This, no good. This, burn.' "

Meredith sold a science-fiction story entitled "Outside in the Sand," about men landing on Mars, to the magazine *Science Fiction Quarterly*. It paid a quarter cent a word, and, after commissions, the check came to $12.60. Sal Lombino was now a professional writer. And he was learning much from Scott Meredith. "He was a brilliant guy, who hit upon a formula that absolutely defined the successful pulp story," Hunter said. "And in today's world of fiction most of the stuff on the market is pulp stuff. John Grisham is pulp fiction. And Scott defined it perfectly."

The world of pulp fiction is now largely forgotten, in spite of Quentin Tarantino's resurrection of the phrase as the title of his 1994 movie. The pulps started around the turn of the century, when the publisher Frank Munsey saw a market for low-priced popular fiction. He published a magazine called *Argosy*, which was printed on low-grade wood-pulp paper and sold for ten cents a copy. It did extremely well, and hundreds of imitators followed. All swiftly organized themselves around genres: Westerns, sports, adventure, science fiction, fantasy, and crime. The format also became standardized: 120 seven-by-ten-inch pages and a wonderfully lurid cover. One of the best of the crime pulps was *Black Mask*, started in 1920 by H. L. Mencken and George Jean Nathan as a way of underwriting their political and literary magazine, *The American Mercury*. Most of the writing was dreadful hackwork, but good writers did emerge—Hammett, Raymond Chandler, Erle Stanley Gardner.

By the time Sal Lombino was starting to write for money, the pulps were past their Depression-era peak, subverted at first by radio melodramas and comic books and, a few years later, by television and *Playboy* and its imitators. Then came digest-size mystery magazines, the best of which was *Manhunt*, and original paperback novels in the pulp genres. (Their great star was John D. MacDonald, who wrote dozens of paperback novels before making the hardcover best-seller lists, in the '70s.) Sadly, just as the pulps were beginning to die (*Black Mask* folded in 1951; most of the others were gone by 1955), the writing was getting better, focusing more on characterization than on brainless action. Still, the pulp formulas remained valuable to fiction writers in search of a large audience, which is to say writers who planned to write for a living. Even today, Hunter can recite Meredith's definition of a pulp story. Meredith's *Writing to Sell*, which remains in print, in its fourth edition, puts it this way:

> A sympathetic lead character finds himself in trouble of some kind and makes active efforts to get himself out of it. Each effort, however, merely gets him deeper into his trouble, and each new obstacle in his path is larger than the last. Finally, when things look blackest and it seems certain that the lead character is finished, he manages to get out of his trouble through his own efforts, intelligence, or ingenuity.

Sal Lombino applied that formula to his short fiction. He began to sell more stories to the pulps, serving the same kind of Grub Street apprenticeship that shaped the styles and work habits of many nineteenth-century writers. Some stories were science fiction. Some were adventure stories, about men lost at sea or forced to battle alligators with their bare hands. "Sometimes they started with the illustration—some heroic guy fighting animals or crazy people—and asked me to come up with a story," Hunter recalled. Some of the better stories drew on his experiences as a schoolteacher. He rose to *Bluebook,* a large-format, higher-class pulp, and to the '50s version of *Argosy*. He climbed from a quarter of a cent per word to five cents per word. Now he left work at the agency at six, took the subway home—he had by then moved to the Bronx—finished dinner by eight and wrote until one. Not one of his stories appeared under the name Salvatore A. Lombino. He used Richard Marsten, Curt Cannon, Hunt Collins, Ezra Hannon. (Some of these were reissued years later under the Ed McBain name.) "I'd sometimes have five stories in the same issue of a pulp magazine," he recalls, "and the editor didn't know they were all me."

Then Meredith came to him with an offer. Lester Del Rey had written a number of plot summaries that were to be developed into short novels for the young-adult market and published by the John C. Winston company, in Philadelphia. Hunter can't remember much about those outlines, but he did remember Scott Meredith's question: Would Sal like to write one? He begged off, saying that he didn't know how to write a novel. Meredith insisted. Hunter remembers the agent saying, "You can do it, you can do it," and then adding, "If you run into any problems, I'll help you."

The publisher was paying $2,500 for each novel, a huge sum for the young writer. The first was called *Find the Feathered Serpent*, a time-travel yarn, which is where Lombino first used the name Evan Hunter. The pseudonym had nothing to do with his alma mater, he says: "It was just a name."

By May of 1953, Lombino had $3,000 in the bank, and he told Meredith that he was leaving the agency to freelance. Meredith was not happy; he was about to offer Sal Lombino a partnership, which would entitle him to a percentage of profits. But Lombino told Meredith, "I don't want to be an agent, Scott. I want to be a writer."

Hunter began his first real novel. The raw material came from his experience at Bronx Vocational. After five months, he had ninety pages and an outline for *The Blackboard Jungle*. The day he learned the novel had been accepted by Simon & Schuster, he told me, "I was in a bakery on Eighty-sixth Street. I don't know what we were doing there—we were living in Hicksville, Long Island. My wife was buying bread or cake and I said to her, 'I think I'll call Scott and see how we're doing on the book.' " His voice began to rise in excitement. "You know, had we heard back from Simon & Schuster?" A pause. "I called, and Scott said, 'They're taking it.' And I hung up the phone and just came dancing out of that booth." He grinned, his hands pumping the air. "There are only a couple of times in my life when I've done that."

The apprenticeship was now part of the past. So was Salvatore A. Lombino. Some years earlier, an editor named Charles Heckleman had told him, "Evan Hunter will sell a lot more tickets." In those years—before anyone had heard of Mario Puzo, or Gay Talese, or Nick Pileggi—there was still much bigotry against Italian-Americans, and it extended to publishing. Salvatore A. Lombino sounded too "ethnic." Lombino legally changed his name to Evan Hunter. When he told his father about the change, Hunter recalled, "he said, 'That's a good idea, let me see what I can come up with.' He came back the next day with two hundred names! All variations on what the name was. He was hot stuff."

A few years later, Ed McBain came into the world. It is no accident that Steve Carella is the most rounded of the characters in the 87th Precinct novels, and the one who serves most often as an alter ego for his creator. In almost every book there are some references to the strength of the Italian family and to Italian values. Here is Carella brooding in *Long Time No See*:

> His grandfather had come to America from Italy because he'd been told the streets here were paved with gold. They were not, of course, and Giovanni Carella learned that almost at once, driving a horse and wagon for the milk company, the horse dropping the golden nuggets anywhere in view. Nor were the streets as clean as those to be found

in Giovanni's native Naples, or so Giovanni claimed, a premise perhaps disputable. But in those days, when Carella's grandfather first got here at the turn of the century, the European sense of tradition and of place caused immigrants like himself to look upon even their slum dwellings as something to be cared for with pride.

The pride is there, but Hunter is clearly not happy with what is now called "identity politics"; he still believes in the melting pot. Carella spoke for him in *The Big Bad City*:

> He never thought of himself as Italian, however, because, gee, you see, he'd been born here in these United States of America, you see, and an Italian was someone who lived in Rome, or was he mistaken? He never thought of himself as an Italian-American either, because that was someone who'd come to this country from Italy, correct? An immigrant? As for example, his father's father, whom he'd never met because the man had died before Carella was born. He was the Italian-American, the hyphenate, the man who'd come all those miles from a walled mountaintop village midway between Bari and Naples, Italian at the start of his long journey, Italian when he'd reached these shores and this big bad city, becoming Italian-American only after he'd recited the pledge of allegiance under oath.

Hunter's writing has one other very subjective distinction, and I think it derives from the disappearance of Sal Lombino. In the 87th Precinct novels, there are dozens of characters with names other than the ones they were born with; usually, they aren't pseudonyms but aliases. There are also countless examples of people who need to wear masks in order to become their best, or most powerful, selves. I remember asking Susan Sontag once if she'd ever thought about writing a detective story, and she said, "First, I'd have to invent the writer who was writing the story."

In important ways, the invention of Evan Hunter allowed Sal Lombino to write novels with a wider focus, exploring in smooth, urban prose a variety of aspects of American life. But the invention of Ed McBain allowed him to dig more deeply into the world that had shaped him when he was a boy in East Harlem and the Bronx. The Evan Hunter novels are about the world of others; the McBain novels are about their creator, a creator who remains Sal from 120th Street, figuring out that you'd better join with friends—a gang or a detective squad—who will help you when you need them. If you are a writer, you freeze time in order to more carefully examine a particular place at a particular time. "I think there are a lot of things in those books, the Ed McBains, that will have some value later on, years from now," he told me. "You can feel the city in them, see it, the people and the places and the weather. At least, I hope so."

We went out for lunch one afternoon, walking along the bright, noisy street outside Hunter's Manhattan apartment. Construction workers shouted at each other, while a crane hauled Sheetrock to the upper story of a new building. "Everything is unfinished," Hunter said. "Everywhere." He was irritated because a new house he was building in Connecticut was still not done, after a year of work. "My books are in boxes, my files, my reference books," he said, walking in a style that was common in the neighborhood where I grew up in Brooklyn: the upper torso still, the legs moving swiftly, the weight heavier on one foot than the other.

We passed women pushing infants in strollers, kids humpbacked with book bags, a tall, angular young woman heading toward the river. As I walked in the company of Evan Hunter—or, more exactly, Ed McBain—each seemed a potential victim of mayhem. At the corner, a squad car moved slowly up First Avenue, and I wondered if the cops in the car knew Steve Carella or Meyer Meyer, or Fat Ollie Weeks. If not, they should. Those characters are part of this New York, too, and the man walking beside me had put them there. When we turned the corner, I asked Hunter how many more 87th Precinct books he thought he would write. He shrugged. "There's one that I have in mind," he said. "It'll be published after I'm dead." He smiled. "I call it 'Exit.' Not bad, huh?" His hands flexed, as if he were anxious to start typing. And we bopped up the avenue together, each of us stepping more heavily on one foot than on the other.

# Honorable Mentions: 2000

"Copycat" by Joan Myers, *Deadly Dozen*.

"The Killing Floor" by Clark Howard, Crippen and Landru.

"Quantum Teleporter" by Michael Burstein, *Analog* September.

"The Stealing Progression" by Tom Tolnay, *EQMM,* August.

"Slave Wall" by Hal Charles, *EQMM,* February.

"Anna and the Players" by Ed Gorman, *EQMM,* November.

"The Bluebird" by Alison White, *EQMM,* February.

"Chatty Patty" by Taylor McCafferty, *Magnolias and Mayhem*.

"The Third Manny" by Terrence Faherty, *EQMM,* February.

"The Fading Woman" by Ed Hoch, *EQMM,* April.

"Blue Wolf" by John M. Floyd, *AHMM,* February.

"The Christmas Mitzvah" by Doug Allyn, *EQMM,* December.

"My Best Fred McMurray" by Rob Kantner, *AHMM,* October.

"Widow's Peak" by Rochelle Krich, *Unholy Orders*.

"The Unborn" by Serita Stevens, *Nefarious*.

"The Consul's Wife" by Steven Saylor, *Crime Through Time 3*.

"Porkpie Hat" by Peter Straub, *Magic Terror*.

"Missolonghi" by Walter Satterthwait, *AHMM,* October.

"Booger" by Beverly Brackett, *Handheld Crime*.

"Lark in the Morning" by Sharyn McCrumb, *Crime Through Time 3*.

"Smoke" by William Sanders, *Crime Through Time 3*.

# About the Editors

Ed Gorman has been called "one of suspense fiction's best storytellers" by *Ellery Queen*, and "one of the most original voices in today's crime fiction" by the *San Diego Union*.

Gorman has been published in magazines as various as *Redbook, Ellery Queen, The Magazine of Fantasy and Science Fiction*, and *Poetry Today*.

He has won numerous prizes, including the Shamus, the Spur, and the International Fiction Writer's award. He's been nominated for the Edgar, the Anthony, the Golden Dagger, and the Bram Stoker awards. Former *Los Angeles Times* critic Charles Champlin noted that "Ed Gorman is a powerful storyteller."

Gorman's work has been taken by the Literary Guild, the Mystery Guild, Doubleday Book Club, and the Science Fiction Book Club.

Martin H. Greenberg is the CEO of TEKNO•BOOKS, the book packaging division of Hollywood Media, a publicly traded multi-media entertainment company. With over 900 published anthologies and collections, he is the most prolific anthologist in publishing history. His books have been translated into thirty-three languages and adopted by twenty-five different book clubs. With Ed Gorman, he edits the 5 Star Mystery line of novels and collections for Thorndike Press, and is co-publisher of *Mystery Scene*, the leading trade journal of the mystery genre.

In the mystery and suspense field, he has worked with at least fifteen best-selling authors, including Dean Koontz, Mickey Spillane, Tony Hillerman, Robert Ludlum, and Tom Clancy.

He received the Milford Award for lifetime achievement in science fiction editing in 1989, and in April, 1995, he received the Ellery Queen Award for lifetime achievement for editing in the mystery field at the 50th Annual Banquet of the Mystery Writers of America, becoming the only person to win major editorial awards in both genres.

Dr. Greenberg received his Ph.D in Political Science and International Relations from the University of Connecticut, and was the founding chairperson of those departments at Florida International University in 1972–1975. He retired as Professor Emeritus of Political Science and Literature after a twenty-year teaching and administrative career at the University of Wisconsin-Green Bay where he served as the university's first Director of Graduate Studies.